# The Kings' Assassin

# The Kings' Assassin

Ed Cannon

**To order additional copies of this book, contact:**
Xlibris
1-888-795-4274
www.Xlibris.com
Orders@Xlibris.com
768152

# Contents

Partial lineage of the Royal House of Rendarick, as recorded in the royal archives of the city of Illicia

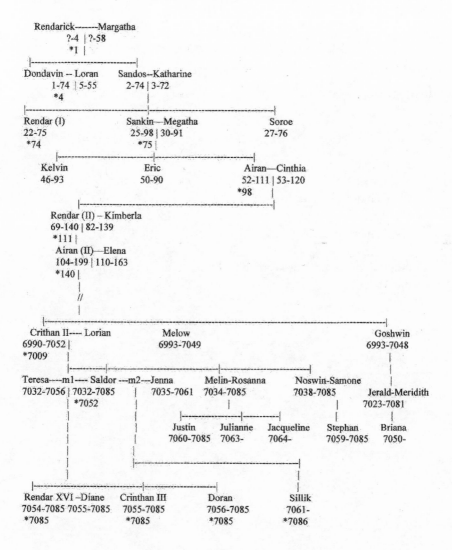

*Marks the beginning of each king's reign.

All dates are relative to the Second Alliance's victory in the second demon war. Illicia officially founded in year 2.

# The Seven Laws

1. Adept
2. Magic
3. Ritual
4. Sorcery
5. Conjuring
6. Wizardry
7. Augury

*A master of the Seven Laws can unite the separate energies and can combine them.

To my wife Vickie and my sister Julie for their endless help and to Charlese for the encouragement to keep going.
To Katherine & David Scraper for their help, guidance and encouragement.

Special thanks to Jenny Wine for the cover and map artwork.

# CHAPTER I

## Homecoming

S ILLIK CLIMBED THE last few steps of the narrow trail. He did not dare to look down at the nearly sheer rock face he had just scaled. With a breath of exhilaration, he stepped out onto the precipice of Soul Crusher. After almost seven years, tonight he would finally be home.

He had survived the desert. For three weeks, all he had seen were its sun-parched cliffs, shifting sands, and stars at night. Now he could see his home, the city of Illicia. It rose from the center of the only major oasis in the Weeping Wastes, which lay directly ahead. The plains of Illicia beckoned him. The green fields and tree-lined approaches stood out in stark contrast to the brown desolation he had endured.

"Praise the Seven Gods," he whispered as he drank from the waterskin on his chest. The Seven Gods of Law were the gods to whom Sillik and all of Illicia had sworn allegiance. They were locked in an eternal battle with the Nine Gods of Darkness.

The pinnacle on which Sillik stood was named after one of the Nine Dark Gods. Eight other mountains surrounded the valley. Every year on the anniversary of the city's founding, the Nine Dark Gods stood on the peaks to terrorize and punish Illicia, and the Seven White Gods surrounded Illicia to protect it and oppose evil.

Sillik glanced at the other peaks. Soul Crusher was the most dangerous to climb, but it had a small, nearly flat summit. The other peaks, such as Sight Blinder and Mind Breaker, offered only jagged summits. He returned his gaze to his home city. Illicia was impressive, as always. Its tall white spires challenged the heavens. Illicia meant "Carved of Stone" in the old tongue. The center of the city had indeed been carved from the granite that permeated the local mountains.

The sun would be setting soon, and the moons were rising on the eastern horizon. There was still time to get down off the mountain and walk to Illicia before the gates closed. The guards on the walls would see him coming. They had the long glass. They might even ride out to make sure he was not a Nomad.

Sillik was surprised to see that all seven moons were rising together. *The Celebration of Kings*, he thought as he smiled. Was it a coincidence that the son of the king was returning on this night? The Celebration of Kings occurred only every seventy-two years. In Illicia, as in most cities, it was cause for celebration. Tonight, he would toast his father, the king, and his half brothers Rendar, Crinthan, and Doran. A part of his mind asked, *Will you? Will you toast your father?*

Nearly two months earlier, Sillik's father had sent a frantic telepathic summons urging him to come home. The message had frightened him, as had the fact that he had been unable to contact his father ever since. Only those who possessed strong magical talents and a deep need could use telepathy. The lack of a response could mean only one thing: his father was dead. Since Sillik didn't know what had happened, he had refrained from contacting his friends in Illicia. If there had been a coup, it was better that no one knew he was coming.

Before he began his descent, he held out his left palm. A misty white light flared and grew quickly. The light banished the shadows near Sillik, revealing the narrow, twisting path to the lowlands. The Seven Laws of Magic, gifts from the Seven Gods, allowed him to do many things that normal men could not. Though sometimes confusing, the seven laws dealt with different branches of magic. A master of all seven laws allowed the user to unite the powers and access vast wells of energy.

Sillik inched down the rock wall. The trail was narrow and covered with loose rocks. He kept his eyes on his feet, his light hovering just in front of him. Halfway down, where the trail widened, he paused and looked around, his magical senses tingling. He was being watched!

He raised his magical defenses, and nearly invisible fireflies swirled around him. His senses sharpened. In the shadows, he could see two shapes hiding before him, and he heard a third breathing behind him.

A click broke the quiet, and the bolt of a crossbow leapt out of the shadows. Sillik's defenses flashed, and the bolt careened into the rocks. He felt the reverberation of the impact on his shields deep in his bones. It hurt, as it always did.

A man yelled, and Sillik whirled while drawing his sword. The brigand's axe flashed, but Sillik's sword caught it. With a quick twist of his sword, he sent the man tumbling headfirst toward the sands below.

Sillik turned back and dodged a second man. He parried a blow, and the man stumbled. When the man turned to run, Sillik grabbed him by the cloak and yanked. Then he released it, and the man tumbled into the darkness.

Sillik saw a third man desperately loading a bolt into his crossbow. Sillik threw a ball of red fire, and the brigand disappeared in a flash of light. Bits of molten metal from the man's armor and weapons sizzled on the cool stone.

Sensing no more threats, Sillik let his magical defenses fade as he sheathed his sword. Tucked behind where the men had hidden was a small metal cage that housed a pigeon. A small tube was affixed to bird's leg. "I wonder what message you were intended to send," he said to the bird.

Sillik removed the pigeon from its cage, opened the tube, and shook out the message. Then he released the bird and watched it fly toward Illicia. He unrolled the message and read the simple message: "It is done." Someone in the city was communicating with those brigands, but who and why? What was to have been done? *Was I supposed to die?* he wondered. *Who wants me dead?*

He hurried down the rest of the path. At the base of the mountain, he saw the mounds of sand where the other two men had fallen. The sand heaved and swirled. Occasionally, dark fins slid into view, only to disappear with a rasping sound. The fins belonged to sandfish, which swam near the base of the rock. They were ferocious eaters and would strip the corpses to bone in a few minutes. He would be safe enough now that the sandfish had fed.

It was almost dusk. The fish grew quiet at night and seldom attacked. Sillik strode quickly across the sand and tried not to look back at the red-stained mounds behind him.

The sandfish were only one of the dangers in the Weeping Wastes. Other menaces included the punishing heat, wildcats, wolves, snakes, and scorpions. As had just been proven, two-legged hazards dwelled in the desert as well. Nomads existed on the fringes of the Weeping Wastes, and then there were the bandits who had fled the cities and now eked out a simple existence on its borders. The Illicians patrolled the desert and tried to keep the lawlessness under control, but there was no way they could eliminate it completely.

As Sillik walked toward the ancient city of Illicia, which had ruled the known world for almost seven thousand years, his stomach churned as images flashed through his mind. He remembered the bitter arguments with his half brothers just before he had decided to leave home. The stress of his brothers' and cousins' endless plots and the turmoil of the court had frustrated Sillik, who was the youngest crown prince.

When Sillik publicly mastered the Seven Laws of Magic, just before his eighteenth birthday, he had upset the political schemes of Rendar, his eldest brother. Like the rest of his half brothers, Rendar had not mastered the magical laws. In an emergency, the laws of Illicia said that a son with magical talent could succeed his father regardless of birth order. Therefore, Rendar viewed Sillik as a threat. Sillik's brothers had beaten him as he progressed through the ranks of magic. Sillik could have easily used the laws to overpower them, but he had restrained himself and endured their torture in silence.

Sillik's father had offered two options to keep him in the city. They had been good choices, fair and appropriate for a younger son with magical ability, but Sillik had declined both and asked to leave Illicia. His father was disappointed, but he had given Sillik his blessing anyway. It was with great sadness that Sillik had taken leave of his father and friends, but he could not bear the hatred and intrigue of his brothers any longer.

Everything had changed, though, when he received his father's frantic, telepathic plea for help. Terror and fear had surged across that link. There was no way he could refuse.

Sillik's armor and weapons marked him as a trained warrior. A sword hung from his left side on a wide, red leather belt. The belt was the symbol of the warriors' guild. It was recognized across the land as a warning to the untrained. The sword hilt was wrapped with gold thread and leather strips. His sheath was simple and unadorned, which was unusual. Normally, a warrior wore the symbol of his city on his sheath. Sillik did not want to advertise his origins, though, so his sheath was unmarked, as was the rest of his armor. The one exception was a carved leather feather on his left shoulder. It connected him with the city of Aceon, home of the giant Herish birds that protected the cliffside city. The symbol wasn't widely recognized, so few knew what it meant. Across his chest, Sillik carried a leather water bag. He smiled as he heard water slosh with every step. It meant he had triumphed over the desert.

As he walked, Sillik unwrapped the desert veil that had protected his face from the sun and sand. The seven crossings of the dense fabric symbolized the protections offered by the Seven Gods. Sillik's face was covered with several days' growth of whiskers. Weeks in the sun had turned the skin around his eyes a deep brown. He folded the veil and tucked it under his belt with reverence. No one could enter Illicia with his face covered. The Nomads who inhabited the desert never uncovered their faces. A state of war between Illicia and the Nomads had existed since the founding of the city.

Sillik took a deep breath and then restored his magical defenses. Tendrils of power spun around him. When he was satisfied that he was suitably protected against the unknown, the fireflies faded away.

As he walked, Sillik remembered the pain that had flashed across the brief link when he last communicated with his father. Sillik had seen magic, felt the impression of battle, seen the face of an attacker, and felt betrayal and a host of other painful emotions. *He is dead,* a voice said. *I hope not,* Sillik replied. It had been centuries since a coup had been attempted. Could someone have killed his father? *Who could have done that?* he wondered. *And how will my brothers react to seeing me?*

The sheepherders were the first to spot him as he passed through the scrubland around the city. They merely watched his passage in silence. Next were the peasants. They were also somber and quiet.

The farms were one of Illicia's greatest secrets. Wind traps caught the moisture and irrigated the land. They were supplemented by deep wells. Water was worth its weight in gold in the Weeping Wastes. Over the years, Sillik's people had learned almost every trick to conserve water and coax food from the ground. The green fields around the city of Illicia kept the desert at bay, and each year, the city expanded the plantings. The land was exceedingly rich and bountiful when water was present.

The farmers' expressions disturbed him. On many occasions while growing up, he had ridden among them. They knew him. He had helped repair their wind traps and the walls around the fields to keep the sandfish out. He had hunted dune wolves and caught sandfish with them. So why would they hardly look at him?

The village was also silent and forlorn. Its buildings were constructed of stone, and every surface was painted with brightly colored pictures. Some were advertisements for a tavern or merchants, whereas others depicted important announcements. One painting that Sillik remembered from his childhood showed a sandfish attacking the walls around the village. The stone presented an impervious wall to the dangerous creatures.

Even the children in the village stopped playing and ran to their mothers as he passed. Sillik smelled dinner cooking in several homes. He smiled, and his stomach rumbled as grilled sandfish, lamb, and other familiar smells infused the air. *Tonight there should be celebrations with wine and music. Yet everyone is quiet and afraid.* The sand crunching beneath his feet was the only sound Sillik heard. The fact that he could not detect a particular threat made him feel even more unsettled.

As he drew closer to the city, he spotted the patrols. Surely they had spotted him by now. Many of the guards knew him by sight. Like any royal son, he had spent his share of nights on the city walls, patrolling the city and guarding its gates. The city walls soared one hundred standard lengths above him, dotted with arrow slits. Towers stood on either side of the main gate and rose periodically above the walls surrounding the city. The towers and walls gleamed crimson in the setting sunlight.

Already Sillik could see dots of light in the city's windows. At night, the towers glowed like jewels. Sillik knew that trebuchets and ballistae stood silently on the walls between the towers. Tall mounds of rocks were piled beside the trebuchets, and pyramids of bolts were stacked beside the ballistae.

He saw the familiar pendants fluttering above the city gate and on top of the towers. The golden eagle symbol was unmistakable. The bird seemed to fly as the pennants rippled in the wind. It felt good to see the pennants after his long absence, but fear tugged at him when he realized they were flying at half-mast. Was his father really dead? And what about his friends–Briana, Kenton, Greenup, and a few others? Were they still alive? If so, what were they doing?

As Sillik drew closer, he saw that more than just the regular patrols lined the parapets. It was as if the city's entire population had turned out to see his approach. Faces peeked out between the battlements. Sillik stopped and smiled up at them. Then, taking a deep breath, he started toward the gates. Farmers and craftsmen lined the road as Sillik approached. He recognized many faces in the crowd, but no one would meet his eyes.

The thick, interlocking granite gates stood open in silent greeting. As he had planned, this was the King's Gate. All of the gates were named. In order of size, the gates were: King, Queen, General, Master, Soldier, Law, and Life. The King's Gate was the largest and most impressive. On this night, it seemed appropriate to use this gate. The rest of the gates were slightly smaller and less ornate. All of the gates were two feet thick and made of polished granite. The gate was wide enough to allow two wagons to pass at the same time. Each half of the gate bore the eagle, which was the symbol of the city.

The gate's lintel and posts were engraved with intertwined leaves, vines, and grapes. Gold leaf covered the designs. Sillik had always thought it ironic that when the city had been built, grapes didn't yet grow in the desert. Even today it took special tricks to grow them. Above the gate, the words "The Hand of Law" were written in a fine script, almost obscured by the leaves and vines.

Carved white marble figures of Rendarick, the city's founder, and his wife Margatha stood on either side of the posts. The stoic figures stood nearly twice as tall as the gates. Rendarick had his feet planted shoulder width apart, his right hand on the hilt of his sword and his cloak billowing around his legs. Margatha stood defiantly with her hands on her hips. A delicate veil covered the lower half of her face, and the faint impression of a smile was barely detectable. She wore several necklaces, and the low-cut dress revealed more than was fashionable today. The hilts of several daggers were carved at her waist. Long skirts covered her legs, and only the toes of her sandaled feet were visible.

Sillik often wondered what Margatha had really looked like. No other drawing or carving of her still existed. Although marble was a soft stone, the Illicians had magically preserved the statues. They were as crisp and clean today as the day they were carved. Sillik smiled at the familiar sight despite his trepidation.

Surrounding the city was a dry moat forty feet wide and thirty feet deep. Sharp rocks and even sharper black iron spikes, taller than a man, jutted up from the bottom. They glinted dangerously at sunset, but during the night, they were nearly invisible. Sillik knew the spikes were designed to intimidate, but in the walls of the moat were still other traps that he did not want to think about.

His feet echoed ominously on the wooden bridge as he crossed the moat. Wood was expensive in the desert, but bridges could be burned if needed to prevent access to the gates. The guards at the gate wouldn't meet his eye. They only pointed toward the keep. Although their veils hid their features, they could not conceal the worry in their eyes.

The captain of the guard saluted as Sillik approached. Like the other guards, he wore a green shirt, black pants, and silver mail. Each guard was also wrapped in a reflective cloak to protect him from the heat. The belts that held their swords glowed blood-red and were highly polished, as were their knee-high leather boots. The Illician eagle engraved on the captain's sword and sheath was standard-issue for all Illician warriors.

The captain of the guard spoke in a gruff, emotion-filled voice. "I have orders to close the city once the prince has entered."

Sillik started to ask who had given the orders but then merely nodded, acutely aware of the unusual nature of the order. The guard had tears in his eyes. Sillik smiled despite his emotion. "What's your name, warrior?"

The captain wiped his hands on his pants before speaking. "Bryon, my lord, of the house Derring." He looked around uncertainly and flexed his jaw.

Sillik nodded. "Derring. I knew a Derring once." He smiled kindly.

Bryon nodded. "My older brother, Your Highness. You and he took first swords together. The damn nomads took his life last year. They wiped out his entire patrol."

"Ah yes," Sillik said. "First swords." Images of a much younger version of himself and dozens of other eight-year-olds swinging their wooden practice swords together and learning how to thrust and parry filled his mind. "I am sorry for your loss," Sillik added sympathetically.

"My lord, the gate?"

Sillik smiled. "Yes, go ahead and do as you were ordered. I will be on my way. Don't open the gates until you have an order to do so."

The captain nodded and ordered all gates closed and guarded. Immediately, guards on the catwalks above pulled the levers and released the counterweights. The counterweights fell free from their restraints, hung suspended in the air momentarily, and then started to fall as the gates began to move. Chain links as thick as a man's torso rattled noisily as the weights fell. Slowly at first and then with increasing speed, the King's Gate rumbled shut on well-oiled hinges. The counterweights hit the ground with a deep *humph*, sending up a shower of sand. The gates slammed shut with a deep, thundering boom. The sound was unique. It was heard daily at sundown, but the tone today was particularly sharp and painful to Sillik. The chains rattled, and the pulleys groaned as the giant steel crossbar fell shut with another deafening crash. The metal portcullis rattled down next. Sparks exploded from its spikes as it slammed into the iron holes in the street. Sillik counted to ten and then heard six answering booms as the other gates slammed shut.

> *Seven gates for the Seven Gods*
> *Seven towers for the Laws of Life*
> *Seven by seven advisors for the Kings of Law*
> *Seven steps for the Throne of Man*
> *Seven branches for the Tree of Life*
> *Seven songs for the Joy of Life*
> *Seven paths to the depths of hell*

Sillik recited the children's song in his head as he heard the answering thunder of the steel locking bars falling into place to lock the other gates. When one gate closed, the other gates were closed automatically, by standing order. Sillik knew that runners would also be sent to all gates explaining that the order to keep the gates closed was a royal decree. Illicia had always been efficient.

Before he turned toward the keep, Sillik watched the guards pull on the ropes to the bellows that fed the twin brass horns suspended above the gate. Three short blasts echoed through the city. Now everyone knew the gates had been ordered closed. One long blast would signify that the city was under attack. In response to that signal, every able-bodied man and woman was expected to go to the walls and defend the city. Two blasts signified danger, and all men-at-arms were ordered to the walls. Three blasts signified that the city was on heightened alert, the gates were closed, and all guard members were ordered to their posts.

At one time, Sillik could have guessed which gate had closed first just by the sound it made. Today, it was more important to know that all them were shut.

Sillik nodded in satisfaction. The city was secure. The guards saluted him with practiced precision, each pounding his right hand against his left shoulder and saying, "Blessed be the Seven Gods." It was the formal salute for the royal family. Hearing it made Sillik relax slightly.

He responded with the formal response. "Blessings of the Seven Gods upon your house."

"My lord," Bryon said hesitantly, "there are chairs waiting for you." He looked to his right. "And we were ordered to escort you. The streets may not be safe."

Sillik eyed the silk-covered sedan chairs with revulsion. Eight men with bulging muscles, silken trousers, no shirts, and shaved heads stood ready to hurry him to the keep. "A lady should ride in those. I will not."

"Yes, of course, my lord," Bryon said, "but we were ordered."

"Did my father or my brothers give you the order?"

"No, of course not," Bryon said, shifting uncomfortably. "My lord, the lord general gave the order."

Sillik smiled. "I will walk then. I do not need or want an escort. I can find my own way to the keep."

Bryon stood straighter. "We were ordered to give proper escort."

Shaking his head, Sillik laughed softly. "No, Captain. I can find the keep. You should stay here and do your job."

"Of course, my lord," the captain said as he bowed and backed away.

Sillik turned toward the keep with a sigh. He would find no answers here. With trepidation, he strode into Illicia. Rendar's Tower, the Tower of Kings, was at the center of the city. All of the monarchs of Illicia had lived in the tower, and beneath it almost all were buried.

The two men standing near the battlements on top of the Red Tower had watched Sillik's approach since he first appeared on their patron's mountain. It always amused them that the early Illicians had named the mountains surrounding Illicia after the Nine Gods of Darkness.

"He will be in the keep soon," the first man said as they heard the seven booms signifying the closing of the gates. "They weren't supposed to attack him." He was lean with a warrior's build. He wore the uniform of the city guard with a lord major's red knot on his shoulder. His round, shaved head glistened in the dying sunlight. A bushy brown mustache covered his upper lip, and two parallel scars ran across his face, ending where his left ear should have been, a sign of his profession and of battles lost. A standard-issue Illician sword, serviceable but plain, hung at his side. One finger was hooked on the red belt from which his sword hung.

The second man stared off into the distance. He wore a gold robe and a seven-pointed gold hat. He was well fed and somewhat portly. His faced sagged with jowls that jiggled when he moved. His black eyes burned with fanaticism. "Yes," he said finally, "yes, I suppose he will. I didn't order the attack. Something else must have happened. Your men must have been clumsy and been discovered."

"We should have attacked him before he ever got this close to the city and certainly not within sight of the city," the first man said as he put his hand on his sword hilt. "He will be guarded now, and it will be harder to kill him. I had men in the mountain passes watching for him. It would have been easy then. A single arrow would have ended this."

"We were directed to let him come into the city," the second man said, a dangerous edge to his voice. "Have you forgotten your instructions? There are *people* who would be very interested in your change of heart."

"I remember," the first man said, suppressing a shudder. His master enjoyed cruelty. She was especially cruel to those who disobeyed. "I helped train this one. He is not like his half brothers. They were gullible idiots and useless dolts. He will be wary. When he learns what we have done, he will begin the hunt."

The second man smiled indulgently as he adjusted his hat. "We were told to wait and announce his arrival, which we have done." He gestured at a square piece of silver on the battlement. "There are others who have other things to do. If they fail ..." His voice trailed off as he contemplated the skyline. "Then other things might be possible. If he is killed outside the city, everyone will mourn but say there was nothing we could do. If he is killed inside the city while they are doing all they can to protect him, the impact will be much more severe, don't you think? I myself was ordered to leave a little surprise for him." The portly man rubbed his chin as he thought. Then he turned to his companion. "Now that the prince is in the city, don't you have somewhere to be?"

The first man nodded sullenly. He looked as if he had something more to say, but then he turned and left without another word, his scabbard grating across the rooftop.

The second man picked up the silver piece of metal. For a moment he fingered it and flashed a quick series of light signals at the Blue Tower with the last of the sunlight. A single answering flash told him where to go. Grunting in surprise, he looked around. The guards on the rooftop ignored him. He waited for the guards to make a slow circuit before he pocketed the silver mirror and left the rooftop.

# CHAPTER 2

## Challenges

INSIDE ITS WALLS, the city of Illicia was as beautiful as Sillik remembered it. Fanciful arches and domes filled the sky. Circular towers soared into the air. Bridges joined the towers above the streets in a maze of crisscrossing paths. Parks, gardens, and reflecting pools were scattered throughout the city. Intricate patterns painted in bright colors glowed everywhere.

Silent throngs of people lined the streets. They were frightened, Sillik realized. Potters, bakers, merchants, warriors, women, and children all watched impassively as he passed. The people were packed so tight that Sillik barely had room to walk. Hands reached out to touch him as he passed, and Sillik let them. He had nothing to fear from these people. Above him, people leaned out of windows, stood on balconies, and lined the overhead bridges to get a glimpse of him.

Tonight was the Celebration of Kings. The scrolls said the rising of the moons symbolized the unity of the Seven Gods. Every city that celebrated the Seven Laws partook in the magic of this night. Under normal circumstances, there would have been dancing in the streets, and wine would be flowing like a river. Sillik felt a shiver of fear. What had happened? It was as if they had no sovereign to celebrate. Sillik had a bad feeling that he wouldn't be toasting anyone tonight, much less the gods. This felt more like Founding, a solemn holiday celebrating the day the cornerstones of the city had been laid.

Looking around again, he tried to distract himself by naming as many guilds as he could. Some guilds wore colors. The winemakers usually wore purple to symbolize their product. The shoemakers' hands were usually stained from the dyes that they used. Some wore hats. The perfumers' guild wore little red hats. Sillik proudly noted the absence of one guild: the slavers. Slavers were not permitted in Illicia, and slavery had been legal in Illicia since its founding.

*What could frighten so many people like this?* he wondered as he quickened his pace. *What else has happened?*

As he walked, he heard scattered voices. "Bless the Seven Gods, he is home," called out one person. "Praise the Seven!" exclaimed another. These were common blessings in the city.

Other comments rattled Sillik's composure. "Avenge us!" someone shouted. "Kill the bastard!" yelled another man.

*What has happened? Who do they want me to kill?*

The shops were open, but the streets were silent aside from the periodic exclamations. Even the smithy near the gate was hushed. Sillik couldn't hear the puff of his bellows or the sound of the hammers on metal. No self-respecting blacksmith would let his forge grow cold while the sun still shone.

Giant oil lamps above the streets cast eerie shadows, which only added to Sillik's discomfort. The lamplighters also stood and watched him pass.

Meats, breads, fruits, and vegetables were abundant in many shops. Fabrics and leathers of all imaginable colors and textures were also displayed proudly before the tailors' shops. Sillik smelled the aromas of tanned leather, bread, roasting meats and nuts, and perfumes. Wine merchants had bottles galore in their shaded racks. The streets should have been alive with sounds and energy as vendors loudly hawked their wares. The musicians who usually played on the streets were in their customary places, but their flutes, harps, and drums were in their laps. Even the bathhouses he passed were quiet, despite this being the favorite time for many in the city to wash away the day's toils.

Sillik saw the veiled figures of Illician women watching silently. Veils were not required, but many women wore them to counter the heat and dryness of the desert. The veils also added mystery. The only exceptions were the women who chose the military or the Seven Laws.

One set of bright blue eyes behind a veil caught his attention as he passed. The woman was standing in the doorway of a candle shop. Her yellow and green silks covered her from head to foot. The only part of her body he could see was her piercing, bright blue eyes. They were sad and crying, and for a moment they reminded him of someone. *No, she is gone,* Sillik thought angrily. *I will not compare someone else to her.*

A few Gold Robes, the teachers of magic and history, were scattered throughout the crowds. Sillik felt their cold, accusing eyes. He shivered despite the heat. *Yes, they will accuse me. They wanted me to stay and join their order, but I did not.* The Gold Robes got their name from the gold cassocks that they wore. The seven red buttons at their necks proclaimed their mastery of the Seven Laws of Magic. *Ignore them*, Sillik thought as he glanced back at the men and women wearing the gold cassocks. *Not everyone who masters the Seven Laws wears the gold robes*, Sillik thought as he fingered the thin braid at the side of his head. At least in Illicia, they all wore the braid.

The road to the keep was narrow and convoluted. Many points along the path could be defended and were overlooked by buildings with arrow slits.

Among the various towers were businesses of all kinds, homes of the great families, and the guild houses. All of the streets were similar, narrow and twisting and barely wide enough for a cart. Why make an invader's task easy? Additional walls surrounded the central towers. There was only one public entrance to the keep. Other hidden entrances existed, but only the royal family and a few others knew of them.

The walls around the keep soared three hundred lengths above the street. By law, no tower in the city proper within arrow range was taller than the inner walls. Behind the walls of the keep, the seven towers stood lonely and silent. The central tower—or as it was sometimes called, the Tower of Rendar—was twice as high as the walls and towers that guarded it.

The three most prominent towers within the keep were the Gold, Red, and Blue Towers. The Gold was for the Gold Robes, the Red for the warriors, and the Blue for the healers. The three towers had been built with colored stone. The three outer towers, called the Brown Towers, housed many other functions. The keep's central tower would be empty except for royal family, Sillik knew with dead certainty. It was the way the Illicians had always treated tragedy, alone and quietly.

The entrance to the center of Illicia was open, as it should have been, but the guards bore a somber expression. The gate was wide enough for a single wagon. Arrow slits were everywhere, as were holes for pouring boiling oil, Sillik noticed with an approving eye. In many other cities, defense was an afterthought.

After he passed, a small group of guards closed and barred the gate to the inner walls. The guards were charged upon their lives to protect the gate, the keep, and the royal family. They wore the uniform of the regular city guard but with the addition of a silver armband to designate their position. They also wore the red belt of the warrior, decorated with additional credentials that noted their skills. The positions were earned through merit and rotated frequently to prevent favoritism.

Sillik was surprised to see rows of guards lining the keep's interior walls. They were stacked shoulder to shoulder, five men deep. The two rows nearest the walls alternately held spears and pikes upright. The setting sun glinted off the edges of their weapons. The guards in the other three rows had bows and multiple quivers of arrows. They stood silent and unwavering. All wore standard-issue Illician swords. The tops of the walls were also packed with outward-facing warriors, their ranks stretching along the curved inner walls. It was as if every guard from throughout Illicia had been recruited to protect the keep tonight. The sound that would have accompanied the closing of the keep's gates was muted magically so that no one knew when the keep was open or closed. In the stillness, a few guards shuffled their feet, and the movement of boots on sandy stone made a loud rasping sound. Here and there someone cleared his throat or coughed.

Sillik took a deep breath and then hurried across the space separating the wall from the Tower of Rendar. Trees and patches of grass dotted the courtyard, softening the hard stone. In his youth, this small segment of the world had been his favorite place to escape his classes, his tutors, the arms masters, and the Gold Robes. In the center of the courtyard was a fountain. The city boasted many reflecting pools, but this was the only fountain. Sillik was saddened to see that it was not flowing. The fountain was turned off only when a king had died. Perhaps tomorrow it would shower water again. At the moment, the pool simply reflected the tower and the sunset.

It was a long walk to the central tower, with all those eyes watching Sillik. Once he entered the Tower of Rendar, he closed and barred the gate. It shut with a mournful whisper. It was also muted magically. The stone arch of the gate was wide enough for four men to stand side by side. The tunnel was short. Sillik heard every one of his steps echo in the silence. The ceiling had many small openings where boiling oil could be poured on attackers. Arrow slits also loomed around him. Sillik looked around nervously. The tower would have been searched, so Sillik was at least semi-confident that no one waited behind those arrow slits with an arrow nocked.

Sillik was surprised to find his father's primary advisors—who were also Sillik's friends—standing quietly to one side of the gate. Briana, Kenton, Greenup, and the Hornsmasher were somber, the dying light reflecting off their solemn faces. General Trandle, Greenup's longtime assistant, stood in the background. Behind them were Lords Grison and Felton, who tried to smile. Lady Viktorie merely nodded.

Briana made a small step toward him and then stopped and stiffened. Her face paled. She tried to smile, but a tear glistened in her eye. Sillik nodded and then inclined his head to Lord Grison, his first instructor. No one spoke. The eyes were pained, and the faces were somber.

None of his immediate family were there to greet him. He didn't even see his uncles, as much as he disliked them. *Could they all be dead?* he wondered.

For a moment, his composure wavered. Tradition required Illician monarchs to have forty-nine advisors, and they were all lined up around the door. His eyes quickly went down the line of faces. He saw men he recognized and trusted as well as people he didn't know or respect. The generals, who were also masters of the Seven Laws, had gold cuffs on their shirts. None of the Gold Robes had a visible weapon. Still, they were armed. Sillik had spent too much time with them to doubt that. The weapons were there, but the Gold Robes were less obvious about their intentions.

The same children's song went through Sillik's head again. He remembered singing it in school.

*Seven gates for the Seven Gods*
*Seven towers for the Laws of Life*
*Seven by seven advisors for the Kings of Law*
*Seven steps for the Throne of Man*
*Seven branches for the Tree of Life*
*Seven songs for the Joy of Life*
*Seven paths to the depths of hell*

*Am I the king? Do I have forty-nine advisors? Will I lead them to hell?* Sillik wondered as he led the procession into the Great Cathedral of Illicia. *I was trained to be a follower. My brothers were supposed to be the kings.* The last line of the poem had always been considered a warning about the abuses of power. But was there more to it? How would he know?

The sound of feet flooding into the keep was overwhelming as the guards resumed their positions. Sillik knew that the cooks, attendants, and hundreds of other people who lived and worked in the keep would also be returning to their posts. Fires would be started, meals would be cooked, dishes would be washed, rooms would be cleaned, and guards would resume patrols. A semblance of normalcy would return, but it was all an illusion.

The large, domed formal throne room was on the first floor of the keep, just a short walk from the main entrance. The walls and ceiling of the throne room were tiled with tan granite. Seven levels of balconies circled the chamber. Above them, large, shield-shaped lanterns hung from the ceiling on chains as thick as a man's arm. Metal mirrors and glass walls reflected their light. The flames danced merrily, casting shadows around the room. In those shadows, Sillik saw faces frowning at him. He recognized some of the faces. For a fleeting moment, he even saw his father's face on the walls.

Statues of the Seven Gods stood around the room. They were cut from white, polished marble and, like the founders' statues, were magically preserved to be as sharp and precise as the day they were carved, the faces of the Seven Gods frozen forever in implacable expressions.

The golden eagle throne sat on a dais to the left of the main door. The high sides were carved to resemble an eagle in flight. Jewels, emeralds, and rubies encrusted the arms and straight back. The precious stones glittered in the light.

While Sillik stared at the throne, the Gold Robes behind him magically enhanced the lighting in the room. As the light grew brighter, Sillik saw the grave of the city's founder in the floor on the opposite side of the room from the throne.

He glanced at the statues of the Seven Gods and took a deep breath. After mouthing their names quickly, he turned back toward the throne. He had never wanted the throne, but here it was, thrust upon him. He would have been content to let his brother rule, but that choice had been taken from him long ago. Now his father was dead, and apparently, so were his brothers. Someone would likely try to kill him as well. *But I cannot give in to fear. I have to become the regal image of a king. I have to give Illicia hope.*

Sillik looked around. Behind him, people milled uncertainly. A few voices whispered. Then, taking a deep breath, Sillik approached the throne. After his first step, he heard a whisper. He stopped, uncertain. He wanted to move, but caution whispered to him like a lover, so he stood still. Something was there. He held his hand up to stop those behind him. He heard their questioning voices, but he blocked them out as he extended his senses.

There it was again, a faint whiff of evil. Dark sorcery had been used here. The stink of it lingered in the air. Sillik could almost taste it. It felt stronger as he approached the throne, like a flicker of movement to the side of his face, always just out of sight.

Sillik felt Lords Kenton and Greenup raise their shields behind him. A moment later, he felt Briana's familiar shields as well. He smiled fondly at the brief caress as her shields brushed his. The Gold Robes behind him would protect the people. No longer concerned about anyone else, he looked at the throne and expanded his senses so that he could examine the magical device. He began to see the layers of what was in front of him. *I got too close*, he realized. *I have already sprung the trap, and it is just waiting for one more event. I can't stop what is about to happen. Who could have done this?*

"This is dangerous," he said to those following him. "It will kill if you are not protected." *Can I disarm it? No, it's too complicated. I don't have the time. It's already starting to fall apart.* Indeed, as he watched, he could see bits of black tendrils of power falling around the throne. The longer he waited, the more dangerous it was becoming.

*Who could have set this?* he wondered as he withdrew his senses from the trap. *Only a master of the Seven or the Nine. Damn, a master of the Nine was here!*

*That is frightening. If a master of the Nine has been here, what else has happened? No wonder my father was in danger.*

If a master of the Nine Black Laws had been here, at the center of Illicia, the implications were staggering. Although the Seven Laws were powerful, the Nine were equally powerful and twisted with evil. Their use would corrupt forever. Could such a master really be here in Illicia? Illicia had always championed the Seven Laws. He scanned the room. *There are other ways into this place,* he thought. *Are they still secret?*

It was obvious now what had been done. His presence–his proximity to the throne–had triggered the magic. It had been aimed at the only person who would have dared to approach the throne. Now that the trap was armed, he couldn't back away. He had to deal with it. He was the only one who could.

Sillik raised his shields and wrapped himself in many layers of protection. He swayed briefly at the sudden, enormous outlay of energy as he melded the layers of protection into a single shield. "Be ready. I'm going to trip this," Sillik said aloud to the room. Then, with a mental nudge and a flick of a finger from Sillik, one of the torches flew across the room and touched the throne.

Sillik cursed as heat and light exploded outward. Tongues of flames surrounded him, and wind buffeted him, threatening to knock him down. His eyes were clenched shut, but he could still see the flames. Pressure tried to crack his shields and to squeeze him as the heat tried to fry his body. *Damn them to the nine hells! Don't try to control it,* he told himself. *Don't touch it! If you touch it, if you control it, they will know you survived this.* Sillik gritted his teeth. *I can survive this. Damn, two attacks in one day. What has happened to my home?*

As quickly as it started, the explosion ended. Sillik straightened up and looked around. "Is everyone safe?"

"We survived," Lord Kenton said with a grimace.

"Did you feel the message?" Sillik asked.

Kenton nodded. After a long silence, he said, "Yes, I felt it. I suppose everyone with magical training in the city felt it. I must think about what that means."

"Your enemies will be warned," Greenup said in his gruff voice. "You were wise to do nothing to deflect the blast. You revealed nothing." Lord General Greenup was dressed in his customary battle armor. He was the chief of the lord generals of Illicia and the greatest military strategist the city had ever produced. His proper title was Lord General Greenup, but most called him "Battle Lord."

Kenton nodded. "But perhaps it was just a test. You survived. I wonder."

"Look what happened to the throne," Briana said. "It's melted. The Seven be praised, you are safe."

"Yes, it is," Sillik said as he surveyed the damage. "The tiles underneath are fused. The throne seems to have melted and flowed."

"The amount of energy was significant. Only a master of the Seven Laws could have set such a trap," Greenup said.

"Or a master of the Nine," Sillik said.

"We will search the keep and make sure there are no more surprises," Kenton said as he motioned to several other Gold Robes.

"If it was a trap, was it supposed to fail?" Sillik asked. "What about those men who attacked me on the way in to the city? What in the nine hells is happening?"

"What men? What attack?" the Hornsmasher asked as he pushed his way into the group. "Hornsmasher" was the hereditary title given to one of the battle lords of Illicia. He had taught battle theory to Sillik and his brothers before being promoted to battle lord. Previously, he had been called Elerson.

"That is going to take some time to explain," Greenup said sadly as he shook his head. "And you must tell us about this attack."

Kenton forced himself to smile. "With your warning, at least we were able to protect everyone else." He turned for a moment to talk to the Gold Robes who had approached him and then turned back to Sillik. "The throne room is safe," he announced. "My people will search the rest of the keep now."

Greenup rubbed his head. "We will let everyone else in now. We have work to do."

Sillik nodded. *Whoever set this trap knows it failed, and they will be warned. Will the assassins be more cautious in their next attempt or even bolder? I didn't reveal anything about my abilities, but I survived, which tells them something. Was the trap supposed to fail? What about the attack on the mountain? Was that also a warning?*

"As I was coming down Soul Crusher, brigands attacked me. Or that's what I thought they were. There were three. I killed them. But they had a pigeon. When I let it go, it flew toward Illicia."

Greenup frowned. "We will retrieve the bodies. Perhaps that will tell us something."

"No," Sillik said, "there is nothing left. The sandfish got two, and one was incinerated."

"Ah," Kenton said, "that is unfortunate."

The Hornsmasher laughed. "Bloody hells, boy. Don't apologize. We taught you well. It's only unfortunate for the dead."

Greenup's frown deepened. "We might have learned something."

"Not likely," Kenton said with a grimace. "Our enemies have planned well."

Greenup nodded. "Aye, that they have. Kenton, can I have a word?" the lord general asked as he, Kenton, and the Hornsmasher stepped away.

Sillik turned to watch the city's nobility and leadership enter the throne room. They stared at the ruined throne. He heard widespread cursing and muttering from those who had not felt the widespread release of energy.

Lord Grison of the Gold Robes strode over to Sillik. Grison, a large man with puffy cheeks, had been Sillik's first instructor in the Seven Laws. "Sillik, my boy, good to see you. Terrible shame about your family, I must say. You look well enough–bit thin and tired, but good."

"Thank you, Master Grison," Sillik said politely as he tried to watch the room.

"No need to call me master anymore, boy," Grison said with a fond smile. "You and I both know my days of teaching you are long past."

"Then Grison," Sillik said with a smile. "Thank you for your concern. But if you will excuse me ..." *Grison will talk my ear off if I don't get away*, Sillik thought, *and he won't say a damn thing of any import.* Sillik turned and found Briana.

Briana had quickly summoned troops and additional guards with the silent Illician battle language. Gold Robes flowed into the room and raised magical shields around everyone assembled.

When Briana paused, Sillik approached her and opened his arms for a familiar hug. To his surprise, she merely curtsied. "My prince, welcome home. I wish it was under happier circumstances."

Surprised, Sillik dropped his arms. "I have missed you, Briana. It has been a long time."

Briana looked around and grimaced. "Indeed it has, my lord. Much has changed."

Sillik studied Briana for a moment. She was a beautiful woman, but she also had a sharp tongue and a fiery temper. She had never wasted time painting her face or styling her hair, but she seemed different now, harder, wound tight as a spring. Sillik frowned with concern as she moved off to coordinate security. He watched her for a few more moments and then shook his head. Much had changed.

The Hornsmasher moved close to Sillik. "A fiery woman, that one," the man said with a nod at Briana. "A man could do worse than her." He smiled. "If you are interested, I could help you negotiate." His voice trailed off, and he grinned again.

Surprised, Sillik looked at the man. "Thank you, Elerson, but not today."

"Ah, I understand, my friend. I am getting ready to arrange a marriage for my son," he said proudly as he stepped closer conspiratorially. "The wench is a Gold Robe student. It will be a grand match: the Hornsmasher's son and a future Gold Robe. My son is a major in the guard now. Who knows? Someday he might succeed me. A grand match. And who knows? The girl might even be a future Speaker." He smiled proudly as he rocked on his heels. "A grand match."

"I am happy for you," Sillik said distractedly. "My best wishes to the happy couple. But please excuse me," he said as he moved to watch the Gold Robes examining the throne.

The Gold Robes had moved toward the throne cautiously and were probing and trying to tease out the remains of the trap. Trying to disguise his interest, Sillik leaned against one of the pillars behind the throne as a dozen soldiers surrounded him; he knew Briana had personally chosen the men to protect him. He recognized them, but for the moment, he chose to ignore them.

Sensing motion at the entrance, he turned his head slightly to see five Illician battle lords marching into the room in precise formation. Their feet stepped in perfect unison. Lord General Greenup was their chief and the seventh battle lord. The Hornsmasher was Greenup's second and the sixth battle lord. These men and women were the reason for the city's military prowess. Standing proudly with straight backs, they arrayed themselves in a semicircle facing the throne. The five wore their battle armor and carried their helmets under their left arms, their right hands tucked behind their backs. Their eyes never stopped on the same spot for more than a moment, and yet Sillik felt like they were watching his every movement. They were always watching and weighing. Sillik smiled as he recalled the battle lord's oath of office.

*To oppose the Nine*
*To fight the darkness*
*To support the Seven Gods*
*To fight for the light*
*To never surrender*

*I could have been a battle lord,* he thought. Sillik had been given that choice; they had offered him a chance to don the black armor. There had been an open shield. One chance—that was all anyone got, battle lord or Gold Robe. *My father would have liked either choice,* he thought. *My brothers didn't like either one. Neither did I. And now I will be king—if I survive.*

As Sillik looked around the throne room, it was like he had never left. The tomb of Rendarick, the city's founder, dominated the floor to his left. Statues of the Seven Gods stood against the walls. The likenesses were amazingly accurate. During the eighteen years he had lived in the city, the Seven Gods, or at least some of them, had appeared occasionally. At least one of the gods had turned up at Founding Day every year since the city's founding to celebrate the city's anniversary.

*Father always said he talked to the Seven Gods on occasion. No one ever believed him,* Sillik thought as he looked at the statues. *No one will believe me either.*

Sillik's father said that all seven of the gods had appeared above his mother's birthing bed the moment that Sillik was born and she died. Sillik remembered his father saying that the Seven Gods had come to welcome his mother to the afterlife. His mother, Jenna, had been a powerful master of the Seven Laws.

Others whispered that the Seven Gods had come to witness the birth of the true king of Illicia. This was just one of the things for which Sillik's older brothers had hated him. Sillik smiled ruefully to himself. *I would like to be free of the gods.*

Turning his head, Sillik regarded the skeleton of the schula to the left of the doorway. It was a relic from the demon wars before the founding of Illicia. The creature, twice the height of a man, had six arms, a large snout, and long, curved teeth. A living schula had not been seen since the end of the demon wars. Four long, curved swords and two long daggers were nestled in its arms. Every Illician warrior was required to study how to fight the beasts. The scrolls said it wasn't easy to kill a schula, but the skeleton on the wall was a clear sign that it was possible.

After she had overseen additional guards, Briana stood between Sillik and the throne, her hand on her sword and her green skirt swirling between her legs as she looked around in anger. Her long, dusty-brown hair flew wildly as she turned. Power and energies crackled in the dry air around her. Her fingers flashed battle commands. Sillik looked around again in concern. Not even she could protect him from what had already happened.

"It was not that way when we closed the keep," Briana said. "By the Seven, what happened?" She did not wait for an answer. "Come with me."

Sillik started to refuse but then succumbed to her demand.

In a small room behind the throne, she pushed a handful of clothes at him. "Change into these, and listen to me. We don't have much time."

Sillik glanced down at the bundle of clothing in his arms. Then he started to remove his cloak. In the bundle of clothing, Sillik found clothes suitable for formal court. Black pants and black polished boots were wrapped in a black silk shirt and a dark green, thigh-length formal coat.

"I had to guess your sizes," Briana said, turning to face the door as Sillik removed his clothing. She bit her lip in worry at what she had to say next. "Sillik, your father and brothers are dead."

Sillik took a deep breath at the suddenness of her confirmation. When he started to speak, she interrupted.

"Wait," she said. "There are things you must understand. Your cousins and uncles are causing problems. You uncles say that they don't want the throne, but they have blocked every move the city council has tried to make. Chaos reigns. Your cousins have all said they do want the throne and are also plotting against everyone, perhaps even their own fathers. Fortunately, your cousins are not on the council, so their power is somewhat limited."

Groaning, Sillik struggled to take his boots off. With his father and brothers dead and Sillik missing, his uncle Melin would have been next in line for the crown. Illician law required the passage of a year and a day from his father's death before Sillik could be declared missing and his uncle crowned. *They will be disappointed that I have come home, but what have I come home to?*

Briana smiled. "I knew you would come back."

Sillik noticed that she didn't say how she knew that, but he let that pass for the moment.

"Your uncles may not want the crown, exactly, but they are siding with different factions of the city, and they do want to be the power behind the winning faction. Things have almost reached the point of civil war." Briana paused and took a breath. "They will want to control you and lock you into whatever is best for them. Also, they would not be upset if an accident were to happen to you. You must be prepared."

"What are the factions?" Sillik asked.

Briana frowned and bit her lip for a moment. "The Gold Robes and the soldiers are somewhat aligned. The guilds have been at odds with everyone over the taxes the council passed last year. The trades seem to keep shifting alliances. We think your uncles are helping the business professions. Everything is causing either stalemates or chaos. Fights have occurred, and people have died. Another complication is the old prophesy of the end of times. Some on the council are using that as a reason to do nothing. The royal council is deadlocked. It would have been open war if we hadn't known when you would return."

Sillik looked up in surprise, but Briana kept talking. *How could they have known?*

Briana turned back to face Sillik. "The council will crown you tonight if you let them."

"No crown, not tonight," Sillik said as his mind staggered. "I need time to sort this out, and I don't need a crown to complicate matters." He buttoned his shirt over his mail.

Briana nodded. "Exactly what I thought you would say. We have planned tonight carefully. Kenton will name you crown prince. You will take everyone's oaths. You do remember the words?" She waited until he nodded. "Good. Say as little as possible, and close court as quickly as you can. There will be time to talk later."

"Can you tell me what happened?" Sillik asked as he pulled the new boots on, grimacing at the tight fit. "You know, to my family?"

"Yes," Briana said, glancing out the door. "Not now, though. They are almost ready for you." She looked back at Sillik and frowned. "When this is over, I will tell you everything I know."

Sillik nodded and then reached for the coat that Briana held up. The Illician eagle was stitched in gold on the chest, and the sleeves were embroidered with gold to proclaim his mastery of the Seven Laws. His clothing was appropriate for solemn mourning and strangely matched his mood. For the sake of ceremony, he would leave his sword in his room, but he did tuck his throwing knives and dagger beneath the coat.

Briana paused before she led him out. "Why did you come in over Soul Crusher? There are easier ways. We had men waiting at all of the checkpoints. It would have been less work to follow the main roads."

Sillik grinned. "I have always enjoyed the view of Illicia from Soul Crusher. I didn't want any special treatment. Last, I wasn't sure what I was walking into."

"But we had chairs to run you into the city."

Sillik frowned. "So I can be a caged pet on display? No, thank you. I prefer my own two feet."

"I will see that everything else is taken to your rooms," Briana said, casting a disdainful look at the clothing and gear Sillik had discarded. "One more thing," she said as she turned to the small table.

For a moment, Sillik's view was blocked, but when she turned back to him, she was holding a crown. Sillik recognized it as the one he had worn during his last appearance at court. "I was told to have this ready for you," she said quietly. "I can tell you about it later."

The crown was gold with seven eagles chasing each other. Their wings made triangular points that reached up to the heavens. Each eagle's beak was locked onto the tail feathers of the eagle ahead of it, symbolizing the united forces of law. Their talons carried swords, inkwells, quills, scales, blindfolds, books, and scrolls. These talismans represented the tools of law. Sillik's father had commissioned the crown when Sillik turned fifteen.

Sillik blinked at the crown. It was a princely crown and clearly not the king's. After a moment, he set it upon his head. A whoosh of dizziness hit him, but he recovered quickly. His head, which had started to pound, was suddenly clear. He touched the crown and felt a magical whisper that faded quickly. "Who has touched this crown?" he asked as he ran his fingers over the gold.

"I found it in your father's rooms. It was clean. Kenton and I both examined it." Suddenly concerned, she looked at him intently. "Why? Did we miss something?"

Sillik smiled. "It is nothing." *What did I feel?* he wondered. *What did my father do to the crown?*

Briana frowned and put her hands on her hips. "You are smiling. That is your tell. You are worried and trying not to show it. Did the crown have magic that we missed?"

"Of course, I'm worried," Sillik said, ignoring Briana's question. "My family is dead, and I don't know why. But I can't let everyone know I'm worried, can I? I must be the confident image of a crown prince." Memories of the lectures that he had received from Lord Norsen during his youth danced in his head. The man had breathed leadership.

"You can confide in me," Briana whispered. "Did we–did *I*–miss something?"

"Something felt like a momentary whisper or a touch of a feather. It is nothing. My head feels better already," Sillik said, grinning. There were many ways to hide magic. His father had been an expert in subterfuge. He'd had too many damn secrets.

Briana eyed him sideways as she considered his words. "You and your headaches," she said dubiously. Then she smiled. "I am glad you are home." To Sillik's surprise she threw her arms around him and hugged him tight.

Sillik returned the hug. When he felt her grip loosen, he let go, and she stepped away, blushing. Suddenly uncomfortable and confused, Sillik looked away.

"I may have overstepped myself," Briana said quietly.

Sillik nodded, but when Briana looked away, his smile faded. The whisper had reminded him of his father. *How strange. What magic could my father have left that Briana and Kenton could not discover? There's magic, and then there is* magic. *Could my father have left something for me in plain sight? Was it a father's love or a royal endowment?* There were subtleties to magic. Some magic could be felt or seen only by the intended recipient.

"Now remember," Briana was saying when he returned his attention to her, "say as little as you can. You don't know the factions yet, and saying too much to any of the factions could embolden them."

Sillik grinned. "Almost feels like old times, conspiring with you." He stretched and felt the clothing bind him. "You guessed right on the sizes. Just a little tight."

Briana's face turned slightly red. "It will have to do. Hopefully, you won't have to fight in it." Briana brushed some lint off the coat. "The coat was your father's. Don't ask where the rest came from." She smiled mysteriously. "Be alert. Oh, I should also tell you that a day of celebration has been declared for tomorrow. There will be a formal feast to celebrate your return tomorrow night. Your council thought it would be a nice touch."

Sillik gave Briana a puzzled look as she led him back to the throne room. How had there been time to plan a feast for his return?

"I will watch your back," she whispered as she kissed his cheek. With that, she stopped to speak to a guard and left Sillik to himself.

Half of the guards eyed Sillik with a mixture of pity and fear. The others wouldn't meet his gaze, preferring instead to focus on what they were supposed to be doing. Sillik felt vaguely out of place as he wandered back into the throne room. He had been away for too many years, and he had never enjoyed court.

Sillik could tell that the men nearest him were alert and watching. Briana had chosen well. The guards leaned forward slightly on the balls of their feet. They reminded him of panthers, coiled and ready to pounce. Their hands were on their weapons. Determination did not seem to describe the intensity with which they surveyed the room.

Lord Kenton hurried over, his tripointed gold hat in hand. He wore a gold square outlined in black on his chest, which symbolized the boxes the first speakers had stood upon when they spoke. Normally, the Speaker of the Gold Robes was an ancient man or woman, and the position was merely symbolic. The fact that Lord Kenton had been elected to the position meant more senior people had been passed over. The political maneuvering and infighting must have been intense for Lord Kenton to reach so high an office. Sillik smiled grimly as he realized his election could also mean that the Gold Robes knew something unusual was happening and had intentionally chosen younger leadership to help deal with the crisis.

"Your Royal Highness," Kenton said in a smooth and polished tone, followed by a formal bow. "Thank the Seven Gods that you have returned safe to Illicia."

Sillik grinned. "How's your family?" He decided against saying anything about his own family.

Kenton grinned with fatherly pride. "Alexis is ready for her master's test, and Kendra is nearing the end of her studies. Alexis has already decided to stay in the Gold Tower. They are here somewhere. Elizabet is also here," he said as he looked around quickly for his wife, who was a Gold Robe healer. "She wears the gold hand now."

"Congratulations," Sillik said. "You must be very happy. Two more masters. I knew your daughters were extraordinary. Alexis will be a good Speaker someday, or perhaps they'll be Co-Speakers?" He grinned. "It has happened before. And Elizabet wearing the gold hand, the leader of the healers—congratulations to her as well."

Kenton nodded with a pleased expression.

Behind Kenton, Sillik saw another familiar face and acknowledged her with a quick nod. He was pleased to see that Viktorie was now the sentinel of the Gold Robes. She wore a gold sword pin, the symbol of her office, at her collar. She returned his smile and nodded formally.

Viktorie was a compact, lean, almost stern woman. She was of Nomadic descent; hence, her skin was a deep brown. Once, her straight hair had been a brilliant black. Now it was muted with streaks of gray. Like most women who wore the gold robes, she also wore a hooped earring in the top of her left ear. A slender gold chain connected the earring to a delicate ring in her nose. Diamonds tattooed on either side of her forehead emphasized the Nomadic tradition into which she had been born. Her robes hung to the floor, where the tips of her black slippers peaked out.

Viktorie didn't need to carry weapons. She was a weapon. As one of the most powerful masters of the Seven Laws in the city, she had a duty to protect the Speaker. The pin at her collar also meant she was second in command of the Gold Robes.

When Sillik had begun his studies of the Seven Laws, she was his watcher. The watcher's function was to mentor new students and make sure they didn't do anything stupid, although it was almost expected that they would do something risky at some point.

The Gold Robes had many divisions within their ranks, and the alliances between the sects had always been fragile, like sand in the wind, always seeking a new pattern. The four sects were the soldiers, the rule makers, the preachers, and the healers. The soldiers were trained in combat as well as the Seven Laws. The rule makers were the teachers and judges; they were the smallest sect but also the most powerful. The healers said they healed the messes created by the other sects. And the preachers taught about the Seven Gods and tried to be neutral in the affairs of the other three sects. Lord Kenton and Viktorie had come from the soldiers' sect, but Kenton's wife Elizabet was a healer.

"Lord Kenton," Sillik said as the two men stepped back, "what did you learn?"

Kenton glanced at Briana before he spoke, anger infusing every word. "Probably no more than you, my lord. It was a trap and a warning to the spell-caster. Now he—or she—knows you are here and has a good idea of your strengths."

Sillik nodded and adjusted his coat as he tried to appear calm.

Kenton continued. "I was worried for your safety. The trap was not here when we left the keep yesterday, and since then the keep has been guarded. I have failed you, my lord, in many ways." Lord Kenton's head hung with shame, and his posture was that of a defeated man walking to the gallows. "I couldn't cleanse the aftereffects of your father's final battle. You should exile me for my failings."

"Nonsense," Sillik said. "Do you know who set the trap?"

An almost musical voice answered, "Not yet, but if I know my husband, we will." Elizabet approached wearing the customary gold robe with a dark blue hem. Her naturally curly black hair was tied behind her head. Her eyes were almost the same color as the hem of her robe. She joked that her sect had been chosen for her at birth. Her earring was gold, and a delicate golden hand dangled from the chain. The healing hand was another symbol of her sect.

Sillik smelled the perfumes of Elizabet and the two women who approached alongside her. The delicate scent of flowers hung in the air. *Purple flowers*, Sillik thought. *Lilacs perhaps? I've never been good with flowers.*

Kenton smiled proudly. "Elizabet leads the healers as of last week."

Elizabet grinned. "Don't talk about me," Elizabet said. "Our prince will want to know about his family. You remember Rebecca and Claudett, of course?"

"Well, we want to know what he has been doing," said a buxom woman with flame-red hair who was standing beside Elizabet.

Elizabet turned to her. "Rebecca, shush."

Sillik grinned in surprise at the women. Rebecca's robes were trimmed with blue, like the robes of all healers. At her waist was a curved black knife. She was the only healer Sillik knew who carried a visible weapon. A blood-red emerald hung from an earring in her right ear. Rebecca was about ten years older than Sillik and had been Elizabet's apprentice and then her assistant. She wore the healing hand on a stickpin near the collar of her dress. Mines a short distance from Illicia were the world's only source of red emeralds. The stones were extremely rare and expensive. Rebecca's family was one of the oldest jewelry families in the city and produced the largest number of emeralds each year.

Claudett, who was a dozen years older than Sillik, was another healer he remembered from his youth. She wore the gold rings in her ear and had two chains. From each chain dangled a small diamond set in a blue hand. Her robes were tight with a plunging neckline, which emphasized her figure. Her specialty was poisons and toxins and the healing associated with them. Her gray-blonde hair fell in golden curls that almost matched her gold robes. Tonight, her blue eyes sparkled with laughter. Her face was square and sturdy. No one would ever describe her as beautiful, but she wasn't ugly. Like many women in the Gold Tower, she had never married.

Sillik smiled and took Elizabet's hand to kiss it, but she brushed it aside and enveloped him in a hug. "We have missed you, Sillik," she said warmly as she held him. "I am so sorry about your family. If we can help in any way, just say the word."

When she released him, Sillik took a deep breath. "Thank you, my lady," he said, his face somber. "Lord Kenton, you were saying …"

Before the Speaker could answer, Rebecca too gave Sillik a bone-crushing hug and a kiss on the cheek. In turn, Claudett also gave him a hug and a kiss on the cheek.

"All of my favorite women," Sillik said with a tired smile.

"He should have a wife of his own now. We must be his second-favorite women," Rebecca said as she laughed.

"Hush," Claudett said with a grimace. "The man is scarcely home, and you go talking wives. Do you want to scare him away? We need to know what happened and why."

"We do not know who did this or how," Kenton said as he glanced nervously at the nearly melted throne, "but we do know who did the rest, my lord. We–"

"We'll discuss it soon enough, I fear," Sillik said. "If you know who killed my family, then you have not failed me. But for now, we have court to hold."

Sillik saw his uncles approaching and groaned quietly.

"I can't protect you from them," Briana whispered as she eyed the men.

"I know," Sillik said, "although I wish you could."

"How bad can it be?" Briana asked.

"Bad," Sillik said in a low voice. Then his face brightened. "Uncles, so nice to see you tonight."

"Spare us the platitudes," Melin said. He curled his lip at Sillik's companions. "The rest of you can leave. We wish to talk to our nephew–prince to prince, you understand."

Surprise flickered across Elizabet and Rebecca's faces. "By your leave, my prince," Kenton mumbled, and then he backed away, deep in thought.

"I am not leaving," Briana said, her eyes like glowing embers.

Melin glared at the swordmaster. "Suit yourself."

Elizabet said nothing for a long moment as she looked at the two elderly princes. "Healers go where they are needed, and none may impede their progress," she said sagely. Then she turned her head to take a long look at Sillik as if appraising him. He discerned worry in Elizabet's expression before she hurried off into the crowd, escorted by Rebecca.

Noswin's face barely concealed his rage. "We had to bury our brother because of you," he said, jabbing his finger at Sillik.

Surprised, Sillik glanced at Briana, who shrugged. "How am I responsible?" he asked.

Melin's mouth compressed into a sneer. "You weren't here to protect him. Before Edwin–the best swordmaster this city has ever seen–died, he told me that options were going to be presented to you," Melin said, with a noticeable jab at Briana.

She stiffened at the mention of her predecessor, but Sillik waved her to silence.

"You could have been a damned Gold Robe," Noswin said, "or the gods knows what. But you couldn't take the pressure of being a prince, and so you ran away."

"I thought you didn't approve of the Gold Robes, Uncle," Sillik said quietly as he felt his anger rising. He glanced at Briana, who was still struggling to hold her anger in check.

"I never approved of half the things you did, boy–seeing you run away least of all," Melin retorted. "But if those Seven Laws of yours would have saved my brother or your brothers, then maybe it has a place."

"How gracious of you after all these years," Sillik said.

"You should never have left," Noswin said. "Your brothers would have been fine kings. They didn't need any of that magic nonsense."

Sillik felt his anger surge as he struggled with a hot response.

Noswin's eyes narrowed. "Hell, you could have been court jester for all I care, but it was your duty to protect your king, and you failed, boy. You failed. If your magic nonsense would have protected our brother, then maybe it would have had value. But no, you had to be noble and leave to become a vagabond. Mark my words, boy: people remember cowardice, and you are a coward."

Sillik looked at his uncles, amazed. He couldn't even begin to defend himself against such insanity. It had not been cowardice. He had received his father's blessing to leave.

Melin snorted. "Now you are the court jester; you just aren't smart enough to know it. Hell, it's been centuries since we've had a real jester. It's going to be fun watching you flop around like a sandfish on stone. We are just going to watch and laugh at Prince Sillik, the court jester."

"In case you forgot, nephew, sandfish don't survive long when they get trapped on stone," Noswin said, his mouth tight with anger. "The vultures come, and they wait till the sandfish is tired. Then they peck out its eyes. Then they—"

"So you are going to be the vultures who feed on your nephew?" Briana asked. Her hand gripped her sword so hard that her knuckles were white.

Noswin laughed. "Not us. But someone is clearly after Illician kings."

"If something happens to Sillik—"

"Then you will be dead, my dear," Melin said. "Remember, I am next in line to the throne, and if my dear nephew does not survive, my first action as king will be to exact the king's justice for the killing of Edwin, the former swordmaster of Illicia, on the current swordmaster. And it will be done slowly …"

Briana bristled, her face full of fury.

"Briana did not kill Edwin," Sillik said as he put his hand on her arm to calm her. "He killed himself."

"She humiliated our friend," Noswin said as spittle leaked out of his mouth. "She took away his pride and forced him to drink. Then she did, in fact, kill him."

"He picked up that bottle himself," Sillik said. "As for his death, your brother absolved her of that. Edwin took that girl hostage. Any one of us would have killed him for that. I would have done it, but Briana was the only one who had the throw. It's unfortunate, but it was necessary to save the girl's life."

"Believe what you will," Noswin said. "I know what's true." With that, Noswin took his brother's arm and led him away.

While Sillik watched them, Kenton moved toward him, his eyes following Noswin and Melin. He looked at Sillik with a worried expression and fingered his chin thoughtfully. "Trouble, my prince?"

"They are acting strangely," Sillik said. "I can't put my knife on it, but I will. As much as it pains me, I might have to spend more time with them, if I can get over the revulsion that I feel for them."

Kenton nodded. "My spies tell me Melin has been making promises about what he would do if he received the crown—repay old debts and promote his cronies, by the sound of it. But at the same time, he says he doesn't want it."

"I can imagine," Briana said dryly.

Kenton shook his head. "No, my dear, you can't or shouldn't."

"Promise me," Sillik said, turning to Briana. "At the first rumor of my death, you will flee. You must get away from them."

Briana smiled. "Don't worry about me, my friend. I have plans and plans."

"There are people, friends of mine," Sillik said.

Briana smiled mysteriously. "Do not fear. I have no intention of being taken by those two. Also, we questioned your uncles after your brothers were killed. Now, Speaker Kenton, are we ready to begin?"

Kenton nodded.

Without a backward glance, Sillik stood before the throne and faced the crowd. He was amazed at all of the people arrayed around the great room. The balconies were full. The generals, majors, and captains of the city stood on his right in front. The warriors stood in ordered rows behind their leaders, with further ordered rows of people in rank behind them. On the left, the Gold Robes quietly watched the proceedings in scattered groups. A contingent of three rule makers stood in a small knot near the back of the room. All of the sects were represented and tended to clump together. The polished marble made the room seem cold. The statues of the Seven Gods seemed to be looking right at him. Sillik suppressed a shiver. He was standing in his father's place.

At least a thousand members of the guard stood quietly in rows around the perimeter of the room. All wore green and black. The golden eagle of Illicia was displayed proudly on their polished, conical helmets, yet Sillik was nervous. Any one of them could be an assassin. All of the guards were armed, as was customary. Illicia had never been a city where the monarchs were afraid to have armed soldiers around them. The guards carried a variety of weapons. Those nearest the doors carried pikes. Dozens of archers stood in the balconies, arrows nocked and ready to fly at the first sign of trouble. All carried swords, daggers, and other sharp instruments. Sillik saw the stripes and curls on their sleeves that indicated their mastery of the Seven Laws or portions thereof.

Lord Kenton stepped forward and spoke in a magically amplified voice. "In the beginning, the Lords of Law created men and women and animals. Some were given the gift of magic, and some were not. In the darkness of night, the Lords of Chaos warped creation and gave each the ability to choose goodness or evil. So says the First Book of Law. Lord King Rendarick, our founder, established this city to be the keeper of the Light. Today we come together to recognize Prince Sillik as crown prince and establish his direct lineage to King Rendarick. So we shall now pray."

Lord Kenton led the traditional prayers to the Seven Gods. The audience recited the rote responses and concluded with the traditional seven bows to the throne. Sillik remembered participating in prayers seven times a day in the Gold Tower. As Speaker of the Gold Robes, Lord Kenton would normally lead the first prayers of the day at Primus, before the sun was above the horizon.

The familiarity of the prayers had a calming effect on Sillik. He took a deep, cleansing breath and settled into a momentary trance. As the prayers neared an end, he looked at the rectangular stone in the floor that marked the tomb of Rendarick, the city's founder. No one would stand on that stone. The stone was not engraved or decorated, but the lack of wear made it stand out. All other Illician kings were buried in the catacombs beneath the city.

Sillik glanced at the wall above the tomb and smiled grimly. The dagger that had killed Rendarick was still where it had been placed thousands of years earlier. It served as a reminder to every king of Illicia. *We are mortal*, Sillik thought. Above the dagger was the schula's skeleton, just one of the creatures from the nine hells that Rendarick had fought against in the demon wars.

As Sillik surveyed the crowd, soldiers, Gold Robes, officers, advisors, and his uncles and cousins stood as if waiting for something. *They are waiting for me to fall over dead*, Sillik thought. *At least some of them are. I wonder how many?* He saw expressions ranging from worship to cunning calculation. Even now, some were considering how to influence events in their favor. Power attracted all sorts. Sillik searched for something out of the ordinary, any sign that the assassin would strike again. An arrow could strike him dead in an instant. A spell might be able to kill him just as easily.

Sillik wrapped his magical protections tighter around himself and poured more energy into them. Casual observers could now see flickers of the tightly wrapped energies around him. To those with training, he would be glowing with power. The Gold Robes frowned in disapproval, but several of the generals nodded and smiled. The Gold Robes had never approved of public displays of power.

Lord General Greenup stepped forward and inclined his head in greeting. He was a mountain of a man, tall and heavily muscled. Gray flecks were scattered through his hair. His face could have been carved from stone. He had been a lord general of Illicia for almost thirty-five years. The sword he wore at his waist was large. Most men considered it a two-handed weapon, but Greenup used only one. His was the highest-ranking military position in Illicia. Greenup had served Sillik's father and grandfather and had been a friend and advisor to Sillik.

Greenup and Lord Kenton quickly pronounced Sillik crown prince of Illicia. Then, on bended knee, they swore allegiance to him. Sillik took their hands as they repeated the traditional oaths. While they touched hands, he used every trick to read the truth in their words. He could feel their heartbeats and the perspiration on their hands. They didn't flinch or try to pull away. Sillik trusted these men as well as anyone, and yet he was anxious. They couldn't lie to him at this moment when they were at their weakest and he was practically glowing with power. When he released their hands, they bowed deeply and then took their places on either side of him.

Then, with little ceremony, Sillik climbed the steps and sat on the royal throne—or what was left of it. He looked at Briana, and she nodded. In her opinion at least, he had done the right thing. Others would have expected him to sit in the chair beside the throne. *To hell with their expectations*, he thought grimly. *I might not wear the king's crown, but I am going to act like I do.*

As Sillik sat on the nearly blasted throne, he shuddered at the implications. He had never imagined such a situation; his brothers and father were dead, apparently by an assassin's hand, and he himself had barely survived a subtle trap. There were traitors in Illicia. He could trust few if any. The challenge had been given. The honor of his people was at stake. He would have to find the assassin and kill him for Illicia's people to accept him as their sovereign.

# CHAPTER 3

## Allegiances

SILLIK RAN HIS hand over the precious gems melted into the arms of the throne and looked up at the eagle's head that had always sheltered the throne. Above his head, the oil lamps burned wildly, their flames tossed by the wind blowing in from outside. A storm was brewing; he could smell the sand in the air. In his mind, Sillik pictured the peasants closing the wind traps to prevent sand from clogging them. Windows would be shuttered, and tarps and awnings would be rolled up and taken inside.

Briana knelt in front of Sillik and swore the oath of fealty. After he repeated the oath, Briana rose and moved to his right and behind the throne. Because she was swordmaster of Illicia, it was her place to stand behind the king.

From that point on, Sillik simply endured the parade of generals, masters of the Seven Laws, and lords who presented themselves and spoke the oaths. Sillik knew most of the people, and he recognized many more. He seethed quietly at the time this took. He had never enjoyed formal court. Today was different from most courtly events, though. This level of activity happened only when a new monarch took the throne.

Sillik masked his emotions with difficulty. He spoke a few words with the people he remembered and accepted condolences from all who spoke them. Many people had changed while he was away, some of them aging considerably. Briana supplied the name and position for every person who knelt before Sillik. Normally, one of his father's advisors would have fulfilled this duty, but Sillik sensed that Briana didn't want anyone else closer to him than was necessary. He was grateful for her memory and support. He would have made dozens of mistakes had it not been for her. A few of the people he had expected were not present, and he supposed they had died. He would have to ask about them later. Sillik knew these people would crown him right here and now if he requested it, but he wouldn't. Illicia was desperate and badly shaken. He had to find those responsible and prove himself worthy first.

The keep was closed to all but soldiers and royal advisors. A few trusted cooks and scribes were the only exceptions. Everything would be run as if the city were under siege. Even more members of the guard were sent to line the walls around the keep. Dozens more were on top of the towers, and hundreds of guards patrolled the city. More guards occupied every level of the royal keep. The Gold Robes had lit the torches lining the walls of the throne room and the great oil lanterns hanging overhead, so there were no shadows in which an assassin could hide tonight. Yet the assassins had breached similar security measures not once but four separate times. He would take no chances, which was why his magical defenses continued to shroud him in layers. Overwhelming displays of force had always worked for Illicia in the past.

When the last of the oaths had been exchanged, Sillik stood and surveyed the silent crowd. "We are adjourned," he said in a loud voice. Without another word, he turned and left, with Briana following at his heels.

Briana had always been a close friend. She was three years older than Sillik and had been marked out from an early age due to her skill with the sword. She had a fiery temper and could explode if provoked. She had also mastered the Seven Laws shortly before Sillik, which had propelled her into the highest levels of Illician leadership. To be both a blade master and a master of the Seven Laws was unusual under any circumstances. Shortly after becoming a master, and after challenging and defeating the previous holder of the position, she had been named swordmaster of Illicia. In addition, she had a bit of royal blood, and a king's interest and patronage had not hurt either. She was next in succession after Melin's and Noswin's branches of the family.

As he walked, he saw Briana's smile out of the corner of his eye. He knew she was relieved that nothing else had happened. Sillik frowned. She wouldn't be smiling in a few minutes. She was commander of the king's guard, and it was her responsibility to protect the king. Sillik knew the conversation wouldn't be pleasant.

To Sillik's displeasure, he noticed that he had acquired an escort of warriors. His new circumstances meant that he would never truly be alone again except in his own rooms. Everywhere he went, he would be followed, protected, and watched. He hated it already. He remembered the feeling of being a prince, like he lived in a gilded cage. *It will be even worse now.*

Kenton and Greenup moved to follow him, but to their disappointment, he waved them off. "We will speak later," he said.

Without pausing, Sillik took the stairs up to his rooms two at a time. He heard Briana hurrying behind him. The guards saluted as he passed. Sillik nodded as he continued to climb without pause. The guards also followed, struggling to keep up. As Sillik climbed, he felt the shields and other protective measures of the keep wrapped tightly around him. His arsenal of weapons was ready, and energies licked the length of his sword.

The long stairs spiraled upward into the darkness. Later in the evening, the Gold Robes would relight the glow balls. Ten men could stand abreast on the lowest step, but the steps narrowed the higher he went. The staircase was lined with tapestries and statues depicting famous figures from Illician history. A statue of Rendarick had watched Sillik from his place of honor at the foot of the stairs. Sillik always felt that the eyes of the statue followed him as he climbed the stairs, and tonight was no exception. Sillik smiled. Upon mastering the Seven Laws, he had learned the secret to those eyes. Being a prince had some advantages.

At each landing, doorways beckoned. The doors led to offices, guard dormitories, storerooms, kitchens, armories, and many other rooms necessary to run an empire. Sillik knew the keep like the back of his hand. Tonight, he didn't stop at any of these places; he merely climbed the stairs in silence. What would he find at the top?

Briana tried to initiate several conversations on the way, but Sillik ignored her. She was eager to explain what had happened, but he wanted time to compose himself before he heard the brutal truth and had to ask the hard questions.

When they arrived on the top floor of the keep, Sillik led them past his old childhood room with its paintings of the founding of the city and the heads of the wolves he had slain. Then he led Briana past his half brothers' rooms and finally to his father's room, which would now be his. At the doorway, he paused and looked around.

A full complement of guards had followed Sillik and Briana to the top of the stairs. They took up their positions a discreet distance away. A dozen more guards had already been waiting uneasily for him. Sillik could feel the source of their uneasiness. The energies from the duel still whispered discord. Fierce energies had been flung across the room and had eventually slain his father. The walls bore the scars of the battle. Burned tapestries and melted stone showed how fierce the fight had been. No wonder his father had tried to summon him.

A full master of the Seven Laws had challenged his father. From the strength of the residual power, his mastery must have been complete. Sillik's father had been a master, but he wouldn't have stood a chance against an opponent like the one he had faced. Of his brothers, Rendar was the only one apart from Sillik who had even studied the Seven Laws. Unfortunately, Rendar had never mastered them. Crinthan had concentrated on weapons, and Doran had studied nothing for very long except women.

Sillik closed his eyes and opened his mind to the traces of dark magic that lingered behind. The Gold Robes had likely tried the same spell he was about to use, but they had failed. Why? Sillik embraced his magic and laid the cleansing spell over the discordant traces of dark magic. When he found what was anchoring it, he was surprised and nearly lost his focus. When his spell had done its work, Sillik opened his eyes. Exhaustion tried to demand his attention, but he ignored it. He had to find out who had slain his father and why. But at least now he knew why Kenton had failed.

Briana gave Sillik a questioning look. She had felt the magic and the cleansing. Sillik was sure she was wondering how he had done what teams of Gold Robes had failed to accomplish. Her eyes narrowed as she evaluated the situation again. Clearly, she noticed the change in him.

Sillik ushered Briana into his new rooms. He smiled. The servants were efficient. A skin of wine and a platter of grilled sandfish were on a table against the wall.

Briana looked at the burned tapestries with distaste. "We left them up so you could see the effects of the battle. I will have Nisha replace them."

Sillik started to say something but then simply nodded. He remembered Nisha. She had been his father's household steward. She was a stern and proper woman with no sense of humor. "Has she learned to smile yet?"

Briana shook her head. "No, never."

Sillik frowned as he looked around the room. *These were my father's rooms. They can't be my rooms now.* The walls of the anteroom were tiled with gold-colored granite. The vaulted ceiling was tiled with gold scale. In the center of the room was a long, rectangular table. Bookshelves and other tables lined the walls. Additional doors led to the bedroom and a small armory. A large balcony took up one entire curved wall. The table was covered with maps, documents, scrolls, and other papers. More maps and scrolls were stacked in most of the chairs.

Sillik walked over to the table and poured himself a glass of wine. It was an Illician red wine and had always been a favorite. He raised a glass for Briana, but she shook her head.

"I insist," Sillik said as he placed a glass in Briana's hand. Then he took a tentative sip. The fruity wine was cool and smooth. Sillik relaxed a little. Then he raised his cup. "To my father, the king." Tonight was, after all, the Celebration of Kings. Sillik tried to relax as he sat down at the head of the table.

"To the king," Briana said in a barely audible whisper as she sipped her wine.

Sillik quaffed his wine again and then looked at her. He gestured to the only other chair at the table that wasn't full of maps and scrolls, but she shook her head. She had a handful of her dress in one hand and was twisting it tightly.

"I failed, Sillik," she said in a rush. "He got into the keep. We had some warning signs that something was wrong. I sent more guards. Your father was certain that something was going to happen to him. He told me he had summoned you a week before he was murdered."

Sillik looked up in surprise but said nothing.

Briana took a deep breath and then continued. "An Illician master of the Seven Laws bluffed his way into the keep and attacked your father. His name was Dernot Lafliar. He received his master title about a year ago. His family has been associated with the wine merchants for centuries. He is young, and the Gold Robes wanted him to join them. Dernot was different, though. He always seemed out of step with what was going on around him."

"You knew him?" Sillik asked, surprised even though he had suspected something along these lines. Briana's words shocked him. He didn't wish to believe an Illician would murder his father.

"In a way," Briana said. "I had spoken to him several times. I don't think anyone really knew him."

"What else do we know about him?" Sillik asked.

Briana shook her head. "Not a whole lot. He didn't have many friends."

"Women, family, other students?"

Briana shook her head. "Sorry, but no. He was an orphan. His parents were merchants and died at the hands of the Nomads in the desert almost ten years ago when their trade caravan was attacked."

"How did he get in?"

"He concocted a story about answering a question from the king and walked right in," Briana said. "The guard had no reason to deny him entry. Sillik, I'm sorry. It wasn't so much a duel as a brutal murder. Your father was outclassed and died quickly." She talked quickly, as if this would lessen the pain. "Then Crinthan was killed during his coronation by a poison dart." She shook her head as tears glistened in her eyes. "We never found the assassin. So from there we took some of the same precautions that we did tonight. Even that was not enough.

"Doran tried to sneak out of the keep after he was crowned—to see his mistress, we think. An arrow killed him a dozen steps outside the keep. He died instantly." She shook her head sadly, and the tears on her cheeks glistened. "He was wearing a hooded cloak, but someone knew it was him. Clearly, they had very good intelligence."

"What about Rendar?"

"He insisted that the assassin who had killed your father was gone, and he walked to the King's Gate with his family the morning after his coronation. My security was good, and I believed the assassin was gone too, but someone shot them all with arrows. Five arrows, and he and his family were cut down. We never found the archers, but we found three bows. They were simple, horn-reinforced recurve bows like those that are used in other cities." She paused and wiped her eyes. "There is more that I must tell you."

Sillik nodded but said nothing.

She took a stiff drink of her wine before continuing. "Before he died, Rendar believed he needed to prove he was ready to be king, so … he took the Shield of Rendarick."

Sillik's head popped up. "It wouldn't have worked for him. He had not mastered the Seven Laws, at least not when I left." His voice trailed off hopefully.

Briana shook her head as the tears flowed freely. "He never did master the Seven Laws. He bullied Lord Kenton into retrieving the shield for him and then carried it with him that morning. He believed it would protect him."

Sillik slammed his goblet on the table. "The fool!"

Briana said nothing for a moment. "It gets worse. In the confusion, the shield was lost."

"Stolen?"

"We think so. Rendar didn't die immediately. He lingered for a moment, and in the confusion, the shield disappeared. One moment it was beside him, and the next it was gone. We searched but never found it. Someone could have carried it out the gate in the chaos. Only the royal guard was close enough at that point. We think a guard stole it, perhaps even killed your brother. We questioned everyone with the Seven Laws. Every one of the guards on duty was questioned."

"That shield was invaluable," Sillik said. "It was one of the few artifacts of Rendarick. I wonder who gave him the idea it would protect him?"

Briana shrugged. "We don't know. Since he wasn't a master, it wouldn't have been part of his normal education. He would have had no need to know about it. Yet he went out of his way to ask for it in particular."

"Someone lied to him," Sillik said. "Surely Kenton told him it wouldn't work?"

Briana nodded. "We all did, but he was determined. It didn't matter what we said. It was as if he thought we were lying to him. As swordmaster, I practiced with it once years ago. It makes you invulnerable to injury while battle rages, but only if you are a master of the Seven Laws."

Sillik nodded. "I have experienced the effects of that shield. But to Rendar, it would have been only an old wooden shield."

"Sillik, I am sorry," Briana said. "You should send me away for failing you, for failing all of you."

Sillik shook his head. "No. Everyone wants me to send them away. First, Kenton wants to be exiled, and now you say you want to be sent on a quest. I won't be surprised if Greenup barges in here tonight asking to be exiled as well."

Briana dabbed her eyes with the back of her hand. "You are in terrible danger. Trust no one. Assassins have killed your father and your brothers. Spies must be everywhere."

Sillik nodded nervously.

"I mean it," Briana said. "You're in danger. Do what you need to do, and then flee. Go to the armories and get the holy sword Avenger. It will come to you if you call. Then flee."

"I can't do that," Sillik said. "I must be the king."

"Then shake up the leadership and appoint new guards. Appoint a new swordmaster. Keltic, Lord General Greenup's grandson, is fast and deadly."

"Keltic," Sillik said, smiling. "I remember when he was but a child."

"He's a man now, or almost. Appoint him as swordmaster of Illicia, and exile me for my failure so that I may hunt your family's killers. A few others are willing to go with me. We can take sand lizards and widen our search."

"No," Sillik said, frowning as he remembered the Illician sand lizards on which his people rode into battle. "I hate the smell of those damn things."

Briana smiled but said nothing.

"You are my closest friend in this city," Sillik said, "and I need your help. Now go. I want to think. We'll talk more tomorrow."

"No," Briana said. "There is more. You need to see this and understand."

Sillik watched as Briana leaned over the table and placed three small pieces of paper in front of him. "We found these in your father's hand the day he died."

"What are they?" Sillik asked as he examined them.

"Map symbols," Briana said, pointing to the pieces in turn. "Colum, Nerak, and the Blasted Hills."

Sillik leaned forward and studied the scraps of paper. The symbols were sharp and crisp, just like his father would have drawn them.

"Lord Kenton has examined them," Briana said. "He found nothing extra."

Sillik nodded. "At this point I assume that so many people have examined the papers that any residual traces of magic would be lost."

"Not as many as you think," Briana said. "We didn't want this information known, so only Kenton, Greenup, and I have touched them. But your father had them in his hand. They were rolled up tight."

"The assassin could have left them," Sillik said.

Briana shook her head. "We don't think so. As soon as they started fighting, the guards heard the noise and came running. I felt the use of magic and ran up the stairs. Dernot was running toward the window when I got here. It was over so fast that I was too late." She wiped her eyes. "We don't think the assassin had time to leave them. I think your father was going to do something with them."

"What?" Sillik asked.

Briana shrugged. "Your father and his secrets."

Sillik smiled. "How did the assassin get out of the keep? How did he get past you?"

Briana's blue eyes flashed dangerously, and she paused as if trying to control her temper. "The guards said he was carrying a package to show the king. Inside the package was an ingenious machine. After he killed your father, he ran to the window. I reached the doorway as he finished strapping something to his back. Then he jumped off the balcony as if he had wings." She gestured with her hands. "He just glided away, and the guards and I could only watch. I was ready to kill him. I had balls of fire like you have never seen, but I couldn't throw them at him because he kept darting in different directions like a dove. I couldn't risk missing, not knowing who or what I would hit. I yelled and screamed, and then he was gone into the darkness beyond the walls of the keep." She paused and wiped her eyes. "We searched the city for days. Searched every caravan leaving the city for a month. He could have sailed over the walls and out into the desert, and we wouldn't have known."

Sillik leaned back, rested his elbows on the arms of his chair, and put his fingertips together as he looked at Briana and the map pieces. "I have to tell you something."

"What?" Briana asked, studying his face.

"He summoned me back in the midst of that battle. Rather than defend himself, he sent me a message. My father had those pieces of paper in his hand, knowing you would find them and give them to me."

Briana frowned in confusion. "He told me a week earlier that he had already summoned you."

Sillik shook his head. "I felt the battle, saw flashes of it. That is why the Gold Robes couldn't cleanse the room afterward. Part of the battle was tied to the speaking spell and to me."

Briana nodded as comprehension dawned on her face. "That explains why they couldn't cleanse the magic. They didn't even want to let you come up here. They talked about moving you to the Red Tower."

"Only I could do it," Sillik said bitterly. "Only I could cleanse the aftereffects of the battle."

"I noticed. I was going to ask how you did something the Gold Robes couldn't."

After thinking for a moment, Sillik stood up abruptly. "Thank you, Briana. Good night." He hated to be so abrupt with such a close friend, but he needed time to think. There had always been things he could do that the Gold Robes couldn't. The question was, why? That wasn't something he wanted to talk about right now.

Anger flashed in Briana's eyes at the dismissal. Sillik was certain he knew her thoughts. They were friends, yet he was dismissing her like a servant. She had merely been trying to tell him what had happened to his father. Perhaps if Sillik had been there, his father wouldn't have died—because he wouldn't have had to divert his energy.

"On a different subject," Briana said defiantly as she stood, "knowing your lack of fondness for your uncles and their offspring, I left orders that they be denied access to the top four levels of the keep. That keeps them out of your kitchens and steam rooms as well as the family levels of the keep." She curtsied. "By your leave, my lord," she said, her voice dripping with sarcasm. Then she turned abruptly, her skirts swirling as if in anger, and left.

Suddenly, it was quiet and still. Only the guards at the top of the stairs made any noise. Sillik's cheeks burned with regret, not only at his words but also at how he had spoken them. How was he going to sort this out? How was he going to find Dernot? The assassins would surely come after him next. They already had.

Unsettled, Sillik made his way into his father's former bedchamber. To make himself feel more comfortable, he threw walls of magic across the windows and doorway. No one could break through them without awakening him. As an afterthought, he threw a warding spell across the door of his closet. It concealed an entrance to the secret passageways. If someone besides Briana knew about it, he had to be careful. He also set wards across the doors to his rooms. If anyone opened the doors, he would be warned. *I have been too trusting*, he thought, *too complacent*.

As Briana had said he would, Sillik found his meager belongings laid out on a small dressing table. He pushed the clothes to the floor. They needed to be cleaned. He was glad to see his sword. He drew it and rubbed his fingers down the length of the blade. It was stained and bore many nicks. He remembered how almost every nick had been acquired. The simple blade had served him well. Anger flared as he felt the wards from the doorway tingle. He slid the sword back into its sheath. *So soon?*

"My lord," said a voice behind him.

Sillik turned and smiled. "Lady Nisha. So good to see you." Inwardly, he groaned. He didn't want to see his father's organizer on his first night back. Anyone who thought the king ruled the city would be correct. But who ruled the king? That would be Nisha.

"Yes, my lord," the woman said stiffly. "There are things you should do. They are important, my lord. I have a list."

"I am sure you do, Nisha," Sillik said as he rubbed his temples. "Have some water sent up. I want to wash the travel grime off first. I don't want to go to the steam rooms tonight."

"Yes, my lord. You need to be measured for appropriate attire as well. You have been gone a long time. Your old clothes will not fit, and you are taller than your brothers."

Sillik smiled at the woman who had been one of the banes of his childhood. "Not tonight, Nisha. I need to feel clean, and then I need sleep."

"My lord, my list has twenty-eight items you must consider." She did not say "tonight," but that's what she meant.

"Give me the list, Nisha. Have water sent up, and see that I am not disturbed until morning."

"We really should—" Nisha stopped when Sillik scowled. "Yes, my lord. Here is the list." She handed a piece of parchment to him. "I will do as you request. Lord Greenup has also requested to see you at your earliest convenience."

"In the morning, at breakfast," Sillik said. "That will give him time to inspect the troops and walk the walls of the keep before he sees me."

"Yes, my lord."

Sillik smiled. Her frown seemed to be permanently etched into her face.

He scanned the document she had given him. *Yes, I should be doing these things, but not in this order. The city council will not be my first priority. Shave and a haircut? What's wrong with my hair?* Sillik almost laughed at the absurdity of the situation when he got to item eleven. It said simply, "Accept marriage proposal." Item twelve was "Meet bride." "Things seem to be out of order," he said as he rubbed his forehead. Item nine, though, was a good idea: appoint deputy. How could he do that? And who should it be?

"Nisha, wait," he said as he picked up a quill. "Here is what we are going to do." When he was finished writing, he handed the list back to her. She glanced at the parchment and then looked up, her eyes wide and a small smile spreading across her face. "Yes, my lord." Then she turned.

Before she could leave, Sillik spoke again. "What happened, Nisha? Dernot had to have help. You know everything that goes on in this tower. Who helped him?"

Nisha paused. "I only hear rumors, my lord."

"What rumors, Nisha?"

"The rumors said a woman helped the assassin. No one knows who, my lord."

"Thank you, Nisha." Sillik said tiredly as he ran a hand through his hair.

Nisha nodded her head and left with a smile.

Sillik watched in surprise. *She was excited! I have never seen that before. When did she learn to smile?*

Sillik felt the wards at the door tingle again as it opened. "Nisha, I thought we were done," he said without looking up.

A lightly musical voice replied, "I am not Nisha."

Sillik looked up in surprise. "Rebecca? It is late. Can we talk tomorrow?"

"I wish we could, my lord," the redheaded woman said as she stepped into the room. "I have things I must tell you that I do not want the world to know."

"How did you get past the guards?" Sillik asked, eyeing the woman with suspicion. She had changed her clothes since their brief encounter in the throne room. Now she wore a dark blue dress of brocaded silk with a high collar. The red emerald still hung from her ear, but the healing hand was missing. Vaguely uncomfortable at her sudden arrival, Sillik watched her carefully. Nisha's words flashed through his mind, and he was suddenly nervous.

"Healers are allowed to go anywhere they need to go," Rebecca answered sagely as she plucked at the pleats of her dress. "You should remember that. Do you require healing after your journey?"

Sillik continued to eye the woman uncertainly. The story of how Dernot had bluffed his way into these apartments was fresh in his mind. "No," he said finally. "I'm fine."

Rebecca looked at him sharply and then laughed. "I am no assassin, my lord. I was loyal to your father, the Seven bless him, and I am loyal to you. I came to offer healing. I can assure you, my healing oaths are refreshed annually as per custom and law. I know that the wastes are unforgiving. I can ease the pains of your journey."

"I am fine," Sillik said, wincing as he spoke. "You should leave."

"Your back pains you, and your right ankle is stiff," Rebecca said. "I can see that much without touching you. You will be dehydrated, and the wine you have sampled"–she glanced at the half-empty bottle on the table–"will only dehydrate you further. You need healing, water, and sleep, in that order. I can help you. I will tell Nisha what to send up for your breakfast."

"No," Sillik said as he sat down. "But I will drink some water," he said in concession. *They will coddle me in kindness if I let them.*

Rebecca smiled. "In that case, I will leave you with some information. I represent a secret sect within the Gold Robes called the Hunters. We support the king and reveal ourselves only to the crowned king. We are making an exception in your case since you are the crown prince, and your father is dead. I may not reveal our members to you or anyone else, but I can say we trace our origins to the days after Rendarick was assassinated."

"How do I know I can trust you?" Sillik asked, even more suspicious now. "A secret sect? I've known you my entire life, and you only spring this on me now?"

Rebecca smiled. "You should not trust me. The question is, will you trust your father?" She slid a folded piece of parchment across the table to Sillik.

Sillik glanced at it and then back at Rebecca. "My father gave this to you?"

Rebecca nodded. "Yes, my lord."

He glanced at the wax seal and recognized the Illician signet. He fingered the seal and then looked up at her. "I will need that ring. Do you know where it is?"

"I'm sorry, but I do not, my lord." She smiled sadly. "I am sorry it has come to this."

Sillik glanced at the parchment. His name was written in a flowing script above the seal. "My father wrote this?"

"Indeed, my lord. He gave it to me over a year ago. Please read it."

*He knew*, Sillik thought. *He knew what was happening and had been planning for it for a long time.* Inwardly dreading what the note might say, he broke the seal and unfolded the parchment.

> *Sillik, trust the bearer of this note. Your mother was a member*
> *of the Hunters, and I have always trusted their advice.*
> *Your father,*
> *Saldor, King of Illicia*

"Satisfied?" Rebecca asked. "I will have to ask that you burn the note when we are done."

His mother had been one of them? Somehow this didn't surprise him. Rather than answer her question, Sillik asked one of his own. "What do you know about the deaths of my family?"

"Not much more than you, unfortunately," Rebecca said. "Dernot did his part. Hired assassins, we think, killed your brothers. We almost caught one, but he slipped away. We think he is still in the city, though." She paused to let that sink in. "Others were complicit, and we are trying to find them. But know this for fact: your uncles and your cousins want the throne. Do not believe what they say on this subject. They are not innocent, but we have not determined the extent of their involvement. You would be wise to avoid them. We also believe there is more to this than simple greed. Someone wants Illicia to remove itself from the world."

Sillik frowned. "So you don't know much more than Briana."

"Only this: After today's explosion in the throne room, we believe that another secret sect may exist within the Gold Robes. There have been rumors of them for centuries, but we believe we finally have evidence. We call them the Killers. We believe they are an offshoot of the healers but sworn to the Nine."

Sillik gave Rebecca a startled look. "The Killers? Healers sworn to the Nine?"

Rebecca nodded.

"Surely the healing oaths would prevent ... Those oaths are unbreakable."

Rebecca smiled grimly. "We have always thought so, but perhaps we were wrong. The healers did the last search through the keep before it was sealed. They were the last in the building. Healers are more attuned to life because of their special healing gifts. Someone among them set the trap on your throne. Attuning the trap to you would have required hair and blood, something the healers could have obtained years ago. One or more of them tried to kill you. Therefore, at least one of them is a traitor and a killer."

Sillik took a deep breath and nodded. "That also means that this has been planned for many years." He rubbed his temples. "If you learn anything more ..."

Rebecca bowed. "I will come straight to you."

Sillik was still struggling to take it all in. "So my mother ... was a Hunter?"

Rebecca paled and swallowed hard. "My lord, I cannot–"

"You knew her," Sillik said. "She died when I was born, so I did not."

Rebecca smiled kindly at the memory. "She was my mentor. She was wonderful. She had a special way of teaching. Now, about that healing ..." She raised a hand, but Sillik waved her off.

"I just want to sleep," he said. "I don't want to dream."

"I can help with that as well, my lord." Rebecca stepped forward and laid her hand on Sillik's neck. "You will sleep. Your dreams will not bother you."

Her hand was cool and smooth. Sillik felt a familiar whoosh of energy and a tingling in his back and legs. He knew when she was finished. The itching that always accompanied healing was mild. He drank a cup of water and then found his way to bed.

Outside the keep, in a lavishly decorated four-story home, Melin and Noswin drank wine and talked in low voices. They had purchased the home with gold and had paid extra to have the room warded against listening ears by some of the Gold Robes who accepted odd jobs on the side for extra money.

The room in which they sat was Noswin's antechamber. It was furnished with expensive carpets and wall hangings. There were no windows and only two doors. One door led to Noswin's bedchamber and the other to a hallway. Melin's rooms were at the other end of the hallway. The wooden chairs on which they sat were inlaid with rare woods and precious gems. The wooden table was also inlaid with gold and amber. Glow balls hanging from the ceiling emitted a steady light. They were the only magical items in the rooms. Their sons had rooms on the floor above. A bottle of Illician red wine stood on the table.

"So our late brother's last son is back," Noswin said as he swirled his wine in a crystal goblet. "Any bets on how long he'll last? I wager a thousand gold sovereigns that he will be dead in a week."

Melin frowned as he toyed with a gold Illician sovereign. The front of the coin bore the Illician eagle in high relief. The reverse bore the face of their elder brother as he had looked upon ascending to the throne. "I didn't think our dear nephew would survive his trip through the desert, much less make it into the city. I thought I would be king tonight." His voice held a note of disappointment and longing. He eyed Noswin uncomfortably. His brother was drunk and unpredictable. "Now I don't know."

The two men had witnessed the assassination attempt. After Sillik closed court, they had ridden back to their home in open chairs with five royal guards running behind them. Noswin had taken pleasure in making the men run faster. He had yelled at the guards to keep up and laughed when they could not.

Noswin spoke again, his words slurred by the wine. "Eh, brother? I wager you a thousand gold sovereigns that you will be king in a week. That whelp will not survive. You will be king, mark my words. Then we can deal with that bitch Briana and the bastard Greenup. I have waited a long time for that."

Melin knuckle-rolled the gold sovereign in his fingers. It glinted in the dim light. "Have we gone too far, brother?" He rubbed his finger on the smooth face of his elder brother's image. The face was young and hopeful. *I remember the day my brother was crowned. Were we really that young?*

"When we were approached," Melin continued softly, "I thought, 'Yes, I would like to be king.' But I am old now, and I thought my son would be a better king than my nephews. What's to say they won't keep killing kings and you and I and our sons won't join our brother and his boys? After us, who's next?" *Are my daughters safe?* he wondered. *They are married and far away, but who's to say what will happen?*

Noswin laughed drunkenly. "That bitch Briana comes after our sons. So high and mighty with her sword. Grandniece or not, she is one I would like to chain and sell to the slavers." He paused to try to drink more wine, but his cup was empty. "Damn them to the nine hells!" He threw his goblet against the wall, shattering it. "That whore humiliated Edwin. He was your friend as well as mine. She drove him to drink, and what does a defeated swordmaster do? He drank himself to death. The knife in his heart was her doing. How much could we sell her for? A thousand gold pieces? Two?" He grabbed another goblet from the table and emptied the wine bottle into it.

Melin nodded as he eyed his drink. Edwin had been very drunk the day he died, and assaulting that mother and her child had been unlike him. Briana had ended the assault permanently. No one blamed her. Hells, the king had praised her, but the king also had given Edwin an honorable funeral.

Noswin took a swig of wine and then spilled some as he set the heavy goblet down unsteadily. "We could have her tortured and cut her throat when we're done."

Melin eyed his brother warily. Sometimes he disliked Noswin almost as much as he had disliked his older brother.

"It is out of our hands now, brother," Noswin said, laughing. "The killing has started, and our nephew, the Nine curse him, is going to die. Then you will be crowned king."

Melin nodded uncomfortably. *But the headsman's axe is in my future if our plans become known.* "With each death, more speculative eyes are looking at us, brother," Melin said. "I feel the questions when they look at me: could we be behind the deaths?"

Noswin sneered. "The only thing we have done is have a conversation in a hallway in the Blue Tower."

"If they find the woman who asked if I would like to be king, they can bloody well trace it to us. That woman will be the death of us. How could we have known she was serious?" Melin's tone softened. "You should go to bed, brother. Sleep this off. Loose tongues will get us and our sons sent to the headsman." He tugged at his collar, suddenly aware of how tight the fabric was on his throat. *And if I become king, will the killing continue? Will my son and I die, and will Noswin then become king like he always wanted? But what if the killing continues? Will my treason dishonor my daughters? Fortunately, they had no part of this and are safely married and out of Illicia. Oh, Lords, what have I done?*

Noswin giggled. "I want to see that bitch Briana put in her place and make her pay for breaking Edwin. You know that's what killed him." He laughed again and grabbed his cup. He tried to drink but spilled most of the wine on his silk shirt. "Damn! Brother, get me some more wine. Wine! I need more wine!" With that, he slumped back into his chair.

"Come, brother," Melin said as he stood up. "I will put you to bed." *Just like I did when we were little,* he thought. *There has to be a way to stop this. Maybe I can talk to Sillik, explain just a little.*

Melin grabbed Noswin's arm and hauled him to his feet. The man was very drunk, and it took some careful maneuvering to get him into his bedchamber.

Noswin laughed hysterically. "Can you just see that bitch Briana begging for food? Naked and begging for food? Hells, maybe she will beg for her life." He continued to chuckle until Melin dumped him onto his bed.

Melin didn't bother to cover him up or take off his boots. *Let him wake up cold and hungover in his own sick,* he thought as he closed the door. *He shouldn't get drunk like that. One careless word, and we go straight to the headsman. Or worse,* he thought as he remembered the woman in the Blue Tower. *If she belonged there, then she would be a healer. But what if she supported the Nine? That would make her ... a what? I really am in too deep. Will the Seven forgive me for what we have done?*

# CHAPTER 4

## Questions

THE NEXT MORNING came too early for Sillik. The normal sounds of the keep woke him shortly after dawn. He stretched in the large bed and, for a moment, enjoyed the touch of the clean sheets. He could not remember the last time he had slept on real sheets.

He got up and splashed some water on his face. Looking at his reflection in the water, he smiled. *Yes, Nisha, I should shave.* Drawing his long knife, he warmed the water with magic and then shaved. He knew from long experience that his father's barber would be standing in the hallway outside. His father had used a barber every day of his adult life. But he didn't want anyone near him with a blade. When Sillik was presentable, he got dressed and then pushed open the doors to his rooms.

Sillik smiled. As Rebecca had promised, he had slept well, and he remembered no dreams. Maybe he would not have that recurring dream again. His back and ankle also felt better than they had in weeks. For now, he felt relaxed and at peace with his fate. Perhaps Rebecca should come more often.

As expected, Lord General Greenup was waiting for him outside, sitting on one of the stone benches that lined the hallway to the king's apartments. Standing to Greenup's right was Sneller, the royal barber. Sneller was a slender, short, balding man. His red silk coat, the symbol of his guild, was neatly pressed.

"No time today, Sneller," Sillik said as he nodded at Greenup, whose face looked pale and lined.

"My lord, I have failed you and your family," Greenup gushed as he stood rigidly erect. "I wish to be punished for my failure. Send me away. Send me to hunt the assassin that has killed your family. My honor demands a response to this crime."

Sillik started to laugh, but seeing the hurt and pain in the big man's eyes, he simply said, "No."

When Greenup began to argue, Sillik held up his hand. "Who has advised the last two kings on military matters?"

Greenup did not answer, so Sillik continued. "Who knows the most about military matters, our military strength, and the name of every guard on duty this morning?" He smiled kindly. "The answer to those questions is you, my friend. I can't exile everyone who thinks they were deficient in protecting my father. With or without your sage advice, my father and brothers would still be dead. We are facing assassins with unknown abilities and an unknown goal. We know that now, and we—all of us—need to figure out how to respond. Now, I am sure Kenton and Briana are lurking around somewhere nearby. Why don't you go get them? I am also sure that Nisha is not far away. Tell her to send in something to eat. Rebecca was going to tell her what to send."

Greenup grinned. "They are already waiting at the top of the stairs. Viktorie is with Kenton. And I already told Nisha to have food prepared."

Sillik smiled. "Bring Viktorie as well then."

Soon, they were all seated around a small table near the balcony. Everyone eyed the energy rippling across the opening. Briana nodded her approval. Today, she was dressed in brown slacks and vest with a white blouse. A long sword was belted to her hip on a wide red leather belt. Kenton and Viktorie wore their customary gold robes, and Greenup wore the same battle armor he wore every day.

Guards knocked quietly at the door. When Sillik nodded, they brought in meat, pastries, fruits, nuts, and a pitcher of juice. Before anyone could ask, Briana announced that the meal had already been inspected and tasted by the Gold Robes.

Smiling grimly at the reality of the situation, Sillik asked the guards to leave and then stood to pour everyone a cup of chilled juice.

"My lord, let me do that," Viktorie said.

Sillik laughed. "In this room, protocol be damned. If I want to pour a drink, I will, and not even the Seven Gods can stop me." As he poured, beads of water condensed on the outside of the metal cups.

When Sillik finally sat down to nibble at some of the fruit and nuts, he looked around the table and saw worried faces. He tried to smile convincingly.

"Briana briefed me on the deaths of my father and brothers last night. So unless you have something else to add, I suggest we move on." He wasn't going to mention Rebecca's visit. He had burned the letter she had given him, after reading it once more.

No one spoke, although several eyes darted to Briana and then back to Sillik.

"Good. Now what is the political situation in the council, Lord Kenton?"

With that, the discussion began and lasted most of the morning. After political matters, Sillik directed them to military preparedness, focusing in particular on Lord Greenup, and then to magical preparedness with Lady Viktorie. When the midday meal arrived, Sillik left to visit the water closet. When he returned, the room was empty except for the guards.

"Forgive me, my lord," said one of the guards. "Everyone else had the same needs and will return in a few moments."

Sillik smiled and nodded and then waved at the wall of magic. An opening appeared, and he walked out onto the balcony. Below him the city was alive with energy. He heard the clash of swords from the practice yards and saw the patrols moving along the walls. Beyond the walls he saw movement in the fields. He noticed that the eagle pennants had all been returned to full mast. The period of mourning was officially over. The prince had returned. Sillik laughed bitterly. He heard Briana behind him and turned to face her. "Does Yardmaster Holden still teach first swords?" he asked.

"Indeed, he does," Briana said with a laugh. "He refuses to stop."

Sillik smiled. "He must be nearly eighty years old by now. He was my first instructor."

"He can still do things with a sword that no one else can," Briana said. "When I became swordmaster of Illicia, I asked him to tutor me again."

Sillik looked at Briana with an appraising eye. "When last we sparred, we tied."

Briana smiled. "As I remember it, we each won a match and then sparred until the sun set, because neither would concede."

"Like I said, a tie. Has Master Holden taught you his secrets?"

"Spar with me, and you'll find out," Briana said, a glint in her eye. Then she changed the topic. "How much longer do you want to talk? There is a lot to discuss, but we don't have to do it all in one day."

Sillik snorted in disgust. "What, so I can go out and inspect schools or road repairs? No, I need to get caught up before I face this recalcitrant council of mine. I have to call a council meeting soon." With disgust, he repeated some of the phrases Lord Kenton had used in his briefing that morning. "There is no profit in war or preparation for war, I am told. The purpose of life is to make a profit."

Briana touched his arm. "Sillik, we all agree that we are at war and that it is a different kind of war than we have faced before. Lord Greenup put it well at the last council meeting. 'There is no honor in ignoring war,'" she said, imitating the lord general's deep voice in a fair approximation. "That silenced them for a while. Now you can break the impasse."

"If only I knew what to do," Sillik said. With a resigned expression, he led Briana back into his rooms and then closed the magical door to the balcony with a wave of his hand.

Kenton, Viktorie, and Greenup were still absent, but Nisha and two women Sillik did not recognize were standing in the doorway.

"The others will be back in a little bit," Briana said. "While we take a break, Nisha thought it would be a good time to augment your wardrobe so you can look the part."

Sillik started to protest, but Briana hushed him. "These women, Roberta and Alissa, are highly recommended members of the seamstresses' guild."

The two women curtsied as they were named.

"They are here to measure you. The more you protest or make a scene, the longer it will take." Briana smiled. "After all, we can't have you raiding all the closets in the keep, looking for clothes."

Sillik nodded grimly. "I see the wisdom, but that doesn't mean I have to like it." Then he turned to the seamstresses and held up his arms. "Ladies, you may approach and do your business." He glanced at Briana over his shoulder. "Did Nisha put you up to this?"

Briana laughed. "Wouldn't you like to know?"

Sillik groaned. With these women overseeing him, there would be no rest. This was Nisha's third item on her list. She was still trying to control him from behind the scenes.

Mercifully, the seamstresses were quick and efficient. Roberta measured and read numbers while Alissa recorded.

"Do I at least get to tell them what I want?" Sillik asked.

Briana shook her head as she suppressed a laugh. "No, I have given them all of their instructions, including to ignore whatever you say. You must look like a king. If we left it to you, you would look like a common ruffian."

Sillik started to say something, but the door opened, and Greenup and Kenton strolled in. They grinned and looked at Briana.

"I am surprised you got him to stand still for so long," Greenup said. He indicated a bundle of maps under his arm. "I thought we might need some reference material."

"Done," Roberta announced as she read off the last measurement. "A good fit is important. Thank you for allowing us to measure you, my lord."

Alissa closed her scroll. "We will have a basic wardrobe in three days. Vestments will take longer. Battle armor will take at least a week."

Sillik nodded. "My thanks to you for making this quick and painless."

The seamstresses bowed to Sillik and then turned to Nisha. "Anything else you need us to do, my lady?" Alissa asked.

"Prioritize some suitable clothing for him to wear here in the keep. He needs that today. Nothing fancy, just functional, and it doesn't have to be a perfect fit," Nisha said with a slight upturn of her lips.

Sillik glanced at Briana, who was trying to hide a grin. He growled.

"Yes, my lady," said Alissa. With that, the women departed, just as Viktorie walked in. Her eyebrows arched in surprise, but she said nothing.

Without another word, Sillik ushered everyone back to the conference table to continue their discussions. He took the largest map from Greenup and spread it on the table. As he studied the map, he considered what he had learned and then asked the question that had been burning in his mind all morning. "Lord Kenton, what can you tell me about the Hunters?"

Kenton grimaced. "An ancient tale to scare the children." He sat back in his chair. "When I was a student, rumors circulated daily about the Hunters. First they existed. Then they didn't. Then they were going to reveal themselves. Once I heard that they were going to take over the city and depose your grandfather." He smiled kindly. "Nothing more than an old story. No basis in fact. Why do you ask?"

Sillik shrugged. "Just a rumor I heard long ago."

Kenton relaxed. "I put them in the same category as the sect of healers called the Killers, who are supposedly sworn to the Nine. We have never found any evidence that they exist either."

Sensing an opening, Sillik asked a prickly question, knowing his friend would react badly. "Who were the last ones in the keep the night my father died?"

Briana sucked in her breath. Kenton's brow furrowed as he thought about it, and then his eyes widened. "My wife and the healers! Surely, you don't think—"

"I do not suspect Elizabet," Sillik said, raising his voice over the sudden protests at the table. "I have known her my entire life. I trust her. I am just looking at everything with a new set of eyes. Since your wife was there, our enemies want me to suspect her in order to sow division within our ranks. But I am concerned there may be a traitor within the healers."

"It is suspicious," Briana said. "We had not thought of that yet. I will look into it."

"We have arranged dinner for you tonight," Kenton said, changing the subject, "that is, if you will allow a small group of friends to welcome you back to Illicia."

Sillik nodded, realizing protest was futile.

"An interesting bottle of Armagnac is about to come on the market," Kenton continued. "They say it is a thousand years old, and there may be as many as seven bottles. Some of the healers are checking the bottles to ensure they are safe to drink. I wanted to buy one, but they are not yet for sale. Can you imagine, a thousand years old? I fear they will be terribly expensive. Anyway, I have procured two other appropriate bottles to celebrate your return."

"That will be fine," Sillik said. "Who will be coming up?"

Kenton opened his mouth, but it was Briana who answered. "All of us, plus Viktorie, Elizabet, Kenton's daughters, and Rebecca."

"Perfect," Sillik said with a pleased smile as they went back to discussing the maps.

Shortly before dinner, the guests arrived and servants brought in trays of fruit and cheese followed by trays of grilled lamb and sandfish. True to his word, Kenton produced two bottles of Illician red wine from a famous bottling. Each bottle was 143 years old. With a little ceremony, Kenton broke the magical seal and removed the cork. He poured glasses all around. When his daughters presented their glasses, he gave them a disapproving glare but filled their glasses anyway.

"Before we drink, I wish to give thanks," Kenton said. The conversation stopped, and heads turned. "May the Seven Gods protect our prince. May wisdom guide his hand. May justice prevail. Amen."

Everyone in the room repeated the "amen" and then spread out around the conference table, which had been cleared of maps and documents. Eventually, the conversation turned to Sillik's plans. Sillik listened politely. It seemed like everyone had ideas about what he should do. Finally, he spoke. "I want to talk to the garrison commanders."

For thousands of years, Illicia had maintained garrisons across the land. Originally, they had been intended to enforce Illician decrees. Gradually, they had changed into peacekeeping forces and then into diplomatic missions and finally to trade outposts. Eventually, towns had sprung up around most of the garrisons. When a garrison was within a city's sphere of influence, treaties were written and signed.

On his way back to Illicia, Sillik had stopped at a few of the garrisons. In each case, the garrison had been closed and sealed with magical wards. Entry had been easy for Sillik, but he had been surprised to learn that his brothers had issued the commands and that the soldiers who had manned garrisons had returned to Illicia.

When his words were met with silence, Sillik looked around in frustration. "Briana said the garrisons had been recalled. I saw empty garrisons on my return. So the garrison commanders are here. I want to talk to them."

Kenton, Greenup, and Briana exchanged looks. "Why?" Briana asked.

"They know things that might be important." Sillik sighed.

"Perhaps," Kenton granted, "but we–"

"I need to get as much information as I can."

"We can tell you everything you need to know," Kenton said.

"And what would that be?" Sillik asked, with a little sarcasm in his voice.

"That Ynak and Peol are soon going to be at war with Nerak," Greenup said.

"Now that's what I'm talking about," Sillik replied, an edge of anger in his voice. "We talked last night about Nerak, but Briana didn't mention anything about war!"

"It wasn't important last night," Briana said, looking around helplessly.

"I get to decide what is important," Sillik said. "Tomorrow, send the garrison commanders to me in twos and threes. Don't tell them why I want to see them."

"It will be done," Greenup said, cutting off Kenton's protest.

"It will upset a great many on your council," Briana warned. "Some will claim it is beneath you to talk to commanders like equals. We are not saying that, but some on your council will."

"I don't care what they say," Sillik said. "But who is it going to upset?"

"Anyone who doesn't believe in you or those who believe everyone's place is fixed and unchangeable," Briana said.

"Your uncles, the bankers, and the merchants," Greenup added.

Sillik shrugged. "I need the information, but we can keep it quiet."

"For a time," Briana said. "The council will expect you to have a full meeting with everyone."

Sillik laughed. "Not for a while. I have things to do first."

"That will not sit well either," Elizabet said.

"Limit who is called to council," Briana suggested.

Sillik smiled and took a bite of lamb. He pointed the rib at Briana. "I like the way you're thinking."

Briana smiled and sipped her wine.

"That will anger many on the council," Kenton said.

Greenup grinned. "It will let them know they do not have Sillik's ear and that their days of self-importance are over."

"Let's go back to Peol and Ynak," Sillik said. "Why go to war now?"

"We believe there was a breakdown in the trade agreements," Briana said. "Both Ynak and Peol accused Nerak, and Nerak, of course, accuses Ynak and Peol. Something happened. Trade has never flourished between those cities, but it was happening. For it to break down now doesn't make sense unless someone wants a war. The commanders will tell you that they even heard that the dragons of Ynak were waking up for the first time in centuries."

"Who would want war?" Sillik asked. "The dragons could make things tricky. A large dragon attack on Illicia would probably destroy the city. Are they after us?"

"We don't know," Greenup said. "Nerak is usually seen as an Illician ally, even if we don't know much about them. As you know, they are very secretive and don't use metal." He laughed. "They believe it is a tool of hell."

"Don't laugh at another's beliefs," Sillik cautioned. "They could be right."

"You can't honestly believe that," Briana said.

Sillik shrugged. "I have seen a lot of interesting things while away. I have met a lot of fascinating people. There are many novel ideas to consider."

"One more thing about Nerak," Briana said. "Do you remember hearing about the blood vow?"

"Of course," Sillik said. "It has some sort of religious or mystical meaning to them."

"We think it will be sworn," Greenup said. "It is rarely used, but this time we think Ynak crossed a line with them, and Nerak will try to destroy Ynak."

"Can they?" Sillik asked. "Destroy Ynak, that is."

Greenup shrugged. "Any city can probably destroy any other city under the right circumstances. That is what keeps the balance of power, more or less. Illicia has been lucky on that score. Our isolation prevents us from being attacked while allowing us to project more force. But can Nerak destroy Ynak? Possibly. If Ynak and Peol are allied, then it is more questionable. Nerak would almost have to destroy each city in turn. But first, it may have to fight the combined forces in the field. I am not sure they can do that."

"And the dragons would be the tipping point in favor of Ynak and Peol," Sillik said.

"No one can stand up to dragons," Elizabet replied.

"Birds can," Rebecca said with a private smile. "The cliff fliers of Aceon. I believe you have been there."

Startled, Sillik looked at the healer.

"I saw the carved feather on your armor," she explained. "I sent your clothing up to your rooms after your arrived. Briana asked me to see that it was done. It was painted gold. An imperial wing commander, am I correct?"

Forcing himself to be calm, Sillik nodded.

Briana looked around the room, but the leather was nowhere to be seen. She had seen that feather, but she hadn't thought about what it might mean.

Rebecca continued. "An imperial wing commander commands how many birds?"

"A thousand," Sillik said slowly. "And the correct title is wing commander of the Queen's Defense." Before any more questions could be asked, he said, "I know you have questions, but trust me when I say, not now. I haven't been in Aceon in two years, not since … well, now is not the time."

"Sillik, you know your idea to meet with the garrison commanders in small groups is a good one," Briana said, eager to change topics. "Perhaps we should do the same with the council–send small groups in to talk to you. We could exclude some of the most obnoxious ones but still let you hear the council members and, more importantly, allow them to see you."

"Do you have any idea where to look for the assassin?" Elizabet asked.

Sillik glanced at Briana. She shook her head.

"I do," Sillik said, "but I don't think we need to talk about it tonight." He stood up. "This has been a pleasant evening, but I am still fatigued. Can we call it a night?"

Everyone else stood and bade him good night. Moments later, the room was clear, except for Rebecca, who still sat at the table.

"You should leave too," Sillik said.

"They should know," Rebecca replied.

"Know what?" Sillik asked, his voice bitter. "There is nothing to know."

She sat there for a long moment and watched him quietly. "I have many sources of information," she said slowly. "I know what happened in Aceon and what happened to the queen's daughter. I believe her name was Nuella."

"Please, Rebecca. Not now. I am not ready, and they don't need to know. At least not yet."

Rebecca regarded him evenly. "I am worried about you, Sillik. Briana should know."

Sillik shook his head. "Not now."

"Of course. Do you require more healing?"

"No dreams tonight, Rebecca," Sillik said sadly. "No dreams. I keep dreaming of that night."

She eyed him with a long appraisal. "Of course, my lord. Drink some water, and then you will sleep." She reached out to touch his head.

Kenton limped through the hallways with Elizabet's hand in his. They had a short walk down five levels and then across the bridges to the Gold Tower. They did not speak, but this close, with their hands in contact, their minds were free to communicate.

"That was certainly interesting," Elizabet said. "Something happened to him at Aceon that he doesn't want to talk about. His heart rate increased markedly when Rebecca mentioned the place. Any healer could have seen it."

"How did Rebecca figure that out?" Kenton asked. "I saw that feather and just assumed it was a strange ornament."

"I gave up trying to figure out how Rebecca does things a long time ago, husband. She just does them, and she is almost always right."

"*Almost* always?" Kenton said, smiling.

"Okay, always," Elizabet said with a laughing tone.

"What did you think otherwise?" Kenton asked.

"Of our prince?"

"Yes."

"He is all we have," Elizabet said. "He is distrustful, believing that we will not tell him everything he needs to know. He has almost a commoner's distrust of power. He doesn't care about politics or whom he upsets. An angry lizard in a wine shop wouldn't do as much damage as he is about to do."

"He is passionate about avenging his father and brothers."

"Granted," Elizabet said, "but at the same time resentful of them for failing and forcing him away from his life abroad. I do want to know what happened to him."

"Did you notice anything about the room when you walked in?" Kenton asked.

"Yes, I was going to ask about that. How did you cleanse it?"

"I didn't," Kenton said, his face betraying his agitation. "Briana said he did it last night when they went up to the rooms–just waved his hand, and it was gone, like a fading kiss."

"How?"

"I don't know," Kenton admitted. "But it appears our prince has acquired some additional abilities. Did you see that barrier across the balcony?"

"Yes," Elizabet said. "How many Gold Robes did it take to build it?"

"None," Kenton said. "He did it himself. It was there when I entered, and he opened and closed doorways in it. Therefore, he must have made it."

"Impressive," Elizabet said. "Our prince must be more formidable than we remember. Either that, or he hid his true abilities. He must have been very worried about getting caught in the spider's web of politics. If he was that strong, you and Reznek never would have let him leave the tower."

"I believe he was that strong, and he was distrustful even that long ago, so he has hidden his true abilities and potential. Or else someone coached him to be distrustful."

"His father," Elizabet said. "But surely he should trust us."

"Perhaps."

"He cannot fail," Elizabet said. "We cannot let his uncles be crowned either. You know as well as I do that they will kill Briana and Greenup. Noswin has never forgiven Briana for killing Edwin."

"No, he hasn't," Kenton said. "If Noswin or Melin gets the crown, Greenup and Briana must flee."

"Yes," Elizabet said. "Plans have been made should that happen."

"I don't want to know," Kenton said with a shudder.

Elizabet smiled. "Nor will you."

"Thank you, my love!" Kenton released his wife's hand to push open the door to their apartments.

The next morning after the first meal, Sillik met with three garrison commanders in the grand receiving room on the first floor of the keep. The room was usually reserved for visiting heads of state, but it had been hastily converted into a small conference room. Its gold and green alabaster walls glowed in the soft morning light.

The three commanders were obviously nervous as they entered. They had not been told with whom they would be meeting. Four chairs had been placed around a small table, upon which sat chilled water and a silver platter of fruit. Sillik relaxed in one of the chairs. He was dressed in the uniform of a city guard, except all rank insignia had been removed. Each commander wore the same uniform, with his golden rank knot on his shoulder. All were armed with swords and long knives.

Briana stood quietly at Sillik's side. She appeared calm and relaxed, but Sillik knew she was poised to strike. Additional guards stood on either side of the doorway.

The commanders stiffened when they saw Briana. Everyone knew the swordmaster, and although they might not recognize the prince yet, there was only one person behind whom she would be standing.

"Come on in, gentlemen," Sillik said, his voice warm. "It's all right. I asked to meet with you." He shook each man's hand as he spoke their names. "Commanders Bollack, Call, and Riedal."

Briana smiled. *He got the names right*, she thought. Greenup had made sure he was prepared.

"You asked to see us, my lord?" Bollack asked suspiciously.

"I understand your concern, gentlemen," Sillik said. "You three men commanded garrisons closest to the cities that seem hell-bent on going to war. I merely want to talk to you about those cities."

The commanders looked at each other. Questions flashed in their eyes.

"Can I get you some water?" Sillik asked as he sat down.

He was trying to put them at ease, but in Briana's opinion, he was doing the exact opposite.

"Now, Bollack," Sillik said, "I understand your posting was near Ynak."

Pursing his lips in confusion, Bollack looked at his companions. "Yes, my lord, but I don't understand how that is important considering what has happened here."

Sillik turned in his chair. "Let me worry about that. Just tell me what you saw."

# CHAPTER 5

## The Yard

SILLIK OPENED HIS eyes with a start. He was standing in a dark forest. Pale white light gleamed between the trunks, and wisps of fog floated between the trees. He heard birds screaming in the night, screaming in anger and fear.

Battle horns sounded in the distance. Screams rent the night as clouds drifted across the dark sky. The moons on the horizon gleamed red between the trees.

He turned toward the screams and drew his sword. The sound of a whip cracking in the distance made his head turn again. He ran. He had to get back. The sound of arrows flying filled the air, and Sillik heard more yells and curses. He saw others moving in the night. He did not fight alone.

Sillik sat upright in his bed. The morning sun was just creeping across the tiled floor. He took a deep breath and tried to slow his heart. He was covered in perspiration. Rubbing his eyes, he threw back the sheet and rolled out of bed.

*Should I tell them I was on my way back? Should I tell them about the new life I made for myself? Should I tell them about what happened? No, it will do no good. I would only have to relive the pain again.*

He put on a red silk robe and tied it with a golden sash. Then he stretched. Frowning, he strode through the wall of power and out onto his balcony to welcome the sun. Far below him, he heard the sounds of the keep awakening.

He remembered having to get up before the sun during his youth to complete his chores before first swords and other lessons. Those had been simpler times.

Rebecca had refused to help him sleep last night. She said one could become addicted to assisted sleep. He would have to learn to sleep on his own. The nightmares had returned, as he feared they would. He had been back in Illicia a week, but in some ways, he still did not feel at home.

"You can go to the practice yard. First swords is still done at dawn," Briana said from behind him as she approached with a cup of steaming tea. "I couldn't sleep either," she added, "so I came up here to wake you and make you suffer with me. But I find that you are already suffering?"

"I couldn't sleep either," Sillik said. "Despite that, I feel …" His voice trailed off as he ran a hand across his temple and through his hair.

"Uncomfortable, restless? Or are you having nightmares? The dream readers would … or the healers could help you. They can prevent nightmares sometimes."

"I'm fine," Sillik said. "I feel more uneasy in a restless sort of way. Like I'm forgetting something, like I should be doing something." *And I don't want to tell the dream readers or the healers about my dreams. The healers won't help me either. You can't heal death.*

"You are," Briana said, her eyes sparkling as she blew on her tea to cool it. "Doing something, that is. You just can't run off into the wetlands without knowing where to go or what you're looking for."

"I need to sweat and use something other than my head," Sillik said as he took a sip of the hot liquid. He grimaced at the bitterness. "I feel confined."

"Then let's go interrupt class," Briana suggested with a wicked grin. "Holden won't mind if the swordmaster and the prince put on a little demonstration for his class. Besides, I want you to meet Keltic. He helps with first swords."

Sillik shook his head. "I shouldn't."

"Yes, you should. You need to act like the king. Drag all the council down there. Let them see the man they are plotting against. Remind them of who you are. I bet some of them will be brazen enough to bet against you if we spar."

"I might bet against myself," Sillik said, smiling as he gazed longingly at the practice yard.

"You underestimate yourself," Briana said. "Besides, you beat me once."

Sillik frowned. "We both know that was luck."

"Yes, but they don't. They just know that you are the only one who has beaten me since I became swordmaster."

Sillik smiled uncomfortably. "Very well. Let me get dressed. By the way, did you plan this?"

Briana laughed. "No, I didn't really plan it, but let's say I had an idea that you might need some physical activity."

Was she blushing? Sillik shook his head. He didn't understand her. He pulled on a pair of pants that had been lying on the back of a chair and let his dressing robe fall to the floor. Briana turned back as he pulled a loose shirt over his head and grunted when his head did not fit through the neck.

While Sillik was changing, Briana spotted a scroll beside his bed. Curious, she picked it up and read the title aloud. "Henderx's Philosophy of the Ethical Use of the Seven Laws." She glanced up at Sillik. "Getting a little philosophical? Doesn't he suggest only using the Seven Laws for self-enlightenment?"

"Ah, so you've read it," Sillik said with a grimace. "Yes, that's what he thinks. And no, I don't agree with him. It was in here, and my father had laid it on a chair. I thought it would be important, but I can't see how." Sillik pulled the shirt back off his head. Exasperated, he wadded it into a ball and threw it across the room.

"Someone should get you measured for clothing that fits," Briana remarked as Sillik found another shirt that was much too large.

Sillik smiled. "You did."

"Then why doesn't it fit?"

A small sound of disapproval came from the doorway, and Sillik jerked his head toward the sound. It was Lady Nisha. She held a silver tray with a pitcher and a cup. Steam curled up lazily from the pitcher.

"My lord," she said, "I have your clothes laid out for you. You have a busy day ahead. You have clothes that fit, if only you would allow me to remove your father's clothing."

Briana chuckled. "He can be so difficult."

Nisha made no comment as she watched Sillik.

"Cancel my morning appointments," Sillik said, ignoring her request. "The meeting at third watch will stay on the schedule." He buckled his sword belt and picked up a throwing knife.

"My lord," Nisha said, rolling her eyes in anger, "you cannot just cancel meetings. People are waiting to meet with you. It is most improper."

"Cancel them, Nisha," Sillik said as he strolled out of his apartment with Briana on his arm.

Nisha's body stiffened with tension, and her mouth compressed into a frown of disapproval.

A short while later, Sillik and Briana emerged in the training yard. A large group of people trailed behind them.

As expected, Holden was watching his first-swords class go through their thrust and parry drills. Sillik nodded to the yardmaster while Briana went and spoke to him.

Ignoring the voices and stares, Sillik walked over and examined the wooden training swords. The mock weapons stood in straight racks by length and weight. Their handles were worn and blackened from the sweat of hundreds of nervous hands. Sillik picked up a sword and tested its weight and balance. As he replaced the weapon, he turned to study the yardmaster.

Holden was a masterful teacher. He resembled a coiled spring wound tight. He knew how to coax the best from every student and never had to raise his voice to do it. Rumored to be the best swordsman Illicia had ever produced, Holden was also an intensely private person. To Sillik's knowledge he had never sparred with anyone, at least not in public.

As Briana spoke to him, surprise flickered across Holden's normally impassive face. With a terse command, he sent his students running to one side of the yard, where they knelt with excited whispers.

Briana approached Sillik. "We can spar. He didn't like us interrupting his class, but he is willing to do it for you."

Sillik looked over at the yardmaster and offered a smile and a nod. Holden's head twitched almost imperceptibly.

Briana and Sillik removed their weapons and their footwear at the edge of the yard and then chose wooden practice swords. Sillik glanced around the yard and saw that it was suddenly full of people. Generals, Gold Robes, courtiers, and everyone else with spare time had crowded into the viewing areas. Kenton and his daughters, Alexis and Kendra, stood apart from the main crowd. Viktorie, as always, stood close to the Speaker. The girls whispered with excitement. A young man stood next to Lord General Greenup. Sillik imagined this must be Keltic.

The Hornsmasher was there with a younger version of himself. Sillik guessed this was the son for whom the Hornsmasher was negotiating a bride. *Good luck with that,* Sillik thought. *He may wear a major's knot, but she'll have to be blind to want to marry that one.* Both the Hornsmasher and his son were squat and wide with wild hair and rough faces.

Briana grinned. "Let's tease them a little. Do you remember your sword forms?"

"Which one?" Sillik asked as the two stepped onto the training stone, which was circular and about thirty feet in diameter. The edge of the stone was engraved with flowing script. Long ago, Sillik had deciphered the words: "Blessed be the Seven Gods, who prepare my hands for war." A large sparring circle was etched into the stone. If a participant stepped out of the circle, he or she lost the bout. Near the center of the circle, Sillik and Briana stopped and stood back to back.

"Let's start with an easy one," Briana said. "How about Dancing Fish?"

Sillik nodded as the image of a fish dancing on its tail on a crystal lake flashed through his mind. This form was like that—slow, smooth, methodical movements interrupted by a sudden burst of activity.

Briana and Sillik went through the first form and then followed it with Bumblebee and Fawn in the Forest. The sword forms were designed to perfect technique and practice skills. The only sound was that of their feet moving on the sandy stone and their breath. It became very obvious that despite his years away, Sillik had forgotten nothing.

When Briana and Sillik completed their forms, the audience applauded approvingly. Two young students stepped up to Sillik and Briana with goblets of water. Sillik took a couple of tentative sips and then quickly downed the entire goblet. Another student stepped up with towels.

"Introduce me to Keltic," Sillik said as he wiped his face. "I remember him as a young boy, but he is your student now." He handed the towel back to the wide-eyed student, who backed away clumsily.

Briana brushed a lock of hair away from her face. "Keltic, come and join us."

Surprise flashed across Keltic's face when he heard his name. As he hurried toward the sparring circle, Sillik saw that he was lean and lanky. His black hair was cut short, and he still had a young man's youthful appearance. However, his movements were smooth and measured. *He will be fast and dangerous.*

"My lord Sillik, may I present Keltic," Briana said, "winner of the city guards' swords competition for the last two years."

Sillik shook the young man's hand. "I am honored. Now come, show me what you can do." He handed Keltic a practice sword.

The crowd murmured in anticipation.

"My lord, I can spar with him. You should not," Briana said.

Sillik looked at her. "Do you trust him?"

"Yes, of course," Briana said, her eyes flashing. "That's not—"

"You aren't going to try to kill me with a wooden sword, are you?" Sillik asked the young man with mock seriousness as he stepped into the sparring circle.

"No, of course not, my lord," Keltic stuttered.

"You are not going to put poison on the random blade that I picked out for you and slice me open?"

"No, my lord," the young man stammered as he bowed and stepped cautiously into the sparring circle.

Sillik looked at Briana. "I think it is safe enough. Besides," he said as he and Keltic began to circle, "I don't think he will touch me."

Keltic finally found his voice. "Is that a challenge, my lord?" He waved his sword in circles on either side of his body, which generated a hum of appreciation from the audience. Then with a leap, he darted in with a surprise thrust.

Sillik parried the move easily. "Whatever you need for motivation," he said, smiling as he casually parried a quick series of attacks. The sound of the wooden swords colliding was loud and clear in the morning air. The noise would bring more observers, which was Briana's plan.

The bout was quick and decisive. Sillik started by simply defending as Keltic pressed attack after attack. Bemused, Sillik observed his style and footwork. When Keltic paused, Sillik began his counterattack.

When it was over, Sillik's heart pounded with excitement. It was obvious that Keltic was a great swordsman and would only get better, but Sillik was the master that day. A smattering of applause congratulated Sillik on his victory.

Briana smiled and stepped forward. Keltic laughed and, with an exaggerated bow, handed her his practice sword. He turned to Sillik. "Maybe the swordmaster of Illicia can show you how it is done, my lord," he said, his voice crackling with excitement.

Briana tested the balance of the blade and nodded with a satisfied grin.

Sillik laughed uncertainly. "Perhaps she can at that, and perhaps she can teach me Holden's secrets." He glanced at the emotionless yardmaster and then waved for Briana to enter the sparring yard. Despite his bravado, he was concerned. He had never really beaten her in a sword fight. When they had last sparred, only a fluke chance had allowed him to beat her once. Sillik knew that Briana was fast and unpredictable. Her attacks could shift and feint. By the time you saw the real attack, it was too late. What had she learned in his absence? What had the enigmatic yardmaster taught her?

Briana stepped up to the edge of the circle and bowed formally, as tradition required. When Sillik nodded, she stepped into the circle and approached him with respect before she assumed a defensive position.

Sillik too assumed a defensive position as he studied her stance. From this position, there were eight possible attacks. Sillik looked at Briana's eyes to see what they might reveal.

Briana was more than a little surprised at how easily Sillik had defeated Keltic. She tightened her grip on the leather pommel of her sword and readied herself. His skills had improved during his absence. Would she still be the better swordsman? She had just seen him perform moves that had not been taught in Illicia. To her surprise, he began to move to his right. Frustration flared as she shifted her position to compensate.

Sillik smiled. Because of the way Briana had moved her feet, she now had only three possible attacks. It was a weakness.

The crowd murmured in anticipation of what was to come. Some people made bets as Sillik and Briana began to circle each other.

*Like a hawk playing with its prey*, Briana thought. *But who is the hawk, and who is the prey?*

Handshakes in the crowd sealed the bets. The circling continued until Briana attacked. Illician rules of chivalry required that while sparring, men couldn't attack a woman first. Briana feinted and then attacked again. Sillik parried and responded with his first attack. Briana parried, and so it began.

What followed was a display of swordsmanship seldom seen in Illicia—or anywhere else, for that matter. In three consecutive bouts, Sillik defeated the swordmaster of Illicia. Had they been fighting with real weapons in a real battle situation, Briana would have been dead.

With perspiration covering her face, Briana conceded that she was no longer the master of arms in Illicia. She tossed her sword back to Keltic as she wiped her face with her hand. Keltic caught the blade with an apologetic expression on his face.

This time the applause was loud and boisterous. Gold changed hands as the gamblers settled their bets. Sillik laughed and tossed his sword to Keltic too. He assured Briana that she was still the swordmaster. He had watched his generals muttering as they absorbed the shock of her three consecutive losses. None of them could defeat Briana even once, let alone three times. Truth be told, most of them couldn't even beat Keltic.

Students ran up to Sillik and Briana bearing more water and fresh towels. Amid the congratulations, Sillik wiped his face and watched those who had placed bets against him. He quickly memorized their faces. He recognized some of them. His uncles were also in the crowd, but they stared pointedly elsewhere. Sillik nodded at Greenup and then at the courtiers.

Greenup smiled grimly and moved his head slightly in agreement. Sillik pulled his boots on slowly as he continued to watch the crowd.

As Sillik talked to a few of the people in the crowd, a man in the back of the gallery spoke quietly to the two men standing beside him. "He is not what I expected," the man, Sanders, said with a grimace. He was tall and slender, almost fragile, but he moved with a sinuous determination. He was dressed as a merchant, but he had never sold anything other than his skill with knives, usually in an alley. "I expected a dressed-up dandy like his brothers, but he is not like them. He seems focused, driven. You said he is a master, but I didn't see anything that revealed he is a master of your Seven Laws. He looks like a common guard."

One of Sanders's companions laughed softly. "I tell you, your plots will not work with this man."

The man in the middle smiled thinly.

"Your plot failed," Sanders said. "It didn't kill him."

"It wasn't meant to kill anyone," the man in the middle said. "What I did in the throne room was simply a test. The fact that he survived tells me many things." The man paused as a white blade of light sprang from his finger, which he used to slice a small fruit. He placed a bite in his mouth and chewed before continuing. "A very great many things."

Sanders sneered. "So what are you going to do, you dressed-up, pompous ass?"

The second man smiled indulgently, but his voice had the bite of iron. "Be careful to whom you speak, Sanders. I can kill you in ways that will leave no trace but will make you suffer incredible pain for months, if not years. You will wish for death a thousand times but be unable to utter a sound or move a muscle. The longer your family and friends care for you, the longer you will suffer. I wonder how much your wife really loves you?"

Sanders blanched and was about to speak again, but only gurgling sounds came from his throat.

Oblivious, the second man continued. "I will tell you that our master has other plans for this one. She is devious. Once he is killed, we shall kill the remaining heirs to the throne in one night's effort. Our mistress has a special treat for the prince's uncles. That message will chill the hearts of every Illician. In the meantime, they will soon figure out who set the trap in the keep. I do not wish to be arrested, so I will be leaving. Our mistress has things for me to do outside of Illicia."

After the practice yard, Sillik led a much smaller group into the steam rooms near the top of the keep. Based on Greenup and Kenton's suggestions, he had added Kenton's daughters and Greenup's grandson Keltic to the list of invitees. Kenton's wife, Elizabet, was away on healer business.

At one time, Sillik wouldn't have thought twice about sitting in the steam rooms and discussing business, but he had been away from Illicia and her customs for a long time. He was self-conscious at first but relaxed when no one else even paused.

By custom, everyone disrobed in the antechamber and hung their clothing on stone hooks. Weapons were placed on smaller shelves near the clothing. The guards who followed Sillik everywhere started to disrobe to join them until Sillik reminded them that there was only one way in and one way out. In addition, he was in the company of the swordmaster, the Speaker of the Gold Robes, the Speaker's assistant, and the Lord General of Illicia. After looking at each other, the guards nodded and took up positions outside the room on either side of the door, crossing their arms menacingly.

Sillik waved everybody into the steam room and then turned back to the guards. "Send word to my rooms that I will need more formal clothing for the appointment at third watch, something very … intimidating." Quietly, he added, "And get something appropriate for Lady Briana."

"My lord, I wouldn't know what to get," the guard said.

A slow smile spread across Sillik's face. "Have Lady Nisha choose something appropriate for the swordmaster, something strong and intimidating. It is time she was given more to do." He laughed to himself as he recalled Nisha's list of what he should be doing.

The guard nodded. "That I can do, my lord."

Sillik turned and stepped into the steam room. It was hot, humid, and dimly lit. There were no windows. Sorcery students heated the stones seven times a day. Servants in short white dresses provided large cups of cool water to everyone who entered. The steam created in the room was captured by vents in the ceiling and recycled.

The small group sat around the hot stones. Briana had left a space for him between herself and Viktorie. Kenton, Greenup, Keltic, Alexis, and Kendra were on the opposite side of the stones.

Kenton looked at the stones and clicked his tongue in disapproval. He held his hands over them and closed his eyes. Moments later, the stones glowed a deep, hot red. "The students are afraid to get the stones really hot," he said. "My knees need the heat."

"Hush, Father," Kendra said with a wave of her hand. "Everyone knows you have bad knees."

Sillik grinned as the fresh wave of heat spread around him. Droplets of perspiration erupted on his skin. He began the cleansing ceremony by pouring the first drops on the stones. "To the Seven Gods," he said in a formal voice.

Everyone in turn poured water on the stones and repeated the words. The water sizzled and turned to steam. Then Kenton dipped a ladle into a bucket and poured more water onto the stones until the chamber was full of steam.

Sweat dripped from their naked bodies in the dimly lit chamber. The only light came from the glowing stones. Since water was such a precious commodity, the only way to bathe in Illicia was to sweat and then use wet towels to wipe down. It was common in Illicia for men, women, and families to sweat together. In the baths, everyone was equal. Many disputes had been settled over the years as people sat and perspired together.

Almost every street in Illicia had multiple steam rooms, and they all had specialties that made them unique. Whether it was the type of stone or the salts, oils, or herbs added to the water, they were all different.

For a while no one spoke as sweat glistened on the skin of those gathered and slid down their faces. Custom dictated that business couldn't start until the highest-ranked person spoke. Today, everyone would wait for Sillik. Sillik sat and enjoyed the heat and moisture. He looked at Kenton, who nodded. Their conversation would be secure.

Sillik studied each of his companions in turn. Greenup and Kenton looked tired. There was a slump in Greenup's shoulders that spoke of age. Briana was still beautiful despite the delicate training scars that crisscrossed her torso. "You can't be a swordmaster without a few cuts," they used to say. At first, she met his eyes, but then she looked away uncomfortably. Viktorie sat in the shadows beside him, but Sillik could still see the terrible scars that marred her beauty. She never spoke of them, and no one ever asked twice. Sillik suspected the scars were what had driven her to leave the Nomads and seek sanctuary in Illicia. She was very protective of her past. She met his eyes with calmness, but she twisted the looped chain from her ear nervously. Keltic had the lanky look of youth. He also bore numerous scars on his arms but none on his hairless chest. Sillik bore his share of scars as well. He rubbed his thumb over a large scar on his forearm. Finally, he broke the silence.

"I want to remind everyone"–he looked at Keltic and Kenton's daughters in particular–"that what is said here will not be repeated."

Greenup smiled. "I will vouch for my grandson."

"And I will vouch for my star student," Briana said as she looked proudly at Keltic, "despite the fact that you beat him today."

"My daughters know discretion," Kenton said. "My wife has healer business today. Otherwise, she would be here as well."

"We shall all miss your wife's advice," Sillik said as he looked around. "As you know, I must be leaving soon."

The announcement was met with silence as everyone considered his words. Sillik could see what Briana was thinking. *You have only just returned!*

"There are things I must do here first," Sillik said. "I must find out all I can about my father's killer. And there are some other things that I must find."

"Like your father's signet ring," Viktorie said in a strange voice. "It is important. I don't know why, but I have seen images of you fighting with it on your finger."

"We haven't seen the ring in years," Briana said. "I asked your father about it, but all he would say is that it was safe."

*He had it when he signed that note he gave to Rebecca*, Sillik thought. *It is not lost, only hidden. I will find it.* Strangely, he found his eyes returning to Briana. She was watching him closely. He nodded, and she looked away uncomfortably.

Kenton cleared his throat. "Your father asked me to look at it once after you left. He was certain there was some hidden magic in the ring. I examined it closely, and while I saw bits and pieces of magic woven around it, I did not find what he thought he saw. He was very unhappy with me."

"Why is it important?" Sillik asked.

Viktorie pursed her lips as she chose her words. "It is tied to the kingship. We do not know how, but all the books on the topic say the success of the king depends upon it being in his possession."

"Books have been written about it?" Briana asked, incredulous.

Kenton chuckled. "In time, there are books written on every imaginable subject. But yes, there are at least three known treatises on the Ring of Kings."

"What else do you seek?" Viktorie asked.

"I am sure my father had notes somewhere."

"He did," Briana and Kenton said at once.

Briana continued, "We looked for them but could not find them. As I told you, all we found was what was in his hand."

Greenup snorted in amusement. "Your father's notes are hidden with his ring."

Sillik nodded but did not say anything as he poured a ladle of water over his head. He had already searched his father's rooms.

"I asked my wife which Gold Robes were the last to leave the keep," Kenton said. "She wanted to know why but soon figured it out. The names she gave were Sulli, Teigan, and Grison. I cannot believe any of these are traitors. Sulli has been a healer for as long as I have been a Gold Robe. Her loyalty is unquestionable. Teigan and Grison have impeccable reputations as healers and have always supported the House of Rendarick."

"Keep an eye on all of them—discreetly," Sillik said. "I dislike suspecting Illicians, but given what has happened, perhaps that trust is misplaced. Dernot had to have help. And if he left Illicia after he killed my father, then who killed my brothers? That assassin or assassins could still be here. I am sure they are still here after what happened in the throne room."

Following a suitable pause, Greenup said, "Before you leave, you should appoint a warmaster, someone you trust. We have admitted that we are indeed at war, even if we don't know whom we fight. The city must have clear leadership."

Briana sat back in thought, brushing a lock of hair from her face. She looked at Sillik. "There hasn't been a warmaster in centuries. A warmaster would report only to you. That person could override the council."

Viktorie tied her hair in a bun on top of her head as she spoke in her quiet voice. "The council has been in a stalemate since your brothers died. Though everyone had his or her idea of what should happen, no one had the authority or majority on the council to implement any ideas."

Greenup smiled. "The council can't take a drink of water without debating for days." He looked at Sillik. "You have seen it. We have all noticed you excluding people as your circle of advisors gets smaller and smaller. You need someone here who can break through the indecision. Once you leave, those people will be back, and no one else can deny them a seat on the council. The council will be mired down again."

"I like the idea," Kenton said. "It would break the impasses."

Sillik smiled. He liked Kenton, but he also knew the man was ambitious. He saw another title he could pin to his chest. *I am sorry, but it will not be you, my old friend.*

With the steam, it was hard to see Viktorie, even though she sat beside him. But when she spoke, everyone recognized her quiet but stern voice. "It must be one of you three," she said. Everyone knew she meant Kenton, Greenup, and Briana. "And it must not be either of your uncles or their sons. They are not loyal to you, my lord, and they would destroy this city."

The door creaked in the dimly lit room, and three servant girls entered, delivering water and fresh towels to Sillik and his companions. The servants would be discreet, but Sillik and his party fell silent while they were close. Sillik smiled as he remembered a piece of advice from his father: "Never say something in front of a servant that you don't want the entire city to know tomorrow."

Sillik gratefully took a towel and held his cup up for more water. The girl was pretty, and she smiled at him while she poured from her pitcher. Her long red hair was pinned to the top of her head. Sillik looked questioningly at Briana and Greenup as he held up the cup.

Briana nodded. "The water was checked earlier. Besides, it is hard to hide poison in water."

Sillik smiled and nodded. He still sniffed suspiciously before drinking it. After a long drink of the cool water, he wiped his face. The idea of appointing a warmaster in his stead was appealing, something he had been thinking about for days. He had already decided whom he was going to select, but he would listen to the debate that was sure to erupt. There was just one more requirement in his mind, and only one of the seven met it.

The servants finished delivering water and towels. With a giggle and a few furtive glances, the girls curtsied and then hurried out.

When the door closed behind the servants, Kenton counted to seven and then poured more water on the stones. The water hissed and became steam.

Sillik leaned forward and held his hands over the hot stones. "Lord Kenton, what does the law say about a warmaster?"

Kenton smiled and looked away for a moment before he spoke. "The warmaster is to conduct war. He or she reports only to the king during the time of crisis. The warmaster is allowed to conduct high and low justice in the king's name. Should the king die while a warmaster is in office, the warmaster will succeed the king, and the usual succession is voided. Should the warmaster die, the succession will pass to his or her heirs. If the warmaster has no heirs, then normal succession is restored."

"What about after the war? What happens to the crowned warmaster?" Alexis asked.

Kenton smiled. "Once crowned, a person cannot be uncrowned."

"My uncles will not like that," Sillik said with a grimace.

"The key is that a state of war must exist," Kenton explained. "Several kings have tried to void the normal succession just by appointing a warmaster and then conveniently dying. In those cases, without a state of war, the Gold Robes voided the declaration and crowned the normal successor."

"So how will my uncles take the news?" Sillik asked.

"I can answer that," Greenup said. "While we don't think they want the crown themselves, they each want it for their sons. Melin, of course, is the elder, and his son Justin would like very much to be king. Stephen, Noswin's son, would also like to rule, so the two would be at each other's throats."

"I know you said you questioned them, but honestly, is there any reason to suspect that my uncles are behind the killing of my family?" Sillik asked. "And do not fool yourself–they want the throne, if for no other reason than to settle old scores. But I think the level of planning and detail is beyond them."

Briana shook her head. "They were questioned, obviously. Your father's assassin was, of course, well known. We didn't catch the assassins who killed your brothers, but your uncles seemed very upset. They did not have the skills to do the actual killing, and their alibis were ironclad. There were no unusual changes in their credit, so it is unlikely they paid someone to do it."

Sillik nodded and then turned to Kenton. "Were they questioned with the Seven Laws?"

Kenton shook his head. "No, we saw no need, but when your brothers died, we thought about it again. This latest attempt on your life is quite beyond them."

"What about my dear, sweet cousins Julianne and Jacqueline?" Sillik asked with a small grimace. The two girls had hounded him mercilessly in his youth and had gotten him into trouble on several occasions.

Briana smiled. "Melin's daughters are out of the picture. They were both married off five years ago. They were also very ambitious. Having decided that neither could be queen here, they sought other opportunities."

"Who were the lucky grooms?" Sillik asked with a smile.

Briana laughed. "Princess Jacqueline married Prince Ametor of Salone. Princess Julianne married the viceroy of Wessten. The viceroy was three times her age, but he intended to crown her. Jacqueline has given Prince Ametor two daughters. So they are both queens in their own right and out of the Illician succession. That just leaves Melin, Noswin, and their sons, Justin and Stephen."

"I know Ametor. I spent some time in Salone after I left here," Sillik said. "The letter of introduction you gave me"–he nodded at Kenton–"got me into the house of Sarac Rish, headmaster of the schools of Salone. They tried hard to get me to stay. I was paraded around and introduced to Prince Ametor and his father, the king. Ametor took me hunting several times. They have bears there that are almost as large as lizards. What about Justin and Stephen?"

Greenup shook his head. "You grew up with them. You know what they're like."

Sillik frowned. "I had hoped things would change."

"Neither of them is suited for warmaster or to be your heir," Greenup said. "Neither has had much military training beyond the mandatory requirements of a prince. Jacqueline has fair magical abilities but married before finishing her master's."

"I suggested Jacqueline meet with Sarac Rish and finish her study of the Seven Laws at the schools, after it was decided she would marry," Kenton said. "Your male cousins have almost no magical abilities," he added. "Justin has a little, but he can barely light a fire."

"What about Julianne?" Sillik asked.

"She tried her master's test three times and failed each time," Briana said.

"So she has the basics but no great control," Sillik said with a frown. "And now we are back to my dear uncles. What do they do then?"

Kenton shrugged. "By birthright, they sit on the council. They spend a lot of time with merchants."

Greenup snorted in derision. "What he means to say is they drink, gamble, and carouse."

Sillik nodded. "So they are unfit and potentially not loyal. Are there any illegitimate cousins out there to further complicate things?"

Briana smiled. "Thank the Seven Gods, no. Or at least not yet."

"That is one less worry," Sillik said as he glanced toward Briana again. *Why do I keep looking at her?* he wondered. "Who should I appoint then?"

At that point, the arguments ensued. Kenton thought Greenup should be appointed, and Greenup argued for Kenton. Viktorie, to no one's surprise, recommended Kenton. If Kenton were promoted, she would become Speaker of the Gold Robes. Keltic and the girls wisely stayed out of the discussion, their eyes wide as they listened. Sillik smiled to himself. The steam was a good touch, and Kenton had cast his magic well. No one could overhear them.

When the debate paused, Sillik looked at Briana. "You haven't nominated anyone."

Briana looked around the small group uncomfortably and then, after a long pause, said, "It is not my position to nominate anyone."

Kenton smiled kindly. "Beware those who seek leadership, but trust those who accept leadership when it is thrust upon them. From the Second Book of Law," he said.

Sillik recognized the words before Kenton gave the reference. "I would like to hear your thoughts," Sillik said to Briana, "please."

Briana looked around, suddenly self-conscious as she realized all eyes were on her. She took a deep breath and spoke in a quiet voice. "I think I should be appointed."

Sillik feigned surprise. Everyone started to talk at once, but Sillik waved his hand to silence them. "Continue." He wanted to know her reasons to see if they matched his own.

Briana wiped her face with a towel. Her face was red from the heat or from the attention or both. Finally, she looked Sillik in the eye. "It comes down to this: Both of you"–she pointed a towel-draped hand at Kenton and Greenup– "represent specific factions of the leadership. You both have minority factions in the council. That is part of the problem. I think the city needs clear leadership. Though I have studied with both of you, I represent neither faction. I am the perfect choice." Dropping her towel on the tile floor, she produced a ball of fire in her right hand. "I am a master, which satisfies the Gold Robes' requirements, and"–the ball of fire elongated into a sword–"I have the necessary skills to meet the lord general's requirements, despite what happened this morning." She smiled ruefully and glanced at Sillik as the sword flashed.

Suddenly, the tip was at Greenup's neck. Tendrils of fires swirled from the blade and then disappeared. Surprised, Greenup pulled away from the blade.

"You both can save face and unite your factions behind me, and together we can control the council." Briana smiled at Greenup. The sword faded quickly, as did her smile, as she turned back to Sillik. "Lastly, I have a bit of royal blood, which should satisfy you."

Sillik raised his eyebrows in surprise. She had guessed his requirement. Her last comment could mean several things. She had enough royal blood to legally succeed him if he did not survive. Also, she had enough royal blood to be an acceptable queen. Sillik felt his face redden, and he looked away from her gaze. *I almost married a woman who would have been a queen.*

Kenton snorted derisively. "After seven thousand years, who doesn't have a bit of royal blood? Why, my great-great-great-grandfather was the third cousin twice removed."

"Father, quiet," Alexis hissed.

Briana smiled as she continued to look at Sillik. "Ah, but Sillik's and my grandfathers were brothers. Is anyone else's as close as mine?" She already knew the answer.

Greenup grinned at Sillik as he touched his neck. "She has my support. But your uncles are going to be angry."

Kenton leaned back and looked thoughtfully at Briana. Sillik was pleased to note that she met his stare with determination. After a long pause, he nodded.

Sillik smiled. He also liked the idea. "Let me think about it," he said. "Now, anything else?"

"Where are you going to go?" Viktorie asked.

Sillik smiled thinly. "I am going to have a conversation with my uncles tonight."

Greenup nodded. "I will bring them. That should make them uncomfortable."

Kenton looked as Sillik. "Are you going to ask them directly? Truth-reading can be difficult."

"That is why I have you, old friend. Help me with the questions."

Keltic started to say something, but a quick look from Briana caused him to close his mouth.

"You still must go to the armories and secure the weapon of your birthright," she said.

Sillik looked at her for a long moment. In the red glow of the stones, she was beautiful. She looked back at him, unblinking. He sighed. "What will I find there?"

"That which you need," Kenton answered. "It has always been the way of Illicia. The armories provide the weapons that are needed."

Sillik turned to the Speaker. "Which weapon do I need?"

Kenton shrugged. "I really do not know."

"This is the gravest challenge Illicia has ever seen," Briana said. "The king and three heirs struck down. You need the sword Avenger."

Everyone looked at Sillik. After a long pause, Viktorie repeated her earlier question. "Where are you going to go?"

There was another long silence as Sillik considered the question. "While I trust this group, I still fear a chance word or flicker in your eyes, and the secrets of where I am heading would be out. No, I think you should remain unaware of exactly where I am heading, for your own safety as well as mine."

Keltic finally found his voice. "Those are interesting scars on your arms. Is there a story behind them?"

Despite himself, Sillik grimaced. It was considered impolite to comment on another's body in the steam rooms since everyone was naked. In this case, though, he would ignore the breach of protocol. He glanced at the pale white scars on his biceps. He frowned as he touched one of the scars. The skin was stretched tight. He closed his eyes and saw the battle again. "Slavers attacked a convoy that I was traveling with." *I don't have to tell them the convoy was coming to Illicia. I don't have to tell them that I chose the campsite and how we were traveling. I don't have to tell them that that's where Nuella died.*

"I killed the man who did this," Sillik said as he opened his eyes and touched his right bicep. "It took a long time to heal, even with help." He didn't elaborate on the kind of magical help, but they all understood. "The slavers managed to capture half of the convoy. It took a long time to track down everyone they had captured and free them. It took even longer to track down the slavers and put them out of business. Many good people were killed that day." He felt the pain of that day rousing like an angry beast, and he clamped down hard on his emotions.

Briana eyed Sillik with concern but said nothing. She knew he wasn't telling the entire story.

Sillik watched Briana out of the corner of his eye. How long would it be before she spoke to Rebecca and the two women compared notes?

Greenup changed the subject, his gravelly voice as rough as his calloused hands. "I am sure you noticed who lost in the betting this morning."

"I did," Sillik said, grateful for the change in conversation. He smiled wryly. "Lord Chanderil still doesn't like me." As he spoke, he pictured the portly guild master in his wine-colored jacket.

Briana chuckled as she wiped perspiration from her face. "I told you your foes might bet against you. I imagine it was hard for him to decide what to do. He doesn't like me much more than you. So given a choice, he bet on what he thought was a sure thing, the swordmaster to beat the king." Briana laughed. "He wanted to crown one of your uncles to spite you after your brothers were killed. I am sure he thought he could manipulate them." She paused thoughtfully and then continued. "In Kings, the game, you can appoint any piece to be swordmaster and move it to attack one time. It can take any piece on its first attack. After that you leave it on the board for ten moves, but you may not move it again. If another piece that is not a swordmaster attacks, it is a roll of the dice to see who wins."

Greenup nodded. "Interesting comparison, Briana. Sillik, remember that Lord Chanderil is no friend of yours. We will keep an eye on him."

Distantly, Sillik heard the chimes ringing the watch. He turned to Lord Kenton. "Third watch."

Kenton nodded and moved to stand up. He grimaced as his knees creaked. "My old bones need more time in the steam rooms. Viktorie, you will need to come with me."

Viktorie nodded and stood gracefully.

Sillik stood with them. "Please excuse us. We need to meet with some people." As everyone else started to move, he continued, "Please stay and enjoy the steam."

Briana looked up with a question in her eyes, and Sillik nodded. "Briana, please come with us."

She stood up and followed Sillik, Viktorie, and Kenton out.

In the antechamber, the servants greeted them with warm, dry towels. Sillik was pleased to receive his towel from the redhead who had delivered water. She smiled as she bowed gracefully in her sheer dress and offered Sillik a towel. Sillik grinned as he saw the laughter in her green eyes. Briana rolled her eyes in derision but refrained from making any comments as another servant handed her a towel.

Sillik was pleased to see his instructions had been carried out. Clothes suitable for formal court were laid out for him.

Nisha stood in the doorway, prim and proper as always. She held several dresses for the swordmaster. Briana started to make a comment but then simply looked at Sillik. He smiled with pleasure. For once, he had surprised her.

Nisha was unhappy, though. "My lord, I must protest. I barely had time to arrange clothing for you and the swordmaster as well."

Sillik smiled. "I am sure all is well, Lady Nisha." He dried himself quickly. "I would take it as a great personal favor if you would assist Lady Briana. She will have important things to do soon."

Sillik saw Briana's back stiffen, but she said nothing as she dressed.

As Lady Nisha considered his words, Sillik began to dress. Once he was finished, he accepted another glass of water from the redhead. "What is your name?" he asked.

"Thelma," she replied as she had handed the metal cup to Sillik.

The water tasted wonderfully cool and crisp. Sillik looked at Nisha, and she turned quickly to leave. He handed the cup back to Thelma and grinned. "You know who I am, of course." He ran his fingers through his hair.

"Of course," Thelma said, her fingers intentionally brushing Sillik's hand, her eyes laughing.

Sillik was momentarily imagining Thelma in his apartments when Briana asked where they were going. Sillik shook his head to clear the images from his mind.

Briana rolled her eyes in disgust. "Men."

"We are going to the throne room," Sillik said. "I have summoned all the people who trained Dernot. In addition, I ordered them to bring all pertinent records." Sillik paused to adjust his sword belt. "I want to use the intimidation of the throne room to get them to tell me something I don't know."

"What do you hope to learn?" Briana asked.

"I don't know if there's anything to learn, actually, but maybe the pressure of me asking questions in the throne room will let something slip. There has to be a reason that an Illician would commit treason."

Kenton stopped at a branch in the hallway. "We will go this way," he said, motioning to Viktorie. "You and Briana should take your time; we cannot arrive together."

Sillik nodded. He and Kenton had been working on this plan. As he and Briana took the other hallway, he explained it to her. "We hatched this plan to put pressure on the Gold Robes. Kenton hasn't been able to get any answers either. Someone is hiding something, so I requested a meeting today. I want it to appear as if I am forcing Kenton to find the answers."

"Will anyone believe that?" Briana asked. "After all, he just shared the steam rooms with you. Everyone knows you are friends, and you studied with him while you were a student in the Gold Tower."

"Ah, yes," Sillik said, grinning. "Greenup left after us and will be briefing everyone else. Kenton and I had an argument in the steam rooms, and he stormed off. You had to take me aside and get me to cool down, by the way."

"I don't know ..."

"I just want to cast some doubt," Sillik said. "I want my enemies to be guessing, and perhaps something will be said. If they are uncertain, then they won't know which way the sand is blowing."

"Are they your enemies?" Briana asked. "This may be a waste of everyone's time."

Sillik stopped and looked out a window at the courtyard below. A dozen Gold Robes milled around outside the entrance to the throne room. As Sillik and Briana watched, small groups broke apart and reformed.

"Someone in the Gold Robes has betrayed this city and my family," Sillik said. "Part of the purpose of today's meeting is to see how close we can get to the truth and if they will react."

"I'm confused," Briana said. "Who is going to react?"

"Kenton and I have set a trap. We are going to poke the bear, so to speak."

"What is a bear?" Briana asked, clearly confused.

Sillik smiled. "Something like a lion."

When Sillik and Briana finally strode into the throne room, the majority of the Gold Robes were almost hostile. They did not like being summoned. Nor did they like being kept waiting. Kenton was playing his part well. His normally friendly, fatherly expression had been replaced with a scowl. Viktorie was as emotionless as always. That was also part of the plan. The Gold Robes were also embarrassed and defensive. Someone they had trained had assassinated the king of Illicia. The crime was dishonorable. It would be a long time before they recovered.

When Sillik first demanded the records, the Gold Robes had objected, insisting they could tell him whatever he needed to know. Sillik had merely reiterated his demand. He wanted to hold the paper in his hand. He wanted to know all he could about the assassin, so he had asked the Gold Robes to search the training records for clues about his enemy. For one thousand years, the tests to become a master of the Seven Laws had been somewhat standard. Finally, in the face of the Gold Robes' obstinacy, Sillik had changed tactics and agreed to let them tell him what he needed to know if they brought the records. Then he had requested this meeting for the purpose of hearing them read the results of their findings.

*There is no way they are leaving with the papers,* Sillik thought. *I will have those records.*

Sillik absorbed every detail he could retain, eager to learn all he could about his foe. He looked for weaknesses and strengths, habits, and dislikes. Everything was debated and discussed in detail. The meeting went long as Sillik sat on his melted throne, which was uncomfortable. He had ordered that it not be repaired until he had been crowned.

The longer Sillik sat, the angrier he became. Briana stood silently behind him, and Kenton stood in front and tried to argue. Sillik glanced at Briana, who had a bemused expression on her face. She had told him this would be a waste of time. Every moment seemed to prove her more correct.

The Gold Robe instructors produced the records and paraded every instructor still living who had ever trained Dernot Lafliar. To Sillik's dismay, he didn't learn much of value about Dernot's arcane talents. The man had excelled in the Seven Laws and had mastered all seven in less time than any previous master, including Sillik. Yet the Gold Robes believed Sillik was still superior. In summary, the Gold Robes had concluded that Dernot was flawed, but they couldn't explain what they meant. Sillik wondered at that as he watched the Gold Robes with more than a little suspicion. They were the teachers of the Seven Laws and had their own agenda and priorities. At times, they had become so lost in academia that he and his father had wondered if their loyalty really was to the city or to their books and scrolls. At other times, the various sects within the Gold Tower opposed each other. Seldom did they all agree.

Sillik also learned that Dernot had favored spells that were technically difficult when easier or simpler methods would have worked just as well. He also favored spells that produced loud, visual effects. Sillik smiled. That was a weakness.

Besides instructors, the Gold Robes brought all of their former students who had known and trained with Dernot. Sillik was not surprised when he was told that no one really knew Dernot. He had been quiet and had kept to himself in the student barracks. He had not gone out drinking with the other students or gone to the gambling houses, and he had never been seen at the lizard races.

Sillik thanked the Gold Robes, and then Greenup brought his instructors into the throne room at fourth watch. Sillik was more pleased with what he learned from them. Dernot had been considered adequate with the sword and superior with the stiletto. His quarterstaff skills had been poor, as were his skills with the spear and bow, and his hand-to-hand combat skills were worse than his ability in archery. He had been rejected by the royal guards for deficient mastery of the sword and had failed the warrior guild ordeal. The only area where it seemed Dernot had excelled was the Seven Laws. Among the useless trivia that Sillik learned was that Dernot preferred his wines cold and sweet. He had received a standing invitation to become a Gold Robe but had never accepted. He liked his women young, lean, and brunette. He tended to wear black despite the heat and liked to use a silver knife to trim his fingernails. It was rumored that Dernot had used that dagger to kill several men. The rumors had never been substantiated, but they persisted despite several investigations.

Sillik shifted uncomfortably on the throne and waved to Tanya. She had been the chamberlain of the keep for as long as he could remember. She came close and bowed. "What do you require, my lord?"

Sillik smiled at her cool, imperious voice. It had invoked fear in every page's heart for years. "Cool wine, please," Sillik said as he glanced at Briana, who nodded almost imperceptibly.

"Of course, my lord," Tanya said as she straightened. Her fingers flashed the message. At the other end of the great chamber, a serving man nodded and darted into a hallway that led to the kitchens.

A few minutes later, a page reappeared bearing a silver platter, on which sat a single white stone cup. As the page approached, Sillik noted that the boy's face was relaxed and almost void of expression. Smiling kindly, while inwardly seething that his enemies had taken the bait, Sillik turned his attention back to the Gold Robes and what they were saying about Dernot.

When the page presented the platter, Sillik reached absently for the cup and handed it immediately to Briana. Briana took the cup and waved at the ever-present guards to approach. With her fingers, she signed for the guards to restrain the page. To his surprise, they each placed a hand on one of the boy's shoulders.

Sillik stood. His expression was sad as he looked down at the boy. Briana sniffed suspiciously at the wine. She looked almost as angry as Sillik felt.

The conversations in the room died quickly as all eyes turned to Briana. Seemingly unaware of the attention, she ran her fingers just over the surface of the wine without touching it. She muttered to herself, brushed her hair away from her face, and then spoke words of power.

As Briana tested the cup, Sillik stood and raised shields around the group near the throne. Kenton nodded approvingly and raised additional shields, merging them into a sphere. The Gold Robes on the floor looked around in confusion as they saw the shields go up.

Briana looked up suddenly, fire blazing in her eyes. She handed the cup to Kenton, who regarded it with the same suspicion Briana had, and then turned to face the guards, her fingers flying with battle commands. Immediately, armed men rushed toward the kitchens. The Gold Robes, now concerned for their own safety, raised defensive shields.

Just then, a stunning explosion rocked the room, knocking most of the people to the floor. Flames and thick black smoke flew out from the kitchens. The Gold Robes acted quickly to raise more shields to protect themselves from the fire and smoke. The guards rushing to the kitchen tried to stop but bounced off the shields blocking the hallway. Sounds of panic added to the noise as more guards poured into the room.

Sillik turned to face the page, on whom the signs of a compulsion were evident. The boy was obviously struggling to fight the compulsion but was unable to disobey.

Kenton waved over two additional Gold Robes, and between the three of them, they began the process to block the compulsion spell.

"We are going to try to help you, young man," Sillik said with a firm voice.

The boy cried out in pain and then sagged in his captors' hands. It was obvious he was dead just by looking at him. Sillik stepped forward in alarm. Somehow, magic had been used to kill the page despite the shields that Sillik and Kenton had raised. His shields flared, momentarily visible in his anger. Despite the breach, there had been no detectable threat.

Briana hissed in anger, and Sillik glanced back at the boy. To his shock, the boy's body shimmered as if surrounded by a fog of power. Kenton cursed and threw wards around the body. Slowly, what had been the face of a boy twisted and stretched, flattening. The skin aged from a youthful facade to that of an old man. When the magic died, Sillik was looking at the face of an ancient man.

"Illusion," Kenton said in disgust. "Always a tool of the dark ones."

Briana stepped forward, her hands on her hips. "I would have sworn he was a boy, barely old enough to shave."

Sillik looked around the room, and his eyes narrowed in dismay. A mountain of weight seemed to settle on his shoulders. *Duty is heavy*, he remembered, *and the duty of the king is the heaviest.* For a moment, he struggled to control his anger. His throat felt choked, and his hand flexed as if in pain. He wanted to lash out, but he held himself rigidly. "Please have the body removed," he said softly. "Bury him with honor. I choose to believe that he didn't want to do what he did."

Briana nodded, her eyes wide with concern. "Perhaps you are right. It took a powerful compulsion to do what they did. And that illusion ... they are displaying more and more skill. You are very lucky." While she spoke, she motioned for two guards to carry out the body.

Sillik watched the recovery effort in the kitchens. Few had noticed what had happened on the dais. "I know," he said in a quiet voice for her ears only.

Kenton, who was continuing to examine the wine, shook his head in anger as he muttered to himself. Sillik wasn't sure if he was cursing or invoking some spell, since the appropriate words were interchangeable.

"Your enemy has planned well," Briana said so only Sillik could hear.

"Yes," Sillik said as he rubbed his hands over the arms of the throne. "Too well." With a sigh, Sillik looked around at the shambles of his meeting. Three healers and a Gold Robe would examine the body of the dead servant. That was standard practice. Additional Gold Robes and healers would examine the fire in the kitchens. Hundreds of guards were running here and there.

"In all the confusion," Briana said as she surveyed the room, "anyone could have escaped."

Sillik nodded. He had come to the same conclusion. His foe had planned well. His meeting had been disrupted, if not destroyed. Dernot's records lay scattered on the floor due to the concussion of the explosion. In some cases, the papers had been rendered unreadable due to the wine that had spilled.

Briana gave Sillik a curious look. "What tipped you off?"

Sillik shrugged. "I felt magic approaching me. It takes a strong compulsion to force someone to do something they don't want to do."

"I didn't feel anything," Briana said in amazement.

"I just knew magic was approaching, not what it would do," Sillik explained. "The servant had a strange expression on his face, and he was the only one moving toward me. It seemed logical to conclude that magic had been used on him."

Briana looked thoughtful. "His expression worried me, but I wasn't overly concerned because Tanya and the kitchen masters have been testing all of your food and drink. I trusted them."

Sillik nodded. "Find out what happened. Who added the poison? Where did the poison come from? Who put the compulsion on the page? If Tanya and the kitchen master are innocent, that is one thing. If one of them is involved, we need to know. In the meantime ..."

"We are going to tighten security again," Briana said. "And you are not to eat or drink anything unless I have cleared it personally. That is an order, Your Highness."

Sillik massaged his neck and stretched. "Agreed. I want a report on what was in that cup, what happened to that boy, and what happened in the kitchens. And I want it by sunset." After looking around one last time, Sillik strode away. Then he stopped and pointed at a guard. "Collect all those papers," he said, waving toward the papers the Gold Robes had provided. "Bring them to my rooms immediately."

The guard nodded. "It will be done, sire."

Briana hesitated momentarily and then, deciding her place was with Sillik, hurried after him. Four guards followed behind her.

Sillik said nothing as he climbed the stairs toward his rooms. He eschewed the elevators that were hand-cranked up and down. *Just another damn way to kill me.*

When Kenton, Elizabet, and Greenup came to brief him, they found Sillik sitting on top of the keep, watching the sunset. Briana and a dozen guards were with him.

"The man was new and had been in the tower only since the solstice, when every new class started," Kenton began. "He came from one of the farms and was proficient with a bow. His name was Ello."

"His mother said he wanted to be an archer," Greenup added. "We don't know how he ended up in the kitchens."

"Who sponsored him?" Sillik asked.

"We don't know that yet either," Greenup said.

"We believe a compulsion was placed on the boy and that he was given the poison," Kenton continued. "Tanya and the kitchen masters swear they tasted the wine. A good red, they said." He paused and looked around. "Dark magic had to be used to compel someone to do something so evil. A master of the Nine had to be involved."

When Kenton paused again, Greenup jumped in. "The fire in the kitchen was caused by two explosions. A fireball dispersed milled flour, causing a secondary explosion. The dual explosions killed thirty-eight people. Tanya knew nothing about the attack in advance and was in tears as she considered what had almost happened. She was in the throne room when it occurred. She escaped with only a few bruises, which the Gold Robes have now healed."

"The poison," Elizabet said, "was a concoction of a few rare plants and seeds that do not grow in the desert. The plants, each one a poison by itself, are rare and expensive. They have been illegal to import into Illicia for centuries. The poisons would have caused euphoria, hallucinations, and then coma and death. Once ingested, there is no cure and no healing to stop this combination."

"Are you saying a healer or someone with knowledge of healing designed this poison?" Briana asked.

Elizabet took a deep breath before responding. "I didn't say that, but yes, it is a reasonable conclusion. We found traces of the poison in a pouch on Ello's belt. But there is no way he could have obtained these materials or mixed them on his own."

"So why the explosion?" Briana asked.

"We think they used the explosion to distract us and cover their escape," Greenup said. "The explosion was also an attack on Sillik's reputation. The smoke was visible from many places in the city. Rumors are already rampant about Sillik's supposed death. The prince must be seen to dispel the rumors, but that will make him more vulnerable. The rumors seem to have started simultaneously all over the city and are surprisingly accurate. More distressing are the rumors that Sillik killed the man for bringing him the wrong kind of wine." Greenup paused. "We can only conclude that this is all an orchestrated attempt to discredit Sillik and further undermine the morale of the city."

"Do we know anything about Ello's family?" Briana asked.

Greenup frowned. "Not much that is relevant. His father died in the Nomad attack, what, ten or twelve years ago? No siblings. His mother remarried, but the second husband already had a large family, so she had no more children. Ello spent time as a shepherd and farmer. He was fair with the bow, his mother said. He came to the city to apply to the city guard. It pays better than being a shepherd." Greenup gave a wry chuckle.

"I know it will look worse," Sillik said, "but if the family is innocent, send them the standard bounty for a life lost in service of the Crown."

Briana started to object but then settled back.

Greenup nodded. "Of course."

"As far as my supposed death and my reputation go," Sillik said, "schedule a series of public appearances so I can be seen." He stood up. "Now, if you'll excuse me, I have to go entertain more people who would like to see me dead."

Briana looked confused.

"Greenup is bringing my uncles to talk," Sillik explained. "Briana, I would like you to be conspicuously absent."

Looking relieved, Briana nodded. "I should have known."

"I apologize," Sillik said. "It was a sudden idea. After they leave, everyone come to my rooms. I am sure we will have plenty to discuss."

Later in the evening, Sillik was studying a report when there was a knock on his door. Greenup looked in and then led Melin and Noswin into the room.

"Your Highness," Greenup said formally, "the Princes Melin and Noswin."

Sillik rolled up the scroll and stood to greet his uncles. Both men were dressed in expensive robes that jarred Sillik's senses and made his eyes hurt. Sillik shook their hands.

"Shall we sit?" Sillik asked as he led the men to the conference table.

Melin looked nervous as he glanced around.

Noswin, on the other hand, remained aloof and did not sit in the proffered chair. "Well, boy, you seem to have made yourself comfortable in my brother's room," he said, sneering as he looked around. "You still like playing the jester? And where is that bitch, Briana? We hear she is spending a lot of time up here now."

Sillik looked at his uncle, resenting the insinuation. The man's eyes were cold, his brow furrowed.

"You should execute her," Noswin said with a grimace. "She failed to keep our brother safe. And why are you keeping Greenup alive?" He glanced back toward the door where Greenup was standing. "You have cause to execute them both, not only for our brother but for your brothers too," Noswin continued, oblivious to Sillik's angry expression. "We heard you killed a page today. Is it true he brought you the wrong wine? Hells, boy, you got a temper!" Noswin laughed. "Hope it doesn't get you killed."

Sillik had been expecting this and had prepared a response. "There was an attempt on my life today. A man died in the process, as did thirty-eight other people. In regard to Briana, she is away on my business. She is still swordmaster of Illicia. You will address her by her title. She is also your niece and deserves your respect and support. As for the lord general, he has done his job. He is a battle lord of the highest degree. You should be thankful for his service."

"So are you bedding her or not?" Melin asked.

Sillik glared at him but did not answer.

"Why are we here?" Noswin asked.

"I wanted to ask some questions."

"About what?" Noswin demanded as he crossed his arms defensively.

Melin looked worried and bit his lower lip.

*I already have them rattled*, Sillik thought. *That's odd. They reacted to the mention of questions. Is it possible they know something?*

"Do you have any knowledge–or did you have any foreknowledge–about the deaths of my brothers or my father?"

For a moment, Melin looked scared, but it was Noswin who answered. "Are you accusing us, boy? Wasn't it that Dernot fellow who killed your father?"

"It was," Sillik said, "but I asked if you had any knowledge or foreknowledge regarding their deaths."

"If that is what you want to know, then we should leave. If you believe your uncles would assassinate their own brother …" Noswin shuffled his feet uncomfortably.

"It has happened before," Sillik said quietly. "If you leave now"–his voice took on a dangerous tone–"then I will send you to the truth seekers in the Gold Tower. That would not be pleasant for you or your families."

Melin's face paled. "That will not be necessary."

"Then answer the question," Sillik said. "Every moment you evade makes me just a bit more suspicious."

Noswin, who had been gripping the high back of his chair, finally pulled the chair away from the table and plunked himself down. "No, we had no knowledge that your father would be killed. That is not to say I didn't think Melin would make a better king."

Sillik shifted his gaze to Melin. After a moment, Melin nodded.

"See?" Sillik said. "That wasn't so hard."

"What else do you want with us?" Melin asked. His voice had a worried lilt that had not been there before.

Sillik smiled. "I wanted to ask your opinion of what my next action should be."

Noswin blinked in surprise while Melin stroked his chin thoughtfully. "We are at war, boy," Noswin said. "Surely you understand that?"

"I do," Sillik said. He kept his elation to himself. This had been so easy.

"Then you understand the kingship has been challenged, and you must go after the assassin?"

Melin picked up where his brother left off. "If you manage to kill the assassin, then you will be deemed worthy to be king." His tone left no doubt as to his opinion of whether Sillik deserved the office.

Sillik smiled. "That might take some time. In the meantime, I need someone I can trust to provide guidance to the council."

Melin sat up straighter in his chair. Noswin was grinning suddenly.

*I have them*, Sillik thought. "Something like an advisor or co-leaders of the council or some other position of leadership."

"We would certainly consider the opportunity," Noswin said.

Sillik appeared thoughtful. "It is only for the duration of the war."

Melin and Noswin exchanged a look. "We agree," Noswin said. "Only for the duration of the war."

"Then thank you, gentlemen," Sillik said as he stood up. "Your advice has been most instructive. One other thing, Uncles." Sillik was barely able to control his distaste. "You may still be in danger. I was told that you moved out of the keep. I would like for you to move back to the keep so we may protect you—you and your sons, of course."

Melin laughed. "You aren't serious."

"I'm afraid I am."

"I am not afraid," Noswin said. "I don't want to move—*again*. And I certainly don't want to move back here."

"I understand," Sillik said, "but we can offer you additional protection."

"No," Melin said.

"Then I shall have additional security sent to you," Sillik replied. "I am told that you already have a small security detail."

The two brothers glanced at each other and then at Sillik. "And if we refuse?" Melin asked.

"Are you arresting us?" Noswin added.

"No, you cannot refuse," Sillik said as he smiled thinly, "and no, I am not arresting you." He turned and raised his voice. "Lord General!"

Greenup entered immediately.

"You may show my uncles out. Oh, and assign a larger detail of men to each of them. They are to do their best to protect my uncles. I won't take no for an answer."

Greenup coughed to suppress a smile. "It shall be done, Your Highness."

The lord general ushered the men out of the room and closed the doors. He returned a short while later with Kenton and Briana.

"How did it go?" Briana asked.

"They do not like you," Sillik said. "But we already knew that. What have you done to them? Anything more recent than Edwin?" He continued without waiting for an answer. "I think they are hiding something. Melin seemed too nervous to be innocent. Have the Gold Robes start doing more research into my dear uncles. Try to isolate Melin. He might talk if offered the right incentive and if he is away from Noswin. Beyond that, I think they were lying, but I don't know about what. They tried to avoid answering a direct question about their involvement and knowledge. We know they didn't do it, but they know something."

Briana nodded. "I don't know what I have done to them recently. Swordmaster Edwin, my predecessor … well, you know that story. You were there. We know they hold grudges and want me dead or worse."

Greenup snorted. "Well, you did kill the man. But it was a long time ago—what, ten years ago?"

"Almost eight," Briana said. "Edwin was threatening that woman's daughter and had drawn his knife. He was going to kill the girl. He was drunk, dangerous, and unpredictable. What was I supposed to do? Wait for him to kill the girl or stop him? He was my friend too, you know."

Sillik held up his hand. "Peace. What else did we learn today?"

"A lot," Kenton said. "We learned that someone is still here and actively trying to thwart our investigation."

Greenup nodded. "They killed good people today."

"You are in more danger every day you stay here," Briana said.

"It is late. Go to bed and get some sleep. We can talk more tomorrow," Sillik said.

Greenup and Kenton stood up, but Briana did not. "I want to look through these papers some more," she said. "I still think we are missing something."

Sillik smiled. "Very well."

"You go on to bed," Briana said. "I can do this. You look like you need sleep."

Sillik nodded gratefully.

"Oh," Briana said, "that redhead from the steam rooms, the one you were admiring. I think her name is Thelma?"

"Yes," Sillik said, not liking where this was going.

"She tried to come up here tonight." Briana's tone was frosty. "She said she was coming to give you a massage." Briana laughed. "And she was wearing that same white shift from the steam rooms, the one you could almost see through."

"I assume the guards sent her on her way? I didn't send for her, if that's what you're asking."

"But of course," Briana said smugly. "I just thought you should know. I am going to have her investigated. I can't believe she would just try to bluff her way in here."

"Thank you and good night," Sillik said. *Just what I need, more women.*

Sillik opened his eyes with a start. He was standing in a dark forest. Pale white light gleamed between the trunks, and wisps of fog floated between the trees. He heard birds screaming in anger and fear.

Battle horns sounded in the distance—urgent, short bursts. *Help needed!* they cried. *Help now!* Screams rent the night as clouds drifted across the dark sky. The moon on the horizon gleamed red between the trees.

He turned as he heard the screams and drew his sword. The sound of a whip cracking in the distance made him turn his head again. Pain flashed across his arms as he felt the sting of a whip. He caught the next stroke with his sword. A useless bit of leather flew off into the darkness.

Ignoring the man with the whip, he ran. He had to get back. The sound of flying arrows filled the air, and Sillik heard more yells and curses. The battle horns sounded again, urgent and more terrifying. He saw others moving in the night. He did not fight alone.

Large birds swept in, and men tumbled out of their saddles. Arrows whizzed past in the darkness, nearly silent until they struck flesh.

Then he heard screams, the sounds of terror. Explosions of magic ripped the night. Sillik ran. Where was she?

Sillik bolted upright in his bed. His body was covered in sweat, and his sheets were wrapped around him. Low sunlight streaked into his room.

Moaning, he crawled out of bed. At the bedside table, he upended a pitcher of water over his head and shivered in the cool morning air. He dried and then dressed and walked out of his bedroom.

In the outer room, Sillik found Briana asleep at the table, her head lying on the papers she had been reading. Her hair was a mess, and ink from the papers was smeared on her face. Sillik put his hand on her shoulder and gave her a gentle nudge. Her reaction was immediate. To his surprise, Sillik found himself on the wrong end of an arm lock, his face pressed against the tabletop.

"Sillik, you shouldn't have," Briana said as she released his arm. "I was asleep, and you startled me. Did I hurt you?" Briana helped him stand. "After everything that's happened ..." She sheathed her knife. "I'm sorry. Let me show you what I found."

Briana rifled through the papers as she explained. "Here are his test scores—Dernot, that is. I couldn't help but notice that they were mediocre at best, until here. His scores went through the roof."

Sillik leaned over her shoulder and looked at the records. "The Gold Robes should have been able to tell us this," he muttered.

Briana nodded. "I started looking for what might have happened in this time, and I found this." She produced a wine-stained piece of parchment.

Sillik took the parchment and read it. One of Dernot's teachers had written a request to Speaker Kenton's predecessor, asking to include Dernot in a trade delegation. He thought it might be a way to reach the student and improve him, by showing him what Illicia did in the world.

Sillik suddenly became aware of how close they were standing as they looked at the parchment. Suddenly uncomfortable, he stepped away and shook his head. "This proves nothing. It is a standard method of motivating students."

Briana had anticipated his argument. "The trade delegation went to Ynak."

Stunned, Sillik sat down in one of the chairs.

Without pausing, Briana stepped forward and leaned against the table so that she could see Sillik's face. "Something happened to him in Ynak. He was turned to the Nine."

"That is a conclusion one could make," Sillik admitted. "Ynak and Nerak are almost at war ..."

"Your father knew this, which is why he directed you to Nerak. The knights usually take the Illician position on most topics, despite the difficulty of dealing with them."

Sillik couldn't fault her logic. Something had happened, and the answer was related to Ynak. He stood up and wandered over to his balcony. The city was awakening. "Someone suspected that there was something to find. That is why the meeting was disrupted yesterday." He turned back to Briana. "We must keep this to ourselves."

Briana was about to argue but then nodded.

"Who requested the trip?" Sillik asked.

"The wine destroyed that detail, but we can keep looking."

"Do so," Sillik said. "That person is likely one of our traitors. I want to know who it is. I don't need to tell you to be discreet. It has to be one of his teachers." Sillik rubbed the back of his neck as he stared out at the city. "We think we know what one of the pieces of paper in my father's hand means. But why Colum and why the Blasted Hills?"

Briana shook her head. "I don't know."

"Let's go back to the basics. Colum is a poor city, a den of thieves. Illicia hasn't been able to depend on Colum for two or three thousand years. Nothing good has come out of Colum in a thousand years," Sillik said. "Nerak has always been an ally. Does this mean that Nerak won't be an ally?" Sillik shook his head at the twisted logic. "Knowing my father, nothing is as expected. The Blasted Hills are a wasteland. No one has been there since the demon wars. And why steal the Shield of Rendarick?"

"The shield is only good for defense," Briana explained. "That shield in particular becomes active during battle. The only conclusion is that someone wants protection because war is imminent, or at least a battle."

Sillik turned away from the city and faced Briana. "A war is going to start. The Blasted Hills were the site of a battle."

Briana nodded. "We haven't explained Colum, but it makes sense."

"Colum is a den of thieves," Sillik said. "It is a trap. Either you evade the trap, or you live through it." Sillik looked at the papers. "Sometimes you learn things in a trap. Sometimes you win. Sometimes in a game, you gain points, or you obtain help."

Briana looked at Sillik in disbelief. "This is not a game. You can't just walk into Colum and say, 'I am the prince of Illicia. Who wants to see me?' You will have a thousand men trying to kill you and another thousand trying to ransom parts of you by nightfall."

Sillik looked out the window and smiled. She was right. It was stupid to walk knowingly into a trap. Yet what if it wasn't a trap? What if there was something or someone in Colum that he needed? What if there was something he needed to learn? His father had thought something about Colum was important. Test or help? Help or trap? *Damn, I don't know.*

"Sillik, you can't just walk into a trap. The point of knowing a trap exists is to avoid it."

Sillik grinned, eager to change the subject. "Now we start our day."

"You can start your day. At least you got some sleep. Me? I am going to my rooms—the back way." She smirked. "We can't have your reputation getting sullied by the sight of my leaving your apartment at dawn."

"My uncles already think we are spending time in bed."

Briana laughed. "That's not going to happen, my prince." She smiled dangerously. "I still sleep with a throwing knife, just in case you get any ideas."

With that Briana disappeared into Sillik's closet. Sillik heard the secret stone door open and close. Then he walked into the closet and drew a warding across the door. It wouldn't prevent entry, but he would at least be warned. The passage led to many places, including Briana's room.

Sillik spent the rest of the day touring the city with the regency council. There were schools to see and other important events to administer. His advisors had stressed the need for him to be seen doing the things that kings did. Despite chafing at what he considered to be a waste of time, he did what was expected. Security was tight, and the trip outside the keep was unannounced. Many smiles greeted him as he walked through the streets. Despite what his council said, he would not allow himself to be carried through the streets on a chair. Throughout the day, his mind kept wandering to Colum and what else his father might have known about that hellhole of a city.

That night, after he and his closest advisors ate dinner together, they began to settle in for another night of discussion. To their surprise, though, Sillik adjourned the conference in his rooms just after moonrise. Briana gave him a puzzled look as he asked everyone to leave the royal apartments. She tried to engage him in a conversation, but he declined and deferred further discussion until the next day. She gave him a long, searching look and then bowed formally and departed. Sillik grimaced at the sarcasm in her gesture but said nothing.

Once all of his advisors had left, he strode down the hall to the guards at the staircase landing. "None are to pass."

They nodded silently.

He returned to his apartment and waved at two guards who had lagged behind after everyone else left, and they followed him quickly. He had known these guards since he was young enough to begin training with the sword. If he couldn't trust them, he couldn't trust anyone.

Sillik stripped off his formal court clothing and shivered in the cool night air. Then he pulled on a pair of black woolen pants and a pair of low black boots. He was about to pull on a rough woolen shirt when he stopped and stared at his mail shirt. He was tempted to wear it beneath his outer shirt, but he decided it would be too obvious at the collar. Finally, he put on a black cloak with a high collar. He checked his appearance in a mirror. Not liking what he saw, he returned to his pile of clothing and picked up two sheathed daggers. One of the guards handed him a short sword with a black belt, which he strapped to his waist.

With his two trusted guards in tow, similarly disguised, Sillik entered the closet just off his bedchamber, the same one Briana had disappeared into that morning. He pushed one stone in the wall and stepped on another. There was a muffled click, and then part of the wall swung open to reveal a dark hallway and a few steps. A blast of cool, stale air wafted over the men.

Sillik felt his own warding alarm, but he ignored it. He motioned for the guards to push the door open, and more of the staircase was revealed. The three men stepped through the door, and then Sillik locked it behind him. The darkness enveloped them. Sillik closed his eyes. A moment later, a ball of smokeless fire began to glow above their heads, illuminating the spiraling staircase that descended into the depths. The passage was barely as wide as a man's shoulders. Sillik sent the light before them as they hurried down the stairs. The spiderwebs glowed and parted as the fire seared the strands before them.

Sillik knew that the previous occupants of the royal apartments had used this passageway for a myriad of purposes. At several points were doorways that opened into rooms throughout the keep. The first entrance they came to was to an apartment directly below the king's. In the past, various mistresses and concubines as well as generals and swordmasters had occupied that apartment. Currently, Briana stayed there. His father had assigned her the room years ago, and Sillik was certain they had used it to discuss many issues. The second entrance opened to the royal library. The third opened into an armory, and the fourth opened into a guard's ready room. The fifth and final exit inside the keep opened into a kitchen. From there, the stairs became very steep as they dove into the foundation of the keep.

Sillik and his companions descended the stairs in near silence. The only sounds came from their feet and their breathing. Occasionally, one of their swords rattled in its sheath. Near the bottom, Sillik felt the air pressure in the passage change subtly. He smiled. She would be watching.

After descending deep into the foundations of the tower, they reached a conference room as well as a bedroom and an armory. Another door and a locked gate blocked the final leg of their passage out of the keep. This door was small and magically locked. Only a few people had the key. Given the recent deaths, Sillik believed that he and Briana were the only two who had keys or even knowledge of this way out of the keep. Sillik knew of two other secret exits from the keep. Those passages didn't come anywhere near the king's apartment. Long ago, he had taught Briana the ways.

Sillik whispered the keyword and gave the lock a touch with magic. The lock snapped open. Sillik opened the door and ushered his light through, followed by his two guards. Sillik pulled the door shut behind them, and it locked automatically. He felt his father's charm on the door and knew that no one else had passed this way. So how had the assassins gained entrance to the keep? Was there another way in that even he didn't know about?

From where they stood, the passage sloped down under the walls. Three other gates were closed and locked. Sillik opened, closed, and relocked each as they passed. At the deepest point were small puddles of water. Sillik grimaced as the cold water soaked through his boots. When, at last, the passage began to spiral upward, Sillik was ready to get out from underground. Only one gate remained.

When they reached a seemingly blank wall, the guards stopped and cast a questioning look at Sillik. He smiled and then touched the wall and spoke an ancient word. Immediately, an archway of white light appeared, revealing a peephole. Sillik used the peephole to verify that the room beyond was empty. Sillik spoke a few quick words in an ancient language, which unlocked the doorway. Sillik's companions pushed the door open, and they all stepped through. Sillik dimmed his light as he went through the door. It wouldn't do to have anyone see him exiting the keep. The door closed behind them, leaving nothing but a blank basement wall. It was now a quick matter of going up a flight of stairs and through a normal door, from which the trio slipped unnoticed into the shadowy streets of Illicia.

Sillik and his guards pulled the hoods of their cloaks up against the chill and looked up and down the street. Several people were out, but no one paid them any attention. Sillik motioned for the guards to follow him and then walked confidently down the street. Sillik managed a quick look at the keep, which was just down the street, and saw that all was normal. Guards patrolled the walls, and the towers were brightly lit.

Sillik headed for an out-of-the-way tavern in a district known for its artisans. The tavern was near one of the lizard stables in the outer part of the city. Fortunately, the stink of the lizards had not permeated everything.

The sign above the door said "The Dancing Champion Grogshop." A foolish-looking man danced above the words. Sillik looked up and down the street and then pushed the door open.

Inside the tavern, the oil lamps were bright. It was warm, and the smells of roasted lamb and fresh baked bread wafted through the establishment. The proprietor waved at them and pointed at a table along the back wall. The stone floors were clean, although the tables bore the scars of countless meals and tankards of ale. A group of musicians played harps, drums, and flutes at one end of the room on a small raised platform. Their tune was lively and full of energy. The audience clapped to the beat and sang along with the chorus in their rough voices. Sillik smiled at the familiar melody.

Serving girls in nearly clean white blouses and long, sand-colored skirts and aprons strode between the tables with platters of food and tankards of ale. They laughingly avoided the occasional grabs and hugs from the patrons.

Sillik had never been here before, but he knew of the establishment. He had intentionally chosen a tavern not frequented by warriors or soldiers. It was known instead for the craftsmen who lived in and frequented the area. As Sillik looked over the patrons, he saw stonemasons, bakers, blacksmiths, carpenters, cobblers, scribes, merchants, a healer, and dozens of other people who did the everyday work that made the city run. Most he could identify from the shape of their bodies or the permanent stains on their hands. The stonemasons looked like the stone with which they worked, with their well-developed muscles and thin layer of stone dust. The blacksmiths had muscles like the stonemasons, but their hands and faces were blackened from the rock they burned and the metal they shaped. The bakers didn't have telltale muscles, but they did have the dusty appearance of their grains. The lone cobbler still wore a leather apron, and his hands were stained black from his work with the shoe dyes. The scribes had ink stains on their hands. The carpenters' hands were scarred, and many had sawdust in their hair. With a bemused smile, Sillik noticed that the various tradesmen didn't mix.

To Sillik's surprise, a cluster of three women sat at one small table. They were drinking Illician red, judging from the bottle and the glasses on the table. They had stopped talking when he and his guards entered the room. Their eyes were cool and calm. *Merchants*, Sillik thought as he examined the women. Their clothing was well-cut but modest, not flashy. They were probably associated with one of the guilds in the neighborhood. One of the women tucked something red into her handbag.

Two of the women smiled with thin, tight expressions. The other frowned. The women whispered a few comments and then finished their drinks. They rose to their feet as one and turned to leave. One of the women dropped a few silver coins on the table from a purse that she then tucked back into the folds of her dress.

*Soldiers—they must not like soldiers*, Sillik thought. He laughed softly. *What can I say? We can be trouble, and I have the look of a soldier no matter how much I try to hide it and no matter what else I am.* He watched them head for the door without another thought until one turned back to look at him. Their eyes met, and he was surprised to see hatred in her expression.

The women marched primly across the room and passed right in front of Sillik. For a moment, he could smell the delicate fragrances they wore. *Something fruity and purple*, Sillik thought as he watched the women leave.

Sillik shook his head as the door closed and then turned to look at the tavern. He had chosen this tavern precisely because he wanted to know what the common folk thought. His guards had specific instructions to listen and talk to people and, above all, to be discreet about their identities. They couldn't hide the fact that they were guards, but for tonight they were in the hire of a merchant who had given them the night off. It explained why they were there and what they were doing. It was a weak disguise, but it was the best Sillik could do.

The tavern master was a fat man with a bushy mustache and at least three chins. His head was bald and shiny with perspiration, and his mustache had streaks of gray. His spotless white apron was tied tightly around his ample waist. "Miri, get these fine gentlemen some ale!" the man yelled at the nearest girl as he strode toward the kitchen. "I will have meat and bread sent to you as well," he said.

Miri, a saucy serving girl, smiled as she brought their ale and a large platter of steaming lamb, bread, cheese, and grapes. "They call me Miri."

"Good evening, Miri," Sillik said. "They call you Miri? So what is your real name?"

The serving girl blinked in surprise. "My mother called me Mirianda, but no one else calls me that. Mirianda is too important-sounding for a barmaid."

Sillik nodded. "Beautiful name, Mirianda. Perhaps your mother named you truly, and you are too important to be a barmaid."

Miri smiled. "Ah, I don't know 'bouts important. But you speak real nice for a soldier. We don't get many of your kind in here. You better not tear the place apart, or Domerick will call the city guard," she said with a glint in her eyes. She plunked three large tankards of ale on their table and then slid the platter onto the table with a practiced move. "If you need anything at all, just ask for me." Then with a laugh, Miri practically fell in Sillik's lap. Behind her, another waitress apologized for bumping her. Miri only laughed as she wrapped her arms around Sillik's neck and kissed him on the cheek.

The guards laughed and lamented that Miri hadn't fallen into their laps instead. But their hands were on their weapons, and Sillik could tell that they were on edge. Sillik smiled at their jokes and pulled some grilled lamb off the platter. It was so hot that it almost burned his fingers. He wrapped the meat in warm bread and took a hearty bite. He could still feel where Miri's arms had wrapped around him. Judging by the grins on his companions' faces, it was obvious they truly were envious.

Sillik made a show of pouring the ale, but he embraced his other powers and tested the food and drink for signs of poison. Sillik's guards also discreetly tasted the food and drink before Sillik was allowed to eat or drink. When the guards nodded, Sillik took a tentative sip of his ale to wash down the hot meat and bread. The chances of poison were always high considering what was happening in Illicia. After they had eaten most of the lamb and the bread, they talked in low voices.

Then Sillik's companions got to their feet. One went to watch a game of cards, and the other to talk to one of the musicians, who were on a break. Sillik sat and watched for a moment, and then he too moved among the tables. He watched a game of dice at one table and listened to several debates. He bought several mugs of ale for the table but never took another sip of his drink. The serving girl blew him a kiss when he flipped her a silver coin for the table.

"To the Seven Gods," Sillik said as he raised his cup in a toast.

Everyone at the table raised their cups. "Praise the Seven!" Then they drank deeply.

After a while, Sillik found himself sitting with a group of stonemasons who were drinking heavily and trying to play a game of stones. When he asked why they were drinking, they said simply, "No mortar." The mortar, they explained, was made of special sands found only in the desert. Since no one could enter or leave the city, the supply of mortar had dried up, and they were temporarily out of work. The stonemasons seemed reluctant to talk to him, so Sillik explained that he and his companions had brought a merchant to the city to buy stone, and now they were stuck here in the city since the gates had been closed. The masons nodded sympathetically.

Stonemasons produced one of Illicia's marketable exports. Sadly, there wasn't much of a market for plain sand, but there was a huge market for carved stone. The mountains provided all the raw material one could want. Basalt, granite, alabaster, and marble were plentiful, and the Illicians produced tons of raw stone for building as well as finished stone statues. If it could be moved, the Illicians produced it, using teams of sand lizards to haul the final product to its destination. Illicia also exported gold, silver, and an amazing variety of jewels. Illician jewelers were some of the best. However, Illicia did not produce enough food or wine to consider exporting it.

When Sillik asked one of the stonemasons about the prince, the mason thought for a moment before answering. "The king," he corrected. "He is the king whether they say the words or not. The king," he continued in a voice slurred by too many drinks, "is being too cautious. Sure, his family has been killed. Sure, whoever did it attacked the family four times. Everyone knows the assassins have fled, don't they? They said some things got stolen, didn't they? Who's fool enough to steal from the royals and not run and hide? They have ways to find you. Their magic can track a man down and find him. They can make a man say he has stolen something when he hasn't." The mason leaned forward. "Now, don't get me wrong. I am the king's man through and through. I saw him once when he was a lad, when I was doing some work in the keep. I still think he is in danger, and whoever did this has it in for the royals, but he has to solve this, or he ain't fit to rule."

Sillik smiled as he listened. Unfortunately, it wasn't as easy as the man made out. For a while, he toyed with his mug. Then he asked what the king should do. Without looking up from his game, the mason said, "Find who done it and kill them."

"Hunt them down like rats and break their backs and leave them for dead," said the mason's opponent, with a voice that sounded like gravel.

"Where should the king look?" Sillik asked.

The mason took a long drink from his mug before answering. "People who could do this are going to cause problems wherever they go. He should look for the biggest trouble."

The other mason nodded his agreement.

# CHAPTER 6

## Thieves

MORROW SLIPPED FROM shadow to shadow. Darkness seemed to emanate from the slender man. He was dressed all in black and had painted his face and hands black so that he could hide in the darkness. A black scarf covered his fair hair. An empty black padded pouch was strapped to his back. He was a journeyman thief, a member of the thieves' guild.

Tonight, he carried a carved black ivory idol of a man's face on a leather cord around his neck. Magic had been used to cut the ivory, and twisting magics had been wrapped around it. Whoever carried it was able to make darkness surround him. The stone had been passed down in his guild for centuries. Tonight, it had been given to him for a special acquisition, an invaluable object currently owned by two wealthy gentlemen.

Creeping along the alley, he skirted from shadow to shadow, searching for a particular wedge of the building. He had hidden in the shadows for three nights previously, just watching, waiting, and counting. The guild master knew that one of the men who lived in this home had acquired something very rare and expensive.

*Ah, this is it*, Morrow thought as he found the crack in the building. Casting a furtive look up and down the alley, he wedged his fingers along the crack and used his feet to push himself up against the wall. Grunting softly, he inched his way up. Near the top of the four-story building, he paused to listen to the sounds coming from the rooftop.

Morrow smiled. *If I succeed, I will earn my master's cut.* Everyone thought thieves used brands, but the thieves had learned long ago that a series of scars on the right hand worked better. If you were caught stealing, the penalty was loss of your right hand and, therefore, your membership in the thieves' guild. There were no one-handed members of the thieves' guild. The rule was harsh but just. The guild had to be smart. *If I earn my master's cut, I can sit on the council. If I get caught, my life will be over.*

Finally, he heard what he was waiting for—the even tread of leather boots on the gravel roof. The footsteps approached and then moved away. Morrow counted to one hundred and then heaved himself over the parapet. The guards on the rooftop were predictable. Each took one hundred steps around half of the building's periphery. When they met, they executed simultaneous about-faces. They neither spoke nor stopped. Every tenth circuit, they walked past each other, neither stopping nor acknowledging the other. Every two hours, two new guards relieved them and then marched with the same exact precision.

Morrow fell into a crouch. The doorways to the lower stories were near. *Not guarded, though*, he thought as he sheathed the small knife he had been holding in case of emergency. Morrow slipped through the rooftop shadows. The two guards were good, but he was cloaked in darkness. Twice, one of the guards looked right at him but did not see him.

At the stairs, he stepped quieter than usual. Another guard should have been at the stairs, but to Morrow's surprise, the post was empty. He touched his dagger. The longer he could go without rendering anyone unconscious, the greater the chance he would be able to escape with what he wanted. Morrow was glad he had never had to kill anyone in the midst of a theft. It happened sometimes, but the guild was never happy when it did. Laughter and music floated up the stairs. He had to go down at least one more flight. The party should be on the main floor.

Morrow twisted the head of the figurine that he carried, and the shadows around him faded away. In lighted rooms, the magic would not work well and would be used up. He would need it to escape.

Morrow padded down the stairs and hallways and into the main sleeping rooms. Sula, the serving girl he had seduced, had sworn that the bottle would be there. She had been a delightful distraction, and Morrow had enjoyed the challenge of gaining her confidence and sharing her bed. It had been easy—arranging a few supposedly chance meetings at the market, following her home as he asked insipid questions, and bringing her a flower that he had plucked off the flower cart. After a week, she had searched this building for him.

It would be a large, heavy bottle of blown glass, she had said, and it would be full and unopened. "They are saving it for something important. They wouldn't even let me dust the bottle, and it was dusty."

Morrow searched the rooms quickly and efficiently. The larger room was the obvious starting point. As he searched, the sounds diminished. The party was breaking up early, the guests leaving. Morrow cursed. Sula had said it would go until early in the morning. *They know,* he thought. *They know, and they are going to catch me.*

Turning, he saw a small table with bottles and crystal cups. He froze as he heard voices coming closer up the stairs. *There!* His excitement flared as he saw the bottle. As expected, a yellow cube sat beside it. They had purchased a cheap protection sphere. Dozens were sold in the back alleys of Merchant Street every day. Morrow laughed. The cubes were sold by the thieves' guild. The buyers usually told the merchant what they needed to protect, and the merchant kept a list of what he sold and what it protected and then sold the list to the guild. Once activated, the cubes were keyed to the person who turned them on. Only that person could reach through the sphere the cube created. But the spheres kept only the honest people honest. Any good thief could get through them easily.

The brass tools that Morrow extracted from his thieving kit were designed to penetrate the sphere. With a delicate touch, he opened the sphere and, using another brass tool, lifted the bottle off the table. As soon as the bottle was clear, he yanked his tools out of the sphere, and it snapped shut.

Morrow slipped the bottle into the padded pouch on his back. His client had been very specific: "Not one coin if it gets broken, and the seal must be intact." Morrow felt the neck of the bottle. Intact. They hadn't tasted it yet; they were probably saving it for a big party. He grinned to himself.

Hearing the voices draw closer, he cursed again and looked around. No windows. Searching madly, he darted into the bedchamber and rolled under the bed. Then he separated a corner of the bed skirt so that he could see back into the room he had just left. He would wait until they went to bed and then leave. For good measure, he twisted the head of the figurine in his waist pouch.

A woman appeared with four men. She was striking in her dark gray cloak. Her back was rigidly straight, and she moved as if she owned the world. *Her face is pretty but more squarish than round,* Morrow thought. *Handsome. Smells pretty too.* She was at least twenty years older than Morrow, but that still made her young compared to the owners of the house. *Older than their sons too,* Morrow thought as the two younger men entered the room with bottles in one hand and glasses in the other. The way they were swaying, they appeared to be very drunk. A bit of golden-gray hair slipped out from the hood of her cloak.

The two older men were gray and almost pallid. Their fine, bold clothing made their faces seem even paler. A servant brought in a glow ball and then backed out of the room hastily, pulling the door closed behind her. *So much for getting out that way*, Morrow thought. *There must be another way out of here. Gods, help me! I'm so close. I can't lose my hand now.*

"The boys ain't part of this. Send 'em to bed," one of the older men said.

"Boys, get," the other man said.

"They will stay," the woman said quietly.

The young men froze.

"They will stay," the woman repeated.

"The boys ain't part of this!" the first man yelled.

"They are your sons," the woman said slowly, as if it made a difference to her. "They are part of this."

The two young men nodded self-importantly, but Morrow knew it was the alcohol talking.

"Can I get you something to drink, my lady?" one of the older men said as he strolled over to the liquor table. Morrow felt his heart flutter in fear. Being caught here would mean the gibbet for sure—or worse.

"No, I don't think so," the woman said.

"Why are you here?" one of the younger men asked drunkenly.

"I heard an interesting bit of news," the woman said. "I thought I would ask if you had heard it too."

"News?" the youngest man asked. "What news?"

"The only news in the entire city is that the prince is back," his brother said.

The woman smiled, and Morrow felt his blood go cold. *That is a dangerous woman.*

"I heard that you and Melin were sent to the prince," the woman said as she sat in one of the stiff-backed chairs. "What did you talk about?" she asked as she flourished a knife from the inside of her cloak. "Be warned," she continued, pointing the knife at the man, "I will know if you are lying. You know what I am and what I am capable of."

The two older men stiffened at the mention of Sillik and looked at each other.

Morrow tried to swallow, but his mouth had gone dry. *Did she say "the prince"? Gods help me, what did I get caught up in?*

"Melin," the woman said as she turned to look at the man. "Tell me what you talked about, and I will reward you."

"He called us," Melin said. "He sent guards to get us; we didn't have a chance to say no."

"And what did you talk about?" the woman asked as she looked at the two younger men.

"He wanted to know if we had any part in his father's death," the other older man said in a rush.

"We didn't have no part of that," one of the younger men said hotly. "They brought it upon themselves."

"Boys, you will be silent," the woman said as she waved at the younger men.

Suddenly, their eyes went wide in fear. It appeared that they were struggling but couldn't move, and their mouths seemed to have been forced shut, as if by an invisible hand.

"Melin, what did you tell your nephew? I will not ask again nicely."

"We said nothing," Melin said.

*They're talking about the killings of the old king and his sons,* Morrow realized with a start. *These must be the old king's brothers. The guild master said these people were rich, but he didn't say anything about them being kin to the king. What did I get stuck in? She acts like she knows who killed the old king. Gods help me.*

"You said *nothing?*" the woman said as she shifted on her chair. Suddenly, Morrow spotted a gold slipper and the hem of a gold dress under her cloak.

*A healer,* Morrow thought as he saw the blue stripe. *May the Seven protect us, she is a healer, but she ain't like any healer I have seen before. She's gonna kill 'em.*

"But you thought about saying something," the woman said as she watched Melin.

Melin stiffened, reddening slightly. "I didn't say anything."

"But you thought about talking." She watched Melin's expression. "I thought so. I will have to think about how to reward your loyalty. I like having loyal servants."

*How can these rich men be a lady's servants?* Morrow wondered. His body wanted to squirm, to run to get away. *If I run now, I will be as dead as they are gonna be.*

"You just asked us if we would like to be king. You never said anything about the murders. I don't want no part of any more killing," Melin said quickly. "There, I said my piece."

"Ah, Melin, you forget who stood to gain the most. Why, you, your son, and Noswin." The woman frowned. "You are implicated no matter what you think."

The man who must be Noswin tried to speak, but no sound came out of his mouth. Morrow could see the man's neck muscles moving, but his jaw seemed to be held shut by an invisible hand.

"I think I will have to reward you," she said mysteriously. "My pet will entertain you."

Morrow gulped as a red creature with spikes and long teeth became visible on the woman's shoulder. *Is that a demon or an imp?* Morrow wondered.

The creature jumped onto Noswin's head and scratched and tore at his face and eyes. He tried to scream, but no sound came out, only blood.

Morrow tasted vomit and swallowed hard to keep from giving himself away as he watched the other men try to yell. No sound came from their mouths.

The woman laughed. "I hope you enjoy your reward. Now, as for your sons ..." Her voice trailed off as she glanced at the two young men. Their muscles strained as they tried to break their invisible bonds. "I think I will spare them." She stood from the chair and walked around the younger men. She stopped to run a finger down the cheek of the first.

Morrow was too afraid to look away. To his horror, each boy jerked and then went limp. "I so despise killing," the woman said as she produced fire to cleanse her dagger. "So messy, don't you think, Melin?" she said as the monster jumped onto Melin's neck.

The man went rigid and then limp. The imp gurgled in delight. *Or did it croon?* Morrow thought. Dread and terror made him keep watching as blood flew everywhere except on the woman.

"Come, my pet," the woman said. "You can come back later and watch them find your handiwork, but I may need you, so I want you close."

The imp shook itself, and more blood flew away. Then crooning again, the creature jumped to the woman's shoulder and disappeared.

To Morrow's horror, the woman walked into the bedroom and looked around. Her eyes moved slowly around the room. Morrow held his breath. *Can she hear my heartbeat? Healers have all sorts of powers. Can she hear me breathe?*

Then she turned and strode out of the room. Silence beat on him. Sweat rolled off his face. His heart beat wildly.

Morrow counted to one hundred before he slid out from under the bed. *Do I have time to put the bottle back? No one will know I was here,* he thought. *I have got to get away. No, I can't fail the guild master. I have to tell him I didn't do this.*

Without looking at the dead men, he started to bolt for the doorway. Partway there, he stopped and looked at the floor. Blood was everywhere, and the woman's footprints were visible. *Damn,* he swore silently. He carefully scooted around the blood splatter and then stopped cautiously and peeked into the hallway. Empty, not even a maid.

At the doorway, he thought about dropping Sula's handkerchief, as he had planned. But if Sula was implicated in murder, those with power might question her, and she might talk about him. Stuffing the white silk into his pants, he darted for the stairs that led up to the roof. No one would believe that she killed those men like that. Theft maybe, but not murder, not her.

Morrow was relieved to discover that the guards on the rooftop had not altered their pattern. He waited until they were heading away, and then he scampered across the roof and down the wall.

# CHAPTER 7

## Daggers

BRIANA HAD ENDURED a long and difficult day with almost no sleep. After what she had discovered, she was angry. Once she had been his friend and confidante. As a young and foolish girl, she had even thought she might marry him. But now Sillik was acting like other men and making decisions based on his gut or whatever else men used to make decisions. Sillik's determination to go after the assassin himself was lizard-headed and wrong. He was safe only here in Illicia.

She snatched up her hairbrush. She had already changed for bed. She was tired and needed sleep–if she ever calmed down enough to go to sleep, that is. Her face was cool from the water she had used to wash her face, but her cheeks still felt hot with anger. She began to brush her hair with long, hard strokes. She shivered in her nightshirt. Illician nights could be cold once the sun went down. A warm bed would feel good. Her anger was just beginning to subside when she felt someone trigger the trip wire.

Briana's anger exploded anew. "Damn that man!"

She yanked off her nightdress and struggled to pull on some pants, a shirt, and some boots. The dark green silk shirt went over her head quickly, but she cursed as she had to lace up the front. It wouldn't be proper to go out indecently dressed. She grabbed her cloak and a throwing knife as she hurried across the room. A bit of silk caught her eye, and she grabbed it. The last things she acquired were a sword and her red belt.

Years ago, she had placed two magical trip wires in the hidden passageway behind the wall of her room. One of the wires was on the stairs above her door, and one was below it. The traces were undetectable but alerted her to someone in the hallway. Sillik's father had used "the ways," as he called them, almost daily. She never believed the king when he claimed that no one else knew of the hidden corridors.

The upper trace had been tripped first, which meant someone was going down. "Damn him," she swore as she stumbled toward the secret door in her bedchamber. Of course Sillik knew of the passages. He had taught her. How could she have gotten so careless? She should have thrown a forbidding across the hallway. She would tonight, she promised herself.

The door to the passageway opened silently. She had worked hard to clean the hinges when she first moved into the apartment. Ages ago, someone had dumped cups of sand into the mechanism. Someone's spouse had gotten suspicious, she supposed. The door was quieter than a lover's whisper now. She had also slid a large trunk in front of the door so that it would make noise if someone opened it from the passage. She didn't mind using the passageways, but she didn't want anyone else using them to get into her room.

Once in the secret hallway, she listened intently and heard the sound of footsteps far below. *Damn, damn, damn. He's going to make me run down the stairs after him.* As she hurried down the stairs, Briana tied her hair behind her head with the bit of silk.

Nearing the bottom of the stairs, she felt a subtle change in air pressure and knew that Sillik had left the protection of the keep. She cursed again.

When she emerged onto the streets a few minutes later, she looked around carefully. He wouldn't have gone far, she concluded, so she started walking casually. The streets were nearly deserted. A few silver coins bought the information she wanted. Three good-sized men had walked down this street a few minutes earlier. Her informant, a companion dressed in revealing silks, had taken her money, laughed, and pointed down the street.

Briana felt her face redden under the woman's knowing smile. She wasn't. She wouldn't. She swore again. *How could the woman think that?* Then Briana reminded herself, *I am running after a man. Of course, the companion would jump to conclusions. She thinks I'm someone's wife or lover running after her man. Damn Sillik!*

Briana hurried down the street and dodged out of the way of a lizard pulling a street sweeper. The man at the reins yelled at her for startling the beast. Briana cursed again and forced herself to slow down. She had to be more alert.

As the street curved, she saw light coming from a tavern, the Dancing Champion Grogshop. Where did they come up with these stupid names? She glanced in the tavern and recognized one of the men inside as Saleen, a guard from the tower. Rather than barge in, Briana looked up and down the street. When she saw the alley, she smiled and hurried up the street.

Once she was in the alley, it was easy to follow her nose until she found the back door to the tavern. The aroma of ale and bread was unmistakable, and the door was open. Taking a deep breath, Briana darted into the brightly lit kitchen. The ovens made the room warm, almost hot. The walls were whitewashed and plastered with various posters. Standard light-ball spells produced the light. The Gold Robes sold the light balls and the service contracts.

The cooks looked up and then shrugged and went back to work. Briana wasn't surprised. They had seen it all, and a woman entering the kitchens from the alley didn't surprise them. Briana edged forward and promptly had to dodge a busty serving girl carrying a platter of empty pitchers. The tray caught her in the side, and Briana and the serving girl went tumbling to the floor in a clatter of breaking stoneware. Briana ended up on top of the serving girl.

"Get off me!" the girl yelled. Briana rolled off the girl as the young woman tried to stuff her breasts back into her blouse.

When Briana looked up, she saw a flash of a dagger in a boy's hand. Her mind tried to react to the fact that the boy was wearing the royal livery. Time seemed to slow as Briana saw his hand go back to throw his knife. Why was he throwing a knife? The target had to be someone she knew.

Suddenly, years of training took over. Her own dagger appeared in her hand and flew at the boy. Time seemed to accelerate as the boy's hand flashed forward. His knife had just left his hand when Briana's knife struck him in the chest. He stood there transfixed for a moment before he turned to face her in surprise, and then three blows struck him in the back. Shock rolled across his face, and his eyes went glassy as he pitched forward.

The cooks stared at her in shock. At least they weren't screaming or yelling. Murder was not common in Illicia, but the cooks were acting like it was. She doubted the Dancing Grogshop Champion had never been the scene of a murder before.

Briana scrambled to her feet and yanked her blade with its monogrammed hilt from the young man's chest. Then she pressed a gold coin into the head cook's hand as she stepped back into the shadows outside the back door. She saw the guards from the keep pick up the body, three daggers protruding from the boy's back. With luck, they wouldn't notice the extra wound until later. She didn't want Sillik to think she had been following him.

When she heard the crowd murmur, it was obvious they had recognized what the boy was wearing. Then she heard Sillik's voice, and she cursed.

With another curse, she turned and hurried out of the tavern and down the curving alley. She would have to be back in the keep before Sillik returned.

# CHAPTER 8

## Answers

S ILLIK THANKED THE stonemasons, bought them another round of drinks, and then, acting drunk, rose unsteadily to his feet. The men laughed at his inebriated situation and went back to their game. They would have forgotten him had not a strange chill raised the hairs on his neck. At the same moment, a loud crash and a muffled oath came from the kitchens. Sillik turned, his cloak swirling, as a dagger flashed through the air where he had just been standing. It thudded into the wall behind him in a shower of stone fragments. The masons looked up in astonishment. Even the musicians missed a beat. Sillik's own dagger was in his hand as he searched for a foe, but in the crowd, he had no clear idea where the knife had come from.

Movement flickered to his left as someone turned in the kitchens. Sillik saw a flash of royal livery. The knife had come from that direction. Livery didn't belong there. Sillik reversed his dagger in his hand and flashed it toward the movement. Two other streaks of silver revealed the positions of Sillik's guards. Three quick thuds were followed by the sound of a body falling and then silence. Sillik drew his short sword and remained on alert for danger, but the rest of the people in the tavern had the good sense to stay put.

Sillik edged forward, but his guards were way ahead of him, and they were not happy. As they bent over to pick something up, they grimaced in anger. Sillik knew he wasn't going to like what they found. The apoplectic tavern master scurried along behind Sillik, asking why they had murdered one of his customers. He yelled for his burly doormen to restrain Sillik and his friends.

The guards dragged the body of a young man back into the common room. Three knives protruded from his back. Any one of the three would have been deadly. He had died instantly. The men retrieved their daggers, and then Sillik rolled the body over. Everyone in the tavern gasped when they saw he was wearing the livery of a royal servant.

"Summon the night guard," Sillik said as he closed the man's eyes. The assassin was older than Sillik. His hands bore signs of rough work, and the livery uniform didn't fit correctly. He was short, which was why Sillik had initially thought him a younger man.

"Never seen him before," Hillself said.

Saleen frowned. "Rumors are going to fly that we killed a royal servant. Ain't gonna be easy to dispel."

"What happened here?" Sillik asked as he tore the man's shirt open, revealing another wound on the man's chest.

"We all hit him in the back, after he threw, when he turned away from us," Hillself said. "Someone else struck him there."

"Someone in the kitchen," Saleen said. "There was a noise. It drew my eyes. What I saw first was a flash of red fabric. Shouldn't have been there."

Sillik nodded. *Bless you, Briana. You do have my back.* "I know who did this, so keep it quiet. There are going to be questions. Lots of them. When asked, tell the truth."

Hillself grunted his agreement.

Beside him, Domerick, the tavern master, was bursting in fear. "The king will have our heads. You killed a royal servant!"

Sillik sighed and then stood up and walked away from the body. Saleen and Hillself followed. They had drawn their swords, and the blades glinted in the light. They hovered protectively on either side of Sillik.

Domerick gulped and backed away. His own bouncers stood beside him, but they eyed the swords warily. Bulky muscles were no match for steel.

Sillik leaned against a table as he waited for the city guard. Now more than any other time, he really wanted a drink, but the assassination attempt made him more cautious than he had been. Even though the patrons around him had been drinking heavily, he dared not run the risk.

When the night guard arrived, Domerick began to plead his innocence and the guilt of the ruffians who had killed the servant. His story had grown to the point where he had caught the murderers. He ignored the fact that Sillik and his companions had made no effort to flee the scene. When the commander of the guard saluted Sillik, Domerick was, finally, speechless.

"I am the guard commander," the man said, "Tomar of the house Slenth. How may I serve, my lord?"

"Thank you, Tomar," Sillik said. "My friends and I were having a drink and talking to the patrons here when a dagger came flying out of the kitchen. We three"—he gestured to himself and his guardsmen—"all saw the culprit, and our daggers each got a piece of him."

Tomar nodded. "I will need more men to escort you back properly, sire. I will summon more guards. You say he threw a knife at you, my lord? Where is it then?"

Sillik looked up at the wall behind him. "It hit the wall over there. Hillself, Saleen, did you pick up the lad's knife?"

"Yes," Hillself said, "it almost got a piece of you. It put a slice in your cloak, it did. The knife is on the table." He pointed at the table.

The knife was plain with a simple bone hilt. Sillik picked it up and felt the weapon. "It's nicely balanced but common. Impossible to determine where it came from. You can buy dozens similar to it from the armorers." Sillik looked carefully at the blade. "It doesn't appear to be poisoned, but be careful."

"We will be careful," Tomar said. "I am having more men brought down. Once you are safely on your way, we will search the patrons and employees of this establishment."

Sillik frowned. He doubted that Tomar would learn anything from the knife. He extended his senses with the Seven Laws to see if he could feel something. Sadly, the only magic he could detect came from the glow balls that illuminated the room. He looked at Tomar. "Do as you must, Commander." Then a thought occurred to him. "Domerick, come here."

The frightened tavern master shuffled over.

"Those women who were here when my friends and I walked in—who were they? Merchants?"

Domerick tilted his head and rubbed a hand over his shiny scalp. "Don't rightly know, my lord … I mean, Your Highness. They came in and been sitting there all evening. Don't serve many high merchants. Didn't want my ale. Made me send a girl to buy them wine. Wanted clean glasses too. Made me wash them again 'fore they would drink. I run a clean tavern, you understand. But clean enough wasn't good enough for them. Secretive lot. Wouldn't even talk while I was standing there. Only I could serve them too. Didn't want to deal with any of the girls. My girls are good—would've taken care of them proper. But no, only me."

"What kind of merchants?" Sillik asked. "One of them looked at me with a peculiar expression, like she knew who I was."

Domerick laughed. "What kind of merchants? Ain't got no idea of that. They were pretty things and smelled nice and paid in silver. Nice tip too," he said as he patted his pocket and rocked on his heels. "They never said what they dealt in."

Sillik nodded. "Smelled nice, you say. Perhaps they were perfumers." He remembered the scent when the women had walked past him. He had smelled that before. *Where? One of them tucked something red into her purse. Was it a red hat? Where have I smelled that perfume before?*

Domerick's eyes widened. "The perfumers' chapter house is a few blocks over. Some of the girls go over every week and buy the lefts. But they wasn't wearin' their hats."

"The lefts?"

"It's a trick some women use. The perfumers mix their concoctions every week. Sometimes they have leftovers after they bottle their wares. They sell it out the back doors, you see. It may be a little strong, so the girls buy the lefts and water it down. They take their own bottles. The perfumers like it 'cause they make money on what they can't sell in the stores. And the girls like it 'cause it makes them smell like highborn ladies. All legal," he said with a wave of his hands.

Sillik looked at Tomar. "Get descriptions of the women. It's a weak lead, but it's all we have. Send men to talk to the chapter house tonight. I would like to know who those women are. And be careful with that knife. Don't press the men here too hard. There are loyal men here, and I don't want to change that."

"By your command," Tomar said stiffly. "I have sent for escorts to take you wherever you wish to go."

"The keep," Sillik said. "Time to go back to the keep."

Within minutes, a hundred guards appeared with torches and bared steel. The torches brought even more attention out on the street as doors and windows opened and crowds appeared to see what had happened.

Word spread quickly that someone had tried to assassinate the prince. People groaned in despair, only to smile when they learned that Sillik not only had survived but also had killed the assassin. They nodded proudly. "He is the one." The fact that three daggers had struck the young man only added to the story. By morning, Sillik assumed the story would be that he had thrown all three daggers himself.

Before Sillik left the tavern, he tossed Domerick a gold Illician sovereign. "For the mess," he said as he waved his hand at the bloody floor. He also tossed a gold sovereign to each of the masons. "For your unemployment and because," he added with a wry smile, "it appears the king is not being cautious enough."

The masons laughed and then gasped in surprise as they looked at the coin in their hands and then at him. A gold coin was equal to a year's wage for some of them.

*So much for a quiet night,* Sillik thought as he turned back to the common room. Still feeling generous, he tossed a gold sovereign to Miri. She caught the coin expertly and stared at it in wonder. It was the equivalent of two years' wages for her.

Two bulky soldiers carried the body outside and dumped it unceremoniously into a cart. Sillik knew the body would be examined for clues before dawn. The Gold Robes would have a report, but it would tell them nothing. Sillik swore to himself. Then with the commander of the night guard in the lead, Sillik allowed himself to be hustled through the streets and back to the keep.

Runners with torches were sent ahead to clear the streets of what little traffic there was. The gates to the keep were open, and hundreds of torches had been lit. Sillik smiled as he marched through the gate and saw the guards staring at him. They knew he had not passed their gate on his way out. Sillik just waved and kept walking.

The entourage followed him through the keep, and a score of them escorted him up the stairs and back to his rooms. Sillik felt like a pet being returned to its cage as he entered his apartments. His tightly controlled emotions were simmering just below a boil.

As expected, Briana and Greenup were waiting for him. Greenup leaned against the conference table, twirling a dagger between his fingers. Briana was pacing back and forth. She was wearing bed slippers and a dark dressing gown. *Or is it a shirt?* Sillik wondered. *Whose shirt? It's too large for her.*

He smiled. She had thrown a cloak over her shoulders, but he could see flashes of her legs as she paced. For a moment, he was uncomfortable thinking about Briana's legs. He shifted his attention to her sword, which was belted at her side. *Her legs have to be cold,* he thought again. Sillik looked away, suddenly uncomfortable with his feelings. He knew that Briana would have been among the first people the night watch awakened. How had she had gotten back to the keep so quickly?

As Sillik took off his cloak, Briana turned to face him. Sillik could tell from her face that she was furious.

"You left the tower," she said, her eyes bright with anger. "With all that has happened and all that I have done to protect you, you repay me by leaving the tower unescorted?" She shook her head incredulously. "You insult me and everything I am trying to do to keep you safe."

Sillik looked at her for a long moment. "I insult you? No, not that. Remember, it's my family that has been killed here, and the city is barely supporting me. They withdrew from the land. It's the city that believes the legend of the challenge. Since they are convinced of their own death, I get to choose how I investigate, and I get to decide what I need to do. Not you or anyone else." He paused and then continued in a quieter voice. "I wanted a different perspective."

Briana looked at him and said nothing. She was more furious than Sillik had ever seen her.

Sillik smiled in an attempt to defuse the situation. "I needed to talk to real people," he said as he ran his fingers through his hair. His neck was stiff, and he felt a headache building. He still wanted that drink, and he wanted to sleep, but anger was fueling him now.

"Real people?" Briana exploded anew, her hand on the hilt of her sword. "We aren't real people?"

Sillik shook his head. He always said the wrong thing to Briana. "That's not what I meant. I meant the common folk. They have a way of saying things simply that makes sense sometimes. I wanted to hear their thoughts. I am tired of the political opinion, the military opinion, and the Gold Robes opinion. The common people can say things simply and truly without guile and without any agenda."

Briana clenched her sword hilt. "And what did the common folk tell you that's different from what we've been telling you?"

Sillik began to untie the laces of his shirt. When he was within arm's reach of his own sword, he stopped. *I must be paranoid if I don't trust Briana. What do I feel for her?* He smiled apologetically. "Much the same as what you and Greenup have said." He paused, choosing his words. "I have to do this myself." He watched Briana closely. She had led the investigations into his family's deaths. She had posted the guards. She had investigated the traitors. If she had been turned, she could have arranged everything.

Briana stared at Sillik in amazement as if she suddenly understood. "Surely you don't suspect me?"

Sillik shrugged nonchalantly, acutely conscious of where his sword was. If she really wanted to, she might be able to draw her weapon and close before he could draw his own blade. Sillik's eyes watched her for any sign of movement. "Right now, I don't think I should trust anyone."

Briana exhaled slowly and then nodded. "Finally, at least you understand that." She turned to leave and then stopped and looked back. "I had nothing to do with what happened. I loved your father as much as I loved my own. I never would have harmed him."

Sillik nodded.

"Your brothers," Briana added, "well, I wouldn't have harmed them either even though, as you know, I didn't care for them. I am loyal to Illicia and the House of Rendar." With that she turned to leave, but she paused again on the threshold to his suite. "By the way, you have a hole in that shirt and in your cloak. The dagger came closer than you think. Had it been poisoned ..." Her voice trailed off as she gave him a stern look. Then, with a swirl of her cloak, she turned to go.

"Thank you," Sillik said. "That throw must have been difficult."

Sillik thought he saw the barest of smiles as she walked away. He turned to face Greenup, who was still leaning against the conference table, but instead of twirling his dagger, he was now spinning it casually on his palm using magic.

"Are you okay?" Greenup asked.

Sillik laughed at the question. "Since I've returned, I have nearly been blown up, poisoned, and stuck with an assassin's dagger. Sure, I'm okay."

Greenup smiled. "I should go with you when you leave. Take a squad of troops with you too."

"As if I could have a low profile with a hundred troops and supplies. Kenton would want to send twenty Gold Robes as well." Sillik laughed. "Then we would have to take lizards to haul the supplies. No, I think my way is better."

Greenup smiled. "Then just you and I?"

Sillik shook his head. "I need you, Briana, and Kenton supporting me. You and I both know the council is going to bog down again."

"Hence my suggestion to appoint a warmaster," Greenup said. "In reality, I am too old, and Kenton is too political, so that really just leaves Briana. Have you given it any more thought?"

Sillik nodded. "I haven't made any decisions yet though."

Greenup grinned. "Don't wait too long. It would be better if you had time to appoint her before court and attend some council meetings with her so everyone knows that you support her. Several factions will attempt to bring her down. As you know, a warmaster will upset the succession, and that will anger many people." With that, Greenup took his leave.

Sillik drank a goblet of warm wine. Then he picked up the cloak he had worn that night and found the hole quickly. He fingered the cloak as he looked at the door and remembered Briana's words. He also found a clean slice in his shirt. The dagger had missed him by the thickness of his shirt. His mail gleamed in the candlelight where he had left it earlier that evening. With a curse, he threw the cloak at the door and stormed into his bedchamber.

A few moments later, he walked out of his room wearing a new shirt. He opened the doors and addressed the guards at the end of the hallway. "Wake the scribes up and send them to me. And have Nisha get me some tea."

They nodded as Sillik turned back to his room. He splashed some water on his face and rubbed his neck. It would be another late night.

"Where is he?" a woman's voice demanded. The doors to his rooms opened, and Claudett strode into the room. "Sillik, thank the gods that you are alive. I just heard."

"Claudett, I am fine," Sillik said. "Really, I am fine. You may go back to bed."

"Let me be the judge of that," Claudett said. "Pardon my appearance. Messy bit of healing," she explained. "Blood all over my dress and shoes, so I had to change."

Sillik glanced and to his surprise saw that she was wearing a dark blue, almost black dress with a narrow gold band along the hem. "I don't think I have ever seen you out of your gold robes," he said thoughtfully.

"Nonsense," she said with a smile. "I do have other dresses. Now let me look at you."

Sillik felt the magic settle over him. He had used the same magic to heal others.

"You need more sleep," Claudett announced a few moments later, "but other than that, you are well enough. You need to let those who support you know what you are doing. You are being unfair to Briana. She does care for you."

A knock on the door made Sillik turn his head. "That will be either Nisha or the scribes. I have work to do before morning."

Claudett gave him a long look but said nothing as she turned to leave. When she opened the door, the scribes and Nisha entered.

Sillik had just closed his eyes after dismissing the scribes, but after two pots of tea, he couldn't sleep. He heard loud voices in the hallway. He groaned as he climbed out of bed and threw on his clothes. Someone was pounding on his door.

"Come!" he said as he buckled his sword belt.

Kenton and Briana rushed in. "Are you are safe?" Briana asked. "You haven't left again?"

"Yes, I'm safe, and no, I haven't left. Why?"

"Your uncles," Briana said.

"What about them?"

Kenton gave him a sad look. "Dead, Sillik. I am sorry. They were out in the city, and someone attacked them. They and their sons were all immobilized and killed."

"I want to see them," Sillik demanded, feeling a surge of anger. He expected an argument from Briana, but none was forthcoming.

"So do we, Sillik, which is why we woke you," she said. "A detail is being prepared to take us. For my peace of mind, please put on your mail and leathers, and then we'll depart."

Sillik pulled on his mail shirt angrily. When his head emerged, he saw Briana was holding his leather. She was already wearing hers. Sillik thrust his arms into his leather overshirt. "Let's go," he said before he had even begun to fasten it on. He led the way out of his apartments and found twenty warriors waiting in the hallway.

In short order, Sillik found himself walking through the twisting streets of Illicia accompanied by over a hundred warriors and more than a dozen Gold Robes. Many of the warriors carried torches. Soon, they were standing before the entrance to an impressive four-story home.

"Where was the detail I assigned?" Sillik asked.

As Kenton answered, his eyes darted around for new threats. "This morning your uncles were in the keep for a meeting. We sent fifty men with them. Your uncles kept them outside."

"So how did the assassin get in?" Briana asked.

Kenton shook his head. "We don't know yet. They are on the third floor."

Briana looked up and down the street. Then she ordered soldiers to search it and take up positions.

Kenton ushered Sillik into a doorway. Sillik entered and took the stairs two at a time. At the third floor, he found more warriors and Gold Robes.

"Out," Sillik ordered.

The soldiers and Gold Robes hurried out of the room without a word as Kenton entered.

As Sillik looked around the room, he felt something was wrong, something evil. There was blood everywhere, but beneath its coppery smell was something else. "There is another scent here," he said.

"Greenup is in charge outside," Briana announced as she entered the room. Her eyes went wide as she felt the foulness and looked around. She stepped sideways to avoid the blood splattered on the floor. "I don't smell anything other than blood."

"No, there was something else," Sillik said as he drew on the Seven Laws to enhance his senses. After a long pause, he found the scent again, and his eyes narrowed. "Lilacs," he said finally. "I have smelled that scent before." *Where?* he wondered. *It is different from what I smelled at the bar.*

"You may be right," Briana said as she stepped close to Sillik. She took a deep breath and held her breath with her eyes closed. When she opened her eyes, she stepped hastily away from Sillik. "But it doesn't prove that a woman did the killing."

"No," Sillik said slowly as he watched Briana. Her face was suddenly red. Why, he didn't know. "It proves nothing," he admitted. *But it is important.*

Kenton said with a grimace, "We will look into it. But there are several women who live in the household."

Sillik examined the room, and his eyes narrowed again as he saw the bodies. It looked like all four had been restrained, but by what? Whatever had restrained them had been removed. They had struggled, and their restraints had dug into their arms. From the wounds on his uncles, it appeared they had been tortured. *But by what?* Sillik wondered.

The floor was covered with drops of blood. The source was obvious, but he knelt to examine a slight arc where no blood drops were evident.

"We saw that," Kenton said, "and this footprint. A woman's shoe."

"Yes," Briana said as she knelt beside the shoe print. "Okay, now we know a woman was here when that happened." She gestured at the bodies.

Nodding, Sillik looked at the strange burns and cuts. *I have seen those signs before.* He shivered despite the heat. The old men's faces had been shredded. What had the assassins wanted? Mercifully, his cousins' bodies bore no wounds other than those that had ended their lives. Each had been killed execution-style with a single knife wound to the back.

Sillik took a breath and closed his eyes. Holding his palms up, he extended his senses again to encompass the room. It did not feel clean. There was a taste of evil in the place. He turned and felt the shadow move.

Kenton felt it too and reacted slightly faster. Together, their magic reached out and caught the squirming shadow creature. Briana's breath caught as she saw the hellish being squirm, but it could not escape. It was an imp, a creature that lived in hell but was a frequent servant of the Nine. She added her strength to the snares, and then the three of them squeezed. Despite its screams, which they felt rather than heard, the creature shrank to a dot and then popped out of existence.

"What was that thing doing here?" Briana asked, breathing heavily.

"It was someone's puppet," Sillik said. "Dernot or his master could not get me tonight, so they got the next best thing. They went after the rest of my family. Damn, I thought I had given them enough security."

"They didn't want it," Kenton said. "They kept the security as far away as possible. There is also another possibility ..."

Sillik looked up as he waited to hear what it was.

"Someone wanted to kill you, your uncles, and your cousins," Kenton said. "Then the next in line would be ..."

"Me," Briana said. "I am next in line after Sillik now."

"Damn," Sillik said. "My uncles should have known better." He stiffened. "Do your investigation. Write your reports. Use the seven laws! Find out what really happened, who was involved, and how the assassin got in here and out. Briana, I want additional security added to you as well. You don't get to go anywhere alone."

"No, Sillik. I–"

Sillik held up his hand. "I don't want anything to happen to you." He reached out and enveloped her in a hug. Then he kissed her forehead. "A full security detail. I will have Greenup take care of the details."

Sillik turned and headed for the door. Then he stopped and looked back. "Have word sent to Melin's daughters, the princesses Jacqueline and Juliann.

They should be warned that their father and uncle have been killed. Tell them … tell them all of it." Sillik looked back at the bodies. "Make the notifications official letters that I can sign before I leave. Oh, and request their cities' support if we need help dealing with the assassins. No, change that–nothing official. I will write the letters tonight. And find those perfumers. I am betting they had a hand in this somehow."

Briana looked uncomfortable, but Kenton pushed her toward the door. "Go with him. Send my people up here."

Briana nodded. When she got outside, she saw the pink of dawn in the sky. *So much for sleep tonight*, she thought glumly.

# CHAPTER 9

## Notes

LATER THAT MORNING, at the beginning of first watch, Sillik opened court in the Golden Cathedral. Runners had been sent throughout the city the previous evening to announce open court. The people of Illicia had lined up before dawn. Security was tight, but Sillik thought the event was important. His advisors had disagreed.

Despite the long night, Sillik bore no outward sign of being sleep-deprived, unlike Briana. She knew he had used the Seven Laws, but she wasn't going to ask. His face appeared as fresh and carefree as if he had had a full night's sleep.

Petitions would be presented. There were eight outstanding cases that needed royal review. It was a longstanding tradition that citizens with legal cases could make a final appeal to the king. Sillik had spent a large portion of the night with the legal scribes, reviewing the cases and precedents and Illician law. Three more cases would be appealed soon. The scribes had wanted to wait for the remaining cases, but Sillik had declined. These people whose cases were ready wanted justice, and he would be the one to give it to them. He wouldn't shirk his responsibility.

Almost five thousand citizens crowded into the Golden Cathedral. Some had come to watch the petitions, and others just to see the "last prince." Sillik knew that was what they were calling him. The stonemasons had said as much the previous night.

The cathedral took up the entire first floor of the Gold Tower. The Gold Robes lived and taught in the floors above. It was named the Gold Cathedral because of the polished, gold granite that covered the floor, walls, and ceiling. Each of the seven walls was dedicated to one of the Seven Gods and that god's branch of magic.

Members of the guard lined the walls, and archers stood quietly in the balconies. Their orders were to shoot at the first sign of trouble. Briana had been firm on that.

Sillik hid a yawn with the back of his hand as he watched the crowds enter. He wore his mail under his regal silk and leather. The seamstresses had delivered a bewildering selection of clothing. He wasn't wearing a sword, but he was wearing his knives. Energies swirled around him, unseen to all except other masters of the Seven Laws. Briana, Kenton, and Greenup stood silently behind him, each swathed in her or his own protections. None mentioned the events of the previous night.

When Sillik stood, the crowd quieted in expectation. He had the scribes call the first case. The people had waited long enough for justice. After he had rendered judgment on the petitions, Sillik confirmed the appointments of over a dozen men and women to positions ranging from steward to watch commander. At first, Sillik seethed at how long this took. Then, as he saw the looks the people gave him, he began to change his mind. This was bringing order to the chaos, and at the same time, he was giving them hope.

Finally, he stood to adjourn court, but before he could formally adjourn, the crowd erupted in applause. It took a while before he could be heard, but he was finally able to close the court. He was genuinely touched by the display of support. It might be a long time before he came back to Illicia, and that saddened him.

When Sillik left the cathedral, his closest advisors accompanied him. Sillik led them back across the courtyard and into the keep. Greenup and Briana were debating some details of one of the petitions, but Sillik wasn't listening. Justice had been done according to the law. When they returned to Sillik's rooms, then they could talk.

Sillik and Briana climbed the stairs while Greenup stopped to confer with the guards. They were halfway up the long, winding staircase when a shadow moved in front of Sillik. Briana drew her blade and stepped forward.

Sillik also reached for his knife until he recognized the woman and her blue cloak. "Rebecca," Sillik said, "do you have any information for me?"

Rebecca glanced at Briana as the latter sheathed her sword. She pursed her lips for a moment before turning her attention back to Sillik. "I do, my lord. Lord Grison has disappeared. He missed two classes he was requested to teach. Guards were sent to look in his apartments. His rooms have not been slept in, and he cannot be found. A sizable withdrawal of gold was made from his accounts three days ago, so it is suspected that he has left the city."

"Lord Grison ... interesting," Sillik mused. "I assume you know he was on a list provided by Elizabet?"

Rebecca's eyes flinched. "I do, my lord."

"Is he involved?" Briana asked, her anger flaring.

Rebecca glanced at the swordmaster. "Indeed, he must be, my lady. To what extent, we will not know until he is questioned."

"Thank you," Sillik said. "What about the other two from the list?"

"They are accounted for," Rebecca said. She then nodded and pulled her cowl back over her head and descended the stairs.

Greenup came up the stairs, stepping aside to let Rebecca pass. "Ah, there you are," he said. "One of my majors has turned up missing. He failed to report to his post this morning. We can't find him."

Sillik and Briana glanced at each other but said nothing until the three were in Sillik's rooms. "Who?" Sillik asked.

"Major Tyier. Remember him? Big fellow, bushy mustache, two scars across his face, and no ear."

Sillik nodded absently. "I remember. We have also learned that the Gold Robe Grison has turned up missing."

Greenup hissed. "We may have figured out who some of our traitors are."

As Greenup examined the food on the table, Briana approached Sillik, her voice low. "Rebecca, she is no ordinary healer. Tell me."

"I am not supposed to tell anyone what she is," Sillik whispered. "For now, just take the information she gave as fact. I will explain when I can."

Briana gave him a reproachful glance but did not say a word.

Servants had left wine and a plate of bread, cheese, and fruits. A dome of magic protected the food, indicating it had been checked for poison. Despite the visual assurances, Briana inspected everything before she would let anyone partake.

When Kenton walked in, everyone sat, and Lord Greenup and Kenton gave Sillik a brief report about the would-be assassin from the night before. According to their findings, the man was an impostor, and no one in the keep had ever seen him before. Nor could they explain the fourth wound. When Sillik asked about it, they merely shrugged. He noticed Briana stiffen and look away, but she said nothing. What they didn't know was how the assassin had found Sillik. When Sillik asked if more were lurking, Briana shrugged.

"What about the women I saw?" Sillik asked. "The merchants?"

Greenup shook his head. "The perfumers' guild was in conclave last night, electing a new leader. The chapter house was locked, and none were allowed in or out."

"So that lead goes nowhere," Sillik said. "Damn."

"Not exactly," Greenup said. "The guild reported that two of the voting members did not respond to the summons to appear in conclave. They gave the names as ..." He paused as he consulted his notes. "Ah yes, a Mistress Jade and a Mistress Blaine."

"Who are they?" Briana asked.

"We don't know," Greenup admitted. "We have scribes looking into their backgrounds, and the guild told us where they lived, so we sent guards to their homes. They were not home, and their housekeepers had not seen them for several days."

"So nothing," Briana said.

"We are still looking," Greenup said, "but it is going to take some time." Pausing to rub his eyes, he continued. "Now to your uncles. Melin made a very large purchase several weeks ago. Nobody thought it strange at the time, but hear me out." He cleared his throat. "Remember the night after you returned, we had a dinner party in your apartments? Kenton brought two bottles of wine. He talked about a bottle of Armagnac that he wanted to buy."

Sillik nodded.

"Last year, a small chest of Armagnac was found. Best estimates were that the bottles were a thousand years old. They had been preserved, of course, and sealed with magic. Seven bottles were found, but the healers certified only one as drinkable. Everyone knew how much Noswin and Melin liked to drink, so no one was surprised when they purchased it. That bottle sold for five thousand double gold sovereigns."

Sillik whistled. "That was probably cheap. Was it any good?"

Kenton smiled. "Everyone said it would be priceless. Elizabet thought I should buy a bottle for you—that is, until we heard what the opening price at auction would be."

"Fine, but how is this important?" Briana asked. "As you said, everyone knows Melin and Noswin liked to drink."

"Ah yes, but they didn't drink it," Greenup said, smiling. "As word got out about their deaths, several of Noswin's friends showed up this morning, trying to buy the bottle. They claimed the brothers had shown them the bottle just days ago, bragging and hinting that they would soon have something to celebrate, and they would drink it then."

"Damn them to the nine hells," Briana said. "They were in on it."

"Yes," Greenup said, "but where is the bottle?"

Sillik looked up sharply. "Where did they keep it?"

"The friends claimed it was in a liquor cabinet in Melin's room," Greenup said.

"We searched and found a liquor tray with an empty space, right where the friends said it should be," Kenton said triumphantly. "A protection sphere covered the bottles, but we all know those are easily breached."

"Who took it?" Briana asked. "The killer or someone else?"

"Good question," Kenton said. "But what we can be certain of is that if we can find the bottle, we'll find the killer or at least someone who might have witnessed the murders."

"Keep this information secret," Briana said. "No one besides us, this group."

"Only those of us here know," Greenup said approvingly. "We told everyone that Melin's personal possessions were being moved to the keep and would eventually be auctioned. We let everyone think we had the bottle."

Sillik smiled. "That's great, but as for the events at the tavern, how did they know I left the keep last night? I told no one but you, Greenup, that I was leaving. Not even my guards knew. So how did they?"

"Could you have been followed?" Kenton asked.

Sillik laughed. "Only by Briana."

Greenup and Kenton turned to the swordmaster, who reddened in exasperation.

"I followed you out of the keep last night," she admitted. "I entered the tavern from the alley. I saw the assassin and used this knife." She drew a monogrammed throwing knife and laid it on the table. "Then I retrieved my knife once the threat was passed. When you summoned the guard, I returned to the keep. I apologize for not telling you."

Sillik smiled at Briana and raised his eyebrows.

Her eyes narrowed. "When did you realize I was following you?"

Sillik laughed. "While we were in the passageway. How did you know we were leaving?"

Now it was Briana's turn to smile. "I put trip traces above and below the entrance to my room."

Greenup looked up. "So the rumors about the passageways are true." He smiled with satisfaction.

Sillik nodded as he smiled at Briana. "I figured it was something like that. I too apologize for not trusting you." He turned to Greenup. "Yes, the keep is riddled with secret passageways and secret rooms. My father showed all of them to me. Most require some kind of magical talent, so my brothers did not know them all. My father made sure I knew them, though. The secrets are kept close; never more than a few know in any generation. The passageways are never acknowledged or mentioned. If too many people know, then everyone will know, or so my father lectured me."

Greenup nodded. "The way you left the keep last night confirmed it for me. Your father always had an odd way of turning up in strange places."

"I knew they existed but nothing more," Kenton said. "Once, long ago, I looked for them but never found anything."

"With all the magical talent in this city, if they were meant to be found, they would have been," Sillik said. The secret ways were not supposed to be a topic of conversation, and yet he was discussing them as if they were the morning meal. "My father said that special rocks and metals were used when the towers were built, which hides them from magic. There is no way to find them using magic." His voice trailed off as his eyes focused on something in the distance.

"Sillik, are you all right?" Briana asked, concern flashing across her face.

"Should I call my wife?" Kenton said. "Do you need a healer?"

Suddenly, Sillik pounded the table. "Damn, it was here all along!"

"What?" Briana asked, alarmed.

"The stone." He pounded the table again.

"You're going to hurt yourself," Briana said.

Sillik smiled. "Please stay here. I'll be back in a moment—I think." With that he stood up and stepped into his bedchamber.

His father had left him a message in a way that only he could. They had discovered the secret together when Sillik was a boy. His father had noted absently that a carved stone panel beside his bed appeared to be out of place because it didn't match the other stones. Sillik had guessed that it held a secret. Months later, Sillik had found the answer and proudly opened the secret panel. "The stone that doesn't move," they had called it. He smiled and pressed the stones around the unique stone carving. The panel opened with a pop, and Sillik stepped forward to look inside the small chamber. He found a stack of parchment and a small black velvet bag. Sillik knew exactly what he would find in the bag.

Sillik reached into the tiny vault and was about to touch the parchments when he pulled back slightly. His father had locked these papers away. He hadn't wanted them to be found. If Sillik had found the vault, others could find it too.

Sillik extended his senses. He found exactly what he had expected would be there. A fire spell was wrapped around the parchments. They would burst into flame unless the password was spoken. Sillik withdrew his hand and leaned back, licking his lips as he tried to figure out the password. If his father had left it for him, only one word would unlock the spell. If he was wrong, the papers would be lost.

Moving close to the vault again, he touched the spell with his mind and spoke the one word that should unlock it. "Jenna," he whispered as he reached out to touch the parchment. The spell popped and then collapsed. Sillik smiled. The password was the name of his mother, the woman who had died giving birth to him. His father had told Sillik endless stories about her. Jenna had been his father's second wife and, according to the note Rebecca had given him, had also been a member of the Hunters. His first wife, the mother of Sillik's brothers, had died in an accident.

Sillik pulled out the parchment and upended the velvet bag. As expected, a large gold ring clinked onto the stone. He flipped through the papers. They were his father's notes, but he saw nothing unexpected. In fact, the notes were almost bland. However, in one corner, a circle had been drawn. On top of the circle sat an Illician eagle. Sillik smiled and turned his attention back to the ring. The Illician eagle on the ring reflected the light. Sillik studied the ring from a distance. He didn't think it was a trap. Just to be certain, though, he wrapped the ring in the velvet bag, closed the panel, exited his bedchamber, and returned to the table where his companions waited.

He laid the ring at the center of the table on a black silk handkerchief that he had previously found among his father's things. He had been very careful not to touch the ring with his bare skin. He moved his hand close to the ring and closed his eyes in concentration as he studied the magic that was wrapped around it. The ring was alive with energy and potential. What had his father done? Was it just the ring, or was something else set to occur?

"Where did you find that?" Briana asked, half-rising to her feet in surprise.

Sillik smiled. "It doesn't matter now." The vault was a secret that his father had not shared with anyone else. *What will the ring do when I put it on my finger?* he wondered. He moved his hand away from the ring and opened his eyes to study it.

After a long pause, he gave up and slid it over to Kenton. "Please tell me what you find."

Lord Greenup nodded in recognition at the ring. "The Ring of Illician Kings," he said, smiling. "Your father believed it predates Illicia."

Lord Kenton looked at the ring and then at Sillik. "Where did you find it? We searched for weeks. Some thought it had been stolen as well."

Sillik smiled but did not answer.

Kenton gazed at the ring thoughtfully. "I knew your father would have tucked it away. I would like to know where, though." He glanced around the room as if the hiding place would reveal itself.

Sillik shrugged. "It's enough that I found it." He looked at Briana and smiled. Then he turned to Kenton. "Is it a trap?"

Briana smiled. "You have started to pay attention."

"I was always paying attention," Sillik said, continuing to look at the Gold Robe.

Kenton examined the ring without touching it. "What did you learn?" he asked, not looking up.

"I don't think there is a trap," Sillik said, "but there are traces of all kinds of things. I don't know what they all do. So no, I actually am not sure if there's a trap. I never handled the thing after I mastered the Seven Laws, so I am seeing it with new eyes today."

Kenton nodded and bent closer to the ring. Muttering to himself, he made notes on a piece of scrap parchment he carried in his pocket. Kenton studied the ring for a long time, turning it over with a small silver dagger as he whispered to himself. Finally, he steadied his hands over the ring and closed his eyes in concentration.

Kenton used several standard spells to examine the ring. Sillik had tried many of the same methods on other objects. After a while, Sillik gave up watching. Refusing to meet Briana and Greenup's eyes, he ran his hand over the carved arms of his chair. He ignored their attempts to draw him into conversation, and eventually they all sat back to wait. He was sitting in what had been his father's chair. The stone was worn smooth from hundreds of generations of kings. It was cold and uncomfortable.

After an annoyingly long time, Kenton looked up with a smile. "It is safe." As if to emphasize this, he scooped the ring up with his bare hand and tossed it to Sillik, who caught it with a surprised look on his face.

He looked down and rolled the ring between his fingers, feeling the ancient engravings that were worn smooth. He pushed the ring onto his ring finger. The gold was cold, but the ring fit perfectly, as if it belonged on his finger. Sillik felt as if he had been wearing it for years. It felt familiar, like something that had been missing. Then he felt a momentary whoosh in his ears, followed by a wave of dizziness. Images flashed through his head in rapid succession. Then the feeling passed, and Sillik took the ring off and tossed it into the air. Smiling, he caught the ring again and placed it in the velvet bag. Three anxious faces watched him carefully. The feeling was similar to what he had felt when he put the prince's crown on his head. Greenup gave him a knowing smile. *Sometime, he and I are going to have to talk*, Sillik thought.

"Did you see them?" Lord Kenton asked.

Sillik smiled but said nothing. His father had never said anything about visions when he first wore the ring. Sillik wanted to understand what he had seen before he talked about it.

"I was here when your father put that ring on for the first time," Lord Kenton said. "He said he saw memories, memories of everyone who had ever worn the ring."

Sillik looked at his advisors. Then he stood up with a sudden burst of energy. "Thank you, gentlemen and lady. You have served me well today, and I have kept you away from your duties too long." Despite their protests and questions, he ushered them out.

As Sillik waved her out the door, Briana produced a small folded letter sealed with gold wax. With a mischievous smile, she handed it to Sillik. He looked at the paper in surprise.

"You should read it," Briana said. "Now that you've dealt with the ring, you can deal with this."

Sillik rubbed a finger over the wax and felt the indentions of the seven-pointed star with crossed swords in the middle. He looked down at the wax and smiled. He had seen the signet years before. Lord Kenton had once used that symbol, a long time ago. He broke the seal and scanned the words. The handwriting was as distinctive as the seal.

*I request the honor of your time. I have information for you.*

*Lady Viktorie,*
*Sentinel of the Gold Robes*

Sillik looked up at Briana. "Please ask Lady Viktorie to join us."

Briana nodded with a small smile and strode to the door. She spoke quietly to the guard and left the door open. Sillik looked at Briana, who smiled knowingly. She wasn't going to tell him what Viktorie wanted.

"The seal," Sillik said. "Only one person in this city can use that seal at a time." He looked up when he heard soft footsteps from the hallway.

Briana made a move as if to leave, but Sillik stopped her. "Please stay."

She nodded with an uncomfortable expression.

*What game are Briana and Viktorie playing?* Sillik wondered.

The guard escorted Lady Viktorie into the room and then closed the door. Sillik suspected Viktorie had passed the note to Briana just recently and had been waiting nearby for his summons. She was dressed in a high-necked, dark green silk gown. She was not wearing her customary gold earring. An intricately detailed necklace of seven eagles hung around her neck. Sillik was intrigued. Something unusual was occurring.

Viktorie started to curtsy, but Sillik waved it off. She brushed her dress nervously and then settled her hands delicately before her. Sillik asked if he could offer her a drink as he poured himself a glass of wine. She smiled but declined. He offered her water or something cool, but she declined again. Viktorie looked at Briana as if wondering why she was present.

"I asked Lady Briana to stay," Sillik said.

When he returned to his seat with a goblet of cool wine, Viktorie took a deep breath and began to speak. "Upon occasion, I have been gifted with the curse of foretelling. My first experience was shortly before you began your studies, before I became your watcher. At first, it was little things. My first significant seeing was the death of Speaker Forbes. At first, I thought it was a bad dream, and when the Speaker died, I thought the dream was just coincidence. He was, after all, very old. I didn't realize what was happening or what I was seeing.

"Over the years, the visions have been infrequent. Sometimes they have shown innocent, happy things, like two people marrying or a woman with child. But the visions are becoming stronger and more frequent. I thought something was wrong when I saw your father fighting things he couldn't control the afternoon he was killed. I saw ravens flying around his head, and in my heart, I knew, but I said nothing. I didn't understand what I was seeing."

Without realizing it, Sillik was leaning forward, hanging on every word. *Foretelling, the gift of prophesies.* He remembered the words in the Second Book of Seven about the gift: "A veil covers the hidden world, which not the strongest man or woman, nor even the united strength of all the strongest men who ever lived, can tear apart. Yet sometimes, a few are granted the opportunity to peek through holes in the veil."

Viktorie continued, "After your brothers were killed, I knew the day you would return to Illicia. I saw you and the moons on the horizon. I knew you would return at sunset, on the Celebration of the Kings. I told Briana, and with her encouragement, I told your council. They were depressed and ready to crown one of your uncles as king. Your uncles were quite happy to know you would return and when." She gave a sarcastic grimace. "So they deferred the crown until after you returned."

"I am sure they were pleased," Sillik said dryly. "And now they are dead. I assume you have a new foretelling, or you wouldn't be here tonight. What do you see now?" *Do I really want to know?*

Viktorie pursed her lips together in irritation, and her eyes flashed with anger.

*Is she disapproving of my request?* Sillik wondered. What was the proper etiquette when asking someone what the future would bring?

"This morning," she said in her most formal and disapproving tone, "I saw fog rolling around your head. Above the fog, I saw nine dragons circling. Then the fog cleared, the dragons fled, and I saw you breaking into an ancient crypt. A demon burst out of the rubble with an army of schula." She paused. "I don't know what it means; very seldom do I understand what I see. I don't interpret what I see."

Intrigued, Sillik sat back and took a long sip of his wine. "Fog," he said. Fog was something most Illicians wouldn't recognize. The word would mean nothing to them. Moisture-laden clouds were unknown in the desert. Viktorie had spent time in several of the garrisons, so she would have experienced it.

"And dragons," he said. The reference was not unexpected. The nine dragons could refer to Ynak or a dark master or both—or worse yet, nine dark masters. The last part, about breaking into a crypt, was interesting. A demon bursting out of the rubble of a crypt? The last demon war had been seven thousand years ago. Demons were real creatures. They varied in strength and abilities, but they were very real. Sillik suppressed a shudder. Viktorie had seen schula as well. Was he going to have to fight schula? No one had seen one since the demon wars ended. They were the stuff of horror stories, except for the fact that Illicia had a schula skeleton.

Sillik ran his hand through his hair. He certainly hoped he wasn't going to be fighting another demon war. His name might mean "demon destroyer" in the old tongue, but he didn't want to test it. "Anything else you remember?" Sillik asked. "Banners, colors, smells, people?"

Viktorie closed her eyes. "You were accompanied by people I did not recognize. Some might have been … well, that is impossible."

"What is impossible?" Briana asked as she moved forward to stand behind Sillik. She put her hand on his shoulder. It felt warm and reassuring.

"I thought," Viktorie said, opening her eyes to look at Briana, "that the people accompanying the prince were knights of Nerak."

Sillik looked at Briana in surprise as Viktorie continued. "I have never met any knights, but some of the men I saw carried staves." She turned and looked out the large window. Her eyes seemed unfocused. "But at the same time, several of the knights bore swords, which is impossible. As we all know, the knights don't use metal weapons." She paused. "A woman was also fighting at your side. She had long brown hair in a braid. In my vision, she was a master of the Seven Laws. I do not know who she is. Then later, I saw Briana fighting at your back as well. I also saw you wielding magic of unimaginable strength. I don't know how you would possess such power. You did not possess abilities like that when I was your watcher." She looked down at her hands. "Always, though, in the background of the vision, a shadow was watching."

Sillik rubbed the stubble on his chin and nodded. At least he was expecting someone or something behind the scenes.

Viktorie stood up primly. "I am now retiring for the night. I have done my duty and now wish to return to my tents. The sun has set, so it is time to sleep or die," she said, quoting a desert Nomad saying.

Surprised, Sillik looked up to discover that the sun had indeed set. "The gods willing, we will meet with the new day's sun," Sillik said, but at the same time he thought, *What am I involved in?*

Briana stepped around the table after Viktorie had left. "She can't control what she sees."

Sillik smiled weakly. "I have only read about foretelling. When she was my watcher, she never said anything about it."

"Would you tell a student you were training about a newly found talent that you had? Especially a talent you didn't want? It is very uncommon," Briana said. "It is also very dangerous. I don't think I would want that talent, to know when someone might die. I will retire now as well." With that she turned to leave for the night.

"No, wait," Sillik said as he turned over the papers from his father's vault.

Briana eyed the papers wistfully, tears glittering in the candlelight.

"My father's notes," Sillik said. "Please sit and join me."

"With all due respect," Briana said somewhat stiffly, "I am tired and would like to sleep. After all, I did spend last night at this table. So thank you for sharing, but I would like to get some sleep. You should, however, read these papers." She touched a pile of letters on her side of the table.

Sillik glanced at the pile of letters and groaned. They were all from the city's nobility. Briana had been reading some of them in her spare time, bursting into laughter on several occasions. When he had asked what was so amusing, she had shown him marriage proposals buried in the letters of congratulations. "We congratulate you on your imminent ascension to the throne and ask you to consider the hand of our daughter, Irene," one had said. "She would be a worthy queen."

"Politics," Sillik snorted in disgust. "If I did what Nisha wanted, I would accept one of those and then ask to meet the bride. No, I can't do that."

Briana looked at the stack of letters more closely. "But this one is different," she said, picking up a small, folded parchment with a wax seal.

"Different how?"

"It is odd," Briana said as she examined the wax seal.

"In what way?" Sillik asked, rubbing his temples.

"This letter," she said. "It has your name on it, but the sealing wax doesn't have a signet that I recognize, and there's something strange about the wax. It wasn't here earlier."

"What is it?" Sillik asked as he looked up. "Lords, I am tired."

Briana grimaced. "It's a dagger."

"Stop!" Sillik said as he jumped to his feet, alarms ringing in his head. "Hand that to me."

Briana handed him the paper.

Sillik cleared a space on the table and laid the folded note carefully before him. Near the middle of the paper was his name. Below his name was a red wax seal with a clear impression. "My father told me a long time ago to watch out for the sign of an upturned dagger," he said as he sat back down.

"What is it, or who is it?" Briana asked.

Frowning, Sillik recalled the conversation with his father. "Tell me," he asked, "do you think there are guilds in the city, secret ones?"

Briana started to laugh but stopped when she saw Sillik's face. "I guess. There have always been rumors of a thieves' guild. But I've assumed they are only stories."

Sillik frowned. "Every time there is an unsolved crime, one the finders can't solve, there are rumors of the thieves' guild. Sometimes they even accuse the crown of being complicit."

"But they're not, and you're not," Briana said. "But what about that?" She pointed at the paper.

"If the thieves' guild exists," Sillik said, "and I think it does, then it stands to reason that other secret guilds exist too."

Briana frowned.

Sillik rubbed his chin. "Assassins' guild," he said finally. "My father warned me to beware of an up-facing knife. He got a note from them right after he was crowned."

"I never heard that," Briana said as she sat down beside Sillik.

"I don't think he told anyone but me and maybe Greenup. I never asked. A few days after he was crowned, he found a strange note, and he couldn't figure out who had sent it."

"What did it say?"

"It said that someone close to him had tried to hire them, but they wouldn't take action against the crown."

"Professional ethics," Briana said, laughing. "Was it real? Who would want to kill your father?" She gulped as she realized what she had just said.

"Loyal Illicians," Sillik suggested.

"Are you going to open it?" Briana asked.

Nodding, Sillik held his fingertips over the paper and extended his senses briefly. "There is no trap," he said absently. "I can't find any poison."

Satisfied, he picked up the letter and broke the wax. Inside the envelope, he found a precise script.

*We had no part in what happened to your family.*
*Guild Master of the Assassins*

Without a word, Sillik handed the note to Briana.

"Interesting," she said. "But hardly proof."

"It is sufficient for me," Sillik said with a smile. "Now how did it get in that stack of mail? Someone must have delivered it."

"The letters have been coming for days," Briana said as she looked at the mound of envelopes. "Anyone could have slipped it in."

Just then, a quiet knock on the door drew their attention. Briana opened the door and was handed another note.

Bemused, Sillik watched her open it as he rubbed his temples. "If it's another marriage proposal, you can add it to the pile. I don't want to think about any more notes."

Briana's expression turned cold and hard as she looked at the wax seal. She handed the note to Sillik. "You will want to read this one."

Sillik was about to question her when he took a closer look at the seal. It was unmistakable. It was stamped with an unrolled scroll. He looked up in surprise.

Briana nodded. "The rule makers wish to see you."

Sillik frowned. "That means Lord Reznek." He fingered the seal slowly and then looked at Briana. "Is Lord Reznek even still alive? He has to be almost one hundred."

Briana nodded. "He turned 101 before High Golden Day. He invited some people to his rooms to celebrate–not that he celebrated. They won't let him drink wine anymore. Said he gets violent and throws things with magic."

Sillik sighed. "You know I don't care for that group. Never did. Too political. They wanted me to become a Gold Robe and then a rule maker. Reznek, I think, wanted me under his wing. I had two choices: become a Gold Robe and a rule maker or let Greenup make me a battle lord." He paused to rub his forehead. "Be a puppet for the Gold Robes or enforce Illician will in battle."

"You never told me," Briana said. "I had no idea."

"Do you know that the lowest-ranking rule maker decides who tests and advances within the Seven Laws?"

Briana had to think for a moment. "I guess so."

"I didn't want to do that for twenty years or so. It is usually about twenty years between rule-maker appointments. The battle lords, on the other hand, seem to die in battle or get injured and are forced to retire. They forced one to retire to make space for me in their ranks. Greenup told me. I thought it was odd that a position in each was suddenly open the day I mastered the Seven Laws. With the rule makers, after deciding who gets to test, then you move up to the appeals court, where five old men sit on the court of arbitration and settle disputes within the city. I don't know if I trust Melin and Noswin's claim that Edwin was making plans for me. You challenged Edwin, what, a month before I tested? And then you had to kill him the week I tested for my master's."

Briana frowned.

"I think my father made the arrangements. He wanted me to have an honorable place. But he never asked me. So how is Lord Reznek, anyway?"

"He has not left his apartments in almost eight years. He could barely move when I saw him last, and his hands and feet are twisted by age."

"He has always been reclusive," Sillik said as he fingered the seal.

Sillik had expected a visit, not a summons. It was said each new king had to be vetted by the rule makers. He rubbed the seal again and tried to remember what else his father had said about them. Frustrated, he broke the seal and read the short note.

*Please come to my rooms when you receive this.*
*Your servant,*
*Reznek*

He leaned back in his chair and handed the note to Briana.

Briana read it and looked up. "You can't refuse him. He holds considerable power, and Kenton cannot protect you if Reznek chooses to oppose you."

"I don't intend on refusing him," Sillik said. "Is he still holed up in the top of the Gold Tower?"

Briana nodded.

Sillik stood up. "Well, let's go see him then. It won't get any easier."

Briana took a deep breath and nodded. "I guess I'm not going to my bed either," she said wistfully.

"Let's see," Sillik mused. "If we go down to the bridges, we can go over and then back up to his rooms."

Briana nodded, her brow furrowed with concern.

"Why so tense?" Sillik asked.

"This is real, isn't it?" she asked. "It didn't really sink in until now."

"Didn't my brothers have to meet Reznek?" Sillik asked.

Briana shook her head. "Reznek didn't ask to see them. So they ignored him. They weren't masters, so they really had no reason to know him."

Sillik nodded as he held his hand out to the door. Briana nodded and then led the way down the hallway. As they passed the guards, the men fell in behind Sillik.

The small group walked quickly to the stairs. When they came to the bridges, Sillik moved into the lead and strode boldly into the night air. Their feet echoed as they crossed the stone bridge. It was about as wide as two men and had a railing. Sillik kept to the middle. The bridges had an emergency pin at each end that could be removed during a siege, if necessary to protect either tower. It was a long way down.

At the entrance to the Gold Tower, the guards saluted with a display of fire and then opened the door. These were the Gold Robes' own guards, and they wore gold armor with gold helmets. Their only job was to protect the Gold Tower and its occupants. Engraved above the door was another ancient message. Sillik paused and touched the words as he recited them: "Blessed be the Seven Gods who train my mind to fight evil." Sillik nodded at the guards' salute and then stepped inside with Briana at his side.

Annias, the tower mistress, met them inside the door. "I will lead you to Lord Reznek. Your guards must stay here." Then she turned to lead the way through the maze of hallways.

Sillik nodded at his guards. "Stay here."

"Lord Reznek has been expecting you," Annias said. Her tone implied that Sillik was late. Then, without another word, she turned and glided down the hallway without a ripple in her robes.

The Gold Tower was a warren of narrow halls that turned at random. Some had speculated that through so much use of the Seven Laws, the tower was now larger on the inside than it was on the outside. When Sillik lived here, there had been stories of new hallways being found and no one knowing where they went. The hallways were lit with a gold glow that seemed to infuse the very stone itself. At one time, he could have found his way through the tower on his own. Tonight, he was content to be led.

After several steep, winding staircases and mazes of hallways, they reached a set of double wooden doors. The men guarding the doors did not salute and kept their weapons blocking the entrance.

Annias turned back to face Sillik and Briana. "Lady Briana will stay here. Only you, my lord, may enter."

Briana started to protest, but Sillik held up his hand. "Very well," he said as he stepped forward.

The guards withdrew their weapons in response to a curt nod from Annias. The doors closed behind Sillik with an audible click.

The room beyond was dimly lit. Candles and oil lamps shared space on every surface with piles of parchment and scrolls. Cobwebs clung to the edges of the room. A haze from the smoke floated everywhere. If there were any windows in the room, they were tightly shuttered. The walls of the keep were magically cooled during the day. Despite the cooler temperatures of the evening, Sillik began to perspire. He looked around, but the shadows were dark.

"So, Sillik, it has been a long time since your master's test," a voice said from the shadows.

"It has been," Sillik agreed. He tried to relax but couldn't.

"What did we last discuss?" the voice asked. This time it seemed to be right behind Sillik.

Sillik smiled at the memory. "We disagreed about my place in the world. You wanted me to become a Gold Robe and then a rule maker."

Reznek stepped into view on Sillik's left.

"You are looking well," Sillik said.

"Phaa," Reznek muttered. He held canes in both of his gnarled hands and was stooped over, his back twisted with age. Most of his once-silvery hair was gone, and his face sagged in long waves. His pallor was gray, but his eyes were still bright. Use of the Seven Laws protected one against some of the effects of age, but age always won eventually, and when it happened, one could age years in a matter of days.

Reznek moved forward slowly. "I was right at the time, but perhaps you were also right."

Sillik looked at the senior rule maker with surprise.

"If you had been here, I have no doubt you would be as dead as your brothers."

Sillik opened his mouth to protest.

"Don't argue with me," Reznek said as he lowered himself into a chair. "I am too old, and I am dying." He sighed as he settled into the throne-like chair and waved for Sillik to sit.

"What do you know about what has happened?" Sillik asked.

"I felt that explosion," Reznek said. "That was sloppy."

Sillik was about to respond, but Reznek continued. "Not you, my dear boy, not you. The trap. I had a full briefing from Speaker Kenton." He chuckled. "You detected the trap and raised shields. That saved lives, including your own. No, the trap was sloppy. Someone was in a hurry."

Surprised, Sillik sat back to listen.

"No one should have been able to detect a trap like that. It was poorly done, and it was too complex. This leads me to two possible conclusions: one, the spell-caster was incompetent, or two, the caster intended you to find it."

"Why?" Sillik asked. "If they wanted me dead, then why warn me?"

"Yes, well, we will have to figure out the 'why,'" Reznek admitted with a wave of his hand. "Now whom do you suspect?"

"The healers were the last in the keep," Sillik said.

Reznek barked a laugh. "They are the last ones you should look at. I do think it revealed more about the people opposing you. They had to have your hair and blood to set that kind of trap."

Sillik thought back to his conversation with Rebecca. "Someone who has access to healers but is not a healer?"

Reznek eyed him carefully. "Yes," he said. "Has someone talked to you, boy?"

"I talk to many people. That is my job," Sillik said, his face relaxed but his heart racing. Would Reznek confirm the rumor?

"Yes, I suppose." Reznek rubbed his chin thoughtfully. "I asked you to see me for other reasons." Reznek pointed toward a pitcher. "Pour me some water," he ordered. "They don't let me drink wine anymore." His voice rose, punctuating his displeasure. "I sure do miss my wine."

Sillik poured the water into a pewter cup and placed it in front of the rule master. "Why did you ask to see me?" he asked as he stepped back and stood behind his own chair.

Reznek laughed. "Straight to the point, are you? You were always direct. I will tell you then." He sipped his water. "It may take a while. There are many reasons. At my age, I don't get out much. I wanted to see if you had become the man I thought you would be." Reznek paused and looked him up and down.

Sillik was uncomfortable under his steady gaze and said nothing.

"Then I wanted to know if you are prepared to be king." Again he paused and looked at Sillik.

Sillik did not look away. He met the rule maker's eyes.

After a pregnant pause, Reznek continued. "Then I wanted to discuss some things that you should know. I think I know why your family was killed."

"You have my full attention," Sillik said as he sat down again.

"What is happening in the land?" Reznek asked.

Sillik smiled tightly as he felt his anger flare. "To put it simply, war."

"But why?"

Sillik shook his head. "If we knew, we could do something about it."

Reznek laughed. "What is the root of all evil?"

"The Nine Dark Gods, of course."

"And their puppets."

"A dark master?"

"Or a group of them," Reznek said.

"There is always more evil."

"Phaa, don't quote scripture to me. Let me ask you another question. How can Illicia do good if we withdraw from the land? And why is there more evil than good? Everything else is equal."

Sillik smiled. "You speak heresy."

"I am long past caring about a little heresy. You know as well as I the legend of the eight."

Sillik smiled. "Is that what this is about? An obscure legend? We discussed this many times before. It is based on some wild conjectures. As I recall, the story is that when the Seven Gods appeared to Rendarick after the demon wars and laid the foundations to the seven towers of the keep, they left room for an eighth tower and forbade construction of any structure on that spot."

Reznek laughed and began to recite from memory. "From the Second Book of Seven, chapter three, stanza nine: And the Seven Gods appeared before Rendarick and the hosts and commanded, 'In this valley you will build our city and support good works forever.' They struck the ground, and water flowed. 'You will turn this valley green, and you will continue to do good.' Then the Seven Gods laid out the seven towers and laid the first foundation stone of each tower. 'Around these towers you will build our city. But on this site, you shall not build any structure here, in memory of what was and what will be again.' Then the great lords sat and spoke to the elders and masters and conveyed great wisdom. On the seventh day, the great lords prepared to depart at sunset when the seven moons rose as one.

"Before the Seven Gods left, the Nine appeared, each on their own peak surrounding the valley. The people were afraid, for they had never seen all of the lords appear together. The Seven were not afraid and said do not show fear and do not be afraid. When they departed, the Nine left as well."

"I know the story. You taught it to me," Sillik said as he shook his head in frustration.

"Illicia has been special," Reznek said. "The Seven Gods favored Illicia, and now we retreat from the world. Now evil can feed again. Who else will profit except forces of darkness?"

Sillik didn't say anything.

"You have been thinking about what you need," Reznek said.

Sillik nodded.

"What does Illicia need?"

Sillik looked at the elder man with a puzzled expression.

Reznek smiled. "I will save you the trouble. Illicia needs to be confident. Its confidence has been shaken. By the Seven, we have had four kings assassinated. The Illician people need to see you being confident and unafraid. All of these half attacks are designed to shake the city's confidence."

Sillik stroked his chin and nodded.

"You don't get it." Reznek's eyes gleamed. "Founding is in a few days."

Sillik nodded but didn't say anything. The city seemed on edge as the holiday approached.

"How many of the Seven Gods will appear?" Reznek asked.

Sillik grimaced. "I was told one appeared last year. So one."

Reznek spat. "Wrong answer. What will the effect on the city be if only one shows up?"

"More depression," Sillik admitted.

"So let it be known that you expect all of them or a majority of them," Reznek said with a mad grin. "Hells, maybe they will listen to you and come."

Sillik smiled despite himself.

"Now enough of that. Listen, I have important things to tell you, son …"

When Sillik emerged from Lord Reznek's room, Briana was pacing the hallway. He signed silence with his fingers as she started to ask what had happened. Without a word, he strode down the hallway.

Annias struggled to catch up. "I should be leading you, my lord."

Smiling, Sillik ignored the woman and continued to lead the way back down to the bridges. He had spent too much time in these halls. As a young man, he had spent time with the Gold Robes during his studies and had been summoned to all of the rule makers' rooms in preparation for his master's test.

At the door to the bridges, Sillik waved his hand with a horizontal cut, and the warded door slid open. The warders tried to conceal their astonishment. They thought they were the only ones who knew the secret of the doors. Sillik chuckled but said nothing despite Annias's protests. Without pausing, he strode into the night air and across the bridge.

Once Sillik and Briana were back in Sillik's rooms, he looked around and, with a dismissive gesture, threw a warding around the room.

Surprised, Briana reached out instinctively and tested the wards. She was even more surprised when she realized they were stronger than any other wards she had felt.

Sillik poured himself a large glass of wine and drank most of it with a few quick swallows. When he saw Briana examining the wards, he laughed. "One of the first lessons I learned was to never show your full abilities. The Gold Robes were always suspicious if you could do things better than they could. I found I could do most things with varying levels of strength, so I learned how to hide my abilities. Now, however, the time for subterfuge is past." Sillik carried the bottle of wine and another glass to the table and poured a glass for Briana.

"What did Reznek want?" Briana asked as she sat down and smoothed her skirt.

"Among other things, he said our conversations here were not secure," Sillik said as he looked around. "They should be now."

"What else?"

Sillik smiled. "We discussed scripture."

"Scripture? That doesn't make any sense. What do the Seven Books have to do with what is happening?"

"From Reznek's perspective, they explain everything," Sillik said as he slumped down into his chair with a weary sigh. In an imitation of Reznek's deep voice, Sillik said, "Attack the heart and soul of Illicia. Response: Illicia withdraws, looking for an enemy within, and can no longer project force. Who wins in that situation?"

Briana frowned. "Illicia doesn't benefit. Whoever is behind this would benefit."

Sillik nodded. "Reznek thinks that there is a dark master—or masters— behind this and that he has agents here in the city."

Briana stood up and walked around the table. "So should we send the garrison soldiers back out?"

"I asked that question too. Reznek said no, and I tend to agree with him." Sillik toyed with his wine glass. "We may need the troops."

Briana gaped. "You think it's that bad?"

Sillik nodded.

Briana stifled a yawn and then fought off another.

"You should go to bed," Sillik said. "I will be safe tonight."

Briana nodded and then stood up and walked to the door. She paused in the doorway and looked back at Sillik. He was already immersed in the papers and rubbing his neck. "I am sorry, Sillik," she said quietly as she closed the door.

Sillik didn't hear her words or the closing of the door. As expected, he found additional notes in the margins of his father's papers. The ring was the key to more than one thing. Sillik leaned back for a moment and rubbed his temples. His eyes throbbed, and his neck ached. Tension. He tried to smile, but the smile faded quickly as he read.

Then with a sudden thought, he stepped to the door and opened it. He spoke a few words to a guard and closed the door again. He had just finished the third page when a knock came at the door.

"Come," he yelled.

Nisha, wearing a thick, pale yellow robe, stepped into his room. "You asked to see me?" she said. "Could it have waited, my lord?"

"Tell me, Nisha—do you wear perfume?" Sillik asked as he rubbed his neck.

She looked up in surprise. "My lord, that is hardly a question a man asks."

"It is a simple one," Sillik said with a grimace. This wasn't going like he had planned. "Please answer the question."

"Yes, my lord, I do," she said stiffly.

"And what does it smell like?" Sillik asked.

"Roses," she said formally. "My father was a flower merchant. It reminds me of him."

Sillik smiled and mentally framed his next question. "Who do I know that wears a perfume that smells of lilacs?" Sillik asked.

"My lord, many women wear perfumes. I can't know what every woman wears," she protested.

"I want you to find out, Nisha. Someone close to me wears something that reminds me of lilacs. I want to know who that is."

"My lord, I must protest. I cannot go smelling all the ladies at court. It is most improper."

Sillik looked down at his papers. "The scent is strong. All you have to do is talk to them." He paused. "You have three days. Now you may go back to bed," he said matter-of-factly. "I have disturbed your rest enough. Also, not a word of this to anyone. No one at all. Your life may depend on it."

Nisha humphed and turned quickly to leave but then paused. "You are leaving then?"

Sillik nodded, and Nisha left. He did not hear the door close behind her as he returned his attention to the papers that his father had left.

He stayed up late that night, reading and rereading the thoughts of his father. What he read, combined with what Viktorie had seen and what Reznek believed, had him worried.

When he finally tried to sleep, his mind kept darting to impossible scenes and people who were long dead. Kings and queens who had worn the ring had all contributed their memories to its magic. Rolling cloud banks were torn to shreds by the thundering clap of dragon wings, which made him sleep fitfully. In the dark corners of his mind, something was blocked. The ring told him he needed to assimilate the memories, but his fear said there was more to it than that.

The next morning, to the surprise of the court, Sillik named Briana king's regent and warmaster. The city had to have clear leadership, as Greenup had observed. He had decided when Greenup first proposed the idea that she would get the job. Her arguments in the steam room had been valid as well.

When she stood in front of Sillik to swear loyalty to him as warmaster, she whispered, "I'm going to hate this job, aren't I?"

Sillik looked at Briana for a long moment and then nodded sadly. "If you do it right, yes. Nothing will be the same, and nothing can prepare you for it." He paused to let his words sink in. "If you like it, then all is lost, and I have chosen the wrong person."

When she laid her hands in his to swear her oaths, he felt her tremble despite her clear, loud voice. "I, Briana Dulcane, swordmaster of Illicia, by my hope of salvation and the love of the Seven Lords, do swear loyalty to Illicia and obedience to the king. I swear that I will faithfully execute the laws of Illicia and do everything in my power to protect Illicia from all dangers. By my desire to walk in the light forever, so may the Seven Gods seal my oath."

Out of the corner of his eye, Sillik saw Kenton and Greenup nod approvingly. They would be swearing loyalty to her next. Sillik almost laughed when he saw Greenup absently rubbing his neck where Briana's fire sword had touched his skin. Viktorie had a stoic expression on her face.

Turning back to Briana, Sillik recited his portion of the oath. When he was finished, he spoke in a quiet voice for her ears only. "You will have to maintain control of this city and the council. That will be hard. They will try to test you. But you have veto authority over everything the council might suggest. They cannot overrule you. Also, should I fail, it will be up to you to carry on the fight."

Briana started to speak, but Sillik interrupted her. "It has to be this way, Briana. You know it as well as I do. The papers are already written and signed in my rooms. Should I not return within seven years, you must be crowned. There are others who have fewer claims to the throne, but you have the most. Something about Rendarick was important. Therefore, it is important that his blood sit on the throne."

"How will I know if you fail," Briana asked, "if I can't go with you?"

Sillik smiled. "I think Lady Silvia will bring you word should I die. She seems to pop in at odd times. At least, she has for me."

Briana trembled, and Sillik released her hands and then raised her up to the applause of the throne room.

As he stood before the court wearing the king's ring, he was buffeted by memories that were not his but were now part of him. He remembered standing on a hill surrounded by sand dunes, laying the cornerstone to this very tower. In other memories he watched the keep and the city being built. The memories were distracting, but Sillik focused on what he needed to accomplish. In his head, he remembered battles, lovers, children, arguments, tragedy, and even death. It was as if every memory of everyone who had ever worn the ring had been imprinted in his mind. Sillik smiled to himself. Margatha, Rendarick's wife, had been beautiful.

That afternoon, Sillik made his trip to the royal armories. He had resisted making this trip, but the time was right. Briana had been relentless, pushing the subject of going to the armories at almost every opportunity. She was right, and her logic impeccable, but Sillik didn't like it. There were dangerous weapons in the royal armories. Finally, he had accepted her argument, but not without question. What did she expect him to find there?

When he asked, Briana had merely shrugged and smiled mysteriously with her typical nonchalance. Sillik wondered what his father might have told her. If his father had summoned him and left a message, then he could have had many conversations with Briana. Briana had been the daughter that Sillik's father never had. Sillik wondered what else they might have said to one another, what plans they had made. She did say, "Wear the ring; it is important." With that enigmatic comment, she had tossed her hair over her shoulder and walked off.

Rendarick's statue in front of the armory held the key. "Stand in the gaze and say the word" was the clue. The word was one known only to the royal family and a few other key individuals. Kenton and Greenup, Lady Briana, and Sillik's uncles all knew the proper word of power.

A host of Illician guards watched impassively as they guarded the entrance. Memories of other times people had stood in this spot enveloped him. They were like voices in his head.

He stood in the statue's gaze and spoke the word of power. Instantly, an archway appeared in the stonework behind the statue, and a door slid open. Sillik smiled as he remembered his first trip to an arsenal as a youth. He had gone not to the usual armories where the common weapons for the warriors of the keep were kept but to the secret armories known only to the royal family and the lord generals. Only the most dangerous magical weapons were stored in the royal armory. When one went to those rooms, one went alone and unarmed, or so the saying went. The magic stored in the armory chose what you needed.

Sillik eyed the words in the lintel warily. Then he announced himself by his royal names and spoke the arming spell. His need was great, and his fear was palatable. "Iron sharpens iron, steel sharpens steel, magic sharpens magic."

The armory was shadowed and cool. A dim light reflected from metallic hangings on the walls. The light source was out of sight. Sillik breathed deeply and smelled the faint scent of oil, dust, and sand.

The ceiling and walls of the room were tiled in a simple gold-colored tile. Fat columns supported the weight of the tower, and the long room twisted and turned in odd, unexpected ways, as if it had been woven into the very fabric of the keep.

He had been here before on his eighth name day. His father and Rebecca had brought him. They had taught him the words to say to enter and the words to the arming. With quiet determination, he had spoken the words for arming, and the illusions had faded away, revealing the weapons concealed in the room.

His father had walked through the armory with him, talking about the weapons. He told Sillik about how he had once seen the sword Avenger–a sword of impossible power, forged by the gods themselves and given to Rendarick, the founder of Illicia. His father had explained that the magic of the room allowed the swords to hide themselves; you could never find the same weapon in the same place twice.

In the present, long, narrow cases revealed themselves, and Sillik began to walk among them. Swords of bewildering shapes and styles glowed briefly as he passed and then faded. These were the great weapons forged with the Seven Laws by master craftsmen.

The weapons had been collected over the centuries by Illicians. Some had been purchased, commissioned for some purpose. Others had been seized in battle. A few of the great weapons still resided in the hands of the great families of Illicia, passed down as family heirlooms. The attributes of the weapons varied as much as the styles. Some carried illusions such as flames. Others never needed sharpening or would never break. A few were impossibly bright and shiny when drawn but all but useless in battle. All but one had been forged by humans.

As Sillik walked, weapons glowed as if showing themselves off but faded when Sillik reached out to touch them. Again and again, he reached for a weapon only to touch what felt like stone. The armory was not alive, but strong magic protected the weapons and evaluated his need. Sillik thought of his father's and brothers' deaths. A tug seemed to pull him forward.

Finally, near the back of the armory, a light glowed and did not dim. Sillik's hand closed around the pommel of a long sword with a slightly curved blade. Three golden eagles with intertwining wings graced the end of the pommel.

A buzzing sound filled Sillik's ears as he pulled the weapon from the case. The tower shuddered, and motes of dust floated down in the dim light. The sword seemed to shake in his hands, and he himself felt shaken as prickles of energy danced over his skin. The pommel suddenly felt warm, as if he had been holding the weapon for years. It was now a part of him. *It feels … comfortable and familiar*, Sillik thought. *Strange*.

Drawing the blade from the sheath, Sillik was surprised to see a tempest of energies flowing around the blade.

"Don't look at it too closely," a voice said.

Sillik turned. "Lady Silvia, so nice to see you again."

The goddess smiled as she regarded the Illician prince. "It is a dangerous weapon," she said with a smile. "I first saw it soon after it was forged. It is old, older than you can imagine."

"Why does it feel so familiar?" Sillik asked as he sheathed the weapon.

"It is magic," Silvia said. "You must use it to learn its abilities. You will face many challenges. But you will find allies that you must bring to the war. Illicia cannot win this alone."

Sillik started to ask another question, but the woman held up her hand. "You must finish arming yourself. You are not done yet, and I cannot answer your questions." With that, she faded from sight.

When Sillik emerged later, the holy sword Avenger was in an unmarked sheath at his waist. Several magical knives were also stashed in sheaths at his hips and in his boot. It was an ominous sign that the most powerful magical sword known to humanity was now at his hip, and the most powerful magical shield had been stolen.

Sillik's generals and advisors saw the blade at his hip and whispered in ominous tones among themselves. They had seen drawings of the sword. It was unmistakable. The grip was long and suitable for two hands. The pommel was a trio of eagles looking outward. The blade was long, slightly curved, and sharp along one edge. Seven eagles were engraved along the length of the blade.

Briana smiled in secret satisfaction when she saw the weapon. Sillik wondered anew at who was pulling the strings. What had his father told her? What instructions had he given her? It was as if she had a hand in the choices being made. Perhaps his father had pulled the strings. Sillik let her draw the weapon and touch the blade. He didn't dare let her spar with it, though. He knew he would never get it back.

If the lord generals were upset when they saw the sword, their reaction was nothing compared to the tumultuous fit the Gold Robes threw when they saw it. They turned red-faced and speechless in anger before they exploded in opposition. Their vocal argument sparked deep divisions between Sillik's advisors, almost evenly dividing them. Rather than argue in the stairwell of the keep, Sillik led everyone, Gold Robes and generals alike, into the council chambers.

He smiled as he watched the generals whisper. They were arguing about whether he should have the sword. Sillik knew that the weapon had been used only twice in all the time the Illicians had possessed the blade; the ring had given him those memories.

General Deluth stood, having been encouraged by Greenup to stand and speak his mind. "I am not a man who speaks much." He paused as he looked around the room, his eyes coming to rest on Sillik. "But I am going to say what everyone is thinking." He was gray and stooped and had not drawn his own weapon in ten years. "I am worried that something is going to happen to you and that the weapon at your hip will fall into the wrong hands. Now I am not a master like you, and I don't know how that thing works. But if anyone can make it work, then it can be used against us. Now, I have always been a king's man, but it has been a long time since that sword has been drawn and used proper. Maybe this is a plot to steal that blade." He paused again and looked around. "Now I've said all I need to say." With that, he sat down abruptly.

Sillik smiled and leaned back in his chair. "General Deluth, thank you for your comments. Only two Illicians that we know about have used the sword, and they were battle-tested kings of Illicia. I know you all consider me untried and untested, but I don't think any of you will dispute my abilities with the sword." He smiled as he looked around the room. "As you are aware, I have other talents as well, so I don't think you should worry about someone taking the sword from me. Now, I submit that I have been battle-tested since I left Illicia." Sillik suppressed the memories that flooded unwanted into his mind as he spoke. "I have led men and women in combat. I will spare you the details of those fights, but I know what I am doing." He looked around the room to impress his words upon them.

A Gold Robe at the end of the table stood up. "You may have led troops in battle, my lord, but I still don't think you should leave with that blade. There, I said what most of us are thinking."

"It should stay here!" another voice chimed in. "If Illicia is going to be attacked, we want that blade here."

Sillik leaned forward, his eyes smoldering. "Illicia has been attacked only a few times in all of its history, if you ignore the Nomads. I don't think that is much of a concern. The sword was a gift to the founders of Illicia during the demon wars. The histories say it came directly from the Seven Gods. I think they will see that it stays where they want it."

"What about its twin?" another voice asked.

Sillik glared. This meeting was getting out of control. He took a deep breath and counted silently to himself. "You refer to the theory of equality—that a tool of the Seven Gods must have an equivalent equal tool for the Nine. In seven thousand years, we have never encountered it. Therefore, I have doubts that it exists. Let's leave that for the philosophers to debate. For the moment, we have a tool, and I intend to use it."

Lord Clement, head of the preaching sect, rose slowly. His flat, jowled face resembled that of an overweight pig. "Sillik, my dear boy," he said smoothly in a high-pitched voice, "I don't think you have thought this through. We have talked about this need that you have to find the assassin, but do you, really?"

Sillik bounced to his feet in anger. "Lord Clement, are you opposing me?"

Shocked, the man met Sillik's eyes with fear. "No, my lord, not I."

"Then I do not understand what purpose your continued arguments serve. If you support me, then surely you want me to have the best tools for the job."

"Of course, my lord," Clement said as his face reddened. He sat down hastily.

"I disagree with you," said Calone, second minister of the preachers, as he rose. "I do not believe this task is as important as you make it out to be."

Sillik frowned. "Then what would you have me do?"

"Why, stay here, of course," Calone said. "Wear that sword if it makes you happy. But you must not use it. It is tied to the demon wars. Using it could lead us back into another war."

"You want me to stay here where there have already been multiple attempts on my life? I was lucky. Someone tried to blow me up. The dagger in the tavern missed me by the thickness of my shirt. The wine in the throne room would have killed me just as quickly had not Briana questioned the page, who was in fact a stranger to Illicia and who had both a compulsion and an illusion placed on him. Also, let's not forget the occasional bottle of poisoned wine or needle in my clothes. Last, there was the attack on me while I was returning to Illicia."

Calone frowned. "Ah yes, but surely those attackers are now dead. There can't be any more."

"Then who killed my uncles?" Sillik asked. "I think I would be safer going after Dernot and then coming back here and cleaning out whatever remnants of his treason remain."

"My lord, you are not suggesting that we ..." Calone looked around nervously.

"You said it, my friend," Sillik said, a hard edge to his voice.

"I will not allow you to insult us," another Gold Robe said, rising to his feet.

"That was very close to a challenge, Lord Symeson," Sillik said, a dangerous gleam in his eyes. He glanced in the mirrors and saw that his guards and Briana all had their hands on their weapons.

"No challenge, no challenge," Symeson said crossly with his hands on his hips. "You have said there is more to this than meets the eye, but you won't tell us why you believe that. You tell us you must take the most powerful sword we know of, but again, you won't tell us why. We have a right to understand."

"Your duty is to do what your king tells you to do," Sillik said, his voice strangely quiet.

"Ah yes, Your Highness, but as you remember, we have not crowned you yet."

Smiling, Sillik straightened. "I was referring to my father, the king, may the Seven bless him. He left me instructions to take the weapon. And you wear on my patience, Lord Symeson, if you continue this conversation."

Sillik sat down again and watched over steepled fingers as the room erupted, with everyone standing in protest. It wasn't long before the arguments degenerated into personal attacks and insults. After a futile attempt to say something, Sillik banged his pewter goblet on the table. The silence was instantaneous. Sillik smiled; his father had loved to do that.

"Enough," he said. "I have heard all points of view, and I am taking the sword. My father wished it, and there is nothing you can do about it. It has been taken from the armory. Only blood can put it back," he said, invoking ancient words from the stories of Rendarick. "I also remind you of Book Seven, chapter nine: 'The Seven Gods gave swords of power in order to protect all of mankind.' This sword is not doing much protecting when it is hidden in an armory."

Sillik stood up and leaned on the table. Briana was sitting beside him at his request. He waved absently at her. He was trying to make the transition easier for her, but he wasn't sure if he was helping or not. "Lady Briana is warmaster of Illicia. While I am away, you *will* accord her all the privileges of her office. You will support her decisions as if they came from me. I also promise you that I will return as soon as I can. I will deal with anyone who cannot support her."

Sillik cast a stern look around the room, making eye contact with everyone who would meet his gaze. A few men looked away pointedly. Sillik stared at them, and slowly, everyone else turned to face the three merchants. One by one, they nodded their heads in assent, but they still didn't meet his eyes.

Once Sillik had their complete attention, he continued. "My uncles, may the Seven Gods receive them with mercy, agreed with me that we are at war.

Lord Greenup can verify this and produce the memory if required. Therefore, my appointment of Briana as warmaster is entirely legal according to Illician law. She is also second in line for the throne, due to my uncles' and cousins' untimely demise. Are there any other questions?"

When no response came, Sillik smiled. "Now, I am reminded that we are below the required number of advisors." A few of the council members stirred uncomfortably. "Accordingly, I have issued letters of appointment. Speaker Kenton's wife, the healer Elizabet, and their daughters Alexis and Kendra are appointed to this council."

The council threatened to erupt again.

"In addition," Sillik said, "I have appointed Lord Greenup's grandson Keltic. The letters were to be delivered at the start of this meeting."

Lord Symeson rose to his feet. "My lord, it is most improper to appoint a healer to your council. Healers do not take lives. Sometimes this council must order that people be killed. It could conflict with her vows."

"Lord Symeson," Sillik said, "I had this researched. It may be unusual to have a healer on this council, but there are many rules that they live with. We all know they cannot kill. But healers have served on this council before, and they will again. I have every confidence that she will serve me well."

Symeson tried a different tactic. "My lord, you could have consulted with us."

Sillik sighed. "Yes, I could have, but to what end? If you are about to say that I lack the authority to appoint members to my council since I don't wear the crown, let me remind you that we are at war, and with the lack of any senior family members, I rule with or without the crown."

Symeson flinched and then closed his mouth angrily.

"With that, gentlemen and ladies," Sillik said with a bow, "I will see you tomorrow. I hope you will remember my wishes." Satisfied for the moment that his decisions would be followed, Sillik turned and left the council room, his cloak billowing behind him. His guards hurried after him.

Briana stayed in the council chamber long enough to deal with a question about the upcoming Shelnor trade delegation, and then she adjourned the meeting.

When Briana found Sillik, he was standing on the roof of the Tower of Rendar. The moons were rising one by one. He had always enjoyed spending time on top of the towers while growing up. He had called these spots the top of the world. The guards had never interfered with him and had kindly not told the king where he was. The stars and the moons were impressive. Equally impressive were the towers of Illicia at night.

"Remember the first time you brought me up here?" Briana asked the shadowed figure.

Sillik smiled in the darkness. He had expected her to find him here. "Of course," he said, grinning. "You were so afraid my father would find out." He heard her cloak brushing the rooftop and her scabbard grating on the stone when she turned to look out at the city.

"I am sorry for what happened," she said.

"I know," Sillik said as he leaned on the battlements lining the rooftop.

"Your father, he was keeping more secrets than usual, even from me. He had spies and secrets. People would visit him—outlanders, moss eaters," she said, using the Illician slang for anyone who lived with an excess of water. "I didn't know who they were or what they were doing."

Sillik smiled sadly. "That sounds like the father I knew. He did like his secrets." Sillik straightened and turned to face her. "What was he doing? What was he thinking? What did he know or suspect?"

She smiled helplessly. "I don't know. He left you his papers and hid his ring for you. It did something when you put it on. He wanted you to find it. He said he had made plans for you, left instructions. So he hid it someplace only you would find," she concluded in a rush of words.

"My father knew something," Sillik said as he turned to look back at the moons. "He didn't tell me what he feared, just notes on the state of the world. Something is happening. What happened here is just a small part of the larger picture."

Briana nodded. "He told me two things the last morning, before ... before he died." Briana looked at Sillik, and even in the darkness, he could see the tears in her eyes.

"He told me to watch for you and to protect your back." She shook off her sadness and tried to smile. "You know what day it is, right?"

Sillik shook his head as he looked out at the dark desert.

"Tomorrow is Founding."

"Ah yes," Sillik said, "the annual night when we remember that we are outnumbered."

"The night we remember that we oppose evil in all its forms," Briana corrected. "Why the pessimism?" She folded her arms defensively. "It isn't like you."

Sillik nodded. "I'm just feeling a bit overwhelmed."

"You can leave on your quest anytime after that," Briana said, "but it will be good for the morale of the city if you are here tomorrow."

Sillik smiled as he remembered Reznek's advice. "What are the bookmakers' odds on more than one of the Seven Gods appearing?"

Briana frowned. "Not good. Last year, the Nine mocked the city for a long time before just one of the Seven appeared. They say it is even odds that at least one will appear. I think it was a thousand to one that more than two would appear. It is two thousand to one that this year none will appear … I mean, given what has happened."

"Did they take into account that this is the first Founding in hundreds of years to follow a Celebration of Kings?"

Briana shook her head.

Sillik smiled. "I want you to place a bet for me. Put a thousand gold pieces on five or more. Spread the word; make sure the city knows. Remind the bookies that we just celebrated the Celebration of Kings. Make sure they know this is my bet."

Briana started to protest, but Sillik cut her off. "There are letters of credit in my rooms. Place the bet."

Briana nodded and then turned to leave.

"When I win the bet, tell the bookies to deliver the winnings to the poorhouses. Spread the gold as far as possible."

"When you win?" she asked. "Do you know something? Has one of the Seven spoken to you?"

Sillik smiled. "I am just hopeful. I remember Lord Norsen and his lectures. 'Confidence is the key to a successful leader.'"

"With that kind of bet, you are going to distort the odds. You might make more with a smaller bet."

"I might," Sillik said, grinning, "but this isn't about making money. It's about inspiring faith in my city and the Seven Gods."

Briana looked at him for a long moment as she considered his words. Then she turned to leave. "You are just a bit crazy," she said over her shoulder.

Shivering, Sillik pulled his cloak tight and turned back to the moons. All he could think about was that his father hadn't sent him that image of pain until the duel in which he had lost his life. *He could have called me back at any time. Damn. He knew he was going to die. He knew something was going to happen, and he waited until the last possible moment to call me home. But if he had called me sooner, could I have stopped it? Or would I be dead too? What was he up to?*

Sillik heard his sheath grate on the polished roof as he shifted his stance. He didn't leave the rooftop until the moons were well overhead.

# CHAPTER 10

## Founding

THE DAY PASSED slowly as everyone in Illicia waited for nightfall. The entire city was expectant. All the trade delegations had left days before, and it would be weeks before another was allowed to enter the city. Outsiders were never allowed to be in the city for Founding Day. This was an edict from before the construction of the city.

Founding Day was a solemn holiday in Illicia. It marked their heritage. At least one of the Seven Gods always appeared. At the same time, the Nine Dark Gods also marked the day, appearing in all of their terrible splendor.

To sacrifice and commemorate all the work of building the city, everyone fasted from sunrise until after sunset. No one except the very young or old could eat or drink. The fast would be broken after the appearance. The Gold Robes were in abundance as they wandered the city and the towers. They spoke to everyone. It was a day to remember and give back to the city.

As twilight neared, the people walked quietly to the walls. The soldiers turned out with precision and lined the inner and outer walls of the city.

Sillik led the council to the roof of the keep. The discussions had been strangely muted all day. Briana said that the Nine Gods of Darkness had hovered on their peaks for a long time the previous year before one of the Seven appeared. Some on the council were predicting that none of the Seven Gods would appear this year. Sillik smiled grimly at the council's pronouncement. If he was wrong, it could undermine his reign for a very long time.

Briana said that today the odds were fifty to one that none of the Seven Gods would appear. It was even odds that one would appear. Sillik's bet had distorted the odds of more than five appearing to two hundred to one.

Sillik noticed an intangible effect of his bet on the people around him. There seemed to be an optimism that had been lacking. The guards stood just a little straighter, and the servants had been quicker.

A thin sliver of sun was still visible when Sillik stepped onto the rooftop. The banners fluttered in the breeze. The council spread out to face the world. Sillik greeted Keltic and Lord Kenton's daughters, Alexis and Kendra. His appointment of them to the council had shocked the keep. For some reason, though, it felt right.

Sillik spent a few moments greeting everyone else on the council. His place was at the center of the circle, at the geometric center of the city. When Sillik stepped into the center of the circle with Briana close by, the last of the sun slipped beneath the horizon.

As if on cue, ghostly figures began to appear over the seven towers of the keep. Sillik and Briana looked up in amazement at the seven ghostly white images of men and women in shining armor and billowing cloaks. The noble figures stood proudly, as tall as the towers themselves. The audible response from the Illicians was one of stunned surprise, and then came a happy roar of approval from every throat. The glow of the Seven Gods bathed the entire city in a pale white light that removed all doubts and fed every soul. The light, unlike that of torches and candles, was strong and steady.

Still in shock at the appearance of all of the Seven Gods, an event that had not occurred in more than a thousand years, Sillik barely recognized that the Nine Gods had not yet shown their faces.

Suddenly, the darkness surrounding each of the nine mountain peaks around Illicia became darker as the Nine Gods of Darkness materialized together. They were as large as the mountains on which they stood. Their eyes gleamed with a red, evil malice, anger etched into their faces. The beards of the five male dark lords moved in the wind of the maelstrom surrounding them. The hair of the female lords whipped like snakes. Lightning flashed in the clouds around them, and thunder rolled through the valley.

Sillik shuddered as he felt the eyes of the Nine bore into him. It was as if they were examining him. The most vile and evil of the Nine, a female form called Nameless, moved forward as if to strike him down.

Then the Nine saw the Seven, and they roared in anger as Illicia trembled. The Seven Gods smiled. One by one, they threw up their arms, and a silvery wall spread around the city. The wall expanded to encompass the fields surrounding the city. The Nine rumbled in disapproval, and a black snake spread between them. It twisted and heaved in the air and then began to collapse like a noose around the city. But when the black snake touched the silver wall, the snake shattered like glass, and the silvery wall glowed brightly.

Another roar of approval went up from every Illician. In anger, the Nine disappeared. The Seven hovered for a moment, looking outward, before turning to face the central keep. Slowly, they floated down to face Sillik. Moments before, the Seven Gods had been as tall as mountains. Now they were just slightly taller than the tallest man. Briana backed away regardless.

The Seven Gods said nothing; they only looked. Their faces were hard, but their eyes burned brightly. Several of the lords nodded in approval. As they faded from sight, one of the Seven made a motion as if crowning Sillik. Briana shuddered. *Lady Silvia*, she thought. Briana had spoken to that particular goddess once. Then the Seven were gone, and the silver wall faded away. Illicia cheered as celebrations broke out in the streets and upon the walls.

Sillik shuddered. In his memory, none of the Seven had ever paused to look at the royal family or even pay attention to the citizens of Illicia. To be singled out and examined was frightening. *We are going to have plenty to talk about tonight*, he thought. More important was the presence of all Seven Gods tonight. It was almost unprecedented.

He waved for the council to follow him. By prior arrangement, Sillik's closest advisors were to dine with him in his rooms, and he would meet with the council again at midday tomorrow. *Time enough for them to sober up and be presentable*, Sillik thought. *People will be celebrating in the city tonight!*

When Sillik stepped into his rooms, he pulled up short, and his hand flew to his sword. Then he recognized the white-cloaked figure standing beside his conference table. He smiled grimly. "Lady Silvia, so nice to see you again," he said in a dry voice.

The woman cloaked in white robes and a glowing white light smiled warmly. She was slender, almost petite. She wore a heavily embroidered dress with a cloak thrust back on her shoulders. A slender dagger was sheathed in a belt at her waist. The buckle of her belt was silver. Everything else about the woman glowed white.

Briana surged forward and stepped in front of Sillik, as if she could protect him from this woman.

"Relax, Briana of House Dulcane, warmaster of Illicia," the woman said, "You know who I am. I bear no ill will to any who fight the Nine. I would speak to the two of you alone." She glanced at Kenton and Greenup and the others behind them. "Speaker Kenton, you will have many questions. We will talk another day."

"Lady Silvia," Briana said, bowing formally.

Kenton quickly ushered everyone else out and closed the door with a reluctant expression on his face. He was missing a once-in-a-lifetime opportunity. "Silvia, the Spirit of the Woods," he muttered wistfully in a low voice as he closed the door.

When they were alone, Sillik turned to face Lady Silvia. "I never expected to find one of the Seven Gods in my chambers," he said, "at least not since Salone or Aecon."

"Ah, levity. You must be uncomfortable," Silvia said with a smile.

"You know I don't like it when you just pop in for one of your visits."

Briana looked surprised. "I thought you were lying, for the sake of Saldor," she said, looking at Silvia. "You were keeping tabs on Sillik?"

Silvia smiled. "I was. Doing a favor. Saldor asked me to look in on our prince from time to time."

Sillik looked from Silvia to Briana. "I am confused."

"I will explain later," Briana said as she turned back to the goddess.

"Hush, child. I haven't much time," Silvia said. "The two of you must listen to what I have to say. Sillik, you are in danger, and you must leave Illicia soon. You have places to go. What have you decided to do about Saldor's papers?"

Briana looked up in surprise.

Silvia glanced at Briana with a cold expression and then looked back at Sillik. "Your father did the research. I may have helped him with some of it, but he found the clues."

Sillik examined the goddess intently. Something odd was happening. "Why are you here?" he asked coolly. "I am tired. It has been a long day. I want to eat, have something to drink, and go to sleep."

Silvia smiled. "To grant your father's dying request."

Shocked, Sillik said nothing.

Briana inhaled sharply but kept quiet.

"He asked for our help." To emphasize her point, she waved a hand. A cold wind blew through the room, and it seemed like all the dust in the room flew to a point over their heads. The ball of dust flattened into a disc of swirling colors that coalesced into a picture of Sillik's father. Saldor was battered and bleeding from cuts on his face. In the background, a man stood straight and defiant.

"The Seven help me, Sillik come to me," Saldor said, and then he pushed himself off the wall with a flash of determination. Power flared in his hands, but before he could attack, a whip-like finger of black smoke struck him in the chest. He gasped, and his eyes glazed as he fell.

Briana turned away as the picture dissolved. When she turned to face Silvia, there were tears in her eyes, and her jaw was set. "Is that what … what he said?"

Sillik had broken into a cold sweat as he watched his father die. Painful memories burned. "Yes, Briana, that is the message he sent me," Sillik said. Turning, he eyed Lady Silvia. "How are you helping him?" he asked, his voice controlled and even. "He is dead."

Silvia frowned. "By helping you survive. He did not ask for any other sons; he asked for you."

Briana finally found her voice again. "Because Sillik was away, and none of his brothers had mastered the Seven Laws."

"Phaa," Silvia said. "Everyone can do magic, but people's minds limit them. No, your father wanted you, Sillik."

"Why?" Sillik asked, crossing his arms.

Silvia smiled as if she knew what he was thinking. "What are you going to do about your father's clues?"

Sillik frowned. "We haven't decided what to do about them. But why are you changing the subject?"

Anger crossed the goddess's face. "Don't lie to me, Prince Sillik. I know you believe Colum to be a trap." The tower trembled, and dust floated down from the ceiling.

"Why is that important?" Briana asked.

"It is important that he deal with the first two clues before the third. The third will shake the foundations of creation and could decide who leads the world for the next ten thousand years."

"No pressure," Sillik said dryly. "I am just going to go after Dernot. What am I expected to find in Colum, Nerak, and the Blasted Hills?"

Silvia eyed Sillik evenly as if considering her next words. "If you stop with Dernot, Illicia will be destroyed within three years, and the world within another four. As for what my enemies plan, even I am not sure what exactly you will find. I know many things but not everything."

Sillik slumped into a chair as Silvia eyed him with a worried expression. "The Nine are behind this convergence of events. Illicia withdraws from the world because of the assassination of its king and most of his heirs. Other leaders supportive of the Seven are killed. War is breaking out in numerous places. Dark masters are actively recruiting from all the cities." Silvia paused as she glanced at Briana. "Even here! There will be tests," Silvia continued, "but they should be within your abilities, and the good they will do along the way will set the path for what is to come. But beware: the Council of Nine has been remade. Remember that there are friends and allies to be found. Illicia needs those allies. Illicia cannot break the Council of Nine by herself."

"What is coming?" Briana asked.

"The future is not yet written, and many things could yet happen," Silvia said.

Briana bristled, but before she could say anything more, Silvia continued. "The destruction of the world or a third demon war could result if things are handled badly. Illicia could be destroyed, not to mention the destruction that could result if a demon and its minions are loosed upon the world. Already a few imps are loose in Colum, and you banished one here not too long ago. Then there are the armies of schula." Silvia paused with a knowing smile and then turned to look at Briana. "You will stay here for a while. You must draw their attention, and then you will rejoin Sillik."

Briana nodded uncertainly as she glanced at Sillik.

Sillik's expression was unreadable as he digested what the goddess had said. Then he stood, walked over to the table, and poured himself a glass of wine.

While his back was turned, Silvia leaned over and whispered in Briana's ear. "When you crown him, he must be wearing the Star of the South. It will find him. Don't ask questions. Remember, he must be wearing it. Say nothing to him!"

Briana looked puzzled but nodded.

When Sillik turned back to face the women, he was about to say something, but Silvia spoke first. "I will give you what aid I can, when I can." With that she started to fade away.

Sillik watched impassively. He was exhausted. "Ask anyone not in the inner council to leave," he said. "What we have to discuss isn't for everyone's ears."

For a moment, Briana's gaze was fixed on the floor. "Sillik, I have to tell you something, something that happened before … before your father died."

Sillik looked up.

Briana took a deep breath. Tears welled up in her eyes. She wiped them away and took another breath. She had to explain what had happened. "More than a year before your father died, I was getting ready to ride patrols with Greenup when Saldor summoned me. Lady Silvia was already here, talking to your father and Rebecca. She said this dark master was making his move, and things were being set in motion. She told us that Saldor would be personally attacked. He scoffed at the notion, but I increased the guards and tightened security throughout the keep. We didn't know it would be an Illician. She said you were connected to the future. She said Nameless herself is aiding the dark master. Rebecca is involved in some way too. Silvia had Saldor write a note and give it to her. I don't know what it says. You should ask her."

Sillik listened quietly as he slumped in his chair.

The pace of Briana's words slowed. "She asked to talk to me privately. She took my hand and led me out to the balcony. I held hands with a goddess! She must have placed a compulsion on me because I couldn't tell anyone what she said even if I wanted to. I can tell you, obviously, so the compulsion must have dissolved, or maybe I can tell you because I did what she asked."

"What did she want you to do?"

"She told me to find your prince's crown and have it ready for when you returned. She said there was something special about it that would help you do what needed to be done. She wanted it here in this room, and she insisted that I put it in your hands and that you put it on your head."

Sillik nodded. "That feeling when I put it on. It set something. Like a door being unlocked." He looked at Briana. "Anything else I need to know?"

Briana shook her head. "No."

"Then let everyone in. Send anyone not in the private council to bed."

When Briana opened the doors, she found Kenton and Greenup along with their children and Viktorie. Lord Reznek stood irritably in front of them.

Without a word, the rule maker strode into Sillik's room on his strange crutches. Kenton followed with a helpless expression. Briana waved everyone else in and closed the doors again. To ensure they were not overheard, she cast a veil on the door to muffle the sounds from within.

Without waiting to be addressed, Reznek started in. "So one of the Seven Gods chose to speak to you, eh, boy?"

"Greenup, would you pour everyone a glass of wine? Let's all sit down," Sillik said.

As the council sat, Greenup floated goblets to everyone and then poured wine for everyone but Reznek, who received water. For once, he did not complain.

Sillik sipped his wine and examined the table for a few moments before he quickly recounted the major points for his audience. Reznek looked pleased as he sat back and rubbed one of his crutches.

"What is the Council of Nine?" Briana asked.

Reznek barked a laugh. "Yes, I thought that might happen. Did she tell you about it?"

"But what is it?" Briana asked. "It sounds like a bad development. I have heard something about it before."

Reznek and Kenton started to answer at once, but Reznek waved for Kenton to speak. "The Council of Nine is a group of nine dark masters in a loose brotherhood," Kenton said in his teaching voice. "Being who they are, they can never agree on a given course of action other than loose goals. If they ever truly unite, the world will be in terrible trouble." Kenton paused to let the point sink in. "According to what was written about the Council of Nine, the last time they worked together, they started the Demon War."

"*The* Demon War, the one that all our histories talk about?" Briana asked. "The war that led to the foundation of Illicia?"

"Yes," Kenton said as Reznek nodded. "The journals say that in that war, the alliance of cities that eventually formed Illicia thought that all of the nine dark masters were killed when the demons were vanquished."

"They were not sure?" Briana asked. "This little bit of history was left out of my education, Speaker Kenton."

Reznek chuckled. "You are not a Gold Robe, my dear. The Gold Robes are taught this once they decide to stay in the Gold Tower. It is thought that no one else need know until the demons come back."

"Bloody hells!" Greenup exclaimed.

"What do we do now?" Alexis asked.

"We fight," Viktorie said. "We fight until we cannot fight, and then we get back on our feet and fight again."

Late that night, after everyone had returned to their beds, a knock sounded at Sillik's door. It opened, and Lady Nisha entered.

Sillik was standing on his balcony, watching the city. "You have a list for me?" he asked.

"Yes, my lord," Nisha said as she fingered a piece of paper. "I made a list of all of the women who have been here since your return, and I have spoken to all of them." She paused. "I hope you do not suspect any of the women on this list for any crime. Surely their perfume is not enough to convict them."

Calmly, Sillik reached for the paper.

Fidgeting, Nisha clasped the paper in both hands. "I circled the names that I could find."

Gently, Sillik took the list. "You may leave now," Sillik said quietly. "No word of this to anyone."

The woman nodded and then surprised him by saying, "You are leaving, aren't you?"

Sillik looked at her and said, "I have to."

Nisha nodded and then approached and kissed him on the cheek. "May the Seven Gods protect you." Then she left without another word.

Sillik looked at the list. There were three names circled. He frowned as he looked at them. Fortunately, in her precise handwriting, Nisha had added details regarding who the people were.

Alissa—seamstress. *She doesn't have the skills*, Sillik thought.

Thelma—bath girl. *She doesn't have the skills either; she has charms, but not magical ones.* Sillik grinned.

The last name on the list drew Sillik's attention. *She does have the skills. And she's a healer. Damn, it can't be. I have known her my entire life. But it makes sense, all of it. Damn her.* Holding the paper in his hand, he wrapped powers around it. A gust of wind compressed the paper, and a ball of fire consumed it. Ash floated to the floor gently.

Turning, he began to compose what he would tell Briana in the message sphere.

# CHAPTER 11

## Warmaster

"WARMASTER!" BRIANA SPOKE the word like a curse as she stormed through the hallways of the keep. Her escorts were nearly running to keep up. Their mail clinked, and their scabbards grated on the tiles. Briana ignored the noise. Servants dodged out of the way as they saw her face. Briana spat the word again. "Warmaster! He was right. I hate this job already."

It had sounded good when Greenup raised the topic in the steam rooms and when Sillik had said it in court. Only later had she learned that it was a curse. Why had she ever nominated herself? *What was I thinking? I wish someone had hit me when I responded*, Briana thought as she cursed again. *I should have stuffed a towel in my mouth. Greenup or Kenton would have been better suited for this. At least they wouldn't have to wear dresses everywhere.*

One of the guards, Saleen, tripped as he tried to dodge a servant carrying towels and sheets. Everything the poor girl was carrying spilled as she and the soldier tumbled to the floor. Briana looked back at the escort and swore again. *What a clumsy oaf!* As warmaster of Illicia, she was the titular head of the city, and as such, she ranked guards to protect her. *Guards that should be able to stay on their feet*, she fumed. Hells, Sillik chose her guards!

Embarrassed, the servant scrambled to her feet and adjusted her dress as she tried to curtsy. Her face was scarlet, and wisps of light brown hair escaped the bun that held her hair off of her face.

Briana laughed irritably. *As if I need protection. I was the swordmaster of Illicia. I am the finest sword in the city. I don't need a protective detail to guard me.*

The servant began to reclaim the clean laundry. One of the guards, Hillself, paused, uncertain whether to help the girl or continue running after Briana. Briana nodded to the servant, and Hillself bent to help the young woman pick up the towels and sheets. Saleen stood slowly and dusted himself off. He was apologetic as he caught Briana's eye.

*This is Sillik's revenge*, Briana thought. *He hated having men follow him around.* She took a deep breath while she waited. *It would be good to make the council wait anyway.* When the servant was on her way again, following a grateful smile at Hillself, Briana took a deep breath and turned to move on down the hallway. The men assigned to protect her were only slightly out of breath and definitely red in the face from embarrassment. Maybe this wasn't Sillik's revenge; maybe he hadn't even thought about it. She shook her head and started back down the hallway, this time a little slower and perhaps a trifle more dignified. *Maybe I'm the problem. Nisha would be pleased, or at least not angry, that I am maintaining my composure*, Briana thought, smiling. It had been a rude shock to her to suddenly have assistants and ladies-in-waiting. Her carefree days were over.

The women had descended on her that morning and had overseen her getting dressed. They disapproved of most of her clothing and even picked out her dress. Several of the women nearly fainted when she reached for her knives and mail. They had even insisted on brushing her hair and would have done more if she had not forcibly ejected most of them from her room. The women seemed to be treating her more like a queen than a warmaster. That was understandable. The city had not had a warmaster in three hundred years. She had checked the records, and the last female warmaster was so far back in antiquity as to have been forgotten. Briana might even be the first, but she scoffed at that idea.

This council meeting would be her first official event. Her stomach did several slow rolls as she paused before the doors. She touched her sleeve and felt the comforting weight of a throwing knife. Her confidence flared.

She tugged discreetly at the high collar of her dress. It itched terribly. She missed wearing her pants and boots. Her mail was uncomfortable beneath the dress. Everything was too tight and constricting. She was hot, and she felt perspiration dripping down her back. She smoothed her dress and stepped forward slowly. Despite all of the clothing, she felt naked without the comforting weight of her sword at her hip. The women had said it wasn't proper for the head of the city to wear a sword even if she was the warmaster. Briana had relented. She tugged at her dress in irritation and then smoothed it again. At least she had a dagger in her sleeve and not one of the useless ceremonial blades that were too dull to cut.

At the end of the hallway, the guards pushed open the doors to the council chamber. Why had they summoned her to this meeting? The room was divided into three distinct camps: merchants, Gold Robes, and warriors. She had met most of the merchants in meetings and various social events. The Gold Robes had trained her, and she had trained with the warriors.

Briana waited at the door while the master of arms cleared his throat. "Princess Briana Duncane, warmaster of Illicia!" he intoned in a deep baritone voice that resonated throughout the room.

Chills went down Briana's back, and she stepped forward stiffly. Everyone rose with a scuffling of feet. The female merchants sank into a minimal curtsy while the male merchants bowed their heads. The warriors saluted with a solid thump of gauntleted fists to their chests, and the Gold Robes applauded. They would not bow or curtsy to anyone.

"Please, everyone, be seated," Briana said as she approached the head of the council table. *Despite the familiarity, they shouldn't be summoning me. I will control this meeting.*

Hillself and Saleen stood impassively behind her. Had she appointed a new swordmaster, he or she would be standing immediately behind her and to her right. She would have to force herself to appoint someone to her old position. Keltic, Lord General Greenup's grandson, was the best choice, as she had told Sillik.

Kenton and Greenup slid into their chairs directly across from her. Viktorie, of course, stood to Lord Kenton's right. Sanhill, the captain of Briana's guard, had been waiting for her in the council chamber and had a dozen men spread around the room. He had recommended this approach to convince any who needed convincing that she was the warmaster.

After taking her seat and arranging her dress, she said dryly, "Crown Prince Sillik left last night at sunset." No one traveled the desert during daylight if they could avoid it. Some of them already knew, but it was her duty to report the king's absence. "He will be back soon to resume his duties."

"Yes, Warmaster, we felt the gate open," Greenup said. Kenton nodded.

The rest of the council had not known, and her announcement and the high lords' confirmation sent them talking in consternation.

She had to pound the table several times to regain control of the meeting. "He wanted the announcement postponed to give him time to clear the city and the surrounding area," she said.

Greenup smiled at what had not been said—namely, where was Sillik going? He had his suspicions, but he didn't want to know for sure. He would have been willing to bet a dozen gold coins that Briana had laid out all the places he should go.

Viktorie interjected. "Your life is in danger, Warmaster. The forces opposing us will come after you now."

Briana nodded sullenly. "I know. Let me draw their eyes, if it allows Sillik to end this." She spoke the words with far more bravado than she felt.

"Can he do it?" Greenup asked of no one in particular. "Can he find this assassin, this Dernot? Kill him and end whatever else is going on?"

Concealing her own feelings, Briana watched the merchants' reaction. Greenup's question had been planned: ask and answer the question that everyone is thinking and then move on.

"He is talented enough, as many of you saw when he beat me in the practice yard," she said, wincing as she said the words. The defeat still stung. *The next person that I spar with will not beat me*, she thought. *I pity that person.* Her response had also been planned, to distract the council. "But," Briana warned, "killing Dernot may not end this."

Several heads at the other end of the table looked up. *That's interesting*, she thought.

"He is strong," Viktorie said in her usual slow, delicate tone.

"I don't like letting him go alone," Briana said.

"We have argued this since his father, Saldor–may he be blessed by the Seven Gods–died," Kenton said.

*Ah*, Briana thought, *he is afraid I am going to reopen that argument today, and he is angry.*

"We cannot interfere," Viktorie said as she held her hands, palms together, before her.

"By the Nine Gods, we should," Briana said as her anger boiled over. "It's our duty to serve our king."

"We have more pressing issues to address," Lord Kenton said. "Someone tried to poison a grain bin last night."

Briana looked up sharply. "Tried?"

"They were caught," Greenup said.

"They?"

"Nine traitors," Greenup said. "Five men and four women. They allegedly tried to bribe their way into a granary with gold. They had several slow-acting poisons on them."

"We don't think they had time to do their job, but we are checking," Kenton said.

"I want to know their plans," Briana said. "And why nine? Nine is a rather obvious reference."

Greenup nodded. "When we know, you will know."

"We will try them by sunset today, as the law dictates," Kenton said with a grimace. "You will have to pronounce judgment if they are guilty."

Briana flinched and crossed her arms defiantly under her breasts. The room felt cold as all eyes watched her. She could feel their thoughts. Would she order these people's deaths? Could she? Was she strong enough to be warmaster? Then in a clear level voice that surprised even her, Briana said, "Hang them if they are guilty."

"It will be done as you command, Warmaster," Greenup said, bowing. "If they can get into a granary, they can get almost anywhere."

"Place additional guards on all water and food storage facilities, including the decoys," Briana added. "Who were they? Illicians?"

"No," Kenton said. "As far as we can tell at this point, they were from a scattering of cities—caravan guards and hangers-on mostly."

"How did they get in the city? The next trade delegation isn't scheduled to arrive for a week."

Kenton shrugged and shook his head.

Greenup snorted with disgust. "Foreigners."

Lord Demar, a large, balding man wearing an extravagant burgundy and leather knee-length coat, stood slowly, and all eyes turned to watch. He was the chief of the merchants' guild and enjoyed all the benefits of his position. When he was assured that all eyes were on him, he spoke. "The same foreigners who buy our stone and sell us many of the things that make this city more comfortable. Trust the military to suspect *all* foreigners."

Ignoring Demar, Briana turned to Kenton. "Your people are working with them?" The Gold Robes didn't torture, but they could ask questions in such a way that the true answer would be spoken quickly.

Kenton nodded with a grim smile. "We will know all that they know soon enough."

"Do we have any more business?" Briana asked.

"You receive petitions tomorrow at midday," Lord Kenton reminded her.

"The trade delegation from Shelnor will be here in three weeks," said Lord Orgon in his reedy voice. A short, balding, nervous-looking man, he wore the insignia of the stonecutters' guild. "It would have been better if the prince had delayed his departure to preside over this agreement, but a warmaster will suffice."

Briana smiled thinly despite the insult as she gave Lord Orgon a sidelong appraisal. To her amusement, he looked around nervously and then sat down without another word. She continued to watch him with an amused expression. The man wouldn't meet her eyes and kept glancing around the room for moral support. It didn't surprise Briana that the first person he looked to for support was Lord Chanderil, chief of the banking guild. Chanderil wisely didn't look at Demar and merely swirled the wine in his cup.

Surprisingly, the second person that Orgon looked at was the Gold Robe Symeson. *That is an interesting arrangement,* Briana thought, eyeing the man suspiciously.

Finally, Briana stood. "The trade delegation is welcome if they come in peace. We have been planning this meeting for a long time. If I remember correctly, there is another planning meeting today. I understand its importance to all of Illicia, and we will do everything possible to ensure its success."

"Petitions tomorrow, Warmaster," Kenton reminded her.

Briana smiled as she looked at the Gold Robe. "I am aware of my responsibilities, and I know my schedule, thank you. I have a meeting with the scribes at midday, when four petitions will be presented. The scribes are to review the applicable sections of our law as it applies to these situations with me."

Briana smiled indulgently as she remembered that she had railed at Nisha for suggesting the meeting. Now, however, she saw the wisdom of her assistant's suggestion. "I am also scheduled to be in the practice yards this afternoon with Holden if anyone wants to spar with me," she said, eyes twinkling. "Any volunteers?" She looked around the table with feigned displeasure. "That is disappointing. After that, as I just reminded everyone, we have another planning meeting on the Shelnor trade delegation. I am looking forward to the debate over what kind of fruit to serve with dinner." She laughed as the merchants paled uncomfortably. "This evening, I have dinner with the Salone ambassador. He is an old friend of my father's, and I have not seen him in years."

Silence greeted her words. They had not expected her response. She saw several eyes narrow as if she were suddenly being reappraised. Kenton and Greenup's eyes were alight with humor. They knew what she had done.

"Now, if there is no other business, I have work to do," she said. "I will summon the council when I need its advice." Briana spoke the last words with a dangerous edge to her voice. "Until that time, we stand adjourned." Then, without waiting for their approval, she turned and strode out of the room. Her guards followed with barely suppressed smiles. They had enjoyed the show.

Once in the hallway, Briana took a deep breath and exhaled slowly. She was so angry that she was shaking from head to toe. This was indeed Sillik's revenge, she concluded. But it was her damn fault! If she hadn't opened her mouth, she wouldn't be in this position. Someone else would be warmaster. He might have picked her anyway, though. She swore to herself as she marched down the curving hallway.

Greenup and Kenton smiled as the rest of the council watched in open-mouthed amazement. Greenup glanced at his grandson, who stood in the background. The young man also had a bemused smile on his face. Once Briana was out of the chamber and the doors were closed, the conversations began.

Later that day, as promised, Briana was performing the Hummingbird in the Forest, a complicated sword form that required extreme patience and deliberately slow moves followed by fast bursts of energy. She was entering the final flight of the form and burst into the air, delivering a sidekick and a slashing strike with her sword. She landed and rolled through the concluding moves of the sword form.

Lords Kenton and Greenup stepped up to the edge of the practice yard and watched, their leather boots crackling on the ever-present sand. Above the practice yard, large awnings provided some shade. The metal rings on the fabric chimed softly in the air as the slight breeze billowed the fabric. Briana's back was to them, but her head twitched a little as she heard the sound of their feet.

She was barefoot on the carved stone circles and wearing a white dobok. The yard was deserted in the late afternoon because most people had returned to the towers of the keep to avoid the heat and to prepare for their evening meal. Holden, the yardmaster, was the only other person nearby. He was motionless as he watched her movements with a critical eye.

Kenton opened his mouth to speak, but Greenup touched his arm and shook his head. His eyes said, *Let her finish.* Kenton nodded and continued to watch. Briana finished the form with the sword thrust behind her back, which symbolized killing the unseen observer, and then stood quickly, her feet together, and bowed.

Greenup clapped in appreciation of the beauty of the form.

"Warmaster," Kenton said tentatively, "we have some bad news regarding the prisoners."

Briana turned to face the men. Perspiration dotted her face and the loose fabric that clung to her body. She wiped the sweat from her face with the sleeve of her dobok. Her breathing was hard but controlled.

Holden hurried up to her with the sheath for her blade. Kenton noticed then that she was using not a practice blade but a real weapon. He suppressed a shudder. That form was hard enough without having to worry about a real blade. Briana bowed formally to the yardmaster and then held the weapon in her upturned palms and offered it to him. Holden accepted the blade with the same ceremony and sheathed it with an elegant flourish. He was the first teacher anyone in the keep met, and he had trained most of the current officers in the city. His courses were difficult by any definition. Students complained that he was exacting and demanded perfection. Most people simply endured his classes and moved on, but Briana had come back to him after being appointed swordmaster. Holden looked at the two lords and then had some quiet words for the warmaster. His leathery face was aged, and he had a stoop, but he was still one of the finest teachers to be found.

Briana looked thoughtful after Holden's comments. Kenton smiled. He imagined the words they must have had after Sillik beat Briana. Although he had seen nothing wrong in the way she had fought, he was sure Holden had been very critical.

She wiped more sweat from her face with the back of her hand as she looked at the two lords. Then she walked to a low bench beside the two men, picked up a towel, and wiped her face again. Her heart was beating quickly, and it wasn't from the exercise. While the men watched impassively, she untied her hair and shook it free. "Go ahead."

Kenton looked down at the sand, his body posture defensive.

Before he could speak, Briana guessed the news. "They are dead, aren't they?"

"Yes, Warmaster," Kenton said. "They were in detention rooms. When the Gold Robes went to talk with them, they were all dead. The bodies are being examined now."

Briana swore. "Were they killed? Did they have some kind of suicide spell?"

"They were under constant guard, Warmaster," Greenup said. "They neither ate nor drank in our custody. They just sat quietly in their cells. But when the Gold Robes arrived to question them, they were dead." He paused. "My men didn't kill them."

"We are examining the bodies," Kenton repeated. "Unfortunately, we just don't know what happened. There is not a mark on them other than what they endured when they were captured."

"Ah, there is Nisha," Briana said as she looked to the side of the practice yard. "I want to know how they were killed," Briana said. "Now I must go get cleaned up and meet with that ridiculous planning committee for the Shelnor trade delegation and Lord Demar. After that, as you know, I have a private dinner with the Salone ambassador. In the meantime, find me some answers. And find them quickly. I don't think we have much time."

# CHAPTER 12

## Sand Lizards

S ILLIK LEFT ILLICIA as the sun was just beginning to set in the sky. He had had the dream again last night. Tonight he would not dream.

He said his goodbyes to Briana and a few others in the keep and then left quietly—no fanfare, no announcements, and no ceremony. He departed quietly through the soldiers' gate with orders that the city remain closed for three days afterward. After that time, the stonemasons would appreciate the opening of the city.

The guards saluted as he passed. "Good hunting," the captain of the guard whispered.

Sillik smiled and nodded solemnly.

Under normal conditions, it took two weeks to ride out of the desert or three weeks to walk, but Sillik set a harder pace. The secret to safely traversing the desert was to know the right path. One didn't simply pick a direction and walk in a straight line. The sandfish would attack in waves, day or night. Exhaustion would set in, mistakes would follow, and finally, the fish would feast. No, the secret was following a convoluted path of rocky outcrops. Sillik had been required to memorize the paths since he was old enough to hold a sword. His warrior's test had demonstrated that he could navigate the desert alone and unarmed and survive. Several of the rocky atolls had wells and storerooms of food and supplies hidden with magic. The Illicians had placed traps on some of the rocky hills in case the unwary tried to rest or hide. The signs and secret paths were another of Illicia's secrets. From the hilltops, he could watch the desert for signs of pursuit.

Sillik raised his desert veil as he walked and pulled the old cloak of his brother up against the warm breeze. He had scavenged what he needed from his brothers' belongings and had left his battle armor on its stand in his room. It was too identifiable, he had told Briana.

The assassins would note his disappearance and try to kill him quickly. He had no doubt that the chase had started the moment he stepped outside the city. He needed a good head start. He had declined the offer of sand lizards because he wanted to avoid notice. Sand lizards left an easily followed trail. Also, they were large and liked to eat, which required additional resources. So he traveled by foot and followed a circuitous route from rocky hill to hill.

At irregular intervals, Sillik doubled back to check his trail and lay false paths. After six days of doing this, he finally saw the signs of pursuit. At first, it was just dust on the horizon. The next day, ravens followed him until he shot them from the sky. Ravens had long been servants of evil and the Nine.

The next day, the dust was closer. He adjusted his path and chose the more difficult trail. The landscape in this part of the desert was rocky with dry riverbeds and low hills. Higher bluffs were scattered around, which provided good locations from which to observe. Sandfish were scarce in this area due to all of the rock.

The attack should have come on the tenth day. The noose was tight. Now it was time to turn the tables. The prey became the hunter.

Sillik strung his bow. His quiver was full of arrows. During the day, he had tracked them. After that, finding their camp had been easy. At sunset, they had eaten a cold meal and passed a water skin around. Sillik had eaten and drunk as well. It might be a long night. One foe ate his meal and then left to guard the sand lizards where they were picketed, and another found a boulder to lean against. Two others sat huddled together, arguing about something. Something was not going the way they wanted. The others lay down to sleep before they took their turn at watch. Once they had wrapped themselves in their cloaks, they were almost invisible.

From where he sat, Sillik could smell the sand lizards. Their stink was truly terrible. It made him hate riding them. However, they were adapted to the desert and were fearsome in battle. The lizards had long, sharp claws that could cut, slash, and puncture. They had long, slender spikes for teeth, and their tails were barbed. Their teeth were used as the points of Illician arrows. The lizards that these men rode were wild desert lizards. They were not as big as the lizards Illicians rode. Only one man could ride these lizards. Illician lizards could carry five or six.

Sillik considered his options. Bowshots were long and difficult. He couldn't be assured of six perfect shots, and without six perfect shots, he risked the survivors mounting their lizards and attacking. With a sigh, he realized he was going to have to do this the hard way. He unstrung his bow and removed everything he wasn't going to need and anything that might make noise. After ensuring his sword and knives were tight in their sheaths, he sat down to watch their camp.

When the moons were at their lowest, he crept toward the camp. It was slow, nerve-racking work with the sentries posted. Move, pause, listen, and repeat. As the perspiration dripped off his face, Sillik was grateful he wasn't in a forest. Dry branches and leaves could sound like kettledrums when amplified by danger, fear, and darkness. For now, he just had to worry about sand or gravel slipping.

Sillik watched the sentry wandering around the lizards. His path was random, and he kept swiveling his head as he searched the darkness. Sillik smiled and then moved to his right. The lizards were silent as they observed Sillik. Their eyes were black pools that seemed to absorb the light. Their tongues flicked in and out, sensing the air.

Sillik was glad he was wearing his brother's old cloak. He had not thought about it at the time, but luck had favored him. The lizards could smell the scent of other lizards. Crinthan had ridden lizards daily, so their scent had been worn into the cloak. Even Sillik could still smell it faintly. He had almost thrown the cloak away, but it was the only one he had found that he liked. Because of the smell, the lizards didn't react to him. If they had, their hisses would have woken the dead. Sillik smiled—the lizards were the blind spot. The sentry apparently assumed that no one would approach from the lizards' position because he never looked toward them.

The hilt of Sillik's dagger made a very effective smack against the guard's head. The man crumpled. Sillik caught him and lowered him soundlessly to the ground. Then he cut the lizards' hobbles and tethers. A few sudden gestures, and the animals scurried away. In minutes, they would be so far away that it would be impossible to catch them.

Sillik checked the sentry. His breathing was slow and steady, and he had a bloody lump on his head. He would be unconscious for the rest of the night. Sillik frisked the man and took the gold in his pouch as well as his weapons. Then Sillik used some leather he found in the man's pouch to tie his hands and feet. He also took the man's boots and slashed them to pieces. He shoved several pieces of boot into the man's mouth and tied the gag in place.

Sillik turned back to the camp. The sentry sitting against the boulder had not moved, and Sillik could tell he was half-asleep. This was much easier than he'd expected. Sillik crept into the camp, still wary. A loose pebble could ruin everything.

After another smack, Sillik helped the second sentry to the ground. Then he reduced the sleeping lumps to unconscious lumps. He confiscated their weapons and tied and gagged all the men. He searched them for any clues as to who had hired them. Sillik knew just by looking at them that they were mercenaries. Men this diverse wouldn't normally be brought together for the same cause unless gold was involved. He found a gold coin on each of the men, but there was nothing to indicate who had paid them. The coins were from several different cities and provided no clues. He took as much of their water as he could carry, but he decided to leave them with one water skin. He poured the rest of their water out onto the rocks. Then he tossed their food onto the fire.

Sillik studied his foes and knew they were not Illicians. It was impossible to determine where they were from, but weaponless, shoeless, foodless, and almost without water, they wouldn't bother him again. When Sillik was finished raiding their camp, he decided to be a little merciful and leave a dagger behind. He buried the rest of their cheap, poorly made weapons in the sand well away from camp.

The following morning, Sillik took a long drink from his water skin as he watched them wake up. The first man who regained consciousness spotted the dagger and scooted close enough to free his hands. Sillik didn't think he cut his hands too badly. Then the man freed his companions and kicked them until they started to move.

With a grim smile, Sillik turned toward Colum. He made good time but still checked his trail often and watched carefully for pursuit. As he neared Colum, the hills leveled out, and at sunset, he paused on the last bluff overlooking the flatlands. Down there, he would be a very visible target. Over the years, Sillik had learned to trust his intuition, and tonight he felt that something was not right, so he ate a cold dinner of dried sandfish and a piece of flatbread, washed it down with water from his pouch, and then stayed low on the bluff.

When the moons rose, he briefly saw a flicker of light on the trail he had followed that day. It wasn't exactly light, but it wasn't fire either. Curious, Sillik kept a close watch, but he saw and heard nothing more. After a long night, he concluded that whatever was out there was just watching. *The desert has eyes,* he remembered Viktorie saying. *Perhaps the Nomads are watching me. They do owe me a favor or two.*

Four nights after his encounter with the mercenaries, Sillik awoke in the night to blowing sand. He struggled into a sitting position as sand drifted around him. He cursed, but there was nothing to do but wait it out. He wrapped his cloak around him like a tent and waited patiently. The storm pulled and tugged at him.

By morning, the storm had passed. After a long hike, Sillik neared Colum. For a few days, he nursed his body at a small oasis before approaching the city.

# CHAPTER 13

## Colum

COLUM WAS AN ancient city on the very edge of the desert. The city was as old as human records. Its towers stood out in stark contrast to the dry, sandy plains. Some of the spires were made of stone, others were adobe, and a few were made of wood. Some of the buildings were stained with guild colors, and others were sand-hued. All were patched and badly painted.

The stone walls glowed red as the sun rose over the waterless land. The city's walls, which had looked formidable in the predawn light, were exposed as cracked and sloppily patched in the brighter light of morning. The city gates opened slowly on their sand-encrusted hinges, creaking and groaning as they were forced into motion. Small, malnourished sand lizards strained in their leather harnesses as they opened the gates. Wooden gates would have been more practical, but wood was expensive out here.

A shallow moat of sharp rocks surrounded the city. Tiny rivers of undefined black ooze seeped through cracks in the walls to puddle amid the rocks and sun-bleached bones scattered at the bottom of the moat. Broken skulls stared lifelessly at the sky. Some of the bones were human, but others were decidedly not. The wind carried the putrid odors of the moat toward Sillik. The smell would nauseate even the most battle-hardened soldiers. Above the towers flew a large, sand-colored flag with the red rising sun, the symbol of Colum.

As Sillik walked, the bottom of his dusty brown cloak whipped around his feet. He had his cloak pulled up and his veil across his face. One hundred paces outside the gates, he stopped and threw back the hood of his cloak and pulled down the veil. With practiced ease, he pushed the cloak over his shoulder so that his right arm, his sword arm, was free. Sillik touched the small pouch that was almost hidden at his waist and smiled. He looked up at the rising-sun pennant of the city fluttering in the morning breeze. He had arrived at Colum. Now perhaps he could get his questions answered.

Sillik counted at least twenty guards at the gate. He didn't even to try to count how many were on the walls. Several were armed with spears or pikes, and all wore swords. A few horn-reinforced recurve bows were visible. Sillik smiled grimly as he recalled what had killed his brother. Someone was making an effort to bring him here.

More guards would be somewhere out of sight. Military tactics were the same the world over. Besides the guards at the entrance, Sillik could see dozens of conical helmets along the tops of the walls. Other guards would be scanning the horizon to see if additional threats were approaching the city.

The guards at the gate would have to be dealt with, Sillik told himself with a wry chuckle. But how? There was little incentive for the guards to let him into the city. A merchant train, yes, but a single warrior? Sillik knew from experience that he could cause trouble. Merchants wanted to buy or sell, and trouble ruined profits. The Colum guards would want to question him about the desert and about Illicia. Standard practice would also suggest questions about why he was there, how long he planned to stay, and what he was doing in Colum. *So how do I avoid being detained or questioned without killing the guards?* Strangely, the thought that he might be killed never crossed his mind.

The answer to Sillik's silent question came quickly as he surveyed the waiting guards. It was a method he wouldn't have used until recently. He smiled as he recalled how he had once bribed his way into a city. The wine had been well worth it. Shaking his head at the fond memory, he reviewed what he suspected about Colum. Illicians tended to avoid Colum since it was poor, out of the way, and a haven for thieves, pickpockets, and thugs. Not even the prostitutes were pretty. There was little law in Colum. Outsiders were always assumed to be guilty, and unwary travelers tended to disappear. Warriors were always challenged when they entered.

If the guards at the gate had their way, the questioning would be painful. According to reports, the guards of Colum liked to break fingers one bone at a time. Sillik had come all this way to find answers to his questions. He wouldn't let them stop him.

The gate was small, considering the height and thickness of the walls. Merchant traffic didn't justify a large gate. *So much the better,* Sillik thought. *The guards will be inexperienced and less wary of strangers.* The main gate was where the peasants farmed and the merchant trains came and went. It was also where the most experienced guards would be.

The guards had watched the approaching man since dawn first showed its red face in the sky. The patrols had reported a lone warrior camped a few miles from the city, and their orders were to observe and report rather than challenge.

The guards' curiosity was piqued. The few people who walked out of the desert were often mad and staggering from lack of water. The guards also knew that the desert hid the city of Illicia. Merchants, entertainers, peddlers, and others who traveled in the desert said the city of Illicia possessed wealth beyond imagination. According to stories, the spires of the city sparkled like diamonds, and the people walked between the needle-like towers on bridges of gold and silver. Some said the walls of Illicia were a thousand feet tall and surrounded by sandfish the size of men. It was also said the city was guarded by unbeatable warriors and demons from the nine depths of hell.

Illicia also produced stone of all kinds. Its stonemasons were without equal in the world. The guards knew that much of the carved stone in Colum had come from Illicia over the centuries.

The guards also knew that Illician warriors who had visited Colum deserved their reputation. Cities had been destroyed for the accidental death of an Illician prince or princess. The death of a single Illician warrior was dealt with almost as harshly. That was, of course, if you could kill an Illician warrior at all. Wars had been ended simply because the Illicians had joined the cause of one city versus another.

The warriors of Illicia were without question the most highly trained in the world. They were experts in armed and unarmed combat and used hands, feet, and multiple weapons in deadly combinations. It was said you could never disarm an Illician until you had stripped him naked, broken his fingers, arms, and legs, cut out his tongue, and shaved his head. Even then, you could only be half sure that you had taken away all of his weapons. To make matters worse, the women were as deadly as the men. Illicia was one of the few cities that allowed and even encouraged women to fight alongside their men. Only the foolish or those wishing to die quickly started a fight with an Illician warrior.

Another important fact was that some of the Illicians were supposed to be masters of the Seven White Laws. Colum had decided long ago that any use of magic was evil. Consequently, anyone suspected of dabbling in the arcane arts, either white or black, was shunned and banished, if not slain. Many who could control the Seven Laws were simply killed by their former friends or associates. They couldn't be trusted. It was a terrible insult in Colum to be accused of being a friend of the Seven or of the Nine.

The thought occurred to several of the guards that they should question the stranger about Illicia before they allowed him to enter their city. Dreams of treasure overrode their fear of him. Perhaps he wasn't an Illician. Maybe he was just a mercenary or an assassin looking for work. There was plenty of blood work to be done here. Merchants were always looking for a permanent solution to their rivals. The guards had not seen an Illician in a long time.

Perhaps even a little "extra" persuasion could be employed to find out what he knew, a few of the more notorious guards thought with wicked grins. He was only one man. Some of the guards fingered their knives in anticipation. One man wouldn't be missed. Unfortunate accidents happened all the time. Unconsciously, several of the guards moved closer to the gate and loosened their swords.

Sillik noted the guards' movements with a grim smile. He quickly assessed their weapons and their numbers. A few wore the red belt of the warrior guild. Those who didn't would be little more than thugs with weapons. Sillik kept his eyes on all of them, but he followed the steps of one guard in particular, a man who had moved to the center of the gate. He would be the captain of the guard. *By the Seven Gods, this might be far easier than I expected.* By pausing outside the city, he had forced the captain to reveal himself.

Sillik formulated his plan and then made the necessary preparations. He would use one of the most powerful of the Seven Laws to compel obedience, but he pointedly kept his hands away from his sword and dagger. His body language and posture were designed to convince the captain that he was harmless, even though the captain probably knew Sillik was anything but.

The captain of the guard was armed with several daggers and a long sword with a well-worn hilt. He wore the red belt of the warriors, but he also had a whip strapped to his side, which was in violation of the warrior code. Sillik eyed it with disgust. Whips were for slavers, not warriors.

Intricately inked tattoos of crossed swords adorned the outside of the captain's biceps. On his forearms, he wore brass and leather plate armor covered in finger-long, triangular spikes. Sillik felt his anger growing. The spikes would produce deep, tearing wounds that were difficult to heal. These were the weapons of bullies and brigands, not warriors. Sillik also noticed that the captain's clothing was dirty and stained, his pants were patched, and his boots were dull and dirty. His shirt might have been red at some point in the past, and his pants were definitely black. Red and black had been the traditional colors of the guards of Colum for centuries.

Sillik grimaced as he looked at the captain's long, black, gray-streaked hair, which cascaded down to his shoulders like greasy rivers. It looked like months had passed since he had seen a bath or even a bucket of clean water.

His chain-mail cap was rusty and encrusted with grime. One corner of the man's mouth was stained brown from chewing leaf. Several half-healed scars adorned his face, and his right eye was almost swollen shut from a recent fight. Sillik noted the eye and thought that if they came to blows, he would attack from the right.

The flicker of dislike that raced across Sillik's face was replaced quickly with a grim smile. *Control your emotions*, he told himself sternly. Had the warriors in Colum sunk to the level of slave masters and bullies? Sillik smiled broadly despite the anger he felt. If the captain of the guard was any indication, he would have no problems in the city. He must find out why this city was important. Why had his father sent him here?

Baldwin, the captain of the guard, stepped forward just outside the gates, his hands hooked on his belt. He licked his lips nervously, spat a wad of chewing leaf from his mouth, cleared his throat, and spat again. Spittle ran down the corner of his mouth, and he wiped it with the back of his hand. He didn't like the feel of the situation. The stranger seemed to radiate authority and power. *Perhaps*, Baldwin thought with a grin, *I could get a bribe from this stranger. It might pay for a night in the taverns.* As he considered the idea, his grin expanded to reveal a mouthful of broken and blackened teeth. He winced. His damn eye hurt. He should have killed the bastard who hit him. Damn royal guardsman! He spat again and studied the stranger.

Baldwin was puzzled. The stranger's stance appeared casual, but Baldwin sensed something. What in the Nine Black Laws was going on? Baldwin might be a poor and unkempt warrior, but he had survived for many years by trusting his gut. Why had this stranger stopped outside the gates? Didn't he want to enter? Without thinking, Baldwin laid his hand on the hilt of his sword, which was loose in its sheath. Baldwin smiled to himself with sudden confidence as he heard the creaking of bows above him. If he drew his sword, his archers would let fly without question. Baldwin had heard his men whispering about Illicia and the city of gold and silver, and he too was curious. Was there gold to be taken? How much gold might the stranger have?

Baldwin tried to estimate how old the man was, but he had too many conflicting impressions. His posture spoke of years of experience, but the lack of gray in his hair hinted at youth. A younger man might outlast him in a fight, but a more experienced man might kill him. The hilt of the traveler's sword looked old and worn. It was too old for a young man, so the sword was old, but the traveler was young. Therefore, the sword must be important, but why? Was it a talisman, a good-luck weapon, or a gift from a father or a sovereign? If a king had given the blade as a gift, this man might be important. Baldwin snorted derisively and shifted his attention to other aspects of the warrior. The man was lean and yet appeared tired. His boots were heavily used, as was his cloak.

Baldwin cursed to himself. He hated contradictions. He prided himself on being a shrewd and savvy warrior. He could read men like the back of his hand. His eyes narrowed as he watched; something about this man bothered him.

Sillik took a deep breath and strode toward the gates, stopping when he entered the blood circle around Baldwin–"blood circle" was an old training term defined by the length of a man's arm and his sword. Apprentice warriors were trained to stay out of a warrior's blood circle until they had drawn their weapon. Sillik smiled nonchalantly. He was not an apprentice, and he had not been one for a very long time.

Baldwin folded his arms across his chest and looked at the stranger. He wanted to step back, but he gritted his teeth and held his ground. Then he noticed a new detail: the sheath of the stranger's sword was unadorned, which surprised him. If he was from Illicia, the sheath should bear an engraved golden eagle. Baldwin's own sheath proudly bore the rising sun of Colum. He frowned in confusion. Was the stranger from Illicia, or was he an outlaw, not claiming any city?

Baldwin had never seen an Illician who wasn't wearing two or three of those cursed eagles. That damned eagle eye was always staring and watching. *By the Seven Gods*, Baldwin swore, *who is this man?* Mercenaries didn't wear the sign of their city. Was he just a mercenary looking for a job? An assassin looking for a kill? Why did he walk out of the desert? Baldwin sniffed. He could smell sand lizards, but anyone who came near one would wear that stink. That alone didn't make the man an Illician. If he was an Illician, why wasn't he riding a sand lizard like most of his arrogant countrymen did? Why was he on foot? No one ever just walked out of the desert. The sandfish would eat someone who walked on the sands. What were his intentions?

It made Baldwin uncomfortable that the stranger had come so close. Both men could draw and attack in a single movement. Baldwin frowned in consternation. *He knows we can both do this, and he knows that I know. So what do I know that he does not?* Baldwin knew that the man who faced him could draw his sword and attack before the archers could let loose a shaft. *We are so close; they will hesitate*, Baldwin reasoned. *He will know that.* His eyes narrowed. Baldwin was feeling greedy and devious. He didn't want this man shot or killed–at least not yet, not if there was gold to be had.

Baldwin knew with a strange certainty that the stranger was a trained warrior. The signs were evident far beyond his red belt. The scars on his hands and the worn leather bore the stains of many adventures. His lean, muscled appearance was a stark testament that this man had followed the warrior code. Yet Baldwin, the victor of more battles and duels than he chose to remember, knew he would die if he had to face this man with naked blades. Despite the morning heat, he shivered. He had never doubted his own skill with the sword before. This stranger wore his leather like a monarch would wear his silken robes. Confidence oozed from the man. Fear made Baldwin tremble.

The captain was suddenly conscious of his own shabby appearance compared to this dust-covered warrior. Baldwin's leather was stained and dirty, but that was from drinking in the taverns. He sniffed and smelled the stale odors of drink and unwashed clothing. His hair was greasy and roughly cut. Remnants of last night's dinner still resided in his gray-streaked beard. He couldn't remember the last time he had visited the city's bathhouses. His clothing was so encrusted with grime, sweat, salt, and sand that it could stand by itself. He tugged at his worn, cracked leather with a sudden lack of confidence. The warrior from the desert smiled proudly. *Damned, arrogant Illician.* Baldwin was about to speak when he met the stranger's eyes. In a flash, he was undone.

Trembling with terror, Baldwin realized that the stranger was a sorcerer, a master of either the Seven White Laws or the Nine Black Laws, one of the rare men who could control the arcane powers of the world. Baldwin had never knowingly seen a sorcerer before, so part of him was shocked. His mind reeled as the stranger's eyes seemed to bore into it like molten daggers. His mind screamed at the invasion, but his body never moved. He wavered for a moment. Blood rushed through his veins. He heard a ringing in his ears and the pounding of his heart. Then it was gone and forgotten.

Sillik worked quickly without moving. In a matter of heartbeats, he was done; the compulsion was set. They would talk, and then Baldwin would let him pass. Normally, he didn't approve of compulsion. But he wasn't forcing the man to do anything he wouldn't have done anyway. This wasn't black, maybe just a bit gray.

Baldwin smiled and made a show of crossing his burly arms. "Who are you, and what do you want here?" he asked with a thick accent.

Struggling to place the accent, Sillik grinned. "You're from somewhere in the north," he guessed aloud. "Rithan or Anon?" The tattoos, where had he seen them before?

"Ain't here to discuss me," Baldwin grunted. "Who are you, and what do you want here?"

Sillik nodded. He was right. He had seen similar tattoos when he passed through the north. "Rithan!" he concluded triumphantly. "I am Sillik. I am simply a traveler passing through."

Baldwin considered Sillik's words. *How did the devil guess where I'm from? Passing through? If I hadn't had that misunderstanding in Anon, I would have passed through Colum too and left this damn desert.* "Passing through, huh? Where you going? How long you staying?"

"No more than a few days," Sillik said. "I need some supplies. Are there any merchants who need a soldier heading north? I don't have any gold, and I might as well earn something if someone is going where I need to go."

"Might be," Baldwin said, not even realizing his questions were not being answered. "Check with the merchants in the water district. Damn water merchants have all the money. Always buying stuff. And no trouble while you're in our city," Baldwin warned, pointing a dirty finger at Sillik's chest. "We don't like troublemakers."

"Of course," Sillik said as he fished a small silver coin out of his pocket and tossed it to the guard.

"Move on," Baldwin commanded as he pocketed the coin.

The guards on the walls, who had watched and tried to listen, relaxed when they saw their captain laugh and smile. Some were envious of the bribe. Gold would have been nice, but silver would buy enough wine for a night in the taverns. Perhaps they would get some of it.

Even at this distance, Sillik noted the disgusting smells coming from Baldwin, the moat, and the city beyond. It was about to get worse when he entered the city. He could at least take care of one of those problems. As he released his controls on Baldwin, he left one last strong compulsion: *Take a bath.*

Sillik stepped forward as Baldwin moved aside. His footsteps echoed ominously as he walked across the bridge and strode confidently into the awakening city. With a charming smile, Sillik nodded to the members of the guard near the gate. The other guards let him pass without challenge since their captain had stepped aside, and they watched in disappointment as the stranger disappeared into the city.

"What are you looking at?" Baldwin asked. "Get back to work!" He swore at the guards with vile, obscene curses that involved their mothers, their fathers, and goats. Then, with a particularly nasty grin, he ordered them back to their posts for a double watch. A collective groan went out from the men. The slaves near the gate looked away, afraid to anger the captain. It would be a bad day for everyone stationed at the gate if Baldwin was in a bad mood.

Then, to everyone's amazement, Baldwin hurried away from the gate, leaving his sergeant in command. He disappeared into the city, heading in a different direction than the stranger, muttering that it was time to clean up. The sergeant shook his head in puzzlement and then turned toward the horizon.

# CHAPTER 14

## Squalor

A S SILLIK ENTERED Colum, he was instantly repulsed by what he saw and smelled. Compared to other cities Sillik had seen in his travels, Colum had little to offer. This crumbling and squalid place didn't even begin to compare to the varied smells, sights, and wonders of the other cities. The streets were narrow and filthy. Residents threw their trash, their leftover food, and the contents of their chamber pots into the streets. Beggars, street urchins, and rats scrambled over the rubbish and fought for each meager find. Rancid smoke hung like a gray, blinding pall in the streets. The heat of the morning promised to turn the streets into a humid, stinking hell. Flies and other winged creatures swarmed through the morning air. Biting insects flew, crawled, and jumped everywhere. Loud, coarse shouts broke the silence as venders hawked their meager wares.

Prostitutes, still groggy from the night and filthy in ragged clothing and cheap perfume, tried to entice customers with lewd comments and seductive poses. Two of the prostitutes raised their skirts and promised delights to Sillik as he passed. The sight of their unwashed skin, missing teeth, and lice-infested, greasy hair made his stomach lurch, but he passed without comment.

The smell of the city threatened to overwhelm him, and he quickly regretted stopping here, but the papers Briana had found in his father's hand demanded explanation, so he'd had to come here.

Eventually, Sillik made his way into a better section of the city where the streets were marginally cleaner, the flies slightly less bothersome, and the prostitutes less obvious. It took him a while to forget the stench, all the same. The people were, on the whole, still rather filthy and poor. Most of them wore clothes cut from gray or brown fabrics. An unfortunate few bore scars or oozing cuts on their faces that could have been delivered by only one weapon—the whip.

Sillik discerned that there were two classes of guards in the city. Both wore the red and black of the guard. The elite guards also wore cloaks of red with gold trim. A few of the common guards wore the red sword belt, but all of the elite guards wore it. Whether they deserved the belt or not, Sillik was in no hurry to find out. For now, he just observed.

Several times during the day, Sillik saw groups of "elite" guards pushing and shoving their way through the throngs of people. They were usually escorting someone who could afford their services. Once they escorted a draped chair carried by four heavily muscled men. The four men were chained to the chair, and Sillik frowned at the use of slaves.

Once, Sillik saw a "common" guard pushed down from behind by one of the elite guards. The angry guard jumped to his feet with a snarl, his long hair whipping around as he turned to face his aggressor, his hand already drawing his blade. When he saw who had pushed him, he released his blade as if it were red-hot. For a long moment, he glared at the other guard and then backed away, much to the delight of the elite guard and his fellows. Both of the guards wore the red warrior belt, but Sillik suspected the odds were not in the favor of the common guard.

As the shadows lengthened, Sillik looked for something to eat. He passed several stalls selling food until he found one that was relatively clean. Using a few copper coins, he bought a large piece of meat, a loaf of bread, and a skin of wine. Then he turned toward the room he had reserved for the night. He had had to pay a high price, even by his standards, for a room that would be considered a hovel in his city. It was almost clean, though, and it was in one of the better parts of Colum.

The skinny and very ill-looking landlord gave Sillik a bored look as he entered the building. Sillik smiled as he deftly dodged a pair of drunks fighting in the common room. Three nearly naked slave girls screamed and ran away from the fight as the drunks drew their knives. Sillik stopped and turned when he saw the flash of metal. One hand was on his sword and the other on a knife hilt. As the drunks tried awkwardly to stab one another, Sillik sighed and strode into the middle of the fight. He pushed the fighters apart, sent one man stumbling backward with a kick to the stomach, and disarmed the other with a few quick blocks. The second drunk cried in pain. His arm was nearly dislocated as Sillik spun him around and planted a foot on the man's backside. Sillik heard someone behind him and whirled to face the drunk he had kicked in the stomach. The man had grabbed another knife and made an angry stab. Sillik spun, hearing the fabric in his cloak tear, and then caught the drunk's arm, twisted it sharply, and felt the bones break. He caught the knife as it fell from the man's suddenly numb fingers. The man fell to the floor, crying out in pain as he cradled his arm.

"That's for tearing my cloak," Sillik said as he scooped up the other knife that had fallen to the floor and threw the knives one at a time into the ceiling beam above the bar. The bartender looked up in surprise at the knives quivering several arm's lengths above his head. The tips of the blades were no farther apart than the width of a man's thumb. A murmur of appreciation came from the patrons as they admired how closely the three knives were spaced. The few sober patrons pounded the tables in appreciation as Sillik turned to leave. Sillik was tempted to set the man's broken arm, but he decided against it when the drunk moaned again. Setting bones without painkillers was a noisy business, and he wanted some sleep. He also was in no hurry to demonstrate his mastery of the Seven Laws.

One of the slave girls gave Sillik a fleeting smile before she hurried off to serve drinks. Another slave girl cried quietly as she knelt beside a customer with a new mug. Fresh welts covered her back. Evidently, she had displeased someone with a cruel temper. All of the girls were filthy, unclean, and unkempt, and all bore signs of recent beatings. At least two were missing teeth. Sillik shook his head. Slavery was a plague that should have been eradicated centuries earlier, but he was not here to free the slaves. He shouldn't have even interfered in the fight. It could draw the wrong kind of attention—or would it bring the kind of attention he was seeking? Without another look back, Sillik climbed the narrow stairs to his room two at a time.

Once in his room, he closed and barred the door behind him. For several moments he considered using a charm to strengthen the door, but he decided against it. He would hear anyone climbing the stairs long before they reached his door. The pair of drunks wouldn't be climbing stairs anytime soon. Indeed, the landlord hadn't even wanted to come up the narrow, rickety stairs when Sillik had asked for a room with a clean bed. The innkeeper had merely given him a key and promised clean sheets.

As he sat in the center of the floor, Sillik looked at the bed and sheets that passed for clean in Colum and shook his head in amazement. He would bet that it had been months, if not years, since the bedding had last seen water. It would be safer to sleep on the floor, wrapped in his torn cloak. He examined the tear in his cloak from the knife fight downstairs. It was long and had ruined what was left of the garment. He would have to find a new one tomorrow. Since he was heading toward forested land, he would look for something in green and brown.

Sillik reached out with his mind and caused the few candles in the room to burst into light. Then he glanced at the balcony and sighed in relief when he saw that the shutters were closed. If anyone had happened to see what he had done, life could have gotten very interesting.

The meat he had purchased was still warm but heavy with grease. The bread was coarse and gritty, and the wine was almost sour. Sillik grimaced as he ate the poor meal. Then he stretched and yawned. The day had been long, and he had detected no sign of his quarry. He was sure he would be able to feel his enemy's presence. Nor had he found any other reason to spend much time here. This city was depraved and grotesque, and he wanted to get away as quickly as he could. Why had his father led him here?

Sillik opened the pouch at his waist and carefully unfolded the papers that had been found in his father's hand the night he was killed. He knew, of course, that one of the Seven Gods had placed them there.

When he had first looked at the rising sun of Colum, Sillik had been surprised to see his name written above it. He had examined the paper with every tool available to him. As far as he could tell, the paper had not been touched by magic, and it contained no secret messages. Two other pieces of paper had been folded inside the rising sun. A single word was written on one piece of paper, and a map symbol was drawn on the other.

"Colum is the closest," Briana had said. Sillik had nodded thoughtfully as he looked at the paper. The handwriting was definitely from Sillik's father. He was sure of that, but he had neglected to mention that fact to Briana.

Lady Silvia had said there would be tests. Therefore, there had to be some purpose to coming to this hellhole. Briana had added that the bows found after the killing of Rendar and his family were similar to those used in Colum. Sillik smiled. The trail was obvious, intentionally so. The papers could signify several things. Sillik's father could have known something about what was happening and had left clues for his sons. Perhaps his father had been part of something and had been killed for it.

Tomorrow, he would leave Colum and head toward one of the other civilized cities before he went to the second city named by his father. Sillik hoped the dragons of Ynak were not awake. They could complicate things. There was nothing here except potentially more drunks and depravity. Perhaps his little demonstration in the common room of the tavern would lead someone to him.

Sillik placed the papers in his pouch and made his way to the balcony. He opened the shutters and stepped outside. He shivered in the cool air. Stars were beginning to appear in the sky along with the moons: Torre, Idin, and Coren had already risen. Tomorrow, he would buy some supplies and a new cloak in preparation for his journey. Perhaps he could find a merchant train heading north and follow along.

He was distracted by the sound of chains rattling and a girl cursing. Curious, he leaned out over the rail. It creaked a warning. Five soldiers had just burst out of the building across from him. Instantly, the street cleared of pedestrians. The men wore the red and gold cloaks of the elite guard. They dragged an old man wearing heavy black chains. One of the guards had a girl slung over his shoulder.

It was the old man who drew Sillik's interest. He wore the rags of a peasant, but he held himself straight and proud. Something about him said "warrior." The girl was also different from the rabble he had seen during the day. As he caught sight of her face, Sillik revised his estimate of her age from girl to woman. He smiled in appreciation. She was cleaner than her streetwise sisters, and there were other differences as well. She was slender and shapely. Her long brown hair was braided and hung nearly to her waist.

Sillik knew just by looking that she was no slave. Her curses also marked her as a well-educated woman. They were inventive and loud rather than salty and coarse. There was something else strange about her, something he couldn't quite see. Despite her position on the guard's shoulder, she had the look of intelligence and cunning as she beat her captor on his back. Perhaps this was what he needed to draw his foes to him.

Suddenly, the guard carrying the woman yelled in surprise, and she rolled off his shoulder and fell to the ground. She jumped to her feet, her brown skirts swirling, and drew a small knife that had been hidden in her bodice. The guard who had been holding her laughed and inspected his hand where she had bitten him. Furious, the woman threw herself at the man. He gasped in surprise and tried to ward her off, but her knife found its way into his chest. The guard stared in horror at the hilt that protruded from his chest. The woman reclaimed her knife as he toppled backward. Shock etched forever on his face, the guard was dead before his head hit the cobblestones.

"No, Renee, don't!" the old man yelled.

Three of the warriors drew their swords as the woman drew the dead man's weapon. They spread apart and moved toward her. The remaining guard held the old man's chains.

The three warriors moved professionally, eyes on her blade. Panic crossed her face briefly as she tried to face all three warriors at the same time. They moved efficiently to keep her contained. Her hair swirled around her face as she looked around, fear flickering in her eyes. The haughtiness that had marked the elite guards all day was replaced with a cold hardness. They had transformed into professional warriors in a heartbeat.

Sillik drew his sword quietly. He didn't want to become involved, but unless he did something, the woman would die. One of the guards slashed at her. She parried. Two of the guards swung their swords. Somehow she managed to parry both blades, but the two quick blows knocked her sword out of her hands. It clattered to the cobblestones. As she reached for it, one of the guards grabbed a handful of her hair and pulled her away from the steel. Her careful braid unraveled with the rough treatment. Then a quick, backhanded blow knocked her across the street. Renee landed in a tangle of dress and travel cloak. For a moment she was still. The guards grinned in anticipation of the fun they were about to have.

Sillik swung his legs over the rail and jumped, catching a rope used to dry laundry above the street. He dangled for a moment before the rope broke. He landed behind one of the guards and sank to his knees. A sword whistled above his head. Laughing, Sillik stood up and parried the guard's blow. Then his blade slid effortlessly through the guard's defense. A tingle raced up Sillik's sword arm as the guard died. Images raced before his eyes. Ideas presented themselves suddenly. Was the sword trying to tell him what to do?

Two of the remaining guards turned to face Sillik. They observed him for a moment and then moved forward together. Their training was evident. Behind them, Renee scrambled for her sword.

Sillik darted to one side, easily avoiding the two blades. As he turned, he parried the guards' blades. One of the guards darted in front of Sillik. The two men exchanged a dozen quick blows while Sillik turned to keep his foe between himself and the other guard. The sound of steel on steel rang in the evening air. The street was utterly deserted as the few remaining residents fled.

*More guards will be coming soon,* Sillik thought as he and the guard circled each other. Behind them, Renee and the remaining guard also circled. Sillik kept turning to keep both of his foes in front of him. His sword felt alive and seemed to fight with a will of its own. This was the first time Sillik had used it in battle. It felt like it was guiding his hand, making each stroke better. Sillik moved to his left and struck. The guard parried in a shower of sparks and an explosion of noise. Then Sillik's weapon slid off the guard's sword and sank into the man's chest. Sillik yanked his weapon free, reversed it under his arm, and turned as his second opponent rushed belatedly to his companion's defense. The second guard died with a surprised expression on his face.

The remaining guard threw down the old man's chains and rushed toward Sillik. He was furious. He had seen four of his fellows die tonight, three killed by a single man. Who was this demon?

The two men fought furiously. Their swords rang with clear notes and bright sparks in the darkness. Sillik knew the sound of their fight would carry in the cooling air. In a few minutes, other guards and curious onlookers would be attracted to the sound. Even now, Sillik saw heads sticking out of windows up and down the street. Sillik had to finish this quickly if he hoped to escape.

In the first few moments, both men realized that Sillik was the better warrior. The guard grasped for a new strategy. He tried to fight a defensive battle, trying to prolong the fight until help arrived.

Sillik heard a sick gurgle. Out of the corner of his eye, he saw Renee's opponent fall to the ground. Impressed, Sillik glanced at her as she went to the old man. She had slain a highly trained warrior. There was definitely more to this woman than met the eye. Sillik's eyes snapped back to his opponent.

The guard began to sweat as he defended himself from an attack that was becoming increasingly difficult to see. Soon, he would feel steel bite into him, and he was scared. He didn't want to die. He had failed to complete his task. Death in battle, though, was preferable to what would await him if he failed. He realized suddenly that there was a way he could succeed in his mission, though it would almost certainly result in his death. He darted to the side. As he saw his opponent's sword descending on his undefended side, he threw a dagger from his belt. A moment later, he was dead, and the woman screamed.

As Sillik sheathed his blade, he saw with his eyes what his mind had already told him. The guard's dagger had struck the old man in the center of his chest and had sunk to the hilt. The old man's eyes bore a tranquility that was harshly at odds with his brutal death. A growing pool of blood stained the stones red. Renee knelt beside the still body. Her long hair was draped around her face, but Sillik could see the tears falling from her cheeks. The street beneath her was dusty, and the tears turned into spots of mud. Her back shook with great, heaving sobs. In the distance, Sillik heard the sound of heavy, booted feet. Touching Renee gently, Sillik pulled her away from the body.

"No," she cried as more tears rolled down her cheeks. "I can't leave him. They will mutilate his body to humiliate him."

"If I take care of his body, will you leave?"

Renee looked up at Sillik with a tear-stained face and nodded.

Sillik groaned inwardly as he withdrew the dagger that had killed the old man. He laid the weapon down quietly, overriding the temptation to toss it away. He held his hands over the locks on the chains, and they clicked open. Renee didn't seem to notice through her tears. Sillik grabbed a cloak off one of the dead soldiers and wrapped the old man in it. Then, hefting the body over his shoulder, he grabbed Renee's hand and hurried into the darkness. He had briefly considered summoning an elemental to accept the body into the earth, but he quickly rejected the idea. Too many eyes would see, and he wasn't sure how Renee would react to such a demonstration of sorcery. More importantly, it was a difficult spell, and he was short on time.

As the pair hurried into the night, a dark shadow followed discreetly.

The two had just turned the first corner when more than a dozen heavily armed elite guards found their comrades' bodies, and Sillik heard more boots nearing. He turned down the first alley he found, and when it branched, he went left. At the next branch he went right. Knowing the general layout of the city, he kept moving away from the scene of the fight. In the darkness, the shape on his shoulder could be anything, and fortunately, few were in the alleys after dark.

When he felt they were far enough away from the scene, Sillik lowered the old man's body to the ground and hid it between two walls, covering it with trash. While Renee kept a lookout for danger, he cast a quick spell to conceal the body. By the time it was discovered, it would be unrecognizable.

Renee turned to face the unmarked grave, her eyes still full of tears. Sillik gave her a moment of quiet and then pulled her down another alley. A few quick turns, and they emerged onto a torch-lit street with crowds hurrying in every direction.

For a while, they lost themselves in the bustling mass of people. After what seemed like an entire night, they took refuge in a small room that Sillik had rented that afternoon for a few silver coins in case of just such an emergency. The room was in one of the sections of the city where silence could be bought with a liberal dose of silver. Once they were safely in the room, Sillik placed a charm on the door. As an extra precaution, he wove a powerful ward around them to prevent anyone from hearing what they said.

When he was finished, Sillik turned to Renee, wiping the sweat from his brow. "Now tell me, why did those guards go to so much trouble to arrest what appeared to be a poor peasant and his daughter?"

"I am not really his daughter," Renee said, "only his niece."

Sillik nodded sympathetically. "Why were they after you, Renee? Why were you and your uncle so important to those jackals?"

For a long moment, she just looked at him. Sillik had the impression that she was considering what to tell him.

Sillik seized the moment to take off his boots. He grimaced with relief and massaged his sore feet. He took of his leather shirt next. He yearned for a soak in hot water but was intrigued by what her story might be. Who knew? Parts of it might even be true.

When Renee finally spoke, her voice was soft, and it cracked as she struggled to control her emotions. "Belliousces, my uncle, and the emperor were the best of friends in the years before the emperor sat on the throne. When the emperor was crowned, he began to change. He became brutal. He seemed to enjoy tormenting my uncle. At first, my uncle ignored his insults. But over the years, his insults got worse. Time after time, I pleaded with my uncle to leave the city, but he wouldn't. He was a man of honor, and he couldn't leave in dishonor. It was then that the emperor began to levy new taxes on the people. As the people complained, the emperor formed an elite corps of warriors to enforce his will."

As Sillik listened to her story, he picked up clues to her background from the way she pronounced several words. Her inflections spoke of different cities. She strung some of her words together like they did in Covenon, yet something in her pronunciation reminded Sillik of Salone. He had spent time in that city a lifetime ago. Salone, Sillik knew, trained most of the masters of the Seven Laws. Perhaps she had been educated in one of those cities. Sillik studied the woman intently. Something else was happening here, something about Salone. A memory tugged at him.

Renee continued her story, unaware of Sillik's contemplation. "My uncle said nothing at first, though it troubled him deeply to let what was happening occur. Then he appealed to the emperor, but nothing would change his mind. That was a month ago. After that, the emperor thought he discovered an attempt to oust him and had the suspected ringleaders thrown into prison. Not one of the alleged conspirators was ever seen again, except for one man and his daughter. During court a couple of weeks ago, the emperor had the pair dragged into the hall. They had been beaten and tortured and were half-starved. For a while, he ignored them. Then he had the girl stripped and a slave brought from the dungeons. She was beaten on the steps of the throne by the slave, and the man was given his freedom. She was dragged away, sobbing. I never learned what happened to her. She has not been seen again."

"What happened to the father of the girl?" Sillik asked softly.

"The emperor had him tortured before the court. Several people tried to leave, but he forbade it. They broke his arms and legs. When they didn't get the answers they wanted, the emperor ordered him skinned." Renee paused for a moment as she recalled the horror she had been forced to watch. She wiped a few tears from her face with her cloak. "During that entire night, my uncle never said a word. When the man finally died, my uncle told me the man was innocent."

"What finally happened?" Sillik asked, though he could probably guess. It was a pattern he had seen many times in his travels.

"Guards stormed our home, but we were forewarned by a friend and escaped through a secret passage moments beforehand. For three days, we hid in a small room near the walls of the city. The entire time, my poor uncle paced back and forth like a caged animal. Finally, I convinced him that we should leave the city. I showed him the small fortune I had brought with me when we fled our home. We had enough gold and jewels to live comfortably anywhere. Finally, he revealed that there was a secret way out of the city.

"The following night, before the second watch, we slipped out and made our way to the Council Tower near the center of the city. Once inside, we avoided the guards and made our way to the lowest depth of the tower. My uncle brushed aside a pile of rotting trash and stepped on a certain stone. At once, a portion of the wall slid aside, revealing a dark, damp stone tunnel."

Sillik noticed with interest that Renee had ignored explaining her accent, her obvious education, what had happened to her parents, how exactly she had come to Colum, and where she had planned to go with her uncle. Sillik didn't believe she would have failed to plan that journey. She didn't seem like someone who would leave things like that to chance. He also noticed that she had not explained her knowledge of the sword. What else was she leaving out? Her story had the ring of truth, though, despite the holes.

Renee continued in her soft voice. "Then we entered the passage, and the door closed quietly behind us. The path he had chosen was not pleasant. It stank, and oily water dripped from the ceiling. Now and then, I heard things moving in the darkness."

Despite himself, Sillik grinned.

"The passage kept descending, and the tunnel grew warmer. The water on the floor began to rise, and soon we were sloshing through calf-deep water. Soon after that, the tunnel sprouted branches. Without hesitation, my uncle chose this branch and then that branch, seemingly at random. I became lost very quickly."

That didn't sound true. Sillik didn't believe she had been lost. With a smile, Sillik wagered that even blindfolded she could have found her way back. She was hiding something. *As if you don't hide things*, a voice in his head said. Sillik cleared his throat and was about to say something when Renee's voice changed.

"Then, without warning, my uncle stopped and blocked me with his arm. He bent down and stared at the water for several moments. With a shaking finger, he pointed at a fine black thread running across the tunnel just above the black, oily water. I remember shivering even though the heat was intolerable and my throat was parched.

"'It's a trap,' my uncle said. After that, he refused to go any farther. He insisted that if we were to leave, we must do it by another route, so we turned back." Renee's tone turned bitter. "We emerged in the tower, and by the time we had avoided the patrols and reached the streets, the sun was already in the sky. We made our way through the streets and found a small room that I rented for a few copper pieces."

"How did the guards find you?"

Renee shook her head, more tears in her eyes. "In this city, most people will sell their souls for a silver coin. A traitor or someone the emperor says is a traitor could earn someone enough gold to live for a year." She ran her hand through her dirt-streaked hair. "They burst into the room at sunset. Before I could move, one of the beasts threw me over his shoulder like I was a slave or a prize while the rest held my uncle at sword point and shackled him like a common thief or murderer."

The anger in her voice made Sillik realize she would be a formidable foe.

"I forget myself," she said humbly, "Thank you for your aid. It was most brave. The men you slew are"—she stopped and smiled—"*were* among the finest warriors in the royal guard."

"You are welcome," Sillik said.

"Who are you?" Renee asked. "You are not from Colum. That much is clear. You wear the red belt of the warrior guild, and I think you did something to hide my uncle when I was not looking, something with the Seven Laws."

*Formidable indeed*, Sillik concluded as he looked at her again. To his surprise, she had noticed but not reacted. This only confirmed that there was far more to this woman than what he saw.

Sillik decided to see just how much she could handle. "Yes, you are correct. I am a master of the Seven Laws."

"A true sorcerer," she breathed excitedly, "not one of those charlatans that I see in the streets." She stopped as she pondered her next question. "Where are you from, and why are you here?"

For a while, Sillik was quiet as he pondered that very question. Why was he here? "Have you ever heard of a people who live in the Weeping Wastes?"

"Yes, of course," she said, pushing her hair out of her face, "the Illicians."

"What do you know of them?"

"They are reputed to be a race of sorcerers and warriors. In the ancient languages of the land, the word 'Illician' is supposed to mean 'resolution carved in stone,' because of their determination to prevail."

"What else?"

"According to legend, they fought and eventually won both of the demon wars under the leadership of their first king. After the wars, it is said that they built a city in the desert, but that's not possible. The wastes are uninhabitable."

"Not true," Sillik replied gently. "Not uninhabitable, only unknown."

"You are one of them?"

"Yes, I am an Illician. I am …" He paused, suddenly cautious. "Related to the royal family."

"Royalty?" Renee's mind seemed to reel at the disclosure. "What are you doing here?" She gestured with open hands to indicate the city. "Shouldn't you be with your people?"

"Yes and no," Sillik said, a lump in his throat. "Some men were killed, and I am searching for the assassin." Sillik believed there was more to Renee's story than what she had told him, so he kept his own story brief.

Renee was quiet for a moment, as if expecting further explanation for Sillik's presence in her city.

Sillik glanced at the window. "Dawn is near. We have talked the night away." Outside, he heard the watch calling the time. Inwardly, he groaned. It was later than he had thought. "We can talk more tomorrow."

While he had been talking, he had considered the end of her story. Despite her possibly feigned awe at discovering he was a master of the Seven Laws, she had been very accepting of that fact, as if she had more knowledge of the Seven Laws than she was willing to tell him. Now that he thought about it, she had also accepted his royal status like one accustomed to dealing with royalty. Sillik's brow furrowed as he looked at the woman. He was intrigued by her obscurations and omissions. There was a polished hardness to her that he had not noticed at first. Her hands, while smooth, were also firm, which indicated that she was not afraid of hard work. Yes, she had left out a great deal. *We are even then*, the voice in Sillik's head said. *You didn't tell her all the truth either. Is this the ally that Silvia hinted at?*

"Yes," she said, smiling for the first time. "No more speech."

She leaned forward slowly, as if expecting a kiss, but perhaps to her dismay, he lay down, threw his ratty torn cloak over himself, and closed his eyes.

As the sun began to show its face in the east, Sillik awoke with a groan. He had had that dream again, and his head was pounding. Beside him, the woman slept. Her long, tousled hair only partially covered her face. She had snuggled beside him in the morning chill. He sat up, careful not to disturb her, and then covered her with his cloak.

Knowing that he must soon go out and finish his business in the city, Sillik slipped with practiced ease into a deep and powerful trance and employed a series of exercises using the teachings of the third and seventh laws in tandem. The exercises would counter some of the mind-disturbing effects of the sorcery he had wrought the night before and wash some of the physical weariness from his body. These were only temporary stopgaps. Eventually, he would have to sleep. But by using these methods, he could function without sleep and without impairment for five or six days. After that, his impairment would increase for three or four days before he finally succumbed to fatigue.

When his mind emerged from the trance, it was as calm as a pond on a windless day. From somewhere nearby, Sillik heard the sounds of pans being rattled. The slaves were awakening and would be cooking breakfast for their masters. Beside him, Renee was still asleep. The fine hairs on her arms were golden in the sunlight streaming around the shutters. Quietly and carefully, he stood up and got dressed.

As he was about to leave, Renee awoke. Her blue eyes were still sleep-fogged. "Go back to sleep," Sillik said gently. "I must take care of some business.

I will return soon with breakfast. Then we will see how to get you out of the city."

Despite her sleepiness, Renee nodded with genuine gratitude.

"Do not leave the room," he warned as she lay down again among the pillows and furs. In moments, her breathing slowed, and Sillik knew she was asleep.

Sillik spoke a quick incantation and lifted his magical lock on the door. When the door closed behind him, the lock slipped back into place. The spell would last only until midday, but he would be back by then.

In the common room, a large fire was burning cheerfully in the fireplace while slaves swept the floor and prodded the drunks out onto the streets. Smiling to himself, Sillik opened the door and stepped outside. Behind, him a badly disfigured slave watched him go, mumbling sullenly under her breath.

First, he went in search of a new cloak. After inspecting several, he told the seamstress what he wanted and paid half the quoted cost in silver and left with the promise that his new cloak would be ready by midday.

He was heading back to their room when he realized he was hungry. *I will need supplies*, he realized. *Everything I had was in that first room, and I can't go back. And I am going to have to help Renee get out of this hellhole. I hope she is the ally that Silvia hinted at.*

He spotted a tavern just down the street. Without hesitation, he walked toward it.

# CHAPTER 15

## The Guild Master

LAZEROS PACED BACK and forth in his study. He was a thin, wiry man, as were most in his guild. But he had long been out of the "game," as he called it. Today, he ran the guild that had fingers in all aspects of Illician life. Some said he had fingers in all of the pockets of Illician life as well. He was dressed in a rich silk burgundy shirt with black breeches and lizard-skin slippers. His complexion was pale because he seldom left his house. Few in the city knew his name, and fewer still would recognize him if they saw him. Once he had been a chameleon, changing his face as often as most women changed their dresses. But that had been a long time ago. These days, gray streaked his temples and his decidedly receding hairline. It would be a race to see if his hair turned completely gray before he lost what little hair remained.

His room was richly decorated with fine leather furniture and wool rugs over gray slate. Real wood paneling covered the walls. Glow balls stood in stands along the curving outer walls of the building. Gossamer-thin silk covered the windows.

In his youth, Lazeros had been a conman, always hatching plots to separate people from their coin. Eventually, the guild had noticed him and corralled his enthusiasm and channeled his skill. The guild had sent him to school, where he learned to read and write. They also had taught him how to dress like a lord and to appreciate some of the finer things in Illicia. Then the guild had used his skills to separate larger prizes from bigger fools.

Lazeros bore no regrets over the life he had chosen. He had been the guild master of thieves for a quarter century. He had had a wife, who had given him a daughter. He smiled. Krista, his daughter, knew everything about his real business and would inherit the business, as they called it, someday. His wife Darlena, however, had never known what he did, but she had been dead for ten years.

His most recent acquisition troubled him, though: a thousand-year-old bottle of Armagnac. Only one bottle in the recently found case was guaranteed drinkable, or so the healers said. His man at the auction had been outbid. Two brothers had bought it, well dressed and strange. Lazeros wanted that bottle and had used his network to find the men who had purchased it. He smiled. That had been hard. He had assigned his most promising journeyman to bring him the bottle.

Morrow had brought it on the day and time he had promised. But he also explained how a woman had murdered its two previous owners. A demon, he said, had killed the two brothers, and the woman had killed their sons. A very strange woman indeed, he had said.

Now Lazeros's daughter Krista was sick—brain squeeze fever, the street healer said. She had gotten sick the very day that Morrow had presented him the bottle. Against his better judgment, Lazeros had sent for a Gold Robes healer. He laughed bitterly. He had worked hard for years to keep his face hidden from the Gold Robes—stayed away from parties, been reclusive. But "send for the best," the street healer had said. *I can afford the best*, Lazeros had thought, so that is what he had done.

Now that Krista was sick, nothing else mattered. He knew he would pay any price to see her laugh again. In a few moments, he would have a Gold Robe in this very room. He would talk to the person, plead with him or her to save his daughter's life. She was too young to die. For a moment, he saw Krista on a funeral procession. *No*, he thought, *there is still a chance. The healer will save her. They must save her.*

A soft knock was followed by a creak as the heavy wooden doors opened. His servant, old and gnarled like a weather-worn tree, led two women into the room. The women were beautiful, as all who used magic seemed to be. They were confident and radiated strength as they strode in. Their chins were high, and their gold robes shone in the candlelight. The blue stripe at the hem of their dresses seemed to reflect their eyes.

"I am Elizabet," one of the women said. "My companion is Claudett." She paused to look around the ostentatious room. "You sent for healers to heal a girl with brain fever?"

"Yes," the guild master said in a steady voice. "I am Lazeros. My daughter is very ill. The street medicine woman said we had to get a healer, the very best," he added.

"Claudett and I should be able to do what needs to be done. As long as the fever hasn't erased too much of her mind, she should survive," Elizabet said in a crisp voice.

Lazeros nodded. "You must save her. She is all I have to live for. I will pay any price."

"We will not speak of fees," Elizabet said stiffly. "Now, if you could show us to your daughter."

"Yes, yes, I will show you to her room. This way," he said as he led the two healers toward the side of the room. "I had her moved to my private rooms." Lazeros touched the wall, and a door opened. They walked through a short hallway and then entered a large bedroom. The floors were covered in red octagonal tiles. The arched ceiling was simple stone painted white.

A large bed dominated the far side of the room. Two nurses sat on one side of the bed beside Krista. Her hair was soaked with sweat, as was her nightgown.

The two healers walked slowly to the bedside and removed their cloaks. Without thinking, Lazeros took the cloaks from them. "You can heal her?"

Claudett turned to look at the man. "You may leave, or you may be quiet. Those are your choices." She turned to look at the nurses. "You may leave to get clean bedclothes and sheets."

The two nurses curtsied and then hurried out. Lazeros backed away from the healers until he felt the wall behind him. When he could go no farther, he stopped. He could not have left if he had wanted to.

The healers eyed him and then approached the girl from opposite sides of the bed. It was wide enough that the healers had to climb onto the bed to get close to her.

A momentary thought flashed across his mind: *three women in my bed*. Then he ruthlessly banned the thought. His daughter and the healers. He shuddered in fear.

The healers held their hands over Krista. Lazeros could see that they were talking, and he tried to listen. When he attempted to move closer, though, he found invisible shackles holding him in place. He tried to speak, but invisible hands held his mouth closed. Panicking, he tried harder to move, to touch his mouth, to move a finger. His heart beat wildly, but then a voice spoke in his head with a hint of laughter. "Do not move, master thief. Yes, we know who you are. By our healers' oath, we will not talk of this. The restraints were put in place to ensure you do not interrupt the healing. Do not struggle, or you will go to sleep until we are done."

Lazeros's eyes widened in surprise, but somehow he forced himself to relax and watch. His heart began to slow. As it did, he found he could take deep, calming breaths.

The healers were fully engaged, their hands touching Krista. At first, she was rigid. Then she began to writhe in pain. *Stop it!* he wanted to scream. *You're hurting her!*

Suddenly, the healers seemed to struggle. Concentration was etched on their faces. Pain seemed to clench the women. Then the expressions on all three faces relaxed, and Krista's eyes began to flutter. With a start, Lazeros knew it was over.

The healers rolled off the bed, and Lazeros found he could move again. He worked his mouth and massaged his jaw. "Is she …?"

"She will be fine," Elizabet said as she picked up her cloak from where Lazeros had dropped it.

Lazeros nodded. "Thank you, my ladies," he said as he considered what he should do.

Claudett laughed as if she could read his mind. "You are worried about what we know. The healers' oath requires that we do no harm and that we do not reveal our clients' secrets. Have no fear on that score."

"Do your oaths prevent you from being paid for your work?" he asked. This had all started when that damn bottle came into the house—his daughter's illness, Morrow's story, the fear. "I have something that I should give you. Something that is appropriate for giving me my daughter's life."

"My lord, we cannot," said Claudett.

"Shhh," Elizabet said. "Whatever you give us, we will give to charity. You know that."

"You will protect my identity?" Lazeros asked. "You know what I am."

"Yes, we cannot violate our oaths."

"Then come with me," he said with a flourish. "Except my daughter …" He looked around, worried.

"She is sleeping," Claudett said. "She will sleep the rest of the day, but she will be fine. Your maids can change her shift and replace the sheets so she will awake clean and dry." As if on cue, the nurses entered with sheets and towels.

Numb in response to what had just happened, Lazeros led the healers back into his office. They watched him with curious expressions as he stood in the center of the room, considering whether or not he should actually do it.

With a sigh, he opened a drawer and pulled out the bottle. "My people acquired this the same day that my daughter got ill. In my line of work, I have to trust luck. This seems like bad luck. My daughter becomes ill, my best … employee disappears. I wish you to take this away—and hopefully my bad luck with it."

Elizabet took the bottle reverently. Her eyes lit up when she saw what it was. "I most certainly will."

The other healer did not say a word and only watched without moving.

# CHAPTER 16

## The Whispering Isles

A TWISTED FIGURE hurried painfully down the street. He stopped and bowed low before the captain of the royal guard. The captain was a proud man with hard, gray eyes and grizzled stubble. He wore the uniform of his city proudly, but he hated what he was doing at the moment. Beside the captain stood a slender man who wore his hair short like a warrior, but the captain knew that his companion was no warrior. The man was thin, and his pale face was drawn, as if he had been deprived of both food and happiness. His gestures were smooth and precise like a dancer.

The captain listened to his informant's information disdainfully and then gave the man a few copper coins. The information was valuable, but he saw no sense in paying what it was really worth. The informant scurried away like a rat. Then the captain turned to face the man beside him for the first time. He had not dared to look directly at him before. The emperor had commanded him, and he had obeyed without question. Now he looked into the man's eyes.

"He is mine," the man said in a strange voice. The captain struggled with the accent. The man's words were strung together, and it sounded like his mouth was full of sand. "Only I have the skills necessary to defeat a man such as he."

The captain looked at the man squarely. He was lean with a sharp face. His nose was crooked as if broken in a fight long ago, but the captain couldn't imagine this man allowing himself to be involved in a barroom brawl. Part of his forehead and the left side of his face were smooth and polished as if melted by intense heat. Both of his eyebrows were missing, possibly seared away when his face was melted. Perhaps whatever had melted and scarred his face had also broken his nose. When he spoke, the melted half of his face was expressionless, as if the nerves had been burned. It was disconcerting to watch, so the captain looked away.

"What if he is a master of the Seven Laws?" the captain asked, not wanting to hear the answer.

The thin man, who was wearing a black cloak, sneered. "The chances of that are slim. After all, he is only the youngest son of a once powerful family, but I will slay him even if he is a master."

"Very well," the captain said, trying hard to keep the sarcasm out of his voice. "I will still have ten of my best men outside. I can't allow such a man to roam the city. Who knows what mischief he could get into?"

"Suit yourself," the man said dryly as they headed toward the tavern.

"Furthermore, five of my men are even now en route to get the girl. The emperor wants the woman," the captain said with a small smile. He wanted the girl too. Five of his men were missing and presumed dead. Renee was involved, and she was going to pay.

"I care naught about the girl," the other man said imperiously, "save that she is desirable and would warm a man's bed nicely. The man, however, is a different story. He is a threat to me as long as he lives, for his ancestors slew most of my ancestors and imprisoned the survivors on the Relinka Islands for two centuries. The blood of my ancestors cries out for vengeance." The man's voice dripped with hatred. To emphasize his point, he spat viciously when he finished speaking. He then raised the hood of his cloak and entered the tavern.

At that disclosure, the captain said nothing and merely signaled for his men to follow him.

Sillik sat down with his back to the wall in the dimly lit tavern. Four naked women scurried around the room carrying serving platters.

"What can I get you, good sir?" the tavern master asked, wiping his hands on a rag that had seen cleaner days. "I have mutton, sweet bread, and cider." His hands rested on his fat belly. The grease stains on his apron danced as he moved. Despite the early hour, he was already sweating.

Sillik tossed the man a silver piece. "That sounds fine. Where can I get some supplies for a trip? Enough for two for several weeks and a small lizard to carry it."

The tavern master eyed Sillik with a practiced eye. "I can supply your needs—if you can pay. Lizards ain't cheap these days, though. Where are you heading?"

Sillik smiled. "I can pay." He laid a small gold coin on the table.

The tavern master eyed the coin. "A lizard alone will cost twice that. The military likes them, so we only get the runts. But they still cost."

Sillik placed two more coins of double weight on the table.

"Several weeks, you say? Dried meat, bread, sausage, water, and wine? They are expensive." The tavern master fingered his chin and eyed the gold hungrily.

Sillik put two more coins on the table. The man grinned and reached for them, but Sillik put his hand on his arm. "I want to leave in the morning."

The tavern master paused and then nodded. "I can have what you need."

Sillik released him, and the man scooped up the coins with a flourish. "Good, then breakfast for two," Sillik said. "I need to take it with me. I will be back at this time in the morning, with two more of those"– Sillik indicated the gold—"if you have what I need by first watch."

The tavern master frowned but nodded. "I can have it."

"No undue notice either," Sillik said with all seriousness. "I don't want the city guard to hear about it."

The tavern master's eyes narrowed. "That will cost you," he said warily.

Sillik nodded. "Another piece of gold for your trouble."

The man nodded, but fear was still on his face as he bent to wipe the table. "First watch," he said. "Three more double-weight golds in the morning." He straightened up. "Annora! Get this man some mutton and bread, and wrap it. He ain't eatin' it here." With that, he bustled off.

Sillik leaned back against the wall as one of the serving girls ducked into the kitchen to fill his order. As he waited, a group of musicians started playing a lively tune in one corner of the room. Immediately, several warriors got up and began to dance. Sillik smiled as he watched one of the serving girls laughingly slip out of an embrace from one of the warriors.

Annora was making her way to Sillik's table when the door opened again. She glanced at the door, and her hand flew to her mouth.

Sillik looked up as a slender, almost dainty man descended the three steps into the tavern. He wore a dark cloak and a silk shirt. The cuffs of the shirt were flared and heavily embroidered. Sillik squinted against the halo effect around the man and tried to make out his face, but the man had his hood up, making his face difficult to see.

With a start, Sillik realized that the man was obscuring his features using arcane magic. As a precaution, Sillik extended his shields and strengthened them. At the same time, he loosened his sword in its sheath. When the man stepped forward, all sounds in the tavern stopped as people turned to look at him. They couldn't help but notice that he was staring at Sillik. The people seated near Sillik moved away quickly. They had seen that kind of look before. The man in the doorway threw back his hood and pushed the cloak back to free his arms.

Sillik felt chills up and down his back despite the comforting warmth of the tavern. He examined the man intently. His clothing was richly fashioned with deep greens and browns. His coat was long with wide cuffs reminiscent of styles not worn in Illicia in centuries. Rows of gold buttons glinted in the torchlight. As one accustomed to wearing rich fabrics, Sillik knew just by looking that they were expensive and richly textured. The man was tall and lean. His precise movements reminded Sillik of a bird.

Sensing trouble, the fat little tavern master rushed between the two men and spoke with a quivering voice. "No trouble, masters." He held a dripping dishrag in his hands, and perspiration dotted his forehead. "Please, no trouble," he repeated in a voice that seemed to suggest that trouble was inevitable.

Sillik stood up slowly and smiled in a vain attempt to defuse the rapidly escalating situation. He touched the pouch at his waist and remembered the three pieces of paper it contained. He was cautious as his eyes took in all the details of his foe. He noted the signs and subtle symbols woven into the man's cloak. The symbols were dark magic and very dangerous. Whatever was about to happen would be settled by arcane methods. With even more reluctance, Sillik made the necessary preparations.

"Move aside, little man," the figure said.

Eyes popping in disbelief, the tavern master backed away like a dog with its tail between its legs.

Sillik stepped away from his low table. "What want you with me?" he asked in the old tongue. If this was going to be an arcane duel, he might as well find out if the man had been formally trained.

The man appeared soft. Apart from his expensive clothing, his hands were smooth and well manicured. His fingers were unscarred and decorated by golden rings. Despite the sword at his hip, Sillik doubted the man knew how to use the weapon.

"I have sought thee out in the name of death, with which I come," he said, providing an equally ancient reply.

"So be it but words until accomplished," Sillik said as he watched his enemy move forward. He had no idea who the man was. He was not Dernot Lafliar, though—that much was certain. The man's aura didn't fit the traditional mold of those trained in the city of Illicia. It fit no mold with which Sillik was familiar, but something about the clothing was familiar.

To the other people in the room, it was obvious that the two men were going to fight. So why didn't they draw their swords and get it over with?

Why were they speaking in such an odd language? It was no surprise that the common folk in the tavern couldn't understand what was being said, for the language the two men spoke had been dead for almost 11,000 years. Some said it was the first tongue of man. That claim was uncertain, but for 5,000 years, there had been but one language in all the land.

"Know me for who I am," the stranger intoned. "I am the Dashlinar of the Whispering Isles."

Sillik looked at his foe with new interest. The Whispering Isles were locked eternally in fog. The souls of the dead who had crashed their ships on the hidden reefs were the source of the whispers. Viktorie's words danced in his memory. She had mentioned fog around Sillik's head.

"I have come in the name of my kindred," the man continued. "We desire to be freed of our bondage to your ancestors. Will you grant us release?"

Sillik reeled mentally as he recalled the names from Illicia's history. His voice took on a biting sharpness, anger blossoming as he spoke. "I know well the reasons that you and your kind were placed on the Whispering Isles. You and yours were ever false and forsworn. Furthermore, your ancestors led and fought many long and bloody wars against your rightful lords. In the name of my city, I deny your request. Furthermore, I charge you to return to your exile forthwith."

As he spoke, Sillik wondered, *How did he find me? How did he know I was the Illician prince? Is this all part of the plots against my family? We haven't had any contact with the Isles for at least two centuries. Is this one of Dernot's traps? This must be one of the tests that Lady Silvia mentioned. Since the trap in the throne failed, this has to be another attempt by Dernot to assess my abilities.*

Grimly, Sillik prepared himself for what he had to do. The Dashlinar looked at Sillik with a shocked expression, struggling for a moment to hide his emotions in response to Sillik's answer. Sillik smiled to himself when he saw the flash of surprise and anger. Clearly, he had not expected this turn of events. Sillik guessed that the Dashlinar had been taught or told that the Illicians had become craven, weak cowards. He had not expected a two-sided fight. That meant Sillik had the advantage.

Sillik thought about the papers in his father's hands. This had to be the trap of Colum. Only someone with knowledge of Illicia and her history could have arranged this situation. Sillik's father had not foreseen the Whispering Isles involvement, but perhaps Lady Silvia had.

The Dashlinar quickly mastered his emotions, but Sillik could still see the dismay in his facial muscles. He had no choice but to play the game and roll the dice.

With a look of resignation on his pale face, the Dashlinar threw his arms up. At once, fire shot from his hands, only to shatter harmlessly against Sillik's shields. The Dashlinar bit his lip with concern as he watched his attack fail. Worry filled his eyes, and his confidence wavered. This was not what he had expected.

Screaming in terror, the people backed away from the battle. When the Dashlinar's first attack waned, Sillik launched his own attack, only to see it shatter harmlessly on his foe's shields. Ignoring the sounds of the terrified people and the smell of lightning, each man traded blow after blow. Sillik felt that he had the advantage, but his victory would be hard-won. His opponent was well trained, as should be expected of a member of the Dashlinar family.

As Sillik and the Dashlinar traded blows, Sillik was distracted by a voice in his head that suggested he draw his sword. Confused, Sillik shook off the suggestion and concentrated on the duel. In the back of his mind, he noticed that his signet ring was on his finger. He did not remember placing it there, but it felt right, so he continued to fight, still fighting the urge to draw his blade. *Why do I want to draw my sword?*

Two hundred years earlier, the Dashlinars, a family of sorcerers, had simultaneously seized control of four cities. The Illicians had arisen immediately to avenge the deposed lords of each city. After six years of war, the Illicians had broken the Dashlinars' power and forced them to surrender. The family's leaders had been executed.

As part of the surrender, the Illicians had allowed the surviving Dashlinars to go into exile on the deserted Whispering Isles far to the south of the land in the summer sea. The islands would support a population of a few hundred without strain. The Dashlinars had accepted the offer gladly. They had fully expected to die at the hands of their captors, just like their leaders. The man had called himself "the Dashlinar," which meant he was the head of their family. He would represent the best, strongest, most highly skilled and trained of their kin. He had come to win their release.

Sillik was sweating now, not from fear but from the fierce energies that darted between the two men and that had set the tavern aflame. The heat of the flames beat down on him like a heavy hand. His eyes were watering from the smoke, and his arms were becoming leaden. Through half-closed eyes, Sillik saw the flames creeping up the walls all around him.

Above the roar of the fire and the battle, Sillik heard the cracking sound he had known was coming. It caused the bystanders to scream anew. Then a sudden idea struck him. He might not be able to end the duel quickly by arcane means, but he might be able to end it by physical means. After a quick glance at the ceiling, Sillik backed up a few steps. As expected, his opponent stepped forward as he though he sensed success. Sillik stepped back again. Overconfidence blossomed in the Dashlinar's face. His fear and trepidation were gone in an instant.

The Dashlinar should have known better, Sillik thought as he sent his next bolt into the ceiling beam. It shattered in an explosion of fiery embers and sharp fragments. The Dashlinar had time to look up just as the wooden beam collapsed and buried him beneath a pile of burning wood.

Sillik surged forward. He drew power into his hand and flung it at his foe. Moments later, the suffering man was dead. With the Dashlinar out of the picture, Sillik used another spell to shield the patrons and staff from the fire. Suddenly free, people streamed out of the room. Once everyone was clear, Sillik collapsed his shield and cleansed the room of magic. The heat of the fire beat down on him as he started toward the open door. Then he heard the first of the screams. Suspecting another trap, Sillik turned and hurried into the fiery remains of the tavern. He would find another way out.

Much later, Sillik emerged from a dark alley. He was covered with soot, grease, and trash and smelled like the sewers. His mood matched his foul physical condition. He turned toward the royal keep, ignoring the stares of the people in the streets. He didn't dare return to the room he had rented. They had waited for him to leave Renee and then sent a sorcerer to the tavern and stationed guards outside. When they did not see him emerge from the tavern, they would assume he had died. He had seen guards searching for something or someone twice that day. He was certain they already had Renee. He would go to the keep and meet this emperor for himself.

Sillik turned a corner and ran straight into a squad of mercenaries. Instantly, swords were drawn. The sword in Sillik's hand was a blur as he waded through his foes, twisting, darting, and turning. Without Sillik having to think about it, the sword moved and parried. Sillik's feet and free hand joined in the fight, but it was the sword that pulled Sillik through the street. He imagined that the weapon was speaking to him. Memories supplied the answers; in a way, the weapon was talking to him.

"By the Seven Gods," he said when the fighting ended as suddenly as it had begun. Twenty bodies lay scattered along the narrow, twisting street. All bore terrible wounds. Sillik was shaken but unharmed. *This should not have been possible. Twenty against one?*

Trembling, he took a deep breath, his face pale. He tore a bit of cloth from the cloak of one of the mercenaries and wiped the residue of battle from his hands and face. In awe, he noted that no blood or gore was on the blade. He shook his head in confusion. Then he dropped the rag, sheathed his weapon, and hurried into the darkness, his scabbard grating and bouncing on the cobblestones as he ran.

# CHAPTER 17

## Spies and Lies

BRIANA SAT DOWN in her room. She had refused to move to the top level of the keep and still occupied the same room she had been given when she was appointed swordmaster. The room was comforting to her despite generations of male swordmasters having lived there. She had softened it over the years. Tapestries done in rich fabrics covered several of the walls, and thick rugs covered large expanses of the floor. In the outer room, she had several real wooden chairs. They had been expensive, but wood was warmer than the stone at night. Eventually, she would have to move, but not until she appointed a new swordmaster.

Beside the chairs, she had a wooden desk against one wall. It had been her father's. She thought of him whenever she sat at it. Her father had been a diplomat for Illicia. He had hauled that desk to all of his postings. It bore the dents, dings, and stains from all of his travels. Nisha, as Briana's steward, had disapproved of the desk and wanted to replace it with a dressing table. Briana smiled in fondness. Her father had written many letters and treaties from that very desk. There was no way she would part with it.

The only hint of her former position was a large sword collection that covered one wall, all "donations" from former swordmasters. When a swordmaster died in office, his or her weapons became the property of the next swordmaster. Over one hundred swords were on display. One of the disadvantages to being a swordmaster was that it seemed like a tradition to die in office. She was one of the few swordmasters to have outlived her position. Of course, there was always the possibility she would die in her new position as warmaster.

It had been an exhausting week. She had sat through countless council meetings where nothing really got decided. Should they send troops to find and support Sillik or not? Today, she had walked the city walls, inspecting Illicia's defenses. Stonemasons had shown her various repairs they had made to the walls and battlements, and she had feigned interest in their work. She had watched crossbow demonstrations and young men wrestling sandfish. She had barely concealed her horror as the men succeeded in wrestling the small fish out of the sand without losing any major body parts. Later in the morning, she had watched advanced student warriors training in swords under the watchful eye of their instructor. She would have given a lot to be able to train with them. After the midday meal, she had met with the Gold Robes to discuss some minor curriculum changes in the schools. They had asked her permission, as if she had all the answers.

Somehow she had imagined the life of warmaster differently, as glamorous and exciting. It was nothing like that. Briana knew she was filling in for Sillik, but unless she was able to persuade the council to support him, she would become the queen in six years, ten months, and a week.

She eased the shoes off of her aching feet. She had done too much walking in too-tight shoes. She rubbed her arches and sighed contentedly.

The knock on the door was polite and quiet. Briana looked up sharply as she continued to massage her foot. "Come," she barked, surprised at the sharpness of her voice.

The door opened, and Sanhill, the captain of her guard, entered and bowed. He seemed surprised to see her barefoot but quickly averted his eyes. "Warmaster, there is a peddler."

Briana caught her breath. "What about him?"

The guard hesitated. "He came to the gate. He has a pass signed by … by the late king, Saldor."

Briana leaned back in her chair. Damn, Sillik had been right. He had said Saldor's network would try to contact her. She breathed excitedly. "If he has a pass, then show him to me."

"Yes, Warmaster." The guard stepped out of her room with another formal bow.

Intrigued, Briana slipped her shoes back on and went over to the window. As she waited, she molded her face into a semblance of tranquility. She didn't want to appear too eager.

There was another knock on the door, and it creaked open. The guard led the peddler into the room and then stepped back to stand against the wall. His eyes were fixed on the peddler, and his hand rested on the hilt of his sword.

Briana waited a moment and then turned to look at the man. He appeared aged and, at first glance, almost senile. He wore the muted browns and golds of a peddler. His large overcoat was threadbare with deep pockets. He was mumbling to himself in a continuous stream of words. Stray locks of gray hair stuck out at odd angles from under the hood of his cloak, which was similar to what Briana had seen other peddlers wear. Every few months the Illicians escorted trade delegations to Illicia. After a week, they led them out of the desert. Peddlers often followed the caravans.

She moved toward him and then quickly moved back, wrinkling her nose in disgust at the odor. She raised her hand to her face, ostensibly to cover a sneeze. He hadn't seen a bathhouse in years.

"You have information for me?" Briana asked as she tried not to glare at the guard. He could have warned her about the smell. At any rate, Sillik had said his father's network would contact her. If the information this man had was valuable, Sillik had left her signed directives on what to do.

"You are not the king," the man said as he looked around. "I do not know you. My pass says to take me to the king." He grabbed a section of his cloak and twisted it in irritation.

Briana decided to be honest with the man and not try any of the tricks she might have considered. "The king was killed," she said. "I am Briana, warmaster of Illicia."

The man cringed at her words and looked around. Then he spoke in a halting, stuttering voice. "My words are for the king. He sent Moleck. Moleck found what he wanted."

"The king is dead," Briana repeated in a patient voice. What had he been sent to find? She decided to try a different tack. "How long have you been looking?" *Is he even sane?* Briana wondered. The way he twisted his head and looked around made Briana wonder if the old man knew where he was or even who he was.

Her question seemed to take Moleck by surprise, and his agitation stopped as he looked shrewdly at her. "Moleck has been looking for eight years."

"Eight years?"

"Moleck speaks to the king," the man said, twisting his cloak in irritation again.

"Can you tell me?" Briana asked. "I can tell the king."

Moleck looked at her, considering her words. He stopped twisting his cloak and simply squeezed it, his knuckles white with the strain. After a long pause that seemed to cause pain, he started to talk. "Moleck, he find what king want."

"What was the king looking for?" Briana asked.

"King ask Moleck find why cities fight, why war happen."

"What wars?"

Moleck barreled on, ignoring her. "Moleck find answer. Answer for all war."

"What answer, Moleck?"

"Master," Moleck said. "Dark masters travel land. Make war ... make trouble."

Briana sat back. "Dark masters," she said to herself, thinking rapidly. Lady Silvia had told them that dark masters were in the land and that the Council of Nine had been remade. This information, though questionable, certainly confirmed what one of the Seven Gods had told them. Briana smiled to herself. She wouldn't doubt a god.

"Moleck hear dark master has friends everywhere, even here." The man fell silent as he looked around furtively. "Many friends here. But dark masters are moving. I followed one—last year!"

"Where are they going?" Briana demanded. "Moleck, where are they going?"

Moleck cringed and cried out in fear. "Moleck not know plans. Just see what they do."

Briana was stunned. It had been a long time since a master of the Nine Laws had raised his head, much less nine of the damn fools. Reznek had warned Sillik of this. So had Lady Silvia.

"What do they want?" Briana asked.

Moleck shrugged. "Moleck not asked why." The man continued to look around the room.

Briana sat back and gave the man a shrewd look. He was talking to himself again. She decided to go back to basics. "Moleck, what is the name of the dark master you saw?"

With agitation and reluctance, Moleck started talking louder to himself. He looked away, angling his head and lowering his chin. After muttering for a while, he said clearly, "Nathalin. His name is Nathalin."

"Where did you see him?" Briana asked.

"He was leaving Colum," Moleck said. "I saw him going north. He said to his followers that he had been to Illicia."

A short time later, Briana stood before the High Council of Illicia, which she had summoned. With little preamble, she announced that a master of the Nine had been to Illicia.

"Where is this peddler?" Kenton asked as he leaned back in his stone chair and pressed his fingertips together. Curiously, Lady Viktorie was not standing behind him.

"I had my guards take him to the kitchens to feed him," Briana answered.

"Do you think he's telling the truth?" Greenup asked.

Briana held her hands up helplessly. "I have no way to tell. He is, after all, a spy. His words have the ring of truth, though. Besides, the late king gave him a pass. Surely, that indicates something."

Kenton cleared his throat. "This spy is dangerous. How did he get into the city?"

"A trade delegation arrived yesterday," Greenup said. "It's been scheduled for weeks."

"I would like to talk to this man," Kenton said.

Briana looked over her shoulder. "Bring him."

One of the guards nodded and left.

After what seemed like a long time, the guard returned alone. He bent on his knee before Briana. "My lady, the peddler is gone. He was taken to the kitchens as you commanded, but none have seen him since, and no one can find him. The keep has been closed, and a search has been ordered."

Kenton stood up, anger flashing in his eyes. "I want him found! I want everyone who saw him to be examined by investigators! If he can walk out of the keep, then he has skills that set him apart."

"Close the city," Greenup suggested.

Briana agreed, knowing in her heart that it was useless. He wouldn't be found. Had this been done to cast doubt on her or to further paralyze the Illicians?

"Be sure to search the trade delegation," Kenton said. "He may try to leave the same way he arrived."

"Gentlemen, please come with me," Briana said as she stood.

In moments, she was leading them up the stairs to the top of the keep. She bypassed the royal apartments and took another small staircase to the roof. Her ever-present guard detail stopped at the base of the stairs, and only Greenup and Kenton took the final steps to the rooftop. A stiff breeze was blowing, and the Illician banners were flapping. Briana walked to the edge of the keep and looked out over the city. The dozen guards who normally kept watch retreated a short distance.

"You know we won't find him," she said.

Greenup nodded grimly.

"For all we know, this was the dark master himself," Kenton said, "and you had him brought up to your rooms."

"I know."

"When the council learns of this, it will further discredit you. They will say you are imagining things, trying to disrupt trade," Greenup said, grimacing at the thought.

"Lord Reznek suggested there was a dark master," Briana said.

"Granted," Kenton said, "but we are choosing not to mention that one of the Seven Gods also made a personal appearance. It would raise additional questions."

Greenup nodded. "If we mention it now, it will appear as if we are creating facts and will further discredit all of us."

"But Reznek," Briana said hopefully.

"Ah yes," Kenton said with a shake of his head. "Whatever Lord Reznek knew, he won't be sharing. He died during the night. My healers are examining his body and his room for evidence. The surviving rule makers will meet at dawn to elect a new senior rule maker. Lord Sandwin should have the votes to succeed Reznek."

Briana looked up in surprise. "Evidence of what? What do you think happened?"

Kenton shrugged. "When I learned of his death, I went to his room. He was in his bed, and his body seemed peaceful enough, but something felt odd. I didn't know what to look for, so I told my healers to be suspicious of everything."

Greenup chuckled. "They will be looking for years. Reznek had his fingers in so many things that it will take a long time to examine everything. But let's return to the subject of this peddler. You had him brought to your rooms. Why?"

"He said he had information for the king."

"It is no secret that the king is dead," Kenton said. "You showed him where your room is. I am afraid that was a mistake."

"I will order additional guards outside your room and on all the routes to your rooms," Greenup said. "Or perhaps you should move."

Briana bit back her retort as she considered her options. "If I move, then I might be consigning someone else to attack."

"You should move anyway," Greenup said. "You are the warmaster."

"If I move, that will also alert our foes." Briana paused and frowned. "And if I appoint your grandson to be swordmaster, Lord Greenup, as I intend, then could he defend himself if attacked?"

"No, he could not," Kenton said. "He did not choose the Seven Laws."

"Then, gentlemen, I am going to stay in my room, at least for now." With that, Briana started toward the stairs.

# CHAPTER 18

## The Keep

SILLIK PEEKED AROUND the corner. In the distance lay the only entrance to the keep. The tall central spire–tall for Colum at least–was heavily guarded, and the keep had its own heavily patrolled battlements some fifty feet above street level.

The gate was closed and barred. Sillik knew he would have to find an alternate route inside. Behind the gate, he sensed more than a score of imperial guards. Knowing that the battlements would provide the only answer, Sillik reviewed what he had seen of them during his stay in the city. How would he get over those walls? Then he remembered the trees that surrounded the keep, including one of the ancient Gridon trees. If one of the branches was high enough, he might be able to make this work.

As he hurried toward the tree, part of his mind argued that even if one of the branches were high enough, the guards surely would have pruned any branches that approached the high walls. The guards were lazy, though. The third branch of the Seven Laws ritual would provide the answer.

When Sillik reached the tree, he looked up and saw that it towered above the battlements. Its trunk was so great that five men holding hands wouldn't surround it. Glancing over his shoulder at the high walls, Sillik made a V-shaped notch in the trunk. Immediately, a rich golden sap oozed out of the shallow wound. Plucking a small leaf from a lower branch, Sillik smeared the sticky sap on his hands and the leaf. Then, holding a small twig in his other hand, Sillik knelt beside the trunk.

Sillik sank into the mental state that was required for any use of the Third Law. Gradually, his breathing slowed, as did his madly beating heart. He was ready to begin. His voice hoarse, Sillik began speaking in a throat-torturing language, the tongue of the Olehim, which was as old as the earth. Sillik's people were the only ones in the world who still remembered it. Even the Illicians couldn't master the tongue. Sillik was no exception. His knowledge of the language was imperfect, but his need was greater than his fear of the consequence of a mispronounced word.

As the strange sounds of the last word faded, Sillik felt the stones beneath him groan and heard leaves rustling above him even though there was no wind. Then there was a grinding pop as the stones shattered.

When Sillik sensed that the branch was the right length, he spoke again and changed the tempo of the spell, letting the branch strengthen itself. Finally, when the branch was strong enough to bear the weight of a man, Sillik withdrew his compulsion and let the spell die. For several moments, Sillik didn't move. Then, with a sudden twitch, his mind awakened from the trance. Drops of perspiration ran freely down his face, and his muscles felt lifeless.

Sillik wiped his face with his arm. He was unused to the varied and demanding sorcery he had performed on this day. Forcing himself to move, Sillik looked up at the tree. The cut he had made in the bark was gone. It was as if the tree had aged years in just a few moments.

Beyond the tree, a guard disappeared around the curving side of the keep. Sillik began to climb the tree. On his way up, Sillik plucked three leaves and placed them reverently in the bag at his side. The leaves had a strange potency and were useful in many things. Soon he reached the newly formed branch and slowly inched his way out. Distant footsteps warned him to be still as another guard walked by.

When the guard was gone, Sillik dropped lightly onto the battlements, landing in a crouch and keeping his hand on his sword hilt, pushing it down low so that the tip of his sword wouldn't hit the stone. Then he ducked into the darkest shadows of the stone and made his way into the keep.

The corridors were cold, dark, and lifeless. They stank with a pervasive odor that was both unpleasant and unsettling. As Sillik slipped through the dim corridors, a dagger gleamed in one hand, and his sword glowed faintly golden in the other.

Sillik avoided the patrols by ducking into empty rooms. The one servant who did spot him was hastily reduced to an unconscious lump as Sillik bounced the hilt of his dagger off the man's head. Sillik tore a sleeve off the man's shirt and fashioned a gag before tying the man's hands and feet. Now where would they take Renee?

After knocking two guards unconscious and leaving them likewise gagged with their own shirts and tied securely, Sillik descended a level. Sillik knew that his risk increased with every person he met. Once too many guards failed to check in, a search would result, and the inevitable alarm would surely complicate his job.

Sillik descended another level. From the number of high-ranking people he had seen entering the keep, he was sure some kind of event was occurring. Given this emperor's propensity to torture people in front of his court, Sillik knew his time was running short. After descending two more levels, Sillik finally heard the sounds for which he was searching. Following them, Sillik wove through the maze of corridors with an intuitive knowledge born from a lifetime of experiences in royal palaces.

Within a few minutes, Sillik sensed that the laughter was coming from a room just around a corner and down the hall. He also sensed four guards at the end of the well-lit hallway. *They will be heavily armed, probably with crossbows and swords*, Sillik thought. *They will be well trained. I will be outnumbered. They will kill me before I get close enough to use my sword. Unless* … He grinned. *Unless I can acquire some kind of protection.*

Knowing what he must do, Sillik retreated down the hall. He would use a branch of the Sixth Law to create an arcane shield. The Sixth Law was the second-most demanding, but it was the most dangerous. He sheathed his dagger. If he were disturbed during the spell casting, he wouldn't need the knife.

The spell came to him easily, but it required extreme patience to weave the layers of energy into something he could handle. It also required more time than was usually available. After several minutes of focusing large amounts of energy and weaving them into a focused disc of power, Sillik had his shield. Beads of perspiration dotted his forehead. For a moment, he relaxed as exhaustion rolled over him. The spell had taken more from him than he cared to admit.

Laughter rose in the nearby room. Above the laughter, Sillik heard a woman wail. He looked at his shield. It was not visible in the ordinary sense. Only Sillik and other masters of the Sixth Law would be able to perceive its area of influence. Drawing his sword, Sillik took a deep breath and then turned the corner.

Immediately, the guards spotted him. As Sillik charged, they brought up their crossbows. Four bolts streaked toward his heart. With a sickening feeling, Sillik realized the bolts were imbued with the seven laws.

His friend from the Whispering Isles—or whoever had sponsored the man—had left Sillik another "favor." Clearly, the events in Illicia and Colum were related.

As the bolts hurtled toward him, Sillik steeled his mind and body for the impact. *Please, Lords, let me survive this.* The shield convulsed sharply as it sensed the approaching magic. *So much for hope.*

The hairs on his arm stood on end as the shield spasmed out of control. At the last instant, Sillik tilted the shield. When the four bolts struck it, Sillik was spun around. The energy in the shield pulsed erratically. While still turning, Sillik threw the shield at his amazed enemies.

The power in the shield detonated with a blinding explosion that killed the four members of the guard and shattered the great wooden doors behind them. Splinters and bits of door flew in all directions, and Sillik winced as a few of the pieces bounced off of him. Smoke filled the hallway as flaming pieces of the door fell to the floor. The music and laughter in the next room faltered and were replaced with screams. *So much for a quiet entrance*, he thought.

Sillik drew a deep breath and cleared his mind. Energy flowed into his body to replenish that which he had just used. As the black smoke cleared, Sillik sheathed his sword, stepped over the bodies of the dead men in the hallway, and entered the brightly lit room. It was roughly circular in shape. The floor was covered with thick, elaborate carpets. Hundreds of people sat behind low tables piled high with meats and candies. Thick, woolen tapestries covered the walls. A score of nude serving women stood and knelt around the room, holding platters and pitchers of wine. Their white bodies glistened with perspiration in the hot room. Torches and candles sent fantastic shadows dancing across the floor and walls. A few people near the doorway beat at flaming pieces of wood that had landed near them. Others began to pluck at splinters that had struck them. Two additional soldiers inside the room were dead, impaled by larger pieces of the former door.

Renee knelt in her torn dress in the center of the room. Sillik noticed with displeasure that her hands were tied roughly behind her back and that she couldn't turn to see him. At least she was alive and relatively unharmed. Dominating the room was the immensely fat form of a man.

Two bare-breasted young women sat on either side of him. They had been feeding him as another cradled his head in her lap. Though they were naked, their hair was coifed elegantly upon their heads, and they wore dozens of golden bracelets on each arm. The man was dressed in bright multicolored silk, and large rings hung from one ear. On each of his fingers and toes he wore large, jewel-encrusted rings. His fingernails were painted bright primary colors. Around his neck he wore a large golden pendant. Sillik assumed the pendant proclaimed him royalty or noble. The man's head was shaved and glistened with oils. As he sat up, rearranging various folds of fat in the process, he motioned for the girls beside him to step back. The women obeyed quickly.

The bracelets on their arms chimed as they moved. Fear was clearly etched on their faces.

A dozen guards rushed toward the door, but the fat man waved them back.

"Come in," he said politely. He chuckled. "Sit down and join our feast, warrior, or should I say 'sorcerer'?" He chuckled again. "Yes, sorcerer, won't you please come in and be seated?"

Sillik glanced around the room. The guard from the gate eyed him intently as he fingered his sword hilt.

"Sorry, Renee. I was delayed," Sillik said as he watched the room and stepped toward the nearest table. Sillik saw the tension in Renee's back disappear like a cool breeze. A score of people scooted away from him. Aware of all the eyes watching him, Sillik reached down and tore a piece of meat from a bird on one of the platters.

The guards kept fingering the hilts of their swords nervously. They expected trouble, and they were ready to prevent it. Sillik did a quick count of guards, stopping at twenty. The odds were not in his favor.

"Try the Chilican sauce, in the bowl just to the left of your hand," the emperor directed. "It is quite good."

Standing upright, Sillik ignored the advice and placed the small piece of meat in his mouth. It was heavily seasoned and had been cooked over special fires. Sillik swallowed, practically choking. "My compliments to the cooks," he said as the meat struck his stomach like a slice of stone.

"Kill him," a guard growled.

Sillik recognized the guard from the gate. "Baldwin, isn't it? Nice to see that you've cleaned up," he quipped.

"Kill him now," the guard yelled as he took a step forward. "He's dangerous. He is some sort of wizard."

"Hush, Baldwin," the emperor chided. "Everything in its own time." Then shifting his bulk, the emperor turned back toward Sillik. "You are, of course, the warrior that the Dashlinar sought?"

"Of course," Sillik said with a small bow and his most charming smile. "I am he." Sillik knew his charm wouldn't work on the emperor, but it might delay the inevitable.

"How is my dear friend anyway?" the emperor asked as he looked around. "I am greatly distressed that he is not here. I hope he is well."

Sillik smiled but said nothing.

"Ah, I see. He is dead," the emperor concluded with false sadness. He tried to frown but giggled instead.

Sillik smiled dismissively. "The Dashlinar should never have left his island."

"So the story of his family's imprisonment was true?" the emperor asked as if genuinely concerned. Surprise and doubt flickered briefly across his face.

"I don't know what he told you, but it is true that his family was imprisoned and exiled from the land for their crimes," Sillik said in his best attempt at haughtiness.

"How did you escape my warriors outside the tavern?" the emperor asked. "They had orders to slay everyone left alive after the duel."

"I, ah, managed," Sillik said, his eyes on the guards who were edging their way around the room.

"Five of my guards were killed last night," the emperor said. "They were among my most loyal men. I assume you killed them? I sent them to find Belliousces." He paused only briefly for an answer and then continued. "Since they failed to capture Belliousces, you saved me the trouble of having them killed for their failure. You see, warrior, I don't tolerate failure."

Sillik shrugged as he looked around the room. The guards were getting closer.

"So you slew five of my finest warriors single-handedly," the emperor mused, "or did you have help?" For a moment, he eyed Renee suspiciously, but then he dismissed her and looked behind Sillik. "Tell me, what became of Belliousces?"

Sillik decided evasion was the best policy and said, "I haven't seen him since last night."

The emperor studied Sillik for a long moment. "If he were alive, he would be here beside you, attempting to rescue his niece. Since he is not, I must assume he is dead or wounded. If he is wounded, he will be found. He loved his niece very much and would return from the dead if he could to protect her."

Sillik smiled as he charted his course through the room. His mentors had always preached the necessity of a battle plan. Sillik knew that if he was to survive this night, he had to have a plan. There was a chance.

"If he is dead," the emperor mused, "I assume you hid the body using some sort of vile sorcery. We should execute you for using evil magic."

Sillik smiled and waved at the destroyed door. "Those guards had magical weapons. Aren't you being hypocritical?"

"We don't ask questions about weapons; they are only tools," the emperor said with a dismissive wave of his hand. "Belliousces thought people could be trusted to use magic. He was so wrong. I wish he had not betrayed me. It's a shame he is dead."

Sillik shrugged, neither confirming nor disputing the emperor's conclusion. He used the move to glance behind him. His heart fell as he saw a platoon of guards enter the room through another door. All were armed, but none wore the royal symbols. They were the common guard. Most wore the red warrior belt, though.

"It seems like you trusted the Dashlinar," Sillik observed.

"He was a pawn," the emperor said. "His entire purpose was to find you and flush you out."

*So this is a game to you,* Sillik thought. *Who is moving the game pieces, though?* He smiled blandly and continued to look around. He noted those wearing weapons and those who were unarmed, the doorways, and the hidden doorways.

"So," the emperor said, "Belliousces is dead. He was a fool, as were they all. But you, my dear, dangerous friend, slew five of my guards. That much I know. The price of their deaths is yours to pay. Now we shall continue with the game and see if we might succeed where our poor soldiers failed. At the same time, we shall invoke the justice of the city. Your head, my friend, shall be placed above the gate before the sun rises."

"Whose justice?" Sillik asked in a mocking tone. "Yours or the gods?"

"Mine, of course!" the emperor shouted.

Just then, a dozen guards filed into the room from several doorways. With them came a man wearing a black mask and carrying a cruel-looking axe in his large, gnarled hands.

"Do you expect me to just kneel before your executioner?" Sillik asked.

"Of course not," the emperor said. His giggles sent his rolls of fat bouncing gleefully. "I expect you to fight, lose, and then be dragged before me. Then after we have skinned you and have you begging for death, as a gift I will allow you to kneel for the executioner's axe."

"We agree on the fight," Sillik responded as he sprang forward.

The three girls standing behind the emperor screamed and ran.

Drawing his blade in one easy move and yelling a battle cry, Sillik met the blades of several of his enemies. Above the sound of battle, Sillik heard the screams of the terrified women and the emperor.

At the first touch of the enemy's steel, Sillik's sword awoke, and he cut down his enemies like a man harvesting grain with a scythe. The sword seemed to be moving his arm. Unnoticed, the wound on his arm began to bleed again. In moments, Sillik had cut his way through the royal guards and, with a captured weapon in his left hand, thrust the blade into the emperor's chest–he didn't wish to sully his own blade. With a choking cry, the emperor died on the blade of one of his own guardsmen. Then Sillik turned and carried the battle to his enemies.

For a brief second, he stood behind Renee. When he had a moment's pause between strokes, he cut the bonds at her back so that she could get out of the way. Instead, she drew the sword of a fallen warrior and attacked another.

In moments, they were back to back, each protecting the other. "You took your time," Renee said.

"I got delayed," Sillik said. "An old family friend stopped by, and we had to have a drink."

Renee laughed. "I would love to hear the story–if we survive."

Sillik nodded as he parried two blades. His foot lashed out to catch one of the soldiers in the face. The man fell backward, his eyes going glassy as his flattened nose started to bleed and then stopped as life fled his body.

Sillik knew that his own death could come at any moment. He was using every tactic he had ever learned just to stay alive. More men were arriving by the moment, drawn by the sharp, unmistakable, metallic sound of swords. Yet this was not a death of which he would be ashamed. His only regret was that he had not avenged his people or his father.

Sillik used his sword, his feet, and magic where he could to influence the odds in his favor. More than one soldier dropped a sword that was suddenly too hot to hold. These men tended to flee once they were unarmed.

Then, through a thinning in the men around him, Sillik saw the executioner. With his great blade, the killer was cutting warriors down on either side of him. He bore the marks of many blades but was cutting down royal guards left and right. It was then that Sillik became aware of the other men fighting with him rather than against him. Renee fought at his back and then at his side. Her skirt swirled around her ankles as she plunged her sword into the chest of a guard.

Suddenly, Sillik was confident. For some reason the chances of his survival had just increased. After another few minutes, the fighting ended as suddenly as it had begun as the last of the royal guard fled. Scores of bodies lay on the floor, their blood staining the carpet a darker crimson. The wounded moaned in pain.

Sillik turned to face Renee as she took a deep breath. A large cut ran across her face and down her arm.

"Look at me," Sillik commanded. She obeyed, and Sillik ran his hand over her wounds, using healing magic to eliminate the cuts. Sillik had never excelled in healing, but he could heal minor injuries such as these. The healers in Illicia could do much more. "You may have a small scar," Sillik said. "I am glad you live."

With a smile, Sillik straightened and surveyed the room. Many of the serving women were sobbing in fear near the walls, their naked bodies splattered with food, blood, and gore. A few of the women were dead. Sillik noticed that one stood unafraid; she was naked and covered in blood but holding a pair of bloody knives in her hands. Sillik had to smile. The next person to suggest that she was a slave would soon be missing important body parts. She was free tonight.

He watched as she approached the royal guards who lay on the floor near her. She prodded each with her foot. The first several were dead, but when she found one who was only wounded, she knelt beside him. Sillik looked away as her knives flashed, and the man screamed. It was Baldwin, he realized, the guard who had stopped him at the gate.

Sillik wiped his face to clear the perspiration from it. By training, he grabbed some cloth from a table but then dropped it when he noticed that his sword was clean, as if it had never touched blood or flesh. His body, on the other hand, was covered in bloody spray and gore.

Sillik spotted a man kneeling near him and said, "My thanks, warrior."

The man shook his head as he struggled to regain his breath. "No, give me not your thanks. It is I who should thank you." Sillik noticed that his companion's sword was covered in gore.

In the distance, Sillik heard a man scream as the former slave woman emasculated another of the wounded. No one moved to stop her. Someone tossed her a shirt, but no one dared to disarm her. She pulled the clothing on warily. The shirt stuck to the blood on her skin, accentuating her figure. It came down to her thighs and covered her like a dress. She smiled through the gore. Sillik saw a spark of light in her eyes.

"My name," the man said, gasping, "is Renunel. I am—or was—a general of this city." The man wiped blood from his face with a piece of torn, stained tablecloth. Sillik didn't want to know what the stains were from.

"For many years, I had hoped Belliousces would agree to lead us, but he always refused until recently, when he seemed to consider the possibility whenever it was broached. When he disappeared, I feared my days were numbered, until I saw what you intended to do. Then my choice was clear. I followed you without fear. Now, warrior, I would ask you. Even as we talk, the killing will have spread through the city. I see in you one who is accustomed to leading men into battle. Please, will you lead us?"

Before Sillik could respond, Renunel knelt and laid his sword before Sillik. "Allow us to follow you and end this bloodbath in our city."

Startled, Sillik looked around the room. All the men who had fought with him, including the axe-wielding executioner, had also laid their weapons on the carpet and knelt. Tears glistening in his eyes, Sillik turned back to Renunel. "You honor me greatly, Renunel, but I cannot do what you ask. Our causes are similar, but they are not the same. It is not my place to lead your people. That place belongs to you. You know your people, and they know you. I am the outsider. Your people might accept me today, but tomorrow they will chafe and whisper about me. They wouldn't understand me." Sillik stopped. He didn't know what else to say. "Arise," he said to Renunel. "Take up your sword, lead your people, and take your rightful place."

"Very well," Renunel said. As he stood, so did the rest of the men in the room. "But know this. We have, even if you will not accept it, pledged to follow you. If in time we should win back our city, then you have only to call, and we shall come to your aid. In days of old, we were feared and respected as warriors, and we shall be again."

"Thank you," Sillik said, genuinely touched.

"One question, warrior," the executioner said in a soft voice that seemed at odds with his size and occupation. "We know that you are a warrior and"–awe crept into his voice–"a master of the Seven Laws, but the world is filled with many men and many warriors and many wonders. While it is true that you must stand among the bravest and wisest, allow us the honor of knowing what you call yourself."

Sillik thought quickly as he looked at the men. If he gave them his real name and identity, the tale would spread. If he didn't, the tale would still spread but more slowly. He chose a third option. "I am but a simple man. My name is Sillik. Now go, take back your city."

With that, the men raised their blades in unison and shouted. The language was indecipherable to Sillik, but the stony walls reverberated the joy of their words. The noise seemed to bring a rush of new people into the room as healers hurried in to administer herbs and bandages to the wounded.

The words of the joyous men broke the spell and strength of Sillik's name. He seemed to be no more than they. He was perhaps a trifle wearier or bloodier, but he was still flesh and bone, as they were.

Renunel began to issue orders like the general he was. There was a quick flurry of activity as the survivors picked up weapons and headed out of the keep. The former slave went with them, her eyes gleaming. Sillik shuddered. He pitied whoever got in her way tonight.

Renunel turned back to face Sillik. "The keep is secure. All the city's leadership was here, and those not loyal to me are dead or worse." He glanced at a moaning, wounded soldier. "It will be a busy night, but we shall recover our city before dawn."

Sillik lifted his sword. "I am ready to help."

Renunel shook his head and smiled. "I will not have it said that we endangered an Illician prince."

"So you know who I am," Sillik said without much surprise.

The general nodded. "The emperor bragged all day that he was going to kill the king of Illicia."

Sillik smiled. "I am a little harder to kill than that. And I'm not the king–yet."

Renunel smiled grimly. "So at least that part was true."

"Did he say anything else?" Sillik asked. "Anything about why he was going to kill me? Illicia has no quarrel with Colum."

"He kept many secrets. The only man who would know"–he pointed to the emperor's corpse–"won't talk again. His steward might have known, but he won't talk either." Renunel indicated another body lying nearby; it had been nearly cut in two by an axe, and the head was twisted obscenely. Sillik turned away. He didn't want to know how the man's neck had been broken.

Renunel acknowledged Sillik's disappointment with a knowing smile. "I must go. I have men to lead. You may search the emperor's rooms for whatever you seek, but I don't think you will find anything."

Sillik started to protest, but Renunel shook his head. "There are rooms through the door to my left that you may use."

Sillik looked in Renunel's eyes. When he saw the resolute expression, he bowed in deference. "Thank you. But I must leave the city at dawn."

"Rest easily, warrior," Renunel said. "The keep is secure. We shall watch you well while you sleep. None shall pass into those rooms but those who are trustworthy."

Nodding, Sillik turned and started to leave. Then he stopped and turned to Renee. "What are you going to do?"

"I am not sure," Renee said. "Give me some time."

Sillik nodded and left the hall, which reeked of death, to seek a well-deserved rest. Behind him, the executioner positioned himself to guard the hallway. His axe gleamed, bloody and dangerous, as he cradled it in his arms.

Renee stood before the executioner, as if uncertain of what she should do. She had heard the entire conversation and had been surprised to discover Sillik's identity. After a brief internal debate, she turned to Renunel and spoke urgently with him.

Sillik smiled as he left the room. He had done what he could. Now it was up to them. More importantly, he had survived Colum. Briana had been correct that Colum was a trap. In the distance, he could hear fighting, but the sounds were much farther away than they had been even moments before.

In the empty corridor beyond the hall, Sillik found five vaulted, nearly identical rooms. A tall, wide balcony took up the far wall, allowing the cool night air to blow gently into the room. To the right of the balcony stood several wooden shutters covered with metal. The shutters could serve a dual purpose. In sandstorms, they would keep the sand and dirt out. In a siege, the metal would stop most projectiles.

On the other side of the room stood a low platform that held a large basin of clear water, large enough to hold a man. Pipes delivered fresh, warm water, and the overflow disappeared into drains in the floor. A smaller basin with water and a shaving mug and razor stood against the wall. A large, elevated bed dominated the other wall. Thick blankets and sheets covered the bed. Sillik looked longingly at the bed and then at the large basin of water.

Thick woven rugs covered most of the stone floor. The walls were unadorned. The room was lit by torches and candles placed at intervals along the walls. In the hearth was a large pile of firestone. Reaching out with his mind, Sillik exerted a slight pressure on the stone in a way he had been taught so very long ago. Moments later, flame burst from the black rock, much to the surprise of a servant who had entered the room behind Sillik with a tinderbox. The servant glanced at the fire and then at Sillik, a look of terror on his face. Then the man fled.

Smiling, Sillik closed the door behind him and stripped off his leather, which he had worn since leaving Illicia. He also took off the cloth shirt, mail, and pants he wore under his leather. The leather needed to be cleaned and oiled, and the cloth needed washing. Everything was splattered with bloody gore and stank from having been worn too long. Sillik piled the clothing outside the door. He hoped the servants weren't too afraid of him to do his laundry.

Feeling much lighter and freer, Sillik approached the water, intending to wash. As he dipped his hands into it, he paused. The face looking up at him startled him. The tangled beard gave him a vaguely ominous appearance. He didn't remember seeing his eyes look so tired before.

The water was warm but not hot, and Sillik sighed. With a guilty look around, he knelt down and bowed his head beside the basin of water. A minor spell quickly heated the water to a temperature more comfortable for bathing. Whispers of steam rose from the surface. Sillik smiled. Then he stepped into the steaming water, sending some splashing over the edge. Sillik sighed in pleasure as he lowered himself into the hot water and leaned back to relax for the first time in weeks.

Moments later, he heard footsteps in the hallway. He tensed. His sword was where he had dropped it. He saw a shadow on the floor outside his door. It paused. As the handle on the door turned, Sillik reached for his sword. It slid out of its sheath and flew to his hand with a wet smack. Grinning, he lowered his hand so the blade wasn't visible. If someone was going to attack, he wanted him or her to be surprised.

The door opened, and Renee entered. Sillik relaxed. She seemed momentarily confused until she saw him. Her eyes widened a little in surprise as he slid the sword away from the tub. Then a halting smile flickered across her face. She was still carrying the sword she had used in the throne room. She looked around the room and then back at Sillik. He smiled. Renee returned his smile and dropped her blade with a clatter. Then she stripped off her own torn and bloodstained clothing.

When her dress hit the floor and he heard the clink of metal, Sillik laughed. He imagined all the knives and other sharp implements hidden in that dress. Briana would be like that, he thought. She must have found some unused weapons after the fight, Sillik decided.

Without a word, she slipped into the steaming water opposite him and breathed a contented sigh. Sillik watched her calmly.

Renee looked around guiltily as she considered what to say. "I wasn't completely honest with you. I didn't know you and withheld some things about myself."

Sillik nodded as she continued in a rush.

"I was born in the city of Covenon. My father was the newly elected governor of the city. When I was born, my parents realized that I carried the same potential for the Seven Laws as they had. They raised me in Covenon until I was eight years old. On my eighth birthday, they sent me to the city of Salone in the Bay of Felin to study the Seven Laws with the masters there."

Sillik smiled at this, and she paused.

"You knew that!" she said slowly with disbelief.

"From almost the moment we met," Sillik said.

"How?"

"Several things. Your pronunciation when we first spoke reminded me of Salone. When I saw you in the street fighting that guard, you were angry. I thought I saw an aura. I could feel magic around you. Last, after I thought about it, I remembered a young woman in the Golden House of Sarac Rish in the City of Salone."

Renee looked stunned as she leaned back in the water. "You studied at the Golden House?"

Sillik smiled. "I didn't say that. After I left Illicia, I traveled around. As an Illician prince, I was entitled to certain, shall we say, privileges. One of my friends in the Gold Robes suggested I meet the masters of Salone. So I went and enjoyed their hospitality for a month or so. But in the end I decided to leave for exactly the same reasons I had left Illicia." Sillik paused as if searching for words. "I had already mastered the Seven Laws, so there was little they could teach me. They knew that too. In the end they wanted me to join their school and teach. I considered it, but as I watched a master class being inducted and noticed a very attractive young woman, I knew I didn't want to teach."

Renee sat back in disbelief. "My master's induction was almost five years ago. We knew there was someone special at the ceremony, but the masters didn't tell us who it was. It was you?"

Sillik raised his hands and shrugged. "I don't know, but the timing sounds about right."

"So you are the Illician king?" Renee said. "Didn't you say 'related to the royal family'?"

"Everything I said was true," Sillik said with a smile.

For a while, they reclined and enjoyed the hot water. The only sound was the gurgle of the water coming out of the pipes and the drip of water into the drain. Then Renee frowned and reached out to wash a spot of blood off his face. Sillik smiled but still said nothing; he just leaned back and let her clean him.

Soon, she shifted her attention and began to massage his neck and shoulders. At one point she got out of the bath and then returned with the shaving supplies from beside the small basin.

She looked at Sillik as she held the long razor. Sillik's eyes seemed to bore into her head, and then he nodded. Smiling, she brushed some shaving soap on his face and then began to carefully shave the beard from his face. Sillik tried to relax but was unsuccessful. It was a new experience, letting someone else shave his face with a long, sharp blade. He forced himself to relax.

When she was finished, she gave him a kiss. "Thank you for coming after me tonight and killing that foul creature. Why did you do it?" She leaned back and let the water cover her shoulders. "You could have left."

"He attacked me, and he sent people to attack me," Sillik said simply. "He was evil. They were foot soldiers in the larger fight. In this fight, I must kill my enemies. I am looking for clues to the larger fight. I have told you about my foe. He is behind this and is testing me through proxies."

"Is it true what Renunel said in the banquet hall, that you are the king of Illicia?"

Sillik smiled. "Not yet."

Renee moved as if uncomfortable in the water, her breasts swaying just below the surface. "There has to be a story there, but you can tell me when you decide to."

Sillik smiled. "There are things you neglected as well."

Renee smiled but said nothing.

Sillik reached out and rubbed some grime off her face. Frowning, Renee submerged her head and madly scrubbed her face and hair. When she emerged, she leaned back opposite Sillik and drew watery circles on his biceps with her toe. "What now?" she asked with a smile.

Sillik stood up, stepped out of the water, and approached the window. Looking out toward the horizon, he said nothing for a moment, water dripping from his face. "Tomorrow, I must leave," he said. "I have business elsewhere." He stretched as the water dripped off him onto the expensive carpets.

Renee watched him for a moment and then rose from the water and stepped to his side. "I know," she said, smiling. "I also have business elsewhere and must leave tomorrow."

The air quickly dried the water from their skin. Sillik stood still and looked out over the dark city. From where he stood, it was impossible to tell that the city below was in chaos and that people were dying. In his mind's eye, though, he could see the fighting and the looting that must be occurring. Families would be barricading themselves in their homes. The fighting would be intense. This was not his fight, though. He had set in motion that which he could.

Shaking his head, Sillik used his mind to touch the torches along the walls, and the light disappeared. Then he picked Renee up and carried her, laughing, to the bed. But the moment his head touched the pillows, he was asleep.

Renee pounded the mattress in frustration. Then, very carefully, she kissed Sillik softly on the cheek and mouthed, "Thank you." Smiling, she snuggled in close, and within moments, she was asleep.

# CHAPTER 19

## The Yana

S ILLIK OPENED HIS eyes with a start. He was standing in a dark forest. Pale white light gleamed between the trunks, and wisps of fog floated between the trees.

Battle horns sounded in the distance. Screams rent the night as clouds drifted across the dark sky, the moon gleaming red between the trees. He turned upon hearing the screams and drew his sword. The sound of a whip cracking in the distance made him turn again. He ran; he had to get back.

The sound of arrows flying filled the air, and Sillik heard more yells and curses. The caravan seemed a long way away. He could see the wagons burning. Magic had been used to light the fires. He felt fire sprites leap for joy. His legs felt like they were mired in mud. He could smell death and smoke. Who had died?

The sharp, metallic sound of swords broke the night. Men yelled.

"Sillik!" a high-pitched woman's voice yelled. He could feel her magic. Arrows whizzed by in the darkness like gnats.

With a start, Sillik awoke, cold and shivering. His eyes felt like they had been glued shut. He was damp with perspiration. He groaned. "Not again," he said as he sat up and rubbed his eyes. He looked around and saw that Renee was gone. *Probably for the better,* he thought. At the same time, he was saddened.

When he looked out the window, he saw that the sky was a predawn gray. Smoke from several fires hung over the city. The sun rose above the horizon in one massive heave and looked down on a city that had seen many deaths during the night.

For several minutes, he sat on the bed and employed minor exercises of the Third Law to refresh his mind. Real sleep should have refreshed him, but the dreams had undone the good.

He remembered carrying Renee to the bed, but with a shake of his head, he realized he had fallen asleep. Throwing aside the sheet, he stumbled across the room to the basin. He noticed that Renee's torn, bloody dress was still lying where she had dropped it the night before. Her sword was gone, though. He grinned as he imagined her storming through the keep naked in search of clothing and carrying a sword. The image was short-lived as he realized that the blanket that had covered the bed the night before was also gone. He shivered again in the predawn air, now realizing the real reason he had awoken. He wasn't as amused at the thought of her taking the blanket. Picturing her wearing a blanket and carrying a sword wasn't nearly as humorous.

Sillik picked up what was left of Renee's dress. It was light. Whatever had clinked when she dropped it last night was gone. He tossed the dress next to the wall by the door. Someone would get it when they cleaned the room.

He splashed some cold water onto his face, which chased away the remaining cobwebs in his mind. Then, using the razor Renee had left beside the tub, he shaved again. It might be a long time before he got another chance. Once he had finished, Sillik began to dress. He shivered again in the cool air.

During the night someone had washed and cleaned his clothing, as he had hoped. The fabric was soft and still faintly warm. His mail had been cleaned and oiled as well. It glinted in the morning light and jangled softly as he inspected it. His fingers found several scrapes in the metal, and he briefly remembered battles past. His leather jerkin had also been cleaned and oiled and smelled faintly of sandalwood, as did the leather belt for his sword. Sillik noted with pleasure that his boots had been polished and buffed as well.

Sitting on a table near his clothing was a platter of food. After checking for poisons, he attacked the meat, cheese, and bread. In moments the food was gone. Afterward, he wondered whether he should have left some for Renee, but seeing as she had taken the blanket, he decided she would have to fend for herself. Feeling much better, Sillik dressed and buckled his sword around his waist. Its familiar weight was reassuring.

Remembering that he had not cleaned his blade the night before, Sillik drew the weapon. The blade was bright and sharp, and he mentally kicked himself. He vaguely remembered seeing that his sword was clean the previous night. Intrigued, he inspected the blade. The edge was sharp and clean as if the blade was newly forged. No sign of the battle could be found. Sillik doubted he could sharpen the blade further if he tried. In amazement, he sheathed it and then glanced around the room to make sure he had everything before he left.

Once he was in the hallway, it took little searching before he found the emperor's bedroom. Sillik knew that because of the man's size, his bedroom would be close to the room in which he had been killed. Physical exertion, including walking, would have been hard for a man that size.

Sillik scowled when he saw the bedroom of the man who had ruled the city. Whether he was an emperor or a city administrator, he should have been able to take care of his room or have others do it. The room was roughly oblong in shape with a vaulted ceiling. At the far end was a large bed that easily could have accommodated the emperor as well as three more people of the same size. At the other end was a long stone table and dusty benches. Three large windows allowed the early sun to enter and illuminate the room. Sillik suppressed a chill even in the sunlight. There was something disturbing about this room, and he looked around warily. Memories tickled his mind.

Robes, blankets, furs, towels, and other bits of fabric were scattered over every surface. The remains of several meals lay on the bed, the floor, and every other surface. The odor of stale beer, sour wine, urine, and other waste made Sillik wrinkle his nose in disgust. He scoured the room for any information that might be important. Reading and writing must not have been high on the emperor's list of favorite activities because parchment and other writing supplies were scarce, and what parchment Sillik did see was mostly small fragments, as if torn from larger documents. Sillik imagined the man tearing offending documents into pieces as terrified servants cowered in fear.

It wasn't until Sillik had almost given up that he realized he was going about his search the wrong way. Dernot had surely been in communication with this man and might even have stood in this very room. He might have left compulsions or other evidence behind. Sillik stroked his chin thoughtfully as he looked around the room, suddenly cautious. He remembered the throne room of Illicia and smiled.

Slowly, Sillik wrapped himself in layers of shielding, much like he had done in Illicia before his throne had exploded. This time, though, he tightened his protections and set a warding around the entire room. If there was a trap, he had no intention of letting a warning go out. His shields were nearly luminous in their intensity. When he was satisfied with the level of protection, he extended his augmented senses around the room. It was as if he could suddenly see the most minute details and unimaginable colors.

As he cast his enhanced senses around the room, he realized that one corner seemed reflective. The more he looked at the corner, the more he wanted to look somewhere else. Sillik smiled. Something was hidden. Gently, he touched the edges of the spell. It was not a trap as he had feared, but something else was concealed.

As Sillik examined the spell, it shifted suddenly to the left. Surprised, Sillik jumped back and threw a bolt of energy at it. Shields flared in response, and a return blow buffeted Sillik. Sillik remembered something the Gold Robes had taught him years ago: if a shadow jumps when you tickle it, then surround it with power and squeeze. It was another imp, just like the one that had killed his uncles and cousins in Illicia.

Memories flooded his mind as he remembered attacking similar beasts in days past. He was ready when the creature changed its tactics. Heat rolled into the room, and shadows tried to form along the walls as the creature called to its brethren. Sillik smiled and produced a ball of light to scatter the shadows. Instantly, the thing in the darkness howled in pain. Reaching out with a mental fist, he squeezed harder. He could feel the hellish creature squirming and fighting, but it was no match for a master of the Seven Laws. As Sillik squeezed it out of existence, he wondered who had summoned it and why. No matter, it had to be destroyed. He could not leave it here to cause more trouble.

Moments later, the creature gave one last wail and then vanished. A puff of smoke was all that was left. Vaguely surprised, Sillik looked around for other threats but found nothing. Then, with a last look around the room, he strode down the hall to the throne room. So much for not letting anyone know he had been here, Sillik thought. Whoever had summoned that thing would know it had been sent back to hell. Another trap, he thought, but he couldn't have just left it there either. Something like that could corrupt a man's soul and eat him for breakfast.

In the throne room, Sillik noticed that the dead had been removed and the torches were still lit, but nothing else had been done. Piles of food still covered the tables. The doors he had destroyed still lay where they had fallen.

In the halls beyond, he met no one. He heard people at several points, but he didn't see them. At the gate of the keep, Sillik sensed more than a hundred people outside. They were all armed, but he detected no signs of hostility.

When he stepped into the courtyard outside the keep, he found himself in the midst of a bustle of activity. Two piles of dead bodies lined one side. One pile was laid out in respect. The other pile was more haphazard and seemed to be dominated by bodies of the elite guards. In another area, soldiers formed up in preparation for what Sillik assumed was a patrol. Members of the guard lined the battlements around the courtyard. They all faced outward. All but one of the flagpoles on the battlements was empty. Only the main pole had a pennant. The rising-sun pennant of Colum had been replaced with an all-red battle flag with a yellow star. Against one wall, several wounded warriors lay on the cobblestones. Healers in white smocks knelt over them, addressing their injuries. Sillik could smell smoke and the stink of death in the air. As battlefields went, though, it was milder than most. The butcher's bill had been light.

Sillik saw many of the men who had been in the throne room the night before. They were all armed, and more than a few were wounded and bandaged. They looked tired and haggard. Many still wore blood-splattered clothing. At the same time, Sillik perceived a quiet confidence. He smiled. During the night, they had fought, and today they had victory. It was then that he noticed the two yana. Stunned, Sillik stopped and stared at the beasts.

Yana were large feline animals with sleek, long brown fur. They were similar to the common stable cat used to control mice and rats, only these were much larger and exceedingly rare. Most of the beasts stood as tall as a man at the shoulder with a proud head that rose far above a man's. Their razor-sharp claws could rend a man in half at the slightest provocation, and their long tails could hurl a man wearing full mail more than a hundred standard spear lengths. Their long, straight teeth could punch terrible holes in the strongest chain or plate mail. They were among the fiercest of all carnivores. From birth they had to be trained to obey men. Even then, they were never more than half-broken. Fiercely independent, they were also courageous allies. When ridden, they wore a thick leather belt around their necks. The belt was used to guide the beast and to enable the rider to hang on, for they tolerated no sort of saddle.

Sillik saw that the exposed tips of the yana's claws were shod with steel. *Battle yana*, he thought with a shudder, the fiercest of the fierce. Yana would eat only what they killed themselves, and yet they were not bloodthirsty, at least no more than any other cat. They would kill only when hungry or provoked, but if an unmounted man met even one beast, and the animal was hungry or angry, then without a doubt, that man was dead.

Sillik was surprised to see two of the animals. They were very rare, living mainly along the coast of the Shining Sea. The pair seemed to be identical. As he looked closer, though, Sillik began to see small differences. Intelligence filled their eyes as they watched the large crowd of men. Both of the beasts knelt, as if waiting for someone to mount them. Their tails whipped playfully on the stained stone. A score of guards armed with pikes and spears watched the animals carefully and formed a half circle around them. The pikes were set to post position, which meant they were leaning toward the yana at about a seventy-five-degree angle. The spears were interspaced between the pikes and also pointed toward the relaxing yana.

"Sillik," Renunel said as he approached. "During the night while you slept, we continued to fight. The entire city is now under our control."

Sillik smiled grimly. "Congratulations."

"When we routed the imperial guards from the royal stables before dawn, we found this pair of yana. We, ah … we ask that you accept them as a gift."

Sillik began to refuse, but Renunel continued. "Please, do not refuse us. There is not a man in the city who would dare to ride them anyway."

"They are worth a king's ransom," Sillik said.

"Which is why we choose to give them to a king."

"Very well," Sillik said, recognizing that the yana would come in handy in his search. "I thank you and accept your gift."

"So shall I," said a feminine voice from behind Sillik. Sillik turned and saw Renee striding toward him with a hot fire gleaming in her eyes. He noticed instantly that she had exchanged her skirt for dark blue woven breeches and knee-high leather boots. She wore a white shirt with a glint of mail underneath. Over the shirt was a brown leather vest that buttoned up the front. At her side she carried a long, narrow curved sword. It was slenderer and lighter than the one she had carried the previous night. A dagger was thrust in the top of her boot, and another peeked out from under her sleeve. Her only feminine adornments were a fine gold necklace and a ruby ring on her left hand. In addition, she had cut her hair to shoulder length and braided what was left.

"I am going with you," she said stubbornly.

"You should stay in your city," Sillik replied.

"I have business elsewhere," she said, smiling. "Besides, it's not my city, as I told you."

"Then ride with me," Sillik said with a grin.

Renunel watched the exchange with sadness. He nodded to Renee and then turned to Sillik. "Where are you going, warrior?"

"I need to see a knight."

Renunel looked puzzled, but before he could say anything, Sillik said goodbye and wished him well.

"Do me a favor," Sillik asked as he stood beside the yana.

"If it is within my power," Renunel said hesitantly. "What do you desire?"

Smiling, Sillik said, "Rebuild your city. Clean it up. Make it something to be proud of."

"We intend to," Renunel said.

"End the practice of slavery," Sillik said. "It is a vile practice. It has led to many deaths." Sillik stroked the yana as he spoke.

Renunel nodded. "We can do that," he said slowly. Then changing the subject, he said, "We assumed the lady Renee would be leaving with you. We have supplied provisions for two—food, water, bedding. It should be enough for weeks."

"I had them cash out some of my uncle's fortunes as well," Renee said with a grin. "So we can purchase additional supplies when we need them."

Sillik smiled and nodded his thanks.

After strapping the bags to the kneeling beasts, Sillik and Renee climbed onto the yana's backs. Then, with a delicate touch of the neck belt, Sillik's yana stood. He tried to instruct Renee, but she quickly copied his movements. Sillik wrapped his veil under his chin as he looked around.

Renee thanked Renunel, and Renunel reminded Sillik that he just had to send word, and Colum would do what it could to help. Sillik nodded his thanks and then turned his yana to leave.

The yana raised their tails and raced out of the plaza. As the yana turned, Sillik saw a sight that made him smile. Around the edge of the keep, men were cutting a long branch from one of the trees.

Sillik and Renee rode through the city streets quickly. For the most part, the streets were deserted and bore the signs of looting and burning. More than a few bodies were lying in the open, all wearing the uniforms of the royal guard. The few living people they saw in the streets were armed and wary. They stared in awe at the yana.

The gates of the city were already open, and Sillik and Renee were not challenged when they reached them. Outside the city, they saw many people camped, waiting for the fighting to end. They were tired and hungry. Many were wounded with poorly wrapped bandages.

As they rode, Sillik thought about the strange scraps of paper that had led him to Colum. The place had been a trap, as he and Briana had suspected and as Silvia had confirmed. Therefore, something about the Knights of Nerak might be a trap as well. His father's notes did not say much about Nerak. They had been concerned mostly with Ynak. Were these really traps or tests? This was more complicated than it appeared—of that he was sure.

During his travels, Sillik had encountered a strange plant called an onion that had several layers. Sillik felt like he was unraveling the mystery like an onion, one layer at a time. There must be some way to cut through the layers to the heart of the matter. Why had Dernot Lafliar led him here? If Dernot wanted him dead, why enlist the Dashlinar of the Whispering Isles? It had to be a test, Sillik concluded. Dernot didn't want to face him until assured of victory.

*If I were Dernot, when would I attack?* Sillik wondered. *If I were without honor, I would attack when my foe had just completed some major working of the Seven Laws or fought a significant duel.*

For five long, hot days and cold nights, Sillik and Renee rode through the land that surrounded the city of Colum. Although they generally went north, Sillik kept changing direction and doubling back to check their trail and study the horizon for clues. Gradually, grass and trees became more common, and by the fifth night, oaks and pines began to dot the landscape.

Each night at sunset, they stopped to camp. Sillik would gather some flat rocks and then hold his hands over them until they were red. They used the heat to warm a bit of water and make tea. In addition to the tea, they ate bread, cheese, and dried meat. Twice they had augmented their meals with berries and small fruits that Renee had found. Sillik also found wild mushrooms one evening and sliced and grilled them while their water heated. After being away from Illicia for only a few weeks, he already missed grilled sandfish. It was something a person either liked or hated. If you liked the fish, you could never get enough. He shook his head with a rueful smile.

Each night after they ate, Sillik heated the rocks again to provide additional heat. The nights were still cold, so they spread out their bedrolls close together. "For warmth," Renee said with a smile. Sillik smiled as well, but each night, sleep came quickly, and dawn too soon. The dreams seemed to come every night as well.

When he awoke after another round of dreams, Sillik struggled to sit up. The sun was just above the horizon. Across the hot stones, Renee was making some tea. She had a worried expression on her face. Wordlessly, she handed him a hot cup.

Sillik took the cup and tested the contents with a quick sip. It was hot and strong.

"These dreams you've been having—what's going on?"

Sillik shook his head. "It is nothing."

Renee laughed softly. "It is not nothing," she said as she handed him a piece of bread and a lump of cheese.

Sillik smiled ruefully. "It is not important."

"Anything that affects you this deeply is certainly important. I need to know. I might be able to help."

"I had a run-in with some people," Sillik said as he ran a hand over his face. "It went badly. I seem to keep reliving it."

Renee gave him a sidelong look as she cut off a piece of cheese. "Do these people have names?"

Sillik rubbed his eyes and shook his head. "Not that I ever knew," he said as he took a bite of cheese.

"What kind of run-in did you have?"

Sillik laughed bitterly. "The messy kind. They attacked a caravan. It took a while to track them down. It was a long time ago, so I'm fine. I just have dreams about the attack."

Renee eyed Sillik uncertainly as he rolled up his blankets and then tied his bedroll to the saddle of his yana. "You're not telling me the whole story, are you?"

"I've told you what you need to know," Sillik said as he finished his tea.

Renee stiffened in anger. Pausing to regard him, she said, "Sillik, I am trying to help you. I am coming with you because I believe we are fighting the same fight. If you don't trust me, I can leave now!"

"I do, and I know," he said tiredly. "I have kept this to myself for so long, it's hard to talk about."

"Let me help."

After a long pause, he began. "I was in the city of Aceon, and the daughter heir was out in the city and slipped on a stair. They have lots of stairs in Aceon."

"Because of the cliffs," Renee suggested. "Isn't Aceon built out of the side of cliffs?"

Sillik nodded. "Anyway, she slipped. No one ever figured out why."

"Assassination attempt?"

"We never figured it out," Sillik said as he rubbed his forehead. "I caught her and saved her life. I had saved her brother's life a few days before that too. That is what really brought us together."

"Another assassination attempt?" Renee asked.

Sillik shook his head. "Just thugs trying to steal some coins. Nuella heard about it and asked for an introduction. We met and developed an interest. After a while, she found out that I was the younger son of the king of Illicia. That got me invited to spend more time with the royal family. We got to know one another, and eventually, we fell in love. We decided we should marry. We were on our way to Illicia to announce the news to my family when we were attacked. Slavers." He paused.

"Slavers attacked our camp. Nuella's brother and I were on the other side of the camp when the attack started. He was injured, and I stopped to heal him. But the real attack was taking place elsewhere. Nuella's maid was captured, and Nuella tried to save her. She succeeded, but she was shot in the process. Nuella died in my arms as I tried to heal her. The arrow had sliced her heart. A real healer might have been able to save her had one gotten there in time. As it was, I saved the crown prince, but I couldn't save the daughter heir. Later, after we returned to Aceon and informed the queen, Nuella's brother and I tracked down all the slavers who had escaped."

"That's how you got those scars on your arms?" Renee asked. "Slave whips? I thought that was what they were."

Sillik nodded.

"Nuella," Renee said. "It's a pretty name. It means snow flower, doesn't it?"

"Yes," Sillik said. "They grow wild on the plains."

"So the nightmares?" Renee asked.

"I dream about it almost every night," he said quietly. "First time I have told anyone."

"It seems to me you did everything you could," Renee said slowly as she hesitantly put her hand on Sillik's. "Come, you are with me today. Let's ride like the wind."

Smiling half-heartedly, Sillik nodded. But before they left, Sillik searched their campsite to remove any sign of their presence. If they were being followed, he dared not leave a trail. It worried him to think about who might be following– or watching.

Villages with tall palisades began to appear, and Sillik steered well away from them. He didn't dare bring trouble down on the villagers. They would also remember the yana for a long time and would tell anyone who passed through about them. He noticed that Renee looked longingly at the villages and the inns, but she didn't question his decisions. Sillik saw fields full of goats, sheep, and bison. He kept a tight leash on his yana. He didn't want them hunting while they were near the villages.

That day, they crossed a small stream. The trees became thicker, almost barring their way. They began to see wild animals as well. In the distance, Renee pointed out the edge of the Mosshavin Forest, ancient home of the last of the Forestals, who had been the protectors of the ancient forests for millennia. At one time, this forest had also covered the lands surrounding the city of Colum, but that had been over ten thousand years ago.

When the day's heat had broken and a cool breeze began to stir the pendants on the rooftops, Kenton stepped out onto the ramparts of the keep.

Briana was standing near the parapet. Her hair was loose and moving in the breeze.

"We have had a development in the investigation into Melin and Noswin's deaths," Kenton said.

"You found the bottle?"

Kenton frowned. "No, sadly, not yet. But I would really like to get my hands on it," he admitted with a laugh.

"Then what?"

"Noswin fired a maid. Very publicly."

"What did she do? Refuse his advances?" Noswin had a reputation for trying to bed every woman who worked for him. Briana wrinkled her nose in distaste at the thought.

Kenton shook his head. "No, not that. She was fired in front of the chief steward for trying to dust Noswin's liquor bottles."

Briana stopped. "He fired a maid for doing her job? That's crazy."

"Not if the bottle cost five thousand double golds," Kenton said with a patronizing smile.

"Oh," Briana said as comprehension spread across her face. "So you found the girl?"

Kenton shuffled his feet. "Ah, well, yes but no."

Briana frowned. "I'm confused."

"Well, I said 'development.' We also found more questions."

"Explain."

"After the maid, Sula, was fired—which was several days before the deaths— she went to live with her sister, whom we managed to track down. The sister had not seen Sula in days and was getting worried."

"And?"

"This morning a report came in. A woman matching Sula's description was found near the lizard pens with a broken neck. She has been dead for days."

"That doesn't give us much."

Kenton brightened. "Actually, that is where it starts to get interesting. Sula's roommate at the household said she had started a whirlwind romance two weeks before Sillik's uncles and cousins were killed. Neither the sister nor the roommate ever saw the man, but one of the guards did. The suitor was described as short, wiry, and nervous."

"Interesting," Briana said as she waited for more.

"I had a hunch and did another sweep around the building. Near the back of the building is a small gap between two buildings, small enough for a short, wiry guy to shinny up to the roof. When we examined the area more closely, we found small black fibers embedded in the wall."

"Thief or assassin?" Briana asked as she brushed her hair away from her face. "Ah, Lord General Greenup, good evening," she said as the man approached.

The lord general nodded. "Warmaster, I am sorry I am late."

"I was just telling the warmaster what we have discovered," Kenton said. "Now to answer your question, thief or assassin? We think thief," Kenton said. "Greenup and I talked to the guards both inside and outside the house. The guards inside reported that a man came to the household during the party. The guards outside reported that a woman in a gray cloak came to the house. The guards on the roof were employed by Noswin. They were sloppy and useless. No one could give a description of the guest who visited other than sex. Hair and face descriptions varied wildly. Greenup and I think that person is the killer. Since everything is inconsistent, we think the killer had magical skills, which is also supported by what you found in the rooms after the murder."

Greenup cleared his throat and said, "It also supports Sillik's conclusion that a woman did the killing."

"We think she got blood on her skirts, which is what caused that strange pattern of blood splatter on the floor," Kenton said. "Either that, or she had shields that left the strange blood pattern."

"And the thief?" Briana asked slowly.

"We think he was there to steal the bottle," Kenton said.

"Very bold," Briana said. "That limits the choices. We have to find him. He might have seen the murderer."

Kenton nodded. "The thieves' guild?"

"Yes, we need to find someone who can put us in contact with the thieves' guild," Briana said.

"Well, about that ..." Greenup shifted uncomfortably.

Briana gave him an amused look. "You know someone?"

"It's not what you think," Greenup said quickly. "I am always on the lookout for recruits. Occasionally, friends tell me about men who might be diverted, who don't have the skills necessary to make a life in the guild."

"Can they find this man?" Briana asked as she turned to face the city and put her hands on the stone battlements.

Greenup shrugged. "I hope so, at least before this mystery killer does."

# CHAPTER 20

## Slavers

AS SILLIK AND Renee hurried through the forest, life settled into a predictable, almost comfortable pattern. At dawn, they rose and ate a cold meal. Then they rode, interspacing the wild rides on the yana with periodic walks, during which they led the animals and stretched their legs. When they came across water, they refilled their water bags. At midday, they ate a quick meal without stopping. At sunset, they made camp and ate another meal. At dawn, they rose and repeated the pattern.

Sillik kept circling back on his path. Renee looked at him questioningly each time, but he offered no explanation. He had the same feeling that he was being followed that he had felt in the desert before he arrived outside Colum. Something was wrong. He felt a prickling sensation that something or someone was watching them.

After several days of travel, they stopped for the night. As the yana walked in circles, preparing to bed down, Sillik prepared to heat some rocks. Suddenly, he smelled smoke and froze. Renee gave him a questioning look. He glanced at her and touched his nose. Renee frowned. All she could smell at first was the clean scent of pine. Then she also picked up the acidic tang of smoke. With a quiet, metallic sound, a dagger appeared in her hand.

"Sometimes you remind me of someone," Sillik whispered.

Renee smiled. "Do you want to unsaddle the yana?"

Sillik turned to look at them and after a moment said, "No, they can fight with their saddles if we have to fight."

Sillik pointed at the forest. Renee searched the forest with her eyes. She noticed that the yana were suddenly alert as well. Their heads were upright, their ears pulled back, and their eyes wide. They crouched low, ready to pounce. Their tails, which were normally bundles of energy, were still and rigid.

Sillik clicked his tongue at the yana. Then he pointed to his left and began to move in that direction. Renee followed. The forest was dense, and once they had traveled a dozen paces beyond the small clearing, Renee doubted she could have found her way back. The smell of smoke continued to increase the farther they walked into the forest. Soon, they heard voices and muffled laughter.

Renee glanced behind her and was surprised to see the yana following. The war beasts crouched low and moved only when Sillik did. From the beginning of their trek, Sillik had had an amazing connection with the yana. He would click his tongue and point his hand, and they would do whatever he wanted. When she had asked about it, he had simply said they were intelligent. The voices became clearer. Renee stopped to see if she could understand them.

Sillik leaned forward and looked into the clearing ahead of them. What he saw chilled him. He motioned to Renee, and she crept forward.

A village, if it could be called that, was in the clearing before them. It consisted of five huts with thatched roofs built around a common cooking area. One of the huts was on fire, but no one was making an effort to put it out. A deer or wild pig was roasting over the fire. Several armed men stood while the villagers lay on the ground.

Renee frowned as she looked at the armed men. For the most part, they were scrawny, even gaunt. Most were dirty and wore mismatched clothing. The apparent leader of the band was balding, with long, greasy hair pushed back over the top of his head. He held a battered sword in one hand and a chunk of cooked meat in the other. Renee looked at Sillik and mouthed, "Slavers."

Sillik nodded grimly, disgust written clearly across his face. He didn't like slavers—no one did—but Renee noticed something deeper. Whenever the subject had come up, he had unconsciously rubbed his shoulder, as he was doing now.

Sillik turned back to the village. Several of the women and children on the ground were whimpering. A slaver kicked one of the women and told her to be quiet. She gasped and sobbed. One man knelt between two of the prisoners and tied ropes around their necks.

Sillik glanced back at Renee and held up five fingers. She nodded and slowly drew another throwing knife. He held a finger to his lips and then clicked his tongue. The yana looked at him. He pointed at one and motioned to the left and then pointed the other animal right. They slinked off the ways he had directed. Renee frowned. *How is he able to control them like that?* she wondered.

Sillik pointed to Renee and motioned to his left. Then he pointed first to himself and then at the village. He next pointed at her, pointed at his eyes, and touched his chest. She nodded and grinned. She was to watch his back.

As he rolled to his right, Renee saw tendrils of arcane energy flowing around him. Knowing that it was overkill, she summoned her own arcane protections. One of the benefits was that it sharpened her senses. She regretted the "improvement" instantly as the breeze sent the sweet, sick smell of an open latrine toward her.

When Sillik drew his sword, she saw it with her heightened senses and couldn't help but gasp. She had not gotten a good look at the weapon the last time he had drawn it. Wrapped around the blade was a swarm of flickering impressions and surprising energies.

Sillik rolled to his feet. Rather than sneak into the village, he strolled brazenly into the clearing. He whistled loudly and clicked his tongue.

The slavers looked up sharply. One scrawny fellow drew a throwing knife and was preparing to throw when one of the yana pounced. Suddenly, the man was staring at a bloody stump where his arm used to be. A scream to the right said the second yana had done its part too.

Renee dispatched a third slaver with her throwing knife as he reached for a crossbow. Then she leapt up and followed Sillik, keeping an eye on his back.

Sillik smiled as he strode into the clearing. The two surviving slavers dashed forward, swords drawn, yelling unintelligible words.

Renee noted that neither of the men wore the red belt or had markings on their sheaths. *Outlaws,* she concluded. *This is going to be a short fight.*

Sillik parried once and then twisted. The first slaver was dead before he hit the ground. He didn't even bother to parry the second man's blade; he just twisted to avoid it. Sillik's blade darted in so fast that Renee almost didn't see it. The man pulled up sharp and saw the blade being pulled out of his chest. In a final effort, he brought his sword up, but Sillik parried it easily. To Renee's surprise, Sillik's blade sliced through the other weapon as if it were wood. It fell to the ground in two pieces. The dying man stared in wonder at the smoldering edges of his broken blade. Then his eyes glazed over, and he fell to the ground.

Movement to her left startled Renee as two more slavers burst out of one of the huts, weapons drawn. Renee yelled at Sillik as she used her second and last throwing knife on one of the men. He went down quickly, a blade in his heart. The last slaver had a sudden change of heart when he saw all of his companions lying dead on the ground. Without a backward glance, he turned and ran toward the forest.

Sillik pointed to the man and clicked his tongue. A yana pounced on him immediately. Renee looked away as the man's screams rent the air. Fortunately, the noise didn't last long.

Renee bent to the grisly task of retrieving her knives. Once she had her weapons back and cleaned, she moved through the villagers, cutting their bonds. The village men stood up as they rubbed their wrists and necks where they had been bound. Renee was amused to note that they collectively took a few steps back from her and Sillik.

The villagers eyed Sillik and Renee warily. The women sent the children for water to put out the fires as the men cautiously picked up their weapons.

Renee stifled a laugh. The villagers were delusional if they believed their hoes and axes could protect them. A quick glance at the two yana told her the slavers they had intercepted wouldn't bother the villagers ever again. They had been torn to pieces. Now that the danger was over, the yana were sitting calmly and cleaning their fur.

Sillik clicked his tongue, and the yana bounded over to him. The sight of the creatures sent the villagers scattering in fear. After having been captured by slavers and then freed, they seemed to think they would now become food for the yana.

Renee looked at Sillik, who sheathed his incredible sword and nodded toward the north. She nodded in agreement and mounted what she presumed was her yana. After all this time, she still struggled to tell them apart.

Sillik looked at the villagers. "We are leaving. Dispose of the bodies. And you might consider building a stockade."

One of the men opened his mouth as if to speak, but his woman beat him to it. "Be silent, Youlsef," she said with a thick accent as she hit him on the arm with a long-handled pan. "Stranger, we thank you for savin' us, we do." She glared at the men of her village and then stated with conviction, "We won't be botherin' you."

"Thank you, my lady," Sillik said as he bowed politely. Then he swung himself onto his yana.

Renee prodded her yana with her heels, and it took off down a trail to the north. She crouched low and hung on tightly as the yana sprinted down the twisting path. Sillik and his yana were right behind her.

As they rode, Renee pondered what had just happened. Sillik's betrothed had been killed by slavers, and now he had gone out of his way to stop some more. Would it be enough to stop the dreams? His actions were understandable now, given what he had told her. When they had ridden far enough to avoid being found by the peasants, they stopped again for the night. Renee noticed that Sillik was moody, but in an attempt to distract him, she said, "Tell me about your family. You got to grow up with yours. I got sent away."

Sillik nodded and began to talk of his father. He talked until he could not keep his eyes open and dozed off. Once he was asleep, Renee snuggled close to him, and with a touch to his forehead, she deepened his sleep. Perhaps it would prevent the dreams for tonight.

# CHAPTER 21

## Messages

BRIANA AND GREENUP had been staring at the maps all evening. Kenton and his daughters had come and gone.

"I really don't understand what you expect to see," Greenup said as he put his wine cup down on the edge of the map. Briana had been marking distances and making notes all evening. "By this time, Sillik could be almost anywhere."

"No," Briana said with a smile. "I know where he is going."

"Really? Would you like to share your sudden insight into our king? Is he following the papers that we found in his father's hand? Has he contacted you somehow?"

Briana nodded. "In a way. Lady Silvia said he must follow the papers. She said she put the papers to his hand."

Greenup looked up in surprise. "You didn't tell us that. What else did she say? Did she give any reasons?"

"Just the end of the world," Briana said. "It is important that he do the first two before the third. The third will shake the foundations of the world and could decide who leads the world for the next ten thousand years."

"Nothing like pressure," Greenup said dryly.

"Exactly what Sillik said," Briana replied, laughing nervously.

"Why didn't you tell us?" Greenup asked.

"Sillik didn't want anyone to know his plans. Besides, I knew, and he told me to tell you and Kenton when I was ready."

Greenup glared. "Did he tell you that in the message sphere that he left?"

For the first time, Briana's composure cracked a little. "You know about that?"

Greenup grinned. "Briana, my dear," he said in a condescending tone, "Kenton and I searched Sillik's room the day he left. We found the message sphere immediately. It wasn't keyed to us, so the only logical answer was that it was keyed to you. We didn't think it was for Nisha."

Briana smiled. "Yes, it was keyed to me." She pointed to the map. "He went to Colum. We thought it would be a trap. Then he was going north toward the Road of Andel. He was going to follow the road toward Nerak."

"What is he going to do about Vouyr?" Greenup asked. "Its evil continues to spread."

"He didn't know," Briana said. "He thought it might be related to everything else."

Greenup laughed. "The evil in Vouyr has been growing for centuries. The Gold Robes have charted it. So was he going through or around?"

Briana shook her head. "I don't know. I don't think he knew."

"Okay," Greenup said, "but what did he say in the message sphere?"

Briana smiled. "He said he had faith in me. He told me to trust you and Kenton."

"And?"

Briana frowned. "He had a name, a person he suspected of killing his uncles."

"That is certainly something. And you chose to withhold that name."

"It is only suspicion. That damn perfume," Briana said. "He thought he recognized it. He had someone compose a list of all the women who wore it."

"Probably Nisha," Greenup guessed. "So who was on the list?"

Briana shook her head. "No, it's only suspicion. I am not going to ruin lives without proof."

"If something happens to you …"

"I thought of that too," Briana said with a frown. "There is a message sphere in the closet," she said. "It is keyed to my death and either of the two of you. It lays out everything that Sillik knew and what I have been able to piece together. It also reveals the name."

Greenup sighed. "What else did Sillik tell you? How to be overly mysterious and ruthless?"

"And nothing else of import!" Briana said with exasperation. "But …" She paused and looked at Greenup. "Lady Silvia said there would be tests."

Greenup snorted. "This, whatever this is, is not going to be easy. We knew that. Someone wants Illicia neutralized, and the best way to do that is to kill the leadership—which *someone* has been successful at doing."

"Ah, but do they know that we know that?" Briana asked smugly.

Greenup gave her a thoughtful look. "Two ways I could answer that. You assume they know what we are doing or that Sillik has done the unexpected. Either has its own risks."

Briana twisted her hair around her finger. "We assume they know everything we are doing, so we keep doing the unexpected. We are going to go after Sillik."

"The council will never go along with that," Greenup said.

Briana smiled. "I am the warmaster. We will be going to war."

Greenup looked up sharply. "Who is going to attack us?"

Briana shook her head mysteriously and changed the subject. "Our guests from Shelnor will be here by midday."

Greenup nodded. "So I've heard."

"I watched the caravan come down through Thunder Pass this morning," Briana said.

Greenup chuckled. "I bet you did. Did Nisha let you away long enough? Did you hear the thunder?"

Briana smiled conspiratorially. "A rider came in last night saying they would arrive today. I had last watch wake me before dawn, so I was on the roof of the keep. I watched the wagons start down the pass shortly after sunrise."

"Do you have to greet them?"

"No," Briana said, "thankfully not. The merchants get them first. They will meet me tomorrow. We will have a reception here in the keep, and I will be updated on the negotiations. They will go out to the quarries tomorrow." Briana pushed back from the table. "Now, I want to change the plans for dinner. Here is what we are going to do ..."

# CHAPTER 22

## The Road of Andel

"THE ROAD OF Andel," Sillik explained as they walked the yana, "once served the cities of Tricon, Lisia, and Vouyr. As you should know, the road predates the founding of Illicia and most of the cities that exist today. The cities were built an equal distance apart, and the road served as a means of trade and mutual defense."

Renee nodded impatiently. "I know my history. The cities are abandoned today, mere ruins, but no one knows why. They say it looks like the result of a battle, though."

Sillik smiled. "But do you know that all three are haunted by something evil? Nothing survives a night within the cities. Illicia tried to cleanse the ruins, but we were never successful. The evil just keeps coming back."

Renee shuddered. "Yes, I have been near Lisia before. We went in a little and then left immediately. It was terrible."

"I have been through all of them," Sillik said. "Vouyr is the worst, it seems." He wondered why Renee had been near Lisia.

"Did you sleep better last night?" Renee asked. "Have you had that dream again?"

"No," Sillik said with a smile as he examined the ground carefully. "Sometimes the dreams comes and go."

"Let's hope they don't come back," Renee said with a smile. "Now, why are we here?" Renee asked. "More importantly, why do I get the feeling we are going *through* the ruins and not around?"

"I think we are being followed," Sillik said, continuing to examine the ground as Renee looked around cautiously.

"Who or what could follow you?" Renee asked, putting her hand on her sword.

Sillik shook his head. "I was followed when I left Illicia. I dealt with the thugs that I found, but the feeling of being followed didn't go away. I have this nagging suspicion that something is still back there. If we go straight through, we get ahead by days. No one will follow us through. I have been through this before, so I know what to expect. I don't think it is men following us this time."

"What is it then?"

Sillik shrugged. "Something that uses scent. Winter wolves—or something worse."

"I've never seen a winter wolf," Renee said quietly. "I have only read about them." She suppressed a shudder.

"I have fought them before. They are large, and if they are in a pack, they are extremely dangerous."

Renee looked at him for a moment. "What will happen—in the ruins, I mean? Lisia radiated waves of disquiet. Within moments we were at one another's throats. Had we stayed longer, we would have killed each other."

Sillik shrugged. "You will be tempted by what you desire most. Trust nothing you see."

Renee nodded, but she was far less comfortable than she looked. What did she desire most? Thoughts of many things flashed through her mind.

Sillik looked around. "The ruins are a good indication of what is going on in the land. Illicia sends Gold Robes every year to measure whether the evil has spread. This is also the shortest route to the Road of Andel."

Renee nodded as she gazed at the ruins. Even the air seemed uncomfortable.

The shift was palatable as they walked. It was as if they had passed through a doorway. One moment, they could hear the normal sounds of the forest, and the next, the sounds were gone. Other than the clink of their weapons and the yana's breathing, Renee couldn't hear anything.

"By the Seven," Sillik swore. He handed his reins to Renee and walked backward a dozen steps until he found the exact spot of the boundary. Kneeling, he drew a line in the dirt. Puzzled, Renee watched as he picked up a handful of rocks, stacking them just outside the boundary.

"It is growing stronger," Sillik said as he took the reins for his yana. He looked around and then headed north. Renee followed.

As they walked, Sillik explained. "Something evil lives here. No one knows for sure, but we think we might have found some clues. Don't stop moving. Don't touch anything you don't have to. Don't pick up anything."

Renee smiled but saved her breath.

"These ruins affect everyone a little differently," Sillik continued. "Animals become difficult to control and can forget their training." He waved at the yana. "Last time I was here, I lost my lizard. It threw me and ran off into the ruins. I don't think it got out. If the yana try to run, let them."

Renee watched the sun. It was already uncomfortably low in the sky. It seemed to be falling toward the horizon. Uncertain of how much farther they had to go, Sillik and Renee pushed on as hard as they could.

Out of the corner of her eye, Renee saw gold and silver and other valuables. She ignored them easily, but the ruins became increasingly tempting. A piece of stone with lettering and a stray thought about what the words might mean brought a shift in tactics. More writing became visible, as if entire libraries had been written on the stone walls. Renee groaned. She loved history. Soon, paintings began to appear. The words turned to flowing scripts, and the paintings seemed to move. Then the images turned to couples and families, children and love. The sun continued to sink, and the shadows grew. Renee pulled Sillik by the hand and increased their pace. Renee tried talking to Sillik, urging him to move faster. Talking also helped to distract her mind from the sights around her. She wondered if Sillik was seeing what she did.

In the dimming light, shapes began to appear. At first, they were indistinct, but then they began to shift. Renee gasped in fear as the shapes became more recognizable—warriors with strange weapons in leather, leaf-like skirts. The women were bare-breasted with wide hats and long skirts that covered their feet.

The warriors motioned at her as if she were a long-lost friend. When she ignored them, they became angry and drew their blades. *They are not real*, Renee kept telling herself.

The shapes shifted faster. Now her father was welcoming her with open arms. Her mother rose to greet her with a scroll in her hand. Then they began to speak. If she could just stop and listen, she would be able to understand the voices. *No, they are not real.* Their motions became more emphatic. Children appeared—her children. They cried and called to her. She wanted more than anything to understand what they were saying.

Renee tightened her grip on Sillik's hand and pulled him forward. The yana were quivering, their ears flat against their heads, their tails rigid. Suddenly, Renee heard a banshee-like wail as the sun slipped below the horizon and disappeared. With a wave of his hand, Sillik threw balls of light into the air above their heads. Seven glowing balls floated above them and moved with them.

When they heard the sound of galloping hooves behind them, Sillik and Renee broke into a run without further prompting. The yana tugged at their leads; they wanted to turn and fight. Renee yanked savagely on their reins, and the yana snarled but followed. The hooves were getting closer. Renee wasn't sure what was coming, but she didn't want to find out. She raised her arcane shields just in case. Shapes to match the sounds encroached on the edge of her vision. They wouldn't come within the circle of light. They screamed in frustration.

Renee saw twisted, humanoid shapes with horns and hooves. They wielded sharp, black weapons. Rocks and other objects began to land near them, including arrows, which fell harmlessly among the stones in their path. Then balls of energy began to fall. Most exploded harmlessly, but a few bounced back into the air and then exploded, buffeting Sillik.

Voices hammered at Sillik's defenses, and he pulled on Renee's hand. Somewhere in the excitement, he lost the leads to the yana. He couldn't see them. Sillik was about to turn and make a stand when Renee pulled on his arm, and he fell into the normal quiet of a forest evening. Renee kept tugging, and Sillik kicked as hands tried to pull him back into the ruins. One last mighty kick, and he was free. The light he had summoned didn't pass through the veil, and Sillik felt the darkness attacking it.

His chest heaving, Sillik lay on his back and tried to catch his breath. Renee lay beside him, also winded. After a moment, he patted her arm. "You okay?"

Renee nodded. When she could finally speak, she asked, "Did you see all that history? Did you see all those books?"

Sillik shook his head.

"What did you see?"

Sillik wiped his eyes. "The last time I was through here, I saw Nuella. This time, I didn't. I saw lots of different things this time, but I also saw the two of us, and I saw fear—naked fear."

Renee waited for him to say more, but Sillik changed the subject.

"I didn't think it would be that bad," he said. It wasn't nearly that bad the last time I was here." As he rolled over, he saw two sets of large eyes staring at him. The yana had made their way out. Stumbling to his feet, he went over to check on the animals. Apart from some singed fur, they were unscathed.

When he returned, Renee was stacking a pile of stones to mark the boundary. Sillik smiled.

"How many times have you been through there?" Renee asked.

Sillik took a long breath. "Three. Now let's move away from the boundary. I don't want to wake up back inside." Sillik sounded somewhat worried. "Illicians have been coming here since Illicia was built. No one has ever reported attacks like what happened tonight, and never has it taken more than half a day to get through."

Renee smiled grimly. "It took us most of the day."

Sillik frowned. "Something very evil is awakening." Viktorie's words came back to him, and he shuddered.

Renee stood up and gratefully accepted Sillik's help mounting her yana. Sillik continued to walk. Now that his eyes had adjusted to the darkness, he could see the road a few hundred steps away.

That night, Sillik built a real fire against the elevated roadbed. After heating water for tea, he kept the fire bright for a long time. The flames were hidden, and there was little chance of them being seen.

Renee tried to ask Sillik some questions as they sat watching the flames, but he was not in a talkative mood.

Sillik smiled, but he wouldn't talk. She grew worried as he repeatedly looked behind them when he thought she wasn't looking. He seemed moody and kept holding his fingers apart and watching energy flitter between his thumb and forefinger as he stared into the flames. For the first time since leaving Colum, they slept on opposite sides of the camp.

When dawn came, Renee looked back toward the ruins. Her pile of stones was no longer visible. She shuddered. Sillik was awake. She wasn't sure if he had slept. He was looking at the road. It was wide enough for two wagons to pass each other easily. Here and there, she could see the fine line of cracks in the ancient stonework, but other than that, the passage of centuries had not touched the Road of Andel.

After a small breakfast, they broke camp and prepared to leave. There was no way to hide the fire they had made. Renee laughed. "One fire won't make a path."

"We will follow the road northwest for a while. We can move quickly on the road. Then we will turn north. I want to skirt the edge of the Plains of Yaw. I think we will find Nerak forces nearby," Sillik explained.

"I am excited to see the Road of Andel," Renee said. "I have heard about it all my life, but I have never seen it."

"Then let's ride," Sillik said with a tired smile.

Sillik's mood seemed lighter this morning. He grinned broadly as he turned his yana and, with a quick jab of his foot, urged the proud animal to jump onto the road. Renee followed a moment later, hanging on tightly. With a laugh, Sillik took off down the road.

Sillik and Renee rode like lightning throughout that day. At night, they camped beside the road again. Using his bow, Sillik brought down some small game. With fresh meat over the next few days, they were able to save the bulk of their provisions. Every now and then, they stopped to fill their water flasks and allow the yana to drink.

Several days after their escape from the ruins, Sillik and Renee stopped beside a small stream as the sun set. They had just eaten, and Renee was filling her water skin. Sillik was leaning against the road when he noticed the yana looking around, on edge. Instantly, he was on edge too. "Renee," he said quietly as he drew a throwing knife.

Renee looked up. When she saw that Sillik was armed, she laid down the water skin and drew her knife. The yana's ears were back, and their tails twitched with excitement. With a hiss, the yana bounded off together into the forest.

"Will they come back?" Renee asked.

"Yes," Sillik said with false optimism as he sheathed his knife. "After they eat, they will return."

"When?" Renee asked. "By morning?"

Sillik paused as he considered what he should say. "To be honest," he finally said, "I don't know when. They go hunting every night."

"They didn't go out last night," Renee said with a smile.

Sillik laughed. "Perhaps. This is the first time they have left in daylight, though." The yana liked to hunt at night. Each time, they had returned before dawn.

"Granted," Renee said as she went back to filling her water skin.

Sillik looked around. They were in a small clearing. The sky was cloudy, and it looked like it might rain. In the distance, he saw figures high in the sky. For a moment, he thought they were dragons. By the time he had begun to use a spell to enhance his vision, they were gone. Viktorie's words came back to him: "Nine dragons circling." When he told Renee what he had seen, she paled in fear.

"You know it is the first day of the new year," Renee said.

Sillik glanced up. "In Illicia it will be year 7086."

"You Illicians count every year?" Renee laughed. "Most cities count the king's reign. It would be year 28 in my father's reign as governor."

*My reign should have begun last year*, Sillik thought sadly. *Or will it begin this year?*

"So while we wait for the yana to come back, what should we do?" Renee asked, raising her eyebrows and grinning.

Smiling, Sillik said, "We can eat and sleep and maybe talk."

Renee laughed. "Men and their stomachs. That wasn't what I had in mind," she admitted with a smirk. She began unpacking some bread and dried meat. "If not that, tell me about Illicia."

Sillik gave her a sidelong look and raised his eyebrows. Then he nodded to himself and began describing the architecture of Illicia.

When night came and the moons rose in the darkening sky, the two travelers ate their small meal and then lay down to sleep. The clouds had faded away, and the night sky was clear and cool. The stars were bright. Sillik lay awake beside Renee for a long time, thinking. Much later, he drifted off to sleep, only to be awakened before dawn by a soft noise.

As he listened, he heard the noise again. Smiling to himself, Sillik relaxed and moved his hands away from his weapons, which lay unsheathed beside him. The yana had returned. Renee lay close to him on her side and breathed softly in her sleep. Sillik watched her for a few moments, pulled the blanket back over her shoulder, and then laid a protective arm over her.

Shortly after dawn, Sillik was awakened again by the sound of birds chirping in the still morning air. Beside him, Renee was still asleep. Her hair lay tangled across her face. Small twigs and leaves clung to her hair and clothing and moved slowly as she breathed. Her dagger lay unsheathed beside her right hand. Gently, Sillik nudged her foot. She awoke slowly, and for a brief moment she looked startled, as if she didn't remember where she was. Then her memory came back, and she smiled and stretched. When Renee saw the yana, her face broke into another happy smile.

Sillik walked to the creek and splashed some water on his face. He saw his reflection momentarily. He looked tired and rough. He needed to shave. Most of all, he needed more good sleep. He splashed more water on his face.

They ate some dried meat and then broke camp. As the sun rose, Sillik walked through the camp and erased any signs of their presence. Then they mounted the yana and headed northwest.

When they stopped at noon to eat some dried meat, hard bread, and berries that Renee had found in the clearing the afternoon before, the River Vivare was in sight. It lay across their path like a silver thread on the horizon. Sillik knew that when the road had been built, there had been a bridge over the river, but centuries of floods and neglect had swept it away. Travelers today crossed by boat. Sillik originally had considered turning due north here, but the previous night he had decided to continue northwest toward the Plains of Yaw.

It took another few days to reach the river. The weather tried to discourage them, with afternoon storms drenching them. The yana hissed in irritation at the rain, and Sillik and Renee fared little better. Their cloaks afforded some protection from the elements, but the driving rain eventually soaked them. The nights were little better. While the yana licked their coats dry at night, Sillik and Renee dried their clothes before the superheated stones that Sillik enchanted with the seven laws.

When they reached the river, the road led to the edge of the water and then disappeared. Sillik could still see the remains of the bridge, which started upward in what Sillik imagined had once been a graceful arc. A series of stone pilings stood in a straight line across the river, each supporting small sections of the old bridge. Today, Sillik supposed, the only travelers on the bridge were the birds that nested there. He could see scores of them flying around the lonely stone towers, fishing and skimming across the surface of the water. The nearest piling was stained white from centuries of bird excrement. Near the water, the piling was green with algae and moss.

Breathing deeply, Sillik smiled. The smell of the water was intoxicating. To a man born in the desert, it was a wondrous sight. It also brought back pleasant memories from his travels. He closed his eyes and took another deep breath. For a moment, he simply looked at the river. Just as he was wondering how they would cross, he saw a small dot far out across the river.

Using the Seven Laws, Sillik focused on the dot. In his mind, the shape exploded into view. It was a barge. He saw a wide sail and slaves rowing great, sweeping oars, in an image reminiscent of the warships that had prowled the seas for a millennium. Turning his sight to his own side of the river, Sillik saw a large camp in the trees a short distance downstream consisting of almost a hundred soldiers. Inside the camp, Sillik saw dozens of large wagons filled with cloth and leather. Shaking his head to break the spell, Sillik calculated how long it would take the barge to reach shore. Considering the present speed and the width of the river, he concluded it would be sometime the following morning.

As Sillik and Renee sat motionless before the mighty river, a yellow-haired man wearing the leather of a soldier walked up the hill toward them. Sillik studied the man as he drew near. The stranger's eyes glittered with a shrewd and cunning intelligence, but he also seemed jovial and relaxed. His tanned face was round, and his nose crooked. He was slightly plump, as if he had spent more time riding in wagons than walking. His hands were scarred. A triangular piece of brown fabric was sewn to his right shoulder, proclaiming him to be a merchant. The belt at his waist was wide, finely tooled, and stained brown. The man's high brown boots were worn and covered in mud. Sillik saw a slim dagger thrust in the top of one boot. Another dagger was strapped to his wrist. He stopped a dozen paces before Sillik and Renee. He had a shrewd eye, and Sillik knew this was someone he would like.

For a moment, the stranger studied Sillik and Renee. Then he held out his empty right hand in the traditional demonstration of peace. "My name is Wolfstein," he said as his eyes flickered to Sillik's belt and sword.

Sillik returned the salute. "I am Sillik. My companion is Renee."

"Ah," Wolfstein said as he bowed with a flourish, "a beautiful woman restores the soul."

"Thank you," Renee said, reddening slightly.

Wolfstein nodded at their mounts. "The beasts you ride are beautiful. Would you be interested in selling them? I can give you a good price. Don't turn me down right away—my price will be fair."

"No," Sillik responded with a smile. This man truly was a merchant.

"For some reason I didn't think you would," Wolfstein said cheerfully, "though I would have given you a good price. Where are you headed, warrior?"

When Sillik hesitated, Wolfstein said, "You have my word by the Seven Gods that you may trust me."

"We need passage across the river," Sillik said. "We can pay." Then with a grin, he threw a leg over the yana's head and slid to the ground.

Wolfstein eyed them alertly. "Some extra coin would not be a bad thing. I can get you across. Your beasts will make it more expensive."

"I have the gold," Sillik said.

"Aye," Wolfstein said appraisingly. "I am sure you do. Ten pieces for each beast and two for each of you."

"Sillik, no," Renee said. "We can follow the river upstream."

Sillik smiled as he held up his hand and looked the merchant in the eye. "Two for each yana and one for each of us."

"It's a wide river," Wolfstein observed with a wide grin. "Eight and one each."

"I can see across the river. I paid less to visit some islands last year," Sillik said as he looked toward the river. "I couldn't see the islands. Four and one each."

"Rivers have currents, and they are hard to row across," Wolfstein said, hooking his fingers on his belt, "and I wager you didn't have those two yana to take to those islands of yours. Six, and I agree to one for you and your lovely companion."

Sillik paused. "Split the difference? Five and one?"

Wolfstein looked disappointed. "I suppose I won't take much of a loss agreeing to that. But you are taking food out of my child's mouth. Now where are you heading?"

"We are heading toward the northern mountains," Sillik responded, careful not to be too specific.

"I am sorry for you, my new friend." Wolfstein shook his head sadly. "You do not know what you do."

"What's wrong?" Renee asked.

"Come with me," Wolfstein said. Then he turned and walked back toward his camp. "I will still see you across the river, but I would rather not."

Sillik and Renee glanced at each other, and Renee dismounted with a worried frown.

Quietly, Sillik said, "It will be okay. Let's see what he has to say." Then they led their yana after Wolfstein.

As they walked, Wolfstein explained the loaded wagons and warriors with a hearty laugh. "I am a merchant, as you know. The city of Suran wants the cloth that is made in Teris. I buy the cloth in Teris, where it is cheap, and carry it downriver to the falls of Siren and then eastward across the land to Suran, where I sell it at a much higher price."

Near the center of Wolfstein's camp, the trio sat down around a small campfire. The guards were watching them, and Sillik felt uncomfortable. They had left the yana a short distance away. Already, the huge animals had curled up in the warm sunlight, licked their fur until they were satisfied with their appearance, and then happily drifted off to sleep. Wolfstein excused himself a moment. When he returned, he dismissed the guards and held up a wineskin.

Wolfstein drew the dagger from his waist to cut the seal.

"Interesting weapon," Renee observed. "I haven't seen one of those before."

"Crystal blade," Wolfstein said as he held up the weapon and looked at the milky-white blade. "I don't use metal." He grunted as he began working on the seal.

"Bren uses crystal knives," Sillik said as he watched the merchant.

"Lots of cities in the north use crystal for knives," Wolfstein muttered. "Crystal is cheap and plentiful. Nothing unusual about it." He poured the deep red wine into three clay cups. As he passed the cups out, he began to explain. "Now about that crossing," he said. "War is abroad. The city of Ynak has declared war on Nerak. Peol is expected to join Ynak within days."

As Sillik's face creased in concern, Wolfstein continued. "Even now the dragons of Ynak are taking wing."

Seemingly unnoticed beside them, Renee paled and looked up sharply.

"The other news is"–Wolfstein looked around the small clearing suspiciously–"I have heard that the Knights of Nerak have sworn the blood vow and are already in the field with large numbers. They intend to reduce Ynak and Peol to ash. Now I know something of Nerak. When they swear that oath, they will do what they say–or damn well die trying."

Wolfstein paused to drink some of his wine. "Now you look like you know how to use that sword of yours. I am always looking for guards in my caravan. I could use an experienced man and woman," he said as his eyes shifted to Renee and her weapons.

"I understand the risks," Sillik said with a sidelong glance at Renee.

Renee raised her eyebrows as she looked at him.

"*We* understand the risks," Sillik corrected.

Wolfstein eyed the two and said, "War of this magnitude has not occurred in centuries. Each of the cities is allied with dozens of others. All could be dragged into this war. Hells, maybe even the Illicians will fight with Nerak."

Sillik nodded his agreement as he sipped his wine. Suddenly, he remembered the shapes he had seen in the sky several days before. If war was really abroad, and the dragons had awoken, they could be in serious danger.

"As I was saying," Wolfstein continued, "the land shall soon be torn by war. It wouldn't be wise to journey north on war-bred yana." He paused and gave Sillik a strange look. "Are you well?"

Sillik was suddenly aware of his pale face and the cold sweat running down his cheeks. "It's nothing," he said as he rubbed his face briskly. "You just surprised me." He drank the wine in his cup. When he had drained the goblet, he held it out for a refill. "Even though war is abroad, I have business in the north."

"The summer has been cool," Wolfstein responded, "and the mouth of the Bay of Felin has not thawed."

"So," Renee explained, "the mouth of the bay is preventing the pirates from raiding. They will move inland since they can't get to the ocean."

Wolfstein nodded, his eyes narrowing. "If I were determined to go north," Wolfstein said as he poured another cup of wine for himself, "despite all the dangers in the land now, then I would head through the Plains of Yaw toward the Blasted Hills."

Sillik started as he thought about the piece of paper from his father with the map symbol for the Blasted Hills. The last battles of the demon wars had taken place in those mountains.

Wolfstein picked up the cap from the wineskin and began absently scoring the wood with his crystal knife. Sillik watched the knife work for a moment as he waited for the merchant to continue.

"But stay toward the center of the Plains of Yaw. Then, in all likelihood, you'll avoid the Knights of Nerak and the dragons of Ynak. Then—"

"But won't that be where the fighting is?" Renee asked. "Both cities are at war. Won't their forces meet in the middle?"

"No," Wolfstein said, "because both cities will send armies to try to destroy the other city quickly. Therefore, the fighting will be fiercest in the areas neighboring each city. Don't you agree, Sillik?"

Sillik nodded. Wolfstein started to say something else but was cut short as a cry of alarm broke the quiet of the camp. Instantly, the color drained from Wolfstein's cheerful face.

"River pirates! To arms, to arms!" someone shouted.

Wolfstein dropped his goblet, and the pottery shattered on the rock, splashing wine on his tunic. Jumping to his feet, he yelled orders to his men. At the same time, several men jumped into one of the wagons and threw weapons to all who passed.

Sillik and Renee declined. They were already well armed.

# CHAPTER 23

## Dinner

A S TRUMPETS BLARED with
bright, metallic fanfare, Briana led
the way into the banquet hall, with Lord General Greenup at her side. Fifty
Illician swordsmen dressed in polished mail marched in step behind her. All of
the swordsmen were also masters of the Seven Laws. Called the Long Knives,
they were the toughest, meanest warriors Briana had ever trained with. In a
one-on-one fight, she could hold her own with them, but they normally didn't
fight one-on-one. They used cooperative fighting techniques that combined
swords, martial arts, and magic. Their armor clanked and rattled as they took
up positions around the room.

The Shelnorans and the merchant guild leaders had been seated earlier
and had been waiting for Briana to arrive. They looked around in surprise at
the overtly militaristic display. Briana smiled to herself. *Keep them off-balance*,
she thought. She glanced at Greenup and smiled. Lord Demar, chief of the
merchants' guild, was furious with Briana over the change. His thin face was red,
and his eyes nearly bulged from his head. Over the objections of the merchants,
Briana and Greenup had changed the format of the dinner. Something about the
visitors from Shelnor had unsettled Briana and Greenup, and so they thought
it wise to take precautions.

Briana sat down and nodded for the feast to begin. Lord General Greenup
sat to her right as her escort for the evening. He was also there to protect her.

Lord Minen of Shelnor sat to her left as a guest. Most of the council was present for the state dinner, as were all of the major merchant guilds. Most of the guild leaders eyed her with thinly veiled anger over the military presence, but Briana did not care. Lord Demar, who had organized the entire week, was standing at the back of the room. He looked at Briana and nodded nervously.

Briana stood again and raised her goblet. Slowly, the faces turned to look at her, and the voices trailed off. It was her job to say a few words, which she did quickly without creating more problems. Then it was Lord Minen's turn to speak. As he stood and looked out at the assembled council members and craft guildsmen, he thanked Illicia for the friendship and the stone. After uttering a few other platitudes, he sat down. Immediately, servants brought out platters of food.

While they waited to be served, Minen put his hand on Briana's and suggested a more intimate touching. Briana forced a smile as she deftly withdrew her hand and rolled her eyes. She stifled her desire to break his fingers, one at a time. The chief of the Shelnor delegation was a short, fat, balding excuse of a man, and Briana felt revulsion every time he touched her. But he was the Shelnor envoy, and she couldn't kill him, at least not yet.

Minen grinned as he looked at her breasts. Nisha had insisted on the formal gown, but Briana felt overly exposed, and she struggled to breathe with the corset. She picked up her goblet with a small smile as she imagined his reaction to hearing his knuckles break one by one. Musicians played a quiet tune in the back of the room. Briana hated the sound. It was distracting and irritating at the same time.

The Illicians smiled politely as dinner was placed before them. The meal was a Shelnor favorite. Those who had been warned ate sparingly. Briana thought the main dish smelled vile and disgusting. It tasted worse. She had liked fish when she had traveled the land, and she liked sandfish, but this Shelnor dish was something else, a salted flat fish on a bed of sweet grain. Accompanying the fish was a plump, yellow fruit that, according to what they had been told, grew along the shore. It was stringy and tough and unlike any fruit Briana had ever tasted.

Fortunately, the Shelnorans seemed pleased and ate heartily. The Illicians, however, eyed the meal with trepidation. Some had already taken a bite and then pushed away their plates.

Lord Minen looked at her as he put a piece of fish into his mouth. "What do you know about these Gold Robes, Warmaster?"

"Excuse me?" Briana asked as she put her goblet down. She grimaced as the water splashed on her hand. In yet another accommodation, the Illicians had not served wine with dinner. Shelnor had outlawed fermented drinks and didn't eat red meat. She had been allowed to sip only water the entire evening.

"You know, these Gold Robes, as you call them, these people who can do magic and other nonsense," Minen said, watching her carefully.

"You think it's nonsense?" Briana asked as she toyed with her goblet.

"You don't really believe the legends about the demon wars," he said, goading her. "And these magicians, these Gold Robes, these masters of the Seven Laws—all they do is trickery." He cut another piece of fish and stuffed it into his mouth.

"Really," Briana said with a forced smile. "Magic always seemed real enough to me." Suddenly, she was glad that she had not revealed her mastery of the Seven Laws to the trade delegation. "I can show you skeletons of schula that fought for the demons in those wars," she continued calmly. "Their bones are very real."

"Pah," Minen said as he crammed more fish into his mouth. "Fabrications to deceive the weak-minded."

Briana bristled with white-hot anger. She wanted to teach this man what the Seven Laws could do.

Greenup moved beside her, his fingers speaking silently. *Calm and provoke?*

Briana glanced at the lord general and then took a deep breath and tried to relax. She nodded as her mind filled in the missing words. *Be calm; don't let him provoke you.*

Suddenly, Minen was caressing the back of her hand. Briana felt her skin crawl as she broke contact.

"Don't put no stock in the charlatans who pretend," Minen said as he leered at her. "His Lordship, Brother Simpsen, the leader of our city, has promised to drive them out of Shelnor."

"In Illicia," Briana said, "the Gold Robes do great good."

Minen put down his utensils and looked squarely at Briana. "We think anyone who deceives is evil, and those magicians deceive."

Briana was shocked at his words. "What about the Nine Dark Gods?"

"Brother Simpsen says not to believe in them. They are stories to tell children," Minen said as he slurped his fruit juice.

"What about the Seven Gods?" Briana asked.

Minen looked at her. "They are no better than the Nine."

Greenup stiffened in anger.

"So why are you here?" Briana asked as she put down her goblet and placed her hands in her lap. "You have to know about Illicia's use of the Seven Laws and our involvement in the demon wars."

Minen smiled. "We need the stone. You have the best price. The stone will be a wedding present from our leader." Minen leered at Briana. "Our king is seeking a wife, but I am not."

Briana did not smile as she looked at the merchant. "I'm sorry. We were talking about stone."

Lord Minen spread his hands innocently. "We buy the best stone, and Brother Simpsen has said the demon wars never happened."

"Really?" Greenup said. "And what evidence does he have?"

Minen smiled. "What evidence do you have that they did?"

Greenup spread his hands. "This entire city."

"A city built by people with an inflated sense of worth, so they write legends in which they do great deeds," Minen said.

Briana laughed and picked up her goblet with her right hand as her left hand signed to Greenup the same "relax" message that he had given her.

Briana leaned back in her chair and frowned. Just a few weeks earlier, on the anniversary of the city's founding, the Dark Gods had appeared on the nine peaks surrounding the city, and all of the Seven Gods had appeared above the city. It was recorded in the Seven Books that all of the Seven Gods had helped lay out the city and helped lay the cornerstone of the keep. The fact that the Nine Gods appeared each year was not spoken of, lest outsiders get the wrong idea.

"So you don't believe what the Gold Robes do is magic?" Briana asked, forcing a smile.

Minen's eyes narrowed. "No," he said slowly. "We do not trust them. They consort with the Nine."

Briana lowered her voice. "In Illicia the Gold Robes consort with the Seven Gods, and we trust them. We trust them so much that they are our teachers, our lawgivers, and our judges. For seventy centuries, that has been fact."

Minen stuffed another piece of fish in his mouth, anger flashing in his eyes.

Greenup signed, *Caution*. Briana felt his unease, as if he were yelling it.

Minen swallowed and cleared his throat noisily. "Brother Simpsen says we should not trust them."

"Do you do everything this Brother Simpsen says?" Briana asked.

Minen snorted. "We owe our sovereign our obedience. But tell me, Lady Briana, how does a woman like you become warmaster of Illicia?"

Briana almost choked and then took a deep breath. "A woman like me?"

Minen smiled. "I mean, you are not a warrior. You were appointed to this position, as I have been told."

Briana started to issue a blistering retort, but Greenup's signed message cut her off. *No truth*, he said. Briana took another breath and, with difficulty, let her anger cool.

Minen took another bite of his fish and washed it down with water. "You must know someone to have been appointed to the warmaster position. What do you know about war? It seems unlikely that he would leave a woman in charge."

Briana leaned forward, purposely exposing a little more of her breasts. "I know the prince."

"Ah," Minen said as his eyes widened. He cut another bite of fish as he considered her cleavage. "Yes, your prince. Where is he anyway? And why did he leave?"

"As we explained, Prince Sillik had urgent Illician business and had to postpone his coronation until his return. He is the prince, and that is good enough for Illicia," Briana said, sticking to the cover story upon which they had all agreed.

"Lord Demar said he is on a blood quest to kill those responsible for killing his father," Minen said, watching Briana over his cup.

Briana stiffened in anger. *I will kill that man*, she thought. "The purpose of Prince Sillik's absence is Illician business and should not concern you, Lord Minen."

Minen eyed Briana as he put his cup down. "I see," he said icily. "But rather than argue, let us watch our entertainment." He waved his hand as a band of acrobats ran onto the floor of the dining hall.

Briana did her best to force thoughts of murder from her mind as she watched the performance.

# CHAPTER 24

## The Walls

LORD GENERAL GREENUP stood atop the keep. In the darkness, the white walls glowed dimly, as did the lights of the towers. He took a deep breath and exhaled slowly. The state dinner with the delegation from Shelnor had been long and tedious. As soon as the dinner ended, he had escaped. The smell of the desert was strong tonight. He sighed with contentment. The stars were bright, but the moons had already set. It would be a dark night.

As he did every morning and night, Greenup walked the keep's walls with his grandson, Keltic. He spoke to the guards and made sure all was well. As he walked, he kept a hand on his sword. Habits learned over a lifetime were hard to break. Greenup and Keltic had begun the tradition of walking the walls on the night that Keltic's father died in combat with the Nomads.

"Briana tells me that she is going to promote you to swordmaster," Greenup said with a smile. "Congratulations."

"Thank you," Keltic said.

"You don't seem excited about it," Greenup observed. "You have worked hard for this."

The younger man frowned. "With everything that's happening, it's hard to be excited about more change."

"Change is the only thing that stays the same," Greenup explained. "It is what life is about. Just remember—do your job, the best you can every day. Protect her. She will need it now that Sillik is gone."

"Is it true that Briana is going to marry the prince?" Keltic asked. "It is what everyone in the barracks is saying."

"I wouldn't believe that," Greenup laughed. "They are both hotheaded. At one time I might have believed that, but not anymore." Greenup paused to greet a guard before he continued. "Something is different now about him. Is that what has you worried?"

"No," Keltic said, "but he does worry me. He attracts danger, and that draws danger to Briana."

"That he does, boy," Greenup said with a chuckle. "He reminds me of your father."

"What did you think of Shelnor?" Keltic asked, steering the conversation away from painful topics.

"Pompous asses," Greenup said with a grimace. "Think they own everyone since they are buying our stone. The warmaster suffered the worst."

"Why?" Keltic asked.

Just as Greenup was about to reply, his skin tingled. The guards who should be ahead were not at their posts! Suddenly alert, he held up his left hand and made a fist as he drew his sword with his right. Dark spots glistened on the parapets. "Guards, to me!" Greenup bellowed.

Keltic drew his sword almost as quickly and turned to guard Greenup's back.

The sound of running feet told Greenup his yell had been heard. The shadowed intruders around the checkpoint heard the sounds too and leapt into motion. Suddenly, the lord general was wrestling two of the figures as they fought for his blade. His sword, forced out of his hand, clattered on the stone. The arrival of additional guards pulled the attackers off Greenup. Lights flared as someone activated the alarms. Horns sounded in the darkness.

Someone dressed in black knocked Keltic to the ground. Greenup saw a face that he almost recognized. In the chaos, a woman squirmed free and lunged at him with a dagger. Greenup twisted and caught the woman's arm. It broke with an audible crack. The woman fell to the ground, crying out in pain.

Another dark figure jumped out of the darkness. Producing a knife, the figure lunged at Greenup, who grinned. *A fair fight*, he thought. He caught the hand behind the knife and then stepped into the attacker, forcing the assailant back over his knee. The attacker shifted, and in the blink of an eye, he was dead. The body fell to the ground.

Greenup threw an illuminating ball of light into the air as he and Keltic surveyed the carnage. One injured woman lay on the ground as well as the dead man who had attacked him. Six guards also lay on the ground.

Guards searched the woman for weapons before administering a sleeping potion designed to prevent her from using magic. The woman would be pain-free but incapable of two successive thoughts for the rest of the night. This would give the Gold Robes time to heal her injuries before they questioned her.

Distantly, Greenup heard alarms ringing from the main walls. He ran toward the keep. As he did, he saw a flash of light in one of the rooms near the top of the keep. "Damn! Seal the keep! Seal the city!" he shouted as he ran toward the stairs.

In the light, he saw a fine wire leading from the walls to the keep. *Damn,* he thought, *they climbed the keep.*

# CHAPTER 25

## Assassins

WHEN BRIANA RETURNED to her room, it was very late. Her guards had stopped in the hallway a dozen steps from her door. She was still angry with Lord Minen. Just because he could afford to buy Illician stone, he thought he could buy her as well. She instinctively brushed her hands against her dress to remove his slime. The sun would be rising soon.

Sillik had been right; she did hate this job. Months of planning had gone into the events of the last few days. Security, travel, rooms, entertainment, food, and countless other details had all been considered. The results of that planning had culminated in today.

The seneschal had been busy throughout the evening. It had been Tanya's responsibility to ensure the evening progressed without a mishap. Briana had seen her hovering in the background all evening, badgering the servers and disappearing into the kitchens between each course.

Dinner had been long and arduous. Briana never would have expected a warmaster to preside over a trade delegation dinner, but as the head of the city, Briana knew what she had to do: smile and ignore the innuendos. Too many people depended on the sale of Illician stone. Lord Demar also had hovered in the background all evening. He was paranoid that some mistake or misunderstanding would cause the deal to be withdrawn.

Briana had smiled in satisfaction as she studied the guests. Most of the men from Shelnor wore pale colors, especially soft blues. The women wore brightly colored silk gowns. On their jackets the men wore family crests that told stories about the families, she had been told. Supposedly, it was possible to deduce ten generations of family history from a single glance at a family crest, but when Briana glanced at a man's crest, she saw only a bewildering combination of symbols and words.

The most common symbols were ships or anchors. One man in particular had a scene of a ship at sea woven on his back. Several of the guards had snickered in disbelief at so much water. Briana had reassigned the men on the spot to guard the lizard waste bins for a month. She would not have the guests shown disrespect. If the lizards smelled, their waste was even worse. The guards would learn their lesson.

Briana was glad that the deal had been signed earlier that day. She laughed to herself as she thought about what might have happened if the signing had not occurred until after dinner. The chamberlain of the keep was also happy. The deal was worth a lot to the city, and the taxes would help.

Briana smiled. She was almost done with these ship-faring fools. Why they wanted stone, she had no idea. But the delegates from Shelnor had purchased seventy-five stone sculptures. It was a large contract by any measure.

Minen, the trade delegation leader, had introduced all of his delegation and then regaled Briana with stories about the personal failings of each of the men and women. She had laughed politely and frowned in disapproval when expected. Meanwhile, she had seethed inwardly. This was no way for a leader to behave. She would have demoted any Illician soldier to garbage disposal, or worse, if he had spoken of his troops the way Minen had spoken of the members of his delegation.

During the evening, she had been introduced to so many people that she was dizzy by the end. Seemingly all the guests had used the opportunity to introduce either themselves or their son to her. Twenty-three notes had been passed to her, according to Nisha. Briana grimaced. Nisha would read them all and tell her what she needed to know.

As expected, offers of matrimony had been blowing in like sand. At last count, there were over sixty offers of one kind or another. One lord had been so desperate to marry off his children that he had suggested either his son or his daughter. Briana had politely declined both offers.

Now, as Briana entered her room, Nisha signaled for the other women to come into the room. Marla, one of her maids, pulled the drapes across the balcony doors. The bracelets on Marla's arm jingled softly as she moved. Briana smiled. It wasn't likely that someone could be watching her near the top of the keep. She could see over the entire city from that balcony. It was an impressive view. Only one floor was higher than hers.

"I would like to retire," Briana said. She had found that she could get the women out of her room quicker if she pretended to be tired. This gave her more time to work uninterrupted on what was truly important.

Quickly and efficiently, the ladies removed her jewelry and unpinned her hair so it cascaded down her back. At the same time, beneath the table, Briana pushed the tight-fitting shoes off her feet. She sighed with relief. Her feet had been hurting all evening. She wiggled her toes in delight.

"Now be still, my lady," Nisha admonished as she and the maids untied and unhooked the formal gown that Briana had been forced to wear for the occasion. If it had been up to Briana, she would have worn pants, boots, a blouse, and of course, her mail shirt. The gown was so tight that it had been impossible to wear her mail, though. She had felt naked without it. She might as well have been topless, the way the gown lifted her breasts and accentuated her cleavage. Minen hadn't minded, though. When the corset was finally loosened, Briana took a deep breath and sighed contentedly. She hated that thing.

True to her word, Nisha produced a cup of warm milk and some warm bread and set the items on the dressing table. Briana had insisted on wearing a weapon and had managed to slip a throwing knife in a sheath strapped to her wrist. Nisha tisked when she saw Briana remove it. She was efficient, but she disliked weapons—especially, it seemed, when women wore them.

Finally, the maids helped her into a sleeping gown. Why did everything have to be a gown? Before she had been appointed warmaster, she had slept in a long shirt or nothing at all.

Nisha shooed the maids out, after which she and Briana went over the schedule for the next day. It would be a busy one. Then Nisha began extinguishing the candles.

"Please leave the candles on my desk, Nisha," Briana said as she suppressed a yawn and then picked up her cup of milk. "I wish to read for a few minutes." She sipped her milk gratefully despite wishing for something stronger—wine perhaps or, even better, whiskey.

Nisha nodded. "As you say, my lady." She left the candles on Briana's desk and a candle beside the bed. Then she bowed and swept out of the room, closing the doors behind her.

Briana listened. In the distance, she heard voices and a hundred other sounds of people, normal for this time of night. The sounds from the city were even more distant and quiet. Any rational person would have been in bed and asleep long ago.

Briana waited a few moments and then reached into her desk drawer and pulled out the papers she had hidden. She had tried to write down every word

Sillik's father had said to her in the months before his death, using the Seven Laws to recall their conversations. There had to be some clues, some hint at what she was supposed to do or what Sillik needed her to do. She had also written down every word Lady Silvia had said.

The candle flames on her desk danced suddenly in the air. Briana felt her heart race. She heard the unexpected sound of metal rubbing on metal. Feeling a surge of excitement, she saw that the doors to her room had not budged.

The throwing knife was still on her desk, but it was too small and delicate for what she needed now. She felt eyes watching her. The hairs on the back of her neck stood on end. She resisted the urge to turn and face the intruder. Slowly, she reached under the desk for the larger throwing knife she had hidden there. The leather sheath was well oiled, so she was able to draw the blade silently. Reversing the knife so it was ready to throw, she marshaled her arcane powers and then stood up and crept toward the door. Her path would take her close to the weapon wall. If she walked slowly enough, maybe she would have time to grab one.

Briana sensed at least three people outside, perhaps as many as five. She thought she could hear breathing. Maybe it was her imagination. No, she was being watched. Her warrior's intuition was on alert. As she walked, she faced the door to her room, as if she intended to leave, but her eyes were watching the drapes across the balcony. Movement would mean her ploy had failed.

She turned her head slightly and saw her battle armor standing on its mannequin against the wall of the room. For a moment she wished she were wearing it. But she knew in the fight to come, agility would be her greatest ally. Armor gave protection, but it reduced mobility. And yet the hard lizard leather spoke to her longingly.

Briana wrapped her defensive energies around herself. First the air shimmered, and then she felt a prickling sensation as the air around her blurred. It would be harder for her foes to see her exact position now. With her enhanced senses, she saw faint outlines of people behind the curtain. They were breathing hard. *Good*, she thought, *they will be winded*.

She took a few more steps and then reached out to touch a throwing knife on the wall, caressing its hilt with her slender finger. Soon it would begin. The candles danced again, and then everything seemed to happen at once.

Four people burst into her room from the balcony, knocking over a vase. Briana drew a curved scimitar from the wall and spun in one move. She saw the drapes tear open. A crossbow bolt exploded against the wall behind her. Then she felt a slicing pain across her abdomen. Her defensive shields crumbled as pain washed over her.

Her mind recognized the faces: they were the Shelnor acrobats from supper. She gasped in surprise as she twisted and threw the dagger. The lead intruder fell over backward and dropped the crossbow. As Briana turned, she threw a ball of light at the ceiling. The room exploded with light, causing the second intruder to shield his eyes. He tried to kill Briana with his sword, but she twisted again, and the man's blade missed.

The second and third intruders raced to the doors to secure them. She threw a ball of fire at them but slipped in the water and broken pieces of vase. The fireball exploded against the tapestry-covered wall with a roar. The tapestry burst into flame, and the stone itself seemed to drip from the heat. Echoes of the explosion rumbled through the keep. *No one will be sleeping now*, Briana thought with satisfaction.

Briana hit the floor and rolled. Pain tore through her feet as she regained her footing among the shards of broken vase. The floor was slippery from blood and water. Her opponent grinned and tried to skewer her. Twisting, she slipped and fell to the floor again. She felt her gown tear as the blade missed her by the thickness of the fabric. Her attacker's sword shattered tiles behind her. She scrambled back to her feet and reached out to her wall. A short sword leapt to her fingers, and she smiled in appreciation. *Magic provides what is required.*

Her guards burst into the room, shattering the wooden door and sending splinters flying everywhere. Together, the two guards fought their way to Briana. One of the guards died instantly, a sword through his chest. Briana thought it was Saleen but had no time to check as she parried another sword thrust.

She heard alarm bells and more running feet. Voices yelled, and time seemed to slow. She killed her opponent in a quick flurry of strokes. *Hummingbird bites,* she thought. She spun and saw Hillself sparring with two of the intruders. As she rushed to his aid, one of the acrobats, a woman, leapt at Briana and grabbed a handful of her hair. It tore, and her scalp exploded in pain. Briana dropped her sword and then spun and broke the woman's sword arm. Her opponent was a slender, almost dainty woman. Briana remembered the moves she had made during the acrobatic performance. *You will not fool me*, Briana thought.

The woman howled in pain and dropped her sword. Her arm dangled at her side at an odd angle, bone protruding from the skin. Her other fist sliced upward at the warmaster's face. Briana felt her nose break. Blood cascaded down her face, and stars exploded in her eyes. Ignoring the pain, she brought her knee up into the woman's stomach and felt her gown tear again. Air exploded out of the woman's lungs, and her head came up. Briana smashed her palm into her opponent's nose. The woman went rigid as the cartilage broke and was shoved up into her brain. Briana grabbed the woman's head, but the light in her eyes faded, and Briana was left holding a dead woman. She let the body drop to the floor.

Briana twirled and scooped up a weapon just in time to see another body fall to the floor. Wounded and bloody, Hillself stood above his opponent. Bleeding profusely from cuts across his face and down his arm, he looked unsteady on his feet. His face was pale, and he was breathing hard. As Briana watched, he sank woozily to his knees.

Just then, a dozen guards burst into the room, weapons drawn. Their eyes took in the carnage and the bodies with surprise.

Briana was quick with her orders. "Find the rest of the Shelnor acrobats. They scaled the keep. Seal the keep if you have to. Hell, close the city until everyone in that delegation is accounted for. Arrest the entire damned trade delegation. I want to know how they climbed the keep and how they knew where I was. Arrest Lord Demar as well and find out if he had any part in this."

She closed her eyes in pain. When she opened them again, she threw a forbidding across the balcony door. No one would get through there. The guards looked surprised, but the captain nodded with approval. The light from her initial spell was beginning to fade, so Briana glanced up and waved her hand. The light brightened and stabilized. "What are you waiting for?" she growled at the captain of the guard.

"Yes, Warmaster!" the captain answered as he glanced uneasily at the glowing wall across the balcony.

"Get Lords Kenton and Greenup. I want them here," Briana added. Now that the excitement was over, she was beginning to feel her injuries.

"They have already been sent for, Warmaster," the captain said. "Are you hurt? Do we need healers?"

"Summon healers for Hillself," she said without thought.

She looked down to assess the damage to herself. The front of her nightgown was plastered to her body with perspiration, water, and blood. It had been ripped in many places, and one of her breasts was mostly exposed. Her scalp screamed, and she saw long strands of dust-colored hair on the floor and in her opponent's hand. Briana knew that her face must be a mess. Her lips were swelling. As she touched her nose gingerly, she could feel that it was broken and swelling. She could breathe only through her mouth, which was filled with the coppery taste of blood from her lips. Her heart still beat wildly. A stabbing pain across her abdomen told her that the crossbow bolt had come too close. She probed the wound gently with her fingers. It was shallow but had bled a lot.

Her feet were covered in blood and screamed in pain. She lifted a foot and found several long cuts where the glass had sliced her. She bit her lip in pain as she pulled a particularly long piece of glass out of her foot. To distract her mind, she shouted more orders. "Check the outside of the keep and make sure more of those acrobats are not on the walls." She swapped feet and found only a few cuts and no glass in the second one.

"Yes, Warmaster," the captain answered. He looked at guards, and they ran to do her bidding.

Lord Kenton stumbled into her room, half-dressed, and immediately paled at the sight of the bodies and Briana.

"Heal me," Briana commanded when she saw him.

"I can have healers here," Kenton said. "I can have my wife, Elizabet."

"No!" Briana said. She pointed at him. "You, now. I have work to do, and I can't do it if I'm bleeding with open wounds." *And in pain*, she could have added, but it wouldn't be right to admit to feeling pain.

Briana knew she could wait for the healers, but she trusted Kenton and didn't want to wait. Another factor right now was the thought of someone she didn't know getting close to her. The healers often had to touch the wounds, and she didn't like that idea. *Damn Sillik for doing this to me*, she cursed.

Kenton looked like he was going to argue but acquiesced. "You are going to have to sit," he said as he took her arm and led her away from the scene. She would have resisted, but Kenton's hand was firm as he led her to her bed.

In the distance, she heard shouts outside the keep. Alarms rang throughout the city. People would be waking up and wondering what had happened. Soon there would be panic. If she weren't seen, people would fear the worst. She needed to be seen tonight and in the morning so that people would know the attack had failed. Distantly, she heard the distinct sounds of the iron bars falling and locking the gates.

She sat on the bed, grimacing at the damage she was doing to the sheets. The sooner he healed her, the better it would be. She reached under her pillow and closed her hand around the hilt of a knife she kept hidden there. The familiar feeling was comforting. Emotions began to flood through her. Anger was the chief feeling. She nearly shook with rage at what had been done to her and to her city.

Kenton bowed his head as he summoned the necessary powers. "Briana, my dear, you must calm yourself and open to the healing."

Briana cursed and told herself, *Vengeance must wait.* Closing her eyes, she said, "I am ready."

Then, starting with the most serious wounds, Kenton touched the injured areas with the tips of his fingers, one by one. She felt the tissues knitting as his hand moved. It itched terribly everywhere he touched. His healing also found glass shards she had missed. Briana hissed in pain as he drew the fragments out. A healer would have been able to spare her the pain, and for a moment she regretted insisting that he do the job. This was battlefield healing, crude but effective.

At least she would be whole and able to do what needed to be done. After her feet and abdomen, he healed her nose and lips. The he found a nasty slice on her arm that, for the life of her, Briana didn't know how she had acquired.

When she opened her eyes, she saw Nisha peering in. The steward looked worried, but when she caught Briana looking at her, she smiled. It was the first smile Briana had seen on the woman's face. Nisha nodded and then turned and left. The guards blocked the exit and did not allow anyone else into the room.

Briana turned her head and looked at the bodies for clues. The acrobats' hands were covered with scratches. *Odd, that*, she thought. *Why?*

In a few more minutes, the healing was done. The pain would still be with her for a while, but the physical injuries were gone. The sites of the healing itched. From long experience, Briana knew it was pointless to scratch.

Kenton looked her over and then nodded and went over to Hillself, who was standing against the wall as Elizabet and three other healers helped him.

Two of the healers stopped to examine Hillself.

Elizabet strode directly to the warmaster. "Briana, you are a mess. What do you need?"

Briana tried to refuse. "I'm fine. Your husband does good work. Please take care of Hillself."

"Your guard will be fine," Elizabet said with a smile. "Let me be the judge of your healing." As she took Briana's hands, she hissed. "My husband missed your broken finger. It will just take me a moment."

Briana looked down at her left hand and was surprised to see that her little finger was obviously broken. The entire length of it was turning purple.

Elizabet wrapped her fingers around it. "Look at me, please."

Briana felt a warm tingling surrounding her finger and a mild itch under her skin.

"Healed," Elizabet announced. "I am so glad you didn't get really hurt."

"Thank you," Briana said as she looked at her finger and flexed it. The bruise was already fading.

"Let me check and see what else my husband missed."

"Thank you," Briana said.

Elizabet did a quick examination and then brushed back Briana's hair, took her face in both hands, and looked into her eyes. She smiled fondly. "You need soap, water, some decent food, maybe some wine, and then sleep. Do not use the Seven Laws to restore yourself. Real sleep." She paused to take a breath. "Don't fight me on this, Briana. If you do, I will put a healing compulsion on you, and you will sleep for an entire day. I will talk to Nisha about the rest." With that she released Briana and went back to check on Hillself.

Briana sat on the bed for a moment and studied the scene. *I need to remember this*, she told herself. *I was attacked, in my own rooms*. She was furious at the invasion.

When she stood, the captain of her guard held out a long, white linen shirt for her to wear. Without batting an eye, Briana let her nightgown fall to the floor—or most of it anyway. She had to peel parts of it away from her skin. Then she pulled the clean shirt over her head. It was too large and extended down to the middle of her thighs, but at least it wasn't torn or bloody. She didn't know or care whose it was. It was clean, dry, and warm. Nothing else mattered.

Sanhill held sandals for her to put on next. Briana put a hand on his shoulder and gratefully slipped them onto her feet. At least they were hers. Now she wouldn't risk cutting her feet again. Sanhill's face was impassive. He had stared straight in her eyes as she changed. She was impressed. Most men would have at least let their eyes wander for a moment. Men were only men, after all. She also noticed that Sanhill had positioned himself between her and the rest of the room. Many feelings raced through Briana, including fear, excitement, and anger, but embarrassment was not one of them. She had just killed three people in her bedchamber. One of her guards had been killed, and another gravely injured. She was furious.

"Report," she snapped as she stepped back into the chaos. Her captain stayed close behind her. Greenup, who had come in while she was being healed, looked up in surprise. His eyes widened when he saw the blood on her face.

*I must be a sight*, Briana thought, *half-naked and still covered with blood despite the healing*. At least she could breathe through her nose, though it itched fiercely. She resisted the urge to scratch it.

"There were twenty acrobats in the show tonight," Greenup said. "We found four here. The watch killed three others attempting to go over the walls of the city. We have reports of one dead acrobat and one wounded woman on the keep walls. We believe eleven are loose in the desert, if they got over the moat. We are checking." He added with a grimace, "Two warriors were killed as the acrobats went over the main walls. Six more warriors were killed atop the keep walls."

*Eight more dead*, Briana thought. "How did they get into the keep?" she asked. "Guests are always escorted everywhere."

Frowning, Greenup shook his head. "We don't know yet, Warmaster."

"Find out!" she snapped.

"We will, Warmaster," Greenup said.

"Illicia was attacked tonight," Briana growled. "Blood demands revenge. By the Seven, I intend to find out who was behind this and let them taste Illician vengeance. Nothing is worse than a woman's curse."

"Yes, Warmaster," Greenup said. "We must catch them first, though. I will have warriors ready to do whatever needs to be done."

Briana nodded as she calmed herself. Then, speaking in a quiet, level voice, she said, "Send lizards after the ones in the desert–tonight. I want them captured before the sandfish can get them. I want to know why they attacked us. I want them alive and interrogated. I do not want them to die in our prison." She looked at Greenup. "The one you captured on the walls must survive and be questioned."

Greenup nodded, his face glowing with embarrassment. They still had not been able to explain how the nine previous prisoners had died simultaneously.

"The rest of the trade delegation?" Kenton asked.

"We will find them," Greenup answered.

"Why would Shelnor attack you tonight?" Kenton asked. "They have been in the city for days, and they have been our trade partners for centuries."

"Shelnor," Briana said as her mind churned. "During dinner they said that several times. Lord General Greenup, I want Shelnor punished for attacking us."

"The council must agree," Kenton said.

Briana snarled. "I am warmaster. Send a hundred lizards to Shelnor. Punish them for attacking Illicia."

Greenup grimaced. "Shelnor could be innocent. It could be a false trail."

"Find out," Briana commanded. "Make sure."

"What should we do with the acrobats?" Greenup asked.

"Question the survivor. Then execute her for violating the peace of business when you are done. Study the dead, learn all you can, and then nail pieces of them above all the gates to serve as a warning. Illicia has always been willing to demonstrate what happens to enemies and traitors."

Kenton smiled. "You are finally acting like a warmaster."

"Prince Sillik said I would hate this job if I did it right," she said. "I want a full report at dawn. I want to hear that a hundred lizards and a full complement of soldiers and Gold Robes have left for Shelnor."

"Do you have any specific punishment in mind?" Greenup asked.

"Yes," she said slowly as a smile came to her face. "It is a seaport. If they are guilty, raze the port. And catch those acrobats; they can't have any desert training. The sandfish will have them by dawn if you don't catch them."

"The orders shall be given," Greenup said.

Briana nodded with satisfaction. "Meanwhile, I am going to wash. Have Nisha find me some water and clothing befitting a very angry warmaster. I will be upstairs, in my new quarters." She paused. "And tell Keltic he has been promoted to swordmaster of Illicia and can move into this room once it is cleaned." She glanced at the wall where she had melted the stone and then at the floor where the tiles had been shattered. "And repaired," she added.

She looked around and saw the papers on her desk. She grabbed them and rolled them up in her hand. "I will want my possessions as well as my weapons moved to my new room." Discreetly hidden within the papers was the throwing knife she had worn that evening. She wasn't going anywhere unarmed.

Briana paused and looked at the acrobats' bodies. "Oh, and I want this back," she said as she extended her hand. The dagger she had thrown wiggled out of the body in which it was embedded and flew back to her hand. Briana held it up, and fire washed over the weapon, cleansing the blade.

"It will be done, Warmaster," Lord General Greenup said as Briana walked out of the room, followed by Sanhill and his men.

The healers and four Gold Robes were the only other people remaining in the room. They were all busy examining the dead. They would spend days piecing the clues together and backtracking the events.

Kenton looked at Greenup, the room suddenly quiet. "She was very lucky. Did you see those tears in her gown?"

"Did you tell her the other news?" Greenup asked. "About Viktorie?"

Kenton shook his head. "I never got the chance."

Greenup nodded. "I will check in and see what we find with the delegation. Meet me back here before dawn?"

Kenton nodded grimly as he rubbed his hands together. "I will look here and then talk to that prisoner. No sleep for us tonight." With that, he knelt beside the first intruder.

When dawn came, Briana was clean and dressed and had even eaten a little breakfast, but she was still furious at the audacity of the attack.

Nisha had ordered a real bath for the warmaster. "People did not know what a bath was," Nisha had said. "I told them to find the largest bucket from the kitchens that they could. Then I told them to bring enough water to fill it. It took five men to move the bucket in here," Nisha said proudly. "Then it took fifty trips to bring enough water. Then I got sorcery students to heat the water. They could not understand why I wanted hot water in a room. They wanted to boil the water. I told them hot, not boiling. We even had to add cold water to bring the temperature down."

Briana had enjoyed the experience immensely and had honestly felt clean afterward. She had scrubbed the blood away and washed her hair. Or, more accurately, the maids had scrubbed and washed her. Afterward, even her sore muscles felt better.

For Briana's next surprise, Nisha had found appropriate clothing. The warmaster was now wearing black wool pants and short, black lizard-skin boots. Nisha had suggested the boots, and Briana had declined until Nisha showed her the softest lizard-skin boots Briana had ever worn. Over her mail she wore a dark green, high-collared silk shirt with gold Illician eagles embroidered on the sleeves. The eagles had swords in their talons. Eagles carrying swords were the symbol on the traditional Illician battle flag.

Over the shirt she wore a long black velvet vest. Her sword hung from her hip, and a throwing knife was strapped to her wrist. Her hair was coiled at the back of her head in an elegant arrangement. Twin ringlets descended on either side of her face. The maids had taken a long time to do her hair. Briana smiled. The pins in her hair were made of sharpened steel and could easily be used as knives. The earrings that chimed softly when she moved completed her deadly attire—Nisha said the eagles in the earrings could be used as throwing stars. Where Nisha had found the clothing and jewelry, Briana didn't care. Part of her wanted to be happy, but reality grounded her emotions.

Her hand still shook a little. Post-battle fatigue had set in. She had not slept and, contrary to Elizabet's advice, had resorted to the Seven Laws to refresh herself.

After she was dressed and presentable, Sanhill arrived carrying a sealed leather pouch. Without a word, he bowed and presented the package to her. It was sealed with the Illician signet ring. Briana's breath caught when she saw the wax seal. Sanhill looked apologetic as he handed it to her.

"My lord, Sillik, charged me to keep these papers safe for you and to give them to you when you moved into this room as warmaster. He said you would know what to do with them."

Briana looked at the pouch. It was obvious to her what must be inside: the papers Sillik had found. She bit her lip in surprise. "Please place it on the table for me," she said as her heart beat excitedly. "I will open it later."

Sanhill nodded and left.

As Briana prepared herself for her next meeting, Nisha approached with a pitcher of what smelled like sangora juice.

Briana had just sat down to watch the bright red sunrise when Greenup and Kenton came to report. Since she was facing east, she could see a line of dust leaving the city. The lizards must be leaving to punish Shelnor. A squad of guards stood at attention around the room. They had followed her when she left her old room downstairs. A nearly transparent forbidding glowed across the balcony. Nisha had demanded the forbidding, and the Gold Robes had agreed. A Gold Robe would maintain the forbidding daily so that Briana wouldn't have to weary herself.

Yes, for now, this was her room. If Sillik survived, then they could sort out which room he would have when he returned. She smiled a little at the thought of him returning and being crowned. It would also mean that she wouldn't be the target anymore. Once a warmaster had been named, the appointment lasted for life, though warmaster life spans were seldom long.

Kenton and Greenup bowed formally. "Warmaster."

"Report," Briana said, barely turning her head to look at them. Two could play at this game, she thought wickedly.

Keltic and Viktorie had accompanied the two, and Sanhill stood impassively with his arms crossed in the doorway.

Keltic seemed self-conscious as he took his place as swordmaster behind Briana. He was nervous, and everyone knew it. His stance was relaxed, but he kept one hand on the hilt of his sword. Briana remembered her first day as swordmaster and smiled kindly.

Greenup began. "We have dispatched 150 lizards and a full complement of warriors and Gold Robes to Shelnor as you directed. Commander Lorarain is in command. She is a good, levelheaded soldier. Her orders are to investigate the situation and punish Shelnor if they are guilty. If they are innocent, she is to warn them and return."

Briana nodded with a tight smile. She had fought in many battles, but she had never started a war before. "How long will it take to get there?"

"Six, maybe seven weeks," Greenup said.

Briana nodded. "About what I expected."

Greenup continued. "Twenty lizards were dispatched right after the attack to find the acrobats. Their trail was obvious. I hope to have news soon. We will catch them unless the sandfish catch them first."

"What about the trade delegation?"

Greenup frowned. "They were all dead in their apartments."

"Hmm," Briana mused. "That does seem to imply they had no part in this. What about Lord Demar?" She didn't want to see that obnoxious man again. He was an Illician and a powerful leader of a strong guild. If he were guilty, it would shake the city.

"We have not been able to find him yet," Greenup admitted. "We have searched his apartments and spoken to his usual associates."

"His family is perplexed," Kenton interjected. "He put so much effort into this delegation that it is unlikely he would have left them."

"He could be with the acrobats," Greenup suggested. "He could be a captive … or a traitor."

Briana was surprised by the news. She took a moment to consider the implications. No one else spoke as they waited for her. "Maybe Shelnor is innocent, and they are going to blame us for the death of their people," she said. "The stonemasons are not going to like the loss of that contract." The stonemasons' guild was a strong force in the city.

Greenup nodded. "It makes as much sense as any other explanation. Lorarain is aware of the death of the delegation and can deliver either a warning or condolences."

Briana wondered if she was being goaded into starting a war or if one had already been started for her.

Kenton seized the moment to give his report. "First, the prisoner. She had a strong memory block. We think the pain of her capture triggered it."

"Pain?" Briana asked.

Greenup smiled. "Ah yes, her arm was severely broken as she was being subdued."

Kenton continued. "We are trying various techniques to get around the block, including hypnotic regression."

"Odds?" Briana asked.

"Not good," Kenton admitted.

"How did they get in the keep?" Briana asked.

Kenton smiled. "That is a little bit more interesting. The acrobats had sorcery traces on their hands and feet. The sorcery allowed them to reach into the stone and make their own handholds all the way up the wall. We have stonemasons repairing the damage, and I have fifty Gold Robes looking at ways to reinforce the stone so it cannot happen again."

"Was it the Seven or the Nine?" Briana asked as she turned to look at the chief of the Gold Robes.

Kenton shrugged and held up his hands in defeat. "Impossible to know for sure at this point since the attackers were killed. My guess is the Nine, since lives were lost. We might know more if we catch the ones in the desert."

Briana nodded. She had reached the same conclusion earlier. "You must assume they have mind blocks in place as well. If they are captured, you must prevent them from experiencing pain."

"Already noted and instructions given," Greenup said. "It's nearly impossible to prevent, though, since any knife cut could be enough to trigger the block. Compulsions will also be in play to make them desperate to avoid capture and to injure themselves if they are."

"We also searched the belongings of the trade delegation," Greenup said. "There might be clues."

Briana smiled. "There might be, but probably not. We never found any clues in any of the other deaths. It's all part of the same script."

Greenup looked at Briana. "Is there something else that we should know?"

Briana shook her head. "No," she said with a trace of bitterness.

Greenup looked at her uncertainly. "We all knew there was a possibility you would be attacked."

She nodded. "How is Hillself?"

Greenup smiled. "He will be fine. He lost a lot of blood, but he has been healed. He was fed and sent to bed. He should be harassing you again in a few days."

Briana smiled. It was the only good news to come out of this. "Saleen died protecting me. He is to be given all honors. He had a wife and child. See that they have no wants."

"Already done, my lady," Sanhill said from the doorway. "Saleen was one of my men. I took the news to them myself and have already arranged for the family in your name."

Briana nodded and smiled.

"I have some additional information," Kenton announced. "Lady Viktorie … has had another foretelling."

Briana's breath caught, and she looked at Viktorie in surprise. The woman's face was pale, and she refused to meet Briana's gaze. Her eyes were locked on something in the distance that only she could see.

"As you know," Kenton said, "Viktorie has the gift of foretelling. She was able to predict when Prince Sillik would return, for example. Last night"–he paused to look around the room–"she saw some rather disturbing things."

"Go on," Briana said.

"Viktorie saw Sillik being killed if we do not support him." Kenton said. "This dark master has established a series of followers. What he is ultimately doing is unknown." Taking a deep breath, Kenton smiled grimly and bowed. "We withdraw our objections to your plan, Warmaster. We will send sufficient forces with you. Senarick, vicar general of the Gold Robes, will lead whatever force you choose to send."

Excitement surged through Briana. She took a deep breath. Lady Silvia had said she would have to ride to his aid. "Summon the council," she said with triumph. Then as an afterthought, she added, "Lord Kenton, I need you to do a little bit of research. Find any information that Illicia has on the Star of the South."

# CHAPTER 26

## River Pirates

$S$ ILLIK HURRIED TO the yana and woke both of the great beasts. As they stood, he jumped onto his yana's broad back. Renee had followed Wolfstein. Sillik strung his bow. Smiling in terrible anticipation, he urged his yana forward. The beast smelled excitement in the air and bounded ahead. The second yana followed.

Renee was waiting beside the wagons and jumped onto her yana as it ran by. Laughing in excitement, she produced a short curved bow and a quiver of arrows.

Wolfstein's men waited patiently where they had spread out along the entire length of wagons. The pirates were already swarming ashore, their ships bobbing gently in the current. Sillik noticed with interest that the barge had reversed direction and was now moving toward the other side of the river.

Wolfstein, Sillik noticed, held a bow and a stave—no metal. Sillik admired Wolfstein's leadership, but he suspected more than simple river pirates. But why would the north erupt in war? The peace had held for hundreds of years. The blood vow of the Knights of Nerak had not been sworn in two hundred years, and the dragons of Ynak had been asleep for five centuries. True, the cities had been traditional enemies for many long and terrible years. Nevertheless, more recently, the cities had healed some of their differences. Both cities had numerous treaties with other cities. If war resulted from this conflict, it could draw in half the cities in the land. That terrible possibility could only aid the Nine Gods of Darkness.

No, Sillik decided, it couldn't be a mere coincidence that war was threatening to engulf the land. Sillik knew that he and his sword were horribly entwined in the ancient and violent affairs of the gods.

While the pirates clambered ashore, Wolfstein had his men ready their bows. Suddenly, most of the pirates charged with a savage cry while a handful of pirates covered their advance with arrows. Over the sound of the pirates, Wolfstein gave the command to fire. It seemed like hundreds of feathered shafts filled the air. None of the arrows were very effective, though, because the wagons absorbed the brunt of the pirates' attack, and the pirates lifted their shields over their heads.

Wolfstein gave another signal, and half of his men fired high as before, and the other half fired low. This tactic slew a score of pirates, and for a moment, the attackers slowed, as if uncertain. Then Wolfstein released his men.

With a loud cry, they drew their weapons and rushed the pirates. In moments, men were fighting along the entire length of the wagons. As the groups clashed, Sillik twirled the yana to face the battle and then rushed the pirates. As he did, on the distant horizon, he saw several black specks that were growing larger.

Sillik shot arrow after arrow at the pirates and had the satisfaction of seeing every one strike its mark. Mere heartbeats before he crashed into the fighting, he dropped the bow and drew his sword. The yana killed the first five opponents before Sillik could draw a breath. One pirate sidestepped the yana's claws though. As the beast turned to face the man, the pirate launched a desperate blow. Sillik saw it coming out of the corner of his eye and prepared for it. At the last possible instant, just when the pirate had begun to have hope, Sillik's sword knocked his blade away. Wonder lined the man's face, and then the yana slew him.

Using his knees, Sillik guided the sleek yana into the growing battle. Together, they slew their enemies. Sillik fought without thinking and became merely an extension of his blood-covered weapon, but a growing feeling of fear awakened his mind, and he realized that the sound of the battle was overshadowed by something new and more terrifying. The bellow of war horns was followed by the intimidating thunder of enormous wings beating down on everyone.

Sillik hazarded a glance upward and saw the dragons descending. A bow hummed near him, but the dragon's breath reduced the arrow to ash before it could strike. The tempest of dragon wings forced Sillik to retreat. He needed to see the field if he was to survive. Arrows rained down, and Sillik resorted to wizardry to make a small shield. Somewhere close, Sillik felt an answering surge of the Seven Laws. There was a master among the dragon riders. That thought sent shivers down Sillik's back. "Renee, there is a master up there!"

"I know. I felt it too!" she shouted over the battle noise.

# CHAPTER 27

## Nomads

"WARMASTER," A FARAWAY voice said.

Briana groaned and tried to roll over.

"Warmaster, you must wake."

Briana cursed quietly and struggled to a sitting position. Her sheets and blankets fell away. She felt her skin tighten in the cool air and shivered. "What?" she demanded as she opened her eyes. The light in the royal apartments was dim, but she could make out the shape of a man near the doorway. Alarm flashed through her veins in a momentary surge of panic. Her hand found her dagger under her pillow.

"We have a development," Hillself said in a patient voice. "A party of Nomads is approaching the city under a flag of truce. They will be at the gates by dawn."

"Nomads? Hells," Briana swore as she rolled to the side of her bed and stood up. "The last time they came near Illicia, they burned half the villages and a third of the fields before we drove them away. That was, what, ten years ago?"

"Twelve," Hillself said. "The carry a flag of peace this time. They wish to speak to you."

"Me?" Briana asked as she strode over to her battle armor.

"Well, the king of the piled rock," Hillself said with a grimace, using the Nomads' term for Illicia.

As Briana dressed, Hillself turned his back. He was already wearing his battle armor.

"The Nomads respect only strength," Hillself said. "We must be prepared for violence. If we aren't, they will be insulted. Relations with the Nomads have always been difficult. Remember, they take no gifts either. Water, salt, meat, and shade are all we can offer them. They have no use for anything else."

Briana cursed. "Where are my damn boots? Where did Nisha hide them?"

"They came through Thunder Pass," Hillself continued. "We stopped them at the top of the pass. The guard sent runners ahead. When the runners got to the checkpoints, they sent light flashes to the city walls."

Briana grunted as she found her boots and pulled them onto her feet.

"They made no aggressive actions and kept their bows unstrung and their blades sheathed," Hillself said. "The guards didn't know what to do."

"What do they want to talk about?" Briana asked as she lifted the breastplate off its stand and over her head. She grunted as the weight settled onto her shoulders and then sighed in pleasure. Illician armor became weightless once worn.

"They did not say," Hillself said. "They carried the flag and walked toward the King's Gate. They brought one of their desert sleds, pulled by a small lizard."

"How many?" Briana asked as she buckled her sword belt to her waist.

"Seven."

"Gods," Briana exclaimed. "Seven of them are worth almost fifty average men. How many masters?"

Hillself smiled as he helped Briana tighten the straps on her leathers. "Masters all," he said, "or at least they all wear the third eye."

"We will have to paint one on me then," Briana said. "It will be an insult to them if we don't tell them who the masters are. We will have to have seven masters in my party as well. Sorry, my faithful friend, but you won't be able to come with me to this. Let's go." Briana grabbed her desert veil and helmet.

Hillself shrugged. "You will be well protected, and Sanhill and I will be close."

Briana smiled. Sanhill, the captain of her guard, was a humorless man but cared deeply about his men and her.

At the bottom of the stairs, Briana and Hillself met Kenton. *His knee is hurting him this morning,* she thought. *His limp is worse. Damn, but it can't be helped. He has knowledge that I need.*

Without hesitation, Kenton used magic to draw an eye on Briana's forehead. "Now you know the Nomads won't enter the city," Kenton said. "They won't pass through the gate. You brought your desert veil?" He glanced down at her hand. "Good, keep your face covered. They only lower their veils to their spouse on their wedding day and never to strangers. A woman is in charge, so it's good that you came."

"Keep talking," Briana said, "but let's walk to the gates and meet our guests. It's been a long time since I have had to deal with them."

As they walked, Kenton told her about the protocol of meeting the Nomads. While listening, she also expertly wrapped the veil around her head with the seven-folded wrap. When she was done, she lowered her helmet onto her head. Only her eyes and forehead were visible. Near the gate, they passed a line of guards blocking access to the city. Some of the people were upset and shouting.

"No use starting a war over a misunderstanding," Briana said. "If the Nomads see unveiled faces, they will pour over the passes and attack. Hillself, stay here and try to explain," Briana commanded. "The sight of all this battle armor should quiet them, if they're smart," she said bitterly. "Now who's going with me to meet the Nomads?"

Kenton held up his fingers as he reeled off the names. "You, Greenup, Viktorie, Browner, Elizabet, Magan, and Rebecca. A battle lord, three Gold Robes, two healers, and you—all masters," he added with a pleased smile. "Now may the peace of the Seven Gods go with you."

Briana nodded and darted past the soldiers barring the street. Rebecca and Viktorie, who were waiting for her beyond the chaos of the soldiers, fell into step with her as she marched toward the gate. The two women wore their battle armor with practiced ease and comfort. The third eye was painted on each woman's forehead. If not for their height, their eye color, and the little bit of hair that was showing, Briana would have been hard-pressed to recognize either woman.

"Do we have any idea what's in the sled?" Briana asked as the Nomads came into view. The seven Nomads were standing or squatting around the sled. It was typical of Nomad sleds, made of two wide wooden runners that supported a leather-covered compartment. Leather straps connected the sled to a lizard, which was crouched in the middle of the bridge over the moat. Two Nomads stood on either side of the creature, holding thin rods that they used to guide the lizard. A white square fabric was tied to one of them.

All of the Nomads were dressed in dusty, brown robes that matched the color of the mountains surrounding the city. Each had a long knife at the waist, a pair of swords strapped to his or her back, and a leather buckler strapped to his or her right arm. A quiver of arrows hung from each person's belt, and all of the Nomads carried a short, unstrung bow. They also carried water gourds on a strap under their arms. The only parts of their faces that were visible were their eyes and forehead. They were covered with a layer of dust.

"No, Warmaster, we don't know what is in the sled," Viktorie answered. "It's not big enough to hide more than two people. If it's a trap, the soldiers at the walls have been instructed to shoot first and not worry about prisoners. Remember, the Nomads do not ride in the sleds. Only children and ancients ride. Everyone else runs. Also take this." She looped a leather water sling over Briana's head. "You will offer water. They won't accept; they have too much pride. Besides, they will take water only from those they consider friends. If for some reason they do accept, you must drink first to show it is not poisoned. Then you will offer it to her. I have checked it, and it is safe."

Briana grunted. Despite the coolness, she was becoming hot under the dark armor. "Well, let's get this started," she said as she waved Greenup and the rest of the group to her side. *I still wonder what drove her away from the Nomads*, Briana thought as she eyed Viktorie.

As Briana approached, the Nomads rose gracefully to their feet. One stepped forward and bowed. She touched her right hand to her chest and then extended it in the Nomad greeting of peace. *Six men and one woman*, Briana thought, based on their heights. Briana repeated the gesture and examined the woman who faced her. *I bet she'd be hard to fight.* The woman's brown eyes studied Briana.

"Briana, Warmaster, we heard a song that you lead the place of piled stone. I wanted to see for myself. I am Caelia. I am the hand of the fist. We are of the clan Rubela, of the high chief."

Briana smiled. *The hand controls the fist, and the hand becomes a fist when necessary. Her voice seems old, tired maybe, but wise. I think I could like her.* "I am Briana, warmaster of this place," she said. No further introductions would be made. It was the Nomad way. Only the leaders would speak.

"Can I offer you water?" Briana asked, producing the time-honored offering.

Caelia regarded her with clear brown eyes and said nothing for several heartbeats. "We are honored. Yes, I will accept your offer of water."

Briana felt Viktorie's surprise beside her. She sensed surprise rippling through Caelia's people as well.

Briana raised the water. "To the Seven Lords and the water of life," she said, using the traditional blessing. She opened the container, slid its round nozzle between her wraps, and took a long drink. The water was still cool from the night and fresh. It reminded her of the mountains in the north to which her father had taken her when she was little. It was a place where water fell from the sky and where water became hard when it was cold. When she was done, she held the sling out to Caelia.

The woman took a long drink. Then, to Briana's surprise, Caelia handed the water to every person in her party. They each took a drink, and then Caelia handed it back to Briana.

Viktorie took the sling from Briana and drank from it before handing it to the rest of the Illician party. While her back was turned to the Nomads, Viktorie whispered, "If everyone doesn't drink, they will become suspicious."

Surprise flashed across what little of Caelia's face Briana could see. *Did we almost do something wrong? Or does she see Viktorie for what she is, a woman of Nomadic heritage?*

Once everyone had drunk some water, Caelia spoke. "Too long have we walked different trails, yet today our paths come together."

Briana's eyes widened. Was this an opening? "How have our paths come together?" Briana asked. She felt Viktorie stir uncomfortably beside her at the breech of protocol.

Caelia's eyes flashed, but she continued. "More than five years ago, one of your men saved the life of Tomas, a man of my fist. He became caught between a desert cat and its cub. It was a clumsy thing to do, and the cat was within its rights to take his life and return his soul to the halls of the Seven Gods. But your man rescued Tomas and was able to avoid killing the cat. Much honor is owed because of his bravery."

*Five years*, Briana thought. *No, more than five years ago. Could it be?*

"Eight days ago, we found strangers in the desert. We do not know how long they had been there, but they came from this place," she said as she looked around. "We were curious, so we followed them. They knew nothing of the desert. The swimmers in the sand took two of the strangers before they found rock. We watched. They did not take any normal trail. They began to walk in circles. They were lost. The heat made them stupid. They saw us because they walked in ways no wise person would. They fought well even though they were stupid with heat and unfamiliar with sand. They could move in unexpected ways." She paused. "Tomas took an arrow that was intended for my heart," Caelia said, touching her chest. "Before he died, I took on his life debt since it was unpaid and he was of my fist. It is fitting that your man saved Tomas and then Tomas saved me. I now owe the man, Sillik, a life debt. The debt must be paid. Honor requires a life debt to be paid tenfold."

Briana's breath caught as she sensed her companions' surprise. "I am sorry for your loss."

"All die. It is the way of the world," Caelia said quietly. "We all return to the Seven Halls at the end of this life. Someday, perhaps, we will get a chance to live again."

"Sillik is not here," Briana said. "He left to settle a blood feud, a debt of his own."

"That is known to us," Caelia said. "We watched him depart this place of stone. His trail was hard to follow, but we managed for a while."

Briana could almost sense Caelia smiling at that accomplishment. "Why were you watching him?"

Caelia's eyes flashed dangerously. "Have I not said? Tomas owed a life debt. We watch all the ways. Tomas made certain that we watched for this man. Tomas looked for ways to repay his debt. We watched over him when he returned to you. We killed most of those that would have stopped him."

Briana nodded. Viktorie had always said the desert had eyes.

"Know this for truth," Caelia said. "We were not the only ones following his trail when he left. We killed one group that followed him and did not belong in the desert. He dealt with another. We watched, and we laughed. He was cruel and harsh yet kind. It confused us. One of them managed to get out of the desert. After Sillik dealt with the second group, we lost his trail."

*She is irritated that they lost the trail,* Briana thought. *Sillik is good; no one is better.* "And what of these strangers you found in the desert?"

"Two survived the encounter. We asked them questions. They looked like wetlanders. We learned very little. They talked of great bodies of water in their lands. We knew they lied, but they did not recant. That confused us, but I think there may be many things we do not know. They told us they had attacked you, Warmaster," Caelia said as she inclined her head. "It is good that you survived. One of the captives did not survive our questions." Caelia said this with a touch of sadness. "He was wounded when we began, and we will not waste healing. We gave him to the swimmers." She laughed. "We brought you a gift. And thus I begin to repay my life debt."

Caelia snapped her fingers, and two of her men pulled a cloth bag out of the sled and dumped it onto the stone roadway. A soft groan escaped the bag, as if from a semiconscious person.

Rebecca stepped forward, but Briana held up her hand to stop her. The bag wasn't large enough to contain a man. *Be careful,* she signed with her fingers.

Rebecca nodded.

"A survivor?" Briana asked, a touch of excitement in her voice. "Where did you find them, these strangers?"

"Southwest of Towering Rocks," Caelia said. "Do you know the place?"

Briana glanced at Greenup out of the corner of her eye, and he nodded slightly. "Yes," Briana said, "we know of it." *She must mean Hell's Gate,* Briana thought as she pictured the two rock formations. *Interesting. Four, maybe five days to get there on foot–hard days at that.*

Caelia nodded. "That is good. The swimmers ate what remained. They were very good fighters, very skillful. Our compliments if you survived an attack by them."

Nodding, Briana touched her chest with her hand and bowed her head at the compliment. Then she studied the blue fabric bag. It moved slightly.

Incoherent sounds came from the lump. "Four attacked me," Briana explained. "My guard killed one, they killed one of my guards, and I killed the rest."

Suddenly, the other Nomads pounded their hands on their bucklers as Caelia nodded approvingly. "We honor you for that. The chukar is our way to compliment. Perhaps in another life you were one of us. We will leave now; we will cause you no trouble. Perhaps we walk paths that are not so different. The winds will reveal the path for both our peoples. Perhaps we will share water again, Warmaster."

"Perhaps they are not different," Briana said. Then, remembering Viktorie's comments, she added, "May the winds take you where you need to be. And yes, I would like to share water with you again, Hand of the Fist."

Caelia touched her heart. "Honor and peace, Warmaster." Then she turned and clicked her tongue while pointing away from the city. The Nomads switched the lizard. It hissed and bared its teeth but sprang to its feet. Its claws scratched the road as it turned around madly.

In no hurry, the Nomads walked proudly away from the gates. Briana admired their calm. Then, without undue haste, the Nomads switched the lizard into a slow run, and the Nomads started to jog.

Once they were out of earshot, Rebecca darted forward and held her hands over the bag. "It's a woman," she announced. "She's alive, barely. Get her out of this thing."

Three guards from the gate ran forward and cut the ropes, revealing a slender woman. She was nude, and her hands and feet were tied roughly behind her back.

Rebecca and Elizabet went immediately into healing mode. Briana watched dispassionately. The woman was similar in appearance to several of the women who had been in the Shelnor contingent of acrobats. But she had a gaunt, almost wasted appearance after her captivity with the Nomads. Her cheekbones and ribs protruded, as if her body had drawn in on itself. Briana doubted she had eaten or drunk much more than was necessary to sustain her life.

Rebecca paused in her healing to ask for water. Viktorie handed the water sling she had been holding to one of the guards. Rebecca told the guard to pour some water in the woman's mouth and the rest on her head. "We need to cool her down."

"Get her to the keep," Briana commanded. "Heal her. I want guards on her around the clock. Drug her so that if she has any talent, she can't use it. I want to talk to her. No mistakes on this one. Rebecca, will she survive?"

Rebecca nodded as she knelt over the woman. "She's weak. She's been beaten, possibly tortured. She needs water, but I think she'll live."

Briana looked around. "Get her out of here, and let's go back to the keep." Briana pulled her veil down. "Open the streets. I am going back. Get everyone up to my room so we can talk about what just happened."

Sanhill met the warmaster around the first curve of the street. The street was silent now except for a few worried people.

Briana stopped. "The Nomads are gone!" she announced. "They brought us a prisoner, a gift. Go about your business." She offered a confident smile.

The people cheered. In the excitement, Briana and her party slipped through the crowd and made their way back to the keep.

Her stomach rumbling, Briana climbed the stairs back to the royal apartments. Greenup and Kenton had gone to oversee the prisoner's guards, and Rebecca was staying near the woman. She said more healing would be required.

Once she was safely in her rooms, Briana removed her sword and breastplate. She kept some of the armor on, though, because it made her feel more comfortable. Plus, it kept Nisha away.

She was standing on the balcony, staring into the desert, when someone knocked at her door. "Come," she called.

Kenton, Greenup, Elizabet, and Rebecca strode in. "We took the liberty of asking Nisha to send food," Elizabet said with a smile. "It was quite an eventful morning."

"Yes," Briana said. "Please sit." She waved at the conference table. "Thoughts?" she asked as she approached. "Pour yourselves some tea, if you wish."

As Elizabet poured tea into the fine Illician cups, Rebecca spoke. "The prisoner is secure in the Gold Tower. She has been healed and should survive. I have trusted guards watching her." She glanced at Greenup, who nodded in assent. "Her name is Bolivie. She has no magical ability, but we have her sedated anyway. So she is no danger to herself or to us. She has been given food, a thin meat broth, and water. The sedative will make her quite compliant once it is fully in her system—much better than the torture those Nomads used on her."

"When can I question her?" Briana asked.

"Give her a day," Elizabet said. "She was treated badly by the Nomads. If we question her now, it will undo all the good work Rebecca has done."

"You know what her fate is," Greenup said. "If she participated in the attack, then she will see the headsman."

"I don't think she participated," Rebecca said. "She is from Shelnor, but she doesn't seem to have the muscles to have taken part in the attack."

"I am more concerned about what she can tell us," Briana said. "I will not send her to the headsman until we are done with her and then only if she is guilty."

"The Nomads told us that Sillik was followed. That's news," Greenup said.

"Not surprising," Kenton said. "The important thing is that he got out of the desert."

"Agreed," Briana said. "Let's see what we get out of this girl. We didn't get anything useful out of the one we caught the night of the attack–just that they had been given gold to attack me."

"And nothing on how they learned how to climb the keep," Rebecca added.

"I would like to lead a small recon force to Hell's Gate and look around," Greenup said. "It's two days by lizard to get there, a day to look around, and a couple of days back. Perhaps the Nomads missed something."

"That would be a mistake," Viktorie said as she entered the room. She had removed all of her battle armor and was now in her customary gold robe. "Caelia will see or hear of our search. She will know that we doubt them. But they did not miss anything."

Greenup smiled. "We trust, and we verify." He looked around the room for support. "I think we can explain ourselves."

All heads turned to look at Briana. "I am going to say yes," she said. "I think Caelia will understand. But Viktorie has a point. She should go with you, in case you have more encounters. You should leave in the morning."

Greenup and Viktorie nodded in agreement. "I will make the arrangements," Greenup said.

"Now I want to change the subject," Briana said with a smile. "I still want to go after Sillik, and I have been thinking about what we will need to do."

# CHAPTER 28

## Student Studies

"FATHER, I FOUND something."

Kenton looked up with a tender smile as Alexis, his oldest daughter, stepped into his library. Bookshelves lined the small, windowless room. The shelves were bursting with rolled scrolls, books, and magical implements and trinkets. The room smelled of dust and dry books. It was a familiar smell that Kenton relished.

The room was adjacent to his apartment in the Gold Tower. He had discovered the room by accident when he found a scroll that talked about a reading room. The door had been magically locked, and it had taken him weeks to discover the key. Once he opened the room, he understood why it had been sealed. Dangerous tomes and treatises were hidden within. Over the years, he had been trying to catalog everything. Only his immediate family knew of the room and how to gain entrance. Glow balls floated in the air near the high stone ceiling. Dust motes glinted in the steady, golden light. Flame was never allowed in this room, which was just big enough for a pair of chairs and a footstool.

It was late. Kenton had been working with Briana ever since the Nomads delivered the prisoner to her. Greenup had left three days earlier to investigate the spot where the prisoner had been captured.

Alexis stepped forward and sat on the stool in front of her father. As Kenton straightened in his chair, he rubbed his eyes wearily. "You remind me of Brie, more every day," Kenton said, admiring his daughter.

Alexis smiled at the reference to her birth mother and brushed a strand of light brown hair behind her ear. Her father's second wife, Elizabet, had raised her, and she had no memory of her birth mother. She folded the pleats of her light gold dress as she waited on her father. Students studying for their master's test wore light gold. Novices wore brown.

"Your mother would be so proud to see you now," Kenton said. "Anyway, what did you find?"

"Kendra and I have been looking at how the acrobats managed to climb the keep, and we think we have found the answer."

"Where is your sister then?" Kenton asked with a knowing smile.

"She has other duties tonight."

"Ah yes, the duties of a new master's student." Kenton smiled. "So tell me, daughter, what have you found?"

"We made the assumption that the magic used came from neither the Seven nor the Nine. Then we went looking for other sources that would allow someone to cut or damage stone."

Kenton leaned forward, intrigued.

Alexis smiled. "Everyone knows the story about how the statues beside the King's Gate were magically stabilized. Those abilities were lost a long time ago. Kendra had the idea to look for stone lore."

"Stone lore?"

"Yes." Alexis nodded, her eyes bright with excitement. "Have you ever noticed that the chief of the stonemasons' guild always has some magical capability? In fact, the same could be said of all the major guilds, save warriors. They all have some magical ability. That observation led us to assume there must be guild secrets. From there it was easy to look back in the training archives before the establishment of the guilds for stone-mining secrets."

Impressed, Kenton leaned back and rubbed his chin.

"We found a scroll in the main libraries that is so delicate it can't be moved. It discusses the ways and methods to harden and cut stone. It also mentions a way to repair stone from an unwise cut." Alexis glowed with the revelation. "The stonemasons can't perform the spell today because it requires more power than they have. I understand how the magic must flow, and I can teach the masters how to repair the keep."

"They will want to study the source," Kenton said, grimacing as he considered his daughter's words. "They will not take kindly to my daughter, not yet a master, teaching them anything."

Alexis frowned. "There was a problem with the scroll. In my excitement, I picked up the scroll to rush here. As a result, that portion of the scroll was damaged and lost."

"I suppose you memorized the information?" he asked, already knowing the answer.

"Of course, Father."

"And you have already tried the magic to repair a cup or a bowl?"

Alexis smiled, and her eyes glittered. "A broken pitcher was nearby. It has been repaired and now cannot be broken. Kendra tried dropping it on the floor. When that failed, she dropped it down the stairs."

Kenton nodded. "I heard the commotion in the hallway earlier."

Alexis grinned, and her face reddened slightly.

"Very well," Kenton said. "We will credit you with the discovery, but the masters will not tolerate a mere student teaching them anything. So you will find a novice instructor and train him in the technique."

"Yes, Father," Alexis said, smiling innocently.

"That was far too easy," Kenton said, suddenly worried. "Why?"

"Because there is more to understand, Father! Since this is a stonecutter technique, it is logical to assume the acrobats would not have stumbled across the capability at random. They must have had help." Alexis took a deep breath before continuing. "Since our stonemasons were perplexed by the damage and the obvious use of magic, the logical answer is that the magical knowledge came from outside the city. Narrowing it down quickly is easy. It has to be a city with knowledge of the Seven Laws and stonemasonry. One city comes to mind," she said with a triumphant smile.

Kenton mulled the clues she had laid on the table. "Ritain," Kenton he said with distaste. "They are Illicia's main competitors for stonework." He looked up at Alexis. "So, my daughter, you have learned that another city is implicated in the attack on the warmaster. That is serious information. Have you told anyone else?"

She shook her head. "Only you, Father. With the intrigue that surrounds you, my sister and I have learned how to be quiet."

"We will have to tell Briana," Kenton said as he stood up.

"I do have one request," Alexis said, standing with him.

"Ah, I expected something in return for your capitulation. What do you want?" Kenton settled back in his chair and looked at his daughter.

"I want my master's test accelerated. You and I both know it is only a formality. Rumor says the warmaster is preparing to go after Prince Sillik. That will require significant resources. I want to go with her."

"I did not expect this," Kenton said. "Any particular reason why you want to go into what is surely going to be weeks of hard riding followed by a battle, if they manage to catch Dernot?"

"I am an Illician," Alexis said. "These may be the defining times of our lives, and I want to be in the middle of the action."

"I wish I could talk you out of this, but you are my daughter, and I know better." He stood up. "Let's go see the warmaster."

Alexis swallowed hard. "I thought you would tell her."

"No," Kenton said. "It's your find, and you want to accompany her, so you get to tell her."

With that, Kenton led the way down out of his rooms. Alexis followed her father self-consciously.

A short time later, they were ushered into the warmaster's rooms. General Hornsmasher was just leaving. He was filling in for Greenup while the latter led the recon to Hell's Gate. He nodded curtly to Kenton but stopped to compliment Alexis.

Kenton was suddenly on edge as he remembered seeing the Hornsmasher in the yard with his son, now a major in the guards. The boy was probably a few years older than Sillik and was probably looking for a wife. What was the boy's name? Damn, he couldn't remember. *A major in the guard and the Speaker's daughter? Damn, damn, damn.*

"Come, daughter," Kenton said as his eyes warned the Hornsmasher to stay away. "We must see the warmaster." "Hornsmasher" was a hereditary title given to one of the battle lords. Kenton remembered that before this man was the Hornsmasher, he had been known as Elerson. *But damn*, Kenton thought, *why can't I remember what his damn son's name is?*

"Yes, Father," Alexis said as Kenton took her arm.

Inside Briana's rooms was a maelstrom of energy and bright light. Alexis's eyes went wide when she saw how angry Briana was as she paced the room. The glow balls had been brightened to the point of brilliance, but Alexis could see the magic in them failing. *They will last the night*, she thought, *and then they will have to be remade.*

"Two more days until Greenup is back," Briana said. "Are you bringing me good news? The Hornsmasher wasn't helpful."

Kenton shook his head. "Perhaps some answers, though. I have brought my daughter, who has information for you alone."

Puzzled, Briana looked at Alexis, and her mood softened.

Alexis knew better than to curtsy to the warmaster if she wanted to be considered an equal, so she stood her ground. "My lady, we have discovered how the acrobats climbed the keep."

Briana glanced at Kenton. "Your masters haven't been able to tell me that yet or how to repair the damage."

Kenton smiled. "No, they have not."

Intrigued, Briana sat down and nodded for Alexis to continue.

When Alexis had finished going over the salient points, Briana got up and walked over to another table and returned with a stone cup. A quick rap on the table broke the handle off the cup. She slid both pieces across the table to Alexis. "Show me this new magic," she demanded.

Alexis frowned. She had not expected a request to demonstrate the magic. She summoned the required energies and wove the spell around the cup. In moments the repair was complete, and she handed the cup back to Briana.

Without a word, Briana dropped the cup onto the table again. It landed hard but did not break. She picked it up and smashed it on the table. When it still didn't break, she smirked. "I don't know who should be more grateful, my servants or me." She tried to break the cup again, but despite several hard raps on the table, she failed to even chip it. She looked at Alexis. "I watched what you did, but I don't think I could replicate it. Are you sure this was a stonecutter spell?"

Alexis nodded. "A simple inversion of the spell would allow someone to wrap the spell around an object like a hand or a foot. Then the person wearing the spell could make his or her own handholds on the outside of the keep for as long as the spell lasted."

"How long might that be?" Briana asked.

"On someone without magical talent, it would start to decay quickly. We know it lasted however long it took to climb the keep, but only traces of decaying magic were left after the battle."

Briana smiled. "You didn't really answer my question."

"I gave the best answer I could, Warmaster," Alexis said.

"So what do we do about it?" Briana asked. "What I mean is, how do we prevent it from happening again?"

"We know the acrobats were able to make their own ladders and climb the outside of the keep," Alexis said. "If we use the repair aspects of this, we can repair the damage they wrought and then harden rings around the outside of the keep to prevent this kind of attack in the future."

Briana turned to Kenton. "Summon your masters. I want Alexis to teach them how to repair the keep and protect it. Might as well consider the walls of the keep as well. The keep first, though." Briana stood up and began to pace again. "After the keep is secure, send some novices to teach the stonemasons how to use this magic."

"We have already discussed how we will disseminate the new knowledge," Kenton said.

"Don't tell me you were going to have someone else teach the masters? Tell your damn masters to sit up and learn. If a young woman learned something first, they better damn well learn from her."

"Very well, Warmaster," Kenton said, clearly displeased.

"Good." Briana turned to Alexis. "I believe I heard that you are up for your master's test."

Alexis nodded, afraid to say anything.

Lord Kenton smiled. "In time, I think my daughter should become one of your advisors."

Briana looked up in surprise, and her eyes narrowed as she looked first at Kenton and then at Alexis. "Lord Kenton, I am going to do something you may not like, but I need someone on my staff now who can think like your daughter, especially when we leave. I am going to give her a royal appointment to my staff. Have her ready to go, as a full master, in two days as my Gold Robes liaison. I am not sure when we leave, but not before Greenup returns. So two days is all you have to get her ready to go."

"Yes, Warmaster," Kenton said, smiling. "It shall be done."

Surprised, Alexis looked from Kenton to Briana. A royal appointment as the Gold Robes liaison? Was it possible?

"One point, though," Kenton said. "Senarick, vicar general of the Gold Robes, will be in command of the Gold Robes. My daughter, whom I entrust to your protection, will report to you and also to Senarick. I cannot appoint Alexis over Senarick."

"Nor should you," Briana said with a small smile. "I agree."

"What will you do about Ritain?" Alexis asked, trying to hide her surprise.

Kenton smiled as he watched Briana.

Briana didn't say anything at first; she just unrolled a map and studied it. "Ritain is out of the way. I am convinced Shelnor is a false lead, but we were obligated to send a response. I would rather treat this differently. Pretend we don't know. That gives us options to deal with them later." She studied the map again and touched the symbol for Colum. "What do you think, Lord Kenton?"

"We can deal with them anytime we choose, but we don't want it to look like we are just eliminating competition."

Briana grinned. "I am sure the merchants would love to see us raze the city. We also must consider the possibility that Ritain is the false lead and Shelnor the real lead. Now have you found anything about that other subject I asked you to research?"

Kenton looked at Alexis. The young woman smiled and pulled out another scroll.

"We found this drawing and a small description," Kenton said.

Briana looked at the drawing and grinned. *So it would find him. Interesting.* "What does the description say?"

Alexis smiled uncertainly. "It is of great age. Once there were seven. Four have been destroyed. The remaining three have been lost. The papers we found predate Illicia. Some of the masters from the demon wars must have had some knowledge of the pendants."

"Any idea what they do?" Briana asked.

"The paper talks about them being a communication tool and …"

"And what?"

Alexis frowned. "They could be used to summon the Seven Gods."

# CHAPTER 29

## Wind and Wings

RENEE STRUGGLED TO wakefulness. Her head was pounding, and the sound of wind was rushing past. Her head and feet felt like they were dangling. Her head hurt, and she couldn't figure out why.

She tried to move, but her arms and legs were immobile. Then she realized her head was rolling to one side. It felt like a thousand soldiers were pounding on it. She felt her hair whipping around in the wind. Slowly, she opened her eyes and gasped. She knew instantly where she was–clasped in the claws of a dragon. The tail of the beast was inches above her head. She couldn't see the ground, which was fine with her. She didn't want to know how high they were.

When she tried to stretch, she felt the dragon tighten its grip. She gasped in pain. Her head rolled, and she cried out again. Her vision blurred, and her body felt like it had been battered with hammers for a week. She reached for the Seven Laws to clear her head and heal her body and felt them agonizingly out of reach. She groaned. This happened sometimes with head injuries. She shook her head, and waves of pain marched behind her eyes. She had obviously been hit in the head. She didn't think she had been injured anywhere else, other than what might result from being grabbed and manhandled by a dragon. As she struggled to think, bits and pieces came back.

She remembered the pirates. She had been fighting them with her yana. Lords, her head hurt. A pirate had tried to stab her with a spear. She had knocked it aside, and then something had hit her. She remembered seeing the yana jump into the air.

She tried to move again. She flexed her hand and felt the rough edges of the dragon's claws. She had never been this close to a dragon before, not that she had ever wanted to. She had no idea where they were going. She turned her head and could almost see the ground. It was a long way down. She closed her eyes again.

The dragons must be climbing, she realized, as the air got colder. She flexed her feet and tried to wiggle her hands. The dragon tightened its grip again, and she gasped in surprise. She closed her eyes and tried to go back to sleep.

Sometime later, Renee felt a sharp descent in her stomach. The air felt warmer, almost humid. She thought she might have fallen asleep, but she wasn't sure. She still couldn't reach the Seven Laws. She had no idea how long she had been carried.

Suddenly, the dragon lurched, and Renee felt a sickening drop as the creature shifted from flight to a hovering position. The dragon's legs dropped, and its head went up. Then she was falling as the talons released her. *I'm going to die!*

She screamed and then hit the ground, gasping in pain as the air was forced out of her lungs. Muscles that had been held motionless for a long period cried out in pain. Her vision swam, and stars burst behind her eyes as her head bounced off the ground. She felt blood under her head. She rolled over and gasped as the dragons landed in a flurry of wind. Grass, sticks, and leaves flew in all directions, forcing her to close her eyes.

When the wind ceased, she heard quick footsteps. Renee tried to raise her shields to protect herself, but her head protested in pain, and she felt a sickening backlash. She couldn't touch the Seven Laws.

"Search her," someone commanded in a rough Ynak accent. Renee had always thought the Ynak accent sounded like someone was talking through a mouthful of mush.

Rough hands grabbed her and pulled her to her feet. For a moment, she saw twice as many dragons as had landed. Slowly, the number of dragons decreased.

Hands searched her efficiently. She bit back a retort as the hands found all the weapons she was wearing, and her face reddened at the intimate familiarity of the search. New hands on her shoulders forced her to her knees. She looked up and saw one of the dragon riders taking his headgear off as he approached.

Renee glared at him. "Why did you abduct me?"

The man sneered. "I am Hensoul, and I will ask the questions." With that, he slapped her hard across the face.

Renee's head snapped to one side, and she tasted blood. She groaned. She was going to have to do this the hard way.

# CHAPTER 30

## Mysteries

ALEXIS MADE HER way through a warren of hallways near the top of the Gold Tower. Her mentor had summoned her. She stopped when a shadow motioned to her.

"I will leave with the war band that Warmaster Briana is taking," Alexis said as she bowed. She was wearing her new battle armor for the first time. It was stiff, and she couldn't quite curtsy in it. She still found it difficult to move in at all, in fact.

"Get up. You don't have to do that anymore. You passed your master's test," the woman in the shadow announced proudly. "Also, don't say that Briana is leaving too loudly. The council has not yet agreed."

Alexis blushed with pleasure and touched the gold swirls on the forearms of her armor. Her new earring from her left ear to her nose glinted in the dim lighting.

"Did your father get you into Briana's inner circle?" the woman asked.

"Yes, he made it her idea," Alexis said, trying to hide her excitement.

"I don't care how he did it," the woman said with a pleased smile. "It is important that you be there. Now listen, and this is very important. You don't have much time. The prince is in danger. I don't need Viktorie's visions to know that."

Alexis nodded, a serious expression on her face.

"Illicia itself is in danger. You must keep me informed of what is happening. You have my tool that I gave you?"

Alexis touched her necklace and nodded.

"Good. Make sure you sleep with it every night. It must be touching your skin to work. It will be easier for me to contact you through your dreams. Now, what are they doing about Ritain?"

"Nothing for now," Alexis said, "just as you predicted."

"Did you train the masters?"

Alexis nodded. "They found a dozen former stonemasons who had grown up in the guilds before studying the Seven Laws, all young like me. Six were able to replicate the magic. I also taught my sister. She can do it as well."

"Impressive for a woman just completing her master's studies," the woman said as she pulled her cloak tight.

"It was your teaching that made it possible," Alexis said in a rush. Alexis smiled and started to say something else, but then the woman moved, and Alexis saw a flash of gold with blue trim. Rebecca had been her secret teacher and mentor for years, and she hid her identity whenever they met in public. Alexis knew her father would not approve of Rebecca being her teacher. Alexis felt vaguely uncomfortable about hiding the truth from her father and mother, but her mentor had a way of explaining magic so much better than her other teachers.

"Now go get ready to tell your sister. I am sure you have told her most of what I have taught you."

Alexis flushed angrily. How had she known? "Yes, ma'am," she said as she bowed her head. Then she spun on her heel and departed quickly.

The woman eyed her student's departure with trepidation. *Will I ever see her again?* "The Seven Gods protect us," she whispered to herself. There was a traitor close to the king, and the leader of the secretive fifth sect of the Gold Robes was worried. The Hunters would not be satisfied until the traitors had been killed and Sillik sat on the Illician throne.

Glancing back down the hallway, Rebecca knew her star pupil was late for her next appointment. Kenton had decided he would take Alexis to the armory to choose an appropriate sword. Alexis had taken the standard classes with the sword and could hold her own. Hopefully, Rebecca thought, Briana would work with her.

# CHAPTER 31

## Unintended Consequences

SILLIK LOST TRACK of time as the battle raged. Then just as suddenly as it had begun, it was over, and the dragons left.

He had been knocked off his yana at some point in the fighting, and he had no idea where the beast was. Sillik walked through the remains of the camp and found Wolfstein near the water, trying to save the life of one of his guards. Sillik knew it was a lost cause, and soon Wolfstein realized it as well. He washed his hands in the muddy river and stood up, but he wouldn't meet Sillik's eyes.

"Sillik, my friend, you must remember that she was the only woman—the dragon riders took her."

Sillik felt sick. He knew he shouldn't have brought her. "How long ago?"

"She was fighting like you were on the yana. A spear killed the yana, and then a dragon swopped in and captured her."

"We must go after her," Sillik said as he looked around.

"I am ruined as a merchant. No one hires a broke merchant," Wolfstein said as he picked up an arrow. "I would like to choke the life out of the men who did this to me," he continued as he broke the arrow.

"There is a way," Sillik said hesitantly. *Maybe this is why Lysander taught me how to use this magic*, Sillik thought. *Lady Silvia made him teach it to me. She told me that, even if Lysander would not.* "There is a way," Sillik repeated with more confidence. "It isn't a way I would have chosen, but it can be done. I will need your help." An old adage went through his mind, and he said it aloud: "The gods help those who help themselves."

"How?" Wolfstein asked. "We have no mounts, and we are alone. We can't even cross the river." He pointed at the burning hulks floating away on the river current. "How can we catch the dragons? It will take weeks to build a raft by ourselves."

"You and I can do it," Sillik said, wondering if they really could. His artificial confidence was transparent.

"Impossible," Wolfstein said. "I am ruined. I would like to kill them, but I do not see how I can."

"I know a way," Sillik said quietly.

"Impossible," Wolfstein said as he threw the arrow into the river.

"Wolfstein," Sillik said, "I could use your help."

"You could indeed," Wolfstein snorted derisively. "You—you are one man. What can one man do against dragons?"

"You have knowledge that I don't have," Sillik said. "You can help me. By tomorrow, we will be able to follow the dragons. Then you can have your revenge."

"You don't even know which way they went. Even if you did, how far did they fly? Is she even still alive? How do you know they didn't simply use her and then throw her to her death?"

"I can make a pretty good guess which way they went," Sillik said with confidence that he didn't feel.

Sillik remembered seeing the shapes resembling dragons high in the air while they were on the Road of Adel. He cursed himself for not taking the proper precautions to ensure they weren't spotted. Through his stupidity, he had caused many needless deaths and the abduction of Renee.

"I can find her. I must," Sillik said with quiet confidence. He was sure she was one of the allies Lady Silvia had mentioned.

"Maybe," Wolfstein said. Sillik noticed that Wolfstein's defense was weakening. "But how? A dragon can fly in one day what would take a man weeks to cover on foot."

"There are other ways to move," Sillik said. "You want revenge, don't you?" *I need him. He knows things that might be important.*

Wolfstein nodded and then stalked away. After a moment, Sillik walked in the other direction. Beside the dead and burned body of one of the yana, Sillik found the leather bags that the animal had carried. At least he still had his supplies.

Drawing his sword like he did after every fight, Sillik inspected it for damage. Once again, the blade was clean and sharp. He put it back in its sheath. Then, using a minor exercise of the Fourth Law, Sillik spoke a quick incantation.

The body of the yana burst into flame. The fire was special, for it gave off no heat and made no smoke. It was a fitting tribute to the noble creature. For a moment, Sillik watched the flames leap skyward. Then he turned to face Wolfstein, who stood behind him, watching the flames.

"Nine of them," Wolfstein said quietly. "They were dark and terrible. They came like giant birds of prey and hovered like dark clouds. Their riders just sat astride the beasts and watched. The dragons' wings beat the air like thunder. The beasts turned their heads this way and that as they hovered, their breath burning anything and everything. Their eyes had a way of burning a man without any flame. And everybody just stood and watched the beasts. Nobody tried to flee. Nobody tried to fight. It was terrible, just terrible. The smell, the smoke, and then it was my turn. I couldn't think. I took a step backward as the beast's mouth opened. I stumbled, and the next thing I knew, I was underwater. My lungs burned. The water above me boiled. I grabbed some roots and pulled myself deeper. My lungs ached. Finally, when I was on the verge of losing consciousness, I let go. The current carried me a thousand spear lengths downstream before I came to the surface. When I looked around, the dragons were gone."

"They can be fought," Sillik said. "It doesn't have to be that way."

Wolfstein nodded.

"Then you will go after the dragons with me?"

Wolfstein nodded again. "May the Seven Gods forgive me!"

"Why shouldn't they?" Sillik asked. "I don't think they will fault you for your decision."

"You cannot be sure of that," Wolfstein replied. Then he walked away.

Sillik turned back to face the fire. It was nearly out. Most of the yana's body had been consumed. After both men had wandered the battlefield for a time, Sillik approached Wolfstein.

"The dead must be honored," the merchant said in a tired voice.

"Very well." Sillik wrapped a cloth around his face and went to collect the bodies of those slain in the fighting. He ignored the pirates and selected only the bodies of Wolfstein's men, dragging them into a pile near the river's edge. Flies had already descended on the bodies and buzzed in irritation.

Sillik could feel Wolfstein's eyes watching him as he worked. Soon, Wolfstein started dragging bodies as well. With two working at it, the task didn't take long. When they had finished, Wolfstein said something about getting some oil and flint to light a fire.

"No need," Sillik said. He waved his hand, and the bodies burst into flame.

"Who are you?" Wolfstein asked as he stared at the flames.

To such a question, there was only one answer. "I am an Illician," Sillik said. It was a matter of honor. He didn't dare reveal that he was a member of the royal family, much less the soon-to-be king. *Don't give answers that require longer answers*, Sillik thought. *Now I know I'm tired if I'm quoting scripture.*

"An Illician," Wolfstein said thoughtfully. "An Illician!" he roared. "By the Wondrous Seven, an Illician!" The gleam in Wolfstein's eyes told Sillik that he suddenly understood many things he had not understood a few moments before. He looked at Sillik with new appreciation. "What is your plan for catching the dragons?"

Sillik smiled. "I could say that my ancestors made many pacts with the denizens of many worlds. In return for aid that my ancestors gave freely, the creatures promised to give their aid to the Illician people as long as the Illicians lived on Earth or until they were released from their service by one of the royal line."

"Is it possible to do what you say—to summon aid from another plane?"

"I could also say," Sillik said with a grin, ignoring Wolfstein's question, "that the cliff fliers of Aceon owe me a favor."

Wolfstein snorted in laughter. "Aceon. I was there once. I have seen the Herish, but I have never flown before. How will you acquire them?"

"I will use the Seven Laws and create a portal."

Wolfstein eyed him uncomfortably. "Is it dangerous?"

Sillik shrugged. "A little."

Wolfstein chuckled. "I see."

"Relax." Sillik approached the water. At the edge of the muddy river, he splashed some water on his hands to remove the blood and dirt. He was tempted momentarily to wash his face but decided to wait until he had cleaner water.

He noticed that Wolfstein had also waded into the water and was splashing water onto his face and arms. Sillik approached him. "You go on," Sillik said. "Light a fire and dry off." Then he pulled a broken lance from under a bush and brushed the moist sand from the glistening blade. "I'm going to see what I can do about augmenting our supplies."

"Splendid," Wolfstein said. The two men went their separate ways to fulfill their tasks.

Wolfstein was sitting beside a fire when Sillik returned. The fire was dying and the former merchant was staring into the glowing embers. Embers popped and rose into the cooling air.

Without a word, Sillik laid two large brown fur–covered bags beside his friend. Then he headed into the darkness and back toward the river.

When Sillik was out of sight, Wolfstein opened one of the bags. A delicious aroma wafted up. Looking inside, Wolfstein saw at least a dozen pieces of meat. Each piece was the length of a man's hand, half as wide, and as thick as a man's forearm. Ravenous, Wolfstein tore off a large piece of meat and relished the delicious taste as he devoured it. He could taste several strange herbs that had been cooked into the meat. Wolfstein also recognized that the way the meat had been cooked meant it would survive many weeks. After he closed the bag and tied it shut, he wiped his fingers on the grass and wondered. He had heard an animal's scream, but he had seen no sign of a fire. As he was thinking, he stroked the fur on the outside of the bag. After a few moments, he realized what he was doing and examined each of the bags.

Wolfstein realized suddenly that he had never seen fur like this before. What kind of beast was it from? The fur was long and soft. If he could sell a few pelts like these, he could retire a wealthy man. It was impossible, he decided firmly, for one man to dress and cook an animal the size of this one in the time that had elapsed. The meat must have been a gift from the Seven Gods. Then he recalled that Sillik was a master of the Seven Laws. Could he have done such a thing? Wolfstein trembled and looked uneasily over his shoulder at Sillik washing in the river. What was he getting himself into?

He looked around, still trembling uneasily. So many things were happening that he didn't understand. A war had erupted between Ynak, Peol, and Nerak. Illicians were wandering the land. There were dark rumors of a forestall in the Forest of Mirath. Then there was the beast Sillik had slain and the assassination of the king of Teris. Wolfstein shivered again.

Opening a wineskin he had been saving, Wolfstein swallowed several large mouthfuls. Red drops ran down his chin as he drank. As the warm wine spread through his body, he began to relax. Feeling sleepy, he wrapped his cloak around himself and lay down beside the dying embers of the fire.

The next morning, Wolfstein awoke, shivering. The sun was already rising in the blue, cloudless sky. As Wolfstein stood, he saw Sillik kneeling beside one of the wagons, facing the glowing sun. Then he heard a strange noise in the air. Or was the sound coming *from* the air?

# CHAPTER 32

## War Band

BRIANA HAD FINALLY won the argument and issued orders immediately. It had taken seven days to prepare for their departure. By midday, more than two thousand lizards were saddled. One rider commanded each beast, and four additional soldiers rode. Two carried pikes, and two carried bows. All of the warriors, whether male or female, wore the red belt and swords. The lizards were divided into ten squads of twenty animals. The golden eagle of Illicia fluttered from every pike, as did multicolored stripes, which marked the squads. Just over ten thousand troops rode to war. One hundred lizards were dedicated as pack animals, carrying food, water, and supplies for the force. They traveled behind the troops.

Briana cursed the fact that the acrobats who had escaped Illicia had apparently all been lost to the sandfish—except for the one the Nomads had brought to her. She had been a legitimate member of the trade delegation and had been treated almost like a captive by those escaping into the desert. It made no sense.

The woman Greenup had captured on the walls had been a different story. But the girl knew nothing useful. Her job had been to get to the top of the wall around the keep, and she and others had used non-magical techniques for that. Ropes and hooks were all they had needed at that point—well, that and a long bow. Others had used crossbows to shoot something at the keep, and four others had crossed the wire and then climbed the keep using ancient magic.

The troops Briana had sent to Hell's Gate had found nothing to prove or disprove the Nomads' story. She hoped the Nomads wouldn't be too insulted.

In the courtyard of the keep, before the council, Briana had delegated Kenton to lead the city in her absence. Kenton had then blessed her and the war band with a prayer from the seventh book: "Do the gods' work and praise their names. They are with you and support you. They will watch over you. If you fall, they will catch you, and you will live with them forever. Praise be the Seven Gods." Kenton had then kissed her on the cheek, and Elizabet had hugged her tightly, before Briana climbed into her saddle.

Briana now pulled up her desert veil and gave a curt nod to the lizard driver. Moments later, they were hurtling down the streets. By prior arrangement, the streets had been cleared, and the shopkeepers had shuttered their doors and windows. Before traffic returned, the street cleaners would make a pass and clean what the lizards left behind.

Briana grinned as the lizards spilled out of Illicia and settled into formation. Twenty lizards and their troops surrounded her as bodyguards. Sixty Gold Robes were in saddle as well. It was the largest force that had been sent from Illicia in living memory and the largest collection of Gold Robes to go into battle in a thousand years. The lizards in her formation carried the golden eagle with borders of gold, the sign of the royal house. If there was a perk to her position, this was it. Forty healers were also in saddle.

Senarick, vicar general of the Gold Robes, rode a nearby lizard. He lived to ride lizards. When he was younger, he had raced lizards in the king's annual races. He was very proud of his victories.

The lizard drivers sat astride their beasts between the lizards' neck and back spikes. The neck spikes in front of them were ground down to make room for the riders. Four saddle baskets hung on either side of the lizards and were riveted to the back spikes. Iron loops embedded in the lizard's cheek scales were connected to reins. Although the spikes near the riders were blunt, the spikes on the lizards' tails were sharpened.

Keltic sat to Briana's left. He had a silly grin on his face and was holding onto a spine for all he was worth. Brian smiled at him as she fondly remembered her first excursion as swordmaster. One bodyguard rode behind Briana. Beside him was Alexis, so that she could be close to the warmaster.

Despite the lizards' speed, it took them five days to reach Colum. As they crested the horizon, the people of Colum panicked. Long-unused and badly out-of-tune battle horns sounded as the gates closed. The few people caught outside the gates ran madly toward the city. It was a comical sight, and if Briana had been so inclined, she would have laughed. Instead, she merely pursed her lips. Had Sillik come this way? That had been his plan. Why, she still couldn't imagine. She had come here once, long ago, and had vowed never to return. He should have avoided this trap.

She raised her gloved fist, and two thousand lizards plowed to a stop. Lances were lowered and arrows nocked as a wall of dust enveloped the troop. When the dust settled, the lizards sank to their haunches, their tongues flicking in and out as they tested the air. The battle drums sounded one final note and then fell silent.

Perspiration dripped from Briana's face. Her leathers were hot, but she didn't feel it. Her heart pounded as a lone arrow arched up from the city. It seemed to move slowly in the sky. Thousands of eyes watched it fly.

Briana smiled. There were no answering arrows. Illician discipline was flawless. Her warriors wouldn't attack unless ordered.

Slowly, the arrow reached its apogee and started its downward trek. It was going to be close. Her driver watched the arrow intently, gripping the lizard's reins in case they had to move. Briana swallowed and gripped her pommel. She wanted it to miss. She didn't want to have to raze the city today. To her relief, the arrow fell short by a dozen paces. Briana lowered her fist and exhaled slowly.

Everyone waited to see what would happen next. In her mind, she could see the leader of the city hurrying out to see what was happening—if he wasn't changing his soiled pants, that is. She smirked at the thought. She could see the consternation and chaos on the walls as guards rushed to their posts and struggled into long-unused armor. How long had it been since they had drilled for an attack?

*I could destroy this city,* a part of her mind whispered. *I am the warmaster of the strongest city in the world. Colum deserves to be eliminated. All I have to do is say the word. No, I can't think this way.* It was tempting though to fall into that trap.

Greenup pointed at a funeral pyre in the distance. "Something has happened here," he observed dryly. "I wonder if Sillik had anything to do with it. Also, I was here about ten years ago. Their emergency response has gotten better. The last time I was here, they couldn't even get their gates closed. Their guards were drunk and asleep."

Briana nodded and seethed with anger as she waited. When the gate finally cracked open and five men stepped out, she gloated. They were on foot. One carried a white flag. Briana grinned and took a deep breath. She could relax a little. It was time to talk.

Briana held her hand up and then lowered it quickly. The bows that had suddenly come up when the gate opened were lowered. Her driver looked at her over his shoulder. She nodded, and he urged their lizard forward. Greenup and Senarick followed on their lizards. Rather than approach on foot, they would talk from their saddles. Illician lizards were twice as tall as a man and very intimidating. It would be impossible for the men from Colum to lie. The lizards looked around in irritation, their tongues darting in and out. They hissed and ruffled their spikes. They could smell fear, and the men from Colum reeked of it.

Once the lizards had stopped and crouched low, Briana announced, "I am Briana, warmaster of Illicia." She removed her battle helmet and lowered her veil.

Even crouched, the lizards towered over the men from Colum. The men's eyes were wide with fear and surprise—fear at what the Illicians might do and surprise at a female warmaster.

She nodded to her left. "Lord General Greenup. He is our battle lord."

Greenup had already exposed his face. He nodded and smiled at the men as he took off his gloves. He twisted in his saddle and hooked a knee over the pommel. Then he casually drew a dagger and began to trim his fingernails. The fact that he was using a throwing knife was not lost on the men.

Briana looked to her right. "Senarick, vicar general of the Gold Robes." Senarick bowed his head stiffly in his battle armor, his bald head glistening with sweat.

She next turned slightly and nodded at the man to her left on the lizard. "Keltic, swordmaster of Illicia." Keltic made no move other than to raise a few fingers. His eyes were fixed on the men from Colum. *Good*, Briana thought. *He is doing his job.*

The man in the center of the small group from Colum nodded respectfully as each individual was named. "I am Renunel," he said, his voice calm despite his obvious fear. "I am the leader of Colum. My apologies for the arrow; the archer will be punished. To my left is Lord Simeon, weapon master of Colum. To my right is Lord Charick, deputy war lord. Now how may we assist our Illician neighbors?" He smiled broadly and stepped forward.

Suddenly, a flash of light struck the ground in front of him, and sand flew upward. "Please, no closer," Greenup said as he held out his hand.

Renunel looked down and saw the hilt of Greenup's dagger sticking out of the sand at his feet. "Of course," Renunel said, raising his hands in compliance. "I meant no offense."

"None taken," Greenup said. He held out his hand, and the dagger flew back into it.

The eyes of Renunel's men widened in fear. "Use of the Seven Laws is illegal in Colum," Renunel said flatly.

"I will keep that in mind," Greenup said, "if I should ever enter your fair city."

"Tell me, Renunel," Briana said. "My reports indicated someone else was in charge of Colum, someone less militaristic."

"Your reports are somewhat out-of-date, Warmaster," Renunel said. "We have made, ah, changes."

"I see," Briana said, leaning forward in her saddle. "We are looking for a man who came this way."

"An Illician?" Renunel asked as he glanced at his companions. His eyes seemed troubled. He looked past Briana and down the Illician lines. "Thousands of lizards," he said, "for one man?" He spread his hands helplessly. "What crime could a man commit that would require such a force?"

"No crime," Briana said smoothly. "We ride to his aid. Have you seen a lone Illician warrior?"

"It must be him," blurted the man to Renunel's right.

"We have seen such a man," Renunel said with a weary sigh. "He lit the fire of revolution here in Colum and killed the former leader of our city. I need your word that you will aid him."

Greenup laughed but didn't say a word.

Briana glanced disapprovingly at Greenup and then nodded. "That sounds like the man we seek. He has a knack for doing the unexpected—and causing some trouble. If it is the man I seek, I swear we will aid him. What name did he give?"

"Sillik," Renunel said. "He said his name was Sillik."

"The king," Briana's driver said, and Briana swore.

Renunel looked up sharply. "He is your liege?"

Briana's eyes narrowed. This man, Renunel, already knew the answer. For the sake of his companions, Briana nodded. "He is. How long was he here?"

"No more than three or four days."

"When he left, where did he go?" Briana asked.

"He said he needed to see a knight," Renunel said. "I didn't understand what he meant. He didn't say any more about his plans."

Briana glowed in satisfaction. It was obvious to her where he was going. "Then we should be able to catch him soon," she announced.

Renunel grimaced, looking uncomfortable.

Briana felt a tickle of fear for the first time since leaving Illicia. Anger and impatience threatened to explode. "You obviously have something else to say, man, so say it, and be quick about it."

Renunel looked at her for a long moment. He saw the gold swirls on the sleeves of her armor and shuddered. He knew what they meant. "We gave him a gift when he left."

"What gift?"

"Yana," Renunel said. "We gave him two yana. So, you see, it will be quite impossible for you to catch him." Renunel's companions shifted uncomfortably and looked away.

Stunned, Briana stared at Renunel. Where in the world had they gotten two yana? Yana could outrun and maybe even outfight a lizard. Rather than being days behind, they could now be weeks behind Sillik.

"Who accompanied him?" Greenup asked. "You did say 'two,' didn't you? Who went with him?"

"Ah yes," Renunel said as he shuffled his feet. "He left with a woman he met here in Colum. She was the niece of one of our former generals. We think her uncle died before the fighting began, but we never found his body. Most strange. Her name is Renee, and she was most eager to go with him. She is beautiful, and more than a few were disappointed to see her leave."

Briana glared at Renunel. "Of course she was," she said dryly and then sat back in her saddle in disgust.

Greenup chuckled, and Briana glared at him. She was suddenly aware of the heat from the desert. Her face was hot, and the perspiration that had been dripping in her eyes was suddenly gone. She hoped her face had not betrayed her emotions.

"Is he in danger?" Renunel asked.

"We think so," Greenup said, finally regaining his composure. "What can you tell us about this woman?"

"She is beautiful and of legal age," Renunel said. "She also has, shall we say, a special fondness for weapons." Renunel looked at Briana. "Like you do, I suspect. Her father was the governor of Covenon, and she was born there. Also, she is well-educated." The way Renunel said "educated" seemed to imply something else, and he had nodded in Briana's direction as he said it.

She didn't understand for a moment but then glanced down and touched the gold swirls on her battle armor. It finally dawned on her what he meant. Briana tapped the gold swirls and smiled at Renunel.

Renunel nodded. "I see we understand one another."

Briana was both stunned and amused. The man had left to find out who was killing his family and had found the only woman with magical training in a thousand leagues. A coincidence? She wondered what Sillik suspected. What did he know?

"To what degree was she educated?" Greenup asked.

"I am told she was trained to the Seventh School."

Renunel's companions looked confused.

Greenup smiled to himself. The Seventh School was the name of the schools in Salone. Since the man had said "to the Seventh," that meant she was a master of the Seven Laws. Greenup shook his head. Even Lord Kenton would be forced to admit that those were impressive credentials. He glanced at Briana, and she nodded at him. She had understood as well.

Renunel changed his tone. "We gave your king our word that should he need help, we would come to his aid." He stood a little straighter and squared his shoulders. "We do not have the resources of Illicia, but we would honor our pledge and send help."

Briana nodded formally. She remembered the words her father had always stressed before he died: "never deny anyone their honor." "We cannot pause to wait for you," she said. "But you may send whatever forces you can muster and honor the treaties of old and your debt to our king. There is war afoot in the land, and we ride fast."

Renunel met her eyes and spoke evenly. "It shall be done, Warmaster of Illicia."

Briana nodded. "Follow our trail; we ride north."

With that, her driver yanked on the reins of the lizard, pulling the animal to the right. The lizard hissed and spat but jumped into a run. Greenup and his lizard were beside her quickly. In moments, the rest of the Illician war band was at a run as they raced to the north.

Briana raised her veil and laughed at the wind.

Renunel and his companions waited for the dust to settle before they raced back into Colum. Renunel was already issuing orders as they ran. There were thousands of things to do before they could leave.

# CHAPTER 33

## The Herish

S ILLIK EYED THE sun carefully as he
began his work. The timing must be
precise. The birds would be ready for midwatch. In his mind, he saw the Cliffs
of Aceon and the aviary. *Level D of the Green Aviary*, he thought. He wanted two
birds in particular. In his mind, he began to twist the required energies. He must
connect the two points. The birds would survive the portal. They shouldn't have
riders on them yet. The men who rode midwatch were arrogant bastards. *The
prince will understand–I hope.*

Once he had the desired locations fixed in his mind, he wrapped the
energies around the points and tore a hole in the air. Lightning flashed, and a
clap of thunder rolled over him. Distantly, he heard Wolfstein yell in fear. He
felt the birds jump through the hole. The other end of the hole closed, but
the opening on Sillik's end twisted and jerked as something else tried to come
through.

"By the Seven!" Sillik swore as he realized what was happening. He
struggled to control the hole. For a moment, he feared he had lost his grip.

Then a voice from beyond the opening spoke to him. "When you have
need, call and I will aid you."

Sillik gasped as he finally slammed the gateway closed. He panted for a
moment and felt the perspiration dripping down his face. He struggled to his

feet and looked around. Wolfstein was standing a short distance away, looking at the two Herish that stood on the riverbank, preening.

"What did you do?" Wolfstein asked as he gripped his spear nervously.

"I opened a portal and borrowed two of the midwatch Herish from the cliff fliers of Aceon."

"Won't they mind?" Wolfstein asked.

Sillik grinned. "I expect the riders are going to be quite upset."

"Is that your plan? Upset enough people so they will come after you?"

Sillik grinned. "I doubt the cliff fliers are going to come after me."

Wolfstein gave Sillik an uneasy look, unsure of what the man meant. "Is it possible for us to go through that portal?"

Sillik shook his head. "No man or woman has ever been through a portal. They go in, but they never come out."

Sillik returned to the remains of their fire and sat down, legs crossed. Wolfstein knelt beside the bags of meat.

"Take one piece," Sillik directed, "and cut it in half."

While Wolfstein did as directed, Sillik explained. "The meat is very sustaining. The secret to it was lost until a hundred years ago, when the proper sequence of spells and herbs was rediscovered. If eaten sparingly, one piece will sustain a man for a week."

Wolfstein felt guilty as he ate his morning meal. He had unknowingly consumed a week's worth of food the previous night. For a while, they ate in silence.

"When will we leave?" Wolfstein asked finally. "I want to get as far away from here as I can."

"Soon," Sillik said. Then he went over the fundamentals of flying on Herish. "The saddle has two straps, one in the front and another in the back. Use them both. Keep them tight but not restrictive. The saddle is pitched forward to keep your head near the bird's neck. It's comfortable. It just takes some time to get used to the position. Keep your feet in the stirrups. To descend, push your toes down. To climb, push your toes up and your heels down. Use the reins to steer left or right."

When the lesson was over, Sillik studied the two birds. The one with reddish-brown plumage was by far the larger. The other bird was dull brown. Their talons gleamed with unholy sharpness. Both wore black leather saddles. Each saddle was held in place by three cinches, one looped around the throat, one in front of the wing, and the last angled behind the wing and under the body.

"It has been a long time, Red Wing," Sillik said quietly so only he and the bird could hear. "There is a silver band near the talons. On the band, the bird's name is inscribed," Sillik explained.

"It is difficult to read," Wolfstein said as he studied the script. "Ah, I see, Brown Death. What is yours called?"

"My bird is Red Wing," Sillik said. "It was foretold a long time ago that I would ride this bird."

"Um, okay," Wolfstein said, but he didn't ask questions.

"Why don't you go get our supplies?" Sillik suggested.

"Good idea." Wolfstein smiled as he trotted up the hill to the campsite.

Sillik studied the high-cantle saddles carefully. Although the leather was shaped for a man, the design was unique to Aceon. Someone had devoted a great deal of care to these birds. *I probably know who groomed them*, he thought as the image of a short man with short black hair formed in his mind. *What was his name? Yes, Remey.* Sillik smiled.

While Wolfstein was getting their supplies and the two spears that had been saved, Sillik greeted the Herish with the customary greetings. Their black eyes gleamed with intelligence.

*The wing leaders will be furious over the loss of their mounts*, Sillik thought. *I hope the aviary master intervenes. They might beat Remey.* It had been a long time since he had flown a Herish, but it seemed like yesterday. *How long has it been since she died? The nightmares have become less frequent. Is it because I am thinking about someone else?*

Wolfstein returned and handed him a bag of meat and a spear. Sillik stuck the point of the spear into the turf next to Red Wing and then placed his boot in the stirrup and pulled himself onto the saddle. He tied his bag onto the saddle behind him.

Wolfstein tied his bag of meat onto his bird's saddle from the ground. He was still nervous, and it showed.

"Your bird, Brown Death, is an expert in aerial combat," Sillik explained. "Trust it."

"Were these the birds you wanted?" Wolfstein asked.

"Yes, they are," Sillik said with a smile of satisfaction. "Yes indeed."

"And you can just borrow the birds?"

Sillik shook his head. "I was taught how to borrow them. There are people there who will understand." *Lysander, I hope you understand*, Sillik thought.

After his other foot found the other stirrup, Sillik looked at his friend. Wolfstein placed his foot in his first stirrup and then paused. The brown beast tilted its head questioningly. Sillik laughed, and his obvious merriment gave courage to the faltering merchant. As Wolfstein mounted his winged beast, Sillik retrieved his spear from the ground. As expected, he found a loop in which the end of the spear could rest. He pointed out the corresponding leather strap on Brown Death's saddle to Wolfstein.

Gently, Sillik goaded Red Wing with his heels. The great creature shook its wings and then threw itself into the air. Wolfstein followed a moment later.

# CHAPTER 34

## Tea Time

BRIANA SAT DOWN beside the hot stones and looked at her companion. The war band had set up camp for the night, and Briana had just finished walking the perimeter of the camp with Greenup. The Gold Robes had just heated some stones for Briana to warm some tea. "Okay, my dear," she said soothingly. "We are alone for a moment. I sent your tent mates off on an errand. I wanted some time alone with you, miss. Now tell me why I appointed you to my staff."

Alexis looked up in surprise as she eased her breastplate off. It was hot and was irritating her skin. Briana, on the other hand, looked comfortable and relaxed in her armor.

"Don't look so surprised," Briana said, a slight edge to her voice. "You and I both know you manipulated your father, and he manipulated me. It was skillfully done. What strikes me as odd is that a master's student could pull off such a trick. So why? And be warned, I will see the truth of your words. That is my talent."

Alexis sat back in surprise as she looked at the warmaster. Her teacher had said this might happen, and if it did, she had to tell the truth. "There are people in the Gold Tower," she said slowly. "My mentor is one of them. They are worried. It was suggested by one of my teachers that I could provide a useful set of eyes. I am to protect you."

Briana raised her eyebrows in surprise. "Do they serve the Seven?"

"Of course," Alexis said, her cheeks flashing red in anger.

Briana scrutinized the young woman. Alexis regained her composure quickly, but her eyes were worried. *Time for the hammer.* "Are you a Hunter?"

Alexis's eyes widened in surprise. Clearly, she hadn't expected the question. "I have been told to tell you the truth," Alexis said with resigned acceptance. She took a deep breath. "Yes, I was initiated into the Hunters the night after my master's test."

Briana nodded as she continued to study the younger woman. "The healer Rebecca—is she your mentor?"

Alexis nodded. "She is the head of the sect. And if you know Rebecca, you know we serve the Seven. She said we should be here to support you and Lord Sillik if that is possible."

Briana smiled. She had found a note to Sillik from his father about the Hunters, and she had guessed that Rebecca had presented it to Sillik.

"We?" Briana asked.

"I am not the only Hunter," Alexis said. "But I may not tell you the names of any others. I have sworn to protect them."

"I do not intend to ask their names. I did some research on the Hunters. A lot has been written, but it is almost entirely speculative. More recently, there have been several unexplained things that I am going to attribute to them." She smiled grimly. "I don't think I really want to know anyway. I do want your oath that if you learn anything important, you will tell me."

Alexis's entire body relaxed in relief. "Of course."

"Now," Briana said sharply, "put your armor back on. This is a war camp. I expect you to have your armor on at all times and be ready to fight. If it is uncomfortable, then you'll need to grow thicker skin."

"Yes, Warmaster," Alexis said as she reached for her breastplate.

"I was asked by your father to improve your swordsmanship. Come to my tent every night before dinner. You are going to go through all the sword forms, and then we will spar." She grinned. "You are going to work harder than you have ever worked before. I don't want you to die on my watch." Briana sipped her tea as she watched the younger woman.

Alexis gulped and paled. "Yes, Warmaster."

"Now I need you to watch my back for a moment. I have a message to send," Briana said as she looked around.

Alexis nodded. "The prince?" she guessed.

Briana nodded as she settled down and embraced the Seven Laws.

When Briana abruptly stood a few minutes later, she swore. "North," she muttered. "Can't even tell me any more than that, can he? Damn man." Ignoring Alexis, Briana headed toward her tent, calling loudly for the lord general. Her guards followed discreetly although more than one cast stern looks at Alexis, thinking the new Gold Robe had upset the warmaster.

Much later that night, Alexis lay awake on her hard pallet, still wearing her armor, and sent her own message back to Illicia. The four other women in the tent were all asleep, and two snored quietly. She had waited until they were asleep so that they wouldn't feel her use of the Seven Laws.

Rebecca responded instantly and absorbed Alexis's information. A pleased and well-done impression came back along with an admonition in the next heartbeat to be careful. Now it was Alexis's turn to be frustrated; she got no new instructions or information as the contact faded away.

# CHAPTER 35

## The Hunt

S WIFTLY, THE HERISH climbed higher and higher. After a few minutes, Sillik turned his bird west, in the general direction of Ynak. Wolfstein's Herish followed instinctively. The whiplike crack of the wings sent a burst of exhilaration through Sillik's veins, as did the rush of the cool air moving past his face. But it also brought back uncomfortable memories of other times and other people. He smiled despite the memories.

"At this rate, we shall catch the dragons by tomorrow!" Wolfstein yelled.

Sillik smiled and nodded.

They flew the entire day, finally landing by a small lake at sunset. The two men stretched out and ate a scant meal while the birds drank from the lake. As the stars appeared and the moons rose, they took to the air again. Calling on reserves of energy, Sillik stayed awake and kept them on course, using the stars as his guide.

While they flew through the night, Sillik had time to think about all he had done since leaving Illicia. In the city of Colum, he had slain the emperor and initiated a coup. Before the coup was over, he had left the city with a beautiful woman, with whom he suspected he had fallen in love. They had gone north, where war was beginning. Armies were moving, and Sillik knew he was flying to battle.

When he felt the tug of Briana's communication, he slipped easily into the link. He nodded at the information she sent. It was hard to concentrate and fly, so he did not say much—he just sent a northward course and nothing else. He felt her disappointment as the link faded.

Sillik was still planning to find Dernot Lafliar and stop the dark masters from whatever they were planning. But now he was racing across the land in a mad pursuit of those who had kidnapped Renee. Sillik wondered if he would ever find her. The land was wide. He was taking a terrible risk by assuming that the dragon riders would return to their city. Even now they might be flying in some other direction, intending to rendezvous with their army in the field. It would be suicide to try to force his way into an armed fighting camp.

Sillik knew everything was happening for a reason, though. The killing of his family had been a brilliant stroke to remove the Illicians from play. The return of the Dashlinar had been a test to measure his skill. Fortunately, Sillik had not revealed much of his strength by ending the battle as he had. The trap in the throne room had set other events in motion. Silvia had said this was about who would lead the world, Sillik reminded himself. *How does the war affect things, though?* he wondered. Ynak and Nerak had been at peace for years. Illicia could have brokered a peace between them again, but it was the outcome of the challenge and wouldn't participate in the events. The theft of the Shield of Rendar also troubled him. And why had the most powerful magical sword in history decided it was finally time to reenter the world? Renee had also hinted at things, but she had not elaborated much.

When dawn began to show its red face in the east, Sillik let the birds descend. As they circled above the dense forest, searching for a place to land, Wolfstein, who had been sleeping, awoke with a yelp.

They landed on top of a small hill that had once served as an outpost for a long-forgotten city. Evenly spaced piles of stones marked the perimeter of a small fortress. The men found a well nearby, and using some sorcery, Sillik raised a bit of water. Both men drank thirstily. When they sat down to eat, Sillik ate a full piece of meat while his companion ate only half a piece. Wolfstein offered Sillik a little wine, but he refused.

As they prepared to return to the sunlit skies, Wolfstein said, "Point the way, and I can lead. You need sleep."

Sillik smiled. "I am fine, and I must lead. We could catch the dragons at any time. I will be ready to fight, and so must you."

Wolfstein nodded, but his eyes looked worried.

They flew all that day. The birds' strength seemed limitless. As they flew, Sillik saw a herd of fleet-footed anil below. With a word, he released the Herish to hunt. The birds wheeled, lining the sun up at their backs. Then they swooped down on the unsuspecting herd. The wind whistled past the men, and they crouched low in their saddles as the birds executed a stomach-wrenching dive. The herd scattered as the birds struck. Each bird chose a large buck and broke its back. They tore the meat from the bones and gulped down large bites.

Then, with great backward strokes of their wings, the birds climbed into the air once again. Sillik steered the birds northward. He knew they should catch up to the dragons in the next day or so—assuming, of course, that the beasts were returning to their caves. If not, all was lost. *I could scry for her,* Sillik thought, *if this doesn't work.*

As the sun touched the horizon, Sillik looked for a suitable place to land for the night. Sillik let the birds land near another small, sparkling lake. Tall pine and oak trees surrounded the water, and they set down on a small, sandy beach.

Sillik slid off his bird. The muscles in his legs were sore. He looked longingly at the water. Without a word, he stripped down and waded in. The water was frigid, and his teeth chattered as he swam out deeper. In his mind, he remembered Renee doing the same thing after a long day on the yana. He had joined her in the water, and he smiled at the memory.

His flesh felt hot despite the cold, and the blood in his ears roared. Holding his breath, he dove underwater. He kicked his sore legs and propelled himself deep beneath the surface. A score of fish darted out of reach. Returning to the surface, he exploded out of the water and took a deep breath of the warm, humid air.

Then he swam to the shore and trudged out of the water. After he had dried himself with his cloak, he found Wolfstein leaning tiredly on his spear. Sillik got dressed and then stopped beside his bird, where he untied the bag of meat and selected his dinner. He glanced at Wolfstein, a question forming on his lips, but Wolfstein answered before Sillik could ask.

"I ate while you were swimming."

Sillik nodded and closed the bag before he began to devour the cool meat, sparing no thought for manners. When he was finished, he wiped his mouth with the back of his sleeve and grinned.

"Would it not be a good idea to sleep for a while?" Wolfstein asked. "Even now I can feel my muscles stiffening. If we are to engage the enemy soon, I need rest."

After a moment's consideration, Sillik agreed. "It would be a good idea. Let's unsaddle the birds so that they too might enjoy the rest."

When the saddles were lifted from the birds' backs, they hopped into the air with a flap of their wings and landed beside the lake. There they began to preen and bathe fastidiously. Laughing, Sillik drew his daggers and examined the edge of each weapon. When he found some spots on the blades, he rummaged through his things until he found an oilcloth. After oiling his daggers, Sillik relaxed and watched the birds bathe. His mind drifted to the impending battle with the dragons. Then a thought occurred to him.

He sat up and looked at Wolfstein. "I have an idea that could help us when we do catch up to the dragons."

"Great. What is it?"

"Would you gather all of our arrows and the two spears?" Sillik asked as he quickly exercised a minor application of the Third Law. The ritual would enhance his concentration and reinforce the direction his thoughts would soon take. As he finished the ritual, he set a series of mental triggers that would activate it when he was ready. He had never used this particular exercise before, but considering all that he had been through in the past few days, he thought it was highly appropriate.

"Spread the arrows before me, points outward, and lay the spears across them, with the points touching in the middle of the configuration," Sillik directed as he positioned himself.

When Wolfstein had finished positioning the missiles, he backed away, suddenly afraid of whatever Sillik was about to do.

When Sillik was ready, he tripped the triggers he had set. All at once, he experienced the profound deepening of concentration and calmness that came with any exercise of the Third Law. It spread quickly through his mind. At once, he began the rune that would make the weapons especially deadly against dragons.

Wolfstein listened intently as Sillik spoke. By concentrating deeply, he found he could understand Sillik's low chant.

"Dragons death and dragons fall. The stone will crack and towers fall. The power makes and power breaks. The power comes to conquer all."

There was more, but Wolfstein tired of the effort and became content with merely watching. After a while, Sillik stopped speaking and made a series of gestures above the weapons. A shimmering light darted from his fingers and sank into the wood.

Moments later, Sillik let his arms drop. Slowly, his body relaxed. When he finally found the strength to look up, he saw a worried expression on Wolfstein's face. "It is done," Sillik whispered.

Wolfstein nodded and then replaced the arrows in their leather quivers. He needed no warning to be careful.

As Wolfstein replaced the arrows, Sillik forced himself to move. He stood up slowly and walked toward the lake to drink. When he returned, his body had regained much of its vitality. Wolfstein was waiting beside the saddles, the birds standing quietly behind him.

"What did you think?" Sillik asked.

"Fascinating," Wolfstein said. "Will it really help us?"

Sillik nodded.

"So that was wizardry," Wolfstein said. "I wish you had spoken louder, though. As it was, I could barely understand what you said."

Sillik's head shot up. "Are you saying you understood some of it?"

Wolfstein nodded. "A little. Why? Wasn't I supposed to?"

Sillik shook his head in amazement. "It doesn't make any sense. Everything I said tonight was in the ancient tongue spoken by my forefathers. Tell me, what did you hear?"

After Wolfstein recited the words, Sillik shook his head in amazement. "Those lines are part of the opening stanzas of all workings of the Sixth Law. I don't know how you understood them. Not only was I speaking in another language; I thought I was yelling. And yet you barely heard me." Sillik shook his head again. "I will have to think about this. You don't have any family members who were masters of the Seven Laws?"

Wolfstein shook his head as he struggled to recollect. "Could you do that again?" he asked. "Enhance the weapons?"

"I could, but not right away," Sillik said. "It is tiring to do. Why?"

"I was wondering if you could make some more, after we find the woman and kill the dragons," Wolfstein said. "I might be able to start again," he added hopefully.

"I am sorry," Sillik said, "but Illicia does not sell or make enhanced weapons for sale. No one does really. After all, they might get used against you."

Wolfstein nodded. "I figured there were rules against it."

Sillik motioned toward the saddles. "Let's go," he said. "Wolfstein, tell me something. You don't use metal. And you have that crystal knife. In the fighting, I saw you using a staff quite dangerously."

"I'm not a bloody knight, if that's what you're thinking," the merchant muttered as he tightened the cinches on the saddle like Sillik had shown him.

"But you know a lot about the knights," Sillik observed.

"Aye, I do."

"Why?"

Wolfstein paused. "Best get to flying."

Sillik did not mount and instead continued looking at the merchant.

After a moment Wolfstein said, "I once was a knight, but I couldn't live that life. I wanted more. So I left. Stay away from Nerak now, I do. They don't like knights leaving, you see. I still try to help in small ways. Getting those dragons is helping. I think you have a plan, and I want to see those dragons dead so they can't kill any knights. That would be bad. Besides, you offered to pay me. I will take one of those fat purses you have. Get me set up again, it will."

"What about metal?" Sillik asked.

"Well, I ain't a knight no more. So I can use metal. Don't like it none, you understand, but I can do it. I can use that spear and those arrows. Won't use no sword or knife, but I got my own knife now, don't I?"

Sillik looked at the man for a long moment and then untied a purse from his belt and tossed it to the merchant.

The merchant caught it and weighed it in his hand. Nodding, he tucked it into a pocket and said, "Best be flying now, don't you think?"

Sillik mounted his bird, and soon they were soon flying through the cold night air. Sillik shivered and wrapped his cloak around his body.

Hours later, the new day dawned cold and cloudy. Then it began to rain. The two men became miserable quickly. The wind streaming past their faces was wet and cold. Their breath steamed. Rivulets of water rolled off their thick cloaks. The Herish seemed impervious to the weather, though, beating their way faithfully through the sky. Sillik's feet were wet and cold inside his boots. Water was soaking through his cloak as well. It dripped down his face and into his eyes. It was then that they saw the dragons.

Ten of the beasts were flying low, barely above the treetops. But where were the others? Judging from Wolfstein's expression, Sillik knew these were the dragons that had attacked their camp. Sillik and Wolfstein were high above the dragons, so high that the dragons looked like fast-moving specks. Sillik strung his bow. It was hard, but there was a trick, a hook in the saddle. The rain wouldn't help the bowstring. *Three or four shots is all I'll get*, he thought.

As he turned his bird into a tight circle, he realized the dragons were fighting. The pattern they were flying was one of mutual defense. But what could threaten dragons from the ground? Occasionally, one of the flying beasts opened its mouth, and a section of green forest disappeared in a flaming explosion of heat and smoke. Sillik drew an arrow from his quiver. He loosened his sword and readied his spear. Whoever the dragons were fighting would be in need of help. Sillik recalled an ancient proverb: "the enemy of my enemy is my friend."

Suddenly, the rain stopped. Sillik heard one of the dragons scream. Its brassy cry indicated terrible pain. Then the beast plummeted toward the ground. Sillik was suddenly curious and cautious. He had seen no sign of a weapon, and he didn't sense sorcery or wizardry. His speculation was cut short as another dragon cried in pain and fell screaming to the ground. The beast's rider tried courageously to revive his beast but failed. The remaining dragons turned from the battle to make their escape. One of the dragons turned too slowly and died. Another flew too close to the trees, and it also died.

Waving for Wolfstein to follow, Sillik urged his bird into a steep dive. The arrow's fletching tickled his face as he drew his bow. He would have preferred to follow the beasts until he found Renee, but these dragons wouldn't return to the others now. It was sound military policy to lead one's foes away from your comrades.

Sillik fired the first arrow. Wolfstein released his arrow a moment later. Both shafts sank into the lead dragon rider's back. The man stood up in his saddle and arched his back. Even as he died, his dead fingers tried in vain to pluck the wooden shafts from his body. The lead dragon, terrified by the death of its rider, turned and collided with another dragon. With a sweep of its maddened foreleg, the frightened dragon beheaded the other rider. Then, screaming in anger and fear, the beasts attacked each other. Wing fouled wing, claws tore flesh, and teeth bit muscle as the two dragons fell from the sky.

The other dragon riders were confused. As they pondered what had happened, they continued flying in the same direction. It was a mistake; they should have scattered. A new dragon took the uncontested lead. Sillik admired their discipline as he took aim at the left-most dragon. His bird pulled out of its stomach-wrenching dive as Sillik's bow hummed. Through the whistling air, Sillik heard Wolfstein's bow sing as well.

Sillik's arrow streaked through the air, its steel point gleaming unexpectedly as a chance ray of light caught the arrow just before it sank into the dragon's skull. The beast shuddered and then folded its wings and fell like a rock from the sky. Its rider tried fruitlessly to make the beast respond to his commands, not realizing that his beast was already dead. Wolfstein also had the satisfaction of seeing a dragon fall as two of his arrows lodged into another dragon's spine, making flight impossible. Considering what they had faced, the two men had done rather well. Seven beasts had died in a matter of a few heartbeats.

As Wolfstein and Sillik streaked toward their quarry, they realized they could no longer use their bows with impunity, so they drew their spears. Suddenly, the advantages of the Herish became apparent as the dragon riders tried to turn their animals. Before the dragons' chief weapon could be brought to bear, Sillik and Wolfstein swooped down like gods of vengeance and attacked.

Sillik's bird purposely overshot the turning dragon, and Sillik's spear darted in as they shot past. The dragon dodged, but a red, bloody gash appeared on its wing. Climbing rapidly, Sillik's Herish easily avoided the incinerating blast and then turned for another pass. Sillik's heart leapt to his mouth as the Herish folded its wings and dove like a falling rock. The dragon rider tore frantically at something tied to his saddle. A forgotten memory jumped through Sillik's mind. The dragon rider twirled the device above his head as his clumsy beast tried to turn and face Sillik.

Too late, Sillik realized what the weapon was—a long piece of leather with heavy metal weights tied to each end. One end of the weapon was held in the hand while the other was twirled in a circle above a man's head. When released, the weapon flew in lazy circles toward its target. If it struck, the weighted ends of the leather would whip around and around the victim, tying his limbs together. Sometimes the leather had tiny blades embedded in it. In the air, such a weapon would be devastating, possibly stunning a dragon and easily breaking the Herish's light bones. From across the gulf that separated the two men, Sillik could read the dragon rider's skill and confidence in his face.

Sunlight broke through the gray clouds, and Sillik saw the unmistakable gleam of tiny blades in the leather. Seeking to do the unexpected, he stood in his stirrups and prayed as he let his spear fly. Then he pulled back savagely on the bird's reins. Red Wing veered sharply and screamed in protest at the rough treatment. Sillik's spear struck the dragon rider squarely in the chest. The death-dealing shock knocked the man from his saddle. As he fell, with the bewildered dragon crying piteously above him, his fingers twitched. The weapon that had been flying madly in tight circles tore itself out of his dying grasp and struck the dragon as accurately as if it had been aimed. The leather wrapped around one wing, crushing it, the tiny blades easily slicing through the delicate membrane. As the weights shattered the bones in the wing, the beast screamed and plummeted to the ground. Sillik watched the falling dragon for a moment and then glanced over to see how Wolfstein was faring. He spotted Wolfstein's Herish and the remaining dragon locked in combat, so he wheeled his Herish to go to the merchant's aid.

Wolfstein and the dragon rider thrust at each other with their spears while both beasts tried to stay in place. As Sillik neared with agonizing slowness, he saw that Wolfstein was bleeding from a score of wounds. He wished he still had his bow, for he could have easily slain the dragon or its rider. But he also saw something that caused him to smile grimly—the glands on the sides of the dragon's neck were flat and deflated. That would give them a few moments to slay the dragon before it could breathe fire again.

With a cry of fury, Sillik's beast crashed into the fray. The dragon screamed in pain and anger as the Herish's talons sliced through its flesh. Sillik drew his sword as the dragon turned its massive head to ward off this new threat. Instinctively, Sillik's Herish attacked the dragon's face with its beak and talons. The dragon was rewarded with dozens of new wounds.

For a moment, Sillik and his Herish were thrown through the air by the strength of the dragon. They tumbled lifelessly, but then Red Wing regained control with a mighty crack of his wings, and they returned to the battle. Wolfstein was fighting against the dragon itself now, inflicting terrible wounds with his spear.

The dragon rider turned his attention toward Sillik, drawing his curved sword. For a moment, the two swords crossed. Then Sillik drove his sword through his opponent. Amazingly, the man didn't die. Gasping in pain and holding his bleeding wound, the man yelled to his beast in an arcane tongue.

The dragon responded by bugling its triumph and then opening its mouth. Belatedly, Sillik realized what was about to happen. When a blast of flame exploded from the dragon's mouth, Sillik's sword arced down. The blade forged by the Seven Laws split the dragon's skull in two. The dragon whimpered once and then plunged toward the ground.

Red Wing cried in fear as he was dragged down as well. The Herish opened its talons, releasing the dragon, and then leapt upward. A charred lump of quivering feathers, Wolfstein's Herish was pulled down with the dragon.

Sillik scanned the cloudy skies for the last dragon, but it was gone. Then, tears running down his face, he descended after the body of the dragon they had just slain.

The atmosphere in the forest was dark and heavy and unusually quiet. Only the faint breeze made any sound. A feeling of doom settled over Sillik as he landed. It was hot, but Sillik still shivered. "Lady Silvia, now would be a good time for one of your appearances," Sillik said, but there was no response.

Sillik found the dragon's steaming bulk without difficulty. Somehow, miraculously, Wolfstein was still alive. He was unconscious, with broken legs and a burned arm. Quickly, Sillik used his healing abilities to heal the man.

Wolfstein's eyes popped open. "Now there is a sight I never expected to see again. I thought I was done for." He sat up, wincing at minor injuries. "Could've sworn my legs were broken."

"They were," Sillik said tiredly.

"There are knights in these woods," the merchant said with a nervous glance around. "Won't do for them to find me here. Like I said, they don't like men who leave. Breaks their laws, you see."

"You are free to go," Sillik said. "Part of my plan was to meet the knights, and that will happen quickly, I suspect."

Wolfstein nodded as he pushed himself to his feet. "Been good meeting you," he said. "Thank you for fixin' my legs. Don't want to be no cripple. But I best be goin'."

Sillik nodded, and without another word, the merchant darted into the forest, heading south.

Sillik approached his Herish. He patted the bird and inspected its cinches. "You are somewhat the worse for wear, but the aviary masters shouldn't be too mad at me. A bit dirty and a little singed, but still alive. The cliffs are a long way from here, but you know your way home, don't you?" He untied his belongings from the saddle and let them drop to the ground. With a sigh, he dropped a note he had written days ago into a saddlebag. "Goodbye, Red Wing. I hope we will meet again." Then Sillik pulled down on the back of the stirrup, and the beast leapt into the air. Sillik stumbled backward against the sand and dirt, given life by the wings of the Herish. "The knights will have to help me now."

As the Herish climbed, a riderless dragon appeared in the sky. Maddened and berserk, the dragon pursued the bird.

Reluctantly, Sillik summoned his strength. The dragon was closing quickly on the unsuspecting Herish. Sillik had no way of warning his former mount. Weak with hunger and fatigue, he began the spell that would hopefully destroy the dragon. Power crackled through the air as he used the Sixth Law. He would have used this earlier, but it took a lot of power, and Sillik had really wanted a prisoner to interrogate.

Flames licked skyward, and yet nothing burned. His hands began to glow with the blue iridescent power. As the spell climaxed, Sillik's hands shot forward, fingers aimed at the dragon. A blazing ball of fire streaked through the air. Sillik's aim was off slightly, but the ball moved of its own volition, curving toward its target, drawn by the life force of the dragon. The unfortunate beast was blissfully unaware of what hit it. It never even knew it had been slain. Its charred corpse plummeted from the sky. Glancing at the Herish, Sillik saw that it was still climbing and heading east.

*Twelve, maybe fifteen days of flying. And then all hell is going to break loose in Aceon. I wonder if the queen still hates me. Lysander will be in a difficult position,* he thought as he remembered his friend, the prince of Aceon. He was confident the Herish would find its way back.

Kneeling, Sillik gasped for breath. His chest heaved. He closed his eyes and let out a long exhale. Then he collapsed.

When he awoke, the sun was just above the western horizon. He stumbled to the bags he had untied from his Herish and fell to the ground. Then he fumbled with the brown leather bag and removed a large slice of meat. He ate, but his mouth didn't taste. He drank, but his mouth didn't feel.

It was then that he heard voices. The sound carried through the forest. Sillik's eyes roamed through the trees. A flicker of movement drew his eyes upward. They were gliding in–that was why he had not heard the sound of their wings. In an instant, he grabbed the brown leather bag and Wolfstein's spear. A slender branch moved slightly and then was still. Sillik was gone.

# CHAPTER 36

## Cold Trails

B RIANA WAS NOT sure how long
they had been gone from Illicia–long
enough for the days to blur together, though. Since leaving Colum, they had
found Sillik's trail difficult to follow, even though two yana made an easier trail
than two people on foot. The trackers were working hard. Sillik had laid false
trails, doubled back, and changed direction. In addition, the thickening trees
slowed their pace. Now as the trackers led them deeper into the forest, they
had not even found signs of a single campfire. Briana was just getting used to
the monotony when one of her trackers jogged into view. She had kept them
on a northerly course, trusting in the one communication.

"Warmaster," the tracker said. "I am Micah. We found something ahead
that you should see."

Briana nodded and then climbed down from her saddle and followed
the tracker. He led her to a small village, where five small huts were partially
burned. A partial palisade had been erected around the village. Micah pointed
at something above the gate.

Her breath caught as she saw the pieces. "Get them down," she commanded.

Micah looked at his men. "You heard the warmaster."

The men climbed the flimsy gate to retrieve the two sword fragments
that had been nailed there. When the men held out the pieces for Briana to
examine, she ran her fingers over the cheap metal. The edges were dented and

dull, and spots of rust were forming. But what drew Briana's interest was where the weapon had been cut in half. The cut was clean and sharp. Briana had seen weapons break but never cleaved without any sign of melting. She held the two pieces together. A section of the blade was missing, exactly the width of a sword blade. Briana drew a sharp breath. Could Sillik's sword have done this?

Briana smiled. "Well done, Micah. You have found the prince's trail. He left this for us to find."

Micah smiled and nodded his appreciation.

"Alexis," she said to the younger woman who shadowed her constantly, "have these taken to my lizard and stowed. I want to examine them tonight." Briana looked around. "Now what else happened here?"

"There is a mass grave over there, my lady," Micah said, pointing toward a mound of dirt as he handed the sword fragments to the young Gold Robe woman. "We think there was a fight, and some people got killed. The Gold Robes looked but didn't find any trace of magic. Four, maybe five bodies, judging by the mound."

"Where are the villagers?" Greenup asked as he walked into the clearing.

Micah shrugged. "We don't know, my lord."

Greenup's eyes gleamed as he glanced at the sword fragments. "It seems you have found the trail that everyone has been looking for."

Micah grinned and bobbed his head. "We hope so, my lord."

Greenup turned to Briana. "From here, north to Vouyr and the Road of Andel."

Briana nodded. "Surely he wouldn't have gone through Vouyr. It is unpredictable and evil."

"We can't take the lizards through there anyway," Greenup said. "We will have to go around and pick up his trail at the Road of Andel—assuming he took the road."

Briana nodded, fear and frustration etched in her eyes. "Let's do it."

# CHAPTER 37

## The Knights of Nerak

A FEW MOMENTS after Sillik disappeared into the brush, two dragons landed beside the corpse of one of their fellows. The beasts had long, slender, sinuous necks and lean, armored bodies. Their heads turned as they looked around suspiciously, their emerald eyes shifting constantly and their long, curved teeth glowing yellow in the sunlight. Convinced they were safe, the dragons made one last flap of their wings and then folded the delicate membranes against their bodies.

As the dragons curled their wings, their riders dismounted. They were small, lean men. Sillik had heard once that large men weighed down the dragons too much, so only smaller, lean men were chosen to ride. Both men wore light leather armor on their chests, arms, and legs. The armor was stained to match the dark green of the dragons' skin. Their cloaks were also painted to look like a dragon's wing and seemed attached to their arms. Sillik noticed that both men wore the red belt, but their belts were a deeper and darker red than the belt he wore. Their swords were curved like the dragons' fangs. The men were clean and well fed, something he wouldn't have expected if they were with the men he was following.

"What's a Herish doing here?" Sillik heard one of them say as they examined the remains of the dragon, its rider, and the burned Herish. "We ain't at war with Aceon."

Sillik cursed. If he started a war between Nerak and Aceon, even his friendship with the prince would not save him.

The dragon riders examined the dragon's lifeless body and then pulled the rider's body free so that they could see his face. One of the riders groaned. "It's Marcum."

The other man nodded noncommittally as he bent to examine the dead dragon's wounds. "The beast, Flame Follower, has several deep cuts." He waved at the beast's underbelly. "I don't know what dealt them, but I know what did this." He pointed at another wound.

The other rider looked up, startled from his grief. "A sword. No knight did that. Do we fight Aceon as well?"

The first rider nodded. "Perhaps."

Sillik debated whether or not to slay the men. He was at a disadvantage. They were fresh and rested. He was not. Furthermore, they were both were wearing mail shirts and leather helmets.

Then the decision was made for him as a score of silver streaks shot from the forest toward the dragons and their riders. The riders never had a chance. Even though they wore armor, something smashed through their bodies, sending them spinning lifelessly into the trees. Sillik got a fleeting look at a blunt stave disappearing into the darkness of the forest.

The dragons fared little better. More than a dozen silver streaks targeted each dragon. One of the beasts roared with pain and jumped into the air as a burst of flame shot from its mouth. It beat the air savagely with its wings. The terrible barrage continued, and in a matter of moments, it was as dead as its companion. It fell heavily to the ground, crushing several trees as it fell.

Sillik was amazed by what he had just witnessed. It had been both terrifying and exhilarating. He decided he ought to move away from the scene of the battle. Before Sillik could take more than a dozen steps, he stopped. Like a trapped beast, he sensed his surroundings. Then his eyes shot upward. Above him, standing on the limb of a large tree, was a man.

The stranger allowed Sillik a few moments to speculate and then said, "You must be the Illician that I was told to look for. I am Handrie, a Knight of Nerak."

Handrie, Sillik noticed, was dressed in loose-fitting leather pants, a thick black belt, low black leather boots, and the black leather shirt that was the trademark of the Knights of Nerak. His face was covered with a thick beard, and he was lean like a trained warrior. In his hands was a long stave of highly polished wood. The veins in the wood were like roots in a tree. His bearing and his countenance radiated power. Sillik had no illusions about whom he faced. The Knights of Nerak—or the Black Shirts, as they were sometimes known—were highly trained warriors despite their aversion to metal. They were reputed to be powerful masters of the Seven Laws as well.

Surprised, Sillik looked up at the knight. "Why in the seven hells does everyone know I am coming, and why are you looking for me?" Then he added, "I am Sillik, of Illicia."

Grinning, the knight jumped to the ground and rolled to his feet with an animal-like grace, but before he could speak, a woman's voice interrupted.

"Because I told his father you were coming," said the voice.

Sillik turned to face the goddess as she stepped into the clearing.

"Lady Silvia," Handrie said as he bowed formally. "So nice to finally meet you."

"I hope you two were not going to do anything rash and try to kill each other."

Handrie grinned. "I hadn't thought about that. He is a warrior and carries a sword. That is usually reason enough to kill."

Sillik rolled his eyes. "Lady Silvia, so nice to see you again," he said dryly. "Tell me, do you drop in on every prince, or do you just have a few favorites?"

Silvia eyed him sternly. "Of course not. Handrie has never seen me before."

"No, but my father speaks of you," Handrie said, brushing dirt from his hand.

Sillik's smile vanished, and he shook his head.

Silvia's smile compressed into a thin line. "Be warned, I am trying to keep you alive."

Sillik bowed his head. "Please forgive me. I forget myself. I am grateful, and I don't want to die prematurely."

Nodding, Silvia said, "Remember, I am on your side. It was not I who killed your family."

"That is all well and good," Sillik admitted, "but I don't understand why you are here. And for the record, Handrie probably saw me fighting the dragons on the Herish, so he probably wants to know more. 'The enemy of my enemy is my friend' sort of thing."

"Exactly," Handrie said, roaring with laughter. "Why were you fighting them?"

"The dragon riders captured my companion," Sillik said with a grimace, glancing at Silvia.

"The woman lives," Silvia said. "She is in no appreciable danger … yet."

Handrie shook his head. "The dragon riders can be hard on female prisoners. Sometimes it is better if she dies quickly."

"I am going after her," Sillik said resolutely. "I was hoping these dragons would lead me to her."

Silvia nodded. "Yes, that was foreseen. You have some time, but you must meet the Knights of Nerak."

"Is that why you are here?" Sillik asked.

Silvia smiled. "In a way," she said as she turned to face both men.

"Why then?" Sillik asked.

Frowning, Silvia said, "I will not have what I do questioned by mere men! Now you must listen. The ancient ties between Illicia and Nerak must be restored. You must ally yourselves to fight what is happening."

Confused, Handrie looked at Sillik. "Ancient ties? I am not aware of any. We generally supported Illicia in the history books, but we had our own reasons for doing so; there is no treaty."

Sillik shrugged. "I suppose you are going to tell us that someone from Nerak in the distant past married an Illician prince. After seven thousand years of Illician history, it is impossible to keep track of it all."

Silvia smiled. "I had not intended this to be a history lesson, but so be it. Tell me, Sillik, who was the founder of Illicia?"

"Rendarick," Sillik said. "Every Illician knows that."

"Who was he before Illicia?" she asked.

Sillik raised his eyebrows. "There it gets a little murky. Some accounts say he was a warlord with the alliance fighting the first demon war. Others say he led the alliance."

"Handrie, have you ever heard of Rendarick?" Silvia asked, clearly enjoying the lesson she had not intended to teach.

Handrie shook his head.

Silvia smiled. "Rendarick was the first son in a pair of twins born to First Knight Dondavin and his queen, Lady Loranda. This was before the knights had given up the sword. The second son was named Sandoes, after Loranda's father. The princes grew up tall and strong. They were taught much concerning weapons and the Seven Laws as well as many other things. They were twenty-one years old when the first of the great demon wars began. The First Knight, forgive him, forbade any of the citizens of Nerak to join the alliance, for Dondavin didn't trust its leaders."

"That is not what happened," Handrie protested. "We fought in the demon wars."

"Only later," Silvia said. "Rendarick left Nerak. He went to join the fight. A small group left with him. First Knight Dondavin named his own son outlaw and erased his name from the records. When Dondavin died a few months later, some said of a broken heart, his second son was crowned First Knight. Although Sandoes sent aid, it was doubtful that his forces would get to the alliance in time. In the end, they did not get through and were turned back by the demon hordes and the schula."

Silvia looked at the men as they processed this information. "I assure you this is correct despite whatever your histories say. I was there; I talked with Rendarick and Sandoes."

"What about Rendarick?" Sillik asked.

"Ah yes," Silvia said, returning to teacher mode. "He joined the alliance and rose quickly through the ranks. The Council of Masters greeted him as an equal. In time, he led the council and then became first lord of the alliance when Tynon, the former first lord, was killed by the demons. Those were dark days, and the defeat of the alliance seemed certain. But Rendarick led the alliance to victories and, in time, defeated the demons at the Falls of Theosa." Silvia smiled. "So you see, Handrie, you owe your crown to Sillik's ancestor, and you, Sillik, owe your existence to Nerak."

"Very neatly tied in a bow," Sillik said dryly.

"You had to reach this point on your own," Silvia said. "Had I told you this in Illicia, it would have meant nothing. Now, standing here together, you two can do some good."

"How much of this did my father know?" Sillik asked.

"All of it is written down in the Illician archives, if you care to look," Silvia said, "all of the battle plans of the alliance, all of Rendarick's orders, a few in his own hand. Your father found them and had them transcribed from the old tongue. There is a book, but you didn't know to look for a book. Even I do not know where he hid the thing. One day you may need that book, if you ever have to fight a demon. Now, what are you going to do about the girl?"

"It is still my intention to find her and free her."

"She is alive," Silvia said confidently.

"I risk much by telling you this," Handrie said, "but we have watched this group of dragons since they landed for the night yesterday. They had a female prisoner. She was tied hand and foot and gagged."

"Where is she?" Sillik asked, unable to contain his excitement.

"Two of the dragons took to the air during the night before we had mustered sufficient strength to attack. When the sun rose and we had the needed strength, the woman was gone."

"Where did they go?"

"That is not known," Handrie said apologetically. "Sillik, be at ease. We have knights searching the forest. If the dragons landed anywhere within a hundred leagues, I shall know by morning."

Sillik was angry. He had come so close. If only they could have started the search earlier. Why was he doomed to never know peace?

"I will leave you now," Silvia said. "Find the girl. She is important. Handrie will support you, and you him. You both have trials ahead." With that, she faded away.

For a long time, Handrie appeared to be deep in thought. Then he finally spoke. "Well, it appears we are kinsmen. I wouldn't have it said that Handrie of Nerak slew a kinsman no matter how far removed. Let us be friends."

"Yes, let us be friends," Sillik said, smiling.

Then, according to the ancient traditions of the land, the men grasped hands and shared salt. According to custom, they were now friends.

Handrie led Sillik through the forest. As they walked, Sillik asked various questions about the people of Nerak, their ways, and their war. "How can you call it a war?" Sillik asked. "It is a slaughter, the way you killed those dragons."

Handrie's face contorted with painful emotions. His shoulders hunched, and he tensed as if he were going to strike Sillik. Then he regained his composure.

"Forgive me if I said anything wrong," Sillik said, aware that he might have committed a grievous mistake.

Handrie's face relaxed, but he still didn't smile. "You do not know all the facts," he said. "Yes, it is a slaughter, but not in the way you imagine–eight score and twelve of my men died this day, and in return, eighteen dragons and their riders perished, including the ones that you and your companion slew."

"By the holy and eternal Seven," Sillik exclaimed. "How? Why?"

"You don't understand," Handrie said sadly. "A neophyte cast his Yrinisan too soon. He missed. His mistake exposed the positions of more than five score of our neophytes. As the dragons descended in anger, with flame billowing from their mouths, a score of adepts attracted the dragons' wrath in the vain hope that a few others might escape and the nearby knights might have a better target."

"Yrinisan?"

Handrie held up his polished staff. "Yrinisan. We gave up the way of iron and steel a long time ago. Someday I will tell you the story, or one of our bards will sing of it. It is a very great tale." Handrie continued his own story. "Distraction was the only way. Otherwise, the dragons would have razed the forest, and more than fourteen score would have died. I was lucky that as many of my men escaped harm as they did. When they regrouped later, they were able to carry the battle to the dragons in relative security, for most of the beasts had already expended their fire venom, and it would be at least a day before it was fully replenished."

"Did any of the neophytes survive?" Sillik asked. He was consumed with a strange desire to know more.

"Yes," Handrie said. "One. Can you guess who?"

"The one who missed?"

"Of course," Handrie said wearily. "When the young man learned of the number of men who had died because of his mistake, he slew himself. He could not live with the dishonor. Honor is very important to a knight, and to have such a dishonor on his soul would have shamed him for life. The only honorable thing left to him was death. Perhaps when he is born again, he will be able to forget the shame."

"It is a dangerous life you lead."

"We live in a dangerous world."

After that, neither man said a word as they walked through the forest. Sillik took the opportunity to study his comrade. Handrie's face was long and lean despite his beard. His expression was as inflexible as if it were carved from granite. His eyes were bright with an inner light and shone with a shrewd intelligence. A faint sheen of perspiration dotted his bare head. His hands were firm and strong. Sillik noticed a strange line of callouses on his right hand. They ran from the tip of the first finger diagonally across his hand and across his palm and along the inside of his thumb. The stave in Handrie's left hand seemed almost alive. It was made of some kind of tight-grained wood and had been polished to mirror-like brilliance. Sillik guessed that Handrie had to be a master of the Seven Laws. At least, he had recognized one of the Seven Gods.

After a while, Sillik sensed that they were nearing the end of their trek. The sun had disappeared below the horizon, but some light remained. At one point he thought he saw a man dressed similarly to Handrie watching them, but in the declining light it was hard to be certain. Suddenly, Handrie stopped and turned to face Sillik.

"I must tell you something," he said hesitantly. "You are a stranger to our ways and traditions. Much has changed since the days when Rendarick was among us. When we began this war, certain vows were made."

Sillik nodded but said nothing.

"But I will tell you this: you must make no reference to the Y'nari-san-tar. To do so is an inexcusable breech of good manners, especially for a guest. It is something that is regarded as highly personal and private."

"Very well," Sillik said. "I thank you for the warning, but I do not understand the word that you used."

"The word refers to what men of other cities call the blood vow," Handrie said quietly.

"I understand. You need say no more."

"Also," Handrie said with a grimace, "you wear bladed weapons. We consider them unclean but permit allies to wear them in our presence. No knight will use them, though, and while you are in our camp, we ask that you not draw them or attract undue attention to them—unless attacked, that is," he added with a smile. "Then feel free to defend yourself. We are not unreasonable. We will not deprive you of the honor of fighting or dying in battle."

Sillik smiled. "Of course."

Handrie nodded thankfully and then resumed leading the way through the forest. They had taken fewer than fifty steps when a large number of men appeared silently around them, seemingly from nowhere. They were all dressed in black. Sillik was surprised at how easily they had been hidden.

The obvious leader was a heavy, stocky man with a black beard and piercing eyes. He stood apart and behind the other men and carried a black staff that seemed to glow.

Handrie stiffened, and his eyes scanned the faces of the men, finally settling on the man standing slightly apart from the rest. "Nordan," Handrie said, "release your men."

"The stranger," Nordan said, nodding at Sillik. "Why do you walk with him? He should be slain."

"He is my friend."

"But he is a stranger?"

"Yes."

Nordan grimaced, and then a slow smile played across his lips. "He wears a sword; it is not allowed."

Handrie planted his staff defiantly. "No."

Nordan frowned. "He violates our laws and wears the red belt. He must be slain."

"No."

"Why? What does he mean to you?"

"I will vouch for him," Handrie said. His face reddened, and the veins in his neck enlarged as he spoke.

"Very well," Nordan said, a gloating tone in his voice, as if he despised Handrie. "On your vow, with myself and my men as witnesses, do you vouch for this man?"

"I do."

"So be it." Nordan barked a command to his men, and they faded into the forest. Then Nordan turned and stalked away.

"He is suspicious," Sillik said.

"He has reason to be angry," Handrie said without further elaboration.

The two men followed Nordan, who soon stopped. He waited patiently until Handrie and Sillik were close. "The weavers closed the net another thirty paces," Nordan said.

Handrie nodded. Then, cupping his hands and bowing his head, he sank into a deep trance. A moment later, light flared in his hands. The light was familiar to Sillik's. It gave no heat and floated in the air. Handrie bent to examine the ground. When he found what he was looking for, he stood and paced off thirty strides. The light followed him. When he stopped, he spoke his name, and a shimmering doorway appeared in the dark air. The edges of the door glowed with tightly controlled power.

Handrie stepped through the portal, and Nordan followed. Once they had passed through the door, Sillik could no longer see them. Then he heard

Handrie's voice. "Come, Sillik. The gate will do no harm. Quickly, though. Holding it open taxes my strength."

Slowly, uncertainly, Sillik stepped through the portal. When his hand first touched the portal, he felt a faint tingling, but that was all. Once through, he turned but could see no sign of it. He stretched out his hand to see if he could feel it again, but Handrie grabbed his arm. "No. The net slays those who try to cross its boundary without the benefit of a portal."

Sillik withdrew his hand. "What is it?"

"Our chief line of defense," Handrie said. "Come. As we walk, I will explain." A moment later, Handrie continued. "The gate is just a neutral expression of power. Are you familiar with a forbidding?"

"Yes."

"The net is very similar in principle. Later, I will introduce you to a man who can instruct you in its construction. Basically, a flat plane of power is formed and then molded around our encampment. It totally envelops us to a height of about seventy-five lengths. Under normal circumstances, we would stretch a wall only around ourselves, but since we fight an airborne enemy, extra precautions must be taken."

"Would the net slay a dragon?" Sillik asked.

"It would slay the rider and at best stun the dragon. But as the net was penetrated, we would be forewarned. No one without knowledge of the proper sequence of words may unlock a doorway through the net."

"How many men does it take to maintain this net?"

Handrie brushed an insect off his neck. "A score of men are needed to establish it initially, but only five men are needed to tend it—unless we come under attack. Then the number needed to maintain the net rises. I have seen fifty men pouring all the power they could into a net, only to have it ripped to pieces under an assault."

As the dense foliage began to thin, Sillik saw a huge fire burning. Its light made the night seem charged and expectant. Then Sillik saw the palisade. Tall wooden walls loomed proudly in the night. Along the walls Sillik saw scores of alert warriors patrolling. It was quite a contrast to Colum.

Upon entering the encampment, Sillik was amazed to see another wall inside the first. Again, warriors manned the ramparts. At the only entrance through the second wall, Handrie was asked to give a password in a language Sillik didn't know. The words sounded long and complex. After passing through the torch-lit gate, Sillik was amazed to see scores of tents all lit from within. The tents were placed seemingly at random throughout the clearing. He would trip on the nearly invisible ropes that held the tents in place more than once as they wandered through the maze of structures.

At the gates to the inner wall, a dozen or more women in diaphanous silk dresses ran up laughing. Several of the women threw their arms around Handrie and kissed his cheeks. As the women moved, their dresses chimed in musical whispers.

One of the women stopped in front of Handrie. "We heard of your patrol's losses, and we are pleased to see you safely returned, Prince Handrie."

Handrie bowed. "Thank you, sister. I must see our father."

The woman laughed in delight as she looked at Sillik. "I like the looks of this one, Handrie. Introduce me, and I will show him Nerak delights." Then with another laugh she darted away with the other women.

Frowning, Sillik narrowed his eyes. Tucked in the woman's belt had been a dagger.

"Sillik, come," Handrie said. As they walked, Handrie explained. "My sister, Miranda, and her ladies. They will sometimes greet all of the commanders returning from patrol. It is their way of helping. She also carries a staff. Most women in our city fight beside the men."

"I thought you didn't use metal," Sillik said. "She was wearing a dagger."

"Crystal," Handrie said. "Very rare in Nerak. My father purchased it for her when she finished school." Grinning, he added, "She knows how to use it too. Sharper than your sword, I'll wager. Care to dance knives with her?"

"I'll pass," Sillik said, grinning. "But is it unusual for women to go to war? It isn't in Illicia, but it is in many places."

Handrie shook his head. "Everyone in my city fights if they want to. Don't let their silks dazzle you. Every one of those women has killed. Many are masters of the Seven Laws, and all are very dangerous."

Handrie kept them moving toward a brightly lit white tent in the center of the clearing. Sillik was impressed with Nerak's defensive strategy. If a foe managed to break through the outer defensive wall—which would be no easy feat—they would still have to fight their way into a virtually walled city. And if they broke through both sets of walls, they would find no clear-cut path to the center of the camp. In the confusion, the leaders would be able to organize the resistance or flee. At the doorway to the large tent, the guards saluted Handrie.

The light inside the tent was very bright, momentarily blinding Sillik. As they approached the center of the tent, Sillik discerned the ancient figure of a man sitting humbly on a small raised platform. Two guards stood quietly at the rear of the platform, and Nordan stood to the left. Handrie motioned for Sillik to stop and then approached the figure, bowing with deference. Sillik watched uncomfortably, acutely aware that he was the only one wearing a sword.

Handrie stood up. "Sillik, I wish for you to meet my father, Ardor, First Knight of my city."

"I am honored," Sillik said as he bowed before the man.

"We understand, my son, that you have sworn to vouch for this man," Ardor said.

"It is true," Handrie said, bowing again.

The old man shifted his eyes to Sillik. "Then, Sillik, be welcome among us, and may your people prosper."

Sillik smiled and said, "Thank you for your welcome."

"Handrie," Ardor said, "the stranger, Sillik, has been made welcome by us, but we would know why you have extended our courtesy to him in this time of war."

"Because I saw him and a single companion slay six dragons."

The silence was thick as every eye turned to Sillik. He didn't flinch under their gaze.

"Where is his companion?" Ardor asked.

Sillik paused. "His Herish went down, and I could not find him."

Ardor nodded in quiet understanding.

"And I extended our courtesy to Sillik because he has the blood in him," Handrie said.

Nordan scoffed, and Ardor glanced sharply at his firstborn son.

"Whose blood?" Nordan said. "All of the sons of our kings are accounted for."

Ardor nodded. "There are no missing bloodlines. My son, you must be mistaken."

"Lady Silvia appeared to us and revealed a connection between Illicia and Nerak."

"Impossible," sneered Nordan. "She lies."

Ardor looked wide-eyed at Handrie. "Interesting. Please tell us this story."

Handrie smiled. "I will tell it," he said as he watched his brother. "I suggest that you summon your scribe to record Silvia's words so that they might be preserved and the royal historians might examine them."

"Very well," Ardor agreed. He nodded at one of his guards, who hurried away to get the scribe.

The men waited patiently for several minutes until the scribe arrived. The man's face was red, and he was breathing heavily. Sillik fought to stifle a laugh. As soon as the scribe was ready, Handrie recited the words that Lady Silvia had spoken.

After the short story was told, Ardor leaned back and nodded to himself. "It could be as she says. It has been long since she visited me. I am glad she has come to you, Handrie." Turning his head, Ardor regarded Sillik. "What part do you play? If you are related to us, then you must be part of the royal line. And so you, Sillik, are a prince of the royal line, possibly second or third in the line of succession and wandering the world alone so that you might take what you learn home?"

"You are correct," Sillik said, dodging some complex issues.

Ardor nodded and smiled. "Sillik, please forgive us," he said kindly. "This is difficult to say, but we must know. How strong a master are you?"

"He has destroyed a dragon with fire," Handrie said, awe in his voice.

"Indeed?" the First Knight said. "And do you know his entire life history?"

"No," Handrie said, smiling, "but we watched and saw this. Then we saw dragons coming and had to prepare for combat."

Sillik nodded slowly in quiet concentration. "It is true that I killed a dragon with fire. I had to protect my Herish."

"Are you a friend of the cliff fliers?" Handrie asked.

Sillik shrugged. "I spent some time there and learned their ways. I was introduced to wind magic and passed the cliff fliers' test when I faced a wind walker."

"How so?" Handrie asked.

"It came through an air portal that I had created and before I could prevent it. It hailed me and asked what aid I required. I couldn't use its aid. To be truthful, I couldn't conceive of how it could help me. So I thanked it and asked it to return to its own plane—which it did, to my surprise."

"You should have slain it," Nordan said.

"Indeed? How do you propose he should have killed it?" Handrie asked, his eyes flashing in anger. "Will the Yrinisan rend its flesh? Can it be exorcised? How can you even see it? Does it possess any kind of sorcery? I can think of a dozen other good questions that I would want answered before I engaged a creature such as that." Handrie's anger was rising. "Furthermore, it had just offered Sillik aid. Would he not have been angering a potential ally if he had attacked it?"

Nordan opened his mouth to speak but decided against it in the face of his brother's anger.

Handrie turned to Sillik. "I assume you were fully protected?"

"Yes." Sillik nodded as he remembered the painful process involved in preparing the Star of Perfection and the Symbols of Dandolian. Yes, he had been well protected.

Nordan said, "I only meant—"

"What?" Handrie asked, cutting off his brother's question.

Nordan glared at Handrie and then, in a fit of rage, spun on his heel and stalked out of the tent.

"He is bitter," Ardor said sadly.

"Yes," Handrie agreed, but he didn't elaborate.

Sillik waited quietly for the conversation to resume.

"I am curious, Sillik," Ardor said finally. "Why were you fighting those who ride the dragons?"

"Because nine days ago, a companion and I were beside the River Vivare with a merchantman whose caravan was camped beside the river. While we were talking, a band of river pirates attacked. During the battle, the dragon men of Ynak arrived. I believe that they were drawn by the presence of the yana. My companion and I had not made any attempt to hide our presence, and we had not known until then about your war. During the fight, the yana were slain, the wagons were burned, and my companion was taken prisoner. The merchant, Wolfstein, and I were the sole survivors. We buried the dead, and I asked Wolfstein to help me pursue the dragons and rescue the girl."

The old man stroked his white beard for several seconds and then glanced at Handrie. "We received word not less than a day ago that two dragons—with a prisoner—were seen streaking toward Ynak, as if possessed. When we heard that the dragons bore a prisoner, we were curious. It is not in their nature to take prisoners. If the Ynak fighters need to interrogate a prisoner, they usually do so in the field. So they must consider the information she carries very important."

"It can mean only two things: that they see the yana as a threat or that they see them as an advantage," Sillik said. "If they—"

"Are able to mount a sizable force on the beasts, we would be at a grave disadvantage," Handrie concluded. "If, on the other hand, we were able to mount even a small number on the animals ... Hmm, I wonder."

"How much does your companion know about the beasts, Sillik?" Ardor asked.

"I do not know," Sillik replied. "They were given to me as a gift in Colum."

"A rich gift," Handrie said, "but that does not help us any."

"Why not?" Sillik asked.

"It doesn't answer the question of whether or not Ynak can acquire any of the beasts," Ardor said, still stroking his beard.

Sillik nodded. "The yana are very rare. For one to be trained, it must be captured within days of its birth and taught to obey. Otherwise, it will revert. And an adult yana will die rather than be broken. I do not believe use of yana could be a threat."

"But we are at war," Ardor said pointedly. "We must consider every threat as real until it can be proven otherwise."

"Would it be possible for us to acquire a few of the beasts?" Handrie asked. "Or failing that, could we make Ynak think we have some?" After pondering the question for a moment, Handrie turned to face his father. "If we can acquire even a few of the beasts, then by making sure they are seen discreetly by the enemy— and maybe with the help of a few illusions—we can make it appear that we have a huge force of the beasts. It might help us make them uncertain enough that we could attack them and destroy them in one sudden lightning blow."

Ardor nodded, deep in thought. "Leave us now, son." With that, Handrie and Sillik bowed and left.

The next several days were very busy for Sillik as he got to know Handrie and the people of Nerak. During this time, he also learned a little about the strange lore of these people, which they had followed for the past three thousand years.

Every male's life was rigidly defined by a complex system of rules and codes. The codes for the various guilds covered every aspect of their lives, from the proper way to eat to the proper way to kill. For several days, Sillik's head swam in confusion as he tried to learn the correct way to do things so that he wouldn't offend his patient hosts.

Sillik also got the impression that their ritualistic life included an intense contempt for all metal weapons. He had not seen a bladed weapon, other than his own, since he arrived in the camp. At the same time, his hosts didn't seem to miss the use of metal weapons. The staves that all of the warrior guild carried could be used as indiscriminately as a battering ram or as delicately as a small knife.

While sitting beside a fire late one night, Sillik finally asked Handrie why his people had abandoned the use of steel.

Handrie leaned back against a fallen log and swirled the wine in his goblet. "The priest guild in our city had always avowed the use of metal as unclean because metal was forged in fire, and fire is the chief tool of darkness. They preferred things born of life. For the most part, the priests were ignored, until about three thousand years ago, when they royal line of kings was discredited under the weak and inept leadership of First Knight Kalen the Sixteenth. Eventually, the situation became so bad that those with any trace of royal blood were forced to flee the city as the populace rose against the king. However, Kalen stubbornly refused to leave and was slain by the leader of the unrest. The usurper crowned himself and assumed total control of the city. He never dared to call himself royal, though, or to sit on the same throne as his predecessor.

"The new king ruled well, if harshly, for twelve years. Then his death came, suddenly and entirely unexpectedly. Since he had no heirs, the city was torn by civil war as various factions fought to gain control. It was during this time that Kalen's exiled descendants plotted their return. They established a network of agents inside and outside the city, and they planted the seeds that would destroy whichever faction gained control. By the time one of the factions achieved a measure of success, the royal family was ready to plot the man's downfall.

"For seven years, they pulled hidden strings and exposed fault after fault while their agents planted conversations about how desirable the kings of old were now. Rather noble blood and a proud heritage than the current tyrant's ravings, they argued. People joined the cry. As support grew, the tyrant became afraid and launched a vicious attack on the suspected haven of the royal family. But all the troops found was a cold fire ring because the royal family had been forewarned. When the people found out, they were angry. Some talked of revolt. In the end, before any blood could be spilled on their account, the royal family revealed themselves. The people were gladdened. The king's men deserted him and went into the hills around the city to find the royal family and to pledge their swords and their lives to the new king. Songs were sung about the return of the royal line.

"And the exiled lineage returned: Sonan, his wife Rebeth, their sons Donalak and Segrin, their daughter Somillia, and his uncle Farthon. All wore simple clothing, and none carried a blade of any kind, for theirs was to be a peaceful and bloodless revolution. Sonan, though, carried a walking staff.

"As they approached their city, the populace welcomed them home. When the current king heard the cheers of the people, he shuddered and began to plot his rival's downfall. So it was that the rightful king entered the city after an absence of almost twenty years without shedding a drop of blood. Sonan led his family and the people through the twisting streets to the center of the city and the palace.

"The usurper met Sonan at the top of the palace steps. The man, obviously insane, ignored the cries of the crowd and attacked Sonan with his sword. Sonan used his walking staff as a shield and was able to defend himself against an assault that had been expected to kill him quickly. Sonan addressed his advantage, and soon the false king was dead. Sonan took the crown from his foe's head and placed it on his own. The crowds roared their approval. Men lifted their infant sons so that they might see and remember.

"As a symbol of their support for the returning king, it became fashionable for men of the warriors' guild to carry a long staff. As men will, whenever they quarreled, they reached for the nearest weapon. By the time Donalak, Sonan's eldest son, was crowned, swords were still carried but seldom used. After the restoration, the priests continued to decry the use of metal. The people also took up the demand. The priests changed in other ways. Instead of leading empty worship and prayer to the Seven Gods, they became militant and began to teach that the strength of the Seven Gods was tied to the strength of their servants."

Handrie passed over the final few words quickly, as if they disturbed him. Sillik wondered what this meant and filed the information away as he became engrossed again in the story.

Handrie said that to ensure the strength of the servants, the priests began to train warriors in the Seven Arts of Combat. To those with special aptitude, they also taught the Seven Laws. "Always, though, the use of the sword diminished in the city," Handrie said. "A new generation grew up ignorant of the sword as the Yrinisan became the chief weapon of Nerak.

"In those days, the Yrinisan were made of wood, as they still are today. In our first war after the restoration, we were beaten badly—routed, in fact—and our city was almost destroyed. If it hadn't been for the discipline the priests had instilled in their training, the city would have fragmented into chaos. The people, especially the warriors, had a dilemma. The symbol of their support for the king had almost become the instrument of their destruction. The sword and the knowledge to wield it effectively had been lost, and the priests didn't have time to reeducate an entire city. The Yrinisan, at that time, was fine for combat with another person similarly armed, but it was terribly ineffective against foes armed with swords, knives, sabers, and other bladed weapons. The staves just couldn't withstand the punishment. The priests even publicly recognized that King Sonan, the head of the restoration, had been incredibly lucky on the day he battled the usurper. An answer was badly needed to solve the dilemma, for tensions were growing again between the cities, and war was expected within months."

Handrie paused to pour himself more wine and then passed the skin to Sillik. The night had become very quiet. The fire was bright, the flames between them crackling comfortably. Sillik poured himself another goblet of wine and corked the skin as Handrie resumed his tale.

"The answer to the dilemma was something that the warriors and the priests—for the two were still separate groups then—had not considered. The only possibilities they had considered were abandoning the Yrinisan altogether or finding a series of tactics that would circumvent the sword's basic advantage," Handrie said, his voice full of emotion as he counted the possibilities on his fingers. "They wouldn't even consider the former suggestion," he said as he folded one finger, leaving one finger in the air to symbolize the one chance his people had had. "So they spent most of their efforts on the latter. They had some success in this endeavor, as attested to by the casting prowess that you so recently witnessed."

Sillik shuddered as he remembered the silver streaks he had seen slay a pair of dragons and their riders. He had not realized that they had been thrown.

"The answer to the dilemma, though, was neither extreme," Handrie said. "It dealt with the properties of the Yrinisan itself. It wasn't even recognized as an answer for several years, until someone happened to notice that the wood used in a certain process of the Fourth Law wouldn't burn and couldn't be cut."

Sillik gasped. Of course. It was so simple. Just as metal was tempered in fire, the Nerakeans had found a way to temper wood using the Seven Laws. "That's incredible," he finally managed to say.

Handrie nodded as he watched his friend's face. "Yes, it is."

"I wonder, sometimes, what other discoveries await the right circumstances to reveal themselves," Sillik said. Then a darker tragedy clouded his mind. His expression became sober. Automatically, he shielded his thoughts, as Handrie had taught him to do.

"I am sorry," Handrie said as he realized what he had said. "I didn't mean–"

"I know," Sillik said. Then he drained the cup of wine he was holding, stood up, and marched away heavily.

The next morning, Sillik and Handrie ate breakfast early. Neither man mentioned the previous night's discussion. Sillik had not slept well, awakening several times. He tried to convince himself it had only been too much wine.

It was Handrie's practice to inspect his troops in the mornings and to confer with his lord generals before the new scouts were sent out. This morning, though, things were different. After eating, Handrie motioned for Sillik to follow him through the maze of tents. He refused to say where they were going. Handrie stopped abruptly before a large white tent and rang a small bell attached to the tent. The bell broke the still air with a clear, crisp note. They heard hurried shuffling inside.

A young boy opened the flap. "First Knight," the boy breathed, clearly surprised at his master's visitor.

"Boy, show them in," a wizened voice commanded from within the tent.

"Yes, master," the boy said as he stepped aside and held the flap open.

Grinning, Handrie entered. Sillik followed him, puzzled by his friend's expression.

Inside, they found a man sitting in the center of the tent. He wore a blue robe that seemed to change hue as he gestured for his guests to sit. The man's face was deeply wrinkled. His hair was white and trimmed close to his scalp, and his eyes glittered with a cunning intelligence. Sillik was reminded of an ancient Illician proverb: "the eyes are the doorways to the soul." Sillik found himself liking the man before he even spoke a word.

"So this is the Illician king," the man said without any preliminaries.

"He is Sillik from the city of Illicia, most honored net master," Handrie said. "Sillik, may I present Lord Morhem, our most skillful and wise net tender."

"I am deeply honored," Sillik said, and indeed he was. He had heard the net tenders spoken of only with utmost respect–almost reverence.

"I thought you might instruct Sillik, my guest, on how one constructs a net," Handrie said. "He is a master of the Seven Laws, so this should be fairly easy for him."

"As you wish, sire," Morhem said.

"Thank you." Handrie turned to face Sillik. "I hope you will forgive me, but I must leave for a day to investigate a report that I received last night."

When Sillik started to protest, Handrie held up his hand. "I know what it seems like, but trust me, and I shall explain when I return."

"Very well," Sillik said.

When Handrie was gone, Morhem dismissed his servant. Sillik's eyes roamed around the tent. It was cluttered with piles of scrolls, clothes, weapons, and many other items that Sillik didn't recognize. Extending his senses briefly, he felt the presence of several small magical items, but he had no time to find out what they were before Morhem addressed him.

"So you would learn how to construct a net," Morhem said, giving Sillik an appraising look.

"Please," Sillik asked. "It seemed that Handrie desired it, and I am interested in all new applications of the Seven Laws."

"Very well," Morhem said, smiling. "Let us begin with some basics. What do you think of when we say 'net'?"

"I got the impression from Handrie that your net is like an inverted bowl covering the camp."

"Very good," Morhem said. "Did Handrie tell you anything else?"

"Only that it takes a score of men to raise a net this size and that once it is established, five are needed to tend it."

"True enough," Morhem said, "but not quite accurate. You are correct in saying that twenty men are needed to establish a net of this size. But the constant attention of five men is not needed to maintain the net. Once established, a net will endure for a while on its own before it starts to decay. The attention of the five is needed only periodically to reinforce it. But though it is not continuously tended, it is continuously monitored. Any and every attempt to pierce the net must be identified. Even now, while I am talking to you, I am helping to monitor the net, as are all of the men who helped raise it. In fact, just before you arrived, a patrol of twenty men passed through the net before my tent. And while Handrie was asking me to instruct you in the art, a bird flew into the net. Furthermore, we can distinguish between living and nonliving encroachments on the net. At present, the net is pierced more times than you or I can imagine by the branches of the bushes and trees that lie on the perimeter. Yet we could, if we so chose, increase the power of the net and seal all of the gaps. But that would serve no purpose other than to identify the perimeter of the net."

"Couldn't those gaps be exploited and an arcane attack forced through?"

"No, the gaps are so small that the surrounding power would neutralize most of the attack. The residue of the attack could then be easily neutralized as well while at the same time the tenders would raise the power of the net in that area."

"What if an attack came from several sides at once?"

"The same thing would occur. As for raising the power in the net to seal all of the holes, well ..." Morhem spread his hands humbly. "I could do that myself with little or no concentration."

Sillik nodded, and Morhem continued. "Your questions are good. Before I teach you how to construct a net, I would like to tell you the history of the net."

Sillik motioned for him to continue.

"The knowledge of how to build a net has existed for at least three thousand years. Tradition has it that a man named Lord Rariel used the net as a means to avoid interruption during meditation. The knowledge had been passed down from father to son by Lord Rariel's ancestors for over a thousand years. During this time, Nerak was engaged in a savage war with the pirates of Anon over a series of trade disputes. It was during this time that Lord General Sandre learned that one of his ablest generals had fallen in a battle not far from the walls of the city.

"That general was Lord Rariel's youngest son. Lord General Sandre was greatly upset and went to Lord Rariel's residence to tell his friend the sad news. Upon arriving at his friend's home, Lord General Sandre learned that Lord Rariel was meditating and was not to be disturbed. Thinking his friend would want to know about his son's death as soon as possible, Lord General Sandre defied the servants and forced his way into Lord Rariel's room. Upon entering, Lord General Sandre perceived a silvery sphere around his friend.

"Lord General Sandre summoned his power and touched the sphere with it. Instantly, the sphere disappeared as Lord Rariel sensed his friend's presence. They never mentioned or talked about the sphere, though Lord General Sandre wrote about his curiosity often in his journals. Finally, as Lord Rariel lay on his deathbed, he taught his lifelong friend how to construct the sphere because he had no one else to teach. All of his sons had died on the battlefields of four different wars.

"Lord General Sandre kept the knowledge to himself until he too lay on his deathbed. He summoned two priests to attend him in his final moments. He taught them the history of the net and how to build one. At his insistence, the priests promised the dying man that they would share the knowledge with all who would learn how to construct a net. Within a year of the lord general's death, the net had become one of the standard spells taught to all sorcerers and wizards. Today, there are more than twenty variations on the technique. But none is as strong as the original. It is one of those rare spells that defy improvement."

Sillik was fascinated. For some reason, this people's entire history was fascinating to him. He wondered why, but he didn't have long to think about it before Morhem suddenly asked him a question. Slightly embarrassed, Sillik had to ask him to repeat it.

"I asked if you were familiar with a forbidding—an exercise of the Sixth Law," Morhem said patiently.

"Yes," Sillik said, "I know the process."

"Good. Then this should be easy, for the two are similar. This is how you construct a net ..."

After half a day and several attempts, Sillik was able to raise a small net around the two men. For a few moments, he marveled at the silvery sphere above his head, but then the net collapsed. The arcane exercise left him gasping mentally. But Morhem assured him it would become easier with practice. Morhem also told him that as he gained experience, he would learn how to control the power so well that the net would be invisible to everyone except him. Then Morhem suggested that Sillik return to his own tent and sleep because the first experience with constructing a net usually left a person very tired.

Sillik agreed heartily and returned to his tent, which wasn't far away. As soon as he lay down, even though it was still light outside, he fell into a deep, dreamless slumber. He slept through the rest of the day and night.

The next day, after learning that Handrie still had not returned to the compound, Sillik returned to Morhem. "I have several questions I would like to ask," Sillik said as the two men sat down on the carpeted floor of Morhem's tent.

Morhem smiled and indicated that Sillik should proceed.

"First," Sillik began, "is it possible to form a net and not be under it?"

"Yes," Morhem said. "I suppose that such a net could be built. But once it was formed, you would lose all control over it. And unless there was someone inside knowledgeable in the art of net weaving, there would be no way for anyone to enter or leave it."

Sillik nodded slowly as he considered Morhem's words. Then in a quiet, measured voice, he asked, "Can a permanency spell be placed on a net?"

Morhem looked startled, the color draining quickly from his face. "A permanency spell?"

"Yes," Sillik said. "Surely, you've ... but no, I see that you are unfamiliar with it. It is a spell that binds spells to a well of power."

"I am sorry, Sillik," Morhem said sadly. "Although I am a master of the Seven Laws, I have never heard of such a spell. If you would teach it to me, I would appreciate the chance to learn." Suddenly, Morhem shuddered as if struck. Beads of perspiration appeared on his face. "Handrie comes," he said through clenched teeth. Gasping for breath, the man groaned. "We are being attacked."

Shocked, Sillik jumped to his feet. He heard alarms ringing madly outside. He saw the effect of the attack on Lord Morhem's face. The man shuddered with each blow. His face became drawn and haggard. Perspiration rolled off his chin. Then he spoke in a low, strained voice. "Sillik, go to Handrie. He is near the outer compound gates."

"Is there anything I can do to help you?" Sillik asked.

"Aid my king. Now go."

# CHAPTER 38

## Delays

BRIANA FUMED AS the war band skirted the edges of Vouyr. To her dismay, Sillik's trail led right through the middle of the ruined city. When they had first approached the city, the Gold Robes had rushed to the front of their lines and inspected the pile of stones inside the edge of the effect.

"It is growing, Warmaster," Kenton had said. "There is no way to tell how wide it has become. We must go around."

Grinding her teeth in frustration, Briana had finally acquiesced. Despite everything, she had been considering a mad dash through the city beginning at dawn. But deep down, she knew she couldn't lead her forces through this ancient den of evil. Someone would fall behind and be lost for no good reason, or worse, they would lose everyone.

It took two days to skirt the perimeter of the ruins. The Gold Robes rode close to the perimeter and guided them around. As long as everyone stayed to the left of the Gold Robes, all was good.

When they reached the Road of Andel, it was time for another decision. Briana bit her lip in frustration. Every head turned to look at her. She felt their eyes. She and Kenton conferred briefly. Every fiber in her being screamed left, northward, toward Ynak and Peol. What if Sillik had done the unexpected? She listened to Greenup's reasoned request to scout for a trail, but it could take days to find traces of Sillik and his yana.

After Greenup finished speaking, Briana smiled. "We go to the north," she said.

Greenup gave her a quizzical look but didn't press his point. She was the warmaster.

Briana gave the order, and her lizard jumped onto the road. It snarled and hissed at the feeling of the stone beneath its feet. With a wave, she took off to the northwest. Behind her, thousands of lizards jumped onto the road and followed her.

It took the Illician war band several days to reach the edge of the River Vivare. To Briana's dismay, there were signs of battle everywhere. What once had been a large camp was now a blackened ruin. The battle had taken place at least a week ago because new grass was trying to grow up through the char.

Greenup pulled up beside her on his lizard.

"Find out what happened," she said. "Send scouts up and down the river to see if there is a trail." She had been so certain that Sillik was heading this direction that she had not bothered to scout the sides of the road. He had to have come this way.

In their haste, they set up camp on the road. They had not slept much. The road was straight and true, and the lizards had very good eyesight.

"Let everyone else get some sleep," she said. "I am sure they are going to need it." Her eyes went to the river. It had been a long time since she had seen a mighty river like this. So much water. She shivered at the sight of it. Some of her soldiers had never seen water like this before. They were not even sure it was real. "Caution the men," she said to Greenup. "Those not familiar with water are to stay away from it."

Greenup smiled. "Yes, Warmaster." He nodded to his driver, who turned the lizard away.

As Briana watched, the Gold Robes walked through the camp. Other groups of riders scouted up and down the river. The majority walked through almost at random. Small groups formed and then spread out again.

Briana stayed in her saddle and waited. It didn't take long. When the Gold Robes returned, she jumped to the ground. *Oh, how my butt aches*, she thought as she stretched and then walked to meet them. Briana looked at the river again. How were they going to cross it without the bridge?

Behind Senarick were four other Gold Robes. Two of the men carried items wrapped in silk. "Warmaster," Senarick said, "we have looked through the battlefield per your command and can present our findings."

She nodded. "Do so."

"This was a merchant camp," Senarick began. "They were attacked by forces unknown, but dragons were used. We found dragon scales, and the writings of old tell us how dragon venom burns. Much was burned by dragon fire."

Briana looked up sharply. Viktorie had said something about dragons.

"Sorcery was used here as well," Senarick continued. "Whose, we cannot say. We know only that we felt its traces. Also, the dead were burned by magic. There were other confusing traces of magic that we do not recognize." Senarick bowed apologetically.

"Anything else?" Briana asked. "Anything to tie the prince to what happened here?"

Senarick smiled. "Of course, he was here. Colum gave him a pair of yana, yes?"

Briana nodded as tension rolled up her back.

"We found what is left of a yana burned behind the wagons."

One of the Gold Robes laid his package at Briana's feet. When he lifted the silk off the remains, Briana saw a burned paw with metal-tipped claws.

"No bodies?" she asked.

Senarick shook his head. "No. As I said, the bodies were burned by magic. There is little left other than a lot of bone fragments. So it looks like the prince arrives here and is attacked, and at least one of the yana is killed. The prince survives and burns the dead. Everything was done to standard Illician battlefield practices. There are two sets of boots leading to the pyre. So someone helped him burn the dead."

"Was it the woman who went with him?"

"No, Warmaster, based on their size, we believe the extra footprints belong to a man. We did not find any footprints for a woman. Either she was killed or captured, or she did not help deal with the dead."

"And then?"

Greenup held up his hand. "There are no signs of anyone going up or downriver."

Senarick cleared his throat. "We have one last finding." He motioned for the other man to present his package to the warmaster.

The Gold Robe handed her a piece of silk. Inside, Briana found a single long feather. "A bird feather?" she asked, suddenly confused.

"Not just any feather, Warmaster," the Gold Robe said excitedly.

"A Herish feather," Senarick said proudly. "There are two sets of talon markings down near the river."

"A Herish," Briana said. "But how? The cliff fliers? Here?" She looked around helplessly. For a moment she felt overwhelmed. How had Sillik pulled this off? "It would take months to get to the cliff fliers from here, and they seldom leave their cliffs."

"Does Prince Sillik know anyone in Aceon?" Alyssa asked quietly.

"He was wearing a gold feather when he returned," Briana said. "Rebecca noticed it and asked him. He wouldn't answer any questions. He must know someone."

Greenup looked impressed. "He was attacked by air. He enlisted servants of the air to assist him. Brilliant."

Briana flashed daggers at Lord Greenup. He grinned.

"*Two* sets of talons?" Briana asked.

Senarick nodded uncertainly.

"He's going after the dragons," Greenup said. "But why? They captured the woman from Colum. Sillik is going after the woman."

"It makes sense," Briana admitted, "but two Herish would not be much help against multiple dragons." She turned back to Senarick. "Vicar General," she said, her tone dangerous as she looked at the Gold Robe. "We need a way across this river, and we need it now."

Senarick wilted, his previous excitement vanishing as he considered his new challenge.

"I am going to get some sleep," Briana announced. "We need a plan for how to get across this river today, gentlemen." Inside, she fumed. Sillik could have this job. She hated being the warmaster. She didn't have the answers. But Sillik seemed to have the answers to every problem, which made her even angrier. *Damn that man.*

# CHAPTER 39

## Alarms

A S SILLIK RAN through the camp, he wondered who could be attacking. They would certainly have to be in large numbers to attack so large a camp.

Overhead, he saw violent flashes of light that marked the various places where the net was being attacked. When he arrived at the gate, he saw Handrie giving orders to his lord generals. Several lesser generals stood nearby, including one frightened grand commander. Sillik felt a brief surge of pity for him. The man surely felt out of place, surrounded by so much nobility.

Nerak, Sillik had learned during his stay, was ruled entirely by the First Knight or his Heir Elect. Reporting directly to them in times of crisis were the lord generals. Each lord general commanded five generals. Each general was in charge of five grand commanders, who were in charge of five commanders. Each commander commanded forty men, called a troop. Therefore, each lord general commanded five thousand soldiers.

"Have your men exit south and come around and attack their western flank and rear," Handrie said. "Lord General Faigen, your men will use the same tactic on the other side. Lord General Ordelin, your men will stay and protect the encampment and the noncombatants. If we should fail, you are to withdraw and regroup with my uncle in the north. Meanwhile, Lord General Calbert and I will lead a direct assault."

Handrie stopped speaking when he saw a young messenger wearing the insignia of a net apprentice running full tilt toward him. The boy skidded to a stop, raising a cloud of dust, and dropped to his knees. "My lord," he said breathlessly, his chest heaving.

"Yes?"

"Lord Varovil sent me, sire," the boy wheezed. "He said to tell you that the drain on the net masters is increasing, and with the deaths of Lords Barmin and Bins last week, he is uncertain whether the remaining masters can support the net for much longer, considering its present perimeter and the strength of the attack. Already, Lords Treven, Dorn, and Kamn have collapsed under the strain—their minds broken."

"Boy," Handrie said as his icy gaze caught the messenger's eyes, "you must take a message back to Varovil or Morhem. Tell them that three will exit momentarily. As soon as they leave, I want the net diameter reduced. I believe that Lord General Ordelin has a few men in his command who have considerable experience with the Seven Truths. They might be able to help the masters maintain the net."

Handrie turned to face a gray-haired man. "Ordelin, will you see if they will do this?"

"Yes, my lord."

"Good." Handrie turned back to the boy. "Now go and tell your masters what I have said."

The boy turned and raced in the direction of his masters.

"Lords," Handrie said, "this is not a major battle, but we will not have an easy victory. I would estimate that we are facing about four thousand warriors of Peol. For the sake of morale, we must devastate the enemy. We will have the advantage of numbers. Be very careful, though. Warn your men. They obviously have a number of wizards with them." Handrie waved his hand at the flashes of light above them to emphasize his point. "Caution your men against unnecessary heroism. I do not want any foolhardy bravery. If at all possible, have them avoid the wizards. Leave them for those experienced in arcane warfare."

Two of the lord generals smiled knowingly. These would be the most dangerous of their adversaries.

"Now, lord generals," Handrie continued, "attend your men and position them. We move on my signal."

Immediately, the lord generals dispersed and spread the word to their generals, who passed the orders on to their men.

Handrie looked at Sillik as though for the first time. "You may stay here," he said.

"No," Sillik said, shaking his head. "I have been idle too long. I would like to accompany you."

"I would welcome your support," Handrie said with an approving smile.

"Where is Nordan?" Sillik asked. "I have not seen him for several days."

"He was sent to lead a reconnaissance party near the city of Ynak. We have reason to believe that the dragons bearing your companion didn't go to the city itself."

"Peol?" Sillik asked as they started toward the edge of the net. Briefly, Sillik felt hope. He might find Renee yet.

"Unlikely," Handrie said. "We believe they are grounded. It is quite possible that in their haste to return, they overflew their beasts. But I do not want to sound too hopeful. There are still many other reasons why they might have disappeared—not the least of which is the possibility that they have landed and met a Ynak army that has eluded our scouts. I would think that ..." Handrie's attention shifted as one of his men approached. "Are we ready, Lord General Calbert?"

The gray-haired man nodded. "The men are in position. When you give the signal, they will exit in small groups through the net. I have warned the net tenders, and they are ready to drop the power at our locations."

"Very good," Handrie said. "Has the outside been scouted?"

Lord Calbert nodded solemnly. "The enemy seems to be waiting about two thousand lengths outside the net. They seem content to let their wizards break it. They know there is no other way in. And if the perimeter of the net is not reduced soon, or at least the assault ended, the net will be broken. Already, two more of the net tenders have broken under the strain. Lord Ordelin's men seem to be helping, but I do not know how much longer they can withstand the stress." His concern was etched on his face.

Handrie nodded. "Thank you," he said quietly. "Prepare to move!"

At once, the knights near Handrie grasped their staves. A few of the younger men wiped sweat from their faces. Sillik opened his mind and prepared his arsenal of arcane weapons. At the same time, he drew his sword. Several of the younger men looked at the blade with reproach, but the older men smiled. They knew the sword could be used as delicately as their staves. Though they preferred their staves, a few had seen good friends die at the end of a sword, and they knew it for what it was—a fearsome weapon, especially in the hands of a skilled swordsman.

Handrie placed his hands as close to the net as he dared. For a moment, he seemed to commune with the net. Then, in a sudden command, he said, "Go!"

Instantly, the net's power dropped near them. Fifteen thousand warriors poured through. Sillik endured a prickling sensation as he passed through the thin barrier. It was quite different from passing through a doorway.

As soon as they were on the other side, the net resumed its normal power distribution and then began to shrink. As it shrank, it became denser and stronger, and the arcane weapons striking it did less damage. Sillik knew the net would survive the assault against it. He also knew that the wizards of Peol would discern the change. However, it was possible that the wizards would be overconfident and attribute the fluctuation to their attack, mistakenly believing that their attack was weakening the net.

Once through, the knights advanced slowly until they were almost in sight of their unknowing foes. Suddenly, Handrie waved a hand above his head. The signal was passed quickly along the lines. After a count of ten, the knights charged.

The warriors of Peol were startled, but they were also highly trained, and their training took control almost immediately as they took up defensive positions.

For Sillik, Calbert, and Handrie the actual physical fighting was very brief. The men were accompanied by forty of Handrie's personal guards, and they passed easily through the enemy's lines. Once on the other side, they searched for the wizards and masters of Peol. They found the men quickly. Handrie seemed to know instinctively where to look. With silent hand signals, Handrie ordered most of his guards back, with the exception of two young knights who Sillik knew to be masters. As the five men observed their foes, another man approached. Sillik recognized the gray-haired man immediately: Lord General Calbert. He smiled grimly at Sillik and then conversed with his liege using hand signals. Handrie glanced at his allies, and then with a wave, he led them toward the eight wizards and the commander of the Peolean army.

As they approached, the five men prepared their arcane weapons and defenses and formed the necessary mental links that would enable them to unite their talents. Sillik was sure of victory. By the strength of their foes' assault, they knew they would face, at best, only four masters and four wizards, plus the army commander. Meanwhile, they had five masters. They were also rested, whereas their foes were nearly spent.

Sillik sheathed his sword. He and Lord General Calbert stood slightly behind and to the side of Handrie. Using their combined strength, they struck with a ruthless, surprise arcane assault. Three of the men of Peol fell before they could defend themselves. After a slight pause, the survivors counterattacked. It was then that their leader revealed himself as a master of the Seven Laws too. Sillik's mouth compressed into a thin line as he realized this fact.

The two sides were fairly matched, even though Sillik and his new allies were slightly outnumbered. Sillik was still certain of victory; it would just take longer. They had to wear their enemies down first. It wouldn't be too hard, seeing as five of the six Peoleans had to be near exhaustion.

The ground between the two groups became charred and black as they exchanged energies. Dread shapes coalesced in the air, only to be shredded moments later. Behind them, Sillik heard the sounds of battle. He pushed the awareness out of his mind as he continued to wage a smaller and more private war.

Suddenly, there was a shout of dismay. Out of the corner of his eye, Sillik saw a young Knight of Nerak running toward the masters of Peol. Before Handrie could stop or warn the young and very foolish man, the knight launched his staff in a maddened attack on the leader of the Peolean masters. The man saw the staff and for a brief moment turned his full attention to it. Brilliant yellow flames leapt from his outraised hand, as they had so many times that day, only this time the flames wouldn't and couldn't be deflected. The raw power charred the staff and was reaching for the knight even as the ashes of his staff fluttered to the ground.

Just before the power struck, the young man realized he was doomed, and calmness seemed to surround his body. Then the power struck him. His flesh turned transparent. A slight smile was frozen on his face. His bones turned yellow and then blackened. Suddenly, the power released him, and his body fell, burned and lifeless, to the ground.

While the Peolean leader turned his attention to the boy, Sillik and Handrie had leapt into action, summoning immense energies and flinging them at the leader. They were too late to save the young knight, but their combined assault, supported and reinforced by the others, slew the Peolean leader. Then Sillik and Handrie turned their attack on their remaining enemies.

Moments later, five more blackened, charred Peolean bodies fell lifelessly to the ground. Without the support of their leader, they had been unable to counter the attack. For a moment, the five men from Nerak and Illicia sagged with exhaustion, the strain of the past few minutes engraved in their sweaty faces. The remnants of power still clung to their tired figures.

As soon as Handrie recovered enough to talk, he cursed the young knight. "I told them I wanted no foolhardy bravery!"

Sillik nodded. He knew Handrie was right, but at the same time, the knight's actions had enabled them to defeat their enemies sooner. One life for eight was a small price to pay.

Handrie turned away from the bodies in disgust, intending to return to the battle. He stopped when he realized he no longer heard the sounds of fighting.

A flash of light distracted Sillik. As he looked down, he saw his signet ring on his finger. He did not remember placing it there.

"We surprised them, my lord!" a lord general named Faigen yelled excitedly as he appeared out of the forest.

"Report!" Handrie snapped, clearly in no mood for festivities.

A flicker of surprise crossed Faigen's face. He continued, a bit more warily. "Five hundred knights dead, eleven hundred wounded. We slew or wounded thirty-eight hundred and took more than a hundred prisoners."

"How many escaped?"

"Maybe fifty," Faigen admitted cautiously.

"I want them tracked down and captured or destroyed," Handrie ordered. "I don't care which. I don't want them telling anyone our position or our strength. They must all be stopped."

"Yes, my lord," Faigen responded.

"Have the patrols resumed in all directions," Handrie continued. "Send messengers to my uncle and inform him of our victory."

"At once, my lord," Faigen said as he withdrew.

"And Lord General," Handrie said, "caution the men. Although we won today, we had several factors in our favor—namely, numbers and surprise. It might not be so next time."

As the man hurried away to do his lord's bidding, Handrie smiled at Sillik. "He is still young and a trifle overeager."

Sillik nodded. He would have liked to defend the young man, but suddenly he felt a strange foreboding in his stomach.

Handrie frowned at Sillik as if sensing something in his demeanor. He was about to ask what was wrong when a hoarse shout drew his attention across the clearing to where a man ran out of the forest. For a moment, Handrie clenched his bloody staff. Then he relaxed, recognizing the man as one of his own.

The man fell gasping at Handrie's feet. He wore a pair of tight-fitting woven pants. His feet and chest were bare. His body was covered with dirt and dried blood. His eyes appeared slightly crazed. A slightly healed wound on his side oozed blood. His staff was blackened, and deep cracks ran along its length. For several moments, the only sound in the clearing was the man's ragged breathing. Faigen, Calbert, and Tasseron hurried quickly to Handrie's side to hear the man's words.

"My lord," the man gasped finally, "I followed the …" The rest of the man's words were unintelligible as a fit of coughing seized his abused body. Someone held a wineskin in front of him. After taking several big gulps, he spoke again. "I followed the dragons, as you directed us. For three days they flew northeast. My companions and I followed on the ground using the spell you taught us. After three days, they landed in a great camp—the main force of the combined cities."

"Go on, man," Handrie commanded.

"I saw more than three hundred dragons."

The onlookers gasped, but Handrie silenced them with a look.

"We counted more than three thousand banners!" the man continued. "Their strength is more than twenty thousand! I watched the dragons land.

They carried a prisoner. She was questioned there beside the dragons. They got angry and cut her throat and threw her body to the dragons."

Sillik turned away, shaking. Why? Another life ended because of him. Why? First his family had been killed, then Wolfstein, and now Renee. Would Handrie fall because he was Sillik's friend? What had he done to make the gods so angry?

Handrie glanced compassionately at his friend and then turned back to the messenger. "What of my brother, Nordan?"

"He led us for two days and then turned north. He said he had business there and that he would rejoin us in two days."

Handrie's eyebrows arched in surprise. He had a sudden fear that his brother might try to betray him to get at the throne. If Nordan did betray his oath, Handrie knew he would lose a fifth of his forces. Lord General Tasseron was intensely loyal to Nordan and idolized the man. Lord General Meers also idolized Nordan but to a lesser extent. *Damn*, Handrie thought. He hadn't wanted the throne in the first place, preferring to be free and unfettered. But now he was the legal heir, and he was being threatened from within and without!

"What of your other companions?" Handrie asked.

"We were surprised. Jharel and Shiaven were killed outright, but Kifferick and I managed to escape. Then Kifferick was sorely wounded when two scouts from Peol attacked us. They had managed to follow us. I slew both of them. Then I exchanged our clothing for theirs. I left their bodies near where we had first been attacked. I wanted the Ynak army to think they had slain us all. Then Kifferick and I hurried to warn you. Kifferick couldn't keep up, though, and had to keep stopping to rest. He was worried he was slowing me down. He kept urging me to leave him behind—which I wouldn't. He died yesterday. He wanted me to warn you of their main strength."

For a few moments, no one spoke. Finally, Handrie broke the oppressive silence. "Were you followed?" He looked troubled as he stared deeply into the boy's eyes.

Wide-eyed, the young man shook his head. "Since the two found us, I have taken great pains to hide our path."

Handrie smiled at the young man, the trance broken. "You have done well, umm …"

"Kashin, my lord," the boy said proudly, "of Commander Ynarick's troop."

Handrie's smile deepened as a thought occurred to him. "Well, *Commander Kashin*," Handrie said, stressing the young man's new title, "you will need some well-deserved rest, and then I am sure that you will want to inspect your new troop."

Several of the men around Handrie cheered the young man's promotion.

Handrie waited for the noise to settle before speaking again. "Lord General Faigen?"

"Sire?"

"When our new commander is rested, please see to his new assignment."

"Yes, my lord."

The young man's eyes glowed as he looked at Handrie. Then Lord General Faigen led him away.

"Hmm," Handrie mused, "the main strength of our enemies. I wonder. Lord General Calbert, have all those with the rank of general and above attend my father and me tonight before the first watch. We must discuss the choices before us and how we shall use this information. Furthermore, I want my uncle to know what we have learned this day."

"I have already dispatched messengers," Lord General Faigen said quietly.

"Dispatch more then."

"My lord," Faigen said, "forgive me if I am too bold, but I don't understand what there is to discuss. Surely, we will attack."

"Lord General Faigen," Handrie said, "the matter is not to be discussed here on the battlefield. We are all tired. Furthermore, we are not under any form of protection. We will consider the matter fully tonight beneath proper shielding."

"Yes, my lord."

Sillik had listened only half-heartedly to the conversation. The pain he was feeling subsided into a dull ache as he and Handrie walked back toward the camp. He decided to ask why Nordan might be committing treason.

"Nordan believes he should be the one to wear the crown after my father," Handrie replied sadly.

"Why?"

"You don't understand," Handrie said. "He is elder, but by tradition and law, the First Knight has always been a master of the Seven Laws and the Seven Arts. Nordan, though, has failed to master the Seventh Law after ten years of trying. He has studied under some of the best minds in our city but still has failed to unlock the secret for himself. This spring, when we began to prepare for this war, my father was forced to declare me as his heir. In light of Nordan's continued failures, it seemed prudent. At the time, my father seemed to believe that he wouldn't live to see peace again.

"When the articles of war were formally declared twelve weeks ago, my father publicly gave me the blessing of the firstborn and the birthright, both of which would have gone to Nordan had he been able to master the Seventh Law. It is now beyond debate. I will succeed my father on the throne—long live the king."

Sillik seconded the oath.

"And when my younger brother masters the Seventh Law next spring, as expected, he will become my heir until I marry and have heirs of my own," Handrie said.

"What if Nordan masters the Seventh Law in the meantime?"

Handrie smiled. "Even if he does, I have received the blessing and the birthright, which cannot be changed. By law and tradition, he can do nothing unless he decides to oppose me. Besides, I do not expect him to master the Seventh Law. He mastered the Sixth Law almost ten years ago. In the years since, he has failed to find his own key to the power of the Seventh Law. As you know, one man's key is another man's poison. Using another's key would confuse and then destroy. Furthermore, he has abandoned his efforts to master it."

For the rest of the walk back to the encampment, neither man said anything, each caught up in his own thoughts. The net stood open for them. A pair of somber men Sillik didn't recognize stood quietly on either side of the gate. They both wore the insignia of a full net tender. They saluted Handrie as he passed through the gate.

Immediately, Sillik felt a sinking feeling in his stomach. Something had happened. Handrie also felt it. The two men exchanged quick glances before hurrying forward.

The familiar walls of the palisade reassured them somewhat, but the two still felt something was wrong. The very air seemed charged and expectant. The trees opened quickly, and the two men saw a lone figure in a pale blue robe standing before the gate. Sillik realized suddenly that no guardsmen patrolled the palisade walls. What was wrong? What had happened?

As they neared the gate, both men recognized the figure as Lord Morhem. When Handrie and Sillik were only a few feet from the man, they stopped. Sillik saw that Morhem's eyes glistened sadly. His hands were clasped behind his back. Then Sillik realized they were surrounded by thousands of warriors. Even as he watched the unfolding scene, Sillik felt a prickling sensation in his mind. He knew that the gate in the net had been closed behind them and that the net was being strengthened, but he didn't know why.

Handrie stood directly in front of his old friend and kept his staff horizontal in a defensive position. His breathing slowed and deepened. He had no idea what had happened. He didn't want to believe that Nordan or any other had corrupted Lord Morhem. Yet at the same time, he was prepared to sell his life dearly if he had been betrayed.

"Your father," Morhem began, as if guessing Handrie's thoughts, "came to me during the battle. On the strength of our friendship, he gave to me the gift of life–he poured his strength around me and into me. He was responsible for the survival of the net. He preserved us, the net tenders, until you and your knights left the net and we could close the perimeter. His actions, though, cost him considerably."

"Is he …?"

Morhem nodded sadly. "He is dead. You are First Knight now, my friend." The tall man revealed what he had hidden behind him—a circlet of seven intertwined bands of gold, the crown of Nerak.

Handrie's eyes focused on the gold, his face frozen in an expression of fear. Then the fear was replaced with resignation. He knelt slowly.

Morhem spoke in a loud voice as he raised the crown over Handrie's bare head. "I crown thee in the same tradition which crowned your ancestors. I also crown thee in the name of the Seven Eternal Lords. May they watch over you and guard you in all your actions. May they temper your wisdom with justice." Morhem looked down at Handrie. "Handrie, do you reaffirm your oath to oppose darkness and tyranny?"

"I do."

"Will you endeavor to defend our city and answer its need as you would answer your own?"

"I will."

"Will you protect the rights, freedoms, and institutions of our city and of its citizens?"

"I shall."

"Whom shall be your heir until you contract matrimonially and produce legitimate heirs of your flesh?"

"My younger brother, Faigen, conditional upon his mastery of the Seven Laws. After him, Rigell, my father's brother."

"Will you obey the creed of the kings and take its teachings as your own?"

"So as I have said before, so shall I do."

"Handrie, I crown thee in the name of the people of Nerak. May your rule be long and wise." Morhem lowered the crown onto Handrie's head.

As the crown touched Handrie, Sillik saw his friend quiver as if afraid. Handrie rose slowly. For a moment, he stood and stared deeply into Morhem's eyes. Then Handrie turned to face the knights around him.

As one, the assembled men knelt, a mixture of emotions on their watching faces. Sillik also knelt and was the first to be raised by the First Knight, a title that was synonymous with "king." Handrie was now entitled to all of the customary signs of respect.

Sillik stood beside and behind Handrie as he looked at the assembled knights. After several seconds, Handrie raised his hands, motioning for the knights to rise. Lord Generals Ordelin and Somack stepped forward. In turn, each man knelt before Handrie and swore eternal loyalty. Then they moved to stand behind their new ruler as nine generals came forward to swear their loyalty.

With the swearing-in finished for the moment, Handrie thanked the knights for their loyalty and announced his desire to pay final homage to his father the following morning. Then Handrie turned and walked inside the palisade. Sillik followed his friend without a word. The two men walked in silence along the curving inner wall until they reached the open gate to the inner wall. Handrie stopped and turned to Sillik. "I will send for you when the council meets tonight."

Sillik nodded. "Where are you going?"

"It is tradition that the heir to the throne stands first vigil over the body of the old First Knight. Relax. Eat and sleep if you can. The council tonight could go very late."

"Very well," Sillik said as a wave of fatigue washed over him. He turned aside to go to his tent, and they parted without another word.

Inside his tent, Sillik found a basin of water and several clean towels. Grinning, he stripped off his outer clothing and then sat down and began to methodically clean off the gore of battle.

Sillik heard the tent fabric rustle and felt a touch of air moving. A faint rustle of silk accompanied the air.

"Miranda, I don't think this is appropriate."

"Hush," the woman said. "I just want to talk to you."

"About?" Sillik asked as he continued to wipe away the battle gore.

"You have spent a lot of time with my brother since coming to us," the woman observed.

"Why don't you come sit down?" Sillik suggested as he finished wiping the blood from his arms and face.

Miranda paused and then sat down before him in a rustle of silks. She had changed into silk again. *That was quick*, he thought.

"Why are you really here?" Sillik asked gently.

"My father just died, and my brothers are at war. One of them must die. I know it must be Nordan."

"I don't think that is why you are here," Sillik said with a gentle smile.

Frowning, Miranda nodded and was quiet for a moment while Sillik wiped down his leather. After a long silence, she said, "It's you. Why is Illicia interested in this war? You are a prince. You wear an interesting sword. I saw you fighting with it. I spent some time at the schools of Salone and know magical weapons when I see them. My crystal dagger has some magic on it, but nothing like your sword. So I have to wonder what a minor prince is doing with that weapon."

Sillik smiled and quickly decided to tell some of the truth. "My father was killed recently by an assassin. So believe me when I say that I understand what you are going through. My father believed that another demon war is imminent." He paused to watch her reaction. "Lady Silvia also believes that a demon war is possible."

Miranda smiled. "All valid information, but that doesn't explain that sword."

"It was believed that to kill my father's assassin, I would need a strong magical weapon," Sillik said with a smile. "Also to deal with whatever else may be coming."

"And the girl you are trying to find?"

"Ah, the real question," Sillik said. "She is important. We met in Colum and had similar interests. It is important that I find her."

"I see," Miranda said with a smile. "Important to you personally or …"

After a pause, Sillik said with a smile, "Yes to both."

"I see," Miranda said with her own smile. "I should go then," she continued as she stood.

Sillik exhaled slowly as the tent flap closed. A hint of the woman's perfume lingered, and he smiled as he sat quietly for a moment.

As he worked, he heard the sounds of life in the camp and knew the knights were returning. He even sensed the reduction of power in the net above his head. It was strange, but ever since he had constructed his own net, he seemed more aware of the net above the camp. *Does every master of the Seven Laws share this awareness?* he wondered. It was something he would have to ask Morhem.

Having cleaned away as much of the gore and dirt as he could, Sillik stretched out on his pallet to rest. When he awoke later, the light in the tent had dimmed. He sat up abruptly. Through the slightly open door, he saw that the sun was still in the sky. With amazement, he also noticed a collapsible tub of steaming water. Sillik wasted no time undressing and stepping into it. Small waves splashed over the edge of the tub. The tub was too small for him to sit, but it was large enough for him to wash off the grime of countless days. He hadn't had a real bath since leaving Colum.

Once he felt clean, he stepped out of the now murky water and dried off with a towel that had been laid beside the tub. He quickly put on his worn leather clothing. As soon as he was dressed, he found a tray of food–hot meat, warm bread with honey, cold cheese, and a large goblet of wine. Afterward, he felt a lot better than he had expected. He was clean, rested, well fed, and secure.

Then he remembered suddenly that Renee was probably dead because she had chosen to follow him, and his good feeling went away. He sat down in the center of the tent and began a series of rituals that would cleanse his mind and hone his powers to their customary sharpness. It was in that position that Levaris, his neophyte servant, found him a little later.

"My lord," the boy said hesitantly. "My lord?"

Sillik's eyes flew open. "Yes?"

"The First Knight has sent word that he desires for you to attend him shortly."

"Very well." Sillik stood up, reaching for his sword.

"The First Knight also bade me to give you this," Levaris said. He held out a black wooden box.

After buckling his sword around his waist, Sillik accepted the box. It appeared to have no opening. Sillik wondered momentarily what it was. He unconsciously followed a design on the lid with his forefinger. Instantly, the lid slid aside, revealing a large golden pendant resting on a bed of red velvet. Sillik lifted it out and examined it. Levaris's eyes widened in amazement as he stared at the gold.

The symbol engraved on the face of the rough pendant was an unusual star. Highly intricate smaller symbols were etched around it. The pendant triggered a dim memory within Sillik. He knew the name. How did he know the name?

Sillik knew that the symbols engraved in the pendant were magical. The pendant was heavy, as if it were made from solid gold. At the same time, it seemed harder than gold. With a little trepidation, Sillik slipped the heavy gold chain around his neck. Instantly, the weight vanished as the pendant settled. He felt as if he had worn it before. He wasn't sure if it was his memory or an ancestor's memory. How could anyone in Illicia have worn this pendant?

"What do you know about this?" Sillik asked as he touched the pendant.

"Only what everybody knows about the great pendants, my lord."

"And what is that?"

"They are reputed to endow several rare arcane abilities on whoever wears them," Levaris said. "They are rumored to be as old as the world. At one time there were seven pendants, but four were destroyed, and one was lost. Of the remaining two, Handrie has one. He wore it last spring when he was declared heir to the throne. This pendant is named the Star of the South. The one Handrie wears is called the Star of the North. It is a great honor that he gives you."

After the boy helped Sillik put on his cloak, Sillik left his tent and walked with quiet determination toward the center of the camp. He had not been in the High Tent since arriving at camp. From the outside, it appeared to be the same, but when Sillik stepped inside, he was amazed at the transformation. Whereas the tent had been plain and austere before, it now seemed regal. Large racks of candles and torches lit the interior. Rich hangings decorated the walls and the tall poles that supported the ceiling. Thick carpets covered the floor. It was as if an entirely new tent had been erected. In the center of the tent sat Handrie. But instead of sitting on a small platform, as his father had, he sat on a high-backed throne. The throne seemed to be made of the same wood as the staves.

It looked hard and heavy yet comfortable. A score of guards stood statue-like around the tent, their eyes roaming intently.

Handrie reclined casually on the throne, his poise casual and bored. A great cloak lay over the back of the chair, and his staff rested against his knees. A large golden pendant hung around his neck. The crown of seven intertwined gold bands was in his hand. One booted foot rested on the seat of his throne. His head rested against the back of the chair, and his eyes were closed. The entire impression was one of power.

Sillik stepped forward. Before he had crossed half the distance to the throne, Handrie's eyes flew open. Smiling at his friend, Handrie stood and stretched, his joints popping noisily as he moved. For a few moments, they talked quietly.

They looked up as two men burst into the tent. The first to enter was Lord General Faigen. Lord General Calbert was right behind him. A flicker of surprise flashed across Calbert's face when he saw the changes to the decor. The surprise was followed by what seemed like a quiet sense of understanding and acceptance of the shift in power. He had not known of Ardor's death because he had come straight from the field, where he had overseen the cleanup while Faigen tracked down the men who had escaped.

Faigen's anger over what he had been ordered to do rendered him oblivious to his surroundings. He stopped abruptly a few feet from Handrie when he finally realized what Handrie was holding in his hand—the ancient symbol of power. Even though Ardor had refused to wear it, Faigen knew what it meant.

Handrie smiled and slowly placed the crown on his head. It no longer hurt to think about his father. He had come to grips with his death. It had not been unexpected. Ardor had even discussed the possibility that he might not see the end of the campaign. And it was typical of his father to do what he had done. Handrie was resigned to the fact that he was the new First Knight.

"When did it happen, my lord?" Calbert asked, more for Faigen's benefit than his own. "When did he die?"

"This morning, during the battle," Handrie answered. "He helped the net tenders preserve the net. Morhem met me with the news when I returned after the battle."

Calbert nodded and then did what law and tradition required—he knelt before his new king and swore his loyalty. "I, Calbert, having been confirmed to the title of lord general by Morgaen, father of Ardor, grandfather of Handrie, do swear loyalty and service unto death by my oath as a knight and by the Seven Eternal Lords to Handrie, the new First Knight of Nerak."

Faigen also knelt—somewhat begrudgingly—and with only slight alterations swore the same traditional oath of service and loyalty. Faigen had just finished his oath when the Lord Generals Ordelin and Somack entered, accompanied by a score of generals.

Somack glanced at his companions and then spoke. "We thought he was already in attendance. He was with me when I received your command for our presence tonight."

Morhem also appeared quietly.

When Handrie saw him, he asked, "Has Lord General Tasseron come through the net?"

Morhem answered the question promptly and sadly, as if he had feared this development. "No, my lord, he has not."

"Double the patrols," Handrie said. "I want Tasseron. His rank and station are forfeit. My brother is missing, and now his most loyal friend has disappeared. I am beginning to fear treason." Handrie glanced at the quiet assemblage of generals standing nearby. "Torloc, are any of Tasseron's generals missing?"

"No, my lord," the man said unflinchingly as he met Handrie's angry gaze. "They are all accounted for. Most are here, but a few are on duty."

Handrie nodded. Then an idea occurred to him. "Verathin!" He had known the man for nearly sixteen years, and he had no doubts about the man's loyalty. "I elect you to fill Tasseron's post."

"Thank you, my lord," the man said as his envious friends slapped him on the back.

Ordelin and Calbert nodded, silently approving Handrie's choice.

"Verathin, come forward and kneel."

Looking impatient, Handrie waited for his new lord general and an accompaniment of generals to swear their loyalty. While he waited, he reviewed a mental list of grand commanders whom he could appoint to fill his empty post of general. When all of this was over, he would talk to Ordelin and see whom he recommended.

As soon as the swearing-in was done, Handrie glanced at Morhem. "Please raise a net."

Morhem nodded and closed his eyes as he began to concentrate. Sillik would learn later that it was standard practice in Nerak to raise a net around those gathered during any policy meeting. In addition to preventing physical spying, a net also prevented arcane spying.

After a few moments, Morhem raised his arms. Instantly, Sillik felt the now familiar prickling sensation as the net formed above their heads. He could no longer sense the outer net. They were cut off from the outside world. The camp wasn't devoid of all of its leadership, though. At least four or five generals were outside the inner net, and one was even outside the outer net. If any emergency arose, they would send an arcane warning that would explode against the net in a certain way. It was a basic requirement that to become a general, a man must have mastered the first four laws. To become a lord general, a man had to have mastered the first six laws. Tasseron was the only one of Handrie's lord generals who hadn't mastered the entire Seven Laws. Handrie's uncle, Sillik understood, had three lord generals who hadn't mastered the Seventh Law.

Once they were under proper protection, Handrie opened the discussion about what they would do with their new knowledge about their enemy. Faigen proposed that they attack immediately. He urged Handrie to unite their strength with Handrie's uncle in the north and to strike quickly and hard.

Somack, though, was adamantly opposed to attacking. "All we have," he argued, "is the testimony of one man. Our scouts have failed to find any sign of this purported camp. And now one man returns with tales of a vast camp. Our list of grievances against Ynak is long and contains testimony from scores of men. Are we to risk our entire effort on the words of one man? Normally, we would be invincible, but we are fighting two cities, not one. And may I remind you of our losses only a few days ago?"

"That is why we must attack now," Faigen said. "We hold the advantage, and we must use it."

While Sillik listened to the debate, he examined the men who would decide what Nerak would do. Lord Generals Ordelin and Calbert said almost nothing. Both wore heavy black leather. Calbert was also wearing a blood-red cloak. He leaned on his staff as he listened to the debate. His silvery hair shone in the flickering torchlight. Ordelin sat on the floor with his legs crossed, his staff resting across his long legs as he watched the debate with interest. Both men wore the golden star that proclaimed them to be masters of the Seven Laws. The other lord generals also wore the golden star of masters of the Seven Laws, but that was the only common characteristic among the men.

Somack wore a long robe of dyed resageris. He stood before Faigen, arguing hotly. He towered over the tallest of men but moved with a strangely feline grace.

Fatten, on the other hand, wore a loose pair of dusty, travel-stained leather pants, sandals, and a cloak. His long face was black with dirt and dried blood from a cut above his left eye. His expression was set and angry. His hands clenched his staff, one end of which was splintered and jagged. The other end was covered with dried blood Sillik wondered briefly what had broken the staff.

Verathin was the youngest of the lord generals and seemed to be self-conscious about his new position. His leather clothes were worn and dusty, but his composure was calm and resolved, as if he already knew the outcome of the debate and agreed wholeheartedly with the final decision. He, of course, also wore the golden star.

Looking around the tent but still listening to the debate, Sillik saw a few more golden stars among the generals. The predominant symbols, though, were the white and brown circles with golden borders, signifying a master sorcerer and a master conjuror, respectively. A silver circle with a gold border indicated a master wizard, but Sillik didn't see any of those. The guards along the walls wore a silver circle without any kind of border, indicating that they were just wizards. In a battle against men who had not studied the Seven Laws, those guards would triumph. But a score of them couldn't stand against a master of the Seven Laws. Even a master wizard would be able to defeat five or six regular wizards easily.

Even though the men in the tent represented most of the power in the camp, Sillik realized it was only one man or woman in a thousand who had the skills to study any part of the Seven Laws. Only a small portion of those ever mastered a single law, and only a far smaller minority ever mastered all Seven Laws.

There were exceptions, of course, such as the royal lines of both Nerak and Illicia. Neither city had ever had a king who hadn't mastered the Seven Laws. Sillik didn't know why this was so. The people had simply accepted it as fact. It was also accepted fact that if other masters of the Seven Laws represented a threat to each other, then the Masters of the Nine Laws represented a threat to everyone.

The Nine Dark Laws were even more hazardous than the Seven Laws. The Nine Dark Laws were reputed to be the gift to humans from the Nine Dark Gods of Chaos, whereas the Seven Laws were the gift of the Seven Gods of Law.

The first six of the Dark Laws were identical to the first six of the Seven Laws. Many times a person had studied the first six and had then changed loyalties and gone on to master the other branch. Sillik noted with a wry smile that whenever someone switched allegiances, it was always white to dark, never dark to white.

The Seventh Dark Law was thaumaturgy, the art of torture. The Eighth Dark Law was necromancy, the art of raising the dead. The Ninth Law united the various laws, much as the Seventh Law did. Once a student began the study of either necromancy or thaumaturgy, his or her destiny was forever locked and unalterable. The study of these dark gifts ate at one's mind and sometimes drove the practitioner mad. Eventually, the person was either totally evil and a fitting servant of the dark lords or dead.

Sillik's reverie was interrupted abruptly as Faigen pounded his broken staff on the ground to emphasize his point. "We must attack! Everything is in our favor. A surprise attack will devastate our enemy."

"Carrion will be picking our bones if we attack," Verathin said. His eyes seemed to be focused on something no one else could see. Faigen glared at him.

As Sillik regarded Verathin, Viktorie's voice seemed to be speaking to him.

"What do you see?" Handrie asked as he leaned forward and looked closely at Verathin. The tent became very quiet as everyone waited for Verathin to speak.

"I see death and darkness," Verathin said. "I see pain and battle. I hear carrion birds squealing over the bodies of dead knights."

Sillik was impressed. A foretelling! Thank the Seven that someone had the talent.

For a while, no one spoke. Then Ordelin stepped forward and outlined a plan that would prepare the camp while at the same time delaying any move to attack. His plan included mobilization of their forces. They would increase the number of their patrols and scouts with an added thrust toward the reported position of the enemy and would send word to Handrie's uncle to do the same. Everyone seemed satisfied with the plan except Faigen, who made one more argument for an immediate attack.

Somack replied with a crushing argument. "No one else has seen this camp or this army," he stated. "Young Kashin has not studied the Seven Laws. How do we know that what he saw wasn't part of an elaborate illusion? You have studied and mastered the Seven Laws, so you know how this could be done."

To this, Faigen had no reply. Indeed, none was possible. It was probable that all of the men present had considered the idea in their hearts, but none had dared speak it until then. Faigen said he had to prepare a new staff. Then he gave Morhem a meaningful glance.

Morhem looked at Handrie. When the First Knight nodded, Morhem raised his arms and dissolved the net. Faigen bowed to Handrie and then left without a backward glance.

"Morhem, please mobilize our troops," Handrie said. "Put the knights in a constant state of readiness. Warn the patrols to watch for my brother and Tasseron. These men are dangerous and will be considered outlaws and traitors until proven otherwise. However, their blood is not to be spilled. If Nordan is apprehended and is found to be a traitor, he shall be punished according to the code."

Sillik shuddered. Although he had no idea what sort of punishment awaited Nordan, it was sure to be unpleasant and deadly. The lord generals made no comment.

Following an uncomfortable pause, Handrie said, "Thank you, my lords." Then with an imperial sweep of his cloak, he strode from the tent, a group of guards following close behind. The remaining guards repositioned themselves along the walls of the tent.

Sillik started to follow Handrie, but Morhem laid a restraining hand on his shoulder. "I would be pleased if you two would partake of food with me," Morhem said to Sillik and Calbert, who stood on Sillik's other side.

Puzzled, Sillik glanced at Calbert, who nodded at Morhem. Without another word, Morhem turned and strode into the night. More than a little puzzled, Sillik followed the net tender along with Calbert.

Soon, Sillik found himself seated on the carpeted floor of Morhem's tent. The tent was brightly lit and strangely warm despite the cool night air. Morhem's servant laid out several steaming platters of roasted meat, along with slices of warm bread and goblets of cold wine. Then Morhem dismissed the servant, and the men began to eat.

Sillik still had not grown accustomed to the long, thin wooden rod–called a *poyasha*–that his hosts used to eat. The wood was tapered yet strong and resilient. It was held in the left hand while bread or wine was held in the right. The thin, sharp end of the rod was used to skewer the square pieces of meat or fruit. As he ate, Sillik puzzled anew over how these people managed to slice the meat so well without a metal blade. When he inquired about it, he was told that the men in charge of preparing the meat used a small wooden blade. Secretly, Sillik believed that the cook had a steel blade hidden in his supplies.

A dull ache became noticeable in his left hand. Unconsciously, he started to lay the rod down but then stopped when he remembered that the poyasha must never touch the ground. He finished his bread and switched hands just as the fingers on his left hand began to twitch from remaining fixed in the same position for too long. Carefully, he returned the poyasha to its rack. Morhem did the same a moment later and then refilled their goblets with wine. Once Calbert had returned his poyasha to the rack, Morhem looked carefully at Sillik.

"What think you of the plan decided upon tonight?" Morhem asked.

Sillik considered the question for a few moments. "It is good considering what we know and what we do not know."

"It was decided," Morhem said as he looked at Calbert, "to increase our patrols."

"True," Calbert granted.

"It was also suggested that Commander Kashin might have seen an illusion," Morhem said.

"How might we see through such an illusion?" Calbert asked.

"You would send someone who has mastered the Seven Laws," Sillik said.

Morhem beamed at Sillik. "Correct. What a shame that we do not have a master of the Seven Laws among our patrols."

Sillik and Calbert smiled. They had been picked. "It seems then," Calbert said slowly, "that someone of higher rank should become a scout."

"Yes, my thoughts exactly," Morhem said, still smiling.

"To be effective, the patrol must be small," Sillik said. "Two men are all we should risk."

"I agree," Calbert said.

"Now," Morhem said, "whom shall we ask to go?"

Sillik and Calbert exchanged a grin. "I'm sure we'll think of someone," Calbert said.

"Yes," Sillik said, "we shouldn't have any problem finding the right people."

"Good," Morhem said. "I was afraid I was going to have to convince you."

"What?" Calbert asked in mock surprise. "You mean us?"

"You are the logical ones," Morhem said. "You have years of experience in addition to being a skilled knight. Sillik is a skilled swordsman as well as the most powerful master I have ever seen. The combination of your talents will help you to succeed where others might fail. We are desperate for information. Tempers are near the breaking point, as you saw tonight. Handrie can hold the lord generals together, but only for a while. Action is demanded, but he must take the correct action. Furthermore, you are both masters. You should be able to determine if what Kashin saw was an illusion or if it was real. This afternoon, I took an opportunity to talk to young Kashin."

Morhem smiled as he reflected on the conversation. "He was, shall we say, tired. I took the opportunity to, ah, probe his mind—discreetly, of course. His memory of the scenes he reported was dim and fuzzy. I suspect something foul. I know not what he saw or what might have happened, but I do not believe he saw what he thinks he did."

"Why did you not speak tonight and voice your fears?" Sillik asked.

"It is not wise to admit we can use our powers to probe men's minds," Calbert said. "It serves only to frighten and anger men. They cannot understand that our gifts are won through rigorous study and practice. To them, the Seven and the Nine are mysterious, something to be frightened of. But back to the subject at hand, Morhem. I see that you are correct, and I will accept your arguments. Before we leave, though, I must give some instructions to my generals."

"No," Morhem said. "They will do quite well without knowing that you will be gone or where you are going." He paused, looking uncomfortable. "You are to depart immediately. We need information as soon as possible. The sooner you depart, the sooner you will return."

Sillik looked at Morhem and weighed what had been said and what had not. Even here in a war camp, people were afraid of spies.

"Very well," Calbert said. "We will leave as soon as we have our supplies."

"I anticipated our discussion and took the opportunity this afternoon to prepare for your trip. I have food, Sillik's meat, wine, and weapons. Forgive my friend, Calbert, but I discovered recently that you know how to use a sword."

Sillik was stunned. Public knowledge that a lord general of Nerak was also a swordsman would ruin his career. He glanced at Calbert.

The older man was pale. "It is true," he said with a quiet voice. "I will not explain. It was a long time ago. May I ask how you found out?"

Morhem smiled. "Suffice it to say that I have my ways. Anyway, I think it would be a good idea if you wore one. They will not be looking for someone wearing a sword. It might also protect you if you are in danger of being captured."

Sillik was reminded of Viktorie's vision in which she had seen people fighting at his side with metal weapons, and yet she had thought they were Knights of Nerak.

Calbert nodded. "I was going to suggest it myself, but my use of a sword was a long time ago, before I was knighted. I will do as you suggest. It seems a wise precaution. But I want your word that this will not become public knowledge."

"Of course," Morhem said. He turned to face Sillik. "I have gathered a selection of other weapons as well: bows, daggers, and lances. I didn't know what you preferred."

"Thank you," Sillik said. He wondered again where Calbert had learned the sword. He was sure he would have plenty of time to find out.

With a sigh, Calbert stood. Sillik and Morhem followed suit.

"Your weapons and supplies are in the back of the tent," Morhem said, heading in that direction.

True to his word, Morhem had a considerable selection of weapons. Most were bloody, and a few were broken. After a little poking and prodding, Sillik found what he wanted: a bow, a quiver of arrows, and a long, slender dagger.

Calbert chose a sword and a dagger along with a wide leather belt and a sheath. Calbert buckled the belt around his waist and thrust the knife between it and his body. He then slung his cloak over his shoulder to hide the sword sheath.

Sillik finished cleaning the dagger he had chosen and sheathed it in his belt. Then he unstrung the bow, slipped it over his shoulder, and attached the quiver of arrows to his belt. He was about to fasten his cloak around his neck when his fingers touched the gold chain. He started to take it off, but Morhem stopped him.

"Handrie wanted you to wear it. It will help you."

"He knows what we are going to do?" Sillik asked, fingering the golden pendant.

"Of course," Morhem said, smiling briefly. "We discussed it this afternoon. It was I who suggested that you be given the pendant for this trip."

"Why?" Sillik asked. "What does it do?"

"It is a communication device. Through it you will be able to contact Handrie."

"How do I use it?"

"Using the Third Law, place yourself into a deep trance and concentrate on what you want Handrie to see. The pendant has other abilities as well, which you should discover for yourself."

"Very well," Sillik said.

"Handrie wished me to warn you, though." Morhem's face became serious. "The procedure I just mentioned is very taxing. It is not uncommon for masters to collapse unconscious afterward."

"I will use it sparingly then," Sillik said.

"We must leave now," Calbert said, "before the changing of the watch."

Sillik nodded, and they walked toward the front of the tent.

"I wish you speed and health," Morhem said as the two men stepped out into the night.

Sillik and Calbert were quiet as they walked through the camp, each wondering when he would see it again. Occasionally, Calbert was hailed, but he didn't reply. At the inner gates, the guards let them pass without a word. As he stepped through the gate, Sillik saw Handrie watching him from the height of the walls. Sillik waved, and Handrie nodded. Then the two men disappeared into the stony darkness.

At the outer gate, Calbert was preparing to give some excuse as to why they wanted the gate opened when the guard cut him off politely. "We were told to let you through, my lord general."

"By whom?" Sillik asked.

"The First Knight, my lord. He said that you were going to take a special message to his uncle, the Lord Rigell."

"Never mind that," Calbert said. "Just let us out."

Without another word, the guard directed his companions to open the large gates, and Calbert and Sillik slipped through. Behind them, the gate closed quickly, and they heard the great bar descend into place. Moments later, they reached the new perimeter of the net. Calbert placed his hands near its surface. Immediately, the power of the net dropped–Morhem had been waiting for them–and they slipped through the glowing doorway.

Once they were beyond the confines of the camp, Calbert cupped his hands and concentrated for a moment. Slowly, light shone from between his fingers. It was dim, but it served to illuminate their immediate surroundings. Then Calbert turned and faced Sillik and asked if he knew the spell to improve one's night vision. Sillik smiled and said that he did. Calbert nodded and extinguished his hand fire. Both men closed their eyes and began the spell. When they opened their eyes, it was as if the sun shone brightly, and they hurried into the forest.

At first, their path was twisted and confusing, for they had to avoid their own sentries. None were to know of their mission. Spies could be anywhere, even in the Nerakean camp. When they were well past the last of the sentries, their path became easier, and they began the warrior run. To an observer, they would have looked like dancers as they leapt gracefully over logs, wove between trees, and ducked under branches. Each foot was placed confidently and without hesitation, aided in part by their night vision and training. They were whispers in the night.

As he ran, Sillik remembered training for runs like this in the desert around his city. It took speed and agility and power to run untiringly for days. Night made it both easier and harder. It was easier to be a shadow at night and hide in the darkness. As one advanced in the Seven Laws, one learned how to power his or her body from the Seven Laws, which enabled one to do things others couldn't. But it was harder because it took more concentration.

The coming war was frightening. Sillik had seen war before. He had fought in several while on his journeys in order to gain experience, but he did not like it. This had a different feel. In some ways, it felt contrived. Sillik wondered what had alerted his father.

The miles flew by. Toward dawn, the moons Idin, Coren, and Maal rose in the sky. By tacit agreement, Sillik and Calbert did not head directly toward the reported position of the enemy's camp. That path would have been too obvious. Instead, they took a longer path that would bring them in from the west.

When dawn showed its rosy face in the east, the men stopped beside a small creek and ate and drank. Calbert made a comment about the meat and then was silent.

They slept most of the day beside the creek. The sound of the water was comforting. They were far beyond the patrols of the camp they had left, in a kind of no-man's-land between the opposing forces.

When the sun was on the western horizon, they ate again and drank a little wine before continuing. Both men sank into a slight trance and used the Seven Laws to improve their vision so they could see as they ran. For eight days and nights, they kept to this pattern.

Dawn was written in the blue sky when they crested a small hill. Sillik was beginning to feel tired. The constant flow of energy to power their run was having an effect. Numbness crowded his thoughts. His only desire was for sleep. They had slowed to a walk some time ago. Suddenly, Calbert stopped and hissed a warning.

Sillik drew his dagger and crouched beside his friend. Calbert pointed to the left with an unsteady hand. Sillik started. In the valley below them, almost obscured by trees, three knights of Nerak lay impaled on wooden stakes. Each man was dressed in loose leather pants. Their bodies bore the marks of bladed weapons.

Sillik and Calbert waited and watched. The knights were obviously dead, so nothing could be done for them. With the rising of the sun, Sillik and Calbert became confident that whoever had done the terrible deed was gone. Slowly, they made their way toward the bodies. Sillik kept watch, bow and arrow at the ready, as Calbert moved closer. A score of carrion birds leapt away from the bodies and into the trees, pieces of flesh dangling from their black beaks. The leering birds were repulsive and ominous.

Whoever had killed these men had been cruel. Trees had been cut down to form the stakes, which had been thrust through the knights' bodies from behind and then stood upright in holes. The knights would have been able to touch the ground with their hands and feet, but they would not have been able to climb off the stakes. They would have struggled for a long time, growing steadily weaker, all the while watching their blood drying on the wood protruding from their bodies. It was a cruel and terrible death. Sillik shuddered as he imagined the screams of agony that would have rent the air.

"This is one of our missing patrols," Calbert said.

"I wasn't aware that any patrols were missing."

"Six patrols are missing–a total of eighteen knights."

Without comment, Sillik searched for any signs that might have been left by the enemy. Whoever they were, they were not careless. He found nothing of use.

Calbert stared at one of the bodies like a man transfixed. An unreadable expression was frozen on his face. "Do you see anything strange about this body?" he asked.

Sillik glanced at the body and then shook his head. "No."

"Look at his hands."

Sillik's eyes narrowed as he studied the dead man's hands. Half of one hand had been eaten. The other hand was clenched in a fist. No, that wasn't right, Sillik thought as his heart began to pump excitedly. One finger was extended–it was pointing! But toward what?

"I see what you mean," Sillik said.

"Do you think we can trust it?"

"A dead man seldom lies. To be sure, we could use augury and find out."

"We don't really have the time for that," said Calbert. "A lot of ritual cleansing would be needed to clean the site before the augury results would be pure." Calbert knelt beside the dead man. "Please consider, the finger could have been positioned to misguide anyone who chanced upon this scene."

"It is possible, but I do not think that is what happened."

"Why?"

"Look at that stake." Sillik pointed at another body. "Note the loose earth and the angle at which the stake leans. That man was trying to escape! It was hopeless—he only would have died faster—but he almost succeeded, which means whoever did this had already left. If they had known, they would have slit his throat to be sure he couldn't escape."

Calbert nodded.

"All we have to do is find out what this man was pointing at."

"Agreed," Calbert said. "But first we need rest. Then we can move on."

Sillik started to protest. A part of him wanted to hurry onward. But Calbert was right. He knew they couldn't take care of the bodies. Any disturbance of the bodies would warn their enemies that forces sympathetic to Nerak were about.

"We need rest first," Calbert repeated.

"You are right, of course," Sillik said.

As they left the clearing, the carrion birds leapt back toward their gruesome meals. On a small hill, well out of sight of the bodies, they stopped and made camp. Both men ate a full piece of meat and drank a little wine. Then, as a safety precaution, they formed a small net above them.

While Calbert slept, Sillik began a long series of ritualistic spells that would cleanse and fortify his mind. He also reviewed what he knew about Peol and Ynak. It left him unsettled. When the sun reached the center of the sky, Sillik awoke Calbert and transferred control of the net to him while he lay down to sleep. While Calbert stood watch, Sillik wrapped himself in his cloak and slept.

Late that afternoon, the birds feeding on the dead men screamed and took to the air. Instantly, the forest became abnormally quiet. Calbert awoke Sillik, and they lowered the net. The silence in the forest was ominous. Normally, the trees were alive with small sounds.

The two men crept toward the execution site. Sillik had his bow strung and an arrow lying across the string, and the rest of the arrows were close at hand. Soon, they heard voices with strange accents. The voices spoke quickly with little pause between words. Calbert mouthed the word "Peol" and gestured toward the voices. Sillik nodded in understanding.

Finally, they reached a spot where they could observe the bodies. Ten warriors stood in a loose formation while six other warriors lifted the bodies off the stakes. One man stood apart from the rest and observed. When one of the bodies was free of the stake at last, the man directed the others to lift the stake out of the ground. Each of the warriors wore the leather belt of a professional warrior and carried the long, slender, slightly curved sword that was the trademark of the Peolean warriors. None of the men wore the red leather of the warrior guild. Peol had never signed the treaty to establish the warrior codes. But Sillik knew they were highly trained warriors. The leader of such men would be ironhanded and a superb leader. His men, though heavily armed, appeared to be young—hardly more than boys. Every move they made broke the stillness and peace of the forest.

Slowly, Sillik and Calbert backed away. Although they undoubtedly had the advantage of experience, knowledge, and surprise, they didn't wish to reveal their presence. As they watched the Peoleans work, Sillik and Calbert made their decision. They would follow the men.

When the Peolean warriors were done with their gory task, they began to walk in the direction in which the dead man had been pointing. However, they hadn't traveled more than a league when they stopped and made camp for the night.

Sillik and Calbert conferred quickly and then decided to continue on. The warriors wouldn't have stopped if they were near their main camp, so Sillik and Calbert decided to bypass the Peolean camp and continue in their quest.

Although they traveled quickly, they were also wary. When dawn began to show its face on the eastern horizon, they found a large thicket and secreted themselves in the tangled brush before once again creating a net above their heads. Calbert lay down to sleep while Sillik stood watch and ate a piece of meat.

Then, on impulse, Sillik entered a deep trance and began to explore the pendant. Soon he found the mechanism that would transmit the message. It was nothing more than an ancient and complex spell that was very similar to a spell Sillik knew for sending messages from mind to mind. The pendant, however, made the sending easier because it required no strength from the sender. Once the pendant was activated, the sender had only to frame the message, and the pendant's magic would do the rest. However, when he tried to contact Briana, he found he was unable to do so for an unknown reason. Sillik filed his suspicions away.

Sillik moved his mental touch away from the trigger and explored the rest of the pendant's abilities. When he felt secure in his knowledge of the pendant and its uses, he broke out of his trance. When he opened his eyes, he found Calbert watching him.

"Did you send word?"

"No," Sillik said as he wiped perspiration from his brow. "We don't know anything yet."

Calbert sighed. "You look like an apprentice sorcerer after his first attempt at a spell. Why don't you get some sleep?"

Sillik nodded. After taking a sip of water, he wrapped his cloak around himself, leaned against the tree, and closed his eyes.

When the sun began to set, Calbert woke Sillik, and they broke their camp and saw to their needs. Then they moved forward cautiously. Soon after the setting of the moons, their patience and care was rewarded when they sensed a man ahead of them. They skirted the forest and moved perpendicular to their path for a while. Soon, they encountered another man. At last, they had found something, but what?

They conferred briefly with hand signals and made the only decision that they could. They would dare the consequences and try to discover what the guards were protecting.

The task was tedious and nerve-racking. The forest was quiet as dawn approached. Every sound the two men made seemed to be amplified. Even the sound of their hearts seemed audible. Sillik remembered the way he had approached the men who were tracking him in the desert. That seemed easy in comparison to this.

Sweat trickled down their faces as they crept through the dark forest. Their senses were stretched to the limits, searching for danger. A sudden sound froze both of the men where they stood. Slowly, they drew their daggers, the cold blades gleaming dimly in the starlight.

Two shapes loomed out of the shadows and moved toward Sillik and Calbert. Each of the approaching men carried a bow slung across his back. Sillik's heart raced. If the men took two more steps toward them, Sillik and Calbert would have to kill them. He willed his heart to slow down as he and Calbert tensed, like animals waiting to pounce.

The shapes conversed softly. Then, with a quiet laugh from one, they parted. Relief rolled over Sillik like a cool breeze. Silently, he breathed a prayer of thanks to the Seven Gods. Then, dagger in hand, Sillik moved forward with Calbert behind him.

Soon, they saw the light of numerous fires. They approached slowly, perspiration dripping from their faces as their eyes searched for danger. The camp was large and extensive, but not nearly large enough to contain as many men as Kashin had reported. There were two possible explanations: one, young Kashin had seen an illusion, or two, someone had tampered with his mind. Sillik had a sinking feeling in his stomach. Morhem had said Kashin's memory was "dim and sketchy"—exactly what would have happened if someone had tampered with his mind.

Sillik and Calbert had reached identical conclusions. In a glance, their eyes said all that needed to be said. Together, they turned to face the camp. It contained several hundred warriors perhaps but no more than a thousand. The main force must be elsewhere.

If Kashin had had his mind tampered with, Sillik reasoned, then Renee might not be dead after all. Sillik was just beginning to feel a glimmer of hope when he heard a twig snap behind him. He whirled in a fighter's crouch, but then a bright light exploded in his head. Pain shot through his limbs. As he fell, he saw dark shapes rushing toward him.

# CHAPTER 40

## Peol

WHEN SILLIK AWOKE, his eyelids were thick with mucus and dirt. His hands were tied roughly behind his back, but he could still move his fingers. Good. That meant he hadn't been out for very long. His head felt terrible, and he felt blood dripping from a wound in his scalp.

Nearby, he heard Calbert moan. Sillik opened his eyes groggily. Then a guard dragged him to his knees. His head spun, and for a moment he thought he was going to vomit. When his eyes focused, he saw a tall man sitting on a throne. Beside him stood a man swathed in black. For a fleeting moment, Sillik recalled the man he had fought in the tavern in Colum. The two bore a striking resemblance.

A long, slender sword hung from the standing man's side. The man on the throne wore a dagger as his only weapon. Glancing sideways, Sillik saw that Calbert was kneeling beside him, similarly bound. His gray eyes were cold and clear.

Suddenly, a guard hit him in the head with the butt of his spear, and Sillik's head snapped forward. His split lips began to bleed. Clearly, the message was that he shouldn't he looking around. Behind the throne, Sillik saw a table. On it were his and Calbert's weapons and supplies. After watching the prisoners for a few minutes, the man in black walked over to the table and examined their possessions. The bag drew his attention immediately.

With scorn, the man opened the worn leather bag and dumped the contents on the table. Then he bent and examined the contents. He placed several of the herbs and leaves in a small pile and then threw the remaining herbs and rare grasses into the oil lamp. Thankfully, Sillik's father's papers, which Sillik had carried with him since leaving Illicia, were still hidden beneath a false bottom in the bag.

When everything from the bag had been destroyed or stolen, the man in black turned to the remaining items but then stopped when he saw a lump beneath the bag's lid. Sillik ground his teeth when he saw what the man had found, and his heart sank. Now they would know beyond a doubt who he was. The man examined his find with a knowing smile and then tossed it to the man on the throne. Without thinking Sillik tried to deflect the path of the talisman with his mind and, with mild surprise, saw that he was slightly successful.

The man on the throne bent to pick up the object, an annoyed expression on his face. Then he leaned against the arm of his throne and examined it—the signet ring. The man's fine features compressed to a state of anger as he recognized what it was. From childhood, he had been taught what the symbols on the ring meant. Now he was afraid, for the gold ring that he held was the ruling ring of Illicia. Its wearer would be the king of those same warriors.

Suddenly, there was a cry of intense pain and the smell of burning flesh.

"Keldan, what happened?" the man on the throne said as he jumped to his feet and hurried to the side of man in black.

By chance, Sillik caught sight of the man's hand. The palm was black and charred, and a few of his fingers were missing altogether. It was as if the man had tried to grasp something of great heat—but what?

Sillik's eyes narrowed. His sword lay across the table. The blade was half withdrawn from the sheath. Had the sword burned him? Sillik's mouth compressed into a thin smile. If he had been revealed by the Ring of Kings, then the man in black, who was named Keldan apparently, had just revealed himself to be a black master, a practitioner of the dark arts, by the way the sword had reacted.

Eyes burning with anger, Keldan wrapped his cloak around his good hand and drew the blade as he held his burned hand against his chest. When the blade was free, the man examined the intricate runes on it with narrowed eyes. He hissed and then quickly slid the blade back into its sheath. "It is the sword Avenger," he said over his shoulder.

The other man nodded wearily as if he had expected this and then returned to his throne. For the first time, Sillik saw a familiar gleam of gold around the man's neck. It was the Star of the South.

The king motioned to the guards. "Release them, and then leave us."

Instantly, Sillik felt the ropes on his hands being cut. He rubbed his wrists to restore circulation. Calbert did the same.

Calbert glanced at Sillik. "You have some explaining to do, my friend," he whispered.

Sillik groaned inwardly. Obviously, Calbert had recognized what the ring meant even from a distance.

"I see before me many questions," the king said. "I see a man who could have been my friend. Lord General Calbert, a Knight of Nerak, wearing a sword. I see him in the company of an Illician, which also poses questions. He bears on his person the Ring of Kings, one of the most closely guarded talismans in the world. And he bears the sword Avenger. No thief could steal both of these treasures, so you must be genuine. You are the king of Illicia. We were warned that such a man would come—tall and dark, and on his hand would be a token of kingship with mighty names of power from the past." The king sneered. "All men have heard tales of Illicia and how it led the second alliance to victory. You Illicians have never let us forget. Your sword was forged in the very strength of law. We were warned of that too. But all believed that the sword would be one of the lesser blades."

"Warned?" Sillik asked, his curiosity overcoming his caution. "Warned by whom?"

"Yes," said Keldan, smiling. "I suppose you would want to know, especially if the rumors we have heard about your people are true. Maybe I will tell you before we kill you. Maybe I should just wait and let my brothers and sisters on the Council of Nine play with you."

"You say too much," the king of Peol said with a sneer. "Even if you kill him, you should not mention the council."

Sillik laughed. "I am actually glad you two are here. I am looking for some dragons. I need a new dragon-hide shield."

The two men glanced at Sillik but ignored his comments.

"So what if he knows that I sit on the Council of Nine?" Keldan asked. "He will not be able to tell anyone. I am more than enough to kill these two."

The king stood up suddenly and reeled. He grasped the side of the throne with one hand, his other gloved hand trying frantically to tear the Star of the South from his neck.

The man in black stared aghast at his king. Then Keldan's eyes grew wide with wonder as he saw the pendant for the first time.

Sillik had no idea what had just happened, but he and Calbert came to simultaneous decisions. As Sillik created a net above his head with a wave of his hand, Calbert launched himself at the king.

Keldan launched an arcane bolt straight at Sillik. Sillik was able to break the spell—barely—and then he activated his full defenses. Swirling red and blue flames surrounded each man, and fingers of flame darted between them as they sought to find weaknesses in each other's shielding. Sillik's mind felt as if tiny insects were crawling over it as Keldan tested his defenses.

Titanic energies surged back and forth between them as each sought to overcome the other. A single touch of the flames would be enough to render a man unconscious, and the full force of the flames would char a man's bones. There was no doubt that Sillik's foe was a dark master. However, Sillik also knew that Keldan was using a sizable portion of his strength to suppress the pain in his hand. Also, his first attack had been his strongest. He evidently had hoped to defeat Sillik with a lightning-quick blow. Now he was weakening, and if he tried to use his full powers for offense, the uncapped pain would flood his mind and body and break his concentration.

Operating on a hunch, Sillik held out his hand, and his signet ring flew to him. He caught it in his right hand, and the ring instantly settled onto his ring finger. Sillik opened his hand again, preparing to produce more magic, and his sword flew into it. Instantly, Sillik felt more powerful than he had ever felt before. The duel would be over quickly.

Keldan also began to sense the inevitable outcome of their fight. His eyes searched wildly for a way out. If he had been whole, he might have had a chance against Sillik. Out of the corner of his eye, he saw Calbert making a bloody pulp out of his king.

Dark shapes coalesced in the air before Sillik as Keldan sought a way to overcome him. The air stank with the carnal reek of the creatures Keldan summoned from the grave. Shadows and mere hints of creatures tried to solidify, but Sillik destroyed every dread thing that Keldan summoned and sent them all crashing back into the eternal abyss.

Furious, Keldan paused to change his tactics. Taking advantage of the break, Sillik launched a powerful blow. Keldan defended himself and returned to the battle. Sillik saw a dangerous gleam in his enemy's eyes. It was the look of a man who had seen his own death and was no longer afraid. Sillik had seen it before. He knew that men were the most dangerous and reckless at such a point.

Keldan mustered his arcane weaponry and launched a fiery assault. Sillik hoarded his own strength and let the ravenous tide of his enemy's wrath slide off him. When Keldan's attack waned, Sillik launched a counterattack. With each blow, he drove Keldan backward. Finally, Keldan could retreat no farther. After a quick series of blows, Sillik sensed his opening. Following a feint, he brought his attack crashing home.

Keldan's shields crumpled as the attack broke his mind. For a moment, he was terrified. Then, in a blinding flash of power, Sillik's last blow consumed him.

As Keldan's ashes floated to the ground, Sillik fell to his knees, gasping. Perspiration rolled from his face and soaked his skin and clothes beneath his leathers. Sillik glanced over at his ally. Calbert had his back to him and was presently engaged in unwrapping the pendant from the Peolean king's throat. Bright blood soaked the ground. When the pendant was free, Calbert dipped it in a pan of water and then tossed it to Sillik, who slipped it around his neck. Then Sillik crawled to his feet, and the two men rearmed themselves.

"We need to find a way out of this trap and then figure out where the main body of the Ynakean army is," Calbert said as he sheathed his sword.

"What about the Peoleans?"

Calbert smiled. "As soon as they find out their king has been slain, this city will erupt in civil war. The guards that held us bore the trappings of four different noble houses. When they and the other five or six noble houses discover that their king has been most foully murdered, they will fall over one another in their haste to be the first to announce the sad news on the city streets and declare that someone from their house is the new king."

Sillik smiled. "So we've reduced our enemies by one."

"Perhaps we have, my friend. But that won't help us in the meantime."

"I may have an idea," Sillik said. "What we need is a distraction, something to distract the camp and create chaos and confusion."

Calbert nodded.

"Then when they discover that their king has been slain, they will undoubtedly send word to the main body. If we could capture one of those messengers, we could find out where the main body of Peol is camped. And if they are following standard military custom, where one army is, the other won't be far away."

"Brilliant, but unless you have a distraction that will help us escape, we won't be capturing anyone," Calbert said flatly.

Sillik thought for a moment. "I think I might have an idea," he said.

"What?"

"A wind roamer."

"Are you sure?" Calbert asked, surprise in his voice.

"It's one they won't expect. We can only try. At worst, it could turn on us, but the two of us should be able to withstand it."

"It's never been done before."

"I don't see any other possibility. We need something big and dramatic."

Calbert nodded. "I agree."

"Will you help me summon it?" Sillik asked. "It will take a lot of power."

Calbert nodded and licked his lips nervously.

The two masters went to work and constructed the symbols that would protect them during the summoning. It was standard procedure among highly trained masters to protect themselves. No one knew for certain what any summoning might bring. A slight mispronunciation of a word might change the entire spell. And the symbols they drew would protect them from most creatures, save perhaps a god or a few major demons. When all was ready, the two men stepped into the star, closed the seventh side, and then spoke the words that activated the symbols.

Then, with Calbert lending his strength, Sillik began the complex formulae that would open the gateway to the principal domain of the air elementals. At once, they felt an answering surge of icy power. They smiled–they would be answered. Within moments, a shimmering plane of power coalesced before them.

With an ear-splitting howl, the elemental stepped through the portal. In their mind's eye, Sillik and Calbert saw a tall, noble, roughly humanoid figure outlined in white standing before them. Parts of the creature's body kept peeling off and disappearing while other parts appeared. Several times, the body blurred and then reformed. From the expression on its face, they knew it was uncomfortable on this plane. They also knew that its pain would increase with time and that it would die eventually, unless its summoner released it. Sillik had expected this, for he had seen the same phenomenon with other elementals and knew that such creatures would fight their summoner with all their strength rather than die on an alien plane. Sillik vowed to save his strength so that he could release the elemental when that time came, for he had no desire to torture it needlessly.

As the elemental grew in stature, the two men were buffeted by the strong winds that accompanied it. The wind howled and sang around them, pounding them mercilessly. But the walls of the tent remained still. No outward sign of the elemental's presence betrayed them.

At once, the winds slackened as the elemental changed its tactics. Sillik shuddered as the being assailed his mind and sought to break the bonds Sillik had placed on it during the summoning. Their wills struggled for control. Sillik's will had broken a wind walker once before and sent it back to its own world. Now, strengthened by his friend's power, Sillik was able to chain the elemental to his purpose. The elemental shrieked at the bonds he placed on it.

Calbert shuddered as the two battled. He had never seen a man wield such might and power. Never before had the immortal air elementals been tamed by humankind. And now two men were binding this elemental to their wills–well, to Sillik's will. All Calbert was doing was lending his strength. Sillik was doing all the work. He was also the genius behind the binding, for he was using tactics that never would have occurred to Calbert. He knew the limits to his strength and creativity. Suddenly, Calbert felt weak and small beside his friend. And then it was done, and the elemental disappeared to await Sillik's signal. The only sound in the tent was Sillik's ragged breathing.

While Sillik rested, Calbert neutralized the symbols and opened the seventh side of the star. He rummaged through the tent until he found two dark cloaks. He donned one and tossed the other to Sillik. As Sillik put his on, he noticed a familiar glitter on his hand. He wondered briefly how the ring and the sword were able to augment his power.

Sillik paused in the doorway of the tent and sent a silent command. All at once, the attack commenced. The wind began to wail, softly at first but rising in volume. Sand and debris swirled in the air. Tents flapped noisily as the wind increased. Shouts of alarm rose from around the camp. Trees bent before the onslaught, and their silent cries sent jagged fingers of pain through Sillik's mind as black clouds rolled across the sky.

Sillik called upon reserves of energy from deep within and summoned the brothers of the air elementals—the fire elementals. These required little energy to summon as they sprang gleefully from the campfires throughout the camp. Fire elementals were weaker than air elementals, but they were still hard to control. With the added threat of the air elemental and the need to conserve his strength, Sillik only dared to summon five of the creatures.

For a fleeting moment, Sillik wished that Calbert's people knew how to control the elementals—at least the minor ones. Sillik promised himself that he would remedy that situation as soon as possible. He struggled to his feet, though couldn't remember falling. Calbert smiled and held out his hand. Sillik accepted the help gratefully and hauled himself up. By the Seven Gods, he was dizzy. He shook his head to clear the clouds that obscured his vision. His mind ached with a dull pain, and his body felt thin and drawn. Gradually, his sight cleared. He turned his thoughts inward and mentally articulated the words to the Fourth Law spell that would banish fatigue. His senses cleared as the spell took effect. He regretted having to use the spell; he would pay a price for it in the long run.

Sillik heard new screams of pain and terror as the wind swept the fire elementals through the camp. By now it would be clear to any masters in the camp that they were under supernatural attack. If they did not panic, they would be able to banish the fire elementals. If they were very brave or foolhardy, they might even attempt to stop the air elemental. However, Sillik was certain that they wouldn't be able to dispel it.

Sillik nodded his readiness to Calbert. Calbert closed his eyes and sought the arcane controls of the net. They had decided to leave the net in place. It would serve to protect the dead bodies in the tent from the elemental. It would take energy to maintain, unfortunately, but it would also let the Peoleans know for certain what had happened to their king.

Calbert opened his eyes and made a series of passes in the air. At once, a doorway opened in the net. Once they left the confines of the net, they would lose all control over it, and the doorway would close. Then, to get into the tent, one would have to either destroy the net at a considerable cost of power or wait at least a day for the net's power to dissipate. Sillik smiled. If any of the masters survived the encounter with the air elemental, they would be forced to break into a nearly impregnable fortress. Both tactics would slow their pursuit.

When the doorway was fully open, the two men drew their swords and stepped out into the night. Behind them, the portal slammed shut–taking the tip of Calbert's cloak with it. Calbert stamped on his blazing cloak until the flames were extinguished. Sillik pitied anything or anyone that tried to go through that power.

As they moved away from the royal encampment, they saw what their sorcery had wrought. The terrible wind was blowing away everything in its path. It was knocking down warriors, tearing tents, uprooting trees, and throwing weapons through the air like toys. Carried along with the wind were the fire elementals. Sillik heard their laughter as they indiscriminately ignited everything they touched–men, animals, tents, and trees all felt the touch of the elementals' fire.

Sillik and Calbert were momentarily stunned at the destruction. They leaned into the wind, their cloaks flapping noisily behind them. They squinted against the grit in the air and tried to ignore the stench.

Calbert pushed Sillik aside suddenly as two arrows whistled past them. Sillik heard a cry of pain somewhere behind him.

"Die!" yelled a pair of berserk guardsmen as they charged out of the darkness.

Sillik rolled back to his feet, and he and Calbert braced themselves in anticipation of the attack. Four blades met. The night rang with the song of steel. It was a glorious and terrible sound. For a man who was supposed to scorn metal, Calbert used his sword like a man born to the blade.

Sillik tried to throw off his growing lethargy. He was tired, and his speed was down. Stumbling, he barely avoided a deadly counterthrust. Out of the corner of his eye, he saw Calbert put an arm's length of steel into his adversary. As the man fell, Calbert quickly withdrew the weapon. He had a terrible gleam in his eye.

With a quick flurry of blows, Sillik exchanged places with his enemy. Then he purposely locked their blades. While their blades were above their heads, Sillik's foot lashed out with a perfect roundhouse kick that landed squarely in his enemy's stomach. Their blades broke free, and the man stumbled backward. Then Sillik's blade crashed down on him. At the last moment, Sillik turned his blade so the flat of it struck the man's temple. Without a sound, the man fell to the ground.

Nearby there was a bright glow from a sudden explosion of flame that then began to fade. Calbert grinned madly. "I had forgotten how exciting a sword fight can be," he said as he wiped a bloody sleeve across his face.

Sillik could only nod as he pulled Calbert aside and caught another slashing blade on his own. Sparks exploded as the two blades met. On the third blow, the lesser blade shattered. Sillik's foe never had a chance to realize what had happened as he fell to the ground.

Then the two men ran. The fire elementals were vanishing, which meant their enemies were recovering and beginning to form a defense. The air elemental still stormed through the camp, but it was also weakening. As each elemental was sent back to its own plane, Sillik shuddered. It was his magic that was being broken, and he felt the pain clearly.

As they ran past a blazing tent, three guards yelled at them. Two of the men were unarmed. The third wore only a dagger. Unwilling to slay unarmed men, Sillik and Calbert struck the men with the flats of their blades. Two men fell stunned. The remaining man cursed and drew his dagger. Sillik grabbed his dagger hand as Calbert grabbed the man's jaw and jerked his face around to look at him. For a moment, their eyes locked. Then the unfortunate man crumpled, his neck broken. A soft sigh escaped from his throat as he fell. Sillik eased him to the ground.

Tents were blazing all around then, and the wind fanned the flames mercilessly, sending them higher. Firelight gleamed on Sillik and Calbert's blood-spattered forms. Their faces glowed as they hurried on. Their estimate of the camp size had been low. It was larger than they had thought but still not large enough to contain the Peolean main force.

At the perimeter of the camp, they met five bewildered guardsmen and fought a quick and bloody battle. When it was over, five bodies lay on the ground, and Sillik was bleeding from three minor cuts. Calbert also had a cut across his cheek. It would forever mar his appearance. Calbert grinned. In the excitement, he didn't feel the pain.

The two exhausted warriors stood gasping over the bodies of the men they had slain. They lingered for perhaps several breaths too long. But fate was a fickle woman. She gave just as easily as she took, and she rewarded bravery.

As their breathing slowed, Sillik heard an ominous sound. Whirling, he raised his sword and parried a pair of blades meant for his back. The clash of steel startled Calbert, and he took a long cut across his arm as he brought his sword up.

Sillik could barely see his opponent in the darkness. However, he could sense Calbert's presence, and when the moment presented itself, he grabbed Calbert and pulled him out of the fray. They left the battle behind them as the Peolean warriors fought each other in the darkness. To avoid the dueling warriors, the two men returned to the camp and skirted its perimeter, the firelight illuminating their path as the air elemental continued storming and screaming through the camp.

Occasionally, they ducked into a tent to avoid mobs of warriors running through the flaming hell that had once been a peaceful camp. Most of the tents were spartan in their contents, but the last tent they entered was markedly different. Oil lamps hung from the beams supporting it, and furs and pillows covered the floor. Multicolored silks hid the walls. Tied to the center pole of the tent was a woman with blonde hair. Renee!

Calbert's face paled as he saw her. What was she doing there? He had last seen her a year ago in the city of Nerak. For a moment, Calbert and Renee's eyes locked. A silent conversation passed between them. Then Calbert turned to watch the door while Sillik released her.

The restraints were ropes, but they were infused with something else, something dark. Hissing in anger, Sillik reached out to untie the magic. He pulled his hands back in shock. Whoever had done this was cruel. Quickly, he eyed Renee. There were dark shadows under her red, puffy eyes. She had been questioned hard. Sillik reached out and grasped the bonds with the Seven Laws. Mentally, he forced the image of a sword into the spell and felt the bonds begin to break and unravel. In moments, it was done. "You can't break magic like this when it surrounds you," he said quietly.

Renee sagged and gasped. Sillik took her hands. Her wrists were bruised, swollen, and raw from the ropes. Tears sprang to her eyes as the blood began circulating again. For several minutes, Sillik rubbed her legs to restore circulation. Once color began to return, he applied healing and watched as the bloody skin healed.

Then he lifted her to her feet. She almost fell, but Sillik caught her and held her until she could stand. When he pressed a sword that he had found in the tent into her hand, she smiled warmly as she tried to master her pain.

Turning, Renee kissed him soundly. "Thank you," she said breathlessly.

Smiling awkwardly, Sillik tried to support the woman.

Calbert smiled. "Let's go. The way is clear," he whispered.

Sillik and Renee followed Calbert outside. Her sword glinted in the firelight. Sillik smiled as he remembered when he had last seen her use a sword. She was still dressed in the riding clothes she had been wearing when he last saw her. She was filthy, but he had healed the worst of her injuries.

The air elemental was still wreaking havoc in the camp, hampering the soldiers' efforts to put out the fires. It slowed everyone's movements and distorted their senses, but it was weaker than it had been. The fire elementals had been banished or destroyed.

Suddenly, Sillik felt pressure mounting against the air elemental. At first, it was only a gentle probing, but it quickly became a series of mind-numbing blows. Amazed, Sillik shuddered and tried to clear his mind. He had not expected to feel the attack against the elemental. Perhaps it was only the amounts of power involved.

Gasping, Sillik realized the true intent of the attack against the elemental. Whoever was directing the attack was not trying to send the elemental back to its own plane. Rather, they were trying to control it, to dominate its will and bend it to their own purposes. To say Sillik was surprised would be a great understatement. What they were trying to do required far more energy than was necessary to send the elemental back to its own plane. There were terrible risks involved as well, for they could just as easily free it of Sillik's bonds without placing any of their own chains around it. If things went badly, it would be set free on this plane, where it would wreak terrible damage as it went mad with pain. Who knew how long it would live before it died—if it ever did. The men working the magic were either very brave or very foolhardy.

The pressure trying to break his magic was terrible. His mind felt like it was being shredded. He felt the creature's pain as it battled the minds trying to dominate it. The elemental shrieked with rage as each new attack commenced. Sillik realized that they were drawing closer to the source of power, exerting pressure with every step. He suppressed a shudder.

The hair on his arms and on his neck rose in recognition of the considerable energy being summoned. At once, Sillik turned inward and drew strength from his reservoirs of energy. At one time, he had believed those reservoirs to be without limit. But now, to his dismay, he felt his very real and finite limits. With his strength only partially restored, he prepared his arcane arsenal as they hurried on. They couldn't hope to delay the inevitable any longer. They had to escape now. Failure would mean death. The last of their diversionary tactics was on the verge of being overcome.

Sillik glanced at Calbert to warn him. The lord general nodded. He already knew. Sillik turned to Renee, intending to give her some reassurances about what they faced and their chances. However, Renee seemed to be cut off from the world, and Sillik couldn't get her attention.

Sillik knew that they had no other choice than to face the men trying to dominate the elemental. Behind them lay the quickly recovering camp. They would be recognized immediately as outsiders if they tried to mingle with those warriors. And now they had a woman with them. Peol believed that women had no place in a war camp and treated women more like possessions than like people. Danger lay in every direction.

Calbert and Sillik weighed their options. Whatever they did could be risky. Even though they didn't know what they would find in front of them, it was easier to move forward. Before them, they might find a score of masters fighting the air elemental or a single master of immeasurable strength. They couldn't avoid the confrontation either, for if their enemy was successful in his attempt to dominate the elemental, it was inevitable that he would turn the elemental on Sillik. Sillik and Calbert knew that if the elemental were dominated, it would have little trouble finding them. They were tied to the elemental with invisible bonds because they had summoned it and bent it to their wills. Sillik also knew he would die if he had to face anyone in an arcane duel in his weakened position.

As they hurried toward the edge of the camp, the pressure in Sillik's mind continued to grow. Calbert was aware of it, but it was not affecting him as badly because of his lesser part in the summoning. Sillik resisted the pressures in his mind as best he could. It was hard to think beyond the imminent encounter, but he tried. He thought in terms of what would happen when they escaped. Despite Calbert's words, he found it difficult to believe there would be no pursuit. At least some faction of the city would be loyal to the dead king and seek revenge.

If any did pursue, it would surely mean his and his friends' deaths. He was approaching mental and physical exhaustion. Calbert seemed to be in better shape despite his age. Then there was Renee. She was another story altogether. The long weeks of captivity had weakened her severely. Only time could heal them all, which was the very thing of which they were short.

Behind them, Sillik heard someone beginning to exert order in the chaotic camp. Sillik sent a silent command to the elemental, urging it to wreak even greater violence on the tents. The elemental shrieked in agony as the two magics sought to command it. For now, Sillik's magic held, but he knew it wouldn't last much longer. Already his magic was fraying at the edges.

Suddenly, they heard voices in front of them. They had been out of the camp and in the forest for several minutes now. Gradually, the forest became denser. The three weary travelers slipped into the shadows and crept toward a torch-lit clearing before them. Perhaps a dozen armed men stood in a rough circle. Four of the men held torches in their mailed fists. The light flickered and danced in the strong breeze. The men were clustered around two other men. As one of the two men turned, Sillik and Calbert started. Renee also caught her breath as she recognized him.

Once, he had been clean-shaven and had worn only the simple black tunic of the Nerak knighthood. Now he stood tall in high black leather boots. His face was covered with the beginnings of a thick beard. His stance was different too. When Sillik had first met the man, he had looked angry and tense. Now he looked relaxed and full of power. Sillik had the sinking suspicion that the man, Nordan, had finally mastered the Seventh Law.

The other man was more of a mystery. He was dressed as a warrior and carried a long, narrow blade at his side. He also radiated power. Something clicked in Sillik's mind when Calbert leaned over and asked in a low voice, "Is he your missing countryman?"

Sillik's stomach did a queasy roll. Icy fingers of dread raced up and down his back, and the hair on his neck stood on end. It was Dernot Lafliar, the man who had slain Sillik's father, murdered his half brothers, and forced Sillik's people to withdraw from the world. Bile rose in Sillik's mouth, and anger coursed through his veins. He barely resisted the impulse to leap out and seek revenge, to see his enemy's blood flow hot and heavy on the grass.

The pressure in Sillik's mind rose again, and he reeled drunkenly. Calbert felt the force pressing against their magic too. His eyes clouded, and he shook his head to clear it. The situation was fast approaching a breaking point.

Renee glanced at each of the men. They were almost incoherent. Then she reached out and touched Sillik's mind with hers. In a moment, Sillik's mind was laid bare for her to read. His mind was clouded by his weakness and the battle of wills, but after a quick search she found what she wanted–the magic that would send the air elemental back to its own plane. The return spell was relatively simple, requiring only energy and steady concentration–two things that Sillik was lacking presently. It was possible, Renee thought, that the masters trying to dominate the elemental wouldn't notice her spell until it was too late. If they did notice, well, she could only hope she would be able to resist them. If they were taken by surprise, it was possible they would be drained of energy. She had seen it happen at other times, so she knew it might work.

She worked her way quickly through the spell. On a physical level, she felt the elemental responding. It was glad to be leaving this plane. It had been subjected to too much pain here. Renee finished the spell with a sudden flourish, and all at once, the elemental vanished. The men who had been trying to dominate it collapsed. Renee smiled, and tears came unbidden to her eyes. *Poor, foolish men.* They had been channeling so much of their strength against the poor creature that its sudden disappearance drained them completely. Many of them felt their life force sucked from their bodies as the elemental vanished. Others, such as Nordan and the renegade Illician, would have been able to stop the flow of energy before their life force was pulled from them. It was a pity. She would like nothing better than to see those two men dead. They had brought far too much suffering to the world.

Smiling through her tears, Renee turned her attention to the men beside her. Calbert recovered relatively quickly, seeing as he had been providing support rather than control. Sillik, however, had borne the full brunt of the creature's summoning and had spent incredible amounts of energy defending his magic. Renee knew he had been lucky. Most people wouldn't have been able to survive the energy drain for as long as Sillik had. Calbert and Renee knelt beside Sillik's unconscious form.

"How much does he know about you?" Calbert asked.

Renee smiled. "He knows everything that is important."

Calbert raised his eyebrows in surprise. "You trusted him that much?"

"Well, he doesn't know that I know you or Handrie, but everything else."

Shaking his head in surprise, Calbert let out a low whistle. "You didn't tell us much when Handrie and I first met you. You must trust him or …" He paused. "Do you love him?" The knight swiveled his grizzled head to look at the woman. "You do, don't you?"

Renee frowned as she considered her response. "Let's help him and get out of here."

Calbert nodded, and they began to pour healing into Sillik's depleted body.

Slowly, Sillik began to respond. He was terribly weak, but he was alive and recovering. His memory came flashing back to him. He remembered the pain, the fear, and …

"Renee?" he asked as soon as he could force his dry mouth to form the word.

"Hush," she said as she continued to pour strength into his tired form.

"I knew," Sillik said haltingly, "you were alive."

"How?"

Sillik smiled tiredly. "I just knew."

"Can you walk? We've got to get away."

"Yes," Sillik said.

Renee and Calbert helped him to his feet. Sillik stood unsteadily for a moment but waved off their helping hands.

"Okay, I'm ready," he said through clenched teeth.

Renee was worried as she looked at Sillik. His face was pale in the moonlight, and his jaw was clenched in pain. Beads of perspiration dotted his forehead.

Dawn was near. The eastern horizon was just beginning to lighten. Slowly at first, and then with increasing speed, the trio hurried away from the scene of death and destruction.

As they left the place where the arcane confrontation had almost occurred, a black-cloaked man with a lifeless arm and a noticeable limp moved cautiously through the forest toward the unconscious bodies of his two newest apprentices. He was well pleased with the experiment. He had finally been able to accurately gauge the strength of the only man capable of defeating him in the end.

# CHAPTER 41

## Real Answers

AFTER GETTING TO safety, the trio stopped to rest and then feasted on roasted jacklinger that Renee had captured while Sillik and Calbert slept beneath a hastily constructed net. They ate in silence, apart from the sound they made when licking their fingers. They threw the bones into the wall of the net. Power flared quickly as it incinerated them.

When they were finished, Sillik turned to face Renee, questions written across his face. Renee knew she would have to answer them or risk losing a valuable ally.

"You know I studied with the masters of Salone," she began. "Toward the end of my many years of studies, word came that the city of Covenon had been besieged and had fallen to the invading armies of Landon and Mariana. The council members were all slain. The governor himself—my father—died before the city's shattered gates. It was then that I was introduced to a group of masters from many cities. At first, I thought that they were rather boring and lifeless. As I got to know them, though, I learned that they were anything but. Some years before, these men and women had become very concerned about the number of dark masters appearing across the continent.

"Accordingly, they had formed a semisecret group dedicated to tracking down and destroying these dark masters. The group had already existed for five years when I met them. That was when I first met Handrie. He had been a member since the beginning. Handrie left the next year to answer his father's summons, but I stayed. I rose in the ranks and became the leader of my group. Shortly after I assumed leadership, we found evidence of a very powerful dark master traversing the land. My group was the only one in a position to try to stop him. The trail was cold when we found it, but it led to Dragurled and then to Posidia, Slarn, and Selnon. And then last year it led me to Nerak. By then, the trail had become hot. I enlisted Handrie's aid, and we set a trap. Somehow the dark master slipped out of my hands and got away. I almost had him. He is recognizable by a limp and a lifeless arm. From Nerak, the trail led to Felean and then to Colum."

Sillik nodded. Much had been explained, but not all. "If your father was governor of Covenon, how did your uncle come to be the emperor's trusted advisor in Colum?"

"My family is originally from Colum," Renee explained with a toss of her hair. "For twelve generations, my family had advised the kings of Colum. My father was the younger son, and when he discovered his potential for magic, his father disowned him. My father was a very young man, and the lure of adventure was strong in him. He hired on as a guard in a caravan and left Colum forever.

"Several years later, he enrolled in the schools of Salone. While there, he mastered the Seven Laws and met my mother, who was also a master. After they left the school, they traveled the continent for several years. Finally, they settled in Covenon, where my father became a merchant. By the time I was born, he had been elected to the governor's council. When I was two, the council elected my father governor."

"You said that you met Handrie," Sillik said, noting the pain in her eyes as she remembered her parents.

Renee's face changed from grief to happiness, but it was Calbert who spoke. "Ardor sent Handrie to the teachers of Salone to be taught the Seven Laws. It is common practice for the nobility of many cities to send their sons and daughters to other cities to be educated. It reduces many of the problems associated with teaching royal heirs."

Sillik nodded. He knew of the practice. His own people had never practiced it, though. They had no need. The Gold Robes were excellent teachers.

"Sillik," Renee said with a pleading expression on her beautiful face, "I want you to believe me when I say that I wanted to tell you everything the first time we met. But my native caution told me to hold back." She paused, looking into Sillik's eyes. "You possess a mastery of the Seven Laws beyond anything I ever imagined possible. And though I could read no deceit in your eyes, I wanted to be sure of you first. I have been betrayed before, and I don't relish the idea of having it happen again. Now the situation has changed. Since you are here with

Lord General Calbert, I know I can trust you. You will also have met Handrie, my friend. Tell me, is he well? Ardor will not like the news of his eldest son's defection."

"Ardor is dead," Calbert said quietly as he watched Sillik's reaction to Renee's words. "Handrie has been crowned First Knight. Nordan has been declared traitor, and Tasseron with him."

Renee's face turned pale. "Nordan was one of the ones striving to master the elemental. He has either mastered the Seventh Law or turned to the Nine. He will be very dangerous. But who was the other man with him?"

Calbert shook his head.

"He was Dernot Lafliar," Sillik said. "A renegade Illician. Of that I am certain."

The others nodded as they processed the news. Then Calbert turned to Renee. "Why did the dragon riders capture you?"

"They wanted to know about the yana," Renee said. "I was in no danger. It was easy to control the minds of those simpletons. They thought they were getting information from me, but actually, the reverse was true. They could hide nothing from me."

"This dark master you mentioned," Sillik said. "Who is he, and where is he from? What does he want? Were you aware that the Council of Nine has been remade?"

"Now who is withholding information?" Renee asked. "We call him Nathalin. As legend has it, he betrayed the Seven Gods a millennium ago and caused their decline. He came seemingly out of nowhere. His ultimate purpose is a mystery, although we do know some of his intentions. He personally converted two of my people to the Nine Laws and killed the king of Posidia. The people of that city have since closed their gates to everyone. All strangers are slain on sight. Nathalin has caused the fall of other kings as well. King Trent of Joen is living in exile. The king of Teris was assassinated before his court three months ago. Nathalin seems to be intent on creating as much chaos as possible. The withdrawal of Sillik's people has very sinister implications."

"What do you mean?" Sillik asked, a chill falling over him.

"I mean Illicians were responsible for defeating the dark lords' designs twice. The dark lords are stronger now than they were then because it seems that the strength of the Seven Laws is declining. Some of the finest masters of this century cannot master spells that were considered routine a century ago—except for you, Sillik. Also, the number of masters continues to decline. Once, entire armies were masters; now barely all of the leaders are. You are a throwback to the days of old when the masters of the Seven Laws were at the very apogee of their power. For seven thousand years now, all that has stood in the way of darkness and chaos has been Illician strength and resolve. And now the Illicians have withdrawn, or worse. The land has erupted in the bloodiest series of wars that the world has seen in nine hundred years. Nerak fights Peol and Ynak. Teris and Landon grapple at one another's throats. Ussengod sacks Felean. Koro is burned by Slarn. Kings and good, honest rulers are deposed for no apparent reason. What does this say to you?"

Renee's eyes were blazing. Sillik's mind was still groggy, but this information was staggering. His mind reeled with the implications.

"You owe us some answers too," Calbert said to Sillik. "We thought you were a prince, but you carry that ring."

Sillik nodded and quickly explained the recent challenges to and attacks on the Illicians.

"And the assassin you were looking for when we met?" Renee asked.

Sillik nodded. "Dernot Lafliar."

"And the men whom he killed?" she asked, recalling what he had told her that first night in Colum.

"My brothers and father."

Renee shook her head as she considered the implications. Then she began to list the factors. "An Illician assassin who killed most of the Illician royal family and then escaped. Illician withdrawal from the land. A member of the Nerakean royal family turned renegade." She shook her head. "Nathalin is assembling his own army."

Sillik wanted to ask more questions, but Calbert stopped him. "The day goes," Calbert said, "and so must we."

"Do we go to Handrie?" Renee asked.

Sillik watched her carefully but said nothing as he ran his fingers over his lips where Renee had kissed him. Briefly, he felt a surge of jealousy but controlled his emotions.

"No," Calbert said, "we go to Handrie's uncle, Rigell. He is closer."

"Do we follow our plan then?" Sillik asked.

Calbert nodded as he stood.

Renee looked at her companions. "What plan?"

"We need to get some information," Calbert explained. "We decided that to gain that information, we have to capture a Peolean and interrogate him."

"What information do you need?"

"The location and strength of the Peolean and Ynakean main bodies," Sillik answered.

"I already know that," Renee said with a satisfied grin.

Calbert and Sillik grinned at each other and then turned to Renee.

"Why didn't you tell us?" Calbert asked.

"You didn't ask," she said as she quickly braided her hair. Once the braid was complete, she wrapped it around the top of her head. Over the years, she had learned the hard way to bind up her hair and wear a leather coif under her helmet. Several times in battle, her opponents had grabbed her hair. She had considered cutting it off, but then everyone would have known she was a warrior wherever she went, as surely as if she wore a suit of mail.

When she was finished with her hair, Renee nodded at Calbert, who raised his hands and broke the net. He wavered unsteadily for a moment as the power shattered.

When the net was gone and all traces of the power had vanished, Renee stood, but Sillik remained seated. Renee and Calbert stood quietly for a few moments. Finally, Renee spoke. "We must go, Sillik."

"They've broken the net," Sillik said, a faraway look in his eyes.

"In the camp?" Calbert asked.

Sillik nodded as he stood.

"What are you two talking about?" Renee asked.

"In escaping from the Peoleans," Calbert explained, "we met the Peolean king and a friend of his. From what you've said today, it seems that the king's friend might be a friend of yours too."

"A friend of mine?" Renee exclaimed. "What would I have to do with a friend of that Peolean scum?"

"Professionally!" Calbert said, laughing.

Renee looked at Sillik and then at Calbert, mystified. "Will one of you explain?"

Sillik grinned. "The Peolean king had a friend by the name of Keldan who was a dark master."

"You slew him?" Renee asked.

Sillik nodded.

"I've heard of Keldan," she said. "He was evil and very powerful. He was also one of Nathalin's captains. We think he came from Ynak. When Keldan is near, Nathalin is sure to be close." She looked around as if she expected him to appear. "It was Keldan who helped Nathalin escape my trap in Nerak."

"We've got to go," Calbert said.

Sillik and Renee nodded and then followed him.

Both of the men were still too weary to move at the pace they had used only days before. And despite her words, Renee had also been weakened by her long captivity. Her mind was strong, but her body was tired.

The first few days, they moved slowly. Each morning, they awoke stiff and sore. Gradually, they became stronger. On the fourth day, Sillik began to utilize some minor rituals. As expected, his reservoirs of energy were refilling. It would still be several days before he had the strength to create a net or use other powerful spells. Since Calbert had played a lesser role in the summoning spell, he recovered far more quickly. Each day thereafter, they increased their pace. On the eighth day, they discovered they were being followed.

Sillik and his friends tried to discourage the pursuit by setting arcane traps behind them and spreading powders that would slay any kind of tracking beast. Each trap was more complex and powerful than the one before. At first, Sillik set the traps to warn and then to wound. They had no desire to slay needlessly. Their pursuers' determination for revenge was admirable but misguided. The Peoleans had no practitioners among them, so the traps were effective–terribly so.

The next morning as they ate breakfast, Calbert observed that they had been wise to discourage pursuit. There was no way they could face the Peoleans in face-to-face combat. It would mean certain death for the trio–they were too heavily outnumbered. However, now that they were within three days' march of Rigell's last reported position, they had no choice but to deal with any remaining pursuers, and ruthlessly.

"What do you have in mind?" Renee asked.

Calbert smiled grimly. "Until now, our traps have been purely physical, designed to maim or kill. What will they do when their minds are attacked?"

"A mind blast?" Sillik asked.

Calbert nodded. "A strong mind-numbing spell. Throw in a few illusions and a powerful trap much like the ones they've already encountered, and they will be decimated."

"Brilliant," Sillik said, though he hated the necessity of the plan.

Renee frowned. "I don't like it."

"The effects will not be permanent," Calbert explained, hoping to appease the woman's morals.

"I know that," she said sharply.

"Would you rather face them in combat?" Calbert asked.

"No."

"Then what's wrong?"

"It's not right to tamper with minds so ... blatantly."

"I share your sentiments, Renee," Calbert said, "but I also recognize the necessity of what must be done. We dare not lead them any closer to Rigell's camp. We have taken a grave risk already by leading them this far. Since we cannot face them in combat, what would you have us do?"

"I don't know."

"Will you help us at least?" Calbert asked. "They are very near, and we don't have much time."

Renee was still for a moment. Then she nodded slowly.

With that, they flew into action. Renee laid the spell that would trigger the trap while Calbert and Sillik went to work on the mind-blasting spell. When they were ready, they tied the two spells together. Any human crossing a line extending one hundred lengths in either direction perpendicular to their path would set it off, and everyone within a hundred-length radius of the breaking point of the spell would feel its full effects. As an extra surprise, they added a few more effects to the trap that would maim or kill a few of the men and trigger a series of illusions. While Sillik prepared the illusions, Calbert created several false trails. Then they hurried away, careful to hide their true path. If all went well, their pursuers would be shattered, disorganized, and demoralized before sunset.

As they moved away from the scene, they set a few time-delayed illusions that would appear during the night, for Calbert knew that any survivors of the mind blast would make camp where their comrades had fallen. They used Sillik's memory of the yana as the main focus of the illusions. They also set a few traps on the false paths. However, they set no traps behind their true trail because as they neared Rigell's camp, the probability of one of Rigell's patrols encountering the trap would increase, and they had no desire to slay any of Rigell's knights. Calbert also gave Sillik his sword to carry. He didn't wish to be seen by his fellow knights wearing a blade of accursed metal. Then he cut down a sapling and began to shape a new staff. When they were a considerable distance away from their main trap, the trio sat down to wait for their trap to spring. It didn't take long.

Sillik, Calbert, and Renee felt a sudden release of their magic. Then screams of pain rent the darkening sky. Sillik shuddered at what they had done. Then the trio slipped through the forest to view their handiwork.

Twelve men lay writhing on the ground. Four more lay without moving, including one who looked like the group's leader. Eight men were scattered about the clearing, trying to stanch their wounds. The six men who still stood were shocked and white-faced.

Sillik's eyes turned hard, and his face drained of color. He reminded himself that this was war. Sillik glanced at Calbert. The lord general's face was hard and grim as he took in the carnage. Renee's face was white as she saw how many men the mind blast had struck.

"The odds are more even now," Calbert said. The others nodded.

As the sun sank slowly below the horizon, their enemies made camp, and the survivors tended to the wounded. Sillik, Calbert, and Renee decided to keep moving. No one wanted to admit it, but all three had a premonition of danger.

As they began the last leg of their journey, Calbert led, his freshly cut staff in hand. Sillik brought up the rear. He turned back constantly and sent his mind questing behind them, seeking to detect further pursuit. As he walked, he kept one hand resting comfortably on the hilt of his sword. The information Renee carried in her mind was very important, so despite her protests, she had been awarded the most protected position. They marched in this fashion for two days. The miles flew beneath their feet as they traveled at the ground-eating pace to which warriors were accustomed. Renee struggled to keep up. Since she had not trained to the warriors' code, she didn't know the breathing techniques or other warrior tricks. Sillik and Calbert worked with Renee to improve her speed.

When the moons were high in the darkened sky on the third night since their last trap was tripped, the trio stopped. While Renee rested, Sillik and Calbert laid a warding spell across their path. It was strong and localized. If anyone following them stepped into the sphere of the spell's influence, Sillik and Calbert would be aware of it. Furthermore, they would know whether it was man or beast (rodents and insects were too small to trigger it). The spell would also give them some idea as to how many people or creatures there might be.

When Renee awoke, she produced from her bag a few wild roots that were extremely nutritious despite their foul taste. The three ate them in silence.

When they were finished eating, Sillik explained to her that they had laid a ward across their path. "That is all," he assured her. "We need to know if we are still being followed."

Renee smiled. She didn't want to show it, but she was relieved. She had feared the worst. She had killed often and violently by blade and magic, but her opponents had always had a chance to defend themselves. These traps were different, though. The men following them had no one in their group who could detect the traps. Consequently, they were struck down like grain before a scythe.

After their quick though meager meal, they resumed their journey. The moons set, and the sun rose. They stopped again briefly at noon to rest. At nightfall, they cooked a pair of jacklinger that Calbert had brought down with his staff. Then they slept under the protection of a net until the moons rose.

Near dawn, Calbert stopped abruptly and sank to his knees. Puzzled, Sillik and Renee did the same. Extending his senses ahead of him, Sillik felt the presence of a dozen men. Curious, he let his mind wander farther ahead. Within moments, he found something so important that he motioned for Calbert's attention.

The two men conversed briefly in low tones. Then Calbert, who was skeptical, sent his mind ranging ahead as Sillik had done. When he confirmed Sillik's conclusions, he sent a powerful thought toward the men hiding ahead of them.

At once, a dozen men arose from their hiding places, and a few approached Calbert and his friends. The rest melted into the forest. All of the approaching men were dressed in brown leather. Their faces were deeply tanned and healthy. In their hands they carried long staves of polished wood. The trio had found Rigell's camp.

Rigell's camp was very different from Handrie's. Both had a powerful net around the outer perimeter, but the similarities ended there. Rigell had guards posted inside and out but had no palisade within. The tents in the camp were made of the same fabric and were the same colors as those in Handrie's camp, but these tents were laid out according to strict military standards, consisting of several sets of concentric circles with wide avenues between the circles and a series of avenues that radiated out from the center, where a large tent stood. This was a position of maximum importance, which meant the war council wouldn't be meeting there. Indeed, they were led to a medium-sized tent near the edge of the camp. It was obvious from the knights present that this was the command center. It was guarded by a score of knights, and many more came and went. Without comment or examination, the guards saluted and then allowed the visitors inside.

The tent was lit as if from a thousand torches, yet not a drop of light leaked out of the tent or shone through its fabric. Sillik blinked in surprise and felt a slick, tingling whisper of a spell caress him as he entered.

The men in the tent were immersed in discussions around a large table covered in maps. Several knights talked and gestured animatedly, but they all fell silent when they saw Calbert. Sillik had no problem identifying Rigell. He was tall and powerfully built despite his age. His presence dominated the tent. Sillik could see a resemblance to Ardor and Handrie in his piercing blue eyes. Rigell's eyes landed on Calbert, and he smiled fondly in greeting. When he saw Renee, his smile broadened. Evidently, she was known and liked. But when his eyes touched Sillik, they narrowed, and his smile disappeared. Suddenly uncomfortable, Sillik called upon his royal training and placed a charming smile on his face.

When Calbert introduced Sillik, Rigell bowed cordially, but Sillik could see the worry behind those calculating eyes. *What problems have I brought him?* Sillik wondered. *How have I complicated this war? Maybe I haven't. Maybe we have the means to end it quickly and decisively.*

While Sillik and Renee stood back, Calbert gave Rigell an outline of their information. Sillik saw a gleam in Rigell's eyes. For a moment, his gaze was transfixed on Sillik, and he lingered for a moment on the hilt of his sword. His eyes narrowed, and his brow furrowed as he leaned on his table for a long moment. Then Rigell summoned food and drink and unrolled a large map. He placed game pieces on the map to represent his location and Handrie's last known position.

Calbert and Renee placed corresponding pieces on the table representing Ynak and Peol. Then Rigell placed another piece on the map—there was another army on the land, he said, moving fast. Stunned, Calbert and Renee looked at Rigell. What wild card was in play? Sillik noted that Rigell's eyes had bored into him as he mentioned the unknown army. Spotters had picked up their trail. They were moving north fast. The group spent the rest of the night discussing strategy and how to coordinate Rigell and Handrie's forces and where best to attack.

At sunrise, the guard changed, and Rigell summoned runners to inform Handrie while Sillik fingered the pendant that Morhem had given him. After a few minutes, he sat down in a corner of the tent. Following the directions Morhem had given him, he concentrated on what he wanted Handrie to see and, more importantly, do.

It took a few minutes, but he felt an answering surge and Handrie's "Well done" flash through the pendant. "We will meet you at the Falls of Theosa in ten days," Handrie said. "We will drive them to you. Be ready."

A little stunned at the ease with which the communication had occurred, Sillik jerked his eyes open. Instantly, he saw Calbert watching him. Sillik hauled himself to his feet and staggered, as if tired. He smiled and paused to recover his senses before he returned to the map.

Rigell was still instructing his runners on what to tell Handrie when Sillik took off the pendant and laid it on the table. Several of the generals gasped when they saw it. Rigell's eyes gleamed. When Sillik spoke, his voice sounded strained. "Handrie will meet us at the Falls of Theosa in ten days. He will be the hammer."

Rigell dismissed the runners and looked from the pendant to Sillik. "Ten days?" He shook his head. "Impossible!"

Calbert smiled. "We will make it possible."

Rigell leaned forward and looked each of his generals in the eye. Last, his eyes met Sillik's. "We break camp as quickly as we can. Leave everything we don't need here, along with a token force of guards and net tenders. If superior forces attack the camp, burn it and retreat. Otherwise, the job of those who stay will be to make the watchers think we haven't left. For those who go, take their rations. It is ten days' hard march to reach the falls. We must travel light and fast, and we must be in position before Handrie drives the cowards from Ynak into the jaws of our trap. Once we get to the top of the falls, we will need ballistae." Rigell's eyes darted to one of his generals, who nodded and rubbed his hands in anticipation. "From the height of the falls," Rigell repeated for emphasis.

Calbert grinned. "We will need someone to bait the trap."

Rigell nodded at Calbert and then turned to his generals. "Organize your knights. We leave immediately." He looked directly at one of the generals, a big man with a barrel chest whose head was clean-shaven and tanned from long days in the sun. "Rubik," said Rigell.

The general looked up.

"I want you to stay and pretend we are still here. We need five days. They have to think we're still here."

Rubik nodded, a serious look in his eyes.

The generals filed out of the tent, and Sillik heard shouts as orders were passed down the line. He knew weapons were being readied and supplies issued. Word of their imminent departure would travel fast.

Calbert took both Renee and Sillik by the arm and led them out. "We have done what we came to do," he said with a smile. Calbert turned and spoke quickly with a guard and then led his friends to the nearest campfire, where cooks provided food and a hot drink.

The three ate and drank quickly. The guard to whom Calbert had spoken returned with three packs. Calbert nodded at the man.

"Standard-issue travel pack," Calbert said between bites. "Food for fourteen days, water for two, and a blanket. We will get more water on the way. After that"—he shrugged—"this should be over."

A moment later, Rigell's tent flap burst open, and a new flurry of activity overtook the camp under his watchful eye.

Sillik, Calbert, and Renee grabbed their packs and then joined the stream of warriors leaving the camp. Sillik felt the net close behind him as they left its protection.

It was impossible for large numbers of men to move through the forest with any kind of stealth, so they spread out into squads, forming a long front. Time settled into a monotonous pattern of high-speed passage through unending forest. At sunset, they stopped to sleep until moonrise. When the moons set, they stopped again and slept until sunrise. The pace was terrible, made worse by the knowledge that they would have to fight when they reached the Falls of Theosa.

Sillik, Renee, and Calbert all retreated into their own minds as they moved through the forest. They spoke little, even when they stopped, and they were quick to grab sleep at every opportunity. Days and nights bled together as the forces hurried through the endless forest. At the halfway point, Rigell called a halt and allowed everyone to sleep the night. Sillik and Renee smiled as they got the word and immediately dropped their packs, unfurled their cloaks, and lay down to sleep.

As Sillik closed his eyes, he felt every muscle spasm and bruise. With a full night's sleep ahead of him, he quickly retreated into a series of rituals from the Third Law that were designed to relax and heal. He knew that Renee and Calbert would be doing the same thing. As soon as he had set the ritual in motion, he fell into a deep sleep.

It seemed like he had hardly slept at all when a jarring scream tore through the night. He awoke, groggy and sore. Another scream sounded, and he was on his feet, sword drawn. Calbert stood up a moment later, staff in hand. Renee struggled to her feet, wavering a little, but with her dagger ready and her other hand on her sword hilt.

A third scream ripped the air, closer and louder. Calbert looked around quickly at the other bundled, sleeping forms.

"Why isn't everyone up?" Renee asked.

"Dragon screams," Sillik said.

Calbert nodded. "Only those who can use magic can hear them. It tears at the soul."

"I thought that was just legend," Renee said.

"No, it's real," Rigell said from the darkness behind them. He paused as another scream sounded. "They are searching. I once saw what was left of a man tortured by dragon screams." He shook his head. "It was terrible. Nothing but an empty shell."

"What are they searching for?" Sillik asked.

"For us," Renee said.

Calbert shook his head. "They can't know we're here. They might think they are being herded by Handrie's attacks, but they should think we are too far out of position to be a factor. So they are scouting. They think they will take the falls and command the high ground. Then they can catch Handrie and his forces and destroy him."

Another scream tore through the night, but this time it was farther away.

"The screams are intended to get a response," Calbert said. "As long as we stay hidden, we should be safe."

"Get whatever sleep you can," Rigell said. "Dawn will come much too soon."

Sillik sheathed his sword and lay down again. He slept, but this time his dreams were of battles, blood, fire, and sorcery.

As he struggled to open his eyes at dawn, he saw that Renee and Calbert had not slept well either. He hazarded a guess that no one who was familiar with magic or any part of the Seven Laws had gotten much sleep.

Sillik ate his handful of rations and washed it down with some cold water. He splashed a little water on his face as well. His stomach growled. Nerak's battle rations, though filling and sustaining, lacked flavor and variety. Sillik almost wished for an Illician lizard. They stank, but at least they could carry more food, which allowed for variety. After five days, the same meal three times a day got old.

After breakfast, the command came down the line to resume the march through the forest. With every muscle protesting, Sillik and the others surged forward into the dimly lit forest.

By afternoon, it had begun to rain, further dousing the spirits of Sillik and his companions. The rain was steady and continuous. Soon, despite their cloaks, they were cold and wet. Worse, the rain made their footing slippery. Sillik saw people slipping and falling on either side of him. Rigell looked worried. He didn't want his fighting force incapacitated before the battle even started. Sillik kept glancing at Rigell, trying to gauge what he would do.

Soon Rigell called a halt. While Rigell consulted with his generals, Sillik and Renee took the opportunity to sink into a trance and repair the damage caused by the forced march. When Renee was done, she opened her eyes and looked around, but Sillik sank deeper into the trance and touched the pendant.

Instantly, it was as if he could see with Handrie's eyes and hear what Handrie heard. They were in a battle. Handrie wasn't worried, but he was concerned. Something was wrong; it was too easy. As Handrie looked around, Sillik also sensed a trap, and it was about to be sprung. Startled, Sillik sent a quick message to his friend. When he received a response, he broke the trance and opened his eyes, feeling refreshed.

"Change of plans," he announced.

Heads swiveled to face him as he stood.

"Handrie has stumbled into a trap. Peol didn't withdraw as we thought. They repositioned their forces here." Sillik drew a map quickly in the mud. "Handrie is here, Ynak and their dragons are moving here, and we are here."

Rigell and Calbert exchanged meaningful looks.

"How far?" Renee asked as she studied the crude map.

"Far enough that even if we ran, we might not save him," Calbert said with a pained expression.

Sillik smiled. "There is a way." He laid out his idea quickly. It felt right to choose this place. Only he knew its significance. Renee might suspect, but only he knew for sure. Memories of other times flashed through his head. The shape of the land was his. Somehow, he knew the best places to place troops.

Rigell leaned back and shook his head. "It is the only way, but what you suggest is impossible."

"Handrie and his men will have to run like the devil to get there," Calbert said.

Sillik nodded. "He knows that, and he was already giving the orders when we broke contact. Instead of driving the enemy, he is going to lead the enemy."

"It will appear as if they are in full flight," Renee said. "Will Ynak take the bait?"

Rigell snorted. "Of course they will. A chance to defeat Nerak and capture or kill the king? Those hotheads will be chomping at the bit to run after him."

Rigell waved two of his generals over and gave the necessary orders. Sillik could see the men melting as they grasped the implications of the orders, but they merely saluted and then turned to spread the word.

Then the four consulted Sillik's map again and chose their bearing. Once they had agreed, they began leading the troops toward Handrie and his fleeing forces. The pace Rigell set was double the pace at which they had been traveling before. Sillik stilled his mind and summoned forth power to maintain the pace. He knew they would have to travel like this for two to three days with minimal breaks in order to save Handrie.

It was then that the knights began to sing. It wasn't a song with words so much as a hum. Sillik and Renee looked around in wonder as they heard it. The strength of the song seemed to bolster every footstep and encourage everyone. Soon, they had doubled the pace. Sillik shook his head in wonder.

# CHAPTER 42

## Battle and Reunion

WHEN SILLIK AND his allies arrived, construction began immediately on what they would need to defeat Peol. Sillik advised Rigell, and orders were issued. Troops were dispersed, and stone axes were produced to cut trees and shape the weapons and defenses that were needed. They didn't have much time.

Handrie's forces arrived a day later. Handshakes and hugs were exchanged, and then Handrie convened a quick war council, during which he reported that Peol's forces were near. Sillik could see the stress and wear he had endured.

If Handrie was surprised to see Renee, he didn't show it. He listened to her as quickly as his uncle and his commanders. Renee and Miranda hugged as if sisters and laughed at some joke, but Sillik could see how tired both women were.

Rigell asked the question that everyone wanted answered. Handrie shrugged and said they had not seen the dragons in several days.

Orders were given quickly and assignments made. Handrie ordered a net established along their lines, and Morhem went to work with his fellow net minders.

It wasn't long before a lookout spotted the approaching dragons on the horizon. "Peol's troops will be just behind them," Rigell said.

The screams resumed in earnest. Sillik shuddered. The dragons were trying to frighten them. Sillik smiled reassuringly at Renee. She smiled back and blew a kiss at him.

The warriors gripped their weapons with sweaty hands. Perspiration dripped from everyone. The rain had abated, but the sun had turned the forest into a humid hell. Flies and other insects buzzed all around them. But this heat was nothing. Soon, the air would be incandescent with dragon fire. Sillik could only stand and watch. He knew what was coming. He had been in this position before.

From ancient memories, he remembered standing in this very spot and directing armies. Tens of thousands of troops had been here. Thousands of masters had worked their spells. The combined forces of thirty-seven cities had been united. The forces arrayed here today were puny and weak in comparison, but they still might win the day.

"You know where we are, of course," Handrie said.

Sillik nodded. Memories flashed through his mind. The ring on Sillik's hand had been here before. Of course, Sillik knew where he was. The ridges looked the same.

"I assumed you knew when you chose this place," Handrie said as he looked around, apparently unconcerned about the battle that was about to occur. "Our ancestors fought here, or very near here." He waved toward the valley. "I read the old books. The younger son is supposed to be the advisor." He laughed. "I thought I would be the advisor. So I read. I memorized all of the old accounts of every war, skirmish, and battle. I learned all that I could so I could be a proper advisor to my brother, the king."

Renee gave Handrie a questioning look but relaxed when she saw he was smiling.

"It was different then," Handrie said. "They were outnumbered. Four or five to one, according to some accounts."

"The trees were not here either," Sillik said quietly.

Renee gave him a sharp look.

"It was not so green. It was winter, and it was closer to eight to one," Sillik continued.

Renee's eyes widened in surprise.

"Our ancestors fought here during the demon wars," Handrie explained. "The first demon war, that is." He smiled. "It's fitting, isn't it, that we fight here today?"

Sillik smiled. "The lay of the land is conducive to what we want to do."

"Do you think they know what is about to happen?" Renee asked.

"I doubt it," Rigell said quietly as he stepped forward.

"I dislike the necessity of what we must do today," Handrie said.

Sillik nodded as thunder boomed in the distance. The air felt heavy with anticipation.

A scout ran up to Handrie and Rigell. He was out of breath, and his tunic was plastered to his lean body. "My lords," he said as he fell to his knees. That was all he could gasp out as he tried to breathe.

Sillik, Handrie, Rigell, Renee, Calbert, and others clustered around the man as he gasped for air.

"Peol," he said, "and Ynak banners have been sighted, my lords."

Stunned silence greeted his words.

Finally, Handrie spoke. "Curse the Nine!"

"And my lords," the scout said, "they are running from something. Someone is chasing them! Herding them!"

Rigell was the first to speak. "The enemy of my enemy is my friend."

The words hung there for a moment.

"We cannot defeat both cities," Calbert said.

Rigell looked at the others. "Do we withdraw?"

"No," Handrie said as he knelt to draw in the muddy dirt. "We are here." He drew a large arc. "Ynak and Peol are coming like this. *If* they are being chased, then we can do what we planned originally."

"And if they are not?" Sillik asked.

Rigell shrugged. "Then we die."

Everyone was silent as they looked at each other.

"Since we are quoting ancient generals, I will add another," Renee said with a smile. "'The survivor does the unexpected.' So said Commander Sihn Lee of the Sel. They will expect us to flee the combined forces, but our original plan is strong. It worked before against superior forces."

"If we split our forces and run, they will still outnumber us," Handrie said. "Our best chance is to stick to our plan, use our high ground to command the air, bottle them into the floor of the valley, and attack from all sides. If anyone comes into contact with my brother Nordan, the traitor, I must be the one to kill him. It is our law." Fire burned in his eyes.

"I ask the same for my traitor," Sillik said. "Dernot Lafliar is mine. I must avenge my city."

Renee smiled. "I imagine they will be together, so I would counsel that you stay together as well. Nordan and Dernot were not chance allies. My foe, Nathalin, converted them. I do not ask to fight him alone, though. I fear I lack the power to kill him myself. So I propose we fight together, for if any of us comes upon Nathalin alone, then that person is lost."

Handrie sprang to his feet. "It has begun."

Sillik felt it too. He detected the use of certain magics. The extreme edges of Handrie's trap had begun to close. Sillik looked up and saw dragons in the clouds. Viktorie's words sounded in his mind: *Dragons dancing above your head.*

Handrie turned to Rigell. "Give the word for the air attack."

Rigell nodded and then turned to his aides, speaking quickly and urgently. His aides took off running.

Somewhere in the forest, strings thrummed, and brown streaks shot into the air, crisscrossing over the battlefield. Some of the streaks were on fire. Others dragged nets, ropes, and wire. Fortunately, the clouds hid most of what happened next.

The skies turned into fire as dragons trumpeted and screamed. Seeing without really seeing, Sillik knew that nine dragons were falling to the ground, and those that had survived were fleeing. The first shots had been fired, and the skies were suddenly clear of threats. Again, Sillik was buffeted by memories that were not his own. In his last memory here, the dragons had fought for him.

Sillik looked at Handrie and Rigell. "It is time."

Handrie nodded and looked at another warrior. The man dipped the tip of his arrow into a strange liquid that Calbert had supplied. Then he loosed his shaft high over the valley.

All eyes followed the shaft. When it neared the top of its flight, Calbert spoke a word of power, and the arrow burst into an explosion of light.

Handrie smiled. "The trap has been sprung."

At once, thousands of arrows exploded against the trees. A nearly unbroken ring of fire surrounded the Peol and Ynak warriors. Successive waves of arrows tightened the noose. Screams and yells came from the forest. Then the flames stopped moving. The next wave of flaming arrows mostly stopped dead in flight and fell to the ground.

Handrie nodded to Calbert, and the next command went out. The ballistae hummed, and a storm of thick bolts crashed into the center of the ring. More explosions detonated. A second wave of arrows launched, followed by a second wave of ballistae bolts. Some of the arrows were stopped, but others got through. All of the ballistae bolts got through and detonated again.

Now the masters of the Seven Laws added their skills to the assault. The shields that Ynak and Peol had raised were ripped to pieces. The next wave of exploding arrows was mostly unopposed. At the height of the assault, Handrie released his men. With a yell, the warriors descended on the remnants of Ynak and Peol's armies.

Sillik was puzzled. This had been too easy. A quick glance at Renee told him she was worried as well. He wanted to be cautious, but Handrie was convinced the battle was over, so he ordered his men to attack what was left.

The memories that buffeted Sillik showed him how the battle had progressed the last time. The battle had lasted for days, attack and counterattack. Sillik suspected something had gone wrong, but he couldn't say what, so he followed Handrie to the valley floor.

It was a ghastly environment. Fires burned everywhere. Smoke hung like fog between what was left of the trees. Bodies lay wounded and burned, but there were far fewer than Sillik had expected.

Handrie looked puzzled. Clearly, he had also expected something different. He was about to order a retreat when they heard the yells.

Instantly, Sillik was also issuing orders. They had been caught in their own trap. Slowly, the word went out, and the Nerakeans turned to face the real threat. Peol and Ynak had sent in only a token force. The rest had held back, waiting until the knights had given up the high ground. Now, with their backs against the cliffs, the Knights of Nerak were the ones at a disadvantage.

The fireballs arched in first. Hastily, Handrie and others threw nets over their men. When the fireballs exploded, the nets trembled. Men cursed. Everyone knew what this meant. The hunter had become the hunted.

"They divided their forces and came in behind us!" Handrie yelled. "Blast the Seven!"

"How do we get out?" Renee asked, worry etched on her face.

"We don't," Rigell said impassively. "We stand and fight."

The tempo of the battle was sliding out of control as Sillik and his friends waited for the attack.

When the overhead assault eased, everyone checked their weapons. Sweat dripped from their faces, and their hearts raced in anticipation. Then the sound started. At first, it was a low, bone-chilling yell, full of hatred and anger. Then it rose into a roar.

When the attack finally started, it was as if there were ten men for every knight. Sillik raced into the battle, his sword singing as he wove terrible magic. Renee, Calbert, and Handrie fought at his side. Everywhere he turned, the enemy died, but it was too few. The knights fought bravely, but they were vastly outnumbered. Sillik felt the collapse of the net, followed by Morhem's scream.

Handrie swore as he batted a sword aside with his staff and killed a Peol soldier with a slashing blow. He was channeling enormous amounts of energy through the staff, using it as a battering ram. The soldier sizzled as he died.

Sillik heard a yell from his left as a dozen enemy warriors rushed toward the dwindling group. Sillik sighed and then used the Seven Laws to incinerate them.

Despite such efforts, the Knights of Nerak were being decimated. The warriors from Peol and Ynak were enveloping them and pressing forward. Sillik knew he could escape, but if he did, many–perhaps all–of the knights would die.

Soon they began to retreat. Handrie was on his right, Renee on his left. Rigell and Calbert were somewhere to Handrie's right. A glance behind revealed the backs of more knights scarcely fifty paces away. Thousands of knights had begun the fight, but only hundreds still lived. If this kept up, none of them would be alive by nightfall.

In the center of the fighting, the Nerak pennant still flew, surrounded by a dozen archers. They fired their bows as quickly as they could. Soon, their arrows would be depleted, and then they would add their staves to the fight.

With startling abruptness, the lines of fighting shifted, and Sillik saw Dernot. The renegade Illician was leaning against a tree, watching. Nordan stood with him. A dozen other men stood behind the two renegades.

Sillik felt his anger surge. He threw a bolt of energy so powerful that it surprised even him. Handrie and Renee responded as well. To Sillik's surprise, his bolt struck a net over the traitors. Lightning cracked, and the net shattered like tiny shards of glass. The renegades ducked as Handrie and Renee's bolts struck, but the bolts killed the rest of the men supporting the traitors.

Heedless of the risk he was taking, Sillik strode forward. He had been reckless with his power throughout the fight, and now he pulled hard on his reserves. To his surprise, he felt them open to reveal power he had not known he possessed. He blinked and saw the signet ring on his hand over his battle glove. He couldn't remember placing it there. Practically glowing with energy, tendrils of lightning sparking from his hands, he attacked Dernot.

The cocky expression that had been on Dernot's face moments earlier was replaced with a look of terror. Then his training kicked in, and he produced a spell that deflected some of the energy that Sillik threw at him.

Handrie had no expression on his face as he wove strings of deadly energy around his brother. Nordan, drawing upon his recent conversion to the Nine, tried to summon creatures from the depths of hell to aid him, but they became ensnared in the fabric that Handrie was weaving.

Uncertain of who needed help most, Renee used her magic to protect both Handrie and Sillik. When she felt a cold chill descend upon the battlefield, she turned and saw a bent, crippled man hurrying toward the battle. Recognition flashed, and she threw all of her anger into one large lightning ball that charged at the dark master.

Exhilaration soared as the ball flew straight and true. However, at the last moment, it was deflected like a fly, and the man continued across the battlefield. He waved his staff, and the magic that Handrie and Sillik had cast was shattered.

Sillik and Handrie shifted at once to the new combatant. Working in unison, they threw previously unimaginable amounts of energy at the man. He shrugged off the attack with a sneer. Renee noticed Nordan and Dernot recovering, so she threw her own attack at them to keep them off-balance.

Sensing the shift in battle, Calbert and Rigell broke off from their combat and hurried to Handrie's aid. Renee kept Nordan and Dernot busy with exploding balls of energy while the four men united to attack the dark master.

Sweat poured from Sillik's face. The energy rolling off this dark master was incredible. He was able to absorb their combined attacks and still counterattack. The battle roared around them as the knights continued to retreat. Only a few hundred knights remained, and they were increasingly outnumbered. Then the wind shifted. Sillik smelled a familiar scent, and his heart soared.

Battle drums sounded. Sillik felt a familiar friend whisper a single word in his mind: "Soon." Suddenly, the enemy's ranks broke everywhere as Illician battle lizards surged into the fray.

Great gouts of fire sizzled the combined forces of Ynak and Peol. Arrows unerringly cut down swaths of soldiers, and the unleashed battle lizards attacked with unrivaled ferocity. Sillik was surprised to see smaller battle lizards enter the battle as well, carrying the rising sun of Colum.

Sillik's emotions soared. He attacked the dark master and saw him stumble. Then the Gold Robes attacked, and the forest erupted again in fire.

Handrie turned back toward Nordan and pelted him with magic as the traitor fled the scene. Sillik saw Dernot throw a knife and kill the driver of a battle lizard. In a heartbeat, the renegade Illician scampered onto the lizard, killed the remaining riders with a searing blast of power, and then rode the lizard into the forest. In an almost hopeless attempt, Sillik sent his own dagger flying at Dernot. He saw the renegade Illician lurch atop the lizard right before he disappeared into the trees.

Renee screamed in frustration as she also lost sight of her quarry. One moment, the dark master had been crawling away from the battlefield. The next, he was gone.

A sand lizard burst into view and skidded to a stop, showering Sillik in dirt, blood, and gore. "By the Seven!" Sillik swore as he struggled to see around the lizard and berate its driver.

A single man wearing Illician battle armor sat atop the lizard. This was unusual since five normally rode. It was then that Sillik noticed the gold patterns on the man's arms, signifying that he was a master of the Seven Laws. Anger bloomed in Sillik. The man should have known not to get in the way. Sillik was starting to sheath his sword when something made him pause. The master still had his veil over his face. Concerned at what was happening, Sillik raised his shields just as the unknown Illician attacked. Surprised to encounter another traitor, Sillik was slow to respond, but his sword dragged his arm up and caught the blast of energy. Suddenly, Sillik felt rested and relaxed, as if he had slept for days. The sword had not only absorbed the malevolent energy; it had also used it to refresh him.

"You should have died in Illicia!" the man screamed as he lifted a large, old shield.

*The Shield of Rendarick*, Sillik thought. "You killed my brothers," he said. Sillik frowned and drew another throwing knife. "You set the traps." *Who is he?* Sillik wondered.

"Of course I did!" the man said as he threw another bolt of energy. "And you were too stupid to figure it out."

Sillik deflected the blow with a nonchalant wave. "Why?"

The man laughed and threw another blast of searing energy at Sillik. "Still too stupid to figure it out?"

Sillik brought his sword up again to absorb the energy. He had never read about the sword having such a talent, but at the same time, it was as if he had always known. Again, he felt refreshed. He had to end this if he were to have any hope of catching Dernot. He moved to his left. *I can't attack him while he holds that shield. Damn, who is this? He knows me, but he won't unveil.*

Laughing, the man on the lizard blocked Sillik's path and threw another ball of energy at him. The lizard hissed. The energy was as black as the deepest night and roiled with evil. Tendrils of dark energy leaked from the ball as it sailed toward Sillik's head.

Sillik sent an answering ball of pure white energy. The two balls shattered against each other and disappeared. Sillik moved to his right, only to be blocked again. He glanced around and saw his friends rushing toward him. His foe also saw the reinforcements and began to throw black balls of energy at Sillik's friends as well.

Frustrated, Sillik blocked the dark energy. The bolts ricocheted into the burning trees. Seeing the trees shake, Sillik had a glimmer of an idea. He began blocking the dangerous energy strategically, aiming the bolts back at the trees behind his enemy.

Trees began to crash down behind Sillik's opponent. Sensing an opportunity, Sillik threw his own bolts into the trees as well, causing more to crash down. Finally, one came down too close, and Sillik's opponent dropped the shield as he leapt out of the way.

Sillik immediately shifted his attack and hammered his foe with arcane energies. After a dozen blows, the traitorous Illician's shields crumpled, and Sillik's next volley incinerated him. As the magic burned, Sillik got a fleeting glimpse of the man's face. Lord Grison of the Gold Robes had always been a fatherly figure, but as his face blackened, Sillik saw it was filled with rage and hatred.

Sillik scooped up the antique shield.

Before he could do anything else, Renee stole a moment and turned to kiss him quickly. "For luck," she whispered throatily. "And for later," she added with a grin.

From that point onward, the tide of battle reversed. The soldiers from Ynak and Peol wanted only to flee the lizards. The Illicians let some of them escape, but they killed as many as they could, quickly and efficiently.

When the Illicians decided the battle was over, the commanders issued quick and effective orders. The standards dipped and swirled in battlefield commands. Horns blared other commands while the drums coordinated the movements like a dance. Gold Robes and healers were sent out to deal with the injured and dying while the warriors secured the battlefield.

One lizard hurried across the field. When it stopped and crouched, the group surrounding Sillik gasped in surprise at the smell. But Sillik smiled and took a deep breath. Nothing had ever smelled sweeter.

When one of the riders jumped to the ground, Sillik noticed that she was splattered with blood and gore and her sword was red and sticky. She took off her helmet and shook out her hair.

"What kept you, Warmaster of Illicia?" Sillik asked with a smile.

# CHAPTER 43

## Coronation

GIVEN THE INJURIES the knights had endured, the Illicians took command of the situation. They would have taken command even if no knights had been injured, but the current situation allowed Handrie to save face. Sillik had supply lizards brought up, and an encampment was set up away from the battlefield on higher ground. The healers were busy lending what aid they could to all who could be saved. The Gold Robes helped those who were dying, removing pain and easing the souls of the passing.

Sillik commandeered a tent to host his allies. The knights were clearly overwhelmed and in shock. Their losses were devastating, but Illicia's cavalry had decimated the combined armies of Ynak and Peol.

As the leaders gathered, Sillik and Renee were surprised to see Renunel of Colum follow Briana into the tent. Briana explained that Colum had sent five hundred troops on their smaller lizards. Colum's cavalry had caught up with the Illicians at the River Vivare. The combined forces had then crossed the river on barges created by the Gold Robes. Sillik smiled and thanked Renunel, who was self-conscious at the attention.

Briana explained that the smaller lizards had worked well and done things that the large lizards couldn't have. Impressed, Sillik ordered Briana to acquire enough smaller lizards from Colum to form a small division and to set up regular trade with the city.

Briana smiled mischievously as she imagined the high council choking over Sillik's orders. Renunel nodded gratefully but still looked uncomfortable in the presence of the senior leadership of two other cities.

Handrie, Rigell, and Calbert had all survived relatively unscathed. To Sillik's amazement, he found not one scratch on himself. Renee had required minor healing, but she soon joined the leadership meeting.

Renee had been suspicious when Sillik and Briana hugged joyfully following the battle. Sillik had lifted the woman off her feet and spun her around. *This could be a meeting between friends–or lovers,* Renee had thought. She had eyed Briana with distrust, and the air between the two women was cold enough to freeze water.

With a flourish, Sillik had turned and said, "Briana, this is Renee. She has been invaluable to me. Renee, this is Briana, warmaster of Illicia."

The two women had eyed each other warily, but Sillik had not noticed in the ensuing chaos.

Later in the day, the Gold Robes learned the art of net casting quickly and threw a net over the entire camp to protect them in case the dragons returned. Patrols and trackers were sent out to hunt down the various traitors. No signs of Dernot or Nordan had been found yet, but Sillik was confident that would change soon.

Handrie and Rigell had dispatched messengers to Nerak, informing the city of their victory and requesting reinforcements. Handrie cursed at the number of knights who had been killed. Nearly three-quarters of his army had been killed or injured.

The Illicians assumed responsibility for clearing the battlefield and burning the dead in huge pyres. They built huge sleds and then attached them to the lizards so that they could drag the dead over to the fires.

Over a hundred prisoners had been captured. Those who were wounded were healed by the Illicians and then cast into a prisoner of war camp. Ynak and Peol prisoners were segregated from one another, officers were segregated from troops, and anyone with magical abilities was also separated from the others. The Illicians followed standard practice and drugged the men with magical ability to the point of stupor. They wouldn't be able to walk, talk, or light a candle until the Illicians decided what to do with them.

"The battle led us here," Briana explained. "Everyone felt the earth tremble at the power that was brought to bear. The Gold Robes were afraid that one of the Seven or Nine had set foot on Earth again. The foundations of the world were shaken. Every master in the world is probably wondering what happened."

As Sillik listened to Briana, he looked at his signet ring. It had been tight on his finger while he wore battle gloves, and it was still tight now even without them. The ring had opened things within him. He had drawn power that he should not have had. Of course, he had also been using the sword–and the pendant. Perhaps the sword, ring, and pendant augmented each other, but he still felt like something was missing, like he was balancing two extremes. He knew he needed something else to provide stability.

Once it was clear that the battle was over, the Illicians had done the next thing they always did after battle: set up steam tents.

Without thinking, Sillik led the way to a steam tent reserved for the leadership. Sillik laughed when Briana's guards seemed uncertain about whether to follow. When Greenup ordered them to stay outside, they nodded gratefully.

Handrie and Rigell paused uncertainly when the Illicians entered the outer tent and began to disrobe. Renee just shrugged and began removing her clothing and weapons as quickly as Briana. Miranda smiled mischievously as she undressed.

The inner tent was slightly taller than the tallest man. It was domed and made from heavily waxed fabric to contain the heat and humidity. A ring of fabric had been laid down, on which the occupants could sit. In the center of the ring lay a pile of rocks. Several wooden buckets of water were spread throughout the tent. The only light came from the red-hot rocks.

Sillik asked Calbert to cast a net over their heads. The older knight nodded, though he was clearly uncertain regarding what was about to happen. Sillik smiled as he tested the net. It would do. It was intended more to mask their conversation than to provide protection.

All through the long march, Sillik had been considering what the results of the battle might be. He had come up with twelve different outcomes. Most of them would have resulted in varying degrees of defeat. Victory of any kind had been an unlikely prospect. But he had not considered Illician forces arriving when they had. In fact, he had not considered Illicia at all, so he was in unfamiliar territory as he considered their partial victory.

For a while, he just sat and thought about what needed to happen next. Multiple paths lay in front of him. Sillik became aware that all eyes were watching and waiting. What were they waiting for? Some brilliance he didn't feel he had? Best to start with the basics.

"To the Seven," Sillik said as he poured ladles of water on the hot red stones. The water hissed and danced on the rocks, and steam boiled into the air. Everyone echoed his words, including Renunel, who was clearly bewildered.

Then Sillik poured water on his face and hands and scrubbed. When he was done, he grabbed a towel and wiped himself down. Then he passed the bucket to Briana.

Briana took the dipper and poured more water on the stones before her. "To the Seven," she said. She ladled water on her face and hands, washed, and then passed the water to Handrie. Briana's breath caught when she saw that Handrie and Sillik were wearing similar pendants. Then she smiled when she recognized the pendants from the drawing Kenton had shown her.

As the ritual progressed around the circle, Sillik pondered how to proceed. They needed more soldiers, they needed to find the traitors, and they needed to kill the dark master. He smiled as memories flashed behind his eyes. Some of the Council of Nine had already been killed, but he suspected replacements were already stepping into vacated positions.

When Renee passed the bucket of water back to Sillik, he addressed the group. "The cleansing after-battle ceremony is an ancient ritual in Illicia. It is meant to physically cleanse the body and to cleanse away the hatred and emotions that led us to do battle." Sillik paused as he envisioned the memories again. "We have won a victory, but it is clearly less than complete. Everything that happened in Illicia was clearly designed to keep the Illicians out of the fight."

Briana smiled at his words. She had been right all along.

"Ynak and Peol were insufficient for the dark master's needs," Sillik continued. "The next time the dark master and his council strike, they will not lack troops. Also ..." He paused, for he hadn't discussed this with anyone except Briana. "There is a foretelling that I will face a demon." Sillik looked around the room. The faces were frightened but trusting. "Therefore, I propose a formal third alliance of cities to deal with this threat."

Silence greeted his words. Handrie was still for a while, a stunned expression on his face, but gradually a smile formed as he considered the implications.

"We need troops," Sillik continued. "Briana will summon the main Illician battle force soon."

Briana nodded eagerly, but there was something else written on her face–concern, perhaps.

Renunel looked around incredulously. "Isn't your main force here?"

Briana laughed. "No, this is just a heavy strike force."

Renunel's eyes widened. Renee covered her mouth to hide her smile.

Sillik smiled at the levity. "Renunel, we appreciate the aid Colum brought and greatly desire your forces to stay and assist us. If you have the ability to bring additional aid, we sure could use it."

Renunel looked pleased at being named. "We will consider it," he said gravely.

"I have already summoned additional knights," Handrie said.

Sillik nodded. "But they will be insufficient for what needs to be done. There is more going on here than meets the eye. Briana," he said, turning to face the warmaster, "send emissaries to all the usual friends and request their help. We will draft a letter signed by me, requesting their aid based upon the treaties of old."

"We can take Shelnor off that list," Briana said.

"Why? What happened?"

Keltic spoke up from the far side of the tent. "Shelnor was implicated in an attack on the warmaster in the keep. A small force was sent to Shelnor to assess their involvement. We haven't heard what they found yet."

"How small?" Sillik asked.

"One hundred and fifty lizards," Briana said. "I told them to find out if Shelnor was guilty before we started a war."

"Damn!" Sillik exclaimed.

Briana started to object, but Sillik quickly clarified. "Not you," he said. "You were attacked; it was the right thing to do. But I believe it's a trap. Our forces are being divided—provoked and divided—and divided we will fall." He fell quiet for a moment and then looked at Briana again. "Recall them. We can deal with Shelnor after this is over." He turned to Renee. "Do you still have any contacts with Covenon?"

Renee smiled and started to speak, but Briana interrupted her.

"Before we go there," Briana said, ignoring Renee's glare, "this—whatever this is—is much bigger than a challenge for the kingship. But first I must know: what is that pendant you're wearing?"

"It's called the Star of the South," Handrie said. "I gave it as a gift to your prince. I wear the matching pendant, the Star of the North." Handrie held it up for her to see. "It signifies the close friendship between Nerak and Illicia."

Briana shuddered as she remembered Silvia's words in Sillik's room so very long ago. She turned to Sillik. "Do you agree that this is much bigger than a challenge for the throne?"

Sillik smiled at his warmaster. "Yes, it is." He knew what she was going to ask next.

"Then allow us to crown you," Briana said. "It will add weight to all your negotiations if you are the king of Illicia rather than the crown prince."

Sillik was quiet for a long moment before he nodded. "Very well, Warmaster."

"Now that that is decided," Handrie said, "we also need to discuss what happened in the battle. We outnumbered them, and yet they held us at bay. Are the Nine that much more powerful than the Seven?"

Greenup responded in a low voice. "It has been a long time since we have faced a dark master. The books say they are just as powerful, not more powerful."

"But *you* were more powerful," Renee said, looking at Sillik.

Sillik smiled. "That is complicated. When I figure out what happened, I will be happy to discuss it. Until then, we need to know what made these three men so powerful that they held us at bay despite our clear numerical superiority."

"I will have the Gold Robe historians research this anomaly as quickly as possible," Senarick said. "But I can tell you right now, there are magical tools out there that amplify magical abilities, much like some that I suspect are nearby. I think they had some kind of help."

"Thank you, Vicar General," Sillik said. "We need the answers yesterday."

"I understand, Your Highness," Senarick said as he wiped perspiration from his forehead. "We will do our best."

"What else do we know?" Sillik asked.

"That Lord Grison was a traitor," Briana said.

"Yes," Sillik said with a grimace, "a lot is explained. I trusted him."

"We all did," Greenup said softly.

"This dark master, he has an amazing ability to recruit," Sillik said. He looked at Renee. "What else do we know about him?"

"We learned about him several years ago," Handrie said. "We heard whispers, nothing more."

"What about Covenon?" Sillik asked, still looking at Renee.

"Yes, I have friends I can contact."

"Would an Illician messenger help them?" Sillik asked.

Renee nodded.

"Good. We can draft some letters detailing what we need."

# CHAPTER 44

## Keys

SILLIK SPENT THE night wandering through the battlefield, accompanied by Renee. They did not speak much, although Sillik shared a few words with the men he passed. Behind them, the ever-present guards followed discreetly. Here in the field, the guards were a combination of soldiers and Gold Robes.

Before sunrise, Sillik stopped on a rock outcropping from which he could see the rising sun and the battlefield. He sat on the damp stone, and his battle armor creaked. "I have not had that dream since we talked about it," he said.

Renee caught her breath but did not say anything.

"We are going to have to make difficult decisions about how to conduct this war," he said. "I have already made one decision that was hard. I never wanted the crown. But I will be crowned today. The one thing that has made things easier is you."

Renee felt her heart skip a beat. *He couldn't mean …*

"I want you to be at my side as events go forward," Sillik said as he held out his hand. "This isn't a marriage proposal. I think that should wait. But I don't want you to leave either. So I thought I had better say something or risk losing you forever."

Renee felt tears in her eyes as she took his hand. *By the Seven Gods, this is really happening.* "You can't marry me," she said as her heart screamed no. "I don't have royal blood."

Sillik smiled as he stood. "Funny thing about royalty. At some point no one was royal. Your parents were on the city council. Your father led Covenon. That counts as nobility. So yes, you can marry me."

Renee turned to face the rising sun. "A new day," she said. "You never asked if I would stay." *Typical man*, she thought. "So I will give you an answer to the question you didn't ask. Yes, I will stay with you. And if the day comes when you want to ask me another question, I will say yes if you ask."

"Very well," Sillik said as he stood. "Let's go get this task done."

Sillik led the way to the center of the encampment, and when they got close, he stopped and stood to silently watch the preparations. Renee stood to his right, and his guards fanned out behind him in an arc.

After morning prayers, the leaders gathered near the battlefield but on high ground from which they had better views. The day had dawned clear, but now rain clouds were gathering. The Illicians were arrayed in circles around a small clearing. Some of the troops had climbed the trees to serve as lookouts. The surviving knights were scattered throughout. Greenup and Briana were at the center of the clearing.

Briana produced a small crate, which held a chest banded with iron. Sillik smiled, recognizing it. Then Briana directed several soldiers to unroll a small silk carpet decorated with red and gold.

There was to be no real ceremony, no formal cleansing or ritual. Clean clothing was nonexistent. Over his armor Sillik placed the Star of the South to cement his relationship with Nerak. Briana had suggested he wear it. The signet ring was on his hand, and Avenger was sheathed at his waist. Sillik had found armor for Renee as well. It had belonged to a female Gold Robe who had died from an errant arrow. The armor almost fit. Briana had helped her adjust it so that it wouldn't chafe too much.

The ceremony would be brief. They all had a hundred other things to do. Somehow, Sillik thought it was fitting to do this here, in this place. It completed a circle in a way.

As Sillik made his way to the center of the clearing, he felt troubled by what was about to happen. He had never wanted to be king. Now it was thrust upon him. When he reached the center of the clearing, he knelt before Briana and placed his left hand on his sword. The Gold Robes had cast a large net to commemorate the occasion. The knights looked a little uncomfortable being under a net they didn't control, but they were intrigued to watch.

Sillik's new friends were standing nearby. Handrie, whose own coronation had happened weeks ago in their old camp, looked happy. Handrie's sister Miranda was not happy, but Sillik suspected that was because of Renee.

Sillik and Briana had agreed that no preamble or other nonsensical rituals were required. They would keep this short. Greenup picked up the small chest and carried it to Briana. She smiled as she opened it. Inside was the Illician crown.

How had she known to bring it? Had it been just a hopeful fantasy, Sillik wondered, or had there been another foretelling? Or had Lady Silvia told her? Sillik did not ask. Some things, he just didn't want to know.

Memories of other kings and queens flashed through Sillik's mind, thousands of men and women who had worn the crown. Illician historians said it dated from the city's founding. The memories paraded in front of Sillik until he was watching the crown being forged. A blacksmith hammered as a man with a golden aura watched patiently. Magic surrounded the gold. Magic had helped make it.

Briana lifted the crown over her head for all to see and then spoke in a loud, clear voice. "Sillik, prince of Illicia, as warmaster of Illicia, I crown thee king of Illicia." With the simple pronouncement, she lowered the crown onto his head.

Sillik jerked with surprise when the crown touched him. Alarms throughout the camp began to ring. Attack! Sillik's thoughts slowed, and he heard the sound of the alarms as if in a dream.

Sillik moved slowly. His hands and head tingled with energy. The tingle became a rush and then a torrent. Power coursed through his body. The weight of the crown seemed to increase, and Sillik wavered. Images flashed through his head, much like when he had first put on the signet ring. Images of the Seven Gods surrounding him added to his confusion. They touched his crown and channeled power into him. The power flow was out of control as the ring, the sword, the crown, and the pendant amplified each other. Memories intruded as he saw new sights.

*I must stand*, he thought as he struggled to control the power flowing through him. He groped like a blind man for a way to control what he felt. He saw his father, watching and smiling. He had known. He saw other kings who had ruled Illicia. They were also watching and waiting. His father nodded his encouragement. Sillik knew that if he failed to control the energy, he would be destroyed. He also realized that he had unwittingly unlocked the magical items in the wrong order. The crown should have been first, yet he had put on the ring first. The sword was intended to be last, and yet he had used the sword second. Now the crown rested on his head, and he was wearing the other three. The pendant also had a part to play, somehow amplifying everything else. And yet there was a way, even though Rendarick, the first king of Illicia, had never trod this path.

Briana's smile faded as she realized something was amiss. In a fog, Sillik saw everyone else step back as they also saw the Seven Gods materializing before them.

Ignoring the image, Renee cursed and stepped forward. She reached up to remove the crown, but power crackled around Sillik. Briana also reached out but was denied. Fearing another attempt on Sillik's life, the Gold Robes moved forward to try to combat that which they could not see.

As if standing apart and watching events from a distance, Sillik laughed. The crown was intended to open the potential. The ring was designed to show the door, the sword was intended to unlock it, and the pendant was meant to shine light through the door. That was the way it had always been. Something in each of the devices was much older than Illicia and showed the way. But to what? As Sillik peered through the door, he saw three more images: a key, a knife, and a scepter. One of the items seemed familiar. Sillik wasn't sure, but he knew he had seen it before.

The memory he had struggled to unlock was now laid bare. Rendarick had used seven items to fight the demon. The dark master was somehow using the demon's power, which was why he was so much more powerful. The remaining items must be gathered before Sillik could face the dark master or, worse, the demon.

"Sillik," a voice said.

Sillik turned his eyes to Lady Silvia.

"You must fight the dark master. He must be stopped before he can summon the demon and bring more schula out of the wastes." Then she retreated to the circle of the Seven. She smiled and waved her hand toward him, revealing a path through the storm. "All will be for naught if you fail to stop the dark master," Silvia said.

He turned the energies, and in a flash, they were his. Then he collapsed, unconscious.

Briana looked up in alarm as the sound of thunderous wings crashed down around them. "Dragons!"

Pandemonium broke out as the dragons belched fire, and the net shuddered overhead. Briana saw the dragon riders' faces as they grinned at the destruction they had brought. She was confused. Should she stay with Sillik or lead the defenses? When she turned back to Sillik, he was already standing with Renee at his side. In Renee's hand was the crown. Sillik's eyes were clear and bright.

*Damn, what just happened?* Briana wondered. *Did Renee revive him, or did the Seven Gods?*

The Seven Gods were fading from sight, smiles etched on their faces.

# CHAPTER 45

## Truths

K ENTON SAT IN a small room. One of
Lord General Greenup's lieutenants
had set up this meeting. He was in a private dining room in a tavern near the
Queen's Gate. The tavern was small, and the occupants seemed to be mostly
lizard men. These were the men and women who worked the lizard stables,
which meant they stank—and the tavern stank—of lizards.

Rebecca stood in the shadows behind him. She had insisted on coming
despite his arguments that he would be perfectly safe.

Kenton sniffed. In his youth, he had raced lizards. But that had been a long
time ago. He wore a black cloak over his gold robes tonight. A pair of goblets
sat on the table along with a bottle of wine. Kenton knew no one would be
drinking, but the tavern master had insisted that he had to serve something.

The door creaked, and two men entered. Both men were slender and
nervous. The older man sighed wearily as he pulled out the chair across from
Kenton and sat. He eyed the wine bottle distractedly, and a brief look of disgust
flashed across his face.

*He is used to better*, Kenton thought.

"I am told that you wished for this meeting," the man said, "and you agreed
to my conditions."

"I wished to talk to you, yes," Kenton said, "and yes, I agreed to your condition of no names and only one person. But I fear you have me at a disadvantage because surely you know who I am."

"I do," said the man, "but surely you understand that a man in my profession and guild cannot be too careful."

"I have no interest in you or your guild," Kenton said, "except as it pertains to a murder." Kenton raised an eyebrow as the second man stirred uncomfortably.

"How do I know I can trust you?" the first man demanded. "My guild has endured for thousands of years."

"Yes," Kenton answered. "But now you are worried. Thieves are turning up dead, all under mysterious circumstances. It is as if someone is hunting them. I believe that someone saw something they were not intended to see, and the murderer is now searching for that someone." Kenton's eyes flicked to the short, wiry man leaning against the far wall of the dining room. "Perhaps someone like our friend here. Perhaps while stealing a bottle of some very old liquor, he witnessed something and can now identify the killer."

"Perhaps," the seated man allowed. "If such an event occurred, then it would make the witness very valuable. My guild would have a price for that knowledge."

Kenton smiled. "Ah yes, prices. Let me talk you through what I think happened and what is happening, and then we can discuss price." Without stopping, he continued. "Several very old bottles of liquor were found, and the men who later died had very publicly purchased the only drinkable bottle. Almost everyone in the city who follows such things knew where the bottle was and who had purchased it. Your man stole said bottle of wine and witnessed the murders. He managed to avoid discovery, perhaps by hiding or by using some magical object. He escaped and delivered the bottle—to you perhaps, so you could sell it or keep it for yourself, since I detect a man of taste. Somehow the assassin learned that the bottle had been stolen and deduced that he or she might have been seen. A hunt ensued. Said hunt has seen scores of thieves killed, all with peculiar scars on their hands. Intelligent minds would then conclude that these were master thieves. Given the difficulty of the theft, only a master thief could have accomplished it—or one just getting his master's rank." Kenton paused while he watched the man against the wall hide his right hand. "The master thieves all report to the guild master, who must be very hard to find—hence my delay in finding you, Lazeros. One would suppose there have been attempts on your life and that you are hiding from the aforementioned killer. That is evident from the state of your clothing, my good fellow." Kenton paused dramatically. "Now to the price. Once we know the assassin, we can bring justice to bear on them, and you can return to your previous life as before."

"You expect us to just name the killer?"

"Yes, I do," Kenton said. "Because if you do not, the killer will just keep killing, and eventually they will kill you and your witness there." He nodded toward the second man. "I, for one, will not lose sleep over the killing of more thieves. But I suspect you might."

Nodding, Lazeros said nothing for a long moment. Then with a sigh, he said, "Tell them, Morrow."

Kenton turned to look at the short wiry man called Morrow.

"It's as you described," Morrow said reluctantly, shifting uncomfortably. "I hid under the bed. I have a figurine that makes shadows darker. I saw it all. They talked about stuff involving the prince, stuff I didn't understand."

Kenton nodded. "How did the older men die?"

Morrow swallowed and turned pale. "She had a creature on her shoulder and turned it loose on them. It wasn't there when she came into the room. She spoke, and it appeared. It just made noises and jumped on them. It ate their faces and necks. They tried to scream … oh gods it was terrible to see. Blood went everywhere. She killed the young men with a knife."

"Describe her," Kenton commanded.

Lazeros looked up in surprise. They already knew the killer was a woman.

Morrow spoke softly as he recalled the event. "Her face was pretty, but more squarish than round. Handsome. Smelled pretty too. She is older than me, but that still makes her young. Oh, and I saw a bit of blue and gold under her cloak. She must be a healer."

His last comment drew a sound from Rebecca, and Kenton looked at her sharply.

"Anything else, master thief? Hair color?"

Morrow shifted uncomfortably. "It was gold like her robes but was faded a bit from gray."

"Did she wear any jewelry, master thief?" Rebecca asked.

Morrow shook his head. "I don't know, good lady," he said, suddenly more afraid. "I couldn't see any."

"Very well," Kenton said tiredly. "Do you have anything else to add?"

"No," Morrow said nervously. "No, Your Highness, um, sir."

"Sir will suffice, and you may go," Kenton said.

"You know who to find?" Lazeros asked.

"We know," Kenton said. "We know."

"How will we know it's safe?" asked the guild master nervously. "How will we know you upheld your side of the bargain?"

"We will fly the kings' pendant above the Queen's Gate," Kenton said tiredly. "The golden eagle in flight will be the symbol you should look for."

The guild master stood, and with a curt nod, he hurried from the room.

Kenton sat in the small room for a long time and fingered his cup. *I must tell Sillik and Briana*, he thought. *Lords, I have to tell my wife.*

Rebecca stepped forward with tears in her eyes. "What are we going to do?"

Sighing, Kenton said, "I don't know."

# CHAPTER 46

## Bubbles

BRIANA SWORE AS she looked up at the sky. The air swarmed with dragons nearly eclipsing the sun as they swooped down and belched fire. The Gold Robes cringed in pain as bursts of flame tore at the net. Black streaks crisscrossed the net as the masters struggled to maintain control.

Handrie shouted for his net tenders to help. "If that net fails, we all die! Shrink it!"

Sillik and Renee stepped forward into the chaos. Sillik grabbed Handrie by the shoulders. "The net will hold," he said with a confidence shared by few. "Is there a way to invert a net and collapse it into a bubble?"

Caught by surprise, Handrie shook his head. "No, it can't be done." Then he paused, a faraway look in his eyes. Suddenly, he saw possibilities he had never considered. "Yes," he said excitedly. "I think it can."

Sillik nodded. "Work with the masters. We need to trap the dragons in a bubble and then pop it. Wait for my signal." He turned to look for his warmaster. "Briana!" Sillik yelled over the din of exploding fireballs above their heads. "Prepare the troops for ground assault. Unless I miss my guess, Peol is going to counterattack as soon as they believe the net is broken."

"The dragons," she protested. "We'll burn!"

Sillik shook his head. "We don't have time to argue. Prepare for an attack." Briana stiffened but then nodded.

Sillik glanced around. "Rigell, prepare your men. Greenup, be ready, my old friend."

The two men nodded. Rigell appeared calm as he surveyed the sky. A small smile curled his lips.

Handrie looked up from his conversation with the net tenders. "We think we can do it. It'll be tricky, though."

Sillik held up his hand. "Just do it. On my mark." He drew his blade.

"We don't have the lizards," Briana protested.

Sillik smiled grimly. "We have to do this the hard way. Handrie, on my count. Everyone else, as soon as the net traps the dragons, I want you leading your troops out. Ynak is out there."

"How do you know that?" Briana asked.

"Because it is what I would do," Sillik said as he raised his sword.

Briana and Renee did the same. Sillik also lifted the Shield of Rendarick. Briana had suggested that he keep it close.

Sillik looked up at the shuddering net and then, with a flourish, dropped his hand. The net convulsed and shook. A myriad of colors flashed through it. The edges began to curl upward, slowly at first and then with increasing speed. As the edges curled, they also seemed to stretch and twist. They extended outward until the net was a flat disk. It glowed and flashed where dragon fire struck. Streaks of black shot through it like lightning. Confused, the dragons screamed. A few tried to escape.

When the edges were above the soldiers' heads, Briana sent her troops streaming outward in all directions. Sillik watched the net masters and the Gold Robes as they tried to control the net. With a triumphant yell from the masters, the edges of the net curled upward and inverted. Sillik smiled as the net closed around the dragons like a bag. It looked like a large bubble in the air.

A few dragons escaped and tried to attack the net, to no avail. As the net closed, the net masters changed tactics and began to shrink it. The dragons flew around inside, panicking and spitting fire. The net turned black but continued to shrink. The dragons collided with one another. Moments later, dead dragons and riders fell through the ball of energy. Then all that was left of the net was a scintillating ball of light that winked out. The net tenders collapsed with relief.

Sillik, Renee, and Briana turned to the battle. Sillik's guards hurried after him into the afternoon sun.

Sillik's first impression was the smell of the battlefield. It wasn't much different than any other battlefield. The acrid smell of smoke hung over everything. The tang of blood and spilled bowels was everywhere, but in the background was the clean smell of the pine trees. *It will be clean again someday*, he thought. Then he heard the sounds: metal on metal, the cries and moans of the wounded, the buzzing of flies, and carrion birds waiting patiently on the edges of the battle.

Then he was running through the battlefield. His eyes saw, but his magical senses felt. His foe was near the edge of the throng. This time Dernot would not get away. Sillik spotted him standing near the enemy's signalmen, who waved their flags desperately to show the remaining dragons where to lay their fire.

Sillik moved forward but staggered as someone tried to contact him telepathically. Pain exploded behind his eyes as the spell tried to form. He fell to his knees as he tried to fight off the spell. *Not now, Kenton,* he thought. The spell collapsed, and Sillik struggled back to his feet.

Briana grabbed one arm, and Renee the other. They were worried.

"I'm okay," he said as he took a step forward. After two steps, he began to run. As he ran, Sillik threw a fireball at his foe. By chance, one of the signalmen stepped into the ball and was incinerated. The flag he was holding fluttered to the ground.

Dernot whipped his head around and attacked.

Sillik pulled the Shield of Rendarick up and felt the spell impact on the surface. The shield hummed, and Dernot's magic shattered.

Sillik threw his own attack, but Dernot had raised his magical shields, and Sillik's magic shattered.

"Attack now!" Renee yelled. With a grimace, Sillik and Renee both threw attacks.

Dernot staggered under the combined attack.

Briana followed with a stunning spell, and Dernot blocked it, but a second one hit him square on. He wavered as three more stunning spells hit him in quick succession. The Illician assassin fell to the ground, unconscious.

Briana ran up to the man and pulled a small bottle with a wax stopper out of her bag. Kneeling over him, she poured the contents into Dernot's mouth. "A drug to keep him unconscious and disrupt his concentration," she said. "He won't be able to light a piece of dry wood for days." She moved Dernot's head to make sure the drug had gone down his throat. When she was satisfied, she let his head drop. "Guard him!" she shouted at some of Sillik's men. "If he escapes, I'll have your hides."

The guards hurried to obey. They had every reason to believe she would be true to her word.

Briana gasped and grabbed her head. Her face paled, and she screwed her eyes shut. "No," she gasped as she started struggling to her feet.

Sillik eyed her quickly.

"I'm okay," she muttered. "Kenton."

Nodding, Sillik rushed back into the battle. A warrior tried to bar his way, and Sillik caught the blow on his shield. The wood hummed, and Sillik felt strength and caught the next blow with his sword. The warrior died quickly.

As the warrior before him fell, Sillik threw fireballs to incinerate the flags. The signalmen had already abandoned their post. He hoped that if he could cut communication between the ground and the dragons, the few remaining dragons would depart. Sure enough, the dragons turned to the west and abandoned their fellows. With the destruction of so many dragons, the ground forces of Ynak were quickly routed.

As the smoke from the fireballs cleared, a figure stepped out from behind a tree. It was a figure from legends and nightmares. The thing was close to twice the height of a man, with six arms and long, curved teeth. The schula grinned, or at least that's what it looked like to Sillik.

Sillik heard Briana curse and Renee take a sudden breath as the schula drew its weapons, seeming to expand as it did so. Each of its six arms held a weapon longer and heavier than a man could carry. It was naked except for a dirty loincloth. Its skin was dark green, almost black. Leather harnesses on its back allowed it to stow its weapons. Heavy leather sandals were laced to its feet. From its muscles, Sillik assumed it was a male. The histories had never mentioned female schula, and the Gold Tower had debated since Illicia's founding whether any female schula existed.

The swords in each of its lower arms were long and deadly, with spikes on the back of the blades. Sillik felt perspiration trickle down his back. *Damn the nine hells. What is this thing doing here? Are there more?*

The schula's middle arms sported knives almost as long as Sillik's sword, and the top arms each carried a long mace.

Instinctively, Sillik threw a fireball that would have incinerated a dozen men. The schula laughed as it deflected the fire. A tree exploded beside him. Its lips curled back in what might be called a smile, revealing rows of black teeth.

A raspy sound came from its throat. Sillik made out two words, "kill" and "eat," and then he stopped trying to listen.

Memories tumbled unbidden into Sillik's mind: Schula had a high resistance to magic. They had the strength of a dozen men. Schula couldn't attack with magic. Always assume the blades are poisoned. Its bite was to be avoided.

How old were these memories? It was no matter because they contained nothing useful. Sillik inched forward, his eyes on the creature's blades. Renee and Briana spread out to his left and right. Then the schula attacked.

Sillik dragged the heavy shield up and gasped as the blow hammered him. The shock of the creature's blow threw him fifteen lengths to the side, and his breath exploded out of him as he struck one of the few surviving trees.

As Sillik shook his head to clear his sight, he saw Renee attack the damned thing and get brushed aside as well. A dozen Nerakean staves flashed out to strike the schula. Snarling, the beast caught one and snapped it in half.

*Damn, it's fast,* Sillik thought. *And strong, No man can do that.*

Arrows flashed into the battle as Sillik struggled to his feet. The arrows thudded home with satisfying thunks. The schula snarled and spun to look for the archers. Suddenly, Sillik was looking at the creature's back. Clearly, it didn't consider him a threat.

Other memories flashed through Sillik's mind. With a sudden burst of energy, he ran forward and swung his sword. The beast turned, and a foot lashed out. The foot caught Sillik's shield and launched him back toward the trees. Sillik's breath exploded out of his lungs as he hit the ground. *Damn, that thing is fast,* he thought again.

More arrows and staves pummeled the schula. It screamed in pain but swung its swords, slicing through warriors who came too close.

Groaning, Sillik scrambled back to his feet and ran back into the battle. Again the schula turned to face him. The schula grinned and raised both swords. Sillik raised his shield above his head to block the weapons. The twin blows rained down on the shield, but this time the magic of the shield caught the weapons.

Sillik swung his sword only to feel it parried. Then the schula attacked with all of its weapons. Sillik felt even more thankful for the shield as it blocked every blow. As if it had a mind of its own, the shield dragged Sillik's arm to wherever it needed to be. At times that seemed to be six places at once, as the schula attacked with every weapon. Staves and arrows continued to pummel the creature and seemed to flow around Sillik. Nothing touched him as he slowly began to wear down the schula.

The schula roared in pain as Sillik cut off one of its arms. Perspiration covered Sillik, and exhaustion flowed over him, and then the schula attacked again in a frenzy. It was frustrated that it could not touch Sillik, and it redoubled its assault. It began spinning and lashing out with its clawed feet.

The battle seemed to slow as Sillik focused only on those flashing black blades and the glint of clawed feet. Sillik blocked another of the schula's kicks, and in a split second, the beast staggered past, and Sillik saw the backs of its legs. He swung his sword and felt his arm jerk as the weapon met resistance.

The schula toppled as its hamstrings were cut, screaming as it tried to turn. Sillik leapt forward and, with a deft swing of his sword, removed the schula's head.

To Sillik's surprise, the creature kept thrashing its weapons around. "Stay clear!" Sillik yelled. His memories said the schula was dead but just didn't know it yet.

"Is that what I think it is?" Renee asked. Her eyes darted around as if she expected more to appear. Blood trickled down her face and arm.

"If you think it's a schula, then you're right," Briana said.

"I thought they were all killed in the demon wars."

"I think they are tied to the demon," Sillik said. "I don't think it has returned yet, so this must be a forerunner or a–"

"Scout?" Briana asked.

Sillik nodded. "When it stops moving, I want the body and head preserved and sent to Illicia. The city needs to know what has happened here."

Handrie appeared a short time later with his uncle Rigell. The sleeve of Handrie's shirt was torn, and he had a bloody gash on his arm and another gash across his chin, but otherwise, he was intact. "We seem to have them on the run," he said, grimacing in pain. His staff was missing, and he carried part of a broken spear. Handrie looked at the twitching beast. "So that's a schula."

A Gold Robe tried to pick up the head, only to almost lose a finger to a bite.

"Go see the healers," Sillik said, nodding at Handrie's wounds. "We captured the Illician assassin," he added with a grim smile. He knew what would happen next.

"I will take him to the healers now," Rigell said. "We wanted to know the news."

"Apparently, Nordan did not stay to fight," Handrie said with disappointment.

Sillik smiled grimly. "We will capture him, eventually."

"This was too easy," Renee said. "Your assassin did not put up much of a fight."

"We surprised him," Briana said hopefully.

Sillik shook his head as he sheathed his sword. "No, he had to know we would be coming after him, and he would have felt what was done to the net. He chose to stay. Or he was commanded to stay."

"Why?" Briana asked. "Everyone knows that after two masters fight, they can feel each other's proximity for a while."

Sillik frowned. "Perhaps to cover the escape of others ... or to hide something else."

# CHAPTER 47

## Execution

S ILLIK KNELT IN a small tent. It was different from all others in the camp. The seven-sided structure had a domed roof. The outside was painted white, and the inside walls were painted to represent the Seven Gods. Small clay statues of the gods rested on stone pedestals. There was just enough room for two people to stand. All Illician war bands had a portable temple. It was important to honor the Seven Gods, especially in wartime. A glow ball was suspended in the center of the tent.

It had been an eventful week since the battle where Dernot had been captured. The man had been questioned for days but had not said a word. His eyes were bright and alert, and he seemed amused but had not spoken.

Every tool of the Gold Robes had been brought to bear on the assassin. They had not exactly tortured him, but they had tried to compel his obedience. Nothing worked. Briana and the Gold Robes believed there was some kind of block that prevented him from responding.

Yesterday, Dernot had been tried and convicted of treason. This morning at dawn, he would be beheaded. Dernot had not participated in his trial. He had offered no defense and had not said a word. His counselor had tried his best, but in the end the seven jurors had voted for death.

Sillik had retreated to the temple tent at sunset. For a long time, he had only sat and thought. He had asked the Seven Gods for guidance, but none was forthcoming. He had hoped Lady Silvia might appear, but she did not.

Later that morning, the forces would be splitting up. He and Handrie would be going to the schools of Salone to enlist their help. Renee thought the teachers might also know about the artifacts that Sillik had been told he must find. Renee and Briana would accompany the two men. Briana had insisted. Rigell would move the battle force closer to Ynak and Peol. Additional forces would be coming from Nerak.

Sillik heard footsteps outside the tent, followed by a polite cough. It was time. He stood and opened the flap and then relaxed the wards he had placed around the tent. The spell had allowed sound into the tent but blocked all sound from leaving it.

Briana stood with the crown. Renee was at her side. The women seemed to have become friends or at least had grown to tolerate each other. He guessed they had been there all night. He took the crown and placed it on his head. This would be a formal appearance, and he must be the king. He took a circuitous path to the center of the camp. The women followed quietly. Behind them, a dozen guards followed at a respectful distance.

The prisoner was already at the center of the site. He was still drugged but at a lower dose. He was aware but unable to use the Seven or the Nine. His hands and feet were bound with heavy chains. The cuffs had been welded shut with the Seven Laws, so there were no locks to pick. Dernot could not even walk with the weight of his chains, and he had been under constant surveillance. Seven Gold Robes and a dozen guards had been watching him constantly. His food and water had also been triple-checked for poison.

A random warrior had been chosen as executioner. Dressed entirely in black, he stood with a large battle-axe in his hands. A mask shrouded his face. No one wanted the position, but sometimes it was required for justice. People avoided looking at the executioner in order to help maintain his anonymity.

The entire camp had gathered to witness the execution. Knights stood shoulder to shoulder with Illician warriors. Gold Robes were interspaced with the net tenders.

Sillik stopped a short distance away from Dernot. For a moment, he simply observed the traitor. Then in a loud, clear voice, he said, "Dernot, you have been tried and convicted of treason. We are here to pronounce judgment. Do you have any last words?"

Dernot merely regarded him in silence. He blinked and then looked toward the sunrise. He seemed confused by the question. The sunrise stained the sky pink. A few clouds were visible.

"Very well," Sillik said. "Dernot Lafliar, you have been convicted of treason and assassination. The penalty is beheading. As king of Illicia, I pronounce judgment. You will be beheaded forthwith. May your soul reside in the nine hells until the end of time."

Dernot's expression flickered, and he did not resist as a wooden stump and a basket were placed in front of him by two grim-faced warriors. Dernot looked at Sillik and without expression put his head down on the stump.

The executioner made a quick swing, and it was over. Sillik averted his eyes at the last moment.

The Illician warriors cheered. They thought this was the end. The executioner pried his sword from the stump and, with a satisfied grin, cleaned the blade.

When the cheering stopped, Sillik turned away without looking at the basket. "Preserve it and send it to Illicia. Send the proclamation that I have been crowned. Illicia needs to know that justice has been done."

Quietly, Renee asked, "Is it over or just beginning? I have never seen a man do what he did—just give up like that."

Handrie smiled grimly. "We hang our traitors, but the result is the same."

Sillik looked at Handrie. "We have to find Nordan and eventually the dark master."

Briana gazed thoughtfully at the blood-soaked basket. "What compulsion would prevent him from speaking? He had nothing left to lose. Yet he just gave up?"

"We may never know," Sillik said.

"You will have to deal with the traitors in Illicia," said Briana. "We know who they must be."

Frowning, Sillik asked, "Did you make contact with Kenton? It must have been important for him to attempt to contact both of us."

Now Briana frowned. "I tried. Renee linked with me. It's like there is a wall between us and Illicia."

Renee smiled. "When do we leave?"

Sillik grinned. "Not for a while. We have injured to heal, and I think more help is on the way. We will wait for them."

# EPILOGUE

"**C**OME TO BED, husband," Elizabet said with a smile.

Kenton stood beside the narrow window. Night had fallen over Illicia. "There was a battle today," he said slowly.

"I know, husband. Every master in the city felt the echoes."

"It will be weeks before we know what really happened," Kenton said.

"Yes, so you should sleep," Elizabet urged.

Kenton shook his head. "I can't."

"I can help," Elizabet said. "Is it your knee?"

"Not that. I want to know what happened, but I can't make contact with Sillik or Briana. I tried today–I felt them, but I couldn't make contact. Now it is like there is a shield over the city, reflecting my attempts back into the city," he whispered.

"I am sure they are fine, husband." She paused pensively. "Briana might not even be involved. She might not have gotten there yet." Elizabet thought for a moment. She glanced behind her and then at her husband again.

"Something important has happened," Kenton insisted. "I know it."

"Husband," Elizabet said excitedly, "I have something to show you."

Turning tiredly, Kenton looked at his wife. *She's beautiful,* he thought, *so lovely. I am so lucky.*

Elizabet looked over her shoulder. "I was saving this," she said. "This was given to me last week. Claudett and I did a tricky bit of healing on a very ill young woman. The girl very nearly died. Her father, a rich merchant, gave us a bottle for our trouble. Normally, I don't accept healing gifts, but I made an exception this one time. I paid the asking price to the healers, so it is legal. But I knew how much you wanted this."

Kenton looked up as Elizabet held out a bottle covered in dust and grime.

"What is it?" Kenton asked tiredly, his eyes downcast.

Elizabet smiled. "One-thousand-year-old Armagnac."


**To be continued in *The King's Death***

Printed in the United States
By Bookmasters